The Singapore Grip

J. G. Farrell was born in Liverpool in 1935 but spent a great deal of his life abroad, including periods in France and Ireland, where he spent much of his childhood, and a prolonged visit to the Far East to research the background of this novel. He went to live in County Cork in April 1979 where only four months later he was drowned in a fishing accident.

His novels include *Troubles*, which won the Faber Memorial Prize in 1970, and *The Siege of Krishnapur* which won the Booker Prize in 1973. *The Singapore Grip* was his last completed novel. *The Hill Station*, unfinished, was published posthumously.

Available by the same author

A Girl in the Head
Troubles
The Hill Station
The Siege of Krishnapur

J. G. Farrell

The
Singapore
Grip

Flamingo
Published by Fontana Paperbacks

First published in Great Britain by
Weidenfeld & Nicolson Ltd 1978
First issued in Fontana Paperbacks 1979
Fourth impression October 1982

This Flamingo edition first published
in 1984 by Fontana Paperbacks
Fourth impression March 1989

Flamingo is an imprint of
Fontana Paperbacks, part of
the Collins Publishing Group,
8 Grafton Street, London W1X 3LA

Printed and bound in Great Britain by
William Collins Sons & Co. Ltd, Glasgow

For Bob and Kathie Parrish

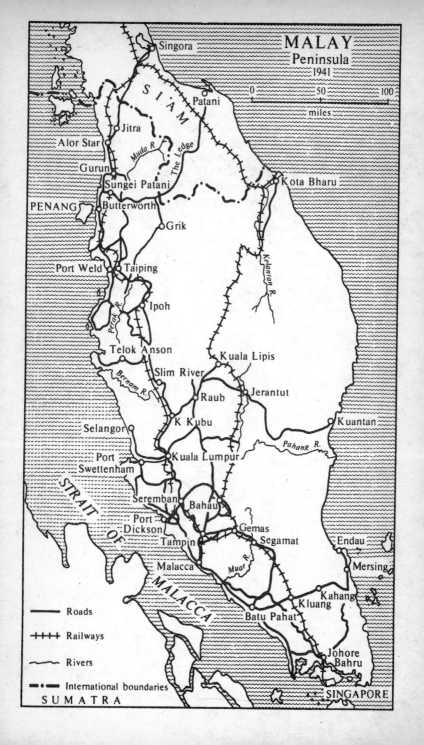

AUTHOR'S NOTE

Odd though it may seem to attach a bibliography to a work of fiction, this novel depends very heavily on primary research conducted by others, as well as on opinions and personal experiences recorded by those who travelled, worked or fought in the Far East before or during the last War. Nevertheless the Singapore of these pages does not pretend to be anything but fictional: although many of its bricks are real, its architecture is entirely fantastic.

J.G.F.

Part One

1

The city of Singapore was not built up gradually, the way most cities are, by a natural deposit of commerce on the banks of some river or at a traditional confluence of trade routes. It was simply invented one morning early in the nineteenth century by a man looking at a map. 'Here,' he said to himself, 'is where we must have a city, half-way between India and China. This will be the great halting-place on the trade route to the Far East. Mind you, the Dutch will dislike it and Penang won't be pleased, not to mention Malacca.' This man's name was Sir Thomas Stamford Raffles: before the war his bronze statue used to stand in Empress Place in a stone alcove like a scallop shell (he has been moved along now and, turned to stone, occupies a shady spot by the river). He was by no means the lantern-jawed individual you might have expected: indeed, a rather vague-looking man in a frock coat.

Although people had once lived there, the island of Singapore, when he arrived, was largely deserted except for a prodigious quantity of rats and centipedes. Rather ominously, Raffles also noticed a great many human skulls and bones, the droppings of local pirates. He wasted no time, however, in negotiating for the island with an alarmed native and then proceeded, his biographer tells us, to set up a flag-pole thirty-six feet high. 'Our object,' he wrote in a letter to a friend, 'is not territory but trade: a great commercial emporium, and a *fulcrum*, whence we may extend our influence politically as circumstances may hereafter require.' As he stood there on that lonely beach and gazed up at the flag with rats and centipedes seething and tumbling over his shoes did Raffles foresee the prosperity which lay ahead for Singapore? Undoubtedly he did.

When you think of the city as it was forty years ago you should not imagine an uncivilized frontier-town of the jungle. You had only to stroll around the centre of the city with its wide avenues and lawns and look at the monolithic government buildings, at the luxurious department stores and at the marmoreal dignity of the banks, to realize that Singapore was the work of a great and civilized nation. True, there were other parts of the city, the various native quarters where Tamils, Malays, and above all the Chinese lived, which were rather less imposing. There, in those 'lower depths' Chinese secret societies undoubtedly performed monstrous crimes, kidnapped their own prominent citizens, fought out appalling territorial battles, stunned themselves with drugs and so forth. If you were merely a visitor, a sailor, say, in those years before the war, Singapore would undoubtedly have seemed no less tawdry, no less exciting than another of the great Eastern sea ports. You would have gone to drink and dance at one of the amusement parks, perhaps even at The Great World itself, whose dance-hall, a vast, echoing barn of a place, had for many years entertained lonely sailors like yourself. There, for twenty-five cents, you could dance with the most beautiful taxi-girls in the East, listen to the loudest bands and admire the glorious dragons painted on the walls. In the good old days, before the troops started flooding in at the beginning of the War, that place could swallow an entire ship's company and still seem empty except for you and the two or three Chinese girls with dolls' painted faces sitting at your table, ready to support you with tiny but firm hands should you look like plunging to the floor full of Tiger beer.

There, too, when you staggered outside into the sweltering night, you would have been able to inhale that incomparable smell of incense, of warm skin, of meat cooking in coconut oil, of honey and frangipani, and hair-oil and lust and sandalwood and heaven knows what, a perfume like the breath of life itself. And from the roof of the Seamen's Institute, or from some other less respectable roof, you might have seen the huge purple sign advertising Tiger Balm and, beside it, once darkness had completely fallen, its guardian, the great sabre-toothed tiger with glowing orange stripes beginning its nightly prowl over the sleeping roofs of Singapore. But there is no denying it, certain parts of the city were tawdry and others were wretched, and becoming more so as the age advanced: already, by 1940, the walls of cheap hotels and boarding-houses, hitherto impermeable except to an occasional muffled groan or sigh, were becoming porous and beginning to leak radio music, twangings of guitars and news bulletins. Every great city has its seamy side. And so let us look for preference at the gentler parts of the city at the elegant European suburb of Tanglin, for instance, where Walter Blackett, chairman of the illustrious merchant and agency house of Blackett and Webb Limited, lived with his family.

At first glance Tanglin resembled any quiet European suburb with its winding, tree-lined streets and pleasant bungalows. There was a golf course close at hand with quite respectable greens; numerous tennis courts could be seen on the other side of sweet-smelling hedges and even a swimming pool or two. It was a peaceful and leisurely life that people lived here, on the whole. Yet if you looked more closely you would see that it was a suburb ready to burst at the seams with a dreadful tropical energy. Foliage sprang up on every hand with a determination unknown to our own polite European vegetation. Dark, glistening green was smeared over everything as if with a palette knife, while in the gloom (the jungle tends to be gloomy) something sinister which had been making a noise a little while ago was now holding its breath.

If you left your bungalow unattended for a few months while you went home on leave, very likely you would come back to find that green lariats had been thrown over every projecting part and were wrestling it to the ground, that powerful ferns were drilling their way between its bricks, or that voracious house-eating insects, which were really nothing more than sharp jaws mounted on legs, had been making meals of the woodwork. Moreover, the mosquitoes in this particular suburb were only distant cousins of the mild insects which irritate us on an English summer evening: in Tanglin you had to face the dreaded anopheles variety, each a tiny flying hypodermic syringe containing a deadly dose of malaria. And if, by good fortune, you managed to avoid malaria there was still another mosquito waiting in the wings, this one clad in striped football socks, ready to inject you with dengue fever. If your child fell over while playing in the garden and cut its knee, you had better make sure that no fly was allowed to settle on the wound; otherwise, within a day or two, you would find yourself picking tiny white maggots out of it with tweezers. At that time, when parts of the suburb were still bordered by jungle, it was by no means uncommon for monkeys, snakes and suchlike to visit your garden with the idea of picking your fruit or swallowing your mice (or even your puppy if you had an appetizing one). But all I mean to suggest is that, besides the usual comforts of suburban life, there were certain disadvantages, too.

Not far from where the Blacketts lived Orchard Road sloped gently down (a gradient that was more psychological than real) almost straight for a mile or so until it lost itself on the fringes of Chinatown and the commercial city where Walter had his headquarters on Collyer Quay and did battle on weekdays. Down there in the city, taking the place of the rats and the centipedes which had once made it their home, seething, devouring, copulating, businesses rose and fell, sank their teeth into each other, swallowed, broke away, gulped down other firms, or mounted each other to procreate smaller companies, just as they do elsewhere in other great capitalist cities. But up here in Tanglin people moved in a quiet and orderly way about their daily affairs, apparently detached from these sordid encounters, detached especially from the densely packed native masses below. And yet they moved, one might suppose, as the hands of a clock move. Imagine a clock in a glass case; the hands move unruffled about their business, but at the same time we can see the working of springs and wheels and cogs. That ordered life in Tanglin depended on the same way on the city below, and on the mainland beyond the Causeway, whose trading, mining and plantation concerns might represent wheels and cogs while their mute, gigantic labour force are the springs, steadily causing pressures to be transmitted from one part of the organism to another ... and not just as that time or just to Tanglin, of course, but much further in time and in space: to you thousands of miles away, reading in bed or in a deckchair on the lawn, or to me as I sit writing at a table.

2

The Blacketts, on the whole, had reason to be satisfied with the calm and increasingly prosperous life they were leading in Singapore in 1937. Only once or twice in the two decades following the Great War had anything occurred to disturb their peace of mind and even then nothing that could be considered particularly serious. True, their elder daughter, Joan, had shown signs of becoming involved with unsuitable young men ... but that is the sort of thing that any family with growing children has to expect.

Although his wife, Sylvia, became greatly agitated, Walter himself was inclined to take it calmly at first. Joan, who had recently returned from a finishing school in Switzerland, had found it hard to settle down in Singapore, separated from the friends she had made in Europe. She was rebellious, contemptuous of the provincial manners of the Straits, as one naturally would be, Walter supposed, after being at such a school (the school, incidentally, had been her mother's idea). Given time it was something that she would get over.

Joan's involvement with the first of these young men, a penniless flight-lieutenant whom she had met nobody knew where, was an act of rebellion probably. Even Joan had not tried very hard to pretend that he was anything but impossible. Besides, she knew well enough that her parents, who took a dim view of the Services, thought of even those generals and air vice-marshals whom duty had called to Singapore, let us not speak of flight-lieutenants. Walter had not set eyes on the person in question because Joan had had the good sense not to try to bring him home. He had waited calmly for her to see reason, explaining with a touch of exasperation to his wife that her tears and her fretting were a waste of energy which she could use to greater profit in some other direction, because Joan would presently come to her senses with or without the aid of her mother's tears. In due course, it had taken a little longer than he had expected, Walter's confidence had been justified. Joan had disposed of the flight-lieutenant as surreptitiously as she had found him. Tranquillity had returned to the Blackett household for a while.

Presently, however, it transpired that Mrs Blackett, testing the material of one of Joan's cotton frocks beween her finger and thumb, felt an unexpected crinkle of paper. Ah, what was this? Something left by the laundry? Mrs Blackett had happened to grasp the light material of her daughter's frock just where there was a pocket. Joan, who was in the frock at the time, blushed and said that it was nothing in particular, just a piece of paper of no importance. 'In that case,' replied Mrs Blackett, 'we had better throw it away immediately, because it does not do to let our clothes bulge out in an ugly fashion by carrying unnecessary things in our pockets.' Quick as a flash her fingers darted into the pocket and retrieved the offending piece of paper (as she had suspected! a love-letter!) before Joan had time to retreat. The ensuing scene, the shrieking and hysterics and stamping of feet, even reached Walter who was upstairs in his dressing-room at the time, brooding on business matters. He gave the storm a little time to blow over but it showed no sign of doing so and at last he was obliged to come downstairs, afraid that they might burst blood-vessels in their passion. His appearance quelled mother and daughter instantly: they gazed at him glassily, breasts still heaving, faces tear-stained. He promptly sent Joan to her room and, when she had gone, reminded his wife that she was under instructions to take these matters calmly.

'The fact is, my dear, that these emotional scenes do no good at all. Quite the reverse. I should like to know how much you have found out about this young man as a result of all this shouting and screaming? My bet is ... nothing.'

It was true. Mrs Blackett hung her head. Joan had declared that she would rather be dead than reveal the least thing about him, where she had met him, where he worked, even what his name was. 'His name appears to be "Barry",' said Walter with a sigh, perusing the letter, 'and I can even tell you where he works, since he has written on his firm's notepaper. As to where she met him, that is of no importance whatsoever. So all you have succeeded in doing is putting Joan's back up. In future kindly consult me before you say anything to Joan about her boyfriends. I shall now go and have a word with the young lady.'

Walter climbed the stairs thoughtfully. The marriage of his daughters was a matter to which he had not yet given a great deal of attention. And yet it was undoubtedly a matter of great importance, not only to Joan, as it would be, in due course, to little Kate, his younger daughter, but potentially to the business as well. After all, if you are a wealthy man you cannot have your daughter marrying the first adventurer who comes along. To allow such a match is to invite disaster. The fact was that Joan would do far better for herself and for Blackett and Webb Limited if she agreed to marry someone whose position in the Colony matched her own.

There were, as it happened, two or three young men in Singapore with whom a satisfactory alliance of this sort could have been made and who, given Joan's attractions, would have asked for nothing better. But when, on her return from her finishing school, such a union had been suggested to her, Joan had been indignant. She found the idea distasteful and old-fashioned. She would marry whom she pleased. Naturally the elder Blacketts in turn had been indignant. Walter had demanded to know why he had paid good money to such a school if not to drill some sense of reality into her. But Joan had been stubborn and Walter had quickly reached the conclusion that patience was the best policy. They would wait and see, tactfully fending off unsuitable young men in the meantime. Despite the scene which had just taken place Walter remained confident that Joan was too sensible a girl to remain permanently attached to someone whom her parents considered unsuitable.

Walter, climbing the stairs, had considered rebuking his daughter and ordering her not to communicate with this young man again. Instead he decided to continue banking on her good sense and merely said: 'Joan dear, I've no objection to you flirting with young men provided you are sensible about it and don't do anything you might regret later. What I do object to is the fact that you have upset your mother. In future please be more discreet and hide your love-letters in some safe place.' Joan, who had been expecting another row, gazed at him in astonishment as he handed her back the letter which had caused all the commotion.

Was Walter taking a great risk with his daughter's future by responding so mildly? Mrs Blackett was inclined to think that he was. Walter, however, reassured her. He was on friendly terms with the chairman of the firm on whose notepaper the young man wrote his love-letters and saw him frequently at the Club. He was confident that if the worst came to the worst and Joan persisted in taking an interest in him, it would require only a nod and a wink to have the fellow moved away from Singapore to a convenient distance (back to England if necessary). As it turned out, this intervention was not necessary: at a certain age nothing can be more stifling to enthusiasm than the permission or approval of your parents. 'Barry', (whoever he was), lovelorn, was allowed to continue his residence in Singapore.

Mrs Blackett now decided that the best way to prevent Joan from carrying on with unsuitable young men was to surround her with suitable ones. True, there was a serious shortage of the latter in Singapore but she would draw up a list and see what could be done ... Joan's trouble was that she never met anyone of the right sort. Mrs Blackett would put an end to that by inviting one or two young men chosen by herself to tea once a week. Joan would be asked to act as hostess and Walter would be there, too, to keep an eye on things. What did Walter think of it? Was it not a good idea?

Walter was dubious. He doubted whether Joan would take an interest in any young chap of whom her mother approved. He was even more dubious when he saw the list that she had drawn up. But in the end he agreed, partly because he saw no reason why his wife should not have her own way for once, partly because he had a secret weakness. This weakness, which was so mild and agreeable it might almost be considered a virtue, was for holding forth, as a man with some experience of life, to younger men just starting out. So it would happen, once these weekly tea-parties were inaugurated, that while Joan sat tight-lipped and rebellious, her green eyes as hard as pebbles, Walter would grow animated and have a jolly good time. Mrs Blackett, meanwhile, would dart glances from her husband to her daughter to the young guest trying to estimate what impression each was making on the other. As a matter of fact, the young man usually sat there looking faintly alarmed as Walter harangued him: after all, this was Blackett of Blackett and Webb, an important man in the Straits, and his parents had told him to be careful not to put his foot in it and to behave himself properly for once.

For a number of years now it had been Walter's agreeable habit to take his visitors by the arm and escort them along the row of paintings that hung in his drawing-room. So it happened that the young man intended for Joan, although on the whole he felt safer sitting down and less likely to knock something over, would reluctantly allow himself to be plucked out of his chair while Joan continued to sit mutinously silent beside the tea-pot, ignoring her mother's whispered entreaties that she should say something to her guest, and even accompany the two men across the room.

Some of the paintings which Walter was showing the young man were primitive in style, painted perhaps by a native artist or by a gifted ship's officer in his spare time: here was a three-masted vessel being loaded with spices or sugar, a line of native porters with bundles on their heads marching in uncertain perspective along a rickety quay surrounded by jungle. In the next painting, by a more sophisticated hand, the ship had arrived in Liverpool and was being unloaded again, and after that

16

would come three or four paintings of the port of Rangoon and Walter would exclaim: 'Look! They're loading rice. Still all sailing ships, of course, and Rangoon's just a sleepy little village. But you wait!'

In the early days, he would explain, while the youth at his side gazed at him uneasily, white rice would not survive the long passage round the Cape and so it was shipped as what was known as 'cargo rice', that is, one-fifth unhusked paddy and four-fifths roughly cleaned in hand-mills. Throughout the East, to India mainly, it was shipped simply as paddy ('The blighters cleaned it themselves.'). Now Walter, unreeling history at a prodigious speed, would guide his guest (well, Joan's guest) to a later picture of Rangoon. 'You see how it's grown in the meantime. And see how steam has taken the place of sail in the harbour (though some ships still have both, of course). And these great buildings with chimneys, d'you know what they are? Steam rice-mills!'

For now it was possible, with the opening of the Suez Canal in 1870, to ship cleaned rice to Europe, thereby cutting out the fine-millers who used to clean the 'cargo rice' in London.

'Ruined 'em,' Walter would remark with a frown. 'They weren't quick enough. A businessman must keep his wits about him.' And if the young man happened to be starting out on a business career himself, as he probably was, Walter might pause to lecture him on how you must always be ready to move with the times, never taking anything for granted.

'Go and join them!' hissed Mrs Blackett to her daughter in a penetrating whisper. 'You're being impolite to your guest.'

'But Mother, I've told you a thousand times ...' And it was true ... she had.

The last picture of Rangoon had been painted after the turn of the century and showed how the thriving rice trade had caused it to spread and grow into a great modern city, now only surpassed as an Eastern port by Calcutta and Bombay. Walter would draw his dismayed captive closer and after a moment's examination of the teeming wharves on the Rangoon River he would put his finger on a fine warehouse and say. 'Our first! The first to belong to Blackett and Webb ... or rather, to Webb and Company as the firm was then called. We still have another exactly similar here in Singapore on the river. Well now, you see how a bit of trade can make a place grow?' And with an air of satisfaction he would lead the suitable young man on to yet more paintings of Calcutta, Penang, Malacca, and of Singapore itself, in various stages of development.

'You see how we made these little villages grow in just a few years. That's what a bit of tin and rubber have done for Singapore!'

There was still another painting to be seen, and one that was more important than all the others, but by now Mrs Blackett was growing impatient and calling Walter and his audience back for another cup of tea. These tea-parties, she was beginning to think, were not having the desired effect. A disturbing thought occurred to her and she eyed her daughter suspiciously. Could it be that the reason for Joan's lack of interest in her guest was that she was already carrying on in secret with yet another unsuitable young man?

3

Walter, after one such occasion, found himself left alone to brood in the drawing-room while Joan, with a sudden friendliness born of relief, conducted her guest to his motor-car and then went to join little Kate who was waiting on the lawn with a warped tennis racket for a game of French cricket. Joan was still just enough of a schoolgirl to enjoy such games. As the young man's limousine crept towards the gates his pale face appeared at one of the windows and he waved, but no one was paying any attention to his departure. He caught a glimpse of Joan, though, dashing joyfully after a tennis ball while Kate clumsily passed the racket round and round her plump little body, and he thought with a pang: 'What a smasher!' And rather well off, too. For once he and his parents were entirely in agreement. Too bad old Blackett was so peculiar!

Meanwhile, Mrs Blackett had seized the opportunity of slipping upstairs to Joan's room in order to set her mind at rest by having a quick read of her daughter's diary. She picked up this little volume and began to flick over its pages. So far, so good. There did not appear to be anything incriminating. She heaved a sigh of relief as the weeks fled by under her thumbnail. But then, just as she had almost reached this very week, she received a nasty shock, for the diary suddenly turned from plain English into a jumble of meaningless letters. What on earth did this signify? It could only be that Joan had taken to writing her diary in code! And that in turn must mean that she had something to hide! Mrs Blackett, seriously alarmed, tried again and again to make sense of those jumbled letters but was quite unable to make anything of them. The only thing that she did discover was that the same name (she assumed it was a name because it began with a capital letter) kept recurring: 'Solrac'!

'Oh dear, he must be a Hungarian this time!' thought Mrs Blackett, raising a hand to her brow.

Downstairs she found Walter still in the drawing-room, musing in front of the most important painting in his collection, the one which he had not had time to show Joan's young guest. He merely greeted her revelations about the diary in code with a shrug, however, and told her to calm herself ... any family with growing daughters must expect occasional difficulties of this sort. It was in the nature of things. Mrs Blackett retired, by no means reassured.

The painting which had pride of place in Walter's vast drawing-room and in front of which he was now standing, was not yet another view of an embryonic city, but of a man. It was a portrait of old Mr Webb himself, a bearded, sharp-featured gentleman of great dignity. Walter, when given the opportunity, would lead his guests up to this portrait and speak with respectful warmth of his former partner, the man without whom he himself 'would never have amounted to anything'. For it had been Mr Webb who had given young Walter Blackett a chance to compete with the giant firms of the Far East like Guthries, Jardines and Sime Darby, by agreeing to merge his own powerful business with Walter's fledgling. And they had got on well together, too, so that in no time a real understanding had been established between them. Besides, growing older now, Mr Webb had needed the energy of a younger partner. In due course Blackett and Webb Limited had been the result.

A lesser man, as he grew weaker, would have held grimly on to everything, with the result that within a few years both the rubber and the agency business would have tumbled about his ears. But old Mr Webb, never afraid to face unpleasant realities, had realized that the years ahead would be too much for him. Perhaps, too, he had dimly perceived some of the approaching hazards of the next decade: in particular, the growing rivalry with Japan in the markets of the Far East. There are few things in life more difficult than for a man to retire from the business he has founded and built up himself. Yet this difficult feat had been managed, at least reasonably well, by Mr Webb when Walter had taken over completely in 1930. And there had still remained a firm bond of mutual respect between the two men.

After his retirement Mr Webb's main interest had been in a small estate business known as the Mayfair Rubber Company which he had kept back, he would explain, as an old man's plaything. He was chairman of this company but his duties were not onerous: the Mayfair was one of the assortment of independent companies whose day-to-day management was handled collectively by Blackett and Webb with an efficiency that neither of them, alone, could have matched. No, it was more likely, if the truth were known, that he had seen the Mayfair as a convenient Old Gentleman's Home. From this point of view there was something to be said for the Mayfair, however slender the yield from its estate in Johore.

When he retires an elderly gentleman needs a pleasant place to live: the Mayfair had maintained its Singapore headquarters for many years back, not in the commercial district as you might expect, but in a rambling, palatial bungalow in Tanglin, adjacent to Walter's own splendid mansion so that only a pleasant stroll through two compounds separated them. A retired gentleman needs the respect and assistance of those around him ... who is more respected and assisted than a chairman in his own company? He needs something to keep him interested in life lest he slip out of it through the inattention that besieges the elderly ... what better than his own rubber company? On the other hand, he needs to be left alone, not bothered by people, because they increasingly irritate him ... whose peace of mind is more carefully preserved than the chairman's? This last point had been particularly important to old Mr Webb.

He had lived alone all his life and did not mean to change his ways simply because he was getting on in years. Surprisingly, he was married. But his wife was in England and always had been. He had married her late in life and never encouraged her to come out to Malaya. Perhaps he had been afraid that people would laugh at him, for she was some thirty years younger than himself (she was dead now, though: he had outlasted her despite those thirty years). More likely, he had simply preferred living by himself and his wife had not seemed to mind, as far as anyone knew. Moreover, he had paid visits to her in England where he was sometimes obliged to go on business. On one of these visits he had even made her pregnant, which speaks for cordial relations. The result of their union had been a son called Matthew who, like his mother, had never appeared in Singapore.

At one time Mr Webb had had the notion that young Matthew should marry Joan. Yes, the old chap had taken a benevolent interest in her as a little girl, showering her with silver spoons, napkin rings and strings of pearls. No doubt Mr Webb, used to his own somewhat despotic family arrangements, had seen no reason why authority should not be exercised to merge families in the same way as businesses. Walter smiled. That might have saved all this bother with unsuitable young men! But by the mid-thirties this union was no longer mentioned, nor had been for some years.

Matthew and Joan ... they might almost had been designed for each other. What a shame! As it happened, neither Walter nor the rest of his family, except for his younger daughter, Kate, had set eyes on Matthew although they, too, had made occasional visits to England. Matthew and Walter's son, Monty, were roughly the same age, yet when Monty had been at school in England Matthew had not joined him ... he had been sent to school in Switzerland, or in Sweden, or in some other country. For, Walter recalled, gazing sadly at the portrait of his former partner, in the smooth and otherwise flawless edifice which Mr Webb had constructed around himself in preparation for a dignified and comfortable old age, a single nasty crack had appeared.

Old Mr Webb, although his faculties had remained unimpaired in most respects, had been assailed by certain progressive ideas about diet and education and Matthew had been brought up in accordance with them. This was surely a tragedy worthy of that ... what was his name? ... that French blighter ... yes, Balzac, that was it. The most progressive of all the schools Matthew had been sent to, so Walter had heard, had taken co-education to the limit of allowing no distinction whatsoever to be made between the sexes. Children were known simply by the title 'Citizen' and a surname. Boys and girls alike wore the same baggy, flowing pantaloons and bullfighter jackets. They swam naked together in the swimming pool, had

21

their hair cropped to a similar length, played the same non-competitive games, and were allowed to unroll their sleeping mats in whichever dormitory they pleased provided it was not in the same one two nights running.

This was undoubtedly the most extreme of several private schools which Matthew had attended. The others had probably specialized in nothing more extreme than vegetarianism and some form of non-coercive teaching. Yet the thought of these schools still haunted Walter to this day. He had done his best to remonstrate, mind you, but the old man was obstinate and had shown himself ready to take offence. The matter had had to be dropped. But what all these schools had done to young Matthew, Walter could only wonder. It seemed to him pathetic beyond words that this old gentleman, whose own life had been an example of rectitude, hard work and self-discipline, should have succumbed to such an array of peculiar and de-bilitating theories, the very opposite of everything that he himself had stood for.

Only too glad would Walter have been if events had proved him wrong, if the fatal vegetarian flaw had not brought about the tragedy he feared. But this was not to be. One of Mr Webb's visits to England had coincided with the General Strike of 1926. Matthew had been a student at Oxford at the time. While his fellow undergraduates had poured cheerfully out of their colleges to lend a hand in breaking the strike Matthew had skulked in his room 'sporting his oak' (Walter understood this to be university jargon for 'keeping his door shut'). Despite the shut door Mr Webb had argued with his son. Very likely the word 'patriotism' had been mentioned.

Walter had received no first-hand account of the meeting but somehow he pictured Mr Webb standing on the lawn of Brasenose College holding up fistfuls of white hair to the icy wind that howled through the quad, while dismal dons, looking up from their books, surveyed this representative of suffering humanity with distaste from leaded casements. He understood that after wandering about for a day or two the old chap had offered his own services as a tram-conductor. They had been refused, of course. No matter how enthusiastic he might be, for the serious business of collecting fares and clubbing trouble-makers off the rear platform he was much too frail. He had retired to Singapore then, having watched the strike collapse without his son's assistance.

At one time it had been understood that Matthew would

take his place in the firm one day. But after 1926 this was no longer discussed. Matthew's mother had died suddenly in 1930 and Matthew himself had seldom been mentioned after that. He was known to be living in Geneva where he had some job connected with the League of Nations. And that, reflected Walter, given the poor boy's peculiar education, is about what one might have expected! Old Mr Webb was still alive, by the way, and on certain social occasions he could still be seen in Walter's garden or drawing-room, looking no less upright and dignified than the old gentleman in the portrait which Walter had just been contemplating. 'Matthew and Joàn ... what a shame indeed. It would have suited the firm nicely.' And with a sigh Walter went to look for his wife who had retired to her room with a pencil and a piece of paper, determined to break the code in which Joan had taken to writing her diary.

Never in her life had Mrs Blackett subjected herself to such mental effort as she did during the next few days in her attempt to make sense of those mysteriously jumbled letters. She tried everything she could think of, she pummelled her brain with one theory after another, she covered the floor of her bedroom with crumpled pieces of paper, she grew thin and haggard, but still without result. At last, however, as she sat defeated in front of her dressing-table gazing at her hollow-eyed reflection and still with a line of Joan's fiendish code gripped in her fingers, chance came to her rescue: she dropped her eyes to the reflection of the paper and found that she could read it without difficulty! It was the simplest of all codes used by children: mirror-writing. She searched feverishly for the other coded sentences she had copied from Joan's diary and held them to the mirror, her lips working ... There was a knock on the door and Walter came in, looking sombre.

'He's not a Hungarian!' cried Mrs Blackett. 'He's a ...'

'A Brazilian, I know. It's even worse.'

'Walter, how do you know?'

'I just asked Joan. What's more, I have a feeling that this time it may be more serious.'

Walter was beginning to think that although difficulties of this sort were in the natural order of things and were such as any family with growing daughters has to expect, a Brazilian was going a tiny bit too far. Weary of his wife's efforts to break Joan's code he had decided to approach his daughter directly. Joan had replied without hesitation that the object of her affections was a secretary at the Brazilian Legation in

Peking who had come to visit Singapore for an extended holiday. They would probably be married in a year or two in Rio de Janeiro, once she had had time to become a Catholic. Although his family did not have much money (they were rather hard up, actually), they were direct descendents of King Alfonso or someone of Spain, or was it Portugal? She was glad that Walter had brought the matter up because she had been on the point of asking whether she could invite Carlos to tea. Oh yes, and if Walter did not mind, it might be best not to show him all the paintings of Rangoon, at least to begin with, until they all knew each other better.

This was serious, undoubtedly. But Walter did not lose his nerve. He knew Joan to have an obstinate streak in her and had quickly decided, in spite of the danger, that the best policy would be to continue as before, counting on her good sense. He believed that given time she would perceive that an impoverished Brazilian was out of the question. Still, this talk of marriage was disquieting. He replied guardedly that he saw no reason why Carlos should not come to tea. In return Joan gave him a kiss.

Carlos, it turned out, wore a monocle, affecting to be a British gentleman. Over tea (this time it was Mrs Blackett's turn to remain tight-lipped and sullen) Carlos explained to Walter that in the Brazilian Legation in Peking there had been nothing whatsoever to do ... nobody there did any work, not a bit, not an ounce, not a scrap! And he uttered a high, bleating laugh, also modelled on that of a British gentleman. One reason nobody did any work in Peking was because the Chinese Government was not there, nowhere near! The blessed thing was miles away in Nanking! In any case, the Chinese and Brazilian governments had nothing whatever to say to each other, not a blessed word! No Brazilian had been near China for centuries! So what could a chap do? he enquired, failing to notice the unfortunate impression he was producing on Walter. What could a chap do but spend his entire day in riding-breeches or tennis flannels and his evenings dancing on the roof of the Grand Hôtel de Pékin? 'A poor show, actually,' he added regretfully, somewhat to Walter's surprise. After a long silence he dropped his monocle glumly into his handkerchief and began to polish. Walter had agreed with his last remark. He glanced quickly at Joan but her face was impassive and he could not tell what she was thinking.

Carlos cleared his throat. Sometimes, when they needed a change from Peking, they would go on leave to Shanghai. He brightened a little. Did Walter know that the Lambeth Walk was now all the rage in Shanghai's nightclubs?

Once he had met Carlos, Walter was reassured. Joan, a sensible girl who knew how important her eventual marriage would be both to herself and to her father's business, could not fail to see how thoroughly impossible he was. Walter was amazed, indeed, that she should have been able to put up with him for a day, let alone a week. But somehow she seemed able to manage it and, presently, the week became several weeks. As time went on, Walter's confidence diminished. He had almost decided to use his parental authority to put a stop to the liaison when he happened to mention the matter to a French friend, a certain François Dupigny, who was passing through Singapore at the time. Dupigny, to whom he had applied for information about the young man's background in the hope of uncovering something discreditable, exercised some important function in the Indo-Chinese Government on behalf of the French Colonial Ministry; he was unusually well-connected in the Far East and had an ear for gossip.

Although, as it turned out, Dupigny knew nothing at all about Carlos he threw up his hands in dismay at Walter's idea that the two young people should be prevented from seeing each other. On the contrary, he declared, nothing could be worse for Walter's cause! The lovers should be not only permitted but *obliged* to spend as much time in each other's company as decorum and chastity allowed. In such circumstances nothing could be better guaranteed to pour icy water over the passion of one young person than intimate acquaintance with the other!

Walter was taken aback by this cynical view, though there might be a grain of truth in it, he had to admit. In all probability, however, he would not have adopted such an unconventional approach to his difficulty had not Joan, at that very moment, asked for permission to visit Shanghai for a holiday in the company of Carlos ... and, of course, of her mother who would have to be persuaded to act as chaperon. Joan naturally expected a refusal and, seeing him hesitate, began to show signs of indignation and rebellion. But Walter's hesitation was less concerned with Carlos than with the political situation in Shanghai and in China generally. He recalled the trouble there had been there in 1932, of which he had been given a vivid description by the manager of Blackett and Webb's Shanghai branch. The curious scene which he had evoked had for some reason remained in Walter's mind: a chilly night in January, the booming chimes of the Custom House clock dying away into silence over the rainswept city, and then the sudden rattle of rifle and machine-gun fire.

As was usually the case with these China 'incidents' the rights and wrongs of the affair had been thickly cloaked in ambiguity. All that one could say for certain was that soon after eleven p.m. an armed contingent of the Japanese Naval Landing Party led by men carrying flaming torches had crossed the border from the International Settlement into Chapei. They had been greeted with a hail of bullets by the bitterly anti-Japanese, anti-foreign, pro-revolutionary Nineteenth Route Army: in no time the streets around the North Station had been littered with dead Japanese Marines. The Japanese had not thought to switch out the streetlights and, with the brilliantly lit International Settlement behind them, had made an easy target for the Chinese in the darkness of Chapei. And since the North Szechuan Road between the Post Office and North Honan Road had remained illuminated and the sound of gunfire could be heard all over the Foreign Concession area, presently taxis and private motor-cars began to arrive loaded with Europeans and Americans in evening-dress who had stopped by on their way from theatres, restaurants and dinner-parties to see the fun. In a few minutes a cheerful, chattering crowd had gathered, champagne was being sipped and neighbouring café proprietors had been roused to supply hot coffee and sandwiches. The general view of this good-humoured, after-theatre audience was that the good old Japs were saving Britain, France and America the trouble of teaching the Chinese a lesson. For undoubtedly the Chinese, with their growing 'anti-foreign' and nationalistic feeling, had been getting too big for their boots. Allow them to continue in this direction and it would not be too long before the various commercial and legal privileges enjoyed by the Great Powers in China would be at an end.

Walter, still hesitating, reflected that the 'anti-foreign' feeling in China had not diminished and could still be a source of trouble. On the other hand, it was now mainly concentrated on the Japanese, who thus acted as a lightning-conductor for Europeans and Americans. This spring (of 1937) had been relatively quiet, apart from reports of increased Japanese troop movements in Manchuria. Besides, the various garrisons of the Foreign Concessions had been greatly strengthened and the Chinese were so busy fighting among themselves that the threat to Shanghai appeared negligible.

'I see no reason why you shouldn't go,' Walter said calmly, 'provided you don't do anything foolish.' And then, though not without misgivings, he settled down to await developments. He was beginning to realize that the marriage of a daughter to the right sort of young man is a matter to which a great deal of attention must be given, whether you like it or not.

4

'But don't you see, Papa dear,' said Joan, reclining on her bed in her underwear and luxuriating in the draught of the fan directly above her, 'how it could come as a shock to a nicely brought-up girl like me who has always been either at home or at school. It was *absolutely* shocking, I mean, and Mama was quite as taken aback as I was, at least she turned as white as milk and I thought she was going to faint. Her eyes got a funny look in them and even Carlos, in his absurd British clothes, looked a bit shaken. Actually, it was a good job Carlos was there because although I don't think he'd seen much of the rougher side of life either, at least his presence was reassuring. He was a *man*, at any rate, even though I know you think he's a bit ridiculous, and his clothes, a tweed suit I think it was, did tremendously inspire confidence. Anyway, without him and his tweeds and his monocle I'm quite sure that Mama would have fainted and think what problems that might have caused in the middle of I think it was called Hongkew and Mama already complaining that she was worn out because we had spent most of the afternoon trailing around the Japanese part looking for this wretched silk shop and being sent on one wild-goose chase after another and it would soon be getting dark and she wanted to get back to Bubbling Well Road where she felt safer and, anyway, I should have felt distinctly uncomfortable, particularly as all the rickshaw coolies vanished the moment they saw there was going to be trouble with Japanese soldiers arriving and, trust him! Carlos had told his chauffeur to pick us up not there, but two or three streets away. By the way, have I shown you the remains of my blisters?

'Well, no, Daddy, I agree that nothing did happen ... We weren't actually molested but we easily could have been. It was more the feeling of being, well, vulnerable. One moment we were strolling along peacefully and the next the street was full of cars and lorries and little Jap soldiers pouring out ... Well, all right then, I admit there was only one car and no lorry and only three or four soldiers poured out of it, the car, I mean, but still it was quite frightening when they started herding us in to the side of the pavement with their rifle butts and there was an officer who looked like a chimpanzee with a sword several times too long for him which he kept tripping over in the most ludicrous fashion. Until then it seemed at least *fairly* amusing, though Mama was getting apprehensive and Carlos was looking helpless and saying something like: 'What a to-do!' which frankly wasn't very helpful of him because Mummy and I could think of that much ourselves. Well, we tried to walk on and they wouldn't let us, and then Carlos suddenly stopped saying 'Bless my soul' and began to rattle away in Portuguese and got quite red in the face because he had seen that they'd blocked off the end of the street and he was afraid that he might be involved in heaven knows what, a diplomatic incident perhaps?

'Of *course*, there was no reason to be alarmed, I'm not saying there *was*! All I'm saying is that it did occur to one that the Jap soldiers could turn nasty and their bayonets looked very sharp, even though there were only three or four of them, and in the meantime the street had suddenly filled with people pressing around the doorway that the soldiers had gone into and some of them looked pretty worked up about something, so unlike the Chinese who are usually well-behaved and mind their own business (or at least they do here in Singapore, don't they?) and I'd never realized before how much smaller they are than us, because our three heads were sticking out of the crowd and it felt a bit like *Gulliver's Travels* or something.

'Anyway, then two Jap soldiers came out of the doorway again carrying someone. All I could see at first was the front man who had a very shiny leather boot gripped in the palm of each hand ... I never did see the rest of him properly, I'm glad to say, just a hand trailing along the pavement and then a glimpse of a shape with its tunic and trousers undone and a horrid mass of red stuff around its middle. He was S-shaped because of the way they were carrying him and he had a sword, too, which scraped tinnily on the ground and kept getting in the way of the man behind who had him by the armpits. But really what gave me such a shock was the Chinese girl they dragged out of the doorway and threw up against the wall ... at least, I thought then that she was Chinese because of her clothes, she was wearing a quilted tunic and black silk trousers and I'd never seen a Eurasian wear anything but European clothes, even though there was something about the colour of her hair which was a very dark red, I naturally thought that she had simply dyed it, which would have been nothing compared to the weird creatures in some of the night-clubs which Carlos had persuaded us to go to the night before. The point is that she looked as if she were about my age or even younger, and then she saw me in the crowd and that is what I found so upsetting.

'Well, it's not my fault that I've led such a sheltered life, is it? I suddenly thought that if I hadn't been English it could have been *me* up against that wall. The little officer was shouting at her and striking her. Her face had gone grey, I mean *literally* grey, the colour of porridge. It gives you a shock yourself to see someone so frightened. Afterwards I couldn't get it out of my mind. I kept thinking that if she were English she'd have only just left school like me.

'I don't know where everybody came from but by that time the street was full of people clustered in a very tight semi-circle around the Japanese officer and the girl and the other two soldiers who had carried the dead man out of the house were having trouble getting through the crowd again to reach them. And suddenly ... he was so busy screaming at the girl and slapping her face that he hadn't noticed the crowd behind him ... suddenly, they pressed forward and swallowed him and the girl up completely. There was some shoving and kicking and I think he tried to draw his sword but he was so tightly packed in with everyone else that of course he couldn't do anything. And at that moment Carlos said: "Now's our chance to beetle off" because the Japanese soldiers who had gone to the end of the street to stop people leaving were coming running back to rescue their officer, and between us Carlos and I managed to drag Mama around the corner and then he went off to find the car, and in no time we were drinking a much-needed cup of tea at the Park Hotel, all back safe and sound on Bubbling Well Road.

'Well, that was that, and even Mama gradually came to see that she had had a little adventure and felt quite pleased with herself, especially when Carlos got hold of a newspaper which said that the officer had been lured into that house by a girl and then murdered by Communists. It didn't say anything about what happened to the girl. Anyway, as I say, that was that and the holiday continued as before with sight-seeing and shopping et cetera and we went to the Moscowa nightclub which was full of the most divinely beautiful Russian girls, all aristocrats, Carlos said, I felt so jealous of them and ... thank you, Daddy dear, but I know very well that I don't though I wish I did, it must be nice ... and so on and then, then it was time to go on board again to come back to dear old Singapore and Mama had to make a fuss about the way her maid was doing the packing, just rolling things up and cramming them into our trunks and, as you know, Mama has only to set *eyes* on a boat to get sea-sick, and so it was really lucky that Carlo was there, even though he was beginning to get on our nerves a bit and we'd privately christened him "The Stage Butler" because he was always so polite and pompous, because otherwise I'd have had to mope about by myself, what with Mama groaning and swallowing tablets in her cabin and all.

'Well, we had lots of lovely dances and games on deck and simply enormous meals and one evening with some other young people we'd met we all got a bit tipsy and decided we'd have an adventure and explore the ship and prowl around in the cabin class and the third-class parts of the boat where one wasn't normally supposed to go. So we set off in a horde, the men in dinner-jackets smoking cigars and us girls in our most gorgeous evening dresses, giggling with champagne and silly jokes and some of the men were even wearing funny hats. Straight away we ran into a hitch. A locked door. Steward won't let us through. "I say, Carlos," said one of the men, "why don't you bribe the fearful little fellow while we look the other way," and we all whooped and shoved Carlos forward and being a Brazilian, of course, he was frightfully good at bribing people and in no time we were pouring through into the other classes.

'Actually, it was then that we began to realize that it was probably rather a boring idea after all to go prowling about in the other classes ... There was really nothing much to *do*! And one of the men who was in the Diplomatic ... He told me his

30

name was Sinclair Sinclair (he had a stammer and he always said it twice and I never found out whether it was really that or whether he was just repeating one of his names) and had been to Harrow and was a great sport and was something like the millionth secretary in Bangkok or somewhere ... he said: "I say, I don't know what you people think b-b-but it seems to me that the other cluh-cluh-cluh ... parts of the ship are just a tiny bit disappointing, if you get m'meaning," and he did rather say what was in everyone's mind. And someone else said: "I mean to say, it's ever so slightly *dingy*, which is not to say that it's not frightfully jolly in its way, and all that.'

'And soon we were all feeling pretty glum which was awful considering how cheerful we'd been just a few minutes before. And by that time we'd come to another locked door and almost decided to go back but Carlos, alias the Stage Butler, had already bribed somebody, sort of automatically, and he was opening the door so we went through that one, too. And that was a mistake because on the other side of that door things were really pretty grim and we found ourselves trooping through a sort of dreadful dormitory with bunks which had a ghastly stuffy smell and was full of half-naked people snoring, and Sinclair Sinclair said: "I think we must be in one of the *holds*," and one of the girls began to feel faint, but the man had locked the door behind us again and we couldn't find anybody else to open it and we were afraid the girl was going to faint or have hysterics or something. So someone said that there must be a way of getting up to the deck ... that there was a law of the sea or something which said even third-class passengers had to have a way of getting on to the deck, and so we decided to wait up on deck in the fresh air while we sent Carlos to bribe somebody to get us back to the first class. Incidentally, when I told Sinclair about the man I'd seen in Shanghai with strawberry jam coming out of his stomach he wasn't at all impressed and said he'd seen lots of things like that and that Asiatics were always killing each other. *It seems they don't mind*. It's been proved scientifically, that's what Sinclair said anyway.

'In the end we found some stairs and got up on to the deck and thank heaven because it was ghastly down there. Someone said that now he knew why it was called the bowels of the ship but nobody laughed because it was vulgar. And even on deck there were people sleeping huddled here and there, Chinese, I think, I suppose they didn't care for it down below either. It was quite warm and there was a lovely moon and a soft breeze. After crawling about down below it was super to be in the fresh air again and one of the men produced a bottle of champagne he'd brought with him and we all took a swig and felt quite merry again. And while we were waiting for Carlos to come back Sinclair Sinclair told us about a game he and his chums used to play in Paris when he was learning French (which they all have to in the Diplomatic) ... it was called *saute-clochard*: evidently all the beggars in Paris sleep in rows over the hot-air vents from the Métro in winter to keep warm and the game consisted in seeing how many you could jump over at a time: it sounds a bit heartless, I must say, but anyway, Sinclair announced that he had decided to beat the world record for *saute-Chinois* which meant the number of Chinamen he could jump over at a time and he said he'd never have a better opportunity than the present. All the other men egged him on and in a flash he'd taken off his dinner-jacket and was pounding over the deck towards a row of sleeping Chinese. Then he leaped into the air and ... oh, incidentally, I've just remembered something I wanted to ask you. When we were on the way out and stopping at ports here and there before reaching Shanghai ... I think it was the morning after we left Canton and we were steaming up a river into Wuchow in Kwangsi Province, anyway, someone pointed out a golf club on the left-hand bank and said it was definitely the most exclusive in the world and when I asked why? he said because it only had four members, the manager and assistant-manager of the Standard Oil Company and the same of the Asiatic Petroleum Company, but that's ridiculous, isn't it? A golf club with only four members. He was only joking, wasn't he? Really! Good heavens! How d'you mean, "Chinese don't play golf?" Now *you're* making fun of me. But sorry, I'll go on: Sinclair leaped into the air and must have jumped over at least a dozen Chinese who were asleep on the deck and luckily didn't land on one ... but not so luckily he did catch his foot against something, a piece of iron or a rope or I don't know what, and took a nasty fall on the deck and grazed his knees and palms and tore his trousers and made a frightful din.

'That's when some of the Chinese woke up and looked at us. I was quite near one of the lights and happened to be looking in the direction of one of the bundles when it stirred and sat up. It was the girl I'd seen in Shanghai shoved against the wall by the Jap officer. I was only a few feet away. I'd have recognized her even if her face hadn't been still all bruised and swollen. And she recognized me, too, I could see that. I smiled at her and said something like I was glad she had got away and was she all right? She didn't say anything at first and I thought, of course she wouldn't speak English and she was obviously shocked to see someone who recognized her. But then she suddenly asked me in perfect English, you know, like an educated person, if I would please not tell anyone about the business with the Jap officer because she was afraid that if people knew about it they might not give her a landing-permit in Singapore and that she was going there to get away from the Japanese. Her name was Miss Chiang, she said, Vera Chiang, and her mother had been a Russian who'd had to leave during the Revolution and then had died and she'd been educated in an American mission in Manchuria or somewhere and that she'd had nothing to do with the man who'd been killed and had never seen him before. Of course, I said I wouldn't tell anyone and I gave her your card with the firm's name on and my name and said to get in touch if she needed help getting work or something. And that, Papa dear, was all that happened except that the Stage Butler started making scenes because he was jealous of me talking to Sinclair Sinclair, but it wasn't my fault if Sinclair was more amusing and I can't bear it when men are jealous and want to have you all to themselves and keep trying to have "serious talks". In the end Mummy and I stopped calling him the Stage Butler and christened him High Dudgeon because of the way he kept stalking about the ship and sulking. Because of him it was quite a relief to see Singapore and the good old Empire Dock and there were the usual little brown boys diving for pennies, but one thing I'd never noticed before was that there were one or two quite old men diving for pennies, or would have except we preferred to throw them for the boys. And that was that except that I forgot to tell you what happened to Sinclair Sinclair. One of the Chinamen he had jumped over turned out to be a very big man and was in a fearful rage about it, and he just picked up poor Sinclair and threw him overboard and there was a terrible splash and he just vanished in the wake ... no, Daddy, you're tickling ... and was never seen again. No! Daddy, stop! You're hurting ... I'm sorry, I'll never tell a lie again! I promise!'

5

Late in September 1940 at a garden-party given by the Blacketts
for a large number of the most influential people in the Straits
a further incident occurred to disturb their tranquil lives. Joan
unexpectedly threw a glass of champagne in the face of one of
the guests. The victim was a young officer from the American
military attaché's office, Captain James Ehrendorf. Fortunately, though, he was more or less a friend of the family and
showed no sign of wanting to make a fuss.

The success of this garden-party (for which, incidentally, old
Mr Webb's birthday had been chosen) was important to both
Walter Blackett and his wife. For Walter its importance lay in
the fact that it was the forerunner of a series of social occasions planned to celebrate his firm's jubilee in the coming
year. Webb and Company had been founded in Rangoon in
1891 and its first office in Singapore had been opened shortly
afterwards. It was hoped that twelve months of rejoicing, symbolized by an occasional garden-party, firework display or exhibition of Blackett and Webb services and produce, would
culminate at the New Year of 1942 in one of those monster carnival parades so beloved of the Chinese in Singapore. The
outbreak of the war in Europe had for a time thrown these
festivities into question, but the Government, it transpired, was
anxious for propaganda purposes that they should continue in
order to combat the ceaseless anti-British ravings from Tokyo.
It was felt that nothing could better demostrate the benefits of
British rule than to recall fifty years of one of Singapore's great
merchant houses and the vast increase of wealth which it had
helped to generate in the community for the benefit of all. As
for Sylvia Blackett, this garden-party was taking place in the
absence of her only serious rivals in the Crown Colony's society
(the Governor and Lady Thomas had departed for eight months'
leave in Europe) and she believed that provided all went well
nothing more was required to consolidate her already well-
established social position.

The Blacketts lived in a magnificent old colonial house of a
kind rare in Singapore, built of brick and dating back seventy

years or more. The ranks of fat white pillars that supported its upper balconies combined with the floods of staircases that spilled out on either side of its portico like cream from the lip of a jug to give the building a classical, almost judicial appearance, and yet, at the same time, an air of ease, comfort, even sensuality. This impression was heightened by the lush and colourful gardens down into which the staircases flowed. Here fountains played on neatly mown aquamarine lawns flanked by brilliant 'flame of the forest' trees. Behind one accurately-trimmed hedge were the tennis courts, behind another the path that led to the Orchid House; in the middle of the largest expanse of lawn was the swimming pool whose blue-green water, casting jagged sparks of reflected sunlight at the white shuttered windows of the bedrooms above, seemed merely to be the lawn itself turned liquid. Beyond the pool a shady corridor of pili nut trees with white flowers or purple-black fruit depending on maturity led to an even more colourful wilderness of rare shrubs. Whoever had planted this part of the garden had tried to escape from the real, somewhat brooding vegetation of the tropics in order to create an atmosphere of colour and brilliance, the tropics of a child's imagination. Here pink crêpe myrtle and African mallow crowded beside the white narcissus flowers of kopsia and the astonishing scarlet of the Indian coral tree and behind them a silent orchestra of colours: cassia, rambutan, horse-radish, 'rose of the mountain' and mauve and white-flowered potato trees until the mind grew dizzy. Scintillating butterflies, some as big as your hand, with apricot, green or cinnamon wings lurched through the heavily perfumed air from one blossom to another. Mrs Blackett, however, no longer ventured into this part of the garden despite the brightness and colour. She found herself sickened by the sweet, heavy smell of the blossoms. Besides, the grounds of the Mayfair Rubber Company were adjacent to this brilliant, leafy grove and she was afraid that she might catch a glimpse of old Mr Webb prowling about naked, pruning his roses with secateurs or, for that matter, doing heaven knows what.

Even before Joan threw the wine at Captain Ehrendorf Mrs Blackett had become aware that she would have to deploy all her social skills to avoid the sort of disaster that is talked about for years in a place like Singapore: this was because Walter, without consulting her, had invited General Bond, the General Officer Commanding, Singapore, while she herself, without consulting Walter, had invited Air-Marshal Babington, the Air Officer Commanding, Far East. Rumours about the rivalry of these two officers had been percolating for some time in the Colony. The open dislike which the General showed for the Air-Marshal was matched only by that which the latter showed towards the former, and on each side was duly reflected, as in a hall of mirrors, by the hordes of aides and subordinate officers who devoted themselves to aping their respective commanders. Air-Marshal Babington, asserted the gossips at the various 'long bars' that sprinkled the city, was filled with envy by the fact that his rival, as GOC Singapore an automatic member of the Legislative Assembly, should have the right to be called 'His Excellency' which he himself did not, although the frontiers of his own fiefdom of the 'Far East' lay infinitely more distant.

Now one of these gentlemen was chatting with his staff officers near the tennis courts while the other, surrounded by his subordinates, held court near the Orchid House, each still ignorant of the presence at the garden-party of the other. It was clear that it would take a miracle to prevent their meeting. Ah, Mrs Blackett recalled with remorse the rule that she had made many years ago and hitherto strictly observed, to the effect that she would not have military men in her house. In her house! On account of the outbreak of war in Europe she had weakened to the extent of putting a literal interpretation on this rule, allowing them into the garden. How she wished she had not! And now, in addition, it looked as if her daughter were about to make a scene.

Mrs Blackett had been conversing pleasantly with a member of the Legislative Assembly. This gentleman had been describing to her how the Japanese were moving into northern Indo-China and the French were not resisting. Why weren't they resisting? she had enquired politely, though really more preoccupied with the question of whether Air-Marshal Babington would move into the Orchid Garden. Because, he explained, of pressure on the Vichy Government by the Germans. And then, all of a sudden, Joan had thrown champagne into the face of one of the guests.

'The Greater East Asia Co-Prosperity Sphere? What's that?' cried Mrs Blackett in horror. Startled, the gentleman explained that it was in the natue of a propaganda exercise by the Japanese who wanted to establish economic dominion over various countries in the Far East.

'Oh,' said Mrs Blackett, recovering her composure.

Joan for some reason was smiling. She had even been smiling, though rather tensely, as she threw her wine into Captain Ehrendorf's face. There was not, it must be admitted, a great deal left in her glass, but there was enough to rinse his handsome smiling features, collect in drips on his chin and spatter his fawn-coloured uniform with darker spots. He only stopped smiling for a moment and then went on smiling as before, though he looked surprised. He took a handkerchief from his pocket and dried his face carefully, patting with particular attention the thin moustache on his upper lip. With his other hand he took Joan gently by the arm and drew her a little deeper into the blue shadow of the 'flame of the forest' tree beneath which they had been standing. As luck would have it, they had been on the fringe of the lawn and only Mrs Blackett herself appeared to have noticed. Joan shook herself free of Captain Ehrendorf's guiding hand and they came to rest again.

'If you're interested in Indo-China,' said Mrs Blackett brightly but firmly to the gentleman from the Legislative Assembly, 'you must have a word with François Dupigny, who escaped from there only the other day with Général Catroux ... and neither of them with a stitch of clothing. You'll find him by the tennis court.' With that, leaving the gentleman looking rather baffled, she moved away towards the 'flame of the forest'.

As she approached, she found Joan and Ehrendorf chatting quite naturally about the band, Sammy and his Rhythmic Rascals, which could be heard playing not far away beside the swimming pool. This band, a daring innovation thought up by her son, Monty, had also caused her some anxiety for she was afraid that it might be thought vulgar. Captain Ehrendorf, the skin around his eyes crinkling into an attractive smile, assured her that it was a great succcess and that he believed he had even seen General Bond's highly-polished shoe tapping to the rhythm. One thing was for sure: the General had moved nearer to the pool ... but that might be because he had an eye for the bathing beauties who swooped and tumbled like dolphins in the blue-green water beneath the dais set up for the band; it had been Monty's idea, too, that the physically attractive younger guests should be invited to bathe. Mrs Blackett, aghast, for this was the first intimation she had had that General Bond had left the comparative safety of the Orchid Garden, glanced towards the band whose metal instruments winked with painful brightness in the late afternoon sunlight, to see four Chinese saxophonists in scarlet blazers and white trousers rise as one man from the back row, play a few bars and sink back again. 'I must find Walter quickly,' she thought. At the same time she wondered whether she might not have imagined the scene between Joan and Ehrendorf. But a glance at Ehrendorf's uniform was enough to tell her that she had not: there were still a number of dark spots on the light fabric though they were fading rapidly in the heat.

'"A nightingale sang in Berkeley Square,"' crooned four of the Rhythmic Rascals, their arms on each other's shoulders and their four heads very close to the microphone. '"I know 'cos I was there ..."'

Mrs Blackett noticed with relief that Walter was moving among the guests not far from the pool. 'Are you *sure* people won't find them vulgar?' she asked distractedly, and again the young people were obliged to reassure her.

'She did *what* to Jim Ehrendorf?' demanded Walter a few minutes later. He had left the pool and taken up a vantage point at the balustrade where the twin flights of stone steps met beneath the portico. From here he had been watching sombrely for some time as General Bond and his staff officers like a small flock of sheep, swagger-sticks under their arms, browsed peacefully on cocktails nearer and nearer to where Air-Marshal Babington and his pack of wolves lay in wait by the tennis courts.

'I can see I shall have to give that young lady a talking to!' But Walter's eye remained on the browsing officers below.

Walter, as it happened, knew a little more than most people in Singapore about the cause of friction between the two commanders. The question that separated them was this. How should Malaya be defended and above all, by whom? Air-Marshal Babington, imbued with the fanatical doctrines of the Air Ministry, considered that only the RAF could handle the task. General Bond believed, on the other hand, as any red-blooded Army man would, that rather than trust to aeroplanes, whose effectiveness was conjectural, the Army should deal with the matter. And now, as ill-luck would have it, both sides of this dispute were represented at his garden-party!

'Did you ask her what the devil she thought she was doing, throwing wine at our guests?' demanded Walter with a scowl which also served to discourage the Bishop of Singapore who was smiling his greeting from the lawn below and perhaps

38

contemplating an approach.

'You know how headstrong Joan is. She's highly strung like me.' Mrs Blackett shrugged her shoulders helplessly.

'Singapore's too small to have her carrying on like that,' grumbled Walter. 'Of course, it may not mean anything.' All the same, it was worrying. Why had she done it?

He had gradually come to see that his early fears, lest Joan should insist on marrying someone unsuitable, had been unfounded. She did not readily attach herself to the men who courted her: he need not have worried about the absurd Carlos. Indeed this, he was now beginning to realize, was just the trouble. She had shown herself to be erratic and unpredictable in her dealings with the eligible young men of the Colony of whom there were, in any case, precious few. The truth was that Walter had not been surprised to learn that Joan had thrown champagne into young Ehrendorf's face (not that he was very much more suitable than Carlos had been, agreeable fellow though he was). In the past three years, while she was shedding the last traces of the schoolgirl he loved and was imperceptibly changing into a young adult, there had been a number of incidents, trivial in themselves but collectively disturbing. One lovelorn young planter she had even invited to step fully-dressed into the swimming pool. He had done so but it had not advanced his cause. Undoubtedly, the marriage of a daughter is something to which a great deal of attention must be given, like it or not.

The band had stopped playing for the moment and his wife had left his side to ask the Rhythmic Rascals if they would mind not emptying the saliva from their musical instruments into the swimming pool. A cloud had passed over the sun and though it grew no cooler a momentary chill seemed to affect the garden-party, an ominous sensation which was, perhaps, only in Walter's own mind.

6

Walter, elbows planted on the stone balustrade, chin in hand, gazed moodily down over his chattering guests, half musing on the marriage prospects of his daughter, half hypnotized by the chicken-wire reflections of sunlight on the surface of the pool, still gently heaving although the last of the bathing beauties, wrapped in a bathrobe and escorted by Monty, was already retreating in the direction of the changing pavilion. Walter himself seldom swam, never in public; he was inclined to be sensitive about the ridge of hairs, so thick that they almost amounted to bristles, which for some odd reason had decided to grow over his vertebrae in a thin line stretching from his neck to the base of his spine. These bristles had a tendency to rise when he was angry and sometimes, even, in moments of conjugal intimacy. His wife had once confided in him that every night of their honeymoon she had been visited by a dream in which she had been led by a boar into the depths of a forest; there on a carpet of leaves, marooned in loneliness, she had been mounted by the animal in the grunt-filled silence of the trees. Walter, at the time, had merely shrugged his shoulders, but his feelings had been hurt by his wife's dream. True, he could have enjoyed a swim with his friends if he had consented to wear an old-fashioned swimming costume with neck and sleeves instead of scanty, all-too-revealing shoulder straps. But Walter was sensitive also about his clothing.

A camera clicked. Walter turned away sharply, aware that his photograph had just been taken. He beckoned to a tall, rather anxious-looking man in his fifties who happened to be passing. This man, whose name was Major Brendan Archer, had been introduced to the Blacketts three or four years earlier by the same François Dupigny who had given Walter such valuable advice on how to detach Joan from her unsuitable young man. Major Archer, who though a civilian had kept his rank as a souvenir, Walter supposed, of the Great War, had become friendly with the Blacketts and with old Mr Webb, too. The old gentleman has responded to the Major's air of rather gloomy integrity, had even paid him the unusual compliment of offering him a partnership in the Mayfair Rubber Company, his plaything, though more likely because he wanted someone to talk to than because there was any serious work to be done. The Major, in any event, had presumably had nothing better in mind and presently had been installed in a little bungalow on the other side of the road. Walter approved of this arrangement. The Major was a discreet and sensible fellow, though sadly lacking in ambition. He was just the man to keep an eye on old Mr Webb who was showing signs of becoming increasingly odd as the years advanced. Nor was it simply vegetarianism and a habit of pruning his roses stark naked: Mr Webb now sometimes invited young Chinese of both sexes for nude physical training and gymnastics 'to build up their bodies'. There was nothing sordid or secretive about this, however, although Walter had heard that the few young women whom Mr Webb had managed to conscript had only agreed to build up their bodies as a result of financial incentives. Mr Webb simply believed that if China were ever to rise again and redeem itself from the shattered and decadent nation it had become, it would be thanks to mental and physical alertness and a generous helping of vegetables. Still, it was sad to see him go like this, and unsettling, if only because Mr Webb still owned a considerable proportion of the company's equity. Walter could not be altogether confident that Mr Webb would not make some drastic provisions in his will following the unfortunate estrangement with his son, Matthew. It was worrying. It would have to be watched. The Major would help in the watching.

Walter and the Major began to pace up and down in the shade of the portico discussing the progress of the war in Europe; at the same time Walter kept an eye on his guests in case of trouble. Presently the conversation turned to the Blackett and Webb jubilee celebrations: Walter wanted to involve the Major more deeply in the planning of the carnival parade in which the celebrations would reach their climax. The Major was just the sort of conscientious individual with time on his hands who can usually be relied upon to volunteer for such things, charity balls, picnics in aid of orphans, Buy-a-Bomber-for-Britain Funds and so forth. But today for some reason he seemed reluctant to step forward.

The jubilee of a great merchant house like Blackett and Webb is by no means as easy to celebrate as you might think. The choice of the form the celebrations should take is a delicate matter and certainly it was one which had greatly exercised the minds of Walter and his board of directors. They had tried to find precedents in the business life of Singapore but with little success: such is the penalty for leading the field, you have nobody to imitate. The festivities to mark the royal jubilee in 1935 had been recalled. On that occasion every bank in Singapore had wrapped its pillars in red, white and blue. Even the Yokohama Specie Bank on the corner of Battery Road next to Robinson's, Walter remembered, had been swagged in

Union Jacks. For the royal jubilee the RAF had lent a hand: as a demonstration they had bombed and set ablaze a construction on the *padang*. Perhaps the RAF could be persuaded to bomb something for Blackett and Webb?

But in the end these ambitious projects had had to be abandoned, because of the war in Europe. It would hardly have been suitable to hold elaborate celebrations when London shareholders were having to fight for their lives. And so they had been obliged to fall back on garden-parties, fireworks and the carnival parade. It was the latter, it seemed to Walter and his board, which offered most opportunity for doing something out of the ordinary, something which people would remember in Singapore, and which would be, as it were, the apotheosis of trade and the British tradition in the Colony combining for the betterment of all races.

In due course a theme for the parade had been found: 'Continuity in Prosperity'. The Government, harassed by Japanese propaganda to the effect that the white man was exploiting his Asiatic subjects as if they were slaves, had responded enthusiastically and had even ventured to suggest that not only Chinese should take part, but other races too. If a few Europeans were to take part the parade would have less the appearance of a performance by slaves to amuse their masters; nor should the Europeans be confined to regal or magnificent rôles, sitting on thrones and so forth: they should not shrink, if required, from the dusty anonymity of the dragon's feet. It was, however, accepted that if old Mr Webb could be persuaded to take part, he should be carried on the ultimate float sitting on the throne of Prosperity. For who better than Mr Webb, the founder of the company, could personify Continuity in his own bony, dignified frame?

In his mind's eye Walter saw a splendid procession of dragons, effigies and floats representing the commercial successes of Blackett and Webb winding through Chinatown to the thump of brass bands and the crackle of fireworks, then up the hill after dark carrying flaring torches to file past Government House where Sir Shenton Thomas would take the salute from the verandah. A Roman triumph indeed! And yet it had to be admitted that so far the response of those Europeans he had approached to take part in a democratic 'parade of all nations' had not been encouraging. Not that Walter would have expected them to leap at the opportunity ... but given the fact that there was a war on, in Europe if not out

42

here, one might have expected a little more support. Walter paused for a moment, having explained this to the Major, in order to give him time to volunteer either for the organizing committee or for the parade itself. But the Major, though he looked oppressed, contented himself with clearing his throat and mutely fingering his moustache.

'Of course, the presence of Europeans in the parade isn't absolutely necessary. We could probably make do with Eurasians, perhaps with chalk on their faces in a pinch. After all, such a parade deals in symbols, not in the real thing. We *do* need Europeans to help in the organization, though.' Again Walter paused and again the Major fingered his moustache and hung back.

'Absolutely indispensable,' declared Walter vigorously, sensing that the Major was weakening.

'Well, I suppose ...' the Major began reluctantly. But at this moment he was saved by a Eurasian newspaper reporter in an ill-fitting white suit who presented himself to interview Walter about his firm. Notebook and pencil in hand the reporter, who was from the *Straits Times*, fell into step with the two men as they paced up and down. Walter, abandoning for the moment his pursuit of the Major, began discoursing fluently on the early days of the company.

When Walter had assumed full command of Blackett and Webb in 1930 he had been faced with grave difficulties, given the Depression. He himself believed that it was precisely the catastrophic decline in business activity which had given him the opportunity to display his ability.

'When trade is booming,' he explained, more to the Major than to the reporter, 'anyone can make money for the simple reason that most things you do turn out to be right. It takes a depression to show you what's wrong with your business.'

'Chairman overcomes early snags,' wrote the young man from the *Straits Times* in his notebook without breaking his stride.

Because of the haphazard way in which Blackett and Webb had grown up the complexity of the business which Walter had to prevent from foundering was such as to numb the mind of an ordinary mortal. But Walter made light of it, insisting that his partner's early exploits should be regarded as the firm's golden age. When old Mr Webb had started out in business in 1890 it had been simply as a merchant in tropical produce. Rice, tea, copra, spices, pineapples, even opium had passed through his hands in those early days. And human beings, too, of course, for like everyone else he had shipped coolies from South China to Malaya and Java, usually as deck cargo. But his principal concern had been with the rice trade in Burma. There, thanks to an agreement with the other Rangoon merchants to keep down the prices paid to the peasants, vast profits were to be made. This trade was not without risk, however, what with forward contracts to fill and a limited supply of shipping.

'Varied trade gets firm off to flying start,' scribbled the reporter.

'Yes, he's the man you should be talking to,' declared Walter as his eye fell on old Mr Webb in the distance: he was sitting bolt upright in the shade over by the Orchid Garden, his back still as straight as a ramrod despite his years. Over there the younger executives of Blackett and Webb approached him in turn, evidently according to some rota system of their own, to exchange a few remarks with him. On occasion, when a young man's name was shouted into his ear, he would reply grimly: 'Knew your father well.' And the faintest twinkle would appear in his steely eyes. At a little distance a cadaverous individual with shoulders so rounded that they amounted, at least in Walter's view, to the beginnings of a hump, was observing these ritual respects with derision from behind a flowering shrub. This was the odious, crafty Solomon Langfield, chairman of the rival firm of Langfield and Bowser Limited. Though Walter could not abide old Langfield he was nevertheless pleased that he had accepted the invitation to attend: evidently Langfield's curiosity had got the better of his desire to ignore the opening of Blackett and Webb's jubilee celebrations, which happened to fall a year or two before his own. Having permitted himself to pause for a moment to sample the pleasure of Langfield's company, Walter returned to the consideration of his former partner, for he was fond of recalling the skill with which old Mr Webb had managed his business in those pioneering days when disaster had seemed always to be just round the corner. In years, for example, when a famine occurred in Bengal, as they did periodically, the peasants in Burma could hold back their crops, secure in the knowledge that the merchants would have to pay what they asked or default on their shipping contracts. Gradually, though, the situation for the merchants had improved. Chettyar moneylenders from India had penetrated the rice-growing delta, entangling the peasants in debt and bringing them to the point where they could no longer hold back their crops for higher prices even when there was a shortage on the market.

At Walter's side the Major had a gloomy expression. He did not like to hear of people being entangled in debt, even for the best of reasons. But Walter, warming to his task, went on: 'You see, the Chettyar money-lenders in Burma and, to a lesser extent, here in Malaya, too, acted on the peasants like saddle-soap on leather. They softened them up for us. Of course, some of the Chetties became rivals in the milling of crops but that couldn't be helped. Without them to get the peasants used to dealing in cash (which, of course, in practice meant tricking them into debts they would have to pay up) rather than in barter of produce the merchants would have all been in the poorhouse, including Mr Webb. One bad crop with forward contracts to fill!' And Walter made his blue eyes bulge with mock horror.

'Pliable peasants bring bulls into rice-market!'

'But that's dreadful,' muttered the Major. 'I mean to say, well, I had no idea ...'

It had taken some time before the Burmese peasants were altogether subdued but by about 1893 the Rangoon merchants had their hands on the key that would lock up the market: namely, control of the rice-mills throughout the country.

'Instantly,' explained Walter, making a chopping gesture with the flat of his hand, 'they cut the price of paddy in half. In 1892 they paid 127 rupees: in 1893 only 77 rupees. How's that for a grip on the market?'

As a result of this forcing down of the price the peasants, ruined by their thousands, had been obliged to leave the land. This was hard luck on the peasants since they had as a rule worked strenuously to clear it from the jungle, but it did have one further advantage, at least for Mr Webb and his fellow merchants. Cheaper methods could now be introduced by the use of seasonal workers, the trusty 'division of labour' which, the Major must agree, had conferred such benefits in prosperity on mankind. To put it bluntly, you no longer had to support a man and his family all year round, you could now bring him in to do a specific job like planting or harvesting. The traditional village communities were broken up and the Burmese had to learn to travel about looking for seasonal or coolie work, from the producer's point of view a much more efficient and much cheaper system. The rice-growing delta had been turned into what someone called "a factory without chimneys",' summed up Walter with satisfaction, wondering what ailed the Major who was looking more chagrined than ever.

'Modern methods increase output. Peasants take to travel.'

'But that's tragic,' burst out the Major unable to contain his indignation. 'It's disgraceful.'

Walter, however, paid no attention to him for that had not been the end of the story, by any means. Even in later years problems still used to crop up for the merchants. The Burmese, certainly, had been largely reduced to the status of coolies by the turn of the century, but Indians and Chinese, who understood western business methods better, had taken to setting up their own mills in the interior of the country and milling rice for export, thereby weakening the monopoly of the big European mills in Rangoon. When in 1920 Blackett and Webb and the other European millers tried as usual to keep the price of paddy down they failed and had to pay up ('Those damned forward sales again!'). So the following year Blackett and Webb had joined the other three main European houses in the notorious Bullinger Pool to harmonize their buying and selling policies.

'Well, that was nothing new. But someone ... don't ask me who! ... used his influence with the railway company to make the freight charges for moving milled rice more expensive than for moving paddy.' Walter chuckled with pleasure at this recollection of twenty years ago. 'Result? The mills in the interior could no longer compete with Rangoon in the export trade. We were back on Easy Street!' The Major muttered inaudibly, clasping his brow.

'What's that you say, Major! Complaints? Of course there were complaints! There always are. Nationalists brought it up in the Legislature in 1929. But that was nearly ten years later and when they held an enquiry it didn't get anywhere. Besides, by that time world prices had collapsed and people had more important things to worry about.'

'Rice sleuths' freight enquiry comes off rails,' scribbled the reporter fluently, stifling a yawn. How had Blackett and Webb come to be involved in rubber? He had to repeat his question because Walter was eyeing his guests to make sure that all was still going smoothly.

The Rhythmic Rascals had started playing once more: this time it was 'Run, Rabbit, Run'. Down below, not far from the pool, one of the browsing military men stiffened for a moment, nose in the air, as if scenting RAF officers on the breeze. But Babington and his men were still safely downwind in the direction of the tennis courts. A moment later he resumed his drinking and chatting, though a shade more warily than before; white-coated waiters passed among the little flock carrying trays of champagne or *pahits*. Joan and Ehrendorf were still standing together, a little way apart from the other guests. Joan had just held out her glass to a waiter carrying a champagne bottle wrapped in a white napkin. Was it Walter's imagination or did Ehrendorf flinch away slightly as she made a move to raise it to her lips?

It was certainly true that rice, explained Walter, turning back to his companions, was only one of many kinds of tropical produce to be handled by Blackett and Webb when the partnership had first been formed. But rubber rapidly became the most important. The years of old Mr Webb's active business life, from about 1880 to 1930, had witnessed a prodigious exporting of capital from Britain to the colonial Empire: this capital's rôle was to take advantage of the high investment returns attending the plentiful supply of land and, above all, cheap labour in the colonies. Already before the Great War Mr Webb had begun to acquire plantations in order to be sure of a steady supply of the various commodities in which he traded. As it turned out, nobody was in a better position to take advantage of the rubber boom which came with the motor-car than a merchant with a good reputation, like Mr Webb whose integrity was beyond question and whose firm was already accustomed to administering plantations. Such a merchant house, instead of risking its own resources (this was a new industry: demand might fluctuate), could tap that huge reservoir of silver which had accumulated in Britain thanks to the Industrial Revolution and which had since grown stagnant. After that, the firm had grown rapidly. The next years had been spent starting plantations or acquiring those started by other people and floating them in London as rubber companies, using Blackett and Webb's reputation and its participation in the issues to attract investors. In due course, as a result, they had found themselves managing-agents of a considerable number of small rubber companies.

'Expanding rubber boom stretches firm's own resources despite elastic demand!' wrote the reporter, warming to his task.

By the early twenties Blackett and Webb had been in a

position to channel business to European companies in return for being made their sole Singapore agents. Shipping lines interested in the freight trade accompanying the rubber boom appointed Blackett and Webb their agents in the Far East. Insurance companies, manufacturers of this and that hoping to find a market in Malaya or the Dutch East Indies, engineering and construction firms looking for contracts ... In no time they were agents for all sorts of business radiating from Singapore over a vast area in every direction, a commercial grip on land and labour of enormous potential resources. And everything, except perhaps for pineapples and the entrepôt business, had flourished. Blackett and Webb could look back with satisfaction on their fifty years of service ∙to the community.

'What's your name, son?'

'Malcolm, sir.'

'Well, you're a bright lad, Malcolm,' said Walter with magnanimity. 'Work hard and you'll get on in life.'

'Thank you, sir.'

The music had come to a stop once more. The Rhythmic Rascals, exhausted by their efforts in the humid heat, were sitting back enjoying a rest. Walter had just noticed something rather odd: old Mr Webb, seated by himself in the shade and temporarily deserted by young executives, was no longer sitting bolt upright as was his custom, indeed he was slumped rather pathetically. Could it be that the old fellow had had too much to drink on this day of celebration? But Walter had never known him to touch alcohol. More likely he was simply too tired to make the effort when he was by himself. Still, he should not have been left alone, today especially.

Walter left the Major and was about to join his former partner when he realized that events elsewhere were beginning to take a disastrous course. One of the staff officers had just spoken to General Bond, evidently suggesting that they should go and have a look at the tennis, for the General and his flock began to stride out firmly in that direction. But they were still some yards away when Air-Marshal Babington and his men, clearly having just made a similar decision to visit the Orchid Garden, put in a sudden appearance from behind the hedge. The two rival groups stopped and glared at each other, bristling.

'Oh Lord!' muttered Walter, hurrying to intercept them.

But again he was diverted, this time by an urgent shout from one of the servants. He was just in time to see old Mr Webb topple out of his chair and roll over on the lawn. At the same moment the first heavy drops of a providential shower of rain began to patter on the lawn and make rings in the pool, scattering the guests who still had not noticed old Mr Webb. The guests took cover, laughing, leaving Walter and the Major, assisted by some alarmed servants, to carry the old gentleman into the house.

'Oh no! Not a death as well!' groaned Mrs Blackett to herself. It was one of those days. Her party had not been a success.

7

Was Mr Webb actually dead or not? It was very hard to say at first. The scurrying cortège that was carrying him into the house made its way, in order not to alarm the other guests, behind the refreshment tent which had been set up on the lawn. From there it made a quick dash for a side door normally used by the servants. Mr Webb's body was extraordinarily light despite its length: the old capitalist was really nothing but skin and bone. The Major had surrendered his share of it to one of the 'boys' and hurried ahead to telephone for an ambulance.

Returning presently to the drawing-room he found that Mr Webb, who was after all still breathing, had been laid horizontal on a sofa which by chance stood so close to the vertical portrait of himself that the heavy shoes he was wearing came within a few inches of the identical shoes in the painting. This coincidence gave the Major the curious feeling that he was looking at a toy soldier that had just fallen over. He rejected this impression immediately, however, and filled with concern, for he was genuinely fond of the old man, he hastened forward to where Walter was unlacing the three-dimensional shoes with respect and taking them off the ancient feet. The Major, determined to be helpful, loosened the old gentleman's stiff collar and then hurried away once more to see if he could find a doctor among the guests.

Presently, though, an ambulance arrived and events took their course. The old fellow had had a serious stroke and was not expected to survive for very long. Walter gloomily rejoined the garden-party. It was not worth sending people home, even if he had had a mind to: they were beginning to go already. By half-past seven the garden was quiet. The 'boys' had finished the task of clearing up after the guests, the caterers had struck their tents, the band had moved on to its evening assignment. Where the rest of his family had got to, Walter had no idea. He suspected his wife had gone to lie down in her bedroom. Having told one of the 'boys' to send Joan to him, he himself retired to brood in his dressing-room from where he had a view over the now peaceful garden.

This tiny, high-ceilinged room was the one place, his family and servants knew, where he must never be disturbed without permission, for it was here perched on the arm of an old leather armchair by the window that he did his thinking. This habit of sitting always in the same place had given the dull leather that covered the chair a deep polish on the arm nearest the window. Teak drawers with gleaming brass fittings, their size according to whether they contained shirts, or collars, or handkerchieves, rose in tiers around him. Beside the door in an alcove stood a vast Edwardian washbasin, also with brass fittings and so deep, so capacious that one could have bathed a spaniel, say, or a child in it, submerging them without difficulty.

Now that the garden-party had come to its sad end Walter had a good deal to brood over and not much time in which to do it. Soon more guests would be arriving, or at least he supposed that they would, unless they were forestalled by news of Mr Webb's stroke. Below in the dining-room eighty places had been laid in silver cutlery on a glistening white table-cloth. A dinner-party had been organized as a preview of Blackett and Webb's jubilee celebrations, to mark the opening of the campaign, as it were, which would reach its climax in the great parade scheduled for New Year's Day 1942. To this party the innermost circle of Singapore's business and governmental community had been invited to offer their congratulations to himself and, in particular, to old Mr Webb whose birthday it was. Walter had instructed his secretary to telephone as many of the dinner-guests as he could find, cancelling the engagement. But undoubtedly at this last minute it would be impossible to locate them all. Well, so much the worse. Those

50

who came would be received and fed. If there were only a few he could leave Monty to take care of them. It would be good practice for him.

Walter gazed out at the insects swirling around the lights by the swimming pool, listening to the tropical night which like some great machine turning over had begun its humming, whirring and clicking, steadily growing in volume as the darkness deepened. And as he listened, he brooded, not on his partner's imminent death (he would think about that presently) but on his daughter's marriage. Walter was considered, and considered himself, fond of his children. But the truth was that he had been disappointed when, after a promising start with Monty, his wife had given him only two daughters, Joan and little Kate. If he had had more sons what could he not have done with Blackett and Webb! He loved his daughters, of course, but he had always assumed them to be a liability. And he had been unable to prevent himself making a bitter comparison between his own family and the Firestones'. It seemed to him perfectly unjust that Harvey Firestone should not only have set up such an effective business but should, in addition, have engendered five energetic sons in his own image with which to expand it. At one time Walter had entertained kindly thoughts of the Firestones and had even sent an occasional Christmas card to their family farm in Ohio. But relations between producers and manufacturers had been soured by the international rubber restriction agreement set up by the British and Dutch rubber producers to stabilize the price. Firestone and the American consumers had launched a political counter-attack ... and now, though there was already too much of the stuff being grown, they had put great areas of Liberia under rubber! What could you do with such people!

'Harvey's trouble was that he was drunk with his own power and just because he used to go camping with the President, who was only a flea-bitten politician anyway!'

Sons are an asset, daughters a liability. This had always been, in Walter's view, axiomatic. But there remained, nevertheless, one time-honoured way in which a daughter could prove an asset: namely, by her marriage. By a judicious match she could accomplish more, at one stroke, than any number of sons might accomplish in a lifetime. What might not have been achieved if Joan had appealed to one of the young Firestones? Walter shrugged the thought away dejectedly: he must not torment himself with such fantasies.

In the past three years a considerable change had come over Joan. She had grown more mature. Above all, she had come to take a serious interest in the business, much more interest than Monty, as it happened. On one or two occasions when Walter had been in need of assistance in some delicate and confidential matter which he did not care to reveal even to his closest colleagues, Joan had done useful work for him, showing a natural grasp of the important issues which he could not help but find gratifying. A sense of reality had come to replace the romantic nonsense she had brought back from her finishing school. Walter now dared to hope that she would no longer find a marriage soundly based on commercial logic quite so distasteful. What worried him, though, was this throwing of wine into young men's faces and invitations to them to step fully-clothed into swimming pools. Nor, it must be admitted, had she as yet shown much interest in the right sort of young man ... or old man, for that matter.

There had, Walter reflected as he left his seat by the window and began dressing for a dinner which he hoped would not take place, only been one merchant's son who had appeared to take her fancy. That had been young Langfield of Langfield and Bowser Limited, heir to a merchant house neither bigger nor smaller than Blackett and Webb. You might wonder who could have been more suitable. Not so. The Langfields were the one family in business in the Straits with whom Walter would have no dealings (none, at least, that he could decently avoid, for he found himself obliged now and then to sit with a Langfield on this or that Government committee). What jubilation there would be among the Langfields when they learned of the disastrous outcome of the garden-party! It had been reported back to Walter that they had already been at work in Singapore insidiously suggesting that there was something vulgar about starting jubilee celebrations more than a year before the date of commemoration. Walter's brows gathered at the thought of the unctuous, salt-rubbing letter of regret which he would receive from old Solomon Langfield in the morning. The old fox was probably hunched over it at this very moment, savouring its hypocritical phrases. He tugged angrily at the butterfly wings of his tie and the knot shrank to the size of a pebble. There was a knock on the door and Joan came in.

'You wanted to see me?' She stopped short at the sight of

her father's scowling face, and then came forward and took his arm: 'Poor Daddy, you must be upset about Mr Webb. I forgot what a blow it must be after all these years.'

'Eh? What? Oh yes, of course, it does come as a bit of a shock. He was certainly a fine man and the place won't seem the same without him. Not that he's dead yet, of course. Hm, but that's not why I wanted to see you, Joan ... What's this your mother tells me about you throwing wine at Jim Ehrendorf?'

Joan smiled. 'Has Mother been making a fuss? It was nothing. Really. He was just getting on my nerves. I'd already forgotten about it.'

'But he's a nice fellow,' said Walter, looking at his daughter in surprise. 'Everyone likes him, even though he *is* American. And he's the least *American* American I know. And there's no one more cultured and with better manners. I can't see why you want to throw wine in his face.'

Joan looked out of the window for a moment with a sly, half malicious, half amused expression on her face which Walter had not seen before. She shrugged. 'I don't know why, myself. I suppose I wanted to see what he would do, whether he would get angry or something. He didn't, of course. He's always so reasonable.' She added with a laugh: 'Even if I kicked his shins he still wouldn't do anything, except perhaps look rather pained and forgiving.'

'Well, please don't kick his shins at my garden-parties, or do anything else to him, if it comes to that. We have a position to keep up in Singapore. Promise?'

Joan nodded and smiled, peering curiously at her father at the same time, or rather at his neck. 'What have you done to your tie, Daddy? It looks most peculiar. Here, let me tie it again for you. I'm expert at tying men's bow-ties. I've had to practise so much on Monty.'

'All right, but I shall sit down if you don't mind.' He held his chin up, gazing at the ceiling while Joan's fingers played deftly about his neck. 'There was something else I wanted to mention. Have you seen Miss Chiang recently? Does she still have a room at the Mayfair? I meant to ask the Major.'

Vera Chiang was the Eurasian girl whom Joan had seen arrested by the Japanese in Shanghai three years earlier and then met again on the boat to Singapore. Nothing had been heard of her for a couple of years during which Joan had wondered idly once or twice what had become of her ... but after all she was just another tiny drop in the flood of Chinese immigrants, legal and illegal, who had been pouring into the Straits Settlements now for three decades. Then some nine months earlier Walter had been visited at his office on Collyer Quay by an official of the Chinese Protectorate. A young Eurasian woman, picked up in connection with the General Labour Union-inspired strike at the Singapore Harbour Board and faced with a deportation order, had given his name and Joan's as credentials. As there was no direct evidence to implicate her personally with the Communist-infiltrated General Labour Union's subversive campaign, and as the name of Blackett carried considerable weight in the Colony, it had been decided not to proceed with the deportation order if the Blacketts were prepared to vouch for her.

Walter had little appetite for vouching for people, even former employees: at best, it was a waste of time, at worst, a source of future trouble. Moreover, he himself did not know the girl and Joan had long since lost interest in her. Above all, he had a great deal of work to do and, as ill luck would have it, old Mr Webb had chosen that particular day to make one of his rare ceremonial visits to Collyer Quay and for the past hour had been sitting in Walter's office, wasting his valuable time. If Walter had been by himself he would have dismissed the matter in a moment: as it was, for form's sake and the benefit of Mr Webb who seemed to be taking an interest in it, Walter had felt obliged to ask if anything else was known about her. Not a great deal, it transpired. She had been the friend or concubine of a Communist sympathizer, deported the year before to an uncertain fate at Chungking; despite the rapprochement between the Communist and the Kuomintang he had most likely been done away with by the latter. Since then Miss Chiang had been scraping a living as a taxi-dancer or, more likely, as a casual prostitute and bar-girl, not a profitable profession to follow these days. The most suspicious thing about Miss Chiang, the man from the Protectorate had declared becoming voluble and oddly intense ('Who on earth is this chump and why must he come and waste my time?' Walter asked himself sourly), was that she was extremely well-educated and spoke excellent English! Walter, who had heard enough, had risen impatiently to escort the fellow to the door, saying that, in the circumstances, he did not think . . .

Walter had been conscious for some time that Mr Webb

was shifting uneasily in his chair but at this point the old chap had suddenly burst out in anger: 'And why shouldn't she be educated? Eh? Tell me that! How will the Chinese ever pull themselves together unless they build up their minds and bodies? Tell me! And you can stop grinning like that, too. I was in this Colony before you were born!'

The old man had stood up, white with anger. The man from the Protectorate, taken aback by this sudden outburst, muttered: 'When they're educated it can mean that they're Comintern agents, that's all I meant,' but at the same time his eyes had narrowed suspiciously, as if he were wondering whether Mr Webb, too, might not be a Comintern agent.

'Well, I shall vouch for her if Blackett won't! Here's my card. Webb's the name. Send her to me if she needs a job. I'll give her one. And another thing, any more impertinence and I shall be in touch with your superior. The first thing you have to learn is to take your hands out of your pockets when you are talking to someone.' With that, Mr Webb had stalked out of the office, leaving the man from the Protectorate, (whose name was Smith, it turned out) with his hands half out of his pockets, licking his lips in an odd sort of way, and grinning at Walter. And that had been that.

Vera Chiang, reprieved, had taken up residence with Mr Webb at the Mayfair. Her duties there were vague: most likely she helped her employer to hire destitute young women whose bodies needed building up. She certainly gave English lessons for on one occasion Major Archer, taking an unsuspecting stroll through the compound of the Mayfair, had come upon her giving instruction to a small, naked class in the use of the verbs 'to do' and 'to make', so he had informed Walter. He had beaten a hasty retreat, needless to say. Strangely enough, despite her past reputation and present employment the Major had taken a liking to her, and so had Mr Webb, though he had never mentioned her name in Walter's presence. As for Joan, though she had visited Miss Chiang once or twice and brought her some of her own clothes which she no longer needed, it would have been difficult for her as a European to become the bosom friend of a Eurasian girl, however well-educated. Such friendships were considered unsuitable in the social climate of Singapore. By a curious coincidence her clothes fitted Miss Chiang to perfection without the least alteration, and Joan had been startled to see how pretty she looked in them. Even Walter, seeing a familiar blue and green dress and a young woman posting a letter at the corner of the road, had slowed his car to give his daughter a lift, only to accelerate muttering to himself a moment later. Walter, in any case, could not have permitted Joan to be friendly with Miss Chiang, given her dubious relationship with Mr Webb.

All this time Joan had been prevented from answering his question by the fact that the moist, pink tip of her tongue was firmly gripped between her strong white teeth, an outer sign of the mental concentration required to tie a bow-tie on the neck of another person, particularly when the tie was of modest length and the neck, like Walter's, resembled the bole of an oak. At last she had finished, however.

'I haven't seen her for some time but I think she's still living there.'

'The point is,' said Walter, going to the mirror to inspect her handiwork, 'that we don't want a young woman of that sort turning up at Mr Webb's hospital bedside. You know how people gossip. If necessary we might have to consider giving her some money to stay out of the way. This, my dear, is a beautiful job!'

8

Walter slowly descended the stairs, brooding again on Harvey Firestone's skill in engendering male babies. How on earth did he do it? Pausing with his hand on the banister, Walter experienced that unnerving feeling which no other businessman had ever produced in him of being outclassed. Not three or four, but five! That was luck of a very high order ... or no, not just luck, it was ... how could one put it? ... from the business point of view, *correct behaviour*, a mixture, very hard to define, of luck, certainly, in large part but also of opportunism, skill and rightness. Walter had been almost overpowered on the occasion of his first visit to Akron, Ohio, by this sensation of *the right thing being done* at high intensity all around him, and not only in the production of male babies but in that of motor tyres and rims, too. Perhaps it was just as well that he and Firestone were on opposite ends of the rubber business.

Walter sank a few more steps and paused again, his mood of self-doubt having passed. Rubber these days was in demand in a way it had never been before. This was, to some extent, thanks to the war and to the fact that the British and American governments were trying to acquire reserve stocks against a breakdown in supplies. But above all it was due to the determination of a few men, Walter among them, who had argued that rubber producers *could* and *must* agree to limit the amount of rubber they released to the market. There was no other answer (except ruin). His brow, which had furrowed like a stormy sea at the thought of Harvey Firestone, returned to more placid undulations as he recalled how the doubters had argued that it had been tried before (they meant the Stevenson scheme from 1922–8) and had failed. Walter had not been daunted. The Netherlands East Indies, the only country to come close to Malaya in rubber production, had not agreed to take part in the Stevenson scheme so of course it had failed. This time the NEI must be made to see reason. They had vast areas of rubber smallholdings; nobody, not even the Dutch administration knew their extent. With all this rubber about to reach maturity and start flooding the market the entire rubber business could collapse. It was obvious that a reasonable price would have to be maintained artificially by a cartel or producers or rubber would become worthless. So Walter and his allies had argued against the doubters, who included, needless to say, old Solomon Langfield, and in the end they had won.

Under the new scheme (somehow Langfield had wormed his way on to the assessment committee despite his earlier opposition) an estimated annual production was established for each country: for Malaya, for the NEI, Indo-China and the other smaller producers. Then an international committee was set up to decide, quarter-yearly, what percentage of the total rubber production of all these countries might be released to the world market without risking a drop in price because there was too much of it about. As a result it had become possible to allot a specific tonnage of rubber to each country and declare that this quarter they might export so much and no more.

Think of this rubber not as the solid elastic sheets resembling bundles of empty flour sacks in which it was actually exported but as the milky latex in which, very slowly, it seeps out of the trees. Walter and his fellow-producers now had a tap in the shape of the restriction scheme with which they could control the flow of latex on to the market. Around this tap were gathered the thirsty manufacturers of the industrial nations, and none more parched than the men from the American motor-tyre industry, the Goodyears, the Goodriches and, of course, the Firestones. Open the tap and they would drink their fill, splashing about as if latex were as worthless as water. Close it, though, and you would soon see their lips begin to crack and their tongues to swell. Let them get thirsty enough and they would not mind what they paid.

Walter had watched the manipulation of the tap with interest. In the years following the Depression demand for rubber had been slack. But by 1936, thanks to an increase in motor-car production and a miserly hand controlling the flow, the price of rubber had begun to rise and there had been a boom in rubber shares. At the end of that year the manufacturers had croaked a request for the producers to release a higher percentage in the coming year. The Restriction Committee had maintained its strict hand on the tap, however, and when criticized by the Americans for the rubber shortage in 1937, had artfully replied that even if it had raised the percentage released there would still not have been any more rubber available. Why not? The manufacturers had been floored by this paradox. Well, because there was a shortage of labour for one thing. For another, from February to April is when the trees are 'wintering' and production always falls. For those who knew the rubber business this was not very convincing but never mind, it would serve.

Walter had now reached the bottom of the stairs and the last traces of scowl had disappeared, giving way to an expression of beatitude. For when the restriction scheme had been set up it had been understood that available rubber stocks should not be allowed to fall below the equivalent of five months' absorption by the manufacturers: this was in order that their businesses, and a possible expansion of demand, should not be put in jeopardy by shortages or delays in supply. And, mind you, the official policy of the Restriction Committee was not to make a killing out of rubber but merely to ensure, in a silky phrase worthy of Solomon Langfield himself, 'a reasonable return to an efficient producer'. It had come as no surprise to anyone in Singapore, least of all to Walter, when stocks fell below the promised five months' absorption and the price began to rise. Presently, the Committee's idea of what represented 'a reasonable return' began to rise, too. Seven pence a pound, eight pence, nine pence ... The scheme was working. Walter had watched, enthralled. Standing at the foot of the stairs he suddenly flourished his fist in the air. That had been one on the nose for the Firestones!

Walter, returning to his senses, now realized that Abdul, his Malay major-domo, had approached silently and was eyeing him with concern.

'What news, Master?'

'Good news, Abdul,' replied Walter conventionally. The fellow clearly wanted to tell him something. He bent an ear.

'A *what*, Abdul? A yogi?' Walter stared in amazement at the elderly Malay who had been in his service for some years and for whom he felt a considerable affection and respect.

The major-domo explained. The yogi had come to entertain the guests. It was the idea of the young *Tuan* Blackett.

'Well, tell the bloody man to go away again. It's supposed to be a dinner-party, not a circus.'

'Yes, *Tuan*.' The old man smiled faintly for there was a bond of sympathy between him and Walter when it came to the behaviour of the younger generation and it was clear that he, no less than Walter, had found the idea of a yogi at a dinner-party outrageous.

'But no, wait, Abdul. On second thoughts we must let Monty make his own decision about the yogi. He'll never learn if we always have to tell him what's what. I shall let him take charge of the dinner-party this evening. There probably won't be more than a dozen guests or so and they can be served in the breakfast-room. Tell him, will you, that I won't appear until after they've eaten. I've work to do.' And as the old servant was leaving Walter added: 'The boy must learn by his own mistakes, Abdul. There's no other way, I'm afraid, no other way.'

Alone in his study Walter was once more preoccupied with his family, this time with his son. Monty had energy and he worked hard. He had done a good job in reorganizing the administration of their estates when business was expanding again after the Depression. He was doing a good job now of pushing through the replanting, very often against opposition from estate managers who could not see the logic of it when rubber was booming. He even had some business sense which, with experience, might be developed. But the boy was erratic, there was no other word for it. Every now and then he would produce some wild idea that made you wonder whether he had understood anything at all. A yogi to entertain at supper on a day like this! True, he had not known that Mr Webb would collapse, but all the same! And they had barely recovered from the Chinese band he had insisted on having at the garden-party.

Moreover, Monty was no longer, strictly speaking, a boy. He was thirty. If he were ever going to learn by his mistakes it was high time that he started. Walter could not help comparing him, unfavourably, with a photograph he had once seen of the five young Firestones, each one as neatly brushed, as smartly turned out in his identical dark suit as his four brothers. And each one, no doubt, with a perfect command of that day's *Wall Street Journal*. You would not catch the young Firestones inviting fakirs to dinner-parties.

Monty had certain good qualities but he was seriously lacking in judgement. Perhaps this would not have mattered if it had been merely a question of the occasional bizarre idea for amusing guests, but alas, it was not. In 1936 Monty had been sent to take charge of the London office for a few months to learn the European side of the business and, while he was there, he had got Blackett and Webb involved in something that anyone with common sense would have avoided. Towards the end of that year Monty had lent the authority of the firm to a great wave of speculation which was being generated by the rubber dealers and brokers in Mincing Lane. Mincing Lane's market analysts, peering into the swirling mists of the future, had perceived not only an approaching shortage of rubber but, stretching beyond that shortage, higher prices as far as the eye could see (that is what they said they had perceived, anyway). The brokers' market reports were in little doubt, they declared, but that the Restriction Committee had decided on maintaining higher prices indefinitely; after all, it could make little difference to the manufacturers who would simply pass the increases on to their customers. And even if the Committee had *not* decided on a higher price it was well known, in Mincing Lane if not in Malaya, that not enough rubber could be produced to meet higher percentage rates of release. Besides, there was a shortage of labour. Besides, it was well known that once the native smallholders, who produced almost half of Malaya's rubber, made a little money, as they would with present high prices, they had the amiable habit of downing tools instead of pressing home their advantage, preferring to doze the day away in hammocks. So, one way or another, a shortage of rubber was inevitable. There was a quick fortune to be made.

Well, promotion of this sort, designed to make your mouth water, is what one must expect of a commodity broker. After all, such a fellow has to make a living somehow and Walter was the last person to hold that against him. But a steady market is not much good to a broker: he wants prices to rise or fall (he does not mind which provided they do one or the other). And if the market declines to fluctuate of its own accord it must be encouraged to do so. A cold night in Brazil and frost has wiped out the coffee plantations. A high wind in Jamaica and it's goodbye to bananas. Fair enough. Walter did not expect the commodity broker to emerge clad in different stripes simply because he was dealing in rubber. But for Monty to give Blackett and Webb's support to such devious special pleading struck Walter as so foolish as almost to amount to the work of an imbecile. Perhaps he had made some money for himself from a judicious trading of rubber shares, yes, perhaps even a large amount, though, if so, he had evidently lost it again gambling. But that was not what he was there for. Fluctuating markets do not help producers because an artificial boom brings with it inevitably its dark shadow, a collapse. And a collapse in prices brings for more difficulties for the producer that the boom earlier brought advantages. But what really angered Walter was something different, something even less tangible. It was the damage which had been done to Blackett and Webb's good name.

Walter got to his feet and stretched wearily. A murmur of voices from another part of the house told him that Monty's guests had arrived. He hoped that the boy would behave in a suitably subdued manner, given the circumstances. Presently, he himself would have to put in a brief appearance. 'Poor old Webb!' he thought as he settled down at his desk and began to read through the bundle of cables which had been steadily collecting on it all afternoon in his absence. But as he sat there, deep below the surface of his working mind, a disturbing thought shifted imperceptibly once or twice. To whom would Mr Webb leave his share of the business?

After an hour he felt hungry and remembered that he had had nothing to eat since mid-day. The clink of cutlery and cheerful conversation came to him faintly from the breakfast-room. It was clear that not everyone was allowing Mr Webb's approaching end to weigh on his spirits. Reluctant to join this cheerful gathering he made his way towards the dining-room, thinking that perhaps there might still be some food set out there.

Entering the dining-room he received a shock, for the servants, evidently uncertain as to the evening's arrangements, had left the room exactly as it was. The long table was still set with eighty places in silver cutlery. Bowls of flowers and silver candlesticks alternated from one end to the other while at each place there stood a little family of wine glasses in which toasts would have been drunk to Mr Webb on his birthday, to himself, to the firm's future prosperity. But what had given Walter such a shock were the four life-size heads fashioned of cake and icing-sugar, crude but recognizable, which had been set up on side tables, one·in each corner of the room. Two of the heads he recognized immediately: one was of himself, benign, dew-lapped, cheeks unnaturally rouged with cochineal, the scalp tonsured with white icing-sugar. The other, more lifelike, represented old Mr Webb's gaunt and dignified features. It seemed to Walter that a cold, almost cynical smile hovered about his former partner's lips, and for a moment he found himself believing that real thoughts might be passing through the fruit-cake brain behind those piercing pale-blue eyes of sugar, that he was thinking: 'So! You thought you had got rid of me at last!'

Recovering from his surprise Walter advanced smiling to read a sugar inscription which announced that these cakes had been presented on the occasion of Mr Webb's birthday and the inauguration of the firm's jubilee celebrations by Blackett and Webb's Chinese employees who had collected subscriptions for the purpose, perhaps, Walter surmised, with the tactful encouragement of the publicity department but nevertheless ... This was unexpected and gratifying, given the troubled labour situation in the Colony. And to think that only a few weeks earlier all work in the rubber godowns had come to a halt and Singapore had trembled on the verge of a General Strike! 'Now who are these other chaps?'

One was clearly intended to be Churchill, but a Churchill with slanting eyes and an Oriental look, manifestly the work of a Chinese pastry-cook. It took him a moment longer to recognize the fourth head, thin-featured, high-cheekboned, facing Churchill diagonally across the room but eventually he realized that it must be Chiang Kai-shek. How patriotic the overseas Chinese remained and, considering everything, how well organized!

In the past three years while the Sino-Japanese war had continued to boom and crash like a distant thunderstorm here and there over the mainland there had been a great multiplication of so-called 'Anti-Enemy Backing-up Societies', not all of them, alas, controlled by the Kuomintang. Sinister letters by courier from Shanghai to the Malayan Communist Party had been intercepted (according to the Combined Intelligence Summary), declaring that 'a victorious war for China will be the overture for an emancipation movement in the colonies.' A memorandum from the Special Branch of the Straits Settlements Police warned against the influence these patriotic societies might acquire with the Malayan Chinese, thanks to their anti-Japanese stand. In appearance, harmlessly engaged in collecting funds to support the Chinese army, many of these 'National Salvation' and 'anti-enemy' organizations were in fact under the control of the Communists.

Finding no other food in the dining-room and unwilling to interrupt his train of thought by summoning one of the 'boys', Walter broke off one of Mr Webb's ears and munched it, pacing up and down. How many of his own employees who had perhaps subscribed to these effigies in cake of hated imperialists were at the same time secret members of, say, the Overseas Chinese Anti-Enemy National Salvation Society or of the even more outlandishly named Youth Blood and Iron Traitor-Exterminating Corps (the latter, to be sure, thought not to be Communist-led and, despite its bloodcurdling title, specializing in nothing more violent than the occasional tarring of a shop in the city for selling scrap-iron to the Japanese), not to mention more conventional gangs like the Heaven and Earth Society? Walter found it disturbing to know so little of where the real allegiance of his employees might lie. 'Not with us, anyway! Or only when it suits them.' The strikes which throughout this summer of 1940 had caused the foundations of the Colony to shake were, moreover, only a local manifestation of an ominous awakening of labour throughout the Far East. Shanghai at this very moment was in the embrace of a transport strike which, as it grew, scattered pollen far and wide. First, the British-owned Shanghai Tramways Company, then the China General Omnibus Company had stopped work. Pollen had been carried on the wind from the International Settlement into the French Concession to fertilize workers of the Compagnie Française de Tramways et d'Eclairage Electrique de Shanghai.

'And the next thing you know they're all at it!' One of the cables which Walter had glanced at a few minutes earlier brought news of a meeting organized by the Shanghai General Labour Union on the 27th at which some ninety-odd unions had been represented. The rubber workers' union, the restaurant workers' union, the weaving and spinning workers' union, the bean sauce workers' union, the silk filature workers' union, the ordure coolies' union, the wharf coolies' union ... and so on and so on. Shanghai, despite its almost incredibly precarious political situation, was important to Blackett and Webb. But Walter was more worried by the general implications of the strikes, for where Shanghai led, the rest of the Far East had a habit of following. Admittedly, workers in Shanghai were in real desperation. All the same Walter did not doubt but that the pollen could be carried across the South China Sea to Malaya and Singapore.

Walter halted in his pacing: again he was aware of a cold, cynical, even bitter expression on the icing-sugar features of his former partner, as if that fruit-cake brain were now thinking: 'This would never have happened in my day!' Well, that was true enough. Malaya's gigantic labour force had been docile in the old man's day when there were always ships to be seen anchoring in the roads crammed every available inch with wretched, fermenting, indentured coolies. In those days there was always cheap labour to be had. It had been the Depression which in the end, here as elsewhere, had brought about a change. Faced with great numbers of unemployed among the Chinese the Government had spent some millions of dollars in repatriating them to China: this display of munificence had been generated by the shrewd calculation that the cost of relief would be even greater if they remained in Malaya. But it had not done the employers any good.

In 1933 the Aliens Ordinance had dealt another blow to the business community for it gave the Governor the power to limit the number of aliens landed in the Colony. Although the intention had been more to check the arrival of Communist subversives from the mainland than to limit the size of the labour reservoir, this had proved, nevertheless, to be its effect. The cost of recruiting in China plus an increase in shipping fares had made it less expensive to recruit *free* workers locally· than to ship those cargoes of *indentured* coolies. The Indian

Government in the meantime, in the belief that Malayan businessmen were exploiting its subjects, had taken steps to limit the flow of Indian workers into the country.

The result? Strikes had begun to break out in Malaya and the Straits Settlements with increasing frequency. The supply of cheap labour had become finite. Many of the estate workers and squatters on pineapple plantations, hitherto isolated from their fellow-workers, had managed to acquire cheap Japanese bicycles: now meetings of widely dispersed workers could be held and collective resistance to low wages had become possible.

'And we didn't even have the wit to sell them the bloody bicycles!' reflected Walter with a wry smile at Mr Webb's effigy.

There had been another development, too. Chinese women, deprived of employment by the collapse of the silk industry in China and not subject to the limitation of the Aliens Ordinance, had begun to arrive by the shipload, whereas before the Depression, apart from women imported by brothel-keepers to stock their establishments, there had been few or none. The result was a sudden sinking of roots. Women had begun to take the cooking and buying of food out of the hands of the Chinese labour-contractors. The workers, who had once been easily abused nomads drifting from one estate or tin-mine to another, had started to settle down and demand the rights of citizens. Old Mr Webb's almond-paste lips might well curl in contempt at the way his younger partner had allowed the initiative to pass to his employees but could he himself have done anything to prevent it?

One of the first strikes, though isolated, had been the most serious of all. In the winter of 1935 Communist miners had taken possession of a coal mine at Batu Arang and set up a soviet to administer it. A soviet in the middle of British Malaya, if you please! Walter had been staggered to hear of it. Of course, it had not lasted long. Even if the Batu Arang mine had not been crucial for electricity and the railway it could not have been allowed to remain as an example to the rest of Malaya's labour force. The police had wasted no time in storming and recapturing it. But the miners' rash action (how naïve they must have been to think that they would get away with it!) had been like a sudden gust of wind which fills the air with thistledown and strips the dandelion of its whiskers. In due course, given time for germination, strikes had begun to spring up all around. Next year it had been the turn of the pineapple factories. The year after that they had spread for the first time to the rubber estates. And what could the old man have done to prevent it? Not a thing.

'Times have changed. That's what the old chap never wanted to see. He thought everything should continue the way it always had. But times have changed, for all that.'

Again that shadow stirred in the depths of his mind: to whom would Mr Webb leave his holdings in the business? 'A businessman must move with the times,' said Walter aloud. And breaking off Mr Webb's other ear, in the interests of symmetry as much as of appetite, Walter departed in search of Monty and his guests, crunching it between his strong yellow teeth as he went.

9

Walter could hear no sound as he made his way along the passage to the breakfast-room and his hopes began to rise. The room, indeed, proved to be deserted, although aromatic cigar smoke still hung in the air. Could it be that the guests had taken their leave already, as a mark of respect to old Mr Webb? If that was the case, then so much the better; Walter was weary after the day's difficulties. But one of the 'boys' clearing the table undeceived him. The party had moved outside to watch the yogi demonstrate his talents. Walter followed them, cracking his knuckles. 'Let the young fool learn by his mistakes then!'

Stepping grimly out of the luxuriously refrigerated air of the house into the sweltering night Walter found that a little herd of guests, men in white dinner-jackets, women in long evening dresses, had collected on that same portico from which, earlier in the day, he had surveyed the progress of the garden-party. On each side flights of stone steps, glimmering white in the darkness, dropped in zigzags to the lawn on which, directly beneath the balustrade, a platform on wooden trestles had been set up for the yogi's performance. Two powerful floodlights smoking with insects had been directed down on the yogi from above. From behind the lights the guests watched him uneasily. Walter passed among them, shaking hands and responding with a few grave words to their expressions of regret over the collapse of Mr Webb. It was true, of course, he muttered, that the old gentleman had had a good innings. Still, one could not help feeling that it was the end of an era. Walter's words, replete with the quiet dignity which the situation demanded, were unfortunately accompanied by a strange descant from below, some monotonous rigmarole in a language no one could understand, spattered from time to time with incomprehensible English. Really, it was perfectly unsuitable and ludicrous.

Monty suddenly came springing up the steps from the lawn where he had evidently been making some final arrangements. He was rubbing his hands together violently and chuckling in anticipation. Walter's heart sank at the sight of him: the boy had such a wild look.

'There you are, Father. I was just going to get you. I was afraid you might miss this fellow. He's really a scream. He does the most amazing things.'

Walter drew his son to one side and said quietly: 'I want you to get this over as quickly as possible. I very much doubt whether it was ever a good idea, but to carry on with it this evening in view of what has happened to Mr Webb, really, you must have lost your senses.'

'Oh, look here, Father ...' protested Monty.

But Walter went on, ignoring him: 'I should have thought that the merest common sense would have told you ... And what d'you think the Langfields will say when they hear about it? They'll waste no time in putting it around that the Blacketts have been dancing on Mr Webb's grave while the body is still warm!'

Walter, becoming excited, had spoken louder than he had intended and the bristles on his spine had puffed up beneath his shirt ... One or two of the guests had begun to show signs of concern at this sudden whispered altercation between father and son. Walter realized that even Monty was looking at him oddly. 'Anyway, get rid of the fellow as soon as you can,' he said sharply.

Monty stiffened. The chanting had stopped. 'OK, Father. Yeah, OK!' he muttered and slid away swiftly towards the balustrade beneath which the yogi was now beginning to demonstrate his powers. Walter continued to pass among the guests, conversing gravely with them as if something unsuitable were not happening, or about to happen, just out of sight beneath the portico. And while he conversed he mused grimly again on the damage done to the firm by Monty's erratic hand in its affairs, for was it not fair to say that the labour trouble on the estates in 1937 had stemmed, indirectly at least, from that great speculative rubber boom which Monty and the London office, in concert with certain unscrupulous brokers of Mincing Lane, had whipped up in the autumn of 1936 with their predictions of a rubber scarcity lasting as far as the eye could see?

Well, the truth of the matter was simple: the swift rise in the price of rubber, and of the employers' profits, had not, unfortunately, gone unnoticed by the Chinese work-force. There had been complaints about low wages in Selangor and Negri Sembilan. On the Bangi estate in Ulu Langat the manager had tried to get rid of his Chinese workers and replace them with Javanese. In no time the workers on half a dozen estates had downed tools. Moreover, other districts soon began to join because the workers from the Connemara estate, who had drawn up a list of demands for the Protector of Chinese, were fanning out on bicycles, those same cheap Jap bicycles which Blackett and Webb had not, until too late, thought of importing instead of the more costly products of Birmingham and Coventry, spreading the news far and wide. Presently twenty thousand or more Chinese had stopped work.

And it had all been perfectly unnecessary. The peaceful atmosphere of Malaya had been riven for no purpose. Ugly scenes had developed. Chinese detectives sent to look for Communists among the strikers, that *idée fixe* of the Chinese Protectorate, had been roughed up. Heads had been broken. In due course over a hundred workers had found themselves behind bars and, to their original demand for a ten cents a day increase in wages, the strikers were now adding two more: the release of the arrested men and compensation for injuries, bound in the end to involve a loss of face for the Government.

And why had it been unneccessary? Beceause that 'almost permanent' rubber boom which Monty and the market analysts had seen trembling in their telescopes at the end of 1936 had proved to be a mirage, as anyone in Malaya or the Netherlands East Indies could have told you it would. The price of rubber, ridiculously inflated by brokers' claims, had collapsed, aided by a recession in America. Sales of cars had declined and by the spring of 1938 the price of rubber had plummeted to about five pence a pound. Hardly had the strikers had their pay increased from sixty to seventy-five cents a day as a result of bitter struggles up and down the country, when workers were being laid off and wages reduced once more. But Monty, the young fool, impervious to the effects on Malaya's estate workers (on Malaya's social fabric even, for once this sort of thing started . . .!) of these wild fluctuations in price generated by the London market, had been unable to see further than the chance of a quick profit. Instead of squashing the brokers' claims he had egged them on. And that, thought Walter more grimly than ever, was another example of the changing times. 'Young men these days have no sense of responsibility to the country!'

The yogi, Walter discovered, gazing down at him with distaste, was a tall, cadaverous individual, evidently a Punjabi. He was clad only in a white *dhoti* and gold turban. In the middle of the turban a large white gem, perhaps a diamond but more likely a piece of cut glass, flared in the floodlights. Thin as he was his naked chest was nevertheless disturbingly equipped with a pair of well-formed female breasts. Some distance to the right of the improvised stage the Blacketts' *kebun* could be seen tending a blazing bonfire.

Meanwhile, the yogi's assistant, a sallow, gold-toothed Eurasian in tattered black evening dress was following in Walter's wake among the guests, proffering for their inspection a box of tin-tacks and a cheap china tea-cup. The guests fingered them uncertainly. When they had satisfied themselves that no deception was being practised on them the Eurasian threw the box of tacks down to the yogi who caught it, opened it and began, rather gloomily, popping them into his mouth one by one and swallowing them. The guests continued to watch him uneasily. The only sound was the impatient cracking of Walter's knuckles.

The box of tacks was a large one and the yogi seemed to be in no hurry, as if anxious to savour each one. Presently the guests began to exchange glances, as if to say that it was dreadfully hot out here and would this go on much longer? Certain of the men, particularly those who considered their time valuable, glanced at their watches with a preoccupied air; one of them, whom Walter recognized as an influential executive of one of the big tyre companies in Singapore, even turned away from the balustrade altogether.

'Yes,' agreed Walter, swiftly taking him by the arm and

compelling him to saunter up and down along the same path which he himself had been pacing earlier in the day, 'it's bound to come as a shock to those who, like you and I, knew him as a younger man. But then, at his time of life ...' Walter shrugged sadly.

'Some time may elapse, I'm afraid, before we see his like again,' declared the man from the tyre company with an air of rather sepulchral piety, but again sneaking a look at his watch.

They began to discuss, in a desultory fashion while the yogi went on stolidly swallowing tacks, the mysterious latex-drinking snails which were said to have appeared on certain isolated estates. Neither of them was inclined to take these snails very seriously. 'Still,' said Walter, 'we'd better not let Mincing Lane get to hear of them or they'll be using the wretched creatures to fuel another round of speculation.' He paused sombrely, having reminded himself of the results of the last speculative boom. These speculators were playing the game of those who, like the Communists, wanted to foment trouble in the Colony. What a lot of strikes Singapore had seen this year already! The Harbour Board dockers had been on strike for three months ... at a time when shipment of rubber and tin was vital, not only for profits but for the War Effort as well. Hardly had that collapsed when, amid violent riots, another one had started at the Firestone factory and then trouble had spread all over the place with rubber immobilized everywhere, a disastrous pile-up of fruit at the height of the season caused by a go-slow of pineapple cutters at the canning factories, and to cap it all, pitched battles between police trying to arrest trouble-makers at the Tai Thong factory and the labour force armed with staves, stones and soda-water bottles.

Walter, despite those heads of cake, began to suffer misgivings about the loyalty of his workers. What if the Blackett and Webb jubilee should be chosen for propaganda purposes not only by the Government to demonstrate 'Continuity in Prosperity' under British rule, but also *by the Communists* to demonstrate the exploitation and disaffection of the workers! The thought of a jubilee procession up the hill to Government House in the teeth of a howling mob was alarming. How the Langfields would laugh!

'Where are they taking Margaret?' demanded Walter's companion suddenly, for the yogi's Eurasian assistant, gold teeth gleaming, had selected his wife from the little herd of guests and with much polishing of hands was leading her down the steps to where the yogi, his meal of tin-tacks finished, was waiting glumly on the platform. Half-way down the steps she baulked and would have returned had not Monty come hurrying down to reassure her. The bristles on Walter's spine began to stir beneath his dress shirt.

All the lady was required for, explained the Eurasian in an ingratiating tone, was to inspect the mouth of the yogi. The yogi, recognizing the signal, opened his mouth wide. The Eurasian promptly grasped the lady's shrinking fingers and stuffed them into the yogi's open mouth. She snatched them out again quickly. No tin-tacks had been discovered. Monty, beside himself with delight, beamed up at the balustrade. In the strong lights he looked wilder than ever.

Meanwhile, the yogi, his appetite returning, had bitten the handle off the tea-cup which had been passed round for inspection earlier and was crunching it noisily between his teeth. When he had devoured the handle he smashed the rest of the cup by rapping it sharply against his own skull, then popped the broken pieces of china into his mouth, crunching them up too. Monty was invited this time to inspect his mouth and was soon able to confirm that the cup had been eaten up entirely. A slight delay followed while the yogi and his assistant peered at something in a cardboard box full of straw, evidently trying to decide how best to deal with it. Walter leaned over the balustrade and beckoned to Monty impatiently.

'Just a moment, Father.'

The yogi dipped his hand quickly into the box and withdrew a thrashing, apple-green snake, holding it up by the tail as it twisted this way and that trying to bite him. He quickly slid his other hand down the body and gripped the reptile firmly behind its head. The assistant began to hammer with his palms on a grimy drum. The guests gazed down at him apprehensively from the balustrade, afraid that something disagreeable might be about to happen. The yogi had opened his mouth and was slowly bringing the snake's head towards it while the rest of its body continued to thrash and flail against his wrists and forearms. 'Oh no!' cried one of the ladies in dismay. Hissing, the snake's head came nearer and nearer the yogi's mouth, its tongue flickering. Abruptly the yogi took the snake into his mouth and bit off its head. There was an audible cracking of bone, a working of the yogi's jaws as he masticated and swallowed it. Then the tip of a pink tongue appeared and licked a few scarlet drops from his lips. Walter stared down at the headless body of the snake which continued to thrash by itself on the platform, smearing glistening red marks on the pale wood which, just for a moment, seemed to resemble Chinese ideographs, as if the snake were trying to make some last furious communication. One or two of the ladies had turned pale and even Walter himself was shaken. He announced loudly: 'If you would like to move inside, coffee and brandy will be served in the drawing-room where it's cooler.'

'But Father, he hasn't finished yet!' exclaimed Monty, dashing up the steps again as Walter began shepherding the guests back into the house. 'He drinks nitric acid. It's amazing. I've seen him do it. He dissolves a copper penny in it first and then he just swigs it! And he's going to walk barefoot through that bonfire before he drinks the acid ... Look, I mean ... since we've got the blighter here!'

Walter stared at his son for a moment, tight-lipped. Then he turned and strode back into the house. Presently, the yogi, left to his own devices, took off his sandals and began to trudge barefoot back and forth through the glowing embers of the bonfire while, at a little distance, his assistant discussed money matters with Monty in a high-pitched voice.

10

Another hour elapsed before Walter had said goodbye to the last of the guests, some of whom had a stricken look. One of the ladies, so Abdul informed him, had been overcome by nausea and had been obliged to lie down: it was that ghastly business with the snake that had done it. He must remember to write a note of apology in the morning. He must also give Monty a dressing-down but that too would have to wait until morning for Monty had prudently disappeared.

Walter climbed the stairs wearily. It was some time since he had given his wife a thought and now he remembered that she had retired with a headache and was doubtless upset by the outcome of the garden-party. Could it still be the same day? That garden-party now seemed to have taken place weeks ago. He found her awake, lying as if stunned against a mound of pillows. She said she was feeling a little better and asked him where everyone was, it seemed very quiet.

'Search me. The only person who seems to be still here is young Ehrendorf. He's in the sitting-room smoking cigarettes. As for the others ...' Walter shrugged. All the guests had gone. Monty had gone. Joan had gone. The yogi had gone, full of china.

'You mean, full of china tea?'

'No, not really, no, I don't,' replied Walter in an edgy sort of tone.

Mrs Blackett sighed but felt too weak to pursue the matter.

'Well, I suppose I should go to the hospital to see how old Webb is getting on.'

Downstairs, Walter found that there was another guest who had not yet departed though now, daunted by the empty echoing rooms, he seemed to be in the process of doing so: this was Dr Brownley, their family doctor. Dr Brownley frequently visited the Blacketts, but more often for social than for professional reasons. Indeed, he was always invited to the Blacketts' parties, always came, was always the first to arrive and usually the last to leave. The Doctor, however, was troubled by the knowledge that he was always going to the Blacketts' but *never invited them back*! Someone less addicted than the Doctor to the grand social occasions in which the Blacketts specialized, where inevitably one found oneself cheek by jowl with the people who mattered in the Straits, might have preferred to soothe his inflamed conscience, or at least to limit the spread of further inflammation, by not accepting any more invitations. Such a remedy, alas, was out of reach of the good Doctor. Though his inflammation throbbed more painfully on each new occasion he simply could not but accept. Now, at the sight of Walter on the stairs he winced visibly, thinking: 'This makes it twelve times in a row and they haven't once been invited to my house!' He had been hoping to slip out of the house while no one was about, thus avoiding the awkwardness of a leave-taking. Indeed, the reason Walter had not seen him earlier was that the Doctor had dodged behind a bookcase to avoid detection. But this time there was no escape and he called out heartily: 'Ah, there you are, Walter. I was looking for you to thank you and, of course, Mrs Blackett for, a delightful ... mind you, one of many such ... I'm just off now. Must be going. Look here, you must come to my place one of these days ... Can I give you a lift? No, of course, this is where you live, isn't it? Ha, ha, well, hm ... You must come to ...' His voice trailed off into a mutter as he prepared to plunge into the friendly darkness outside. Issuing invitations, the Doctor had found, provided a little welcome relief in awkward situations like this ... but you felt correspondingly worse later when faced with the prospect of redeeming them!

'What's that?' demanded Walter, puzzled by the Doctor's habit of muttering to himself before departure. The Doctor flinched. 'I was just saying that you must come to my place one of these days,' he was obliged to state in a clear and unequivocal tone.

'Oh, all right. Why not?' said Walter. 'Good night, Doctor.' And with that he returned to the drawing-room.

Walter, who had a horror of hospitals, had been contemplating a quiet *stengah* before paying a visit to old Mr Webb. He had forgotten that young Ehrendorf was still there and was not altogether pleased to find the room full of cigarette smoke. 'These days you really have to winkle out your guests one by one,' he thought as Ehrendorf stood up politely, trailing a newspaper from his fingers. However, on the whole he had a good opinion of Ehrendorf and even felt, as one male to another, some sympathy for him in his predicament with Joan. But there it was, women were peculiar and there was not very much one could do about it. If some woman had thrown wine in Walter's face as a young man he would have fetched her a clout. Ah, but then he had never pretended to have the exquisite manners of an Ehrendorf and could very well see that, equipped with polished manners, one could not go about clouting women at garden-parties.

'You haven't seen Joan, have you?' Ehrendorf enquired, resuming his seat but sitting, Walter was glad to perceive, on the edge of his chair as if ready to stand again.

'Not for some time. I have an idea that she may have gone out for the evening.'

'Well, in that case it seems,' said Ehrendorf with a rather strained smile, 'that I've been stood up. Well, never mind, it's not for the first time. I'll just finish my drink if you don't mind and then I'll be on my way.'

'No hurry.'

Walter called for his *stengah* and sank back in his chair, glad enough after all to have Ehrendorf's company and to delay his visit to the hospital for a little while. Walter did not greatly care for Americans these days: the acrimony aroused over the Rubber Restriction scheme and the subsequent counter-attack by the American consumers had left its mark. But when one day Captain Ehrendorf, posted to the US military attaché's office in Singapore and armed with an introduction to the Blacketts, had presented himself at their house, neither Walter nor the rest of his family had been able to find fault with him. This had been partly because his introduction had come from none other than Matthew Webb and the Blacketts were curious to learn more about Matthew and the way he lived (incidentally, he must soon do something about sending the poor boy a telegram about his father's illness), but most of all because Ehrendorf himself was unusually charming and good-looking. He might, indeed, have been specially constructed to topple all Walter's prejudices about Americans.

Americans, thought Walter, are vulgar: but no one had better taste than Ehrendorf. They are loud: no one more soft-spoken. They have no culture: Walter had yet to meet anyone more cultured, better educated, better mannered, more tactful and well-informed. The fellow, amazing though it might seem to Walter's jaundiced eye, was quite simply a gentleman. Walter had found it hard to think of him as an American at all. Why, he even spoke English like a civilized person.

Ehrendorf had wasted no time in telling the Blacketts what he knew of Màtthew, whom he had first met at Oxford. He himself had been a Rhodes scholar at the university (here he paused for a moment but the Blacketts had stared at him blankly) for a couple of years. Then, five or six years later, they had bumped into each other again, this time in Geneva in 1932 where he himself had been posted as a very junior military assistant to Mr Norman Davis in the long, tortuous and exhausting discussions on the Disarmament Conference. Matthew had not been working for the League Secretariat itself but for some other-organization whose name escaped him, connected with it in some way. There were so many! Was it the International Peace Bureau, or the Red Cross Committee? Was it the Permanent Secretariat for War Veterans and War Victims? Or the Union for the Assistance of Calamity-Stricken Populations? Of one thing he was pretty sure, he laughed: it was not the International Humanitarian Bureau for Lovers of Animals, whose rather odd programme was 'to extend to the animal kingdom the sentiments and duties of humane justice'. He had a suspicion that it might well have been the International League for the Protection of Native Peoples; that was certainly the field he was interested in, anyway. But no matter! How glad they had been to meet each other again!

Geneva in winter was the most depressing town on earth, the international community was cliquish and segregated grimly by nationalities, the Genevese burgher himself was the most narrow and xenophobic animal on two legs. He and Matthew, whom he considered 'the most wonderful person in the world' and 'a wonderful human being' (young Kate tittered when he said this and clasped a hand over her mouth), casting aside the depressing and Jesuitical, even Jansenist, shackles of Disarmament had resumed their own much more interesting discussions on art, sex, Freud, the existence or otherwise of God, chattering away, as young men will, he added with a smile, about the causes of the Thirty Years War and whether the Defenestration of Prague was instrumental in the downfall of the Palatinate and of the Bohemian church, and countless other matters of this kind which they had been unable to settle to their own satisfaction during the time they had spent together at Oxford. Matthew, 'a very delightful person', had been the ideal companion in this dull and provincial Swiss town. They had even managed to make a quick trip to London that winter to see Gielgud's production of Rodney Ackland's magnificent play, *Strange Orchestra* at the St Martin's Theatre. Then, alas, all too soon, the call of their respective duties had caused their paths to diverge once more. In the years that followed they had only managed to meet again once or twice, for a hurried meal in the nearest restaurant to this or that railway station in some European city where the threads which each was unreeling behind him on his way through Life's maze had happened briefly to intersect. But they had at least kept in touch by letter, just about.

Walter was sufficiently accustomed to American hyperbole to realize that Ehrendorf might not literally consider Matthew to be 'the most wonderful person in the world'. Americans, he knew, were inclined to use such expressions about any acquaintance they found moderately inoffensive. Still, it was encouraging. The poor boy's bizarre education might not have completely ruined him, after all. Mrs Blackett had reacted more cautiously: gossiping about the Defenestration of Prague, whatever that was, did not seem to her such a good sign. As for Ehrendorf, he really was delightful. The Blacketts were charmed by him. Not even young Kate, who was passing then through a stage when she detested all men, could quite resist him.

Ehrendorf had become a frequent visitor at the Blacketts' house and he would call without performing any of the preliminary social manoeuvres which were still customary among the older Singapore families. Instead of making use of the box fitted to the gate with a tiny slit for visiting cards, and then retiring, as the ritual required, to wait for an invitation, he would have his staff car drive him boldly up to the front door and wander in unannounced. He never stayed for long, though. He was always on his way somewhere ... to Government House, perhaps; the Blacketts would not have been surprised to learn, such was Ehrendorf's disarming ease of manner, that he wandered in on the Governor and Lady Thomas as casually as he did on them, and he was certainly on friendly terms with the Governor's ADC and staff ('the servants' hall' as it was known at Government House) ... or to a reception at some legation, or further afield, to a conference in Manila, or Saigon, or Batavia. Sometimes, if he were going to a party nearby and Joan was at a loose end, he would courteously invite her to join him and together they would be whisked away in the staff car to some elaborate reception or beach party. It was clear, of course, that Ehrendorf, despite his accomplishment, was a long way from being an ideal, or even a possible, suitor for Joan. But his manifest good-nature inhibited the elder Blacketts from objecting for a time to the attentions that he was paying to their daughter and, in any case, it very soon became clear to Walter that no objections were likely to be needed. Her delicate appearance notwithstanding, Joan's tender womanhood was clad in a tough hide. The distressing day which this young man seated opposite him had evidently just experienced would have been further proof of it, if he had needed proof.

'Perhaps you would tell Joan that I waited for her,' Ehrendorf said calmly and without resentment as both men got to their feet. 'I guess it slipped her mind that she had a date with me.'

'I expect so,' agreed Walter blandly. 'Well, I must be on my way over to Outram Road. I could drop you off in Market Street if you like?' But Ehrendorf had a car waiting and each went his separate way.

The night was very hot and still, but clear. Walter found it refreshing to sit there in the back of the open car beneath the stars, surging through the empty streets. And how peaceful the low, tiled roofs of the shophouses along Orchard Road looked in the starlight! Noticing that the California Sandwich Shoppe on the right-hand side was still open he remembered that he had eaten nothing, apart from Mr Webb's ears, for some hours. For a moment he considered telling the *syce* to stop, but no ... he no longer felt hungry. The heat and weariness had robbed him of his appetite. At the bottom of Orchard Road the Bentley turned to the right into Hill Street, past the white Moorish façade of the Oriental Telephone and Telegraph Company trembling in the starlight like a vision from the Arabian Nights, and then glided on its way south-west under the looming blue-black shadow of the police barracks, over the river (Walter, holding his breath against the stench, briefly glimpsed the silhouette of Blackett and Webb's godown at the bend of the river and closer at hand on the water itself the huddled lighters and *sampans* where prodigious numbers of Chinese were fated to live out their lives), and then on along New Bridge Road towards the General Hospital, Walter brooding now about the Chinese once more.

'We in Singapore may have our share of overcrowding and child-labour and slums, but at least it's not like Shanghai!'

For Walter, Shanghai was a constant reminder, a sort of *memento mori*, of the harsh world which lay outside the limits of British rule. The population of Shanghai's foreign areas had already been excessive before the war had broken over the city in August 1937. But within a few weeks the influx of refugees to this sanctuary had brought it to more than five million. Moreover, these were people who, even in peacetime, had been living on a level of bare subsistence that all too often dipped into total destitution: then a man's only means of supporting his family was to sift through rubbish bins or dredge the flotsam from the ships along the wharves. 'You would think the Chinese here would be more grateful considering what their relatives in Shanghai have to put up with!' There existed, Walter was aware, a macabre thermometer to the state of health and well-being of the Shanghai population (of other cities in China, too): namely, the 'exposed corpse'. Even in relatively good times, such was the precarious level of life in China, vast numbers of 'exposed corpses' would be collected on the streets ... six-thousand-odd in the streets of Shanghai in 1935. In 1937 more than twenty thousand bodies had been found on the streets or on waste ground in the city. By 1938 with the help of the war the number of corpses collected had risen to more than a hundred thousand *in the International Settlement alone*! 'The cremation of six hundred corpses,' the Health Department report for that year declared encouragingly, 'takes only four hours, though a greater number must have from six to eight hours for complete combustion.'

Well, no wonder that labour in Shanghai was so cheap and productive when the worker was accompanied everywhere by his grim *doppelgänger* the 'exposed corpse'! 'Our workers in Singapore may sometimes find it hard to make ends meet but at least they don't have that sort of thing to cope with. And why not? Because men like old Webb saw fit to devote their lives, not to a lot of political bilge about nationalism, welfare and equality, but to the building up of businesses which would actually produce some wealth! Perhaps one day we shall see what sort of fist our rabble-rousing friends the Communists make of feeding people but I only hope I don't have to depend on them for my next meal!'

Righteous indignation welled up inside him at the prospect until he remembered that, for the moment at least, the Communists were dropping their anti-British campaign, so people said, in order to concentrate all their efforts against the Japanese.

'Well, Mohammed,' asked Walter leaning forward in the rush of air to speak into the *syce's* ear, 'are you happy living in Singapore?'

'Very happy, *Tuan.*' Walter could not see the man's features in the darkness beneath the black outline of the cap he wore, but he glimpsed the flash of white teeth as he smiled.

Presently, soothed by the vastness of the night sky, his thoughts turned to Mr Webb again and not, this time, with the lingering resentment of the old man's rigid ideas which he had felt earlier in the evening (those contemptuous marzipan smiles) but with sympathy and gratitude. And for the first time he began to feel a real pang of sorrow, that painful sense of absence, of being deserted almost, when someone whose life has been closely intertwined with your own suddenly disappears. For in spite of his age, Mr Webb's collapse had come as a surprise: it was only when you had a hand in picking him up that you realized that there was nothing much to him any more but skin and bone and the undimmed presence of a powerful personality, what weight there *was* consisted largely of his heavy English shoes. He had, after all, continued hale and hearty throughout the decade that followed his retirement. Only in the past year or two had he shown some signs of failing: at one time he had come to believe that his fellow directors of Blackett and Webb were trying to poison him, in the gruesome

Malay fashion, with needle-like bamboo hairs coiled like watch-springs which then unwind to puncture the intestines or lodge undetected in the mucous membrane of the bladder. Fortunately, he had forgotten about it after a while.

Next, there had come a final flaring-up of the entrepreneurial fires which had been banked up peacefully since his retirement. He had demanded that Walter should expand Blackett and Webb into a great vertical combine like Lever Brothers or Dunlop. A vast amount of rubber was already under their control and there was still time to get a foothold in the palm-oil business. Why should they not go into the production and marketing of motor-tyres and margarine in Europe and America? Walter, though he considered the idea ridiculous, had murmured soothingly that it was worth thinking about. But old Mr Webb had become querulous, demanding a proper response to his plan. Gently Walter had explained that the opportunity for such an expansion was long since past: the competition was too powerful, capital and European executives too hard to come by, even if business had not been so sternly regulated by Britain's war economy. Mr Webb had been bitter and disbelieving, had denounced Walter as 'a mere tradesman' ... but presently the fires had died down again; in the last few months before today's fateful garden-party at which he had tumbled out of his chair and into the strange twilit ante-room to death, neither his dreams of a huge combine nor his fears of bamboo poisoning had caused him any distress. The question of palm-oil, though, had lodged in Walter's mind like a coiled bamboo hair: insignificant at first, it was coming imperceptibly to irritate him. Blackett and Webb should have become involved in palm-oil ten years ago. A businessman must move with the times. How often, recalling the fate of the fine-millers of rice in London ruined by the opening of the Suez Canal, had he not warned young men against thinking that a business could be maintained in a changing world without constant change!

The Bentley, having skirted the teeming, narrow streets of Chinatown, ill-lit and even at this hour apparently bubbling with sinister activity and subversion, had now almost reached Outram Road. The several buildings of the hospital were scattered on a small hill among trees; first-class, second-class and third-class buildings respectively housed patients occupying corresponding positions on the social ladder. Mr Webb, naturally, had been taken to a building from which he would be able to leave the world in a suitable manner. The Bentley, therefore, drew up beside the half-dozen cream pillars which formed the entrance to the main building: Walter remained in the motor-car while the *syce* went to make enquiries about Mr Webb. The man was gone some time and, presently, Walter got out to take a stroll beneath half a dozen tall palms on the lawn opposite the building. Above, on the roof, he could see the silhouette of a clock tower but it was too dark to make out the time. He supposed it must be well after midnight by now. Through the open windows on the ground floor he could see into what was evidently a general ward, dimly lit. He stared into it for a moment, half fascinated, half repelled: he was just able to make out shadowy figures stretched motionless beneath the silently whirring fans. So, this was how it ended for a man who had once had the Rangoon rice trade by the throat: in essentials not very different, he thought sombrely, from the way it ended for one of Shanghai's 'exposed corpses'.

A crunch of gravel. Walter turned away. The *syce* was approaching accompanied by Major Archer. The Major had come earlier on a similar mission to Walter's. Old Mr Webb was still in the same condition, unconscious and paralysed. Walter could no doubt look in on him for a moment if he wanted.

'Perhaps tomorrow,' said Walter, moving back towards the Bentley, reprieved. 'I really just came to find out how he was getting on.' He lingered, however, for a moment with the Major, explaining that Mr Webb's collapse meant that a number of difficult decisions would have to be taken. What were they going to do now about the theme of 'Continuity' in the jubilee procession? That was just one of many new problems that were zigzagging their way to the surface like bubbles as Mr Webb drew nearer to death. And should he make arrangements for young Matthew Webb to come out to Singapore? 'After all, it seems a long way for him to come if he's not going to inherit.'

The Major showed surprise. But surely. Why, Mr Webb had happened to mention only the other day that Matthew would be his heir! He had even asked the Major some months earlier to witness his signature on the appropriate document and at the same time had spoken warmly of those who devoted themselves to the rehabilitation of native peoples.

'He said nothing to me about it,' muttered Walter, thankful for the darkness which helped to mask the shock which this news had caused him. Until this moment he had allowed himself to entertain some hopes that, in default of an heir, he himself might be left at least a substantial part of Mr Webb's holdings in the business.

'Surely he would have told me if he had changed his mind?' He stood for a moment with his hand on the door of the car looking up at the stars.

'Well, perhaps I will go and look in on him after all,' he said finally and with a nod to the Major made his way heavily towards where his former partner lay on his death-bed.

11

The medical opinion had been that Mr Webb would not survive more than a few hours. But the hours and the days and presently the weeks went by and still the old fellow lingered on. An era had ended, Walter was right about that, and no doubt a new era had begun. But Mr Webb somehow managed to survive this jolting passage over the switched points of history and live on into the spring of 1941. Most likely, if his feeble hold on life had been shaken loose and he had died then and there, which probably would have been best for everybody, Walter would not have thought it worth while to summon Matthew merely to attend a funeral. But Mr Webb continued to cling on stubbornly and, besides, if Matthew was to inherit his father's share of the business Walter preferred to have him in Singapore where a clear idea of the serious responsibilities attached to his inheritance could be the more easily printed on his mind. After all, they knew so little of Matthew. He would have to make up his own mind, of course, whether or not to come out. Was he even in Europe still? A number of the more affluent people in Britain, according to J. B. Priestley's wireless broadcasts, were prudently moving to Canada and the United States, leaving the lower classes to defend their estates against the Germans. Walter knew nothing of Matthew's financial situation but assumed that he must be, at least, comfortably off.

As a child Matthew had once or twice written dutiful letters to 'Dear Uncle Walter', thanking him (his little fingers guided by his mother's hand) for some Christmas present or other. In the years that followed the General Strike one or two more letters had arrived. Their purpose was not stated but Walter had not found it hard to guess. The young man, filled with remorse by the estrangement from his father, was seeking some word of him. Naturally, Walter had replied with reassuring descriptions of the old man's comfortable days at the Mayfair Rubber Company. Matthew had continued to write an occasional letter to the Blacketts throughout the thirties, though his letters had grown shorter and the information they contained somewhat random, as if he merely wrote down whatever caught his eye as he looked around his hotel room or out of the window (he never seemed to have a home of his own). These letters had come not only from Geneva but occasionally from other cities, too. There had once even been a picture postcard from Tokyo, showing what appeared to be a sheep standing up to its knees in a lake. 'What is supposed to be the purpose of this?' Walter had wondered, amazed, staring at the sheep and trying to penetrate its significance. It seemed that the boy had paid a visit to the Far East, after all.

One of Matthew's letters in 1939 had mentioned that he would soon be in London on some unspecified business. As it happened, Kate, then aged almost twelve, had been there at the time, staying with an aunt for a few days before returning from school to Singapore for the summer holidays, holidays destined to be prolonged by the outbreak of war. The Blacketts' curiosity about Matthew was considerable. Why should Kate not go and have a chat with him?

Walter had wasted no time in cabling his London office, instructing them to telephone every hotel in London until they found a Matthew Webb. In the meantime poor Kate, who had not been consulted and who naturally dreaded the meeting in prospect, had waited praying that he would not be found. The principal cause of her despair was the thought of being seen 'by a man' in her school uniform, a fate which she and her school-friends agreed was the ultimate humiliation. But in due course, after on or two false alarms, Matthew had been unearthed in a shabby boarding-house in Bloomsbury. The London manager of Blackett and Webb had packed Kate into a taxi and rushed her across London.

The meeting had not been a great success at first. Matthew had been lying on his bed in his underwear reading a book while his trousers, which had just been soaked in a cloudburst, were drying over a chair in the window. Without his trousers he was reluctant to let a young girl into his room although, as

Walter later observed, one might have thought that this was one of the few contingencies in life that his progressive education had prepared him for. Moreover, at first he appeared never to have heard of any Kate Blackett and could not think what she wanted of him. Kate had had to shout explanations through the door, arousing the interest of the other lodgers. Meanwhile, the landlady's suspicions had been awakened by the telephone drag-net which had caught Matthew in her establishment and she had become convinced that he was a malefactor or pervert of some kind. So Kate's mortified explanations through the door had been punctuated by instructions from the landlady for him to leave her premises immediately. Finally, however, Matthew had dragged on his sodden trousers and opened the door.

Kate was later asked to describe the person who had confronted her as the door opened. Well, he was quite nice, she thought. She could not think of anything else to say. Oh yes she could, he wore spectacles. Chiefly what she remembered was that his shoes squelched when he walked: they had evidently been soaked, too. He had walked straight out of the boarding-house, ignoring the landlady and the London manager, who was rubbing his hands in consternation at the way things had turned out. Kate, dreadfully embarrassed by the furore she had caused, had followed Matthew to a tea-shop round the corner. She had felt so self-conscious that almost the only thing she remembered about their conversation was that when, at the end of it, Matthew had risen from his seat there had been a wet patch where he had been sitting. And yet they had got on very well really, she assured her father. He was quite nice, she thought.

Why stay at such a wretched place? Why travel with only one pair of trousers and shoes? It could hardly be that he was short of money. He presumably had a salary of some kind and Walter was certain that despite their estrangement old Mr Webb had not ceased to provide a generous allowance for his son. 'I'm afraid,' Walter had said when discussing Kate's revelations with his wife, 'that all those half-baked schools have had their effect on the lad, whatever Jim Ehrendorf may say to the contrary.'

As it happened, the Blacketts had been unable to learn much more from Ehrendorf than they had from Kate. Ehrendorf was perfectly well able to tell them what Matthew *thought* about a number of matters, many of them abstract. He could tell them where Matthew stood on 'socialism in a single country', on

J. W. Dunne's 'serial time' and suchlike. What he could not do was to give the Blacketts any real idea of what he was *like*. Was he married? How did he dress? Well, if he wasn't married where did he eat his meals? Smiling, Ehrendorf had to admit that they had been so busy talking that many of these questions had not crossed his mind. Now that he thought about it he had come across Matthew once or twice in restaurants in Geneva, eating by himself with a book propped against a jug of wine or beer. But there was not much else he could remember. He agreed with Kate that Matthew wore glasses, however. He was sure of this because once, while they were strolling under the plane trees on the Quai Wilson, he had broken them.

'How?'

'Sir?'

'How did he break them?'

But Ehrendorf could not remember. Perhaps he had dropped them. They had been discussing Locarno at the time. Matthew had strong feelings about such treaties and soon Ehrendorf was sharing them with the Blacketts: it seemed that as a good League man Matthew did not believe in the Big Powers settling things behind closed doors.

'And so,' smiled Walter, 'all you can tell us is that he wears glasses, which we knew already.'

'And that he's a wonderful human being,' added Ehrendorf with warmth.

Kate had taken to giggling whenever Ehrendorf spoke warmly of Matthew. This time, when she giggled, Ehrendorf suddenly sprang across the room and seized her before she could escape. He picked her up bodily, although she was getting to be quite a lump, and brought her back under one arm. This time he was going to find out why she was laughing. In the end Kate had to confess: it was because he was always calling Matthew a 'wonderful human being' and she kept thinking he was calling him a 'wonderful Human Bean'! Her parents exchanged exasperated glances at this: Kate had recently discovered that she had a sense of humour and they had suffered greatly in consequence. But Ehrendorf seemed to find it amusing. Thereafter Matthew became known to the younger Blacketts as 'the Human Bean'.

Well, since old Mr Webb continued to cling on stubbornly Matthew had to be sent for, whatever he was like, and influence used on his behalf to overcome the difficulties of war-time travel. Fortunately, rubber was a priority cargo these days and the Ministry of Supply listened sympathetically to Walter's request that Matthew should be sent out to take his father's place in the Mayfair Rubber Company. It took time before Matthew could be located through his solicitors (it turned out that he had not made a prudent bolt for it with the stampeding herd of well-to-do), and more time before the details could be arranged. The result was that not just weeks but months had passed since the unlucky day the old gentleman had fallen out of his chair at the garden-party before word eventually reached Walter that Matthew had started out on his journey. But these days unless you were a brass hat or a Minister nobody knew when you would arrive, or even if you would arrive at all.

Mr Webb, though severely paralysed and still unable to communicate, had in due course been moved back to the Mayfair with a nurse in constant attendance. Walter, who himself had a secret dread of dying in hospital, had overborne medical advice to the contrary and had the old gentleman returned to his home. There he could more easily take a few minutes away from his business affairs to lift a corner of the mosquito net and give a comforting squeeze to the cold knuckles which lay on the sheet.

Once or twice Mr Webb had tried to say something. Something to do with the sun, apparently. It could hardly be that the light was bothering him because the blinds of split bamboo chicks had been unrolled and allowed only a muted glow to enter the room. Perhaps the old man had been thinking of agreeable evenings spent prowling with his secateurs and watching the sunlight gleam on the skins of his naked gymnasts as they swooped and swung and balanced, growing stronger every day. Walter found it disturbing, nevertheless, to see his friend lying there, breathing noisily in his tent of white muslin. Mr Webb's eyelids were half open but his expression was vacant for the most part and he showed little sign of being aware of his surroundings. 'This is how we all finish,' mused Walter grimly.

'It's the end of an era,' he said aloud to Major Archer who stood beside him in a respectful pose at his dying chairman's bedside.

Because presently Mr Webb again tried to say something about the sun Walter decided that Miss Chiang should be recalled.

Perhaps he would find her presence soothing. After Mr Webb's collapse the gymnasts and body-builders had been dispersed with a bonus added to their emoluments. Miss Chiang had declined indignantly when offered an additional reward for staying away from her former employer while he was in hospital. Now the Major was given the delicate task of running her to earth in some tenement in Chinatown and persuading her to return to visit the patient. She agreed without fuss and her presence did indeed seem to exert a soothing influence on the old man. She was still wearing one of Joan's cast-off dresses and Walter, glimpsing her one day as she was leaving the Mayfair was taken aback, as much by her good looks as by the thought of her dubious relationship with old Mr Webb. 'Who would have thought that Webb would end up like this with a half-caste holding his hand!'

Walter, these days, had little time to spare for visiting the sick. Business had never been more hectic and besides he was becoming increasingly preoccupied with the problem of finding a husband for Joan. Now that it had become clear that he was unlikely to inherit Mr Webb's share of the business it had become more important than ever that she should make a sensible match.

'What are your feelings for Jim Ehrendorf, if you don't mind me asking?' he enquired mildly one day, finding her alone.

'Oh, he'd put his hand in the fire for me,' she replied with a laugh.

Walter was silent for a moment, contemplating this reply which, though interesting, did not answer his question.

'Don't you believe me?'

'Of course I believe you,' said Walter, laughing in turn. 'What I wanted to know was what you feel for *him*?'

Joan shrugged, gazing out of the window, her eyes like green pebbles. 'He's all right. He gets on my nerves though, I'm thinking of chucking him one of these days ... in fact, the sooner the better.' Walter was satisfied with this reply.

Some days later, however, he thought of it again in a rather different light. For it happened that one day, in the course of a casual conversation while waiting for Joan to come downstairs, Ehrendorf said something which Walter, as a rubber producer, found unusually interesting, and which placed him in something of a predicament if he were to pursue his policy of replacing Ehrendorf in Joan's affections with someone who would make a more suitable husband.

Walter's predicament stemmed indirectly from the successful operation of the Restriction scheme's tap for controlling the flow of rubber on to the market, of which he had originally been one of the chief plumbers. As a result of the recession of 1938 and the fall in price to five pence a pound the Committee had given the tap a savage twist, shutting down the flow to forty-five per cent of capacity. Thereafter in the reservoir of rubber stocks the level began to sink and the price to creep up again. By the beginning of 1939 the level had fallen once more below the danger mark which had released the previous boom, but the Committee still showed no sign of opening the tap.

As it had turned out, it was neither the idleness of the native smallholders nor the lack of capacity of the producing countries which had now set the price of rubber on its long, steady climb, but the declaration of war in Europe. At the end of 1939 with the level in the reservoir very low (a mere two months' absorption) the price had been standing at a gratifying shilling a pound. This, patriotism apart, had been a tense period for Walter and his colleagues. What effect would war have on the use of rubber? Their experience during the Great War had been of little help: in those days the industry had hardly got under way. But they had not had long to wait. Despite a grudging increase in the amount released to the market the level continued to sink. Rubber was being used more than ever.

At this point the Committee began to come under heavy pressure, not just from the manufacturers but from the United States Government and the British Ministry of Supply. More rubber must be released! And it was, but still not enough. The German attack on France and the Low Countries the preceding spring (May 1940) had alarmed the Americans about their future supplies: they wanted to build up a reserve in case it should be needed for their defence programme. And so they had established the Rubber Reserve Company to buy the 150,000 tons they thought they would need at a decent price of up to twenty US cents a pound; the Committee had agreed to increase the flow so that there would be enough rubber on the market for them to buy. Presently the Americans had decided to make it 330,000 tons.

Alas, against all expectations the amount of rubber used by private manufacturers continued to rise and, despite the increased rate of release, there was still not enough to go round. The United States Government's twenty cents, which at one time would have been considered bountiful, was being resolutely outbid by private manufacturers who, often as not (Walter had to smile at the thought of it) were themselves the chaps who had been appointed as buying agents for the Government and who were now in the satisfactory position of bidding against (and naturally outbidding) their official selves! How poignant it was when the Reserve Company found that after six months of effort its cupboard was still almost as bare as it had been at the beginning! Even when the Committee had at last reluctantly agreed to raise the rate of release to one hundred per cent for the first quarter of 1941 there was still no sign of the market reaching saturation point. The spreading Japanese influence, moreover, was diverting rubber from Indo-China and Siam away from Britain and the United States. There could no longer be any serious doubt about it, in Walter's view: the producers' wildest dreams were being realized. This time they had a *genuine* shortage of rubber, not just the wishful thinking of a fast-talking London broker.

Now in February 1941 while he was chatting idly with Ehrendorf about Japan's need for raw materials and the powerful grip that this gave the Western nations on her wind-pipe (where on earth had Joan got to, by the way, she surely hadn't stood him up *again*!) the young man happened to remark that his countrymen were planning to acquire a further 100,000 tons of rubber for the Reserve Company.

'What did you say?' asked Walter casually, doing his best to conceal his surprise: this was the first he had heard of such a deal. He was certain that none of the other producers or dealers in Singapore was aware of it. Nor had he heard anything from his friends on the Committee. In fact, he could hardly believe that it was true; it seemed more likely that Ehrendorf had made a mistake. Ehrendorf repeated what he had said: he had heard it from someone at the consulate. 'By the way,' he added cheerfully, 'it's supposed to be a secret so please keep it to yourself. Careless talk can cost jobs as well as lives.'

'Of course,' agreed Walter blandly, and then to change the subject asked: 'What did you do to your hand?' Ehrendorf's left hand was bandaged.

'Oh, it's nothing. Just a burn.' Walter was on the point of asking him now he had done it but, on second thoughts, decided not to pursue the matter. An uncomfortable silence prevailed for a few moments until at last Joan's footstep was heard on the stairs.

In March Ehrendorf's prediction was proved correct when news came that the Committee had agreed to an offer for a further 100,000 tons. This gave Walter food for thought. A day or two earlier Joan had confided in him that she had now definitely decided to see no more of Ehrendorf. He was getting on her nerves! She was going to clear the decks! And yet, Walter realized, this might not be altogether convenient for himself because it so happened that there was something about the American attitude to the buying of rubber which he badly wanted to know. And it seemed possible that Ehrendorf might be able to tell him.

For some months Walter had been aware that sooner or later difficulties would arise over the fact that the Reserve Company, though given the job of piling up vast quantities of rubber, was being constantly outbid by the big American companies. Why, of 140,000 tons at present afloat for America, the Reserve Company's share was a paltry 5,000 tons! This situation, with the American Government increasingly biting its nails over its reserve stocks, could not be expected to last. Already the first hints were reaching Singapore that the American authorities were on the point of taking some remedial action. Walter was anxious to know what that action would be before it was actually taken.

There was only one thing to be done. Though he did not like to interfere in Joan's private affairs (except, of course, where a potential husband might be concerned) Walter decided to explain his predicament to his daughter. She listened carefully to what he had to say and once again he was pleased by her quick grasp of business matters. 'I can't promise, of course, but it might just happen that we learned something that would do the firm a power of good.'

'A reprieve has been granted!' declared Joan, smiling. 'What a lucky man he is to have you pleading his cause!'

12

Walter did not consider himself a person easily given to self-doubt and discouragement: vigorous initiative was more his cup of tea. But sometimes these days he could not avoid the feeling that his familiar world was crumbling away at an alarming rate. No doubt the Japanese were at the root of a great deal of the present trouble in the Far East: since 1937 a veritable blizzard of edicts designed to cripple European and American interests in China had come from their puppet Government in Peking. Foreign trade had been progressively frozen out and replaced by Japanese monopolies. Look at the huge cigarette factory currently being built in Peking by the Manchuria Tobacco Company, a sinister edifice indeed when you remembered that non-Japanese cigarettes were already subject to a special discriminatory tax throughout Inner Mongolia! Or consider the way the Japanese had taken over the Peking–Mukden and Peking–Suiyan Railways without paying a cent of the interest these railways owed to the foreign bondholders who had financed them, not to mention the havoc they were wreaking throughout China with their military currency. Nor had Blackett and Webb been spared: their import–export trade with Shantung, which had once gone through Tsingtao, had been driven from there by penal anti-Western restrictions to Weihaiwei, only to have the same restrictions follow hot on their heels. Walter did not particularly blame the Japanese for taking what they could get, but he did blame the British Government for allowing them to do so with impunity.

But even without the Japanese Walter believed that his familiar world would still have been crumbling. The strikes of the past decade had changed the whole complexion of Malaya. Serious strikes had continued: Walter doubted now whether they would ever stop. The rise in the cost of living brought about by the outbreak of the war in Europe was the present cause: the workers were aware that profits had risen, too. Five months ago (December 1940) two and a half thousand tappers in the Bahau Rompin area had struck, claiming a daily rate of $1.10 for a task of 350 to 400 trees. The estate manager had promptly paid them off, which meant that they lost the barrack accommodation on the estate that went with the job. They had set up a makeshift camp in Bahau Town. When the police had come to arrest the ring-leaders a few days later crowds sympathetic to the workers had confronted them. Ugly scenes had developed in the course of which the police had opened fire, killing three workers.

Nor was that the end of it, nor likely to be for years to come, in Walter's view. At this very moment, while he sat eating lunch in the Cricket Club with a colleague, Indian workers in the Klang District were on strike. If you had tried to tell old Webb that one day Indian estate workers would take to this strike game he would not have believed you. Indian workers, though paid less than Chinese, were habitually docile and respectful of authority. And yet now they were having to quell them with police and troops! Many of Walter's friends at the Singapore Club were amazed at this change of spots by the Indian workers, but not Walter. He had been expecting it for some time. Because now, he knew, the changed atmosphere in the country would permit such things to happen. The old order of things was as dead as a doornail. Walter sighed and dipped a silver spoon into the pudding which crouched on his plate, a solid moulding of greyish tapioca with coconut milk and a thin, dark syrup. *Gula malacca!* How that cool taste stirred memories of the old days in Singapore!

His thoughts were interrupted by the appearance of a 'boy' with a telephone message which had been relayed from his office: Mr Webb's condition had taken a turn for the worse. Would he come at once? Walter, perhaps in the grip of nostalgia, had drunk several beers and, unusually for him, did not feel altogether sober. He glanced around the room as he stood up: many of the other diners were in uniform and he thought: 'I'd better not fall over and make an ass of myself in front of this crowd!' But he managed without difficulty to negotiate the door and the hallway in a dignified manner. It was outside on the steps, beneath the red-brick Victorian portico, that he almost had a serious collision with a tall, thin and rather chinless Army officer who was entering the Club. The officer's disapproving expression intensified into a grimace of annoyance as Walter, to prevent himself plunging head first down the steps, grasped a thin arm in its rolled-up khaki sleeve. A glance at those blue eyes and tentative moustache was enough. Although Walter, for preference, did not consort with military men he recognized this one immediately. For it was none other than General Percival who had recently taken over the military command from General Bond (Bond's rival, Babington, had been replaced, too). But this General Percival, to Walter's bleary eye, looked a scarcely more encouraging prospect than his predecessor.

'Silly fool! Why don't you watch where you're going?' muttered Walter under his breath as he let go of the General and hurried on down the steps in search of his car.

Before he could find it, however, he recognized a familiar figure also in uniform approaching from the direction of the Victoria Memorial Hall. It was Ehrendorf. Walter hailed him and they exchanged a few words; Walter was barely able to conceal his impatience. He declined Ehrendorf's offer of a *stengah*, explaining that he must hurry to Mr Webb's bedside as it seemed that the old man's long resistance might now be coming to an end.

'By the way,' Walter permitted himself to enquire at last, 'did you hear any more about the new buying arrangements for the Reserve Company?'

'Why, yes, as a matter of fact.' Ehrendorf looked somewhat uncomfortable at the question. 'I guess I can rely on you to keep it to yourself!' Walter reassured him, trying to seem casual.

'Buying is to be centralized ... no more private deals. All rubber exports to the United States are to be licensed. Licences will only be issued for shipping through the central buying agency and for fulfilling any outstanding forward contracts.'

'I see,' said Walter. 'That's interesting. Outstanding orders will go through? When will it begin?'

Ehrendorf did not know. 'In a few days, I suppose.'

Walter said goodbye to Ehrendorf and climbed into the back seat of the Bentley. 'Mohammed,' he said presently to the *syce*, 'I would like you to drop me at Collyer Quay and then to go to the Mayfair with a message for Major Archer. Tell him that I have been delayed by a very serious matter but will come as soon as I can.' He sat back, satisfied with his decision. It was one, he knew, with which old Mr Webb would have been in perfect sympathy.

As it turned out, although it was evening before Walter had at last finished sending cables and reached the Mayfair, there had been no particular need to hurry: his old friend and partner still had not succumbed. Nor, for that matter, did there appear to have been any great change in his condition. Mr Webb still lay there, breathing noisily in his illuminated tent of white muslin. The Major explained, however, that the old man had gone through a crisis of some sort about mid-day, had appeared restless, and several times had repeated the word 'sun' and a number of other words too garbled to be understood, at least by the Major.

'But the interesting thing was,' he told Walter, 'that Vera Chiang, who was here at the time, thought she understood that he was trying to say: "Sun Yat-sen".'

'Nonsense!' cried Walter. 'The old boy just wanted to go and prune his roses in the nude. He didn't give tuppence for Sun Yat-sen.' And clapping the Major cheerfully on the back Walter strode off, chuckling, through the compound in the direction of his own house; but as he went a grim thought came stealing after him through the hushed garden and pounced on him before he had reached the safety of his own walls: 'This is how we all end up, mumbling rubbish to people who interpret it as they want!'

On the evenings that followed, while Mr Webb, now mute again, continued to lie there, and on through June, July and August of 1941, Walter's nostalgia for the old Singapore became acute. Perhaps this was paradoxical for in the old days, about which he was less and less able to resist holding forth to Major Archer at his dying partner's bedside, business had never boomed the way it was booming now. But in those days the atmosphere had been different, more relaxed ... no, it was not simply youth, though being young undoubtedly had something to do with it. No, it was the place itself. Singapore had been different in those days. Business had been an adventure, not the grim striving for advantage it had become latterly. They had been as if on a different time scale: everything had seemed to happen more slowly, more comfortably.

Walter paused, staring up as if for enlightenment at the grey metallic blur of the ceiling fan and then down again at the billowing cocoon of the mosquito net within which lay old Mr Webb (soon to be hatched out into a better world). At one time in Singapore everyone had known everyone. Those were the days of great rambling colonial houses where the tradition of lavish hospitality lingered on from the nineteenth century. Ah well, all that had gone with the wind. In the course of time the bachelor messes, too, which the merchant houses kept going for their young chaps, had been replaced by blocks of flats. And once they had disappeared all the fun that young men used to have in the tropics had disappeared with them.

It was the development of Singapore as a great naval and military base which had started the rot. People who had no real connection with the country had flooded in. The Military had their uses, he went on, forgetting that the Major himself had been a military man in his day, but they were nomads, here today and gone tomorrow, never bothering to get to know the people or the country. What was the result of this influx? Simply that the old feeling of space and tranquillity which used to make Singapore such a pleasant place to live in had gone, and gone for ever.

'Sylvia and I used to motor thirty or forty miles sometimes in our pyjamas to have supper with friends in Johore. That's what I call a comfortable way to live!'

And the Major, though he would have preferred to discuss Japan's increasingly threatening attitude in the sphere of international politics, was obliged to confess that going to a dinner-party in pyjamas did sound to him the very model of a life of contentment: obviously in those days there was no risk of meeting maddened hordes of strikers waving *parangs*.

The Singapore Club in the old days was not, declared Walter on another visit a few weeks later (forestalling the Major's attempt to ask him what he thought of Roosevelt's proposal, just announced, that French Indo-China should be considered a neutral country from which Japan could get food and raw materials; the Major had got on well with old Mr Webb and sorely missed his chairman's forceful views on perplexing world topics), no, it was not the mixing pot of all ages and conditions it had since become, no sir! Nowadays you might find yourself rubbing shoulders with any young twerp just out from England or some other fellow whose too careful public school accent might slip from time to time exposing heaven knew what dubious origins. But then it had been truly exclusive, the sort of place frequented by the older and more influential men in the Colony, reserved exclusively for males, of course, except for New Year's Day when ladies were invited for lunch to eat the traditional dish: Pheasant Lucullus! Yes, the Singapore Club used to be the lair of the *Tuan Besar*, like this poor old chap here, and it was quite a daunting prospect for a young man to go and visit him in it.

A mere two days later, as the Major, perfectly disconsolate at being deprived of his chairman and unable to settle down to the paper work awaiting him in a very empty-seeming office, was roaming the bungalow like a dog without its master, he once more came upon Walter who had somehow stolen into the building without being seen and was lurking at the old man's bedside.

'Singapore had a pride in herself in those days,' declared Walter, spotting the Major in the doorway, but then he hesitated, perhaps realizing that as an opening remark this might be considered odd. After a moment he cleared his throat and added: 'Everything is all right here, is it, Major? If you need any help let me know and I'll send someone down from the office.'

The Major agreed that everything was in order. Indeed, since Blackett and Webb managed the day-to-day running of the Mayfair there was little for him to do except play cards with

Dupigny (for the Frenchman, now penniless and a refugee in overcrowded Singapore, had been given shelter in one of the Mayfair's many rooms) and at fixed hours to open up the recreation hut which old Mr Webb had patriotically built in the grounds for the troops flooding into the Colony (fortunately, no troops ever put in an appearance to make use of it). But though life had pursued its usual uneventful course at the headquarters of the Mayfair Rubber Company, there had been some alarming developments on the international scene: in response to the reported occupation by Japanese troops of the whole of Indo-China, America, Britain and Holland had frozen Japanese assets. One did not have to be an economist to see that this put Japan in a serious plight. Would this action make the Japanese see reason or would it light the blue-paper to a Far Eastern war? The Major was anxious to have Walter's opinion about this (he had already had Dupigny's which was deeply pessimistic, but then so were all Dupigny's opinions), but Walter, brushing aside this prospective clashing of continents, was impatient to give the Major some idea of the pride that Singapore had had in herself. Lifting one corner of the mosquito net to peer at the grey, rigid form of his old friend he exclaimed: 'My word! Before the Great War we came second to none. After it, too, for a time.'

Taking the Major's arm he explained with a chuckle how the great Russian dancer, Pavlova, had come to Singapore expecting to find herself dancing at the Town Hall theatre, only to find that it had already been booked by the Amateur Dramatic Society. Her manager had suggested that the Amateur Dramatic Society would not mind postponing its performance of Gilbert and Sullivan so that the great ballerina, before whom grovelled the most refined, most perfumed, most diamond-glittering, evening-dressed audiences in the world, might dance on the best stage available in the Straits. Ah, but as it turned out the Amateur Dramatic Society did mind! They had their pride. They had been founded over a hundred years ago. They saw no reason why they should surrender the Victoria Hall to a foreign artiste ... and so she had to go off and make the best of a cramped little stage at the old German Club. And Walter laughed so long and loud that the ceiling rang with his laughter and even the melancholy Major looked amused ... but had Walter's laughter concealed a muffled cry from the direction of the mosquito net? The Major cast an uneasy glance in that direction. A strange rictus was twisting the old man's lips. A mumbled cry broke from them which might have been: 'Sun Yat-sen!' (or might not, it was hard to tell).

The Major freed himself from Walter's grasp. It surely could not be ... or could it? With an exclamation the Major sprang to his chairman's side, whipping aside the film of mosquito netting. But too late! That smile or grimace, whichever it had been, that strangled cry, whatever it had meant, had been his last.

'Young Matthew will be too late after all,' observed Walter sadly. 'And he's due to arrive any day now.'

'If you have an hour to spare,' Walter said to Joan on the following day, 'I should like to show you something.'

Together father and daughter installed themselves in the back of the Bentley. Walter had evidently already given instructions to the *syce* for they set off without more ado in the direction of the river. Walter was more silent and subdued than usual and Joan found this whole expedition somewhat mysterious. 'Where are we going?' she asked.

'To look at a warehouse,' he replied briefly but said no more. Only when the motor-car was nudging its way along the crowded streets beside the river did Walter again break his silence, to ask Joan if she had seen Ehrendorf.

'No. I've finished with him,' said Joan with a smile.

'Ah,' said Walter. 'Good enough.' He leaned forward to tap the *syce* on the shoulder. With considerable difficulty on account of the lorries being loaded and unloaded at the wharves where lighters and *tong-kangs* clustered several deep they had reached a tall brick godown at a bend in the river. Apart from the fact that it was built of brick in a conservative style and bore an inscription in white letters: *Blackett and Webb Limited*, recently repainted for the jubilee celebrations, there was nothing very remarkable about it.

'You may wonder why I brought you here,' said Walter, smiling now. 'As you see, it's just a godown, nothing very special. But to me this building is rather important because it's the first we put up here in Singapore and, incidentally, an exact replica of Webb's first building in Rangoon. I used to come here a lot and day-dream as a young man. Not that old Webb used to give me much time for day-dreaming. There's a little office up above ... Let's go up if you don't mind getting your frock dusty.'

They stepped through a small door cut in the massive wooden

gates facing the road. After the heat and sunshine of the road it seemed dark and cool inside. Dust sparkled in a shaft of sunlight which blazed at their feet and cast a dim light back over the rest of the cavernous building, illuminating the bales of rubber which rose around them.

'I used to think I'd bring Monty here one day but I doubt if he'd understand what the place means to me.'

They climbed a swaying ladder, Joan going first, to a dim ledge that hung in the shadows above them. As he followed her Walter noticed his daughter's strong thighs beneath her frock and thought: 'Yes, she's a real Blackett. She has pluck. Her mother would never climb a ladder like that.' When he had reached the ledge Walter led the way through a maze of rubber bales to a little store-keeper's office with a window over the river. 'Here we are,' he announced. 'This is my little nest. You have the chair. I'll sit on the table. Well, my dear, the reason I asked you to come here isn't only sentimental, though that may be part of it. The fact is that the business is at a crossroads now that Mr Webb is dead and I am going to need your help. As you know, Matthew Webb who is due out here shortly will inherit his father's share of the business. Well, we don't know what he's like exactly but as far as I can make out he's a somewhat muddled person. We don't want him rocking the boat, therefore ... No, Joan, just let me finish ... therefore it would suit me, putting it in a nut-shell, and I hope you won't mind me suggesting this ... it would suit me if he found you as attractive as, let's say, his chum Ehrendorf does ... Yes, in a moment, Joan, but please let me have my say first. Now I want you to understand that I'm not asking you for anything more, though I shall be pleased if you find a good husband one of these days ... Just make him find you attractive, I'm sure I don't have to tell you *how* although ... and this is something that I have never told anyone, not even your mother ... the one sure way that a woman can make a man lose his head is by *blowing hot and cold*, you know the sort of thing, loving one moment, indifferent the next, that sort of feminine way of carrying on is something, let me tell you straight, that a man finds irresistible Well, there you are, but before you give me your answer just let me repeat two things. Firstly, the business could well be vulnerable to foolish behaviour by Matthew Webb and, secondly, you don't have to marry him if you don't want to. It will be enough if you get him under your thumb for a couple of years. There!'

'But Father!' exclaimed Joan, laughing and jumping up from her chair to give her father a hug. 'How old-fashioned you are to deliver such a speech! I took it for granted long ago that you'd want me to marry Matthew for the sake of the firm. And the answer is "yes", of course. I don't care what he's like! You took such a long time to pop the question. I was beginning to think you'd never ask!'

Part Two

13

On account of the hazards of war-time, the convoys that were diverted without explanation, the passenger vessels that were commandeered for the movement of troops, the seats on aeroplanes usurped at the last moment by august officials, not to mention the spies that lurked everywhere and studied every mortal thing that moved on the face of the earth through field-glasses or kept their treacherous ears open while quaffing pints in dockside pubs, Matthew Webb had been frustrated again and again in his efforts to reach Singapore. The result was that the month of November was already well advanced before he found himself on the last stages of his journey. By that time, though his impending arrival had not been forgotten by the Blacketts (Walter brooded on it constantly and so, presumably, did Joan), it had assumed less momentous proportions than in the first days after Mr Webb's death. Walter could see the matter now more in perspective, for the old man had been buried for almost a month, sad news which had been conveyed to Matthew in Colombo where he had been stranded interminably until Walter could pull a string or two with the RAF. Moreover, in the frenzied commercial atmosphere of Singapore at the time, exacerbated by the bewildering arrival of more and yet more troops from Australia and India, who could manage to spare time for such domestic, or dynastic, matters, or even, if it comes to that, think of the same thing for two moments running? But at last Matthew was about to arrive.

The Avro Anson which for an hour or more had been following the wandering dark-green edge of the coast now swung out to sea before turning north-west in a wide curve that would bring it back over Singapore. For a few moments nothing could be seen but an expanse of water so dazzling that it hurt Matthew's eyes as he looked down on it from the cabin window. Then, as the Anson floated in over the harbour in which lay three grey warships and a multitude of other vessels, over the railway station with its track curving away across the island to the Causeway, and over a number of miniature buildings scarcely big enough to house a colony of fleas, it began to wobble in a dreadful, sickening fashion, and to lose height. Presently, the Singapore River (which was really nothing but a tidal creek) crept from under the wing, ominously bulging near its mouth like a snake which had just swallowed a rabbit and then trailing back inland to the thinnest of tails on the far side of the city.

Next there came an open green space on which a fleas' cricket match was taking place and then the toy spire of a cathedral, aptly set at the intersection of diagonal paths forming the cross of St Andrew, with one or two flea-worshippers scurrying over its green sward to offer up their evening prayers, for the sun, though still brightly fingering the cabin of the aircraft, was already casting deep shadows over the cathedral lawns ... But again the plane dropped sickeningly and the wing on one side tilted up in the most alarming way, so that even though Matthew continued to look *down* he could still see nothing but sky. This dismaying sensation continued until the plane had completed a full circle and was coming in from the sea again with level wings. But even so, every few moments the floor would seem to drop away and when Matthew tried to interest himself, as a diversion, in MacFadyean's *History of the Rubber Industry* which lay open on his lap, he was promptly obliged to jettison even this light work from his thoughts, simply to keep the plane airborne.

By now they were distressingly near the surface. He saw waves, then a junk floating past the cabin window with a thick-veined sail, then a flotsam of human heads and waving hands. Somehow or other the wheels cleared the roof of the swimming club at Tanjong Rhu (Matthew would have thought they were too low to have cleared anything at all). A few more perilous wobbles and the wheels consented to touch down with a bump and a brief howl, followed by another bump as the tail touched. The journey had been a strain: he had never been up in an aeroplane before. But now he felt relieved and pleased with himself; soon he would be describing the experience to his earthbound friends.

'Don't forget to watch out for the Singapore Grip!' shouted one of the crew after him in a clamour of cheerful goodbyes and laughter as he jumped stiffly to the ground.

Now he found himself standing on the tarmac, a little unsteadily on account of the equatorial gale from the still turning propellors. Uncertain which way to walk he peered around in the haze of evening sunlight. The heat was suddenly stifling: he was clad in it from head to toe, as if wrapped in steaming towels.

A figure in a white flannel suit was hurrying towards him into the slip-stream, trouser legs flapping, jacket ballooning and one large hand clapped on to a khaki sun-helmet to keep it on his head. The other hand was held out even from some yards' distance towards Matthew who, a moment later, found himself shaking it.

'You're Matthew Webb, aren't you? I'm Monty Blackett. I expect you've heard of me ... Hm, now let me see, I don't think we have met before, have we? Never mind, anyway. It doesn't make any difference. We'll get to know each other in a jiffy, I expect. Can't very well help it in a hole like this.' Monty was a burly young man about the same age as Matthew but his face had a heavy-set appearance which made him look older: an impression reinforced when he removed his sun-helmet for a moment to scratch his head by the fact that his hair was receding. Matthew wondered whether the black tie he was wearing, which had been blown back over his shoulder, was a mark of respect for his father or merely conventional Singapore attire.

After the two young men had exchanged greetings, which they had to shout because of the noise from the engines, there was an awkward pause between them.

'Look, it's been raining,' Matthew shouted, nodding at the shivering pools of rainwater that lay here and there on the tarmac; at the same time he smiled at himself, thinking that that was not what he had meant to say at all.

'What?' bellowed Monty, stepping forward and giving Matthew an odd look. 'Yes, I'll say it has, it rains almost every bloody day at the moment, I'll have you know. Come on now,' he added, 'enough of the weather.' He took Matthew's arm to steer him away from that whining aeroplane which only then agreed to arrest its motors with a few last chugs and swishes. 'Well, well, same old Matthew,' he chuckled cautiously, though, strictly speaking, he could not have known very much about the 'old Matthew' at all, since they had never met before. Once more he darted an odd, sideways look at Matthew as if trying to weigh him up, while, still chuckling vaguely, he conducted him to the terminal building, a surprisingly up-to-date

102

construction with control tower and observation decks, somewhat resembling a cinema. Matthew remarked on its modern appearance. Singapore must be quite ...

'Oh yeah,' agreed Monty indifferently. Brightening a little, he added: 'They have a restaurant there. You don't feel like some oysters, do you? They fly them in from Hawkesbury River in Australia. Look, that's not such a bad idea ...'

'Well, not just at the moment, thanks,' said Matthew, surprised. Monty's enthusiasm subsided with a grimace. Matthew, still groping for a topic of conversation, said: 'I must say, I don't know how you stand this heat.'

'Heat? This is the coolest part of the day. Wait and see how hot it *can* get here. I say, is something the matter?' For Matthew had suddenly stiffened.

'I think that man is making off with my bags.' Like many people whose natural inclination is to think the best of people Matthew found it necessary, when travelling, to remain dramatically on the alert to defend himself against malefactors.

'He bloody well better had be,' grinned Monty. 'Otherwise he'll get hell from me!'

'You mean ...?'

'Of course. He's our *syce* ... you know, chauffeur. Now don't worry, old boy. Just trust old Monty. Everything's organized. Come on, Sis is waiting for us in the car ...' And with that he led the way out of the building uttering a strange, smothered groan as he went. Matthew hurried after him, filled with pleasure at the prospect of seeing little Kate, to whom he had taken a considerable liking in the course of their one short meeting.

'Monty, I must thank you for getting me on that plane. Otherwise I might have been stuck in Ceylon for ever, what with the war and so forth.'

'Think nothing of it. We just pulled a few of the right strings and it was a stroke of luck that there happened to be an empty plane coming our way. You see, the point is this ...'

Now they had reached the motor-car and Monty broke off to give the driver some instructions. The latter murmured: 'Yes, *Tuan*,' and stowed Matthew's suitcases in the back of the vehicle; this was a huge open Pontiac with white tyres, a wide running-board and deep leather seats. A young woman whom Matthew failed to recognize was half reclining on the back seat, holding a cigarette holder in a studied pose. She was wearing a simple white cotton frock and a green turban with two knots which stood up, Hollywood style, like a rabbit's ears. The haft of a tennis racket was gripped between her bare calves and its glimmering strings between her pretty, pink knees. She ignored Matthew's greeting and said to Monty: 'Let's scram before I die of heat.' Matthew, disappointed to find this person instead of Kate, tried not to stare at her: this must be Joan Blackett, Kate's elder sister. Kate had spoken of her as of a superior being, sophisticated beyond measure, terrorizing the young men of the Colony with her irresistible appeal, breaking hearts with as little compunction as if they had been chipped dinner-plates.

'But the point is this ...' Monty was repeating, a trifle more sonorously than before, now that they were comfortably installed in the Pontiac one on each side of Joan. There was another pause, however, while the young men each lit a Craven A.

'The point is this,' he said yet again, puffing out an authoritative cloud of blue smoke. As he did so, Matthew found himself wondering whether Monty Blackett might not on occasion be ever so slightly ponderous and self-important, and though, of course, it had been kind of Monty to come and meet him, nevertheless, an ungrateful voice whispered in Matthew's ear: 'What *is* the point?' and he glanced quickly at Joan to see whether she was sharing his impatience. But she was looking moodily in another direction ... towards the wind-sock waltzing impatiently in the breeze at the end of the aerodrome, or towards a large American limousine with Stars and Stripes fluttering from its bonnet which had come into the airport drive at great speed with a squeal of tyres as it negotiated the bend but was now nosing uncertainly in the direction of the terminal building while the driver made up his mind which way to go. Presently, she turned her turbaned profile and her grey eyes fixed themselves intently on his face. He stirred uneasily.

'The point is, Matthew, that at the moment the blighters are so anxious for our rubber that they go out of their way to help whenever they can. They're not usually so helpful, I can assure you. And it doesn't stop the bloody bureaucrats, those clever merchants in Whitehall, making a nuisance of themselves whenever they get the chance. We're constantly battling with pen-pushers in some ministry or other a few thousands miles away.' He added sententiously: 'You'll soon find that out when you have a look at the files in your father's office. Now what's all this? What does this cove want?'

While Monty had been speaking the American limousine which had been prowling about uncertainly for a while had at last made up its mind to approach the Pontiac. It came to a stop beside them and an American soldier slid out from behind the wheel and held the door open.

'Oh lumme, it's him,' said Monty, glancing at Joan.

'Great Scott!' exclaimed Matthew. 'I know that bloke. We were at Oxford together. His name's Jim Ehrendorf ... He's a really wonderful fellow, you must meet him. I was meaning to try and look him up when I got here and now ... but wait a sec ... Of course, you already know him, don't you?' And Matthew clapped a hand to his brow.

'Yes, we do,' said Monty. 'The thing is ...' But without waiting to hear what the thing was, Matthew had leaped out of the Pontiac and was warmly shaking hands with the smiling Ehrendorf. They exchanged a few words, both talking at once. Joan and Monty watched them blankly from the motor-car.

'I thought I wouldn't get here in time,' Ehrendorf was saying as they turned back towards the Pontiac, 'and I'm tied up for the rest of the day. In fact, I wouldn't have heard you were arriving at all if it hadn't been for the chance of meeting up with Walter downtown. Hiya Monty, Hiya Joan!'

'Hiya,' said Monty. Joan showed no more sign of acknowledging Ehrendorf's presence than she had Matthew's. She looked irritable and said again: 'For God's sake, let's scram ... It's so hot.'

'How pretty you look, Joan, in your *vêtement de sport*,' said Ehrendorf in a way that managed to be both casual and rather tense. ' "Shall I compare thee to a summer's day?" '

'I'd far rather you didn't, if you don't mind,' replied Joan sullenly. 'Let's go, for God's sake.'

'I know his type,' said Matthew. 'Next thing, he'll be trying to tell you you're "more lovely and more temperate".' Both he and Ehrendorf laughed but the two Blacketts did not share their amusement; indeed they both looked rather put out.

Ehrendorf continued to stand uncertainly beside the motor-car, gazing at Joan, who looked away petulantly. Matthew took out a handkerchief, removed his glasses and mopped his streaming face. The heat was dreadful, despite the breeze and the approach of night.

'I've got it,' said Ehrendorf. 'Why don't I ride in with you guys. I'll tell my driver to follow and then I can go on from there.' Without waiting for approval Ehrendorf spoke to his driver and then installed himself in the front seat of the Pontiac. Matthew climbed in beside Joan again.

Now the Pontiac was in motion at last; an air of interrogation, of words unspoken, formed over it as it swung out of the aerodrome gates. From near at hand there suddenly came a clamour of music, laughter and singing. A thousand coloured lights twinkled in the gathering dusk through a grove of trees that lay just to their right in the fork of the two roads. Keeling over like a yacht tacking against the wind the Pontiac turned away from the lights on to the Kallang Road.

'That's one of the sights,' Monty said, pointing back with his cigarette shedding sparks. 'A sort of funfair called The Happy World. They're going to catch hell, though, unless they do something about blacking out those lights.'

'There's a better place called The Great World on Kim Seng Road on the other side of town,' said Ehrendorf, turning to grin at Matthew. 'You'll be able to dance with lovely taxi-girls there. Twenty-five cents a throw.'

Matthew decided not to ask for the moment what a 'taxi-girl' was. Instead he said: 'You didn't have that natty moustache in Geneva, did you, Jim? And what have you done to your hand?' For Ehrendorf, though he no longer wore a bandage, still had plaster around his fingers. But to Matthew's surprise these questions only seemed to embarrass Ehrendorf (was he sensitive about his moustache?) who murmured vaguely that it was nothing, he'd stupidly burned himself a few weeks earlier, and then, without further comment, turned his evidently sensitive moustache to face forward again while he examined the road ahead through the windscreen.

Meanwhile the Pontiac had howled over a bridge and was careering through the twilight at an alarming speed. Every now and then as an obstruction loomed up the driver would brake and swerve violently. The horn blared without pause. The blurred forms of rickshaws, motor-cars and bullock-carts receded rapidly on either side. Once, to avoid a traffic jam which suddenly presented itself, they mounted a verge and without slackening speed thrashed through some sort of vegetation, evidently someone's garden.

'Good God!' thought Matthew. 'Do they always drive like this?'

'People in Britain seem to find it amazing,' Monty was saying, his thoughts still on their earlier conversation, 'that we should know more about running the rubber business than they do in Whitehall. What they don't seem to realize is that if we suffer here in Singapore, everything suffers, and that includes their wizard War Effort. It's so hard to get anything done with these bloody civil servants. Sometimes I wonder if they haven't all got infantile paralysis!' And Monty bent his wrist, hunched his shoulders and twisted his face into a highly amusing imitation of a cripple. But Matthew found it hard to smile: he had somehow never found imitations of cripples very entertaining. Monty did not notice this lack of response, however, and shed a great bark of laughter into the humid, sweltering twilight.

Becoming serious again Monty said, pointing at a group of dim buildings on the left: 'That's the Firestone factory where last summer's strikes were started by the Commies. Thanks to the bungling of our little men in the Government they very nearly turned it into a general strike.' Matthew, who had been beginning to fear that he and Monty might have no common interest, became attentive and ventured to remark that he was interested, not only in political strikes and the relations of native workers to European employers, but also in ... well, the 'colonial experience' as a whole. But Monty's response was disappointing.

'Oh, you're interested in the "colonial experience", are you?' he mumbled indifferently. 'Well, you've come to the right place. You'll get a basinful of it here, all right.'

Ehrendorf glanced round quickly but without catching Matthew's eye. His glance, indeed, got no further than Joan's tennis racket still tightly gripped between her knees as she lolled back against the leather seat: he stared at the racket with great intensity, but only for a moment. Then his moustache was dividing the breeze again.

For some time the spinning back and forth of the Pontiac's steering-wheel as they swerved to avoid other vehicles had caused the three young people on the back seat to sway from side to side. Joan, because she was in the middle and had less to hold on to, tended to slide more than the others and already once or twice Matthew had found himself pressed against her soft body while she struggled to recover. Now, however, as the Pontiac negotiated a wide curve with muttering tyres and Joan was once more thrown up against him, she appeared to abandon the unequal struggle: she simply lay against him with her head on his shoulder. Matthew wondered whether to push her off but decided it might not seem polite: better to wait for a curve in the opposite direction to do the job for him. In a few moments the car straightened its course again, which should have allowed her to slide back towards her brother, but to his surprise she remained where she was, sprawled against him. And even when, presently, off-side tyres howling like souls in torment, they entered a curve in the opposite direction, she still remained firmly glued to his side, as if all the laws of physics had been suspended in her favour. Then he really did begin to wonder, because that surely could not be right.

Matthew licked his lips, perplexed. He was not quite sure what to make of it all. The truth was that he felt too hot already without having someone pressed against him. He was very much tempted to shove her away to allow the air to circulate. Not that he found the sensation of her body against him altogether disagreeable, he had to admit. But still, it was a bit awkward. Ah, now he caught a tantalizing breath of French perfume on the rushing tropical evening.

'Watch out for that tennis racket, Sis,' said Monty with a leer.

Matthew glanced at the turbaned head beside him but Joan showed no sign of having heard her brother's remark. Nor had Ehrendorf apparently. At any rate, only the neatly barbered back of his head continued to be visible.

Thinking that perhaps some conversation might revive Joan sufficiently to unglue her from his side Matthew asked: 'Does anyone happen to know what the Singapore Grip is? The RAF blokes in the plane kept telling me to watch out for it but they wouldn't tell me what it actually *was*!' But as a conversational opening this proved a failure. Nobody replied or showed any sign of having heard. 'How deuced odd they all are!' thought Matthew crossly. 'And what's the matter with Jim Ehrendorf?' He was tired from his journey, too tired to make an effort with people who were not prepared to make an effort *back*.

Monty, meanwhile, had pulled the brim of his sun-helmet over his eyes, turned up his collar, stuck his cigarette in the corner of his mouth and was saying in a hoarse, gangster voice: 'Keep your heads down, you guys. The men from the Ministry of Supply are after us!' Again the Pontiac shed a great bark of laughter as it raced on into the city, leaving it to float behind among the padding rickshaw coolies who formed a slow stream on either side of the road.

14

Weariness caused Mátthew to give up the struggle for a while; he merely lay back against the sighing leather-clad springs. He could not think what was the matter with Ehrendorf who might have been hypnotized the way he continued to gaze stolidly at the road ahead: this was quite unlike the gay and talkative person Matthew had known in Oxford and Geneva.

'I suppose everyone here is worried about these talks with the Japs in Washington,' he said presently, hoping again to initiate a conversation. But Ehrendorf still made no reply and Monty, who did not appear to have heard of them, merely asked: 'What talks?'

Surprised, Matthew explained that Admiral Nomura, the Japanese Ambassador in Washington, had been having talks with the American Government. The Americans wanted the Japs to move their troops out of Indo-China and to agree to peace in the Pacific; the Japs wanted the Americans to stop helping Chiang Kai-shek in their war against China and to unfreeze their assets. Things would look grim if they didn't agree. That was why he had expected that people in Singapore might be worried.

'I suppose some people may have the wind up,' said Monty indifferently.

Matthew decided to give up once more and let events take their course. While he lay slumped in the corner of the seat with a young woman sprawled on his shoulder like a hot compress, one curious picture after another trembled before his eyes, reminding him of the 'magic lantern' he had played with as a child. One moment the Pontiac was grumbling and nudging its way through a narrow street hung with banners of Chinese ideographs, the next it was speeding down a wide avenue between silver slopes which flashed and winked at him and proved to be great banks of fish (Matthew was glad of the speed: the stench was so powerful it made you clutch your collar and roll your eyeballs back into your brain). He peered in wonder at the glistening naked bodies of the men working by oil lamps to gut and salt these silvery Himalayas of fish but the next moment again the Pontiac had transformed itself into a stately barge forging it way over a smoky, azure river ... Here and there Chinese waded head and shoulders above the blue billows, which presently grew transparent and correspondingly thickened into a darker blue empyrean hanging a few feet overhead; through this blue canopy, like cherubim, disembodied Chinese heads peered down from balconies at the Pontiac making its slow progress beneath.

'This is the street of the charcoal burners. The bloody Chinese live fifty to a room here in some places.'

Now the clouds of smoke had rolled away to reveal that they were in another, quite different street where from every window and balcony there swung pots of ferns and baskets of flowers. Strings of dim, multi-coloured lanterns hung everywhere. 'It's time this lot got weaving with their black-out, too,' said Monty, and his eyes glittered like cutlery as they roved the balconies above. Suddenly Matthew saw that in the heart of each display of lanterns and flowers there was a beautiful woman set like a jewel.

'Did we have to come this way, Monty?' grumbled Joan, removing herself from Matthew's shoulder. 'Why didn't we go along Beach Road?' Ehrendorf stirred at last and looked around with an uncomfortable smile; meanwhile, the Pontiac continued to advance with Joan firmly sandwiched between the two perspiring Englishmen on the back seat. Certain of the women on the balconies above stuck languorous poses, or stretched out a slender leg as if to straighten a stocking. One idly lifted her skirt as if to check that her underwear was all in order (alas, she appeared to have forgotten it altogether); another forced a breast to bulge out of its hiding and palped it thoughtfully.

'Look here, Monty,' Joan protested, 'this is a bit thick. You did this on purpose.'

'Did what on purpose?'

'You know perfectly well. And it's not very clever.'

'In Singapore you can see things they don't mention at posh finishing schools,' exulted Monty, 'but that's no reason to get in a bate.' He added for Matthew's benefit: 'This is respectable compared with Lavender Street yonder where the troops go. You could have a "colonial experience" there all right!'

So wide was the Pontiac, so narrow the streets of this part of the city, that it was a miracle they could pass through them at all. Even so, they frequently had to slow to a walking pace while the *syce* made some fine decisions, an inch on this side, an inch on that. On one such occasion a figure sprang suddenly out of the twilight and landed with a thump on the running-board causing Matthew to flinch back, startled. But the figure proved to be only a small bundle of skin and bone wrapped in rags, a Chinese boy of six or seven years of age. This child clung to the side of the motor-car with one small grubby hand while he cupped the other under Matthew's nose, at the same time dancing up and down on the running-board with a dreadful urgency. But more distressing still, the boy began a rapid, artificial panting like that of a wounded animal.

The Pontiac had cleared the last of the narrow streets and could now accelerate ... but still the child clung on, panting more desperately than ever. Meanwhile, the *syce* was steering with one hand and using the other to reach behind Ehrendorf and hammer at the little fingers gripping the chassis.

'Stop!' cried Matthew to the driver. 'Stop! ... Make him stop!' he shouted at Ehrendorf. But Ehrendorf sat as if in a trance while the Pontiac hurtled through the dusk swaying violently, the child panting, the *syce* cursing and hammering.

'No father, no mother, no *makan*, no whisky soda!' howled the child.

Monty had calmly selected a couple of coins from his pocket and was holding them out, almost in the child's reach, and making him grab for them with his free hand. Having enjoyed this game for a little he negligently tossed the coins out of the speeding car. A moment later the boy dropped off the running-board and vanished into the rushing darkness in their wake.

'That's one of their favourite tricks. The word *makan* means "grub" by the way, and you could probably do with some yourself, I should think. We thought we'd take you first to the Mayfair to leave your things and then on to our house for some supper.'

They were now on a wider thoroughfare; in front of them rattled a green trolley-bus: from the tips of its twin poles a cascade of blue-white sparks dribbled against the darkening sky. Despite the advance of darkness the heat seemed only to increase. The sun had long since dropped out of sight somewhere behind Sumatra to the west but in the sky it had left a vast striated blanket of magenta which seemed to radiate a heat of its own like the bars of an electric grill.

Soon they were on a long straight road, still lined with Chinese shophouses but with here and there an occasional block of European shops or offices. This was Orchard Road, Monty explained, and that drive that curved away to the right led up to Government House. The large white building a little further along was the Cold Storage: in there homesick Britons could buy food that reminded them of home.

Presently they turned off Orchard Road and found themselves in a residential district of winding, tree-lined streets and detached bungalows with now and then a small block of flats set amidst tennis courts. They lurched up a sharply curving slope past a tiny banana plot.

'It may not be much ... but given the hordes of brass hats commandeering living quarters in Singapore these days one is lucky to find a roof at all. Here we are, anyway.'

The Pontiac keeled over sharply and pulled off the road with groaning tyres. The Mayfair Building was a vast and rambling bungalow built on a score of fat, square pillars. Because the ground here was on something of a slope these pillars grew taller as they approached the front of the building, exaggerating their perspective and giving them the appearance of a platoon on the march beneath an enormous burden. The bungalow itself was encased in louvred wooden shutters and open balconies, along the sides of which partly unrolled blinds of split-bamboo hung beneath the great jutting eaves. The apex of the bungalow's roof of loose red tiles was left open in the manner of a dovecot to allow warm air to escape, and was crowned by a second, smaller roof of red tiles. Despite the metropolitan grandeur of its name the Mayfair Building had a slightly decrepit air.

While Joan performed a quick and efficient inspection of herself in a hand-mirror, Matthew got out of the car and prepared to follow Monty.

'I won't come in with you, Matthew,' Ehrendorf said. 'I'm busy right now but I'll see you later. We'll get together real soon, OK?' Now that he, too, had got out of the car and stood there, an elegant figure in his uniform, it seemed to Matthew that he looked more his former cheerful and confident self. They shook hands, agreed to telephone each other and then Matthew followed Monty around the side of the building to the main entrance. Here he glimpsed a tennis court, disused, from whose baked mud surface giant thistles had grown up and now waited like silent skeleton players in the gloom. Beyond the tennis court the compound was walled in on each side by a powerful tropical undergrowth and the encroaching jungle.

Gesturing in the darkness Monty said: 'There's a recreation hut and a lot of gym stuff over there. I expect you know that your father was keen on that sort of thing? What? You didn't?

112

He was very partial to rippling muscles and gleaming torsos.'
Monty chuckled cautiously. 'This way. Watch your step.'

They made their way up protesting wooden steps to a front
door that stood open and was plainly two or three inches too
big for its frame. As Monty dragged it open further the hinges
shrieked. He went inside. Matthew, having paused to polish his
glasses, was about to follow him when he heard a faint scuffling
sound from the darkness on the other side of the house. He
heard the sound of heavy, indignant breathing, then silence
followed and, after a few moments, a long, melancholy sigh,
barely audible against the hum of the tropical night. In another
moment he heard footsteps and Joan emerged from the gloom.

The interior of the bungalow exuded the unloved air of
houses that have had to endure temporary occupation by a
succession of transient lodgers. Matthew surmised that his
father had not taken a great interest in his material surroundings.

'What a dump!' said Joan, wrinkling her perfect nose as she
peered in.

'It's seen better days, I admit,' agreed Monty. In the obscurity
Matthew sensed rather than saw that the furiture was chipped,
the paintwork peeling and the woodwork so warped that drawers and cupboards would no longer quite open, nor windows
altogether close. He was surprised to think that it was in these
modest surroundings that his father, a man of wealth, had
spent so much of the latter part of his life. 'Perhaps the old
chap was not such an ogre after all.'

As he advanced into a wide verandah room scattered with
darker masses which might be furniture, two floorboards sang
in counterpoint under his shoes. A middle-aged man who had
evidently been brooding by himself on the verandah in the now
almost complete darkness came on a serpentine course through
the sagging rattan furniture to meet them, snapping on a light
switch as he passed and bathing the room in an electric light
which at first flickered like a cinema projector but presently
settled down to a more steady glow.

'Major Brendan Archer,' said Monty casting his sun-helmet
away into the shadows. 'This is Matthew Webb.' He added to
Matthew: 'The Major has been more or less running things
since your father's illness.'

Matthew and the Major shook hands. The Major came vaguely
to attention and said indistinctly: 'I'd like to say how sorry
... hm ... your father ...' With a muffled bark indicating

emotion he stood at ease again The Major had a mild, vaguely worried appearance. His very thin hair had been carefully smoothed with water and brushed straight back, revealing only the finest of partings. It was supplemented by a rather doleful moustache.

'I see you're looking at my moustache,' the Major said, causing Matthew to start guiltily. 'That blighter Cheong got at it with the scissors. He said he'd be careful but of course he got carried away. Took too much off one side.' It was true. The Major's moustache, when you looked at it, was definitely lopsided. The young people peered at it respectfully.

'How sensitive people are about their moustaches out here,' thought Matthew. 'It must be the climate.'

'Why don't you prune the other side a bit?' suggested Monty. 'Even it up?'

'Mustn't look like Hitler.'

'No, of course not,' agreed Monty. To Matthew he explained: 'The Major's been trying to re-enlist for active service. He can't be bothered with the Japs. Defend the old homeland, eh, Major?'

'Oh, I'm afraid the war will be over by the time I get back to England. One worries, you know, about people at home in the air-raids. I have a couple of young nieces in London ... well, not really nieces ... more god-daughters than nieces, in South Kensington, actually, though strictly speaking ...'

Monty interrupted: 'You don't say so, Major? I've heard that the entire might of the Luftwaffe is being thrown against South Kensington.' To Matthew he said: 'Come on, I'll show you around quickly and then we'll beetle off.' They left the Major looking baffled.

'Old bore,' said Monty.

As they made their way round the bungalow Matthew was conscious of Joan's blank eyes and neatly plucked eyebrows turning towards him from time to time, but she still had not addressed a word directly to him. Swinging louvred shutters divided one room from the next, there seemed to be no doors here except for the bathroom and one elaborately marked 'Board of Directors'. They peered into his room which contained nothing except a long, deeply scratched table and a dozen or so chairs. Above the table a huge electric fan laboured noisily. Monty switched on the light at the door. A wiry, middle-aged man clad only in shorts lay stretched on the table, asleep

114

with his mouth open. Monty led the way over to inspect him, saying: 'This is Dupigny. I gather he's supposed to have some sort of job here, God knows what, though. Hey, wake up!' Monty shook him. 'François is what is known as a "sleeping partner",' he jeered. 'Come on, wake up! The Japs have landed in the garden!' But the man on the table merely uttered a groan and turned over. They retreated, Monty saying over his shoulder: 'François used to be a big-wig in the Indo-Chinese Government until Pétain booted him out. He's convinced Jap parachutists are going to land any moment.'

Now at last they were approaching the rooms which had been set aside for the Chairman: a swinging door upholstered in green felt had once divided this part of the bungalow from the rest but now, removed from its hinges, it was merely propped against the wall. Beyond it, nevertheless, one could discern an improvement in the quality and condition of the furnishings. First, they came to an outer room used as an office. Matthew had expected a room that was perfectly bleak and bare of ornament, to match his own view of his father's character. To his surprise the walls were crowded with pictures and photographs of all kinds. He barely had time to glance at them; besides, the presence of the young Blacketts inhibited him. But what was he to make of this sepia photograph showing his father perhaps thirty years ago, holding a tennis racket and with his arm cheerfully around the neck of his smiling partner or opponent? Or of this one of his father good-humouredly presenting something to a group of neatly suited Chinese, each of them with his trousers at half mast? Surely the old tyrant had not smiled more than once in his entire life!

They peered into the bedroom which lay beyond, a great high-ceilinged room which contained two massive Edwardian wardrobes, a narrow iron bed with a mosquito net hanging knotted above it like a furled sail, and a bedside table on which medicine bottles still crowded around the stem of a table-light. Matthew, harrowed by the sight of these medicine bottles, withdrew to the office once more. Joan had remained in the background plucking with finger and thumb at the back of her turban. The driver had brought in Matthew's suitcases and now carried them into the bedroom.

'There should be a Chinese boy around somewhere. He'll unpack for you. Let's go and get something to eat.'

A balding young man was hovering diffidently at the door of

the office as they passed through. He cleared his throat when he saw Monty and said: 'Monty, I wonder could I have a quick word with you?'

'No, you bloody can't. I'm busy. And what are you doing here, anyway? You're supposed to be out on the bloody estate. We don't pay you to hang around Singapore.'

'I just came in this evening, Monty. You see, it's rather important and I had already mentioned it some time ago to Mr Webb before his illness . . .'

'You just came in this evening, did you, Turner? Well, you can bugger off back this evening, too. If you aren't satisfied with your pay you can send us a letter of resignation and join the bloody Army. Got it?'

'But I've just spoken to Major Archer and he . . .'

'I don't care who you've spoken to. I'm telling you to hop it. Get going. Scram!'

'I could eat a horse,' said Joan suddenly, addressing Matthew for the first time and even smiling at him. 'I only had a sandwich at the Cold Storage for lunch. Actually, I'm trying to lose weight. How much do you think I weigh? Go on, have a guess.' Matthew could only blink at her, however, too astonished to reply.

The young man's face had turned very pale and his forehead glistened with perspiration: there was clearly nothing for it but for him to depart, and he did so, but without making any abrupt movement. His image seemed gradually to grow indistinct until presently one could make out pieces of furniture where he had been standing and then he had faded away completely.

'Eight stone exactly!' exclaimed Joan in triumph, clapping her hands. 'I knew you couldn't. Nobody can. You see, it's partly the way I dress.'

'That miserable cove,' Monty explained in a self-satisfied tone, 'is Robin Turner, the manager of your estate in Johore, though you'd hardly think so the amount of time he spends in Singapore. That little so-and-so and I were at school together and I pulled a few strings to get him a job out here when jobs weren't easy to come by. What d'you know? Within a couple of years he'd got himself married to a *stengah* and his career out here was as good as finished.'

'A *stengah*?'

'Half one thing and half the other . . . a Eurasian . . . a mixed drink! You can tell 'em by their chichi accent . . . sing-song like Welsh. He's been trying to get her a job as a governess in a white household but nobody wants their kids to end up with that accent ... no fear! In this part of the world, Matthew, people don't mind who you have your fun with, provided you do it discreetly (they're pretty broad-minded about that), but they get shirty if you try to mix things socially. Quite a few young fools like Turner have lost their jobs or missed promotion with European companies because they thought they could suit themselves. Young Turner had to resign from the clubs he'd joined, of course, double quick. I warned him it would happen but no, he knew better.' Monty heaved a sigh: his good-nature had been tried to the limit. 'Anyway, you've seen the set-up. Let's go and get something to eat.'

Matthew glanced at Joan. Her moment of animation had passed; now she was looking down her nose and plucking delicately at her chest, evidently rearranging whatever she wore under her frock. 'Isn't François supposed to be coming?' she wanted to know.

On their way back to the verandah they came across Dupigny, now clad in a billowing white suit, tying his tie by the light of a candle. He was a gaunt, dignified man in his fifties. He said in careful English: 'I shall follow you, Monty. I look forward with delicious alarm to discover what your cook has prepared for us.'

15

'My dear boy, it gives me great pleasure to welcome you at last to this house and, I should say, to these Straits Settlements which your father did so much to build up in his lifetime.' Monty and Joan had slipped off to change, leaving Matthew to introduce himself as best he could to the elder Blacketts whom he had with some difficulty located in a palatial drawing-room. He had often tried to picture Walter Blackett: he had supposed him to be someone very large and commanding. As it turned out, the man with whom he had just shaken hands was certainly commanding, but only his head was large: it loomed over a compact body and short legs and was covered in thick bristles of white hair which had collected here and there like drifts of unmelted snow on a stark mountainside; further white bristles supplied moustache and eyebrows: from beneath the latter, eyes of an alarming pale blue examined Matthew with interest. 'Come,' he said, 'and meet Sylvia.'

In her day Mrs Blackett had been considered beautiful, but all that now remained of her good looks were a pair of cornflower blue eyes, a shade or two darker than Walter's, set in a puffy, handsome, disappointed face. She still retained, however, some of the mannerisms of a woman accustomed to being admired for her appearance: a habit of throwing back her head to shake away the ringlets which had once tumbled charmingly over her smooth cheeks, or of opening her eyes very wide while you were talking to her, as if what you were saying was of enthralling interest. It made little difference whether you spoke about the emergence of a Swahili literature, about training schemes for electrical engineers, or about the best way to stuff a field-mouse. She would still gaze at you as if fascinated, her lovely eyes open very wide. Sometimes this automatic fascination could have a numbing effect on her interlocutor.

Looking at Mrs Blackett's disappointed, once-beautiful face, Matthew suddenly recognized that Joan was a beauty, though until this moment her appearance had not made much impression on him. It was as if, looking into her mother's faded features, he was confronted by a simplified version of Joan's and could say to himself: 'So that's the sort of face it's supposed to be!' It was a process not very different, he supposed, from thinking a girl was beautiful because she reminded you of a painting by Botticelli: if you had never seen the painting you would not have noticed her. But wait, what was it the Blacketts were saying?

For some moments the Blacketts, each ignoring the other's voice as only a married couple can, had been raining statements, questions and declarations of one kind or another on the already sufficiently bewildered Matthew. In the course of the next few minutes of incoherent conversation they touched on the war, his journey, rationing in Britain, his father's illness, his father's will (Walter took him by the arm and steered him away down the other end of the room, thinking this as good a time as any to remind Matthew of the responsibilities which would accompany his inheritance, but his wife uttered shrill complaints at being abandoned on her sofa and they were obliged to return), the Blitz, the approach of the monsoon, the rubber market and his journey again. Then Walter was summoned to the telephone. While Walter was absent Mrs Blackett took hold of Matthew's wrist: she wanted to tell him something. 'I think you met my children, Monty and Joan, earlier this evening, didn't you? You know, I hardly think of them as my children at all. We are more like three friends. We discuss, oh, everything together as if we were equals.'

Matthew, who could think of no reply to this confidence, scratched his ear and gazed at Mrs Blackett sympathetically. But where was Kate? he wondered aloud. He had been looking forward to seeing her again. Was she away somewhere?

'Oh, she was here a moment ago,' said Mrs Blackett vaguely. There was silence for a few moments. Walter's voice, speaking emphatically, could be heard from the adjoining room. 'Yes, just three friends,' added Mrs Blackett despondently.

Presently she groped for Matthew's sleeve and with a tug, drew him to his feet. She wanted to introduce him to the people who had just come into the room. But these newcomers, on closer inspection, proved to be merely her children, or 'friends', Monty and Joan. She had evidently thought they might be someone more interesting for at the last moment she hung back, murmuring: 'Oh, I thought it might be Charlie.'

Monty and Joan, ignoring their mother, subsided into arm-chairs and ordered drinks from a Chinese servant who moved silently from one person to another. They both looked hot, though the air here was pleasantly cool. Joan had exchanged her white cotton frock for a dress of green silk with padded shoulders and leg-of-mutton sleeves. Now that she had removed her turban her sable ringlets tumbled charmingly over her cheeks. Matthew, however, could not help staring at her legs; if he feasted his eyes on them so greedily it was not because they were unusually well shaped (though they were) but because she was wearing silk stockings which had become a luxury in England in the past year. Unfortunately, both Monty and Joan had noticed the direction of his gaze: he saw them exchange a sly glance.

'Kate!'

Kate had been hovering for some time in the next room anxiously awaiting the right moment to make a casual entry. She had been allowed to wear her best dress for besides Matthew an important RAF personage had been invited to supper. Now here she was, looking self-conscious. There was a moment of awkwardness, then she and Matthew shook hands. Kate blushed furiously and, stepping back, almost fell over a chair she had not noticed.

'You know *what*?'

'What?'

'If we were having steak for supper we could grill it on Kate's cheeks.'

'Mother, will you make him *stop*!'

'Really, Monty,' said Mrs Blackett wearily.

Snatching up a magazine Kate went to throw herself down on a sofa at the other end of the room. She did not open the magazine, however, but instead picked up a Siamese cat which had been curled up on the floor and began stroking and kissing it, ignoring the rest of the company.

'It's so nice to have a chance to talk,' said Mrs Blackett, 'before the others arrive.'

There was a murmur of assent but then silence fell again. Monty glanced at his watch; Joan yawned behind scarlet finger-nails. Kate continued to stroke the cat at great speed, occasionally planting a kiss on the wincing animal.

Walter came back presently and took a seat beside Matthew, explaining that he had invited Brooke-Popham, the Commander-in-Chief, Far East, and a member of his staff to supper; earlier in the day he had attended a meeting with them about rice distribution. For the truth was, he went on, that in the event of hostilities in the Pacific, Malaya could find her food supplies in jeopardy, at least in the long run, because the greater part of the country's rice had to be imported. Ten years of effort (he himself had served on the Rice Cultivation Committee set up in 1930) still had not induced the native smallholders to grow rice instead of rubber. They were too idle. What could you do with such people?

'I suppose they think that rubber is more profitable,' suggested Matthew.

'I suppose they do,' agreed Walter.

'And they're right, aren't they?'

'Oh, I wouldn't say *that*, exactly.' Walter's tone was casual but he glanced sharply at Matthew as he spoke. 'There have been great variations in demand, of course, for rubber. Point is they can't eat it in bad times. Otherwise it would be the perfect crop for a country like this. Rice involves too much hard work. Anyway, there it is, we have to import it in vast quantities to feed the estate workers.'

'Perhaps the estates should grow rice . . .' murmured Matthew. 'It seems unfair to expect the smallholders to grow a less profit-able crop simply to allow the estates to go on growing the more

120

profitable crop ...'

'Ah, but we haven't agreed that rice is less profitable.'

'In that case why do the estates ...?'

'Drat!' exclaimed Mrs Blackett, hearing a distant bell. 'They're arriving already and just as we were beginning to have a nice talk.'

Walter had risen before Matthew had time to finish what he was saying. But even so, Mrs Blackett reached the door before he did. It opened to admit Dupigny in his billowing white suit. He and Mrs Blackett exchanged greetings. As she made to lead him deeper into the room she said: 'You, François, who always keep so well in touch, must tell us what you think.'

'Of what, Mrs Blackett?'

'Of the situation,' she replied vaguely.

'My dear Mrs Blackett, if you want my opinion the Japs will overrun us in a twinkling. First they exhaust us in the jungle. Then they seize us by the throat.'

'You terrify me, François, when you say such things. Except for Matthew you are the first to arrive so you must pay the penalty and come and sit down here with us for a few minutes ... though I can see that what you have to tell us will scare us out of our wits.'

'My apologies,' murmured Dupigny with the exquisite tact of the diplomat and man of the world. He was evidently apologizing not for having cast Mrs Blackett into a state of alarm but for having arrived too early, for thus he had interpreted the words 'first to arrive'.

Mrs Blackett, leading the way across the room, said over her shoulder: 'How smart you look, François! I'm so glad to see you are managing in spite of your difficulties.'

In the meantime, Monty had slipped into the chair beside Matthew vacated by his father, and in a malicious whisper explained to him that Dupigny was penniless! a beggar! a total pauper! and that his mother, of course, knew very well that she was being pursued across the drawing-room not only by Dupigny but by his entire wardrobe as well, for the fellow was still clad in every single garment he had been wearing when he had slipped away from Saigon with General Catroux, give or take the odd pair of shorts or shoes he had been able to borrow off Major Archer who luckily for Dupigny happened to be an old chum of his from the Great War.

While Matthew listened to all this and watched Dupigny stoop to brush Joan's knuckles with his smiling lips, he could not help wondering whether he would ever find anything in common with Monty. Dupigny looked up, still smiling, his attentions to Joan's knuckles complete.

'Well, François, what's the joke?'

'I smile because I remember that yesterday for the first time in my life I have been mistaken *pour un maçchabée* ... for a corpse.'

'For a corpse?' cried Joan, suddenly becoming vivacious again. She was evidently a willing victim of Dupigny's charm and polished manners. 'I don't believe you, François. What a terrible liar he is!' she grumbled to her mother.

'But precisely, for a corpse!' Dupigny struck an attitude. 'I am just leaving the bungalow when a Chinese gentleman approaches and says to me: "*Tuan*, are you dead?" I assure him that to the best of my knowledge I am still alive ...' Dupigny paused to acknowledge the smiles of his audience.

' "But, *Tuan*," says our Chinese friend, "are you not then seriously wounded?" On the contrary I tell him that I am never feeling better in my life ... "But then, *Tuan*," he says, almost in tears, "you must at least be 'walking wounded' otherwise you would not be here in this street!" '

'I know, it was an air-raid practice!' exclaimed Joan. 'I bet your Chinaman was wearing an ARP armband and a tin hat. But I thought that for corpses they always used Boy Scouts. Does this mean that they are now using grown men?'

'*Hélas!* Every day they grow more ambitious!'

New arrivals had been shown into the room in the meantime and Mrs Blackett set off once more towards the door, stumbling against a low foot-stool on the way, for the truth was that her lovely blue eyes were far-sighted and she should have worn glasses. Two officers had just entered. One of these newcomers was Air Chief-Marshal Sir Robert Brooke-Popham, a solidly built gentleman in his early sixties whose appearance suggested slightly baffled good nature. He had a square head, bald on top and with very thin hair plastered down at the sides above large, protruding ears. Beneath his white walrus moustache his open mouth lent him the air of wary incomprehension one sometimes sees in people who are not quite sure they have heard you correctly. Each of his powerful forearms cradled a shaggy bundle of documents which he was now trying to shuffle into a single bundle so that he might grasp the hand of Mrs Blackett. But in doing so a few sheets detached themselves and subsided in a series of gentle arcs to the floor. As he stooped to retrieve them, a few more slipped from his grasp and his air of bewilderment increased. At his side a tall, saturnine staff officer in the uniform of a Major-General watched without expression as the Commander-in-Chief scrabbled on the floor to assemble his papers. 'You'd better let me, sir,' he said taking the bundle and stowing it firmly under his arm. Then he put his swagger-stick down on a side table; an instant later he neatly scooped it up again as Mrs Blackett, turning, failed to notice the table and stumbled into it. She smiled her thanks to Brooke-Popham who had kindly steadied her with a hand to her arm. After a moment's hesitation the General put his stick down again.

Matthew's attention was now diverted by Monty's voice in his ear, whispering a further malicious commentary, this time on the Commander-in-Chief himself: it was common knowledge among those 'in the know' that despite his grandiose title Brooke-Popham had frightful difficulty finding anybody who was actually subject to his authority. Certainly not the Navy. And the Governor, too, if he wanted could go his own sweet way. And even General Percival and Air-Marshal Pulford who had replaced the dreaded Bond and Babington still took many of their orders from the War Office and Air Ministry respectively leaving poor old Brookers in his office at the Naval Base with nothing to do but stick flags in maps and, to make things worse . . .

But Matthew had to struggle to his feet to shake hands with the Commander-in-Chief. Brooke-Popham shook hands firmly with Matthew and gave him a somewhat rabbity smile. Then he moved on to greet Walter and his place was immediately taken by a dapper gentleman who was following in the Commander-in-Chief's wake: this was Dr Brownley, the Blacketts' family doctor. The Doctor was somewhat distraught this evening for, earlier in the day, after weeks, even months of inner struggle and deliberation, he had purchased an article he had seen in John Little's window in Raffles Place, an article he had longed and lusted for with the passion of a lover. But now that it had at last become his, somehow the expected consummation had not taken place. Since buying the wretched thing, which he could ill afford, he had scarcely given it a thought. The joyous fever to which he had been subject for months had suddenly left him. 'What's wrong with me?' he wondered, surreptitiously taking his own pulse. And now another distressing thought occurred to him: 'This makes eighteen times in a row that they've invited me here and I still haven't invited them back!'

'You must come to us one of these days', he muttered as he shook hands with Matthew, rolling his eyes in a rather odd and desperate way ... (but fortunately the fellow didn't seem to hear).

'D'you really think the Japs will attack us?' Joan was asking Dupigny.

'Without a doubt,' replied Dupigny emphatically, and an expression of surprise and dismay passed fleetingly over Brooke-Popham's honest features as he overheard these words.

'My dear, François is in a most macabre mood this evening,' said Mrs Blackett to her daughter. 'I advise you not to listen to him. He has already had me shaking like a jelly.'

'Ah, but it is not amusing, I assure you,' said Dupigny, seeing that his words had caused Joan to smile, for with Dupigny it was often hard to tell whether he was joking or not and he frequently said the most outrageous things with a perfectly straight face.

'But I understand, François, that the Japanese specialize in chopping the heads off Frenchmen. They raise a sword above their heads and go ... chop! And Monsieur's head is rolling in the gutter. They say it is quite a sight. I think I shall take my knitting like Madame whatever her name was.'

'You think I am joking, Joan. Not at all! You forget that I know something of them, the Japanese. But what is the good?' he added, turning to Matthew as Joan went off laughing. 'You British are so serious. And when you think of France it is always in the manner of that *grand emmerdeur*, Charles Dickens. As for your self-confidence, that is something miraculous! Did you know,' he pursued, taking Matthew by the arm and leading him aside, 'that your Governor, Sir Thomas, went on holiday for eight months despite the outbreaking of war? That is an example of your phlegmatic British behaviour which fills a poor Frenchman like myself with awe, with admiration and, it must be admitted, with alarm!' He surveyed Matthew with an ironical smile.

'But never mind about that. Let me explain to you instead about this Air-Marshal. Sir Popham, for he is a most unusual sight. I refer not to his appearance, which is, I agree, awe-inspiring ... but to his very presence here in this room. It is something quite unusual.' And Dupigny went on to explain to Matthew in an undertone (how fond everyone seemed to be of whispering assessments of each other's behaviour behind their backs!) that years of living in Singapore had, it was well known, instilled in Mrs Blackett a deep contempt for the Armed Forces. It had been, in peacetime, a most surprising sight to see her heaping abuse on the old and respected profession of arms, members of which she had for years resolutely refused to invite to her table. Why, even Major Archer, the least martial of men, given an introduction to the Blacketts while making his first tour of the Far East in 1937, had had to be warned to demobilize himself before calling. The poor fellow would otherwise have left a card on which, printed in spidery script for all to see, was his guilty secret: *Major Brendan de S. Archer*. And Dupigny laughed heartily at the thought.

The fact was, he went on, that Mrs Blackett, though charming in every way, was something of a snob and this very drawing-room was the meeting-place of one of the most exclusive circles on the island, scarcely even rivalled by Government House. For, as Mrs Blackett willingly used to admit, she had one advantage over the Governor. She was not obliged, as he was, to invite the rabble of dignitaries, military and civilian, whom the war was bringing to Singapore. She could invite whom she pleased. 'All those depressing generals!' she used to exclaim sometimes in the presence of her own more carefully selected guests. 'Poor Lady Thomas!'

And yet, not even the Blacketts, as it transpired, had been able to prevent the invasion of their circle by the War. Since the beginning of hostilities in Europe there had been progressive signs of weakening. He, Dupigny, had been there in person on one occasion when Mrs Blackett had asked Walter whether she should not relax this prohibition of military men from her dining-room 'in the interests of the War Effort'. An admiral or two, perhaps?

Walter had stroked his chin as he pondered his wife's difficult question, groping for the reply of a frank, straightforward sort of man. Well, no, he did not think so. After all, one's principles don't change simply because there's a war on. The problem, after all, was not that the odd admiral was short of food, but that he was tedious company. This had not changed. Very likely it had become worse. With a war raging in Europe the admiral would doubtless feel encouraged to discourse interminably on military and naval matters at the expense of ... well, of the more important things in life.

And so Mrs Blackett had continued for some time to exclude the Forces (except for the Major, of course, who was in any case masquerading as a plain civilian and who had had no

125

connection with the Army in twenty years). But then, little by little, as Hitler had advanced through Europe, the Allies had made corresponding advances into the Blacketts' exclusive circle ... a colonel here, an air commodore there, in civilian clothes at first but, presently, in uniform. 'Until today we have the pleasure of seeing an Air-Marshal and a General sipping their *pahits* among us as if it were the most natural thing in the world!'

Matthew had listened with interest and amusement to this discourse. Dupigny was an entertaining companion and he would have liked to hear more about the Blacketts. But at this moment a distant gong sounded and supper was announced. Joan had disappeared for a few moments but returned just in time to catch her father's eye as they were going into the dining-room. Walter raised his eyebrows as if to enquire: 'Well, what do you think?' Joan did not have to be told what her father's raised eyebrows referred to. She had just slipped into the dining-room ahead of the guests to rearrange the name-cards by the various places, allotting herself a seat where she knew the light would fall to particular advantage on her long neck and delicate features, casting a special sheen on her sable curls when viewed from a certain other place. She smiled at her father and discreetly raised her thumb. Walter, in turn, did not have to be told that his daughter expected to make short work of the task she had set herself.

16

On his way into the dining-room Matthew, attempting to demonstrate to the Doctor the width of a stream where he had once caught a number of trout, struck Mrs Blackett a blow in the stomach that robbed her of her breath for a moment or two. A fuss then took place. Matthew fell back, disgraced, while the other guests crowded around to help her to a chair, offering her drinks of water and telling each other to move back and give her air. She sat there, gasping. Matthew watched her from a distance, discomfited and surprised: it had not seemed to him that he had struck her very hard. The impression left on his knuckles by the blow was already fading but he was pretty certain that it had never amounted to a good, solid punch, the sort that one might have expected would drop one's hostess to her knees. The unworthy thought occurred to him that Mrs Blackett might be putting it on a bit. But women were, after all, members of a gentler sex. It was distressing, whichever way one looked at it. He had been hoping to start off on a better footing with the Blacketts.

Meanwhile, Dr Brownley, at Mrs Blackett's side, kept saying: 'Highly interesting ... Highly interesting' as if to himself; this caused Walter to look at him askance but actually the Doctor had been saying 'Highly interesting' to Matthew before the blow had been struck and was now merely repeating it. Sometimes a word or a phrase would get stuck in the Doctor's mind and rattle around in it for hours without any apparent reason. Occasionally, if by misfortune the phrase expressed some powerful image, it might stay in his mind for days or weeks. Once, for example, he had heard a dentist admonishing a patient who was inclined to neglect her teeth: 'Your nose will meet your chin!' For several weeks this phrase, alien, violent, rapacious, eating up all other thoughts, had whirled around his mind like a rat in a refrigerator. 'Your nose will meet your chin!' He had thought he would never get rid of it. In the end only the desire for an article he happened to see in Whiteaways had been sufficient to suffocate it. 'Highly interesting,' he murmured as Mrs Blackett, getting to her feet with a sigh, declared herself sufficiently recovered for the dinner to proceed.

This incident, fortunately trivial, did serve a useful purpose, however. It reminded Matthew that he must keep a stern watch over his comportment while at the dinner-table. It was not simply a question of table manners, though years of eating by himself with his eyes on a book beyond his plate rather than on the plate itself (how often had he been roused from his thoughts by something hot and slippery, a grilled fish, say, or a great bundle of spaghetti, dropping into his lap from an incorrectly angled fork!) certainly left room for improvement in that respect. No, it was more a tendency to grow over-excited in the course of what he knew should be an urbane discussion, to utter great shouts of derision at the opinions of his table companions, to gloat over them excessively when he found them guilty of faulty reasoning or some heretical assumption. Next day he would realize, of course, that he had behaved boorishly and would be filled with remorse, but next day it would be too late. Alas, more than once in Geneva he had found a door closed to him after he had allowed himself to get carried away. With the Blacketts he must watch his step!

Often had the Blacketts wondered precisely how Matthew had spent the years since he had left Oxford. Why had his infrequent letters been sent from hotels in remote corners of Europe? What was it, at a time of life when most young men decide to settle down in a home of their own, that had kept him flitting across frontiers like a lost soul? While these questions were being put to him Mrs Blackett, looking tired after her ordeal, glanced around the table to make sure that everything was in order; her gaze lingered for a moment on an unoccupied chair next to Joan and a shadow of concern passed over her features. Meanwhile, a bowl of soused fish was being proffered by the 'boys' to each guest in turn.

Oh, the answer to that was simple, Matthew explained, fishing in the dark tide of vinegar and peppercorns. He had been working for a charitable organization in Geneva called the Committee for International Understanding, vaguely connected with the League of Nations.

'My dear boy,' said Walter, 'I'd be surprised to learn that a single one of those charitable organizations ever did a damn thing that was any practical use to anybody. Geneva, if you ask me, is a city of hot air and hypocrites and that's all there is to say about it.' Walter hesitated, glancing at Dupigny who appeared to be rolling his eyes in horror at this opinion of Geneva, uncongenial, perhaps, to a former functionary of the Ministère des Colonies: but it might simply have been that Dupigny was flinching away from the fumes of vinegar rising from the bowl of soused fish which had now been offered to him in turn. He somewhat grimly captured a piece of fish on the serving spoon, inspected it for a moment, sniffed at it, then dropped it back into the dish, indicating to the 'boy' that he did not want any.

'These idealistic committees are a waste of time and as for the League itself ...!'

Matthew chewed his fish calmly even though such a remark would normally have provoked him to vociferous argument: lucky that he had been reminded of his weaknesses a few moments earlier! Moreover, in a sense Walter was right. It was true that the Committee for International Understanding, which was merely one of hundreds of such idealistic barnacles clinging to the hull (already low in the water) of the great League itself, had not achieved any visible success in all the years he had worked for it. In the early days he had spent hour after hour writing letters to politicians urging them to good behaviour in the interests of the 'world community'. Invariably these letters had been answered in vague but polite terms by private secretaries who hinted that there were grounds for optimism. But as for any concrete improvement, well, that was another matter! All that one could say for sure was that 'out there' (Matthew had spent hours during his first winter in Geneva gazing out through the rain-rinsed window of his office in the direction of the lake), in the real world there was a sort of counter-Committee composed of private secretaries whose letter-writing labours exactly mirrored his own and, it had gradually dawned on him, were equally without significance.

And what a dismal place Geneva had been! The steadily falling rain through which one might occasionally, if one were lucky, be permitted to see the brooding mass of the Grand Salève across the lake, the bitter wind from the Rhône valley churning the waves to a grey cream beneath the low blanket of cloud, the sensation of oppression which lay over the city during its never-ending months of winter, Geneva was no place for the experiment that was taking place there, the most daring, most idealistic, the grandest, most thrilling and sublime effort to introduce reason and equity into the affairs of nations. And gradually, so it had seemed to Matthew, the proceedings of the Assembly with its myriads of committees and sub-committees emitting a thick fog of quibbling resolutions and differing points of view, which thickly cloaked its good intentions just as mist clouded the Grand Salève, had come to resemble the Geneva weather. For month after month you could see nothing through the curtains of rain tumbling out of the sky but then abruptly, like a miracle the clouds would disappear, the sun would shine and Mont Blanc would appear white and glittering in the distance across the water. Yet how rare it was that the fog lifted from the Assembly's proceedings! On those rare days, the opening of the great Disarmament Conference in 1932 had been one of them, Matthew had believed himself to be present at one of the great turning-points in the history of mankind. He had been wrong as it had turned out and now he was sadder and certainly older, if not much wiser.

'Did someone mention Geneva?' asked Brooke-Popham who, at first busy with a large helping of fish, had now got the better of it and was free to enter the conversation. 'Met a young chap only the other day who'd been a couple of years there. Said it was a deuced awful hole. What was his name now? M'memory isn't what it was. American. Capital fellow. Very obliging. Let's see now. Colonel ... no, Captain Erinmore. No. D'you know the chap I mean, Walter? Said he knew you and your charming daughter here. Herringport. No ... Now let me see ...'

'I don't believe I've had the pleasure, Sir Robert,' said Walter somewhat stiffly, exchanging a quick glance with Joan. The whole table, including Matthew, gazed at Brooke-Popham as if hypnotized.

'I know ...' said Brooke-Popham. A tremor ran through his audience and Joan turned a little pale as she waited for the Commander-in-Chief to speak. There was silence, however, until it became clear that Brooke-Popham, worn out by his long day, had momentarily dozed off. However, his staff officer, the General whose name Matthew had failed to catch, now smoothly took control of the conversation in the place of his slumbering superior and launched into a lengthy reminiscence, not of Geneva but of Lake Maggiore where he had been on holiday in 1925 with his wife, who was a god-daughter of Chamberlain's wife. And this, by the most fortunate coincidence, for he had never been to Lake Maggiore before or since, had happened to be the historic October of Locarno! What an extraordinary scene he had witnessed! The peasants, their clothes white with dust, tramping in from the surrounding hills with vast hood-shaped baskets of grapes on their backs. And Chamberlain himself, a bizarre figure among these sons of toil. Ah, the General could see him still as if it were yesterday, his monocle glinting in the autumn sunshine as he lolled among the scarlet cushions of his red Rolls-Royce whose long silver horns like trumpets occasionally cleared their metal throats to scatter the rustics from its path: this machine, once the property of a maharajah, had been hired locally, it seemed.

'But ...' began Matthew, becoming indignant despite his good intentions.

The General, however, had not yet reached the high point of his reminiscence, which amounted to nothing less than an invitation from the Chamberlains to join them for the excursion in celebration of Mrs Chamberlain's birthday so charmingly thought up by Briand and his friend, Loucheur: they had hired an Italian lake steamer, the *Fleur d'Oranger* for the occasion. On that delightful, extraordinary trip on the lake the General and his wife had mingled with all the chief delegates to the Conference, with Skrzynski and Benes, with the bearded, bespectacled, floppy-hatted Belgian, Vandervelde, with the shaven-headed, thick-necked German, Stresemann, his duelling-scarred cheeks set on fire by the sun and champagne ... what a day to remember! In his mind's eye he could still see Loucheur with his round pop-eyed face and the curling black moustaches of a Victorian waiter, chuckling as the champagne flowed. And then, to cap it all, Mussolini, ostentatious as ever, had made a dramatic dash by racing car from Milan to Stresa and from there by speedboat to Locarno!

And then, the General's voice became solemn at the recollection, on the following day a great crowd of peasants had gathered in front of the town hall as the autumn twilight thickened. The word spread quickly through the crowd. The Treaty had been signed! Like a holy relic the document was carried to the window and shown to the crowd. A great cry had gone up. The church bells had been rung and women had wept and prayed. The Treaty had been signed!

'But just look at the result!' cried Matthew, his kindly face transfigured with emotion.

'Eh?' said the General, taken aback.

'Just look at the result! "By our signatures we affirm that we want peace," Briand declared and yet within fifteen years France and Germany were at war again and the rest of Europe with them. And the reason was this: Locarno was the *old way of doing things*! Behind-the-scenes diplomacy between the Big Powers. Whitehall and the Quai d'Orsay and the Wilhelmstrasse up to their old tricks again ...'

'I know, his name was Herringdorf,' exclaimed Brooke-Popham waking up suddenly, but nobody paid any attention to him and presently he dozed off again.

'And so it goes on. So it has always gone on. If the League failed to prevent this war it was because Britain, France, Italy and Germany, while paying lip-service to the idea of an international assembly to settle differences between nations, were never prepared to submit to its authority. Nor give it the power it needed. Who could take the League seriously when the real business was not being transacted in Geneva at all but aboard a pleasure steamer on Lake Maggiore! The Big Powers have brought this horrible destruction down on their own heads because their half-baked foreign ministries staffed by upper-class dimwits, who have more in common with each other than with the people of their respective countries, preferred to make cynical treaties rather than give real meaning to their membership of the League.'

'Steady the Buffs!' said Walter, not in the least concerned by Matthew's unfortunate harangue.

Matthew's face had grown flushed as he spoke. In his excitement he had wound a napkin round his clenched fist and delivered a terrible uppercut to the under surface of the table with the result that a miniature earthquake accompanied his final words, causing the glasses to dance on the table. Mrs Blackett, painfully surprised by this outburst for which she could see no sane explanation, glanced significantly at her husband to warn him against pursuing the argument. But Walter, calmly reaching out a hand to steady the tinkling cutlery beside his plate, said with a smile: 'Strong nations, Matthew, will always take advantage of the weak if they can do so with impunity. This is a law of nature. After all, as you must agree, the disapproval of the League did nothing to inhibit Japan from taking over Manchuria ... '

'Well, exactly!' shouted Matthew. 'Because the League was given no support. Because Sir John Simon and the Foreign Office preferred to turn a blind eye to the crying injustice done to China and give tacit support to Japan!'

'Even without Britain's tacit support Japan would not have acted differently. Well, François, you're the expert at this sort of thing, what d'you think?'

'It is, I'm afraid, very simple. Powerful nations will have their way with the weak. They will see that their own interests are served. No doubt life would be better if both nations and people were guided by principle rather than by self-interest but ... it is not the case. It is foolish to pretend otherwise.'

'Self-interest? But surely a government has a duty to act in the *moral* as well as the material interests of its people!' This last assertion, however, was received only with sympathetic smiles. The matter had already been settled to the general satisfaction.

Matthew was still in a state of dangerous excitement and these cynical views might well have caused him to deal the delicate rosewood dining-table another and perhaps even terminal blow but with an effort he managed to control himself. He was aware that in any case he had already made quite an exhibition of himself. Besides, he had heard this sort of thing so often before. He unwound the napkin from his fist and nudged his spectacles further up his nose, peering sadly round the table at his companions. Kate, who was bored, was overheard asking her mother in a whisper what would be for pudding. Everyone chuckled and relaxed at this, even Matthew, though he was still distressed. He became aware that Joan was gazing at him from across the table and he could not help thinking how beautiful she was, the way the light caused her hair to glow and modelled with shadow the delicate contours of her cheekbones. He found it strange and disconcerting how this good-looking but impassive and perhaps even rather dull girl would suddenly brighten up and radiate a strong sexual attraction all around her, just as fireflies, mating at dusk in a warm climate, light up at intervals to signal their presence to a potential mate. No wonder, then, that according to Kate her elder sister was always breaking the hearts of the young men of the Colony: she evidently could not help it, any more than a firefly can stop itself lighting up at intervals.

'Your nose will meet your chin!' muttered the Doctor to Brooke-Popham at his side.

'What!' demanded Brooke-Popham waking up abruptly and staring at the Doctor in astonishment.

'Your father and I often used to discuss these matters,' said Walter who could not resist putting a few finishing touches to their argument, 'and I think we both felt that misplaced idealism had sapped the nation's strength badly in the last twenty years. The pacifism which has been vaunted since the end of the Great War by our friends of the socialist persuasion has resulted in the decline of British prestige and, even more serious, of her forces, too. Our enemies have been encouraged to try their luck.' Noticing that the Commander-in-Chief was awake again Walter added: 'What d'you think, Sir Robert? Am I talking through my hat?'

'Most certainly not, Walter,' said Brooke-Popham, using his napkin to dry his moustache where a few drops of vinegar still glimmered. 'You need only take the example of the year 1932. Is it a coincidence that the same year should see a mutiny of the British fleet and an aggression by the Japanese against the International Settlement in Shanghai? Most certainly not. One clearly suggested the other. Moreover, our socialist brethren were not without influence even at the War Office. Naval parities with Japan and the foolish doctrine of "No war for ten years" were the sad result of listening to their siren call.' The Commander-in-Chief beamed around the table to show that his views should not be taken amiss, even by those whom they happened to contradict. Nor did his friendly gaze omit the joint of roast beef which had just been brought in and set down for carving in front of Walter.

'All in all,' went on Brooke-Popham, 'it's perhaps just as well that the Japanese don't have a fighter to match our Brewster Buffalo, otherwise they might be tempted to try something on in this part of the world.' He hesitated. 'Not, of course, that we can afford to be over-confident,' he added, and his brow clouded somewhat; reports had been coming in of increased shipping at Camranh Bay for the past few days and even of landing-craft being loaded at Saigon. Well, he had not been nick-named 'Fighting Popham' for nothing. He sighed, thinking how difficult modern warfare was. Not like the old days! He was tired: ready to return to his quarters at the Sea View. Perhaps he would take a stroll on the hotel's lawn by the sandy beach (bristling, though, nowadays with barbed wire and machine-gun nests), just to settle his mind before retiring. He wanted no landing-craft forging into his dreams and bursting there like ripe pods.

17

Now for some reason an air of melancholy settled over the table like a gentle fall of snow on an avenue of statues in the park, collecting in white drifts on heads and shoulders and blurring individual features. Matthew was contemplating Geneva again as he served himself with two delightfully lacquered roast potatoes, musing not without bitterness on the years he had spent travelling as the envoy of the Committee for International Understanding. For the truth was that those who governed the destiny of nations had remained as remote when he appeared in person as they had when he had written letters. Years, he remembered, had been spent roaming the corridors of palatial hotels (all the doings of the Committee had been attended by the most drastic luxury, as if the merest suggestion of economy would have blighted its high ideals) waiting to be summoned by some minor official of this or that Chancellery. On the rare occasions when he had found himself face to face with the statesman himself, it had always turned out to be because the statesman was in exile or disgrace, or because the Committee had been thought to be more important than it really was, or on account of some other such misunderstanding. In Japan, where he had gone in 1937 to recommend caution with respect to the 'China Incident' he had had an interview with a senior officer of the Japanese Army. This man had listened politely to what he had to say but had, himself, refrained from comment. Matthew had asked him whether he thought a war between Japan and America was probable. The officer had replied that he shared the view of the Emperor on that question. And what, Matthew had wanted to know, was the Emperor's view? Unfortunately, the officer had replied without blinking, the Emperor's view was something about which he was completely in the dark.

From about that time, perhaps, had dated Matthew's growing feeling of hopelessness concerning the Committee's task. After this visit to Japan he had taken to reading a good deal on his travels and though he still performed his duties conscientiously, of course, his spirit was no longer quite as deeply engaged as it had once been. It had become his habit to take books with him when visiting government offices: unimportant visitors were sometimes left to cool their heels in desolate ante-rooms for long periods. On more than one occasion he had become so engrossed in his reading that when finally informed that the dignitary in question would now receive him he had looked up in surprise, unable to think for a moment what the fellow might want of him.

Opposite Matthew, Brooke-Popham sat with his shoulders up to his ears, frozen in an attitude of weariness; he was remembering the old days. What fun it had been when they had first gone over to France in 1914! Not like today when every initiative was frustrated by some administrative detail. In those days the Flying Corps had only had to take care of reconnaissance: they had moved about the country like a travelling circus looking for a suitable field which they could use as an aerodrome wherever it was needed. In the course of the retreat from Mons it had been even more like a circus: he would set off in the morning in the Daimler in search of a suitable field and then the aeroplanes would follow and land on it later in the day, while the ground staff trailed across country after them with the fuel and the field work shops loaded into the most extraordinary collection of vans, solid-tyred lorries and pantechnicons, borrowed in London from different businesses ... the van they had borrowed from Maples, the furniture people, had kept breaking down for some reason ... As for the Daimler and the other motor-cars, they had been lent by various officers and civilians. One day, he remembered, he and Maurice Baring had set off in the Daimler on a misty autumn morning and about lunchtime had found a field on some table-land above a village called Sailly: and they had set to work then and there to carry stooks of corn to the side of the field so that the machines could land; and then on the way to Senlis he had bought a brass bell with a beautiful chime for the Mess. It had grown dark before they reached Senlis and a great yellow harvest moon had risen over the misty fields and the poplars. Baring had said it reminded him of a Corot. What a fine autumn that had been in 1914! A clear golden light lay over the reaped fields and the farms and the gardens full of fruit. He had only to close his eyes to see a little group of pilots at Saponay, lying in the straw and chatting after a reconnaissance sortie, or to see the heat-distorted air rising above the stubble at midday.

'A penny for your thoughts, sir,' said the General, hearing him utter a sigh.

'Oh, water under the bridge, Jack,' replied Brooke-Popham, clearing his throat dejectedly.

Matthew, accustomed to rationing, had found the roast beef extremely appetizing and was even wondering whether it was likely that he would be offered some more. At his side, however, Dupigny was eyeing his plate dubiously, prodding the meat here and there with his fork.

'It's roast beef,' said Mrs Blackett firmly.

'Nevertheless,' Dupigny said to Matthew in an undertone, 'it is sometimes possible to eat well here. Today, no, we are out of luck. But sometimes, when Walter invites his fellow merchants of Singapore the cook makes *un petit effort*. Then, ah! you would think you are in Italy of the Renaissance seated at a table surrounded by merchant-princes. You see, here in Singapore there are many people of this kind. The names of their commercial empires have the ring of glorious city-states, don't you think so? Sime Darby! Harrisons and Crosfield! Maclaine Watson and Company! Langfield and Bowser! Guthrie and Company! And the greatest of them all, brooding over the Far East like the house of Medici over Tuscany: Jardine Matheson! Nor should we forget Blackett and Webb for there, in his usual place at the end of the table, a merchant-prince in his own right, Walter Blackett presides over this reunion of wealth and power as if he were Pope Leo X in person! That is a sight worth seeing!'

Dupigny's flight of fancy was interrupted by a sudden crash outside the door. Walter half rose to his feet but before he could make a move the door opened and a man lurched into the room backwards, as if he had just eluded the grasp of someone he had been struggling with in the corridor outside. For a moment he seemed to be expecting a further onslaught from his invisible assailant, but none came so he straightened himself and smoothed down his hair; the door was closed quietly from outside by an unseen hand. 'Sorry I'm late, Walter,' he said in rather slurred tones. 'Where am I sitting?'

'*Quelle horreur!*' whispered Dupigny, his eyes glinting with malicious pleasure. '*C'est Charlie, le frère de Madame Blackett. Et ivre mort, en plus!*'

Charlie was wearing merely a cream flannel shirt, open at the neck, and grey flannel trousers. On his feet he wore tennis shoes with the laces undone. His dishevelled appearance and the fact that he was panting slightly suggested that he had just come from some energetic sporting event. Matthew could see no family resemblance to Mrs Blackett in Charlie and he was clearly some twenty years younger. Like her, though, his face framed by blond curls bore the traces of youthful good looks. He was badly in need of a hair-cut.

Monty swiftly rounded the table and took him by the arm, steering him towards the empty place beside Joan. Charlie surveyed the table with watery blue eyes as he went, muttering half to himself: 'I'm glad to see you haven't polished off all the grub.'

'We've just been hearing, Charlie,' declared Mrs Blackett, 'that Matthew has recently come from Geneva where he has been working for the League of Nations.'

'Has he, indeed?' mumbled Charlie over the roast beef which had been hastily placed before him. 'And I'm sure a fat lot of good ...' The rest of the sentence was muffled by his first bite of roast beef.

'Well, not *recently*,' said Matthew with a smile, and explained that the Committee for International Understanding, with Europe crumbling about it, had closed down in 1940, naturally dismayed by the amount of misunderstanding the outbreak of war entailed. 'As a matter of fact, for the past year I've been working on a farm. Because of my poor eyesight they didn't

137

want me in the Army.'

'*Le* "Digging for Victory", *alors?*' suggested Dupigny. 'It is evident that the supply of food is no less important than the supply of munitions,' he added reassuringly.

Meanwhile Walter, swallowing the irritation caused him by the unorthodox arrival of his brother-in-law, had engaged Brooke-Popham in conversation, for the Commander-in-Chief had shaken off his melancholy and, though comatose, was still awake. For someone like himself, Walter was explaining, whose job it was to run a merchant business, a war with Japan was not a vague possibility for the future, it had already been in progress for some time. In this war, which was being fought invisibly and in silence by means of quotas, price-cutting and a stealthy invasion of traditional markets, Blackett and Webb had found itself not only in the front line but fighting for its life. Since the end of the Great War there had been a steady encirclement of British commerce in the Far East. By 1934 Japanese assaults on British textile markets had caused Westminister to introduce import quotas on cotton and rayon goods destined for Malaya. No wonder Walter and other Singapore merchants had protested to the Colonial Office that their mercantile interests were being sacrificed for no better reason than the inability of Lancashire to survive intensive competition from Japan. Walter paused and the faint grinding of his teeth became audible in the silence. He had reminded himself of the fact that Solomon Langfield, a big importer of Lancashire cotton, had been in favour of the quotas. That unprincipled blackguard! The bristles on his spine stirred beneath his Lancashire cotton shirt.

Walter surveyed his family and guests sullenly, as if somehow they had been responsible for this lamentable state of affairs. They gazed back, as if hypnotized. Only Monty, who had doubtless heard all this before, twiddled his fork and smothered a yawn.

'What I would like to know is this: can one really blame the Japanese?' enquired Walter. His guests exchanged puzzled glances, as if to say: 'Of course one can blame the Japanese. Why ever not?'

'After all, they too are fighting for their lives. They depended so heavily for their survival on silk and cotton that, naturally, they would do whatever they had to in order to sell them. In 1933 the average Japanese price for textiles was ten cents a yard while Lancashire's was eighteen or nineteen cents, almost

138

twice the price! Mind you, the Japs got up to every trick in the book to evade the quotas. For example, since cotton piece-goods were not included in the quotas in no time pillow-cases big enough to put a house in began to arrive here in Singapore ... pyjamas to fit elephants ... shirts that twenty people could have got into ... and all designed to be swiftly unstitched and used by our local manufacturers instead of the Lancashire cotton they were supposed to be using. Frankly, I admire their ingenuity. Can you blame them?'

'Business is all very well, Mr Blackett,' said the General rather brusquely. 'But you surely do not mean to condone the way they grabbed Manchuria and invaded China. Your own firm's business must have suffered as a result of the way the Japs have been closing the Open Door.'

Walter nodded and smiled. 'That's true. We have suffered. But look at it from the Japanese point of view. Can you blame them for extending their influence into Manchuria and China? After all, the demands they have been making since 1915 ... for the lease of Port Arthur and Dairen, for the South Manchuria and Antung–Mukden Railways and for the employment of Japanese capital in Manchuria and Eastern Inner Mongolia, what do they remind you of?' Walter, smiling now, gazed at his baffled guests. 'I can tell you what they remind *me* of! They are an excellent imitation of the sort of economic imperialism through demands for special privileges which Britain herself has been making in Asia since ... well, since this young man's father started our business in the 1880s.'

'But was that a reason for Japan to invade China?' the General wanted to know.

Walter shook his head. 'As a businessman I understand very well why the Japanese had to invade China in 1937. China, from the point of view of trade and investment, was chaotic. No reasonably hard-boiled businessman looking at Nationalist China would have seen much to give him confidence. The Kuomintang wanted to put an end to foreigners' privileges. They wanted to see the foreign concession areas at Shanghai, Tientsin and so on handed back to China. They wanted to stop foreigners having their own courts and raising their own taxes in China. No, business must go on, whatever the price. And a businessman needs security. So can one blame the Japanese?'

'Security for business doesn't give people the right to invade and kill their neighbours!' protested Matthew.

'My dear chap, I couldn't agree with you more. But there

comes a point where the justice of the matter becomes irrelevant. You must look at the situation from the Japanese point of view. For them it was a matter of life and death because while the Kuomintang was putting their investment in China at risk they were faced at home by the disastrous effects of the slump. In 1929, forty per cent of Japan's total export trade was in raw silk. It only needed the collapse of American prosperity and a consequent plunge in the demand for silk to bring the Japanese economy to catastrophe. Raw silk exports were halved almost overnight. Sales of cotton and manufactured goods joined the slide! What were they expected to do? Sit at home and starve? Let's not be naïve, my boy. Justice is always bound to come a poor second to necessity. Strong nations survive. Weak nations go to the wall, that has always been the way of the world and always will be! The point is, can one blame them for taking matters into their own hands? From the business point of view they were in a pickle. And now, mind you, with their assets frozen and their difficulties in getting raw materials their pickle is going from bad to worse. I believe the Americans should give them the raw materials they need. Otherwise what can they do but grab them by force?' Noticing that the Commander-in-Chief was looking taken aback by this suggestion, Walter added tactfully: 'Not that they'd get very far in this part of the world.'

'The reason the Japs are so touchy and arrogant is that they eat too much fish,' said Brooke-Popham. 'It's scientific. The iodine in their diet plays hell with their thyroids. They can't help themselves. So, no, I suppose one can't blame them.'

18

Now the last course had been placed on the table: a thoroughly satisfactory baked bread-pudding. Matthew, for his part, eyed it with concern, afraid that it might prove too unusual for the taste of Dupigny. He need not have worried, however, for Dupigny surprisingly proved to have a craving for it, ate two helpings liberally coated with bright yellow custard and even went so far as to ask for the ingredients. Mrs Blackett, mollified by his enthusiasm, gave them: stale bread, raisins, sugar, an egg, a little milk and a pinch of nutmeg.

'Incredible,' murmured Dupigny, eyebrows raised politely.

Brooke-Popham's thoughts had wandered back to August 1914 again, recalled to France by Dupigny's presence. He chuckled inwardly at the thought of how primitive all their arrangements had been that first summer. He had carried a small, brand-new portmanteau full of gold everywhere he went, paying for everything out of it, from new flying-machines to spares, to chickens and wine for the HQ Mess. The hours he had spent guarding that portmanteau! Once he and Baring had driven into Paris in the Daimler and gone to Blériot's factory there to buy a new flying-machine. Then, later, they had bought new tyres and headlights for the Daimler. He had paid for them in gold to the astonishment of the chap in the shop. 'The English are amazing!' he had said in French to Baring, who spoke the lingo. Yes, those were the days! Brooke-Popham folded his napkin, stifling a yawn, beckoned home now by the nodding palms of Katong and the Sea View Hotel. 'Life is good,' he reflected.

The great dish of pudding had been removed. The meal was over. A large white pill and a glass of water had been set in front of Charlie, who had been eating doggedly with his mouth very near his plate and making no effort to join in the conversation. Since he had finished eating, however, he had been practising backhands with an invisible tennis racket over the table-cloth. In the process his wrist caught and knocked over a glass of water. There was a moment of startled silence.

'I leave you to deal with him,' Walter said to his wife with unexpected anger, rising from his chair.

'Oh, really, Uncle Charlie, what have you done now?' Kate said, putting a comforting hand on his shoulder. 'And you haven't taken your pill.' The guests filed out in silence, leaving Charlie staring sulkily at the saturated table-cloth.

Matthew would have liked to retire to bed at this point: he had had a long and tiring day. But it seemed that the Blacketts had not yet finished with him for Monty suggested a quick stroll in the garden. Together they stepped out into the warm, perfumed night accompanied by a dull-eyed Joan, yawning again behind scarlet fingernails. Birds uttered low cries, insects clicked and whirred around them and once a great patch of black velvet swooped, slipped and folded against the starry sky. Some sort of fruit bat, said Joan.

Although flanked by the young Blacketts, Matthew found himself peering uneasily into the vibrating darkness: he was not yet accustomed to the tropical night. As they sauntered through the potentially hungry shadows in the direction of the Orchid Garden he tried to recall whether he had once read something about 'flying snakes' or whether it was simply his imagination. And did fruit bats only eat fruit or did they sometimes enjoy a meal of flesh and blood? He was so absorbed in this speculation that when, presently, he felt something slip into his hand he jumped, thinking it might be a 'flying snake'. But it was only Joan's soft fingers. To cover his embarrassment he asked her about fruit bats. Oh, they were perfectly harmless, she replied, despite their frightening, Dracula-like wings.

But, Monty was saying with a laugh, what did Matthew think about another weird creature, namely their Uncle Charlie? Did Matthew know that he had been a cricket Blue at Cambridge? For he had been, though one might not think so to look at him now.

'Does he work for Blackett and Webb?'

Monty and Joan hooted with laughter at this idea. 'Father wouldn't let him within a mile of the place. No, he's in the Indian Army, the Punjabis. That was OK while they were stuck on the Khyber Pass or wherever they normally spend their time. But then, disaster! Charlie's regiment gets posted to Malaya. Father can't abide him, as you may have gathered. He has to put up with him, though, because of Mother who insists on inviting him to stay whenever he has any leave. She's afraid he will go off the rails if she doesn't watch over him. She may be right at that. Once he spent a week in Penang and we kept getting telephone calls asking us if we were prepared to vouch for a Captain Charles Tyrrell who was running up bills right left and centre. Then he started tampering with someone else's wife and there was the most frightful palaver over that. Father had to go up and straighten it all out. You can imagine how delighted he was. Because, of course, we're well known in this country and gossip spreads like wildfire.'

'Oh, and he's a poet, too,' said Joan, giving Matthew's perspiring hand a little squeeze.

'That's right. He wrote a poem about a place in Spain ...'

'Guernica.'

'Yes, that's it, about the place Joan just said. Mother had to warn us all not to laugh because he took it so seriously. He's quite a card.'

Matthew had only been able to give part of his attention to what he was being told about Charlie because of the sensations that were spreading up through his body from the hand which Joan was holding. Not content with the damp, inert clasp of two palms, Joan's fingers had become active, alternately squeezing his own and trying to burrow into the hollow of his palm. He could not help thinking: 'If Monty weren't here ...' and his heart pounded at the thought of what he and Joan might get up to. But Monty *was* there; and he showed no sign of noticing the delicious hand-squeezings that were going on in the darkness. Presently he said: 'We'd better be going inside. They'll be leaving soon.' With a final squeeze Joan's hand abandoned Matthew's as they passed back into the light.

They found the elder Blacketts and their guests drinking coffee and brandy in the drawing-room. Relations between Walter and the unfortunate Charlie had evidently been somewhat restored while they had been in the garden for, as they entered, they heard the tail-end of an argument that had been taking place.

'You expect young men being paid next to nothing to die defending your property and your commercial interests!' Charlie was asserting vociferously. He was still a little drunk but had tied his shoe-laces in the interim and his appearance was less dishevelled.

'I don't know about dying,' replied Walter good-humouredly. 'All you've done so far is drink.' And that proved to be the end of the discussion and of the evening, for the Air-Marshal and the General announced that it was time that they were on their way. They politely insisted on shaking hands with everybody on their way out, even with little Kate who, overcome by the momentous occasion, got mixed up and said: 'Thank you for having me.' This caused smiles all round and poor Kate wished she were dead. How could she be so childish! She blushed furiously and tried to smile, too, though she really felt like bursting into tears.

'You must come to our place one of these days,' muttered Dr Brownley to a semi-circle of glassy-eyed Blacketts who seemed to have gathered for no other purpose than to stare after him in mute accusation as he escaped into the darkness.

Dupigny suggested to Matthew that they walk back to the Mayfair by way of the road rather than the garden, to see if the Major had retired to his little bungalow on the opposite side of the road. Matthew said goodnight to the elder Blacketts. On the way out he found Monty and Joan on the steps by the front door. Monty held out his hand, saying that he was off to bed and would wish Matthew good night.

'Monty, I'd like to thank you for your help in getting me out here.'

'Think nothing of it, old boy. After all, we couldn't leave you to be raped by all those strapping Land Girls, could we?' And with a wave Monty disappeared inside.

After a moment Joan came forward. He thought she was going to say good night, too, but no. 'Hello you!' she said, lighting up like a firefly in the darkness. He peered at her uncertainly. 'You always look so serious,' she added, putting her shoulder against his and shoving him a little off balance.

'Do I?' he asked cautiously.

'Come on, I'll walk down the road a bit with you and François.'

They set off together down the drive but almost immediately Joan was called back by her mother who was standing at the front door. She wanted to know where Joan was going.

'Oh Mother!' Joan said irritably.

'Why can't you leave the girl alone?' Walter wanted to know, equally exasperated. A hurried conference took place.

While they were waiting for her Dupigny asked: 'D'you like women?'

'Well, yes, of course.' To Matthew this seemed a rather peculiar question. After a moment he added: 'I'm rather keen on D. H. Lawrence, as a matter of fact.'

There was a pause while Dupigny turned this over in his mind. Presently he said: 'Out here, you know, there are many young men but few young women ... I mean, European. There are, *bien entendu*, the Asiatical women, ah yes, but in Singapore, you see, although the young men make terribly love in a physical way to the oriental ladies and sometimes even to the mature European ladies (those who have, as we say, *la cuisse hospitalière*), still, alas, they are not satisfied. They sigh for companions of their own age and race. They are encouraged, moreover, by their elders who wish to preserve the purity of the race, a desire of which Hitler himself would not disapprove. With us in Indo-China it is different. We do not worry like the British when one of us decides to marry the daughter of a prosperous native. Such marriages have very often a great utility, both commercial and political.'

'Well, I must say ...' began Matthew, but his tired brain declined to furnish him with any suitable observation.

'You like Joan, perhaps? Yes, she is a nice English girl, healthy, full of virtues, plainly but solidly built in the English

manner, made (*comme le bread-pudding de Madame sa mère*)
entirely of good things, but, alas, without either the ravishing
innocence of a child or the serious attractions of a mature
woman. Personally I believe the only one of the Blackett ladies
to my taste is *la petite* ... Miss Kate, and even she is becoming
a trifle *trop mûre* ... She is already in my opinion a bit too ...
how d'you say ... *bien balancée* ... *bien foutue* ... Yes a bit
too well-endowed, thank you.'

'But she's only a child!'

'I agree she has that in her favour. All the same, the rot begins.
I speak physically, of course.' Dupigny suppressed a yawn.

'Of course,' agreed Matthew hastily, feeling the tide of the
conversation carrying him swiftly out of his depth. 'But what
I meant was ...'

'Ah, Joan is returning at last.'

The night air seemed very humid: the breeze had dropped,
increasing the impression of heat. An hour ago there had been
a brief, heavy downpour and water still gurgled busily in the
deep storm-drain beside the road, but overhead the sky was
clear. Matthew and Dupigny sauntered along hands in pockets;
Joan walked between them, humming a song beneath her
breath. As the road curved towards the Mayfair, however, she
dragged the two men to a stop and disengaged herself. She had
promised her mother she would not stay out long. Matthew
shook hands with her stiffly: he thought it best not to attempt
a more intimate embrace for the moment. As for Dupigny, he
collected her slender fingers in his own and conveyed them to
his lips but, despite the darkness, Matthew could see that he was
using them to mask the remains of the yawn against which he
had been struggling while speculating on the sensual qualities
of the Blackett women.

'How romantic you are, François! Why can't Englishmen be
like you? Well, good night!'

Matthew and Dupigny walked on towards the Major's bungalow which seemed, as far as Matthew could tell in the darkness,
to be no less ramshackle than the Mayfair Building on the other
side of the road. They called at the verandah but there was no
reply, except the soft cry of a night-bird from somewhere in
the undergrowth. Matthew produced his packet of Craven A
and they each lit a cigarette, lingering in the road while they
smoked: indoors the heat would be suffocating.

'D'you happen to know what the Singapore Grip is?' Matthew
asked. 'Some people I met said I should watch out for it.'

'I believe it is what they call here a certain tropical fever, very grave. Certainly, you must watch out for it.'

'Oh?' But why, wondered Matthew, would the RAF men have found it so amusing if it was a serious illness? This was a mystery.

Matthew would have pursued the matter but Dupigny was asking him how well he knew his old friend Major Archer. 'What? You have been introduced only? You must make his acquaintance better ...' And he went on to explain how fond he was of the Major. The Major, indeed, was one of the few people on earth for whom he, Dupigny, had any affection at all. They had first met in France during the Great War. In those days he had been a liaison officer with a British regiment. He and the Major had hardly known each other then. After the war he himself had gone to Indo-China, the Major had gone to Ireland. But then, one day in 1925, on a visit to London to see his tailor during his European leave, they had bumped into each other at a restaurant in the Strand, chez Simpson, perhaps? With enormous difficulty they had succeeded in recognizing each other, they had exchanged cards, they had renewed their acquaintanceship. Then, in the course of his next visit to Europe in 1930, they had met yet again, this time on purpose, and in 1935 yet again.

Dupigny had watched his English friend with the utmost curiosity. It had taken the Major time to settle down after the war. For a while he had been in hospital. And then he had evidently witnessed some unpleasantness in Ireland which had affected his peace of mind. The terrible unemployment of the post-war years had further unsettled him. In those days, too, he had perhaps still been yearning to capture a suitable young lady as a bride. There had no doubt been some woman in Ireland ... but that Dupigny suspected only. For the Major himself never spoke of such matters.

Over the years Dupigny had noticed the Major becoming more private in his habits and, in some ways, undoubtedly a bit eccentric. If you had gone to take coffee with the Major in, let us say, 1930, you would have witnessed a strange ritual. The housekeeper would first appear with a silver jug containing just-boiled water. The Major, still chatting to you politely, would whip a thermometer from his breast pocket, plunge it into the water, remove it, read it, dry it on a napkin and, with a nod to the housekeeper, replace it in his pocket. The coffee could now be made! Ah, that was the bachelor life for you!

146

And there were other things, too. He had taken to grumbling if his wine glasses did not sparkle as clear as rain-water ... yet at the same time thought nothing of piling his cigar ash on the polished surface of his mahogany dining-table, or of dropping it, without ceremony, on the carpet.

You might also, if the Major had ushered you into his drawing-room in Bayswater about the year 1930, have found it hard to discover a satisfactory seat, since all the more comfortable chairs and the sofa were occupied by slumbering dogs, refugees for the most part from Ireland's fight for independence and by now growing old. If you did find a seat it would be covered in fine dog hairs: these animals were always moulting for some reason. The Major himself would merely perch on the arm of a chair while the dogs gazed at him with bleary devotion from their cushions. Sometimes, if a bark was heard in the street outside, they would give answering barks, though without moving an inch from their chairs. Dupigny had known few more strange experiences than that of sitting in the company of the silent, withdrawn Major towards the end of a winter afternoon and hearing those dogs erupting round him in the gloom.

'Eh bien! So all is up with the Major!' one might have thought in 1930, looking at him perched on the arm of a chair across his penumbrous, dog-strewn drawing-room. 'Nothing surely can save him now from the increasingly private comforts and exacting rules of his bachelor life.' One by one over the next five years while he, Dupigny, was again in Indo-China the dogs had dropped away and were not replaced. The Major, perhaps, was no longer very fond of dogs and had kept them mainly from a sense of duty, just as he had kept the drawing-room itself exactly as it used to be when his aunt was still alive. By this time, without a doubt, he had become a confirmed bachelor. The marriages of his contemporaries no longer filled him with such envy. He had begun to see that being married can have drawbacks, that being single can have advantages.

Not, of course, that the Major had not continued to fall in love at regular intervals. But now he tended to fall in love with happily married women, the wives of his friends and thus, for a man of honour like himself, unattainable creatures who personified all the virtues, above all, the virtue of not being in a position to return his feelings. The love he bore them was of the chivalrous, selfless kind so fashionable among the British in late-Victorian and Edwardian times, perhaps because (selon l'hypothèse Dupigny) it handily acknowledged the female principle

147

in the universe without incommoding busy males with real women. Still, Dupigny had had to admit that his poor friend had a life which suited him very well, *y compris les amours*.

Agreed, the Major's reward in these encounters was not the tumultuous one of illicit embraces between the sheets: it was the glance of gratitude on a pure maternal brow, the running of a moustache as soft as ... *blaireau*, how d'you say? (badger? thank you) ... the running of a badger-soft moustache over fair knuckles, the reading of unspoken thoughts in bright eyes. These small moments, remembered late at night as he sprawled in his lonely bed smoking his pipe in a bedroom that smelled like a railway carriage (*Fumeurs*), were the Major's only but adequate reward.

If, however, perhaps hoping for a deeper relationship, the lady should pay him a visit one afternoon bringing her children (Dupigny had witnessed one such occasion) the Major would become cross. Young children would totter about the house knocking things over and trying to hug the elderly, malodorous dogs, themselves grown short-tempered with age. Older children would chase each other from room to room and would keep asking him if they could play with certain important possessions of his (a gramophone, a pair of Prussian binoculars, a steam-powered model boat or electric railway) without realizing that these objects could only be handled with elaborate ceremony and precautions. These children-accompanied sentimental visits, Dupigny surmised, had never failed to be disastrous, passion-damping.

On such occasions, no doubt, faced with a terrifying glimpse of what a real marriage might entail, the Major could not help congratulating himself on his escape. A white marble statue of Venus, it was true, still glimmered, seductively unclothed, at the foot of his stairs. But having turned forty the Major must have reflected that by now he was over the worst. He had come through the years of emotional typhoons battered, certainly, but all in one piece. It was wonderful how a human being could adapt to his circumstances. The Major knew in his heart that he could not have endured marriage, the untidiness and confusion of it.

And so, there the Major had been, about 1935, fixed in his habits, apparently suspended in his celibacy like a chicken in aspic. But one day, abruptly, he was no longer satisfied: he had decided to give it all up, this comfortable life, to travel and see the world before he was finally too old. A man has only one life! How surprised Dupigny had been when one day he learned that the Major was making a voyage to Australia, and then to Japan, even to visit him in Hanoi and later in Saigon! Why had he done this? Another love affair that had gone wrong? The Major never spoke of such things. Why had he then settled in Singapore, opportunely for himself as it now turned out? This was something which Dupigny had not understood. And neither, perhaps, had the Major!

Matthew and Dupigny, having finished their cigarettes, approached the entrance to the Mayfair Building: a little way into the compound a stiff, dignified old *jaga* in khaki shorts and a yellow turban watched them sleepily from his *charpoy* but all they could see of his face in the darkness was a copious white moustache and a white beard. Dupigny asked whether the Major was still in the bungalow. The *jaga* raised a skinny arm to point towards the building behind him.

'It seems the Major has been here all the time. Let us go and wish him good night.'

After the starlit compound the darkness on the verandah seemed almost complete. It was agreeably perfumed, however, by the smoke of a Havana cigar whose glowing tip Matthew had no difficulty in locating as it danced for a moment in fingers raised in greeting.

'Not yet in bed, Brendan? Old gentlemen must take care of themselves.'

'I'll be going to bed in a moment,' the Major said, but Matthew had already been informed that the Major, harassed by insomnia, was just as likely to sit here on the verandah smoking cigars until first light. 'Did you hear anything? Were there any military big-wigs there?'

'Brooke-Popham and a General. They appear confident.'

Matthew and Dupigny groped their way across the verandah to the Major's side. There Matthew collapsed with a shriek of bamboo on to a chaise-longue. How tired he was! What a lot had happened since he had last been in bed! 'Very soon now I shall go to bed,' he thought wearily. From where he sat he had a view of the Major's silhouette. He could see the outline of his 'badger-soft' moustache, recently outraged by Cheong's scissors. He could even see the corrugated wrinkles mounting the slope of the Major's worried brow, growing smoother as they reached the imperceptible line of hair neatly plastered down with water.

'What fools those men are!' exclaimed the Major, and the

149

tip of his cigar glowed fiercely in the darkness. But after a moment he added humbly: 'Of course, they may know things that we don't.'

19

At the end of the first week of December a little group of men wearing overalls or boiler-suits or simply shorts on account of the heat gathered one afternoon in the shade of the tamarind tree in the Mayfair's compound. They belonged to the Mayfair Auxiliary Fire Service unit (AFS for short) and they had been summoned, although today was Sunday, to an urgent practice. The morning newspaper had carried news of a convoy of un-identified transport ships heading south from Japanese-occupied Indo-China and the Major, who was in charge of the Mayfair AFS unit, feared the worst. The Major, at the moment, was not under the tamarind tree but in the garage beside the house, struggling with a tarpaulin. Matthew, who had just been en-rolled in the unit, was assisting him. There was no ventilation in the garage and the day's sun, beating down on the corrugated iron roof, had made it like an oven inside. Matthew had already been suffering from the heat: now he felt the perspiration running down his legs and collecting in his socks.

The Major had dragged the tarpaulin off a large box-shaped object which proved to be some sort of engine, gleaming with steel and brass pipes and fittings. Matthew stared at it blankly. It had two large dials on a sort of dashboard and, instead of wheels, two carrying-poles like a palanquin.

'It's a Coventry Victor,' declared the Major with pride. 'Brand new!'

'But what does it do?'

'It's a trailer-pump. The trailer is over there. I've had a bracket put on the back of my car so we can tow it about if need be. Give me a hand and we'll carry it outside. We're going to have a drill with it when our instructor gets here. He's an ex-London Fire Brigade man and when he's sober he knows his stuff ... which isn't always, unfortunately.'

Presently, the instructor arrived. He turned out to be a short, bald and red-faced man in his fifties called McMahon. After a lengthy altercation with the taxi-driver who had brought him he advanced swaying towards the Mayfair Building. The Major had explained to Matthew that Mr McMahon, like many firemen, had started life as a seaman. It became clear, however, as he collided with a bush, shouting, on his way round the house, that this was not the explanation of his rolling gait.

The Major had drawn up the members of the Mayfair AFS unit in a line beside the tennis court ready to be inspected by their instructor. They stood at ease, waiting uncertainly, while Mr McMahon weaved his way towards them, cursing. Apart from the Major himself, the unit consisted of Dupigny, a Mr Sen and a Mr Harris, both clerks who were occasionally lent to the Mayfair by Blackett and Webb (the former was Indian, the latter Eurasian), Mr Wu, a friendly Chinese businessman, the Chinese 'boy', Cheong, who had surprised the Major by volunteering and who, though his face remained perfectly impassive in every situation, had proved easily the most efficient of the recruits, Monty Blackett, who had volunteered (the lesser of two evils) to avoid conscription into the Local Defence Force but was still hoping to achieve, if not a complete dispensation, at least, a more agreeable position in Singapore's active or passive defences, and finally, a handsome young man called Nigel Langfield, the son of Walter's arch-rival and enemy, Solomon Langfield: Nigel was wearing a very new blue boiler-suit with AFS prettily embroidered in red on one of its breast pockets; from time to time he would lower his nose to sniff the satisfying new-cloth smell of this garment.

These would-be firemen eyed their instructor with concern as he waded towards them, as if through a swamp. Before reaching them, however, he unexpectedly changed course to embrace the trunk of another tree not far away. Then, with his arms still round the tree and still cursing, he slithered to the ground, eventually struggling around to use it as a back-rest.

'God help ye, y' blithering lot o' helpless bastards!' he babbled, fighting for breath. 'Let's see another dry drill then, you perfumed bunch o' pansies or, God help ye, the fists'll be flyin' or me name's not McMahon! Get on with it ... A dry drill, I'm tellin' ye!'

'I thought we were going to do a wet drill today,' said the Major, looking dissatisfied. 'That's what you said last time.'

'*This* time I'm sayin' it's a dry drill, y'bastard, so hop to it and see that ye run the bleedin' hose out without a twist in it

151

or ye'll catch it hot, I'm tellin' ye ...'

'Well, we might just do *one*,' said the Major, 'in order to get the feel of it before we do a wet drill. I'm afraid McMahon's not going to be much help to us today by the look of it,' he added in an undertone to the rest of the unit.

'I heard that, y' pissin' old goat,' yelled McMahon, quivering with a fresh paroxysm of rage and struggling ineffectually to get to his feet, evidently with the intention of exacting retribution.

'Shut up or we'll bash your silly brains in,' said Monty languidly, sloping off in the direction of the bungalow.

'Look here, Monty, where are *you* off to? We're just going to begin,' said the Major indignantly.

'I'm just going to find an aspirin, old boy, if you don't mind.'

'Well, hurry up about it. I'll try and explain the basic drill to Matthew in the meantime.'

There were, the Major explained, two types of hose: suction hose for picking up water from an open source such as a canal or a river, and delivery hose, for relaying water to the fire. Suction hose had a wide diameter and was reinforced to keep it cylindrical; it also had wire strainers to prevent stones or rubbish being sucked up into the pump. 'Have you got that?'

'I think so. This other one, then, is the delivery hosepipe, is it?'

From under his tree McMahon shrieked with laughter. '*Hosepipe!* He thinks he's a bleedin' gardener!'

'Hm, I should have mentioned that, we say "hose" rather than "hosepipe", and ropes are known as "lines" and the rungs of a ladder are called "rounds" ... I don't suppose it matters particularly, as we're just a scratch team, but McMahon seems to prefer it.'

Delivery hose, the Major continued, was wound flat on a revolving drum and came in fifty or a hundred-foot lengths with a diameter of two or three inches; at the business end there was a tapering brass tube called the 'branch', not the nozzle! The drill was that the number one man ran off in the direction of the fire with the branch, unreeling a length of hose as he went; meanwhile the number three man laid out another length of hose and dealt with the couplings. These couplings were what were known as 'male' and 'female', that was to say ...

'That fat pansy wouldn't know the difference if ye took up y'skirts and showed him!'

'That will do, McMahon,' said the Major sharply. He turned

back to Matthew. 'The idea is that the male coupling plugs into the female on the previous length of hose. The male plugs into the standpipe, if that's where the water is coming from, or into the engine pump. Meanwhile the runner takes hold of the lugs on the "female" end around which the delivery hose is normally wrapped and he uses them as an axle round which the roll of hose unwinds. Here, Nigel will give us a demonstration.'

Nigel obediently took the roll of hose and holding it a little way from his body went loping gracefully away with it, laying it down neatly on the turf behind him as he went.

'It's not as easy as it looks. Nigel's rather good at it.'

It was true. Everybody watched in admiration and even McMahon was temporarily silenced by this display of skill. There was still no sign of Monty so Cheong was sent to look for him. Meanwhile Mr Wu, who with Dupigny and Cheong had been tinkering with the engine, was called forward to show Matthew how to climb a ladder which had earlier been set up against the roof of the Mayfair.

'When climbing radder glasp lounds not side of radder,' explained Mr Wu to Matthew.

'What?'

'Glasp lungs!'

'Good heavens! You mean, your own? Or someone else's?'

'That's right,' said the Major, approaching swiftly. 'You should always hold the rungs, or the "rounds" as we call them, rather than the frame of the ladder. And incidentally never step on to a window-ledge: they tend to collapse. The drill is to put one leg right into the window. Ah, thank heaven for that, it looks as if McMahon has gone to sleep,' he added. 'Perhaps this would be a good time to get the pump working. After all, we may not have much more time to practise.'

A gloomy silence had fallen on the Mayfair AFS unit. Even McMahon, muttering in his sleep, looked discouraged. Staring into the distance where the white wedding-cake mass of the Blacketts' house glimmered above the trees, the Major said: 'Still, with luck we may never be needed.'

As soon as the afternoon's drill was over Matthew with a sigh of relief made for the bathroom, which as he had already discovered, had one serious disadvantage: the absence of any running water. A vast green and yellow earthenware jar with a copper ladle stood in one corner. This was a Shanghai jar. The procedure was simple: you dipped the ladle into the jar and poured the water over yourself. Matthew stripped and began sluicing himself; he found the water in the jar tepid but refreshing, nevertheless.

'An Irishwoman will be fired from a cannon, Monty? Whatever for?'

Monty, who had followed Matthew into the bathroom with an invitation, explained. It was some special show being put on at The Great World in order to raise money for the war against the Japs in China. The Irishwoman was a human cannonball making a tour of the Far East. And there was also a group of singers called the Da Sousa Sisters. Anyway, Joan had said she was keen to go. That meant they only needed another woman and they could make an evening of it. 'You don't happen to know any women, do you?'

'Monty, I've only just arrived.'

'Never mind then. I expect I'll be able to scrape one up somewhere. I'll see you over at our place in a couple of hours, OK?'

'Oh look, while you're here, Monty, I'd like you to explain something about our Johore estate that I don't understand. Why are we replanting at a time when it's so urgent to produce rubber? I don't get it.' The previous day Matthew and the Major had driven over the Causeway and into Johore on the mainland so that Matthew could inspect the Mayfair estate. They had discovered that in a number of places mature trees were being replaced with saplings. When they had questioned Turner, the estate manager whom Matthew had glimpsed on his first evening in Singapore, he had not known the reason for it. He had simply been instructed to replant by Blackett and Webb who, as managing agents, were in control of planting policy.

'Well,' replied Monty, sighing heavily, 'it's nothing to worry about. It's all under control.'

'I'm sure it's under control. I just want to get the hang of things, that's all.'

'Rubber trees don't last for ever, you know. And as they get older they get brittle. They break in the wind ...'

'But they last for thirty years or so, don't they? And the trees that are being replaced aren't that old. Besides, it's not just an odd tree here and there. It's being done in sections.' There was no sound in the bathroom except for a steady splash of water and Monty's rather laboured breathing. Matthew began to ladle water over himself again.

'Look here,' said Monty finally in a rallying tone, 'I have to admit that your question has stumped me. We have so many estates that it's hard to know everything about each one. The

Mayfair is small beer compared with some of the others. But I tell you what. I'll get the facts straight before your next Board meeting and we'll thrash it out there, OK? Now don't worry about a thing. I'll be on my way now ...' However, he continued to stand in the doorway watching the water coursing over Matthew's plump body. Did Matthew know, he enquired with a leer, that in the East there were many stories of beautiful girls who, in order to be cool, climbed into Shanghai jars and then could not get out, so they had to call a manservant to break the jar? Matthew could probably imagine what happened next! With that Monty departed, licking his lips, to bathe in the greater comfort of his parents' house.

Later, refreshed by his bath and wearing a light linen suit, Matthew was on the point of leaving for the Blacketts' house when the telephone rang. It was Ehrendorf. In the few days which Matthew had now spent in Singapore the two friends had so far managed only one brief meeting. The reason, undoubtedly, was that Ehrendorf was extremely busy. With the rapid decay of the political situation in the Far East his services, Matthew surmised, must be in constant demand for the assessment of British military strength and strategy. However, Matthew was aware of a new feeling of constraint in his friendship with Ehrendorf. How different it was now from the way it had been before! He could not help contrasting that strained meeting at the aerodrome and the subsequent drive into Singapore with their previous meetings in Europe. Matthew, though by nature unobservant, was well aware that Joan was somehow at the root of this new awkwardness. He supposed that Ehrendorf and Joan had had some sort of affair; he remembered the melancholy sigh he had heard from the darkness at the Mayfair on the night of his arrival. But why should that affect his relationship with Ehrendorf?

On the telephone, Ehrendorf sounded more friendly and cheerful, more like his old self. He asked Matthew how he was going to spend the evening, suggesting that they should have a meal together. Matthew explained that Monty had just enlisted him to watch an Irishwoman being fired from a cannon. Perhaps Ehrendorf would like to come, too? As a 'military observer' it could almost be considered his duty.

'OK, I'll meet you at The Great World. There's a place where they sell tickets at the main gate, something like the lodge of an Oxford college (inside you'll find it's more interesting, though!).' And Ehrendorf rang off. It was only on his way to the Blacketts' that Matthew remembered ... Joan would be there, too. And that might cause some difficulty.

Presently Matthew found himself in the Blacketts' drawing-room, waiting for Monty and Joan. While the elderly major-domo went off at a dignified pace to alert some member of the family to his presence Matthew took a quick look at the portrait of his father which hung at the end of the room, then he went to sit down on a sofa. A Chinese 'boy' came and placed a packet of cigarettes and some matches at his elbow and then silently withdrew, leaving him alone except for a long-haired Siamese cat curled up on the floor: this was Kate's beloved pet, Ming Toy. He scooped it up and sat it on his lap. It opened its eyes for a moment, then closed them again.

'Are you a tom-cat, I wonder?' he asked the cat, lifting its magnificent tail to inspect its private parts. He began to rum-mage about in the animal's fur, peering at it closely for signs of gender. The cat began to purr. Matthew was in the middle of this careful inspection of the cat's hindquarters (its fur was so long and thick one could only guess at what it might conceal) when Walter came into the room. He gave Matthew a rather odd look. Matthew hurriedly let go of the splendid tail and put the cat back on the carpet.

'You're just the man I wanted to see,' said Walter. 'I want you to look at some of these paintings of Rangoon and Singapore in the early days.'

20

'So there you are, my boy, is that not an achievement to be proud of? Over this great area of the globe, covered in steaming swamp and mountain and horrid, horrid jungle, a few deter-mined pioneers, armed only with a little capital and a great creative vision, set the mark of civilization, bringing prosperity to themselves, certainly (though let's not forget that the croco-diles of bankruptcy and disgrace quietly slipped into the water at their passage, ready to seize the rash or unlucky and drag them down into their watery caverns), but above all, a means of livelihood to the unhappy millions of Asiatics who had been faced by misery and destitution until their coming! Such a man

156

was your father!'

Over the years Walter's rhetoric as he conducted his guests on a tour of his collection had grown more solemn and impressive. Here and there fanciful touches had crept in (the crocodiles, for example, which nowadays forged after his intrepid capitalists): if they earned their keep he allowed them to stay; otherwise they were discarded. He had grown more convinced himself of the rightness of what he was saying and more indignant at the absence from history books of the great men of commerce. Surely it was unjust that history should only relate the exploits of bungling soldiers, monarchs and politicians, ignoring the merchant whose activities were the very bedrock of civilization and progress!

On the whole Matthew was inclined to agree with Walter: he, too, considered it odd that great commmercial exploits should have been so neglected in the list of man's achievements. Both courage and a creative intelligence were certainly needed to set up a great commercial enterprise, even one on the scale, relatively small by international standards, of Blackett and Webb. Why, then, did History hesitate? Could it be that History was unhappy about the motives of the great entrepreneurs, or about the social ills that accompanied the undoubted social benefits flowing from these enterprises? Matthew, listening to Walter with one ear, began to ponder this interesting question.

Walter, who had been inclined to fear the worst on first acquaintance with Matthew, had been surprised and gratified to discover that Matthew was quite well-informed about economic conditions in the Far East and in other backward countries of the colonial Empire. Agreed, it was theoretical knowledge, culled from books so that facts and statistics and ideas lodged in his head in a Russian salad of which it was unlikely that any practical use could be made. But still, it was clear that Matthew was interested, as opposed to Monty who was not. Walter even dared to hope that given some experience of the real world of the market-place, and a little time for Joan to make him familiar with the unaccustomed snaffle and bit, something might be made of Matthew, after all. He explained in ringing tones the importance for the morale of Malaya's native masses of Blackett and Webb's jubilee celebrations. Soon these native peoples, like the inhabitants of the British Isles, might find themselves having to fight for their country. They needed an idea to fight for. By a happy chance that idea, by general consent, had been found to be embodied in Blackett and Webb's jubilee slogan: 'Continuity in Prosperity'! And it was here, went on Walter enthusiastically, that Matthew would have his first opportunity to make a contribution to the War Effort; for the jubilee procession planned for New Year's day, after a sequence of floats symbolizing the benefits conferred on the Colony by Blackett and Webb, was to have culminated in the founder sitting on a chair borne by grateful employees. Thus the image of Continuity would be stamped indelibly on the native mind. But, alas, Mr Webb's death had left the chair empty. Who better to fill it than his son, Matthew?

'Oh well,' murmured Matthew vaguely, 'I'd like to help, of course, but that sort of thing isn't really my cup of tea. Not at all. Hm, why don't you try Monty? He'd be much better.'

'Well, we'll see about that,' replied Walter somewhat testily, disappointed by Matthew's lack of enthusiasm. He decided to have a word with Joan: he could see it was high time she started producing some results: 'Are you and Joan going out this evening?' he asked after a pause.

Matthew explained about their proposed trip to The Great World.

'Really, Monty's the limit,' Walter muttered to his wife who had just entered.

At this moment Monty and Joan burst into the room, laughing over something. They both stared at Matthew as if surprised to see him there ... But no, that had been the arrangement.

'Well, let's get going,' said Monty. 'We don't want to miss the show. Besides, Sinclair is waiting in the car.'

'But Duff and Diana are coming,' said Mrs Blackett, 'aren't you even going to stay and say hello to them?'

But Monty regretted that they had not a moment to spare. Yes, he would see that Joan was not home too late and, yes, he did have the keys of the Pontiac. If you once got stuck with those 'talkative buggers' from Westminster, he explained to Matthew on the way out, there was no getting away from the 'dreary sods', the evening was as good as ruined.

Standing, for some reason, bolt upright on the back seat of the Pontiac and shading his eyes with his hand, or perhaps saluting although there was nobody in the vicinity except the Malay *syce*, was a tall, thin Army officer of about Monty's age. This was none other than that Sinclair Sinclair with whom Joan had enjoyed such an agreeable voyage from Shanghai some years earlier; in the meantime he had exchanged his career in the Foreign Office for a commission in the Army where, thanks to family connections and the dearth of regular officers which attended the outbreak of war, his rise had been swift; now here he was, instead of fighting Jerry in North Africa, called to put his experience of the Far East at the disposal of Malaya Command and pretty fed up, too (as he had explained to Joan), at finding himself a member of the 'Chairborne Division'!

'Thank heaven!' he cried while they were still at some distance. 'I thought you'd never come. I was beginning to feel like a ca ... ca ... ca ... person abandoned on a desert island!' and he uttered a shrieking laugh, like the working of a dry pump, and with the same sort of hollow gulping coming from his midriff.

'I'm Matthew Webb,' said Matthew, since the young Blacketts, intent on dismissing the *syce* and installing themselves in the Pontiac, had not bothered to introduce them.

'Suh ... suh ... suh ... suh ... suh ... suh ...' Matthew was obliged to pause with his hand in the officer's while this long string of redundant syllables was dragged out of his mouth like entrails, and his smile grew a little fixed as he waited. But finally, with a gulp and a snap of his teeth, the officer was able to bite off the string and exclaim: '... inclair Sinclair!' Matthew, who had taken an immediate liking to him, nodded encouragingly, wondering whether Sinclair was his first name, last name or both at once. It seemed better not to risk an enquiry.

This time Monty was driving, but no less recklessly than the Malay *syce* had done on the previous occasion that Matthew had been in this car. As the Pontiac surged down the drive into humid evening and then turned with screaming tyres on to the road, Monty thumped the steering-wheel jubilantly chanting 'Run, rabbit, run!' Joan sat in front with her slender, sunburned arm gracefully resting on the back of the seat behind her brother. She was wearing a plain, short-sleeved dress of blue cotton, beautifully ironed. How fresh she looked! 'She toils not, neither does she spin,' thought Matthew, gazing in wonder at the beautiful creases in the starched cloth. She turned, her hair tossing in the wind as they hurtled down Grange Road, and gave him a quick, sly smile.

'I'm going to have to duh ... duh ... dash off early this evening,' shouted Sinclair. 'I go on duty at midnight.'

'I knew it,' said Monty. 'You're going to be a bore, Sinclair. I feel it in my bones.'

'No, I'm not,' protested Sinclair. 'Must watch out for the jolly old Jap, though.'

'You *are* going to be a bore then.' Monty fell into a moody silence until they were approaching The Great World. 'It looks as if we'll have to leave the car and walk. It's been like this every night for the past few weeks with the bloody troops arriving.'

'By the way,' said Matthew, 'Jim Ehrendorf wanted to come so I said we'd meet him at the gate.'

'Oh no! That's all we needed,' grumbled Monty exchanging a glance with his sister. 'What did you do that for?'

They parked the Pontiac in River Valley Road and proceeded on foot. Women shuffled along in the crowd carrying on their backs doll-like babies with shaven heads, some asleep, some peering out in wonder at this strange world with black button eyes. Already by the time they had reached the corner of Kim Seng Road the crowd had thickened considerably.

'Is all this for the human cannonball?'

Monty shook his head. 'Everything goes on here. You'll see. People here are crazy about dancing. They bought the dance-floor out of the old Hôtel de l'Europe which used to be the swanky hotel on the *padang* and had it put here. They sometimes get the orchestras from the P & O boats in dock (or they used to, anyway). Makes a change from Chinks and Filipinos.'

Presently they came to the entrance beneath an archway on which was written in streamlined neon script: *The Great World*. Here a dense crowd of men and women struggled for admission; among them several men in uniform. Suddenly a man in a lighter uniform caught Matthew by the arm: it was Ehrendorf. 'I just got here this moment,' he said cheerfully. 'Hi there, Monty! Hiya Joan!'

'What a surprise,' said Monty without surprise.

'Jim, I'm not sure that you know, ah, Sinclair ...' said Matthew.

'Let's get inside before we get crushed to death,' said Joan, ignoring Ehrendorf. 'These soldiers smell like pigs.'

'Look, I just want to hire someone to watch my car while I'm inside so could you wait a moment?' said Ehrendorf, his cheerfulness evaporating. 'I'm afraid the local gashouse gang will have it stripped down if ...'

But the young Blacketts had pressed on through the entrance dragging the hesitating Matthew and Sinclair with them.

'Look, shouldn't we wait for Jim?'

'Don't worry, he'll find us all right.'

Matthew had a last glimpse of Ehrendorf's face as Monty propelled him through the entrance and was harrowed to see the expression of suffering on it.

'See you in a minute then,' Ehrendorf called after them and hurried away.

21

Matthew now found that he had been shoved into a great circular concourse in the middle of which stood a thicket of bamboo and palms. On one hand was an open-air café whose tables were thronged with rowdy troops drinking beer, on the other a billiards saloon through the tall open windows of which Matthew glimpsed green pyramids of smoke-filled light above the tables and oriental faces glimmering in the surrounding darkness. Farther along was a great hall from within which there came the regular thump of drums and sighing of saxophones.

Together they struck off through the crowd which in some places was so thick that they had to shoulder their way through, passing along a street of stalls with corrugated-iron roofs and flimsy, brightly lit fronts. Some of these stalls were open-air eating-houses festooned with lurid, naked, pink-eyed chickens hung by their necks on hooks, lidded eyes closed in death; beside them were piled varnished ducks and lumps of meat swimming in grease and studded with fat flies gorging themselves; next to the meat laboured a wizened specialist in fish dumplings, and next to him a family of plump Malays beside bubbling cauldrons of *nasi padang*, giant prawns, curried eggs, nuts and *ikan bilis* (dried fish no bigger than your fingernail), all being shovelled on to plates or twisted in cones of leaves. Here a groaning lady was being sawn in half, there another was being put through a mincer with blood horribly gushing out underneath; next came a shooting-gallery where an Australian sergeant in his wide-brimmed hat was using an air-rifle to smash blackened light-bulbs to the jeers of his comrades, and a strip-tease stall; a neighbouring stall displayed a sign warning of *Waning Virility*: 'Please swallow our Sunlight Pill for Male

Persons, Moonlight Pill for Female Persons. Guaranteed.' Beneath the sign was a display of medicine bottles together with a crude and alarming diagram in coloured crayon which was evidently intended to represent sexual organs.

As Matthew paused to study it his arm was suddenly taken by a tall and slender Tamil girl with a pigtail (in which jasmine flowers were intricately braided) hanging to her waist. He nudged up his spectacles to see her better, gazing with surprise into her dark face where a silver stud gleamed in the whorl of each nostril. She was very pretty and he would have liked to talk to her, but the others were already disappearing; and so he disengaged himself apologetically and hurried after them, his heart thumping. How exciting it all was, how much more interesting than Geneva!

Now, hurrying through the crowds in search of his friends, he almost ran full tilt into a makeshift stage (merely boards and trestles) on which a Chinese opera was taking place. Actors and actresses in glorious costumes were declaiming in a penetrating falsetto, impervious to the scene-shifter in khaki shorts and singlet and with a cigarette dangling from his mouth who was rearranging the furniture around them. One of them, with a forked beard reaching to his knees, stalked off into the wings, rolling his eyes in histrionic rage, and a murmur went up from the crowd of Chinese who had gathered to watch. On his way round the side to rejoin the alley which he had left Matthew found himself gazing into the dressing-room, for the sides and back of this miniature theatre were covered only by cloth hangings blowing about in the breeze and allowing him a glimpse of the actresses making-up for the next scene: elaborately rouged and pink-powdered faces glared at mirrors while tweezers prepared a further assault on already well-plucked eyebrows. Several tiny Chinese girls clung to wooden spars also peering in at this arresting sight.

Afraid that he had lost his friends altogether, he pressed on; his progress was slow, nevertheless, for his attention was captured by various wonders which sprang up one after another: a man selling bunches of dried frogs tied together by their legs, a family of acrobats turning somersaults, a stall selling the juices of unfamiliar fruits by the glass, a wizened cashier in a bamboo cage, *satay* morsels skewered on hundreds of bamboo spills roasting over charcoal, sellers of *soto* soup, and *won ton mee*, and apple fritters fizzing in rancid-smelling oil, and *nasi goreng*, and heavenly ice-cream flavoured with mango and durian, and the durian itself, so desired and so dreaded for its peculiar odour, piled in pyramids like cannonballs ... and other astonishing sights and events beyond description, taking place, too, in a street crowded with them and women of every shape, size and colour, from a family of performing pygmies, to the graceful, delicate Chinese, to floury, bucolic British and Dutch in voluminous khaki shorts; and accompanied by a cacophony of musical instruments and gramophones in an atmosphere heavy with perfume, incense, sandalwood, sweat and tobacco smoke in the soft, humid air of the tropics.

Matthew recalled the conversation he had had earlier in the evening with Walter and began to ponder the commercial enterprise which had brought about this extraordinary mixture of races and cultures. It was as if the sudden appearance of Western capital in Malaya had created a vacuum which had sucked in people from all the surrounding countries and from much farther away. Would this nation of transients who had come to seek a livelihood under the British Crown one day become a nation with a culture of its own, created somehow out of its own diversity? It had happened in America, certainly, but would it happen here where the divergences of culture were even greater than they had been among the American immigrants? Was a colony like Malaya, as the Communists claimed, a mere sweat-shop for cheap labour operated in the interests of capitalism by cynical Western governments? Or was Western capital (which included his own capital, too, now that his father had died; he must not forget that!) ... or was Western capital, as Walter insisted, a fructifying influence bringing life and hope to millions by making hitherto unused land productive? Or was it perhaps both things at the same time? (Had not Marx himself suggested something of the sort?) To what extent were the affairs of the Straits Settlements and Federated Malay States directed by Britain with the welfare of their inhabitants at heart and to what extent with British commercial interests? that was the root of the question! Matthew had halted again, perturbed. He could see Monty and Joan and Sinclair not too far ahead and he wanted to think this out before rejoining them. But at this moment something odd happened.

Among the strollers, diners and revellers Matthew had been aware, while sinking his teeth into these weighty problems, of a number of painted girls, Chinese or Eurasian, unusually graceful and attractive in their high-collared, straight-cut Shanghai gowns, slit at the side to above the knee. These girls wore their blue-black hair short and marcelled in the Western fashion, but as Matthew stood there, immobilized by thought, he could not help noticing that one of them, strolling arm in arm with another girl, was not only wearing a Western summer frock but also wore her hair long and loose. And even more surprising, for she seemed to be Chinese, when she passed in front of a brightly lit food-stall her hair, which had seemed to be as black as her companion's, glowed dark red around the edges, like a bottle of red ink held up against the light.

She was saying something to the girl beside her and accompanying her words with a sweet smile which revealed a glimmer of white teeth. Matthew, captivated by her appearance, could not help staring at her. Looking up, she noticed his glance and gave a start of surprise, as if she recognized him. With a word to her companion she came boldly up to him, still smiling, and said in a low voice: 'Matthew, I knew your father.' Then, since Matthew merely goggled at her, she went on: 'He was very kind to me. I was so sorry when he died! My name is Vera Chiang ... I saw you when you came to the Mayfair with Mr and Miss Blackett, who has also been kind to me ... and she is beautiful, too, don't you think? just like Joan Crawford she reminds me of, so lovely ... and now, Matthew, you are all alone in the world ...' Her eyes had filled with tears of sympathy.

'Good gracious!' murmured Matthew and continued to peer at her in astonishment. He cleared his throat, however, in order to say something more adequate and was about to nudge his glasses up on his nose, but she took hold of his hand and clasped it feelingly in both of hers, saying: 'I was in trouble and your dear father, like a saint of heaven, from the depths of my misery gave me "a bunk up" (please excuse my slang expression of speaking!) and now he has died, it is so sad, it really does give me "the blues" when I think about it and sometimes at night I cry by myself, yes, but forgive me, for you it must be very much worse than for me!' And with emotion she clasped his hand tightly to her chest with both of hers.

'Actually, my father and I weren't all that ...'

'Yes, I *know* how you were feeling when you heard this news and I thought "Poor Matthew" because your father had shown me a "snap" of you when small baby and I wondered: "In whatever country in the world will this news reach him?" and your father had told me that when one day he was no more,

164

you, his only son, would be left alone in the world because your dear mother had "kicked the bucket" long ago and there was no one else to look after you.' On an impulse she flicked open a button of her frock and gently slipped his hand through the opening, clasping it with both of hers more tightly than ever to comfort him, with the result that Matthew now found his rather damp palm moulding what appeared to be, well, a naked breast: whatever it was, it was certainly silky, soft, plastic, agreeably resistant and satisfying to the touch. He continued to stand there for some moments enjoying this unusually pleasant sensation, though distinctly bewildered. Meanwhile, they gazed into each other's eyes, hypnotized, and currents of feeling flowed back and forth between them.

At this moment a torrent of inebriated Dutch sailors, their arms on each other's shoulders, half running, half dancing the remains of a drunken hornpipe, scattering the crowd right and left, suddenly came bearing down on them. One moment Matthew was standing there, immobilized by the question of colonial welfare and progress, with the damp palm of his hand neatly moulding a young woman's naked breast, the next he was being jostled by a crowd of chuckling Chinese as they fled before the hornpiping sailors. He was pushed this way and that. He and the young woman were sundered ... the hand through which such agreeable sensations had been flowing was brushed away, his spectacles dislodged from his nose and swung perilously from one ear as he struggled to keep his balance. Now a gale of deep-throated laughter blew in his ear, his wrists were grabbed and slung around enormous damp necks, powerful hands closed round his chest, and the next instant he had been whisked away as part of a giant spider's web of sailors from which one or two diminutive Chinese were struggling like flies to extricate themselves. Matthew found himself carried along in a blur of rushing lights and figures, swaying and horn-piping at a terrifying speed, his feet hardly touching the ground, until at last the spider's web's progress was arrested by crashing into a tent where what might have been some rather intimate massage seemed to be taking place. By the time that he, too, had managed to disengage himself and adjust his spectacles, which by a miracle he had not lost (he would have been helpless without them), he was some distance from where he had seen the girl. He went back a little way, looking for her, but the crowd had surged over the place where they had been standing and he could no longer even be quite sure where it had been.

He felt a hand on his arm. He turned and found that it was Monty.

'We thought we'd lost you. What have you been up to? Come on, it's this way.'

'Monty, I must tell you, a really strange thing just happened...'

But Monty was anxious not to miss the beginning of the show and without waiting to hear any more had set off again towards a distant spot-lit enclosure. From that direction, too, there now came a high-pitched, piercing laugh, like the creaking of a dry pump, or perhaps the lonely cry of a peacock in the dusk.

22

A considerable crowd had assembled to witness the unusual sight of a European lady being fired from a cannon; canvas awnings had been erected to screen the event from those reluctant to pay the price of admission but here and there the fabric was torn and small boys fought for places at peepholes. Inside the enclosure an elaborate scene had been set: on the right stood the cannon, its long barrel, mottled with green and brown camouflage in the best military manner, protruding from a two-dimensional cardboard castle on which was written *Fortress Singapore*. Behind the cannon loomed the giant papier-mâché heads of Chiang Kai-shek and King George VI, the former with a legend hung round his neck: 'Kuo (Country), Min (People), Tang (Party). World friend with all Peace-loving Peoples!' together with a similar legend in Chinese ideographs beside it. 'God Save King' said a more prefunctory legend around the King's neck.

On the left, at a distance of some fifty yards, stretched a large net and, in front of the net, an impressively realistic armoured-car constructed of paper and thin wooden laths. From its turret there reared, like snakes from a basket, a fistful of hideously grinning bespectacled heads in military caps; towering above these heads, like a king cobra ready to strike, was yet another bespectacled snake's head which was surely, thought Matthew, intended as a caricature of the young Emperor Hirohito. Any doubt but that this was intended to be the cannon's target was dispelled by a sign on the armoured-car which declared: 'Hated Invader of Beloved China Homeland.'

'But where are the Da Sousa Sisters?' demanded Monty. 'I thought they were part of the show.' The programme he had bought consisted of a single folded sheet, on the outside of which was a blurred photograph of a bulky, helmeted figure, presumably the human ammunition; inside, it read:

1 Advance of atrocious enemy.
2 Cannon fires.
3 Miss Olive Kennedy-Walsh, BA (Pass Arts), H Dip Ed, TCD will hurtle through air towards advancing disagreeable aggressor.
4 Treacherous aggressor smashed. (Mgt not responsible.)
5 Voluntary contributions to China Heroic War Effort gratefully received.
6 God sake King.
7 End.
8 Please to exit. Thank you for custom.
Paper model supplied courtesy Chou & Son, Undertaker and Funeral Preparation. All Religions catered for. Sago Lane, Singapore.
    'End as you wish you had begun.'

'Oh, that's nothing,' said Monty to Matthew, who had remarked on the excellence of the imitation armoured-car. 'You should see the Cadillacs and houses and ocean liners and whatnot they make for rich *towkays* to take away with them to the next world. It's a skilled profession. The Chinese can be pretty simple-minded,' he added with a sneer.

'Where *are* those suh ... suh ... suh ... sisters? This is a duh ... hm ... liberate swindle, don't you think so, Monty?'

But a pink-faced young planter nearby, overhearing Sinclair's complaint, assured him that the Da Sousa Sisters had already made their appearance. They had sung a number of songs, including 'Chocolate Soldier' and, of course, their signature tune: 'Halloa! halloa! 'halloa!' He doubted whether they would appear again that evening.

'Just our luck,' grumbled Monty.

'I don't think Jim will ever find us,' Matthew was saying, but at that moment he saw Ehrendorf shouldering his way into the enclosure. Meanwhile, a portable gramophone was being vigor-

167

ously wound by one of the stage-hands. Another Chinese in a white dinner-jacket took the microphone. 'Just in time,' said Ehrendorf cheerfully. 'I wouldn't have missed this for anything.' Joan was sitting at the end of the row and he sat down next to her. But she stood up immediately, saying to Monty and Sinclair: 'Move along. I want to sit next to Matthew.' With some confusion, because the gap between the rows of seats was narrow, she struggled to the place which opened up between Sinclair and Matthew. Ehrendorf flushed and stared grimly down at the arena.

Now the star of the performance, Miss Kennedy-Walsh, was being announced: she was a strongly built woman in her thirties, dressed from head to foot in an aviator's suit of white silk which perfectly modelled her impressive figure: the audience murmured in appreciation of her well-formed thighs, her generous breasts, her strong jaw and pink face.

'Will she ever squeeze down the barrel?' joked Ehrendorf tensely.

'Big ah blests number one!' remarked a smartly dressed young Chinese beside Matthew giving the thumbs-up sign. Matthew had already noticed by the pin-ups displayed at the 'virility' stall how the Chinese seemed to admire big-bosomed women.

Miss Kennedy-Walsh, indeed, was not finding it easy to insert herself in the barrel. Her splendid thighs she fitted in with comparative ease; somehow, aided by the slippery material of her suit, she also managed to cram her hips into the muzzle. But her breasts remained obstinately stuck on the rim and with her arms pinned to her sides she was helpless. Stuck! Her face flushed with irritation. A murmur of concern arose from the audience. 'Glory be to God, will ye give us a shove, y'lazy gombeens!'

A hasty conference of the Chinese organizers was already taking place. They scratched their heads and stared at Miss Kennedy-Walsh's too ample bosom and then they stared at the cannon and scratched their heads again. The master of ceremonies put his hands on her shoulders and shoved politely, but that did not help. If anything it made things worse. Miss Kennedy-Walsh slipped down a few inches but her bosom remained on the rim and her face grew redder.

'Will we be stayin' here all the night or what?' she demanded furiously. Her mouth could be seen working but her further comments were drowned by the martial music which suddenly started up. Matthew, who had been watching with interest and concern, stiffened suddenly as he felt Joan's hand creep into his own and his pulse quickened.

In the meantime someone had had an idea and a Chinese lady had been invited on to the stage. She was heavily made-up and, despite the heat, wore a brilliant feather boa round her neck. She had evidently been hastily summoned from other duties and appeared flustered. The master of ceremonies, explaining what he wanted her to do, made kneading motions and pointed at the recalcitrant breasts. A sheet was modestly thrown over the muzzle and Miss Kennedy-Walsh's protruding head and torso. The lady with the boa vanished underneath it; the gramophone continued to play martial music. When, after a few moments, the sheet was whipped away again, there was no sign of Miss Kennedy-Walsh. A ripple of applause echoed around the enclosure.

Now the show was beginning in earnest. The master of ceremonies, first in Cantonese, then in Malay, then in English, asked the audience on a given signal to count down from ten. A spotlight was directed on a man by the breech of the cannon holding a lanyard: he smiled nervously; a wheel was spun and the barrel elevated. Another spotlight was directed on to the model armoured-car with its wavering, two-dimensional Japanese effigies. Long ropes had been attached to the front of the armoured-car which now began to move very slowly, dragged by two Chinese stage-hands, from behind the net and on towards 'Fortress Singapore'. A high ramp had been set up in front of the net and the armoured-car obligingly diverted from its course and, instead of continuing to advance directly on the Fortress, started to climb it. The martial music had come to a stop, replaced by a long roll of drums. The counting began. Ten ... nine ... eight ... The armoured-car had almost reached the top of the ramp ... Three ... two ... one ... Fire! The man holding the lanyard jerked it, but nothing happened A gasp of dismay went up from the spectators. In the silence that followed, muffled comments could be heard from inside the barrel of the cannon. Monty consulted his programme: 'We seem to have got stuck on number 2: "cannon fires".'

Another hasty conference took place, this time around the breech. While it was taking place the men with the ropes, somewhat apprehensively, darted up the ramp under the eye of the cannon, seized the armoured-car and carried it back to its original position; then they took up their stations once more with the ropes. Presently, after another roll of drums and a few adjustments by a man with a spanner, they were again given the signal to start pulling. The armoured-car began to climb! Ten ... nine ... eight ... The nervous strain was clearly telling on the men with the ropes: the vehicle was advancing jerkily, now halting, now bounding forward. Three ... two ... one ... Fire! A tremendous explosion echoed around The Great World and a white projectile went winging its way in a glittering arc beneath the black vault of the sky. Swooning with excitement, the men with the ropes gave a great pull: the armoured-car shot over the top of the ramp and down the other side just as Miss Kennedy-Walsh hurtled by where it had been standing an instant before; on she went to land helmet first in the net; there she jumped and arched and flapped like a netted salmon.

Missed! This was not a contingency for which the men holding the ropes had prepared themselves. They looked at each other helplessly. What were they to do? Even the most perfunctory realism required them to continue pulling. The armoured-car turned its nose hesitatingly towards 'Fortress Singapore' and continued, slowly but steadily, to convey its wavering cargo of grinning, bespectacled Japanese towards where the cannon loomed, bereft of ammunition. A roar of indignation went up from the crowd. The master of ceremonies hurriedly intervened and the armoured car was whisked away, Miss Kennedy-Walsh took a bow. A collection in favour of the Nanyang Anti-Enemy Backing-up Society was announced.

'Let's go and have a drink,' said Monty, who seemed satisfied with the way the show had turned out despite the non-appearance of the Da Sousa Sisters. As they made their way towards the exit the crowd was beginning to sing: 'God save glacious King!'

They set off down another alley; the crowds strolling up and down had grown even more dense than they had been earlier. Monty, Joan and Sinclair walked in front. Matthew followed at a little distance with Ehrendorf; he wanted to think of some way of comforting his friend who was still clearly upset by the way Joan had changed places in the enclosure. Moreover, he was worried that if he walked beside Joan, she might not be able to resist the temptation of holding his hand in full view of the others, thus causing Ehrendorf further unnecessary chagrin. Matthew could not help thinking it curious that she should find him attractive. Very few other women ever had. He had tried to accept this, as he tried to accept everything, philosophically.

But above all Matthew simply wanted to talk with his old friend and to recover their former intimacy, for Ehrendorf was one of those rare people who could be interesting whatever he talked about. Matthew enjoyed argument and speculation the way other people enjoy a game of tennis. Furthermore, although he did not mind the particular, it was the general which really stirred him. It was not enough for him to know, for example, that two Catholics were pitched out of a window in Prague in the interests of the Jesuits and Ferdinand of Styria early in the seventeenth century (as it would be for you and me), Matthew immediately wanted to investigate the general implications of the deed. And he would speculate lovingly on whether or not it had been *necessary* (not merely a coincidence) that a period of intolerance should follow the Emperor Rudolph's liberal reign, or on some other quite different aspect of the matter ... on religion as against economics as a cause of war, or (even more far-fetched) on the effect of windows, and of glass generally, on the Bohemian psyche, or on the marriage of physical and mental enlightenment (windows, lamps, electric light advancing hand in hand with rational thought) in the progress of humanity.

Of course, people change. Matthew and Ehrendorf had both undoubtedly changed in the years since they had argued into the night in Oxford and Geneva. Matthew had realized even in Geneva that he himself was beginning to change: he no longer enjoyed arguing with his friends, above all those who had embraced the academic life, quite as much as he had once done. It was not simply that these friends had tended to adopt the lugubrious and self-important air which distinguishes academics: surrounded by the paralysing comforts, conveniences and irritations of university life what else could they do? He sensed that what distressed him was a gap which had opened up between thought and feeling, the remoteness, the impartiality of his friends to the subjects they were teaching or studying. Objectivity, he had had to agree with them, was important obviously. But what was required, he had declared, striding up and down with their vintage port inside him while they eyed him dubiously wondering whether he would wake the children, was 'a passionate objectivity' (whatever that might be). He had usually found himself taking the last bus home feeling muddled and dissatisfied with himself as well as with his friends. Yet with Ehrendorf it had always been a little different, perhaps because, coming from a military family, he had chosen to

171

become a soldier rather than an academic, though more likely it was simply a difference of personality. Whatever the reason, in Geneva he had always found it delightfully easy to discuss things with Ehrendorf.

Now, just as if they had been strolling along the Quai Wilson instead of through 'a pulsing, perfumed, malodorous, humid, tropical evening, Matthew brushed aside some trivial enquiry from Ehrendorf about Sinclair (who was he? how long had Joan known him? were they particularly close friends, perhaps even childhood friends?) and reverted to the important matter which had stopped him in his tracks earlier. Could the coming of western capital to the Far East be seen as progress from the natives' point of view?

'I'm sure you've heard Walter's lecture on how he and my father and some other merchants transformed Burma from a country, where, unless a coconut fell off a tree, nobody had any supper, into a modern rice-exporting nation ... I gather he delivers it to everyone he comes across ...'

'Well,' sighed Ehrendorf, automatically falling into his old Oxford habits, 'it all depends what you mean by ...'

'Progress? Or natives?'

'Well, by both, I guess,' Ehrendorf smiled faintly, 'since there was massive immigration of Indians and *their* situation must have been different from that of the Burmese. Walter certainly exaggerates. Burma was a fertile and prosperous country before the British took over. But you mustn't think that a barter economy is like Paradise before the Fall: a cash economy has more resources to survive floods, typhoons, and whatnot, even if it does introduce certain difficulties of its own which were not there before.'

'Difficulties! Why, the rice merchants knocked Burma for six! The whole culture was destroyed. The old communal village life collapsed. Almost overnight it became every man for himself. People started fencing off grazing land which used to belong to the whole village and so forth. Profit took a grip on the country like some dreadful new virus against which nobody had any resistance. When the Burmese were reduced to becoming migrant seasonal workers in the paddy fields the old village life was finished off completely ... and with it went everything that made life more than a pure money-grubbing exercise. At one time they used to hold elaborate cattle races, and water festivals, and village dances and theatricals and puppet shows. They all vanished. And what replaced them? A huge increase

172

in the crime rate! To be happy people need to live in communities. If you don't believe me you can read it in the government reports!'

'Sure, I believe you,' said Ehrendorf rather vaguely. 'But still, this is a partial view. You must look at the whole picture.

'By the way, just look at that Indian bloke over there in his striped tie and cricket blazer, modelled on some fatuous English tradition that has no *real* meaning for him at all. He's borrowed a culture that doesn't fit him any better than his jacket.'

Ehrendorf, while looking at the whole picture, had also had his eye on the Blacketts and Sinclair some way in front of them; perhaps he, too, was no longer as keen as he used to be on abstract discussions, or perhaps he was preoccupied with other matters. He had grown thinner since he and Matthew had last met in Europe and had developed one or two hesitations in his manner which had not been there before. Once or twice Matthew had been on the verge of that nightmare sensation when you suddenly find yourself thinking: 'But I don't know this person at all!' and the person in question happens to be your closest friend. But now a glance at Ehrendorf reassured him: it was the same old Ehrendorf, except for the moustache; a little older, of course, and not quite so cheerful and self-confident as he had once been. But then, he himself had aged, too.

Ehrendorf's fine eyes rested on Joan's botttom as she walked some distance ahead between her brother and Sinclair; the light blue, neatly ironed cotton of her dress picked up the glow of naphtha lanterns as she passed each stall so that, from a distance, it seemed that her figure flared and died, flared and died, almost hypnotically. Very often a girl's bottom begins to sag in her twenties (which does not matter particularly since few people notice or care whether a bottom has dropped or not) but Joan's had not done so; from behind you might have thought that she was simply a mature adolescent. Nor had she developed those over-bulging cones of tissue at the top of the thigh which sometimes bestow even on a slender woman a saddle-bag effect. 'Her bottom is too perfect,' Ehrendorf might have been thinking as he stared ahead in a trance. 'It's too beautiful to get a purchase on, like everything else about her, it simply slips out of your hand.'

Matthew, however, could not be expected to notice this sort of thing. Besides, it was doubtful whether, even if he had been interested, he would have been able to see far enough without taking off his spectacles and polishing them : in the course of the evening a thick film of dust had collected on the lenses.

'Sinclair must be a new arrival in Singapore, I should think,' remarked Ehrendorf. 'Although he seems to know his way round OK.' This was undoubtedly a statement rather than a question but, nevertheless, a vague air of interrogation lingered about it. Matthew, however, paid no attention : he was evidently still too busy trying to express what was in his mind.

'Let me give you an example, Jim, of what happens when cash and the idea of profit strike root in a country unaccustomed to them like Burma. It seems that's there a ghastly Darwinian principle of economics known as the Law of Substitution which declares, more or less, that "the cheapest will survive". This has all sorts of unpleasant consequences, one of which is that non-economic values tend to be eliminated. In Burma they used to build beautiful, elaborately carved cargo-boats which looked like galleons : these have been entirely replaced over the past fifty years by flat barges which can transport paddy more cheaply. And it's the same everywhere you look : native art and craft replaced by cheap imported substitutes, handlooms have disappeared, pottery has given way to petrol tins. Even the introduction of new crops by western capital has tended to impoverish rather than enrich the life people lead. In Burma the natives used to cook with sesamum oil, now they use ground-nut oil because, though it doesn't taste so good, it's cheaper. In Java people have taken to eating cassava instead of rice because it's cheaper ...'

'If it's cheaper,' protested Ehrendorf, 'then they have more wealth to spend on other things.'

'Not so! If they can live more cheaply it stands to reason that they can be paid less, provided there's no shortage of labour. Yes, exactly, it's our old friend "the iron law" up to its tricks again! What additional wealth may be generated by the use of cheaper methods and cheaper foods doesn't cling to the natives : the extra saving goes to swell the profits of the western businesses which control the land or the market ... like Blackett and Webb! The native masses are worse off than before. For them the coming of Capitalism has really been like the spreading of a disease. Their culture is gone, their food is worse and their communities have been broken up by the need to migrate for work on estates and in paddy fields. Well, am I right?'

'But Marx believed, did he not, that such a stage is necessary in the progress of society from feudalism to Communism and therefore even saw the British in India as a force for progress.'

'You can't have it both ways! What you and Marx say is fine ... that is, if Communism is what you *want*. But what if we reach this stage where the poor are made poorer and organized into gangs of coolies and then ... lo and behold, *there is no revolution*! Are the natives not worse off than they were in their traditional communities? Of *course* they are! You still have to show me what advantages the coming of western capital has brought, in Burma at any rate.' After a moment Matthew added: 'In any event, my bet is that in practice Communism would be scarcely any better than Capitalism, and perhaps even worse.'

Ahead of them Monty, Joan and Sinclair had disappeared into the Wing Choon Yuen Restaurant whose palatial entrance was partly screened from the alley by a substantial brick and pillar wall: on top of this wall neat rows of palms had been set in brown earthenware pots decorated with dragons. Ehrendorf said: 'This is still a partial view, Matthew. No doubt there is something in what you say. But in the West, too, craftsmen have been unable to survive mass-production, capitalism and the Law of Substitution. That's life, I guess.' He shrugged and added with a smile: 'There's another principle which I shall call Ehrendorf's Law which is now in operation in all prosperous Western countries and which asserts "the survival of the easiest". Twenty years from now coffee beans will have disappeared and we'll drink nothing but Camp Coffee, not because liquid coffee tastes better ... it tastes worse ... but because it's easier to prepare. Pretty soon nobody will read books or learn to play the piano because it's easier to listen to the radio or phonograph. Mark my words! Ehrendorf's Law will do just as much damage in the long run! All the same, Matthew, I can't agree with you because you neatly avoid mentioning all the benefits of western civilization, the social welfare, education, medicine and so forth. But let's discuss that another time. And by the way, it has just occurred to me, if this guy Sinclair *had* been an old family friend of the Blacketts I'm sure I'd have seen him or heard of him in the last couple of years ...'

'Let's not bother with the Blacketts ... I want to discuss my theories,' said Matthew.

It was then that Ehrendorf suddenly went silent and looked rather upset. It had occurred to him that Matthew, far from being too preoccupied with his own ideas to discuss Sinclair and his mysterious relationship with Joan, had all this time been deliberately keeping the conversation away from the Blacketts.

Matthew had not noticed his friend's reaction and, following him into the restaurant, muttered grimly: 'Oh, education and medicine. Don't worry. One could say something on that score, too!'

23

Monty, Joan and Sinclair were seated at a table set among foliage on the *terrasse*. As Matthew and Ehrendorf approached, Sinclair got to his feet saying: 'Got to duh ... duh ... ash off, I'm afraid. Got to do my duh ... duh ... duh ...'

'Of course you haven't,' said Monty. 'Sit down, Sinclair, you're being a bore. It's nowhere near midnight yet. You said you didn't go on duty till midnight. Well then?'

'Got to duh ... duh ... duhoo ... well, a whole lot of things, a fearful amount, in fact. So, have a nice time and I'll be suh ... seeing you,' he added in a fluent rush. He kissed Joan's hand, rolling his eyes for some reason, waved to the others and departed.

The young Blacketts had ordered *ikan merah* (fish, Matthew understood) and chips and a large bottle of Tiger beer between them. Matthew and Ehrendorf ordered the same. While they waited a rather tense silence fell over the table: even Monty, not usually at a loss for words, seemed disinclined to speak. In the dark shadows behind Joan glowed a shower of delicate, speckled marmalade-coloured orchids, framing her perfect face and shoulders. Ehrendorf snatched a quick glance in her direction and then, though he had already given his order, buried himself in the menu. While his eyes moved silently over *won ton* soup, crab sweetcorn soup, sweet sour prawn, Taoist fish ball, cornedbeef sandwich, lychee almond beancurd ... his face took on a strained and innocent expression, as if he were thinking: 'The trouble about such perfection is that you can't get a grip on it, it slips away. There's no perspective.'

'Will you kindly stop that!' said Joan suddenly and with anger.

'Stop what?'

'Looking at me in that stupid way.'

'I wasn't looking at you at all. I was reading the goddam menu, if you don't mind.' Ehrendorf's voice had grown shrill and his accent, which normally might have been taken for English, suddenly became that of an American again. Matthew took off his dust-filmed spectacles, polished them on a rather grey handkerchief, put them on again and stared unhappily at Ehrendorf.

'What. I wanted to say, Jim, about education and medicine . . .'

Silence, however, fell over the table once more. Matthew examined the wall and the dragons which decorated the earthenware pots; from beyond the palms which grew out of them came the constant murmur of voices and laughter and the throbbing of music. Presently, a Chinese girl appeared with a bowl from which she took a steaming face-flannel with a pair of wooden tongs and placed it in Joan's hands: she then offered one to Monty, Matthew and Ehrendorf in turn. Matthew mopped his perspiring face: the sensation of relief this afforded was extraordinary. More waiters presented themselves, bringing fish and chips and beer. As they began to eat the atmosphere grew more relaxed. Matthew, knife and fork raised and ready to pounce on his fish (he was hungry), cautiously raised the subject of education. Admittedly, he had yet to delve deeply into the matter as it affected Malaya but he did know what the British had managed to achieve in this line in India . . . namely, a prodigious number of unemployable graduates. 'The Indians have always had a tremendous desire for education. The only trouble is that there are hardly any actual *jobs* for educated men to do, unless they want to be clerks or lawyers, and there are already several times too many of *them*.'

Monty had taken knife and fork and begun vigorously to chop up his fish, first laterally into quarters, then diagonally, as for the Union Jack, but most likely this was not the mute response of a patriot to the drift of Matthew's argument so much as a convenient way of reducing the fish to pieces small enough to deal with; he speared one of the pieces together with a bundle of chips and stuffed the lot into his mouth.

'All we needed in India were Indians educated enough to serve as clerks and petty officials: in no time at all there were enough of them, and several times too many. Curzon did his best to launch vocational and technical education and I gather it's been tried here in Malaya, too. But with miserable results. You may well ask why.'

None of Matthew's listeners seemed, as it happened, to be on the point of putting that or any other question to him. Monty, breathing heavily through his mouth, seemed completely occupied in masticating fish and chips. Joan and Ehrendorf simply stared at Matthew, looking tense and dazed; Joan had not touched her knife and fork but now picked up a single chip in her fingers and snipped off the end with her perfect teeth, without taking her eyes from Matthew's face.

'The fact is that in most tropical colonies the only work available is agriculture, and sometimes a bit of mining. What we really want is cheap unskilled labour. What skilled jobs there are in a country like Malaya don't go, it appears, to Malays, but to Eurasians, Chinese or sometimes Europeans. No cheap unskilled labour is what western capital came here for and that's what it gets ...!'

'But ...' began Monty. He was silenced immediately, however, by his own right hand which, spotting its opportunity, had raised another forkful of fish and chips and now crammed it into his mouth as soon as it opened to speak.

'As I expect you all know there was talk of starting an engineering school a couple of years ago at Raffles College here in Singapore. What happened? A commision reported that it was pointless because there'd be no jobs for the graduates. So you see the idea that we British are educating our colonies in our own image simply won't wash. That may be what we'd like to do, and certain attempts have been made no doubt, but that's not what is actually happening.'

'Oh, look here,' said Ehrendorf mildly, but to Joan not to Matthew. 'This is a bit ridiculous.' Joan, her eyes still on Matthew snipped off another inch of the chip she held neatly between finger and thumb, but otherwise ignored him.

Matthew went on: 'And yet there still persists this sad belief that a man can better himself by education. At this *very* moment here in Singapore, according to the official figures, there are more than ten thousand clerks, most of whom live in the most dreadful conditions earning ten dollars a month if they're lucky, not even a living wage, simply because their numbers far exceed any possible demand for them. Ten thousand clerks for a city of this size! It seems it's a regular practice for older clerks to be replaced by younger men at lower salaries and yet that doesn't stop the schools turning out another seven hundred boys every year with qualificatiohs for clerical jobs. And all because of this pathetic, unfounded belief that education leads to lucrative jobs!'

'Really, you can't expect me to put up with this,' said Ehren-dorf suddenly.

'Well, clear off then! Nobody invited you, anyway.'

'As it happens, Matthew did.'

'Frankly,' said Monty, pushing away his empty plate and selecting a toothpick, 'I don't think it matters a bugger whether they work as coolies or anything else so long as they have jobs. That's precisely what they don't have in South China and India. They come here because they think it's better, and they're damn right. It is.'

'I thought you said you were going. If so, what're you waiting for?'

'That's just what you'd like, isn't it?'

'Monty, surely we have a *responsibility*,' went on Matthew doggedly, 'to the people living here when we arrived; even more so to those we encouraged to come and work on the estates. One of the most astounding things about our Empire, when you come to think about it, is the way we've transported vast pop-ulations across the globe as cheap labour. Surely we must have their interests at heart, at least to some extent, as well as our own. Otherwise it's not much better than the slave trade.'

'We do have their interests at heart: we're giving them employment which they didn't have where they came from. Besides, almost half our rubber in Malaya is produced by Asiatic smallholders, people who probably came here originally as coolies and then set up in business for themselves. They produce pretty piss-awful rubber but that's their business.'

'Let's go and dance,' said Joan. 'Monty, pay the bill and let's go.'

Monty summoned the waiter and produced a roll of blue dollar bills, saying: 'Without British capital there wouldn't have been any rubber business.'

'But don't you think, given the huge returns on money inves-ted in Malaya that something more should be done for the people who actually do the work on the plantations to produce it ...? Otherwise, the British Empire is nothing more than a vast business concern ...' But Matthew's last words, though intended for his companions, had been transformed into a soliloquy by their sudden departure, Joan in the lead, Ehrendorf striving to walk beside her and speak to her, and the burly figure of Monty not far behind. Matthew hurried after them, nudging his glasses up on his nose.

As they approached The Great World's dance-hall the

atmosphere seemed to thicken, as if the very dust which hung in the air was quivering with the percussion of drums and wailing of saxophones. Monty dropped back for a moment, indicating that he had something he wanted to say to Matthew. No, it wasn't about the colonial question, he muttered confidentially, it was more of a proposition he wanted to make. He'd thought it over quite a bit and consulted his two chums who were also very, very interested (that went without saying, actually, because in its way this was a bargain such as one didn't often come across and so *of course* they would be interested) and, well, the upshot of it was that he and his two chums had decided unanimously to invite Matthew to join them in ... the point being that he was a chap from the same sort of background as they were, a factor one had to bear in mind in a place like Singapore where gossip got around in no time ... anyway, in short, they'd decided that Matthew should be given the opportunity of making up the fourth ... No, nothing like that, he hated all card-games himself, couldn't abide them, in fact, well ... in a nutshell, instead of risking heaven knows *what* dreadful diseases with the sort of women one was likely to pick up here at The World or anywhere else in Singapore he and his chums had decided to club together and they'd found a very nice Chinese girl called Sally who had her own flat in Bukit Timah. She was clean and not the kind who'd get drunk or make a fuss. She was ...

'Oh, but really, Monty...'

'No, just listen a moment. You aren't a bad sort of bloke, Matthew, in your way (in fact, I quite like you), but you're the sort of chap who rejects things out of hand without even listening and weighing up the pros and cons. And this is just the kind of arrangement that would suit a bloke like you who isn't very good at getting women, if you don't mind me saying so, and besides, *it's not expensive* ...'

'Monty, I can assure you ...'

They had now joined Joan and Ehrendorf in the queue of people, many of whom were in uniform, waiting for admission to the dance-hall. Monty lowered his voice a little so that his sister should not hear what he was saying. She was clean, she had imagination (which was something one didn't often find), she was good-tempered and sober, she was not narrow-minded in her approach (in fact, you could do almost anything you liked) and it would only come to $17.50 a month per person. It was such a bargain that Matthew probably thought he meant

American dollars, but not a bit of it! He meant Straits dollars. It was an incredible opportunity! For $17.50 Matthew would have, at least to begin with, one evening a week *guaranteed* and the possibility of another, if one of his three partners did not exercise his option for two evenings in that particular week, as would most likely very often happen because of some social occasion they couldn't get out of, OK? Because Matthew was the last to join it was only fair, after all, that the others should have first choice but he, Monty, for one would be most surprised if it did not work out that Matthew found he had two evenings on most weeks ...'

'Hey, Yank! Why don't you join in the bloody war then?' demanded a perspiring, drunken Tommy, waving a beer bottle at Ehrendorf.

'Because we don't want to make it too easy for you guys,' replied Ehrendorf cheerfully.

'Give us some gum, chum!' shouted someone else and there was a cackle of laughter.

'Because you're a lot o' pissin' cowards, that's what!' shouted the first man belligerently.

'Who needs the bleedin' Yanks anyway? Old Adolf would only give 'm a spankin'!'

Raucous cheers greeted this remark but Ehrendorf, still smiling good-humouredly, had reached the bamboo cage and handed over fifty cents for himself and each of his companions. Then he waved to the boisterous crowd in khaki behind him and vanished into the throbbing darkness followed by a medley of cheers, insults and ribaldry.

'Yankee ponce!'

'They 'ave 'em 'orizontal wi' teeth in 'em 'ere, sir!'

'Can I do yer now, sir?'

Blundering after his friend, Matthew presently found himself at the edge of a dance-floor, covered but open at the sides for ventilation, gleaming with French chalk in the semi-darkness like a subterranean lake. So this was the famous dance-floor taken from the old Hôtel de l'Europe which, Joan was now whispering huskily into his ear, at the turn of the century had been the finest in Singapore. No doubt his father, together with the wealthy and influential in the Colony, in his day had waltzed or fox-trotted on those very boards! But now the *beau monde* had been replaced by that bewildering array of races and types he had noticed earlier in the evening in the open air, even two members of the family of pygmies could be seen executing a perfect tango close at hand. Matthew gazed enchanted at the teeming dance-floor. Abruptly, he realized why this sight gave him such pleasure. He tried to explain to Monty who had taken Joan's place at his side: *this was the way Geneva should have been*! Instead of that grim segregation by nationality they should have all spent their evenings like this, dancing the tango or the quick-step or the *ronggeng* or whatever it was with each other: Italians with Abyssinians, British with Japanese, Germans with Frenchmen and so on. If there had been a real feeling of brotherhood in Geneva such as there was here (the Palais des Nations turned into a *palais de danse*) the Disarmament Conference would not have got stuck in the mud the way it did! 'It was the feeling, perhaps even the *confidence* that men of different nations and races could get on together that was so tragically missing. And yet here is the evidence! Men are brothers!'

'Yes, er, I see what you mean,' mumbled Monty cautiously, 'but about that other matter we were discussing. I mean, well, you think it over. There's no need to make a snap decision, Matthew. On the other hand we do know plenty of blokes who would jump at the chance if we offered it to them, so you can't keep us waiting indefinitely.'

'But I'm not keeping you waiting, Monty. I've told you, I'm not ...'

'No, well, you think it over,' muttered Monty hastily. 'No need to make a snap decision.' And he started to explain to the rather bewildered Matthew how to set about dancing with a taxi-dancer. You first of all had to buy a book of four twenty-five-cent dance tickets from the bloke over there. Then when music started you made a dash for the one you liked the look of. But you had to make it snappy or someone else would grab her. At the end of the dance she took you back to her table and you handed over a ticket. You weren't allowed to sit with them unless you paid a special fifteen-dollar fee for taking them away from the taxi tables.

'Thanks Monty, but I think I just want to watch.'

'You would!' murmured Monty inaudibly.

Meanwhile, however, the tango had turned into an exhibition by a Filipino couple who were chased somewhat haphazardly round the floor by a white spotlight; the man was a foxy-looking individual in a white suit, the woman, a sinuous person in sequins with flashing eyes and raven tresses. The music changed tempo and they began jitterbugging violently, shoes flashing.

the grinning members of the band were also from the Philippines; clad in dazzling white blazers and orange trousers they formed a shallow bank against the far wall, harmonizing satisfactorily with the lurid, unlikely birds which had been painted on it. Overhead, painted on the ceiling, Matthew could just make out the shape of a gigantic golden dragon whose bulging eyes, faceted with mirrors, showered reflected sparks like confetti on the swaying dancers below. Now the spotlight, outguessed by the movement of the dancers, strayed for a moment to the edge of the floor and hesitated there by coincidence on Joan and Ehrendorf. He was talking intensely into her ear while she stared unseeing at the polished floor, tapping her foot moodily to the beat of the music. He looked up for a moment, dazzled and bewildered; Joan shook her head, tossing her hair. The spotlight moved jerkily away in pursuit of its quarry.

Saddened by the look of desperation on his friend's face, Matthew shifted his attention to the taxi-girls sitting at tables beside the floor, wondering whether the girl whose breast he had found himself clasping earlier in the evening might not be among them: these girls, too, appeared to be Chinese or Eurasian for the most part, with a few Malays, Siamese and Indo-Chinese; undoubtedly, thought Matthew, these women from further up the peninsula towards China were the loveliest and most graceful of all with their glistening black eyes and delicate features: beside them even the delicate Joan looked clumsy, heavy and rough-skinned. Ehrendorf, however, did not seem to think so for he had taken Joan by the wrist and was trying to persuade her to join him on the floor which, temporarily deserted, now began to fill up. The band set to work on another tune. Men of all descriptions, from diminutive Chinese clerks to enormous tipsy Australians, swarmed across the floor to secure the services of the taxi-girls. Ehrendorf tried to lead Joan on to the dance-floor but she resisted, snatching her hand away from him. Ehrendorf then seemed to give up hope all of a sudden: his chest deflated, his shoulders drooped, he passed a hand over his forehead as if dazed.

'Well, have you thought it over about that nifty Chinese girl I was telling you about?'

'Monty, I told you before: it's not my line.'

Monty looked taken aback: 'There's no need to decide right away, old boy. I don't want to rush you. And look here, if you have only one evening a week we could probably fix it so you don't have to pay quite so much. After all, that's only fair, isn't it? How about fifteen dollars a month? It's really worth it, you know. God, boy, she goes at it hammer and tongs, I can tell you!'

'It's not the price, for heaven's sake. It's the idea of it.'

Monty stared at Matthew, baffled. It had not occurred to him that Matthew would drive such a hard bargain. Or could there perhaps be some other explanation? And then an idea struck him.

'If you think you'll get it from her,' he said warningly, indicating his sister who was standing a few paces away, 'I'm afraid you're barking up the wrong tree. I know lots of blokes who've been out with her and she doesn't.'

'Doesn't what?' asked Matthew. And then added hurriedly: 'Oh, sorry, I see what you mean ...'

But Monty, nevertheless, uttered the heavy sigh of someone whose patience has been tried beyond endurance. 'She doesn't,' he repeated. And then, just to rub it in: 'Not even *occasionally*!'

24

Matthew's head was reeling as he and Monty and Joan passed out of The Great World and into Kim Seng Road; for a moment he felt quite giddy and had to steady himself with a hand on the wall. Ehrendorf, shattered, had left half an hour earlier by himself; before leaving he had said to Joan: 'We must have a serious talk. I'll look in this evening if you're not back too late.' Joan had replied that he could do what he liked. She was accustomed to young men wanting to have serious talks with her. After a moment Matthew felt well enough to remove his hand from the wall and proceed: it was doubtless the effect of the unaccustomed heat and the crowds which had caused that moment of dizziness. Outside the gate there were fewer people to be seen; the stars shone brilliantly and the night seemed less oppressive.

They had only taken a few steps in the direction of River Valley Road when Joan said grimly: 'I'm going home. I've had enough for one evening.'

'But it's not even ten o'clock yet!' protested Monty indignantly. 'We can't turn in at this hour, particularly now we've got rid of Romeo. Besides, we're supposed to be showing Matthew the town.'

Matthew announced that he, too, felt he had seen enough for one evening. His spell of giddiness a few moments earlier had left him with a feeling that everything he had witnessed was utterly unreal. But Monty would not hear of another defection. He said to Joan: 'Why don't you take the Pontiac if you aren't going to come with us? We'll take a taxi.'

Presently, Matthew found himself in a taxi with Monty and heading, not for Raffles Hotel which Monty said would be full of stuffed shirts and only open till midnight anyway, but for some more interesting destination which Monty knew of. The taxi was a little yellow Ford 8 with springs that chimed and wheezed at every bump in the road. At the end of Grange Road they came into Orchard Road again, then into Bras Basah Road. Now they were drawing near the sea and a great white building loomed up on the left: Raffles Hotel, Monty said. As they passed the brilliantly lit entrance on the landward side Matthew glimpsed an elderly couple leaving, the man in a black dinner-jacket, the woman in a long glittering evening-dress and stole. Monty chuckled at the crowd of natives who had gathered on Beach Road to watch the Europeans dining on the lawn beneath the tall pencil palms. 'That's the nightly show for the Asiatics. They think white women are whores the way they wear back-less evening gowns. They come here every evening and lick their lips.'

At Monty's direction the taxi turned away from Raffles Hotel along the sea-front. On the right now was the starlit expanse of the *padang* and beyond it, just visible against the sky, the dignified silhouette of the former Grand Hôtel de l'Europe, the benefits of whose dance-floor Matthew had longed in retrospect to transfer to Geneva. The driver evidently knew what was expected of him without having to be told, for their progress had slowed to a crawl and he had half turned in his seat await-ing further instructions. Monty was peering intently at the shadowy figures of women sitting in rickshaws or standing idly in groups of two or three beneath the trees which lined the road. 'Stop!' he said, and the taxi drew in to the kerb.

Hardly had they come to a halt when there was a great stirring in the darkness; from what had seemed to be empty rickshaws shadowy figures emerged. Further shapes could be seen shifting in the obscurity beneath the trees; beyond, anchored at sea in the inner roads, were a great number of ships of which only the lights were visible. In a moment, to Matthew's surprise, the open windows of the taxi were entirely filled with women's faces, piled one on top of another like coconuts; shortly the windscreen, too, was blocked by the faces of yet more women leaning over the bonnet. A soft murmur filled the air from which an occasional word in English detached itself.: 'OK John!' ... 'Nice!' ... 'Back all same flont!' 'Whisky soda!'

Meanwhile, the driver, an elderly Malay with a brown face and the white hair of a grandfather, had groped for an electric torch and shone its beam on one window after the other.

'Can these be real women?' wondered Matthew as the beam wandered unsteadily over the serried painted masks. Yet on many of these masks the wrinkles stood out despite the paint and powder; the angled light etched them all the more harshly, replacing sunken eyes with a blob of darkness. At the same time, here and there skeletal arms had stretched through the open windows to trail about in the interior of the cab, floating and flickering like sea-weed, plucking weakly at his shirt and trousers, palping his arm or thigh.

'Hags!' declared Monty. 'Drive on!'

The driver raced the engine and the windscreen cleared. One or two other faces showed themselves fleetingly in the places of those that had gone: younger, weaker, more innocent, but no less desperate, trawling unhopefully with this brief glimpse of their younger faces for the twin male lusts which they knew were swimming back and forth like sharks somewhere in the depths of the cab. The hands groped more desperately, pleading, tugging, pinching. Then the taxi moved off in a hail of curses and vociferation. One or two of the women even tried to follow in rickshaws, hoping to catch up at the next traffic lights. But in no time they were left behind.

Monty explained, with the weary condescension of an expert, that certain of these women had their own permanent rickshaw coolies, usually ancient, hollowed-out skeletons of men, excavated by the pursuit of their shattering trade in the Singapore heat, who could no longer compete with younger rivals but might still, now and again, whip their broken limbs into a trot to reach some likely looking prospect with their fair cargoes of flesh ... by which he meant, he added with a chuckle, those leathery harridans whose services you could always purchase for a few cents. And they weren't all Chinese, Malay or Tamil either, by any manner of means. Sometimes you came across

Europeans, yes, women who had 'gone wrong' in some Eastern city, who had found disgrace through opium or alcohol in Calcutta, Hong Kong or Shanghai ... He, Monty, as a student of human nature, took a pretty keen interest in the stories that some of these women could tell you ... there were even aristocratic women driven out of Russia in penury by the Revolution. And more recently, as a matter of fact, things had been getting better in Singapore as far as women went. Young Chinese girls had been arriving in droves, refugees from the Sino-Jap war escaping from Shanghai or Canton ...

'Not *better*, Monty!' cried Matthew indignantly. 'How can you be so heartless!'

'Oh, I just meant younger, you know,' muttered Monty sullenly. 'No need to get worked up, old boy. After all, it's not my fault...'

'But it's all our faults! It's disgraceful! This is supposed to be a prosperous country. We send huge profits back to our fat shareholders in England and yet we can't even provide for a few refugees without them having to go on the streets.'

'It's no good taking this high moral line out here in the East, you know. People don't go in for that sort of thing out here. It's not our cup of tea. You just have to accept things the way they are. In the Straits it's every man for himself, if you know what I mean, and it's as well not to over-do the pious remarks. Personally, and I think I can speak for a lot of chaps who have been out here a while, I don't care for moralizing, in fact it binds me rigid.' Monty sounded irritated. The evening's entertainment, which had started promisingly with the woman fired from the cannon, had proved the dampest of damp squibs. And now, would you believe it? he could hardly say a word without getting a sermon in return.

'I'm sorry, Monty. I don't mean to sound prudish. It's just that I think we have a rotten way of doing things when it comes to anything but making money,' replied Matthew absently for, of course, Monty could not be blamed for the plight of Chinese refugees on the sea-front in Singapore. But where then did the fault lie? While Matthew mused on this problem the little yellow taxi turned about and headed north again. It rather looked, said Monty gloomily, as if they would have to settle for a massage somewhere.

25

Among the painted masks which had peered in through the cab's open windows Matthew had noticed one or two younger faces : he remembered one in particular, of a Chinese girl aged perhaps no more than fifteen or sixteen, rather ugly than pretty, but with a pleasant, homely, elfin ugliness like that of a bulldog, if you can imagine a delicately featured bulldog. Supposing that this girl, as seemed likely, was one of the new recruits that Monty had been talking about, he wondered at what precise moment during the past ten years it had become inevitable that she should be uprooted from her village somewhere in South China, or from a slum in Shanghai, and flung down on the streets of Singapore, obliged to sell herself if she could find a buyer? Surely, suggested Matthew to the passive figure of Monty beside him, one must connect this child's desperate face with the long series of failures he himself had witnessed at the League of Nations in Geneva, with the ever-recurring inability of the Great Powers to commit themselves to a world organized on international lines, with the ever-present cynicism of the Foreign Office, and the Quái d'Orsay, and the Wilhelmstrasse where no opportunity was ever missed for showing the diplomats' professional distaste for open diplomacy or for sneering at the idea of a world parliament. What chilled the blood was the thought that this girl's plight and a million other tiny tragedies had been brought about by suave, neatly barbered, Savile Row-suited, genial, polite, cultured and probably even humane men in normal circumstances who would shrink with horror from themselves if they could be made to see their responsibility for what was happening!

Monty's only reply to this suggestion was a grunt or, possibly, a groan. What the point was, in this sort of speculation, he could not for the life of him see. He yawned and smacked his lips. What an evening! First one thing, then another. Well, the only consolation was that this business about which Matthew was getting so steamed up did sometimes produce mouth-watering opportunities. Perhaps he would manage to lay hands on some newly arrived little Chinese piece before the evening was out. It was sometimes on the cards these days, though one had to be lucky.

Encouraged by Monty's grunt of interest in what he had been saying, Matthew went on to explain that his own arrival in Geneva had coincided almost to the day with that fateful explosion beside the South Manchurian Railway in 1931. He had seen it all at first hand, from the first angry denunciations by China's representative, Dr Sze, of massacres by Japanese troops and the reply of Yoshizawa (the same chap who had just recently been in Java demanding oil and minerals from the Dutch) that the troops were merely defending Japan's enormous interests ... to what had happened much later: to the devious hypocritical, perfectly disgraceful support given to the untenable Japanese position by Sir John Simon and the Foreign Office, not to mention the British Press. Only the *Manchester Guardian* had condemned the Japanese and their British supporters.

Monty, peering out at the shadowy streets of Singapore as they fled by on either side of the cab, mumbled that he had been 'in the dark' about all that side of things. He belched dejectedly (perhaps he should not have bolted his fish and chips and beer so greedily at The Great World).

'You see, Monty, so much depended on how the League reacted. It was the first time the Council had had to deal with a quarrel involving a major power and it set the style for everything that has happened since ... for everything that will happen, even if one day they manage to revive the League, *for years to come*. Because at that time people all over the world still believed in the League. When the Manchurian crisis broke out it was almost like some medieval tournament. People flocked to Geneva to see the respective delegates do battle. Each side spent vast sums of money, which their countries could ill afford, on propaganda and entertainment to try and win people over to their side. The Chinese took over a luxurious suite on the Quai Wilson, got hold of a French chef and some vintage wines and started giving magnificent dinner-parties.

'Meanwhile, as a sort of counter-attack the Japs staged a colossal reception in the Kursaal at which tons of food and gallons of wine were funnelled into the open mouths of the plump burghers of Geneva as if into Strasbourg geese ... In return they made everyone watch a dreary propaganda film which they showed in the empty, echoing opera-house next door (both places had been shut down for the winter) all about

189

the benefits of the South Manchuria Railway Company. Dismal isn't the word. It did no good, anyway, because of the Lytton Report. You know all about that, I expect?'

Hoping to forestall further revelations Monty murmured that, as a matter of fact, he was rather well-informed on that ... er ... particular subject ... er ... But Matthew willingly set to work to refresh his memory, just in case. 'This fellow is a serious menace,' thought Monty, glancing at the stout, bespectacled figure of his companion.

What had happened was that the League, this was actually a temporizing device, sent a commission of enquiry composed of a German doctor, a French general, an Italian count and an American Major-General under the chairmanship of Lord Lytton to Manchuria to establish the disputed facts of the matter. It had taken them a year but when they finally published their report, they made no bones about it: Japan was roundly condemned ... no doubt to the horror of Sir John Simon and his ilk. They concluded that Manchuria was an integral part of China, that the Japanese action could not be justified as self-defence, that Jap troops should be withdrawn and a genuinely Chinese régime restored. 'That really set the cat among the pigeons, as you can imagine!'

Whether Monty could imagine or not, all he said was: 'This place is usually full of troops at this time of night. It's funny, there must have been a police raid or something.'

The taxi had come to a halt in a sleazy rubbish-strewn street lined with the usual two-storey shophouses but wider than the streets they had come through. Matthew, still in Geneva, stared out in a daze. Washing, hanging over the street from a forest of poles, tossed and billowed in the light breeze like the banners of an army on the march. Here and there dim electric lights glimmered, emphasizing the darkness rather than shedding light. Monty was speaking.

'Sorry, what's that?'

'I said I thought we might have a beer before going home.'

One moment the street was deserted except for a few shadowy figures playing mah-jong under a street-lamp, the next it suddenly began to fill up; men were scurrying out of doorways, pedalling up on bicycles, galloping towards them in the shafts of rickshaws, even slithering down drainpipes. Nearby a manhole cover where the pavement spanned the storm-drain popped up and men began to pour out of that, too. All these men were converging on one place, the taxi in which Matthew sat in a trance with his thoughts struggling back like refugees from Geneva. He roused himself at last. 'What's all this?'

'They're just looking for customers for their girls,' said Monty who had been paying the taxi-driver. 'Come on, and hold on to your wallet.'

Before they could set foot on the pavement they were surrounded by dim, jostling figures. Words were whispered confidentially into Matthew's ear as he waded after Monty ... 'Nice girl' ... 'Guarantee virgin' ... 'You wantchee try Singapore Glip? More better allsame Shanghai Glip!' ('Do I want to try *what?*' wondered Matthew unable to make head nor tail of this rigmarole.) ... 'Oil massage number one!' ... Hands flourished grubby visiting-cards. 'You want very nice pleasure!' bayed a giant, bearded Sikh, placing himself menacingly in their path. 'You coming please this way.' But Monty brushed him aside and dived into a lighted doorway beneath a sign reading: 'Dorchester Bed and Breakfast. Very select. All welcome. Servicemen welcome.' Matthew, one hand anxiously gripping his wallet, plunged after Monty. His head was reeling again. 'I must be ill,' he thought giddily as he clambered up a smelly flight of stairs. 'What am I doing here? I should be at home in bed.'

At the top of the stairs an Indian with oiled black hair and a dark, pock-marked face was waiting to greet them. His smile revealed very white teeth among which nestled here and there a glittering gold one; the glitter of his teeth was echoed by the glitter of a row of gold-topped fountain pens and propelling pencils in the breast pocket of his shirt, by the fat gold rings on his fingers, and by the steel watch on his wrist: all this combined to give him a disagreeably metallic appearance. Around his waist he had wound what at first appeared to be a white *sarong*; on closer inspection it proved to be merely a bath towel with the words *Hotel Adelphi Singapore* in blue. Was this his normal attire or had they just surprised him in his bath? For a moment it was hard to be sure.

'Very kind lovely gentlemen,' he said, putting his palms and long, delicate, glittering fingers of both hands together in graceful gesture, 'please coming this way please.'

They were shown into a small, dimly lit room. An elderly and very fat Indian lady, who had evidently been asleep there on the floor, was making a hasty exit and dragging her bedding with her. Monty ordered beers and they sat down, Monty on a bamboo chair, Matthew on a broken-backed couch. The Indian had disappeared down a passage. Matthew stared round the room uneasily. What strange places Monty frequented!

On the wall there were two calendars: one, for 1940, advertised the *Nippon Kisen Kaisha* and showed an enormous ocean liner with Mount Fuji rising improbably out of the mists behind it; the other was for 1939, advertizing Fraser and Neave's soda water: a healthy-looking European girl, whose rather blank, flawless face bore an odd resemblance to Joan's, was holding a tennis racket in one hand and a glass in the other: two men in tennis flannels in the background, very much diminished by perspective, whispered together beneath her outstretched arm and eyed her with interest. Nearby was another picture, this time a photograph torn from a magazine and framed. Matthew gave an exclamation of surprise when he saw who it was: for how often had he not seen that familiar face coming or going in the lobby at the Hôtel Beau Rivage in Geneva! For what hopes and, ultimately, for what despair had its owner not been responsible when he had faced Mussolini over the Abyssinian crisis! With excitement he summoned Monty to join him in gazing at the foxy, handsome features of Anthony Eden.

Monty, however, declined to move. Either he was an *habitué* of the establishment and had already seen the picture, or else he had no particular interest in Anthony Eden; it might be, too, that he feared another discourse on world affairs for he winced visibly as Matthew, reminded of Geneva by the picture of Anthony Eden, suddenly resumed his harangue on the Lytton Report.

'As I was saying, it set the cat among the pigeons, of course it did! The Lytton Report condemned Japan. Result? China could now demand action under Article 16 according to which the other members of the League could be asked to sever trade and financial relations with Japan. This was something that the Big Powers did not want to do: both Von Neurath, for Germany, and the bald baron, whatever his name was, for Italy, made it quite plain in the Assembly debate on the Lytton Report that they wouldn't put up with any positive action. For three days the matter was thrashed out by the whole assembly in one of the larger rooms of the Disarmament Conference Building, where, as I expect you know, another long-running tragedy was playing at the same time, but among the Big Powers it was our man, I'm afraid, Sir John Simon, who really took the biscuit ...'

While Matthew, who had sprung up from the couch again and was striding up and down the room making the floorboards creak, had been discoursing the Indian had reappeared with two bottles of beer with straws in them. He looked unsurprised to find one of his customers striding up and down shouting; odd behaviour was by no means unusual under his roof, but he was inclined to take it philosophically, reflecting that every profession must have its disadvantages. He handed one bottle to Monty and the other to Matthew who took it without noticing.

'Simon, believe it or not, managed to give such a selective interpretation of the Lytton Report that anyone who hadn't read it might have wondered whether it wasn't the Chinese who had invaded Japan instead of vice versa. Not surprisingly, the smaller nations were indignant. Before their very eyes all the fine words and noble undertakings were proving to be gross hypocrisy. "If the League does not succeed in securing peace and justice," the Norwegian delegate declared angrily, "then the whole system by which right was meant to replace might will collapse." And he knew what he was talking about, as it has turned out. One of the Finns then wanted to know if the League was merely a debating club. I don't know if you can imagine, Monty, the shock and anger and disappointment we all felt at the way Simon and our Foreign Office destroyed, with the help of their cronies, what was without doubt the best chance the world had ever had to institute a system of international justice!' Matthew, making a violent gesture with his beer bottle, had caused the liquid inside it to foam out of the neck and spill over his hand. He paused for a moment to brood and lick his knuckles.

In the meantime the door had opened and half a dozen women had been shown in; they went to sit in a glum row on a bench against the wall.

'You picking please woman at your disposition,' said the Indian politely.

Four of the newcomers were middle-aged Chinese women with scarlet cheekbones; two of them started a whispered conversation in Cantonese, a third puffed smoke-rings from green lips, a fourth took out her knitting. The other two women were much younger, mere girls; one was a flat-nosed, round-faced Malay, the other a plain, pallid Chinese with neat pigtails; this latter girl took out a school exercise book and a text book and began to do her Latin homework. Monty looked them over without excitement and belched: the beer seemed unusually gaseous this evening. He was uncomfortable and out of sorts, no doubt about it. He felt, in particular, that there was still another bubble of air lodged distressingly inside him. Would it soon rise to the surface? He waited, surveying himself internally and thinking what a wretched evening he was having.

Suddenly, from some other part of the building through the thin walls there came a drunken Scandinavian voice. 'You say you are a wirgin. I say you are *not* a wirgin!' This was followed by an alarming crash.

'But,' said Matthew, who had taken a gulp of beer and was striding up and down once more (he was sweating copiously and felt by no means sober though he had had little to drink all evening), 'the Report was there and there was nothing they could do about it. That Report had stuck in the gullets of the Great Powers. They could neither swallow it nor spit it out. In fact, the only thing they could think of to do was, of course, what they always did in Geneva when they found themselves at a loss: they formed a committee ... this one was to *report on the Report*! Ludicrous! It was called the Committee of Nineteen. It wasted no time in settling down to the stern task of fostering sub-committees of its own in the best Geneva tradition, in particular a sub-committee for conciliation. What a farce! At one time the cynics were saying that they would soon have to have a report on the report on the Report. And yet the Report itself was plain enough. In due course the Committee of Nineteen produced its report on the Report, however. They even went so far as to broadcast it from the League's new wireless station in Geneva. And yet again the Big Powers found themselves with egg on their faces! Japan was plainly condemned. Chinese sovereignty should be restored. Members of the League should not recognize Manchukuo. But ironically enough, at the very moment that Japan was being condemned at Geneva she was preparing to invade Eastern Inner Mongolia as well.'

'I say you are *not a wirgin*!'

'But even so, most likely the Western powers would not even have made the effort they did make to condemn Japan's aggression, had the Japs not attacked Shanghai ...'

The young Chinese girl with pigtails, on instructions from the management, had unfastened her bodice, allowing a small lemon-nippled breast to shudder free of its constraining buttons. Meanwhile, its owner pouted over a perplexing sentence she was invited to translate: 'Romulus and Remus, you are surely about to jump over the walls of Rome, are you not?' (Question expecting the answer 'Yes'). What did this mean? Was it gibberish deliberately planned as a snare to the unwary, perhaps designed to make one lose face in some subtle occidental way? Surely it could be nothing else? (But wait! That, too, was a question expecting the answer 'Yes'. She had the feeling that an invisible net had been thrown over her and that an unseen hand was beginning to pull the cords tight.) Well, she could not spend all night trying to penetrate the mysterious workings of the occidental mind so, with a sigh, she passed on to the next question.

'To be frank, Monty, outside Geneva who cared a damn about Manchuria, or a music-hall place called Eastern Inner Mongolia? But Shanghai was different. When the Japs sent in troops from the International Settlement and bombed unarmed civilians in Chapei, people began to realize that Western business interests were threatened. There were limits, after all. But in the end what action did the Big Powers take?'

Again a dreadful crash! This time it was against the very wall of the room in which they were assembled: the whole building seemed to shake and the framed photograph of Anthony Eden cantered clippety-clop against the wall for a few seconds. 'I give you "wirgin"!' came a hoarse voice accompanied by a woman's cry.

The row of women stared at Matthew with dull eyes. The Indian, disappointed with the effect they were having on his two customers, had encouraged them to unbutton their blouses and undo their skirts or *sarongs* in order to present themselves more advantageously. The young Chinese girl, having finished her Latin as best she could, had turned to arithmetic. Now she was sitting, stark naked, sucking her pencil over a problem which involved the rate at which a tap filled a bath. What, she wondered, was a tap? And what, come to that, was a bath? She would have to consult her aunt who was one of the older women with scarlet cheekbones.

The Indian was hurrying along beside the stout gesticulating figure of Matthew, trying to draw his attention to the enhanced appearance of his girls. The far door opened a crack and the fat Indian lady, his mother, peered in. She was still holding her bedding and anxious to resume her slumbers. He motioned her away crossly.

'Uh ... uh ... uh ...' Monty could feel that bubble of air rising.

'Very young! Soft as rising moon! Or perhaps nice gentleman preferring experience lady with wide knowledge all French and

Oriental techniques? Are they, sir, not what doctor ordering?'

'What?'

'Experience lady ... wide knowledge ...'

Matthew, sweat pouring off his brow in torrents, gripped him by the arm and said, blinking fiercely: 'You may well ask! As a gesture the British, several months too late, declared an arms embargo ... but on *both* sides, as if both had been equally guilty. In a couple of weeks it lapsed anyway because the arms manufacturers were big employers and there was a lot of un-employment at the time. So, the Japs had plainly broken the Covenant and got away with it. They left the League, of course, or at least Geneva, the following day. I watched them go myself in a great procession of motor-cars from the Metropole where they'd been staying ... There was something horrible about it because it meant the end of everything. I was standing near the Pont de Mont Blanc as they went by on their way to the Gare Cornavin. They went by in silence. Each car that passed was like another support being pulled out from under the League. That was the last we saw of them in Geneva but they left the League in ruins ... they and the Big Powers between them. Why? Because this sad defeat of principle at the hands of ex-pediency, this old way of having things settled behind the scenes by degenerate foreign ministries had set a precedent from which we never recovered. Ah, you say that History will find them guilty? Nonsense! History is too muddled and nobody gives a damn about it anyway. Disarmament! Abyssinia! Spain! The same thing was to happen again and again!' Matthew re-leased the Indian and staggering to the couch, sat down with his head in his hands.

Another crash shook the wall and Anthony Eden went clip-pety-clops once more.

'Uh ... uh ... uh ... aaaaaaah!' Monty belched deafeningly. His expression, which had been careworn, brightened a little and he looked with more interest at the row of women. The Indian, however, was already signalling them to be on their way. Evidently they were not what doctor ordering.

Now he approached Matthew with a large leather-bound album of photographs and beckoned Monty to come and have a look, too. These pictures were of his better, high-class girls, he explained. Matthew gazed at them in wonder. The photo-grapher had surprised many of them in intimate moments and some of them had prices pencilled against them, as on a menu. In a few cases there was the instruction: 'Client must ordering in advance' or 'Miss Wu (20 mins.). She weighing one hundred pounds of tropical charm.' Or even 'Miss Shirley Mao (2 pers.)'.

The Indian, seeing Matthew reading with interest, pointed with a grubby finger and said: 'She personally recommending, sir.'

'Are some of these girls refugees from the war in China?' asked Matthew.

The Indian's eyes narrowed as he tried to penetrate the signification of this remark. 'You wanting refugee-girl?' he asked carefully. And he, too, studied the album, wondering which of the girls would best accommodate this special interest. 'I finding Japan-bombing-Chinese-refugee-cripplegirl. Very interesting. You drink beer waiting ten five minutes. I find.'

'Let's go,' said Monty. 'Give the man a dollar for the beer and a couple of dollars for the girls. Otherwise we'll be here all night.'

'You staying, please, nice gentlemen,' cried the Indian. 'No, you going out,' he shouted at his mother who was trying to sneak back in again with her bedding. 'No, you must signing police book,' he howled as Monty made for the door. He produced a grimy ledger. Monty made a quick scribble in it and handed the pencil to Matthew who signed carefully, looking at the list of other signatures.

'Good heavens!' he exclaimed, hastening down the stairs after Monty. 'Did you see whose names were in the Visitors' Book? The Archbishop of Canterbury and Sir Robert Brooke-Popham have both been here tonight!' He paused dizzily to steady himself against the wall. Monty rolled his eyes to heaven and plunged out into the night, saying over his shoulder: 'People don't sign their own names in places like this, you idiot!'

'I say you *are not* a wirgin!' echoed after them into the empty street. A distant crash, a faint cry, and all was quiet. Singapore slept peacefully under the bright, equatorial sky. The shadow of a cat slipped through the street. A child cried. A weary coolie dragged his rickshaw home. An old man sighed in his sleep somewhere. Presently, in two or three hours from now would come the first faint drone of Japanese bombers approaching from the north-east. But for the moment all was quiet.

26

The taxi-driver (it was still the grandfatherly Malay with white hair who had been driving them earlier in the evening), seeing Matthew stagger as he got out of the cab at the gate of the Mayfair, assumed him to be drunk and asked him if he would like a massage because he knew of a certain place ... But Matthew shook his head. He felt weak and dizzy: all he wanted to do was to plunge into bed. He said good night to Monty and set off up the short drive towards the Mayfair Building; with a growl of its engine the taxi was gone, leaving only a deep sigh of relief floating in the empty air where it had been standing. Monty, bound on pleasure, this time did not intend to be thwarted.

'I must have caught some fever,' Matthew thought as he climbed the steps and dragged open the protesting outer door to the verandah. This thought was followed by another, still more distressing: perhaps he had caught the Singapore Grip! Certainly an illness of some kind had taken hold of him. He had half expected to find the Major smoking a cigar on the verandah, but though an electric light was burning, there was no sign of him. Nor was Dupigny anywhere to be seen. So tempting, however, was the prospect of resting his weary body without delay that Matthew allowed himself to be diverted into the nearest rattan armchair, where he lay panting and perspiring while he recovered a little of his strength. Almost immediately his eyelids dropped and he fell into a doze.

But in only a matter of moments he was woken again by the screeching hinges of the outer door. Someone was coming in. He struggled to sit up and look alert but his eyes seemed to have slipped out of focus and for some moments only presented him with a grey blur. Then he found himself face to face with Joan who was saying: 'We saw the light from the road as Jim was on his way home and we thought we'd just call in to say good night.'

'That was nice of you,' said Matthew warmly. Ehrendorf had come in with Joan but was sitting on the arm of a bamboo chair half in the shadows of the door.

'And Jim wanted to have a word with you,' Joan went on.

'If it's about what we were discussing earlier,' said Matthew, aware that his eyes were trying to slip out of focus again, 'about, you know, the colonial question and so forth, well, the point I was trying to make is that we must allow the *whole* country to develop. At the moment what it amounts to is that we only allow the native people to work in agriculture because we insist on selling them our own manufactures. Let me give you an example . . .'

'No, no, it wasn't about that,' cried Joan hastily. 'Jim will tell you. Go on, you said you would,' she added accusingly while Ehrendorf stirred uneasily on the edge of the circle of light and perhaps contemplated whatever it was that he had had in mind to say to Matthew.

In the meantime another layer of gauze had been removed from Matthew's memory of what had gone on earlier in the evening, so that now at last he began to think: 'What a miracle that they should have made it up after the row they were having an hour or two ago!'

'Go on, you *did say* you would.'

Ehrendorf's pale, handsome face continued to stare mutely at Matthew from out of the semi-darkness and he sighed. A motor-car passed up the road with a deep, chugging sound; the reflected light from its headlights glowed in thin slices through the unrolled blinds of split bamboo. Finally Ehrendorf said: 'I just wanted to say, Matthew, that I expect I shall be leaving Singapore in a day or two . . . Another posting, I guess you'd call it. Not yet sure where *to*. I realized this evening that Joan and I . . . Ah, no future in our relationship . . . Best of friends . . . Hm, wish each other well, naturally . . .' He fell silent.

'There,' said Joan.

'What? You're leaving? And I've only just arrived! That really is a shame!' exclaimed Matthew, distressed. Ehrendorf had sunk his head briefly in his hands to give his face a weary polish. 'It's time I was getting home,' he said. But whether he meant to America or to his flat in Singapore it was impossible to say.

For some moments Matthew had been aware that there was something odd about Ehrendorf's appearance. It was this: his uniform clung to him as if it were sopping wet. Indeed, staring more closely at it Matthew saw that it was several shades darker than it should have been and clung to his skin. His hair, too, was plastered down as if a bucket of water had been emptied over him. Moreover, a pool of water had collected round his shoes and was advancing slowly into the circle of light.

'We shall both certainly miss you,' said Joan brightly.

'I guess it's about time I packed my grip and moved on some place else,' said Ehrendorf with a wry, bitter smile.

Matthew, on the point of bringing up the question of Ehrendorf's sodden clothing, was diverted by this last remark into asking if, by the way, either of them happened to know what a Singapore Grip might be, was it a fever of some sort? Ehrendorf seemed taken aback by this question: after a moment's consideration he said he thought it was a suitcase made of rattan, like a Shanghai Basket, as they were called, only smaller. If that was what they were he had one himself. Joan, however, said no. In an authoritative tone she declared it to be a patent double-bladed hairpin which some women used to curl their hair after they had washed it. This brief excursion into lexicography served to add a further element of confusion to a scene which Matthew had already found sufficiently puzzling. There were questions which must be asked, he felt, to straighten everything out. And he must think of them immediately for Ehrendorf, plucking dejectedly at his wet trousers, was already getting to his feet. He must ask about the pool of water where Ehrendorf had been sitting, and about his departure and Joan and the Singapore Grip. But his eyes chose this critical moment to become a blur through which nothing could be seen, though his mind remained as keen as ever and he heard a voice which reminded him of his own saying a cheery good night to some people who were leaving. Some moments went by while he sat quietly waiting for clear vision to be restored. When it had been, he found himself sitting opposite an empty chair beneath which was a little pool of water. Something else glistened on a rattan table not far away: it was a small handbag of white leather which Joan must have forgotten.

'I must be quite seriously ill and undoubtedly I should call a doctor before it's too late.' But again he closed his eyes and, again, within a few moments, was obliged to open them, this time because he had heard a crunch of gravel and a creak of the wooden steps which led up to the house. The Major, perhaps, or Dupigny returning home, he surmised. They would certainly help him to make contact with a doctor. It was Joan, however, in excellent spirits.

'It's me,' she cried gaily. 'I forgot my handbag. Come for a walk outside. It's lovely. The moon's just rising or perhaps it's the starlight. You can see as clear as day and it's getting cool at last. Come on, stop day-dreaming. You'll be telling me next that you want a "serious talk". But I've had enough "serious talks" for one evening. Well, come on, let's enjoy ourselves.' With that she grasped his hand and pulled him up out of his chair, ignoring his protests and pleas for help. Soon, with his head spinning, he was blundering down the steps beside her. Once in the fresh air, however, he felt a little better and decided that perhaps he was not so ill after all. Joan was right. It was cooler and the heavens were so bright that two shadows accompanied them across the lawn, past the gymnastic equipment, unused since the death of old Mr Webb, the vertical bars, and the high bar like a gibbet with a background of stars, into the denser shadows of the little grove of flowering trees and shrubs which lay between the Mayfair's grounds and the Blacketts' and then on through the dark corridor of pili-nut trees.

'I want to show you something,' Joan said as Matthew shied away from entering this funnel of darkness. Despite his dizziness he was aware that voracious animals might be lurking there and he did not intend to dispense entirely with prudent behaviour. Joan tugged him through the darkness, however, and presently they reached the open space of the lawn with the swimming pool and the house behind it rising white and clear in the moonlight. But instead of heading towards the house, Joan now drew him aside into the blue-black shadow of a 'flame of the forest' tree. There, to his surprise, she slipped into his arms and he felt her lips on his. His arms tightened round her convulsively and the blackness around them became drenched in magenta with the pounding of his blood. He felt her teeth begin to nibble at his lips; her hand found its way inside his shirt and began to travel over his damp skin, leaving a trail of awakened desire wherever it went. He released her to unbutton the top of her cotton dress. But as he did so she slipped away from him laughing, deeper into the shadows.

'Matthew, are you in love with me?' she asked.

'Well, yes,' he muttered, blundering in the direction from which the voice had come. But he found the shadows were empty and again he heard her laughter from where he had just been a moment before; and her voice asked mockingly: 'Are you in love with me, Matthew?'

'Please,' he said. 'Where are you?'

'First you must answer. Are you in love with me?'

'Yes, oh, that is . . .'

'How much?'

'Well ...' Matthew found a handkerchief and mopped his steaming brow. He felt somewhat unwell again.

'Here I am, over by the swimming pool. Come and look at the moon's reflection. That water is so still tonight!'

Matthew left the shadow of the trees and went to where she was sitting on her heels at the edge of the pool gazing down at the bright, motionless disc of the moon stamped like a yellow wax seal on the surface of the water. He attempted to put his arm round her but immediately she drew away, saying that there was something he must do first. She told him but he did not understand what it was.

'What?'

'Yes, you must jump into the water with your clothes on.'

'I must do *what*?' cried Matthew in astonishment. 'Are you joking?'

'No, you must jump in with your clothes on'

'But really ...'

'No, that's what I want you to do.'

Matthew said crossly: 'I wouldn't dream of it. I'm going to bed now ... goodnight!'

'Wait Matthew, wait!' pleaded Joan. 'Wait!'

Matthew paused. The edge of the pool was rounded and raised a little, like the rim of a saucer. Joan was now walking along it, arms outstretched like a tight-rope walker. As he watched she allowed herself to lose her balance and fall backwards into the moon's reflection. There was a great splash and a slapping of water against the sides of the pool. Joan, smiling, lay back against a pillow of water and did one, two, three strokes of a neat overarm backstroke which caused her to surge out into the pool with a bow-wave swirling back on each side of her head. Matthew shook his head in bewilderment, scattering drops of perspiration, as if he himself had just stepped out of the pool. But really, this was the limit! He was invaded by a feeling of unreality. Moreover, the moon and the stars had begun plunging and zooming in the heavens. Any moment now he would collapse if he did not reach his bed and lie down. He plodded back over the moonlit lawn which tilted now this way, now that, like the deck of a ship in a storm, and on through the dark corridor of trees, pausing only to vomit into the shrubbery.

'Wait, I'm coming too,' came Joan's distant voice. 'I still haven't got my handbag.'

But when he had wearily clambered up the steps of the Mayfair Building and once more dragged open the creaking door of the verandah he found another surprise waiting for him. So slippery had reality become to his grasp that, for a moment, it seemed to him quite likely that the young woman who came forward, smiling, to greet him, was Joan who had somehow managed to rearrange time and space to her convenience and arrive back there before he did. It was not Joan, however, but the Eurasian girl with dark-red hair whom he had met earlier in the evening at The Great World, Miss Vera Chiang. At the very sight of her the palm of one of his hands began to tingle deliciously.

'You are most surprised, I expect, to see me here, are you not? (You remember, yes, Vera Chiang.) Well let me put things straight for you, Matthew, and then you won't be any longer looking in such a condition. You see, I still have in this house the bedroom which your dear, dear father gave to me when I was "on my uppers". Your father, Matthew, was such a good, kind and generous man. You can be pretty sure I'll always say one for him for the help he gave me ... And so here I still have some of my precious bits and pieces, such things like my books (because I always have my "nose in a book") and "snaps" of your dear father with no clothes on and of my family (all now having "kicked the bucket" I'm sorry to say) who were very important in Russia and obliging to leave in Revolution and so this evening, when we were split up by those rowdy sailors, I remembered I must look at them again, which I haven't for some time and I heard you come in and I thought Matthew will also enjoy looking at my "snaps" ... There! And, are you all right, dear? You look rather "hot about the collar", I must say.'

Matthew, who was very hot indeed and distinctly unwell despite the pleasant surprise of finding Miss Chiang again so soon, had been obliged to steady himself against a table as the bungalow gave a lurch. After a moment, however, he felt sufficiently recovered to say: 'As a matter of fact, I'm not feeling very well. I seem to having an attack of the Singapore Grip, or whatever it's called.'

It was Miss Chiang's turn to look surprised at this information and she even went a little pink about the cheeks, which made her, thought Matthew, look prettier than ever. For a moment she appeared nonplussed, though. What a pretty girl she is, to be sure, he mused, and what a pity that everything seems so unreal.

'Matthew!' called a voice from outside and in no time there came the by now familiar sound of the door being opened. Joan stopped short when she saw that Matthew was talking to Miss Chiang. She raised her eyebrows and looked far from pleased.

'D'you know Miss Chiang?' Matthew managed to say. 'I think she said she was going to show me some photographs ...' he hesitated and eyed Miss Chiang's face carefully: it had occurred to him that she might already have shown him the photographs, in which case what he had said would sound rather odd. Miss Chiang agreed, however, that that was what she had been about to do and Matthew gave an inner sigh of relief.

'Gracious, Miss Blackett, you're all wet! Let me get you a towel.'

'No, thank you, Vera, I shall have dried out in no time. Besides, I find it pleasantly cool.' And Joan slipped into a cane-chair not very far from where Ehrendorf had sat and dripped only a few minutes earlier. As she did so, despite his fever (or perhaps even because of it), Matthew could not help noticing how the thin cotton of her dress stuck to her body, outlining its delicious shape and revealing a number of things about it which he had had no opportunity to notice before. In the meantime, Joan, who still had not quite swallowed her irrita-tion at finding Vera and Matthew together, was asking super-ciliously whether Vera was pleased with the dress which *she* was wearing. Was it not lucky for Vera, she asked turning to Matthew, seeing that the poor girl was penniless when she came to work for Mr Webb, that *her* cast-off clothing had proved to be a perfect fit?

'Oh, it was terribly lucky for me!' exclaimed Vera, clapping her hands. 'I had never worn such lovely clothes before, Matthew. Except, of course, when I was a baby in Russia, I suppose, because my mother's family was of noble blood, princesses at least ... and my father was a wealthy tea-merchant, definitely "well thought of" in the highest circles, so I understand ...'

'In our family,' said Joan, 'it has always been our custom to give our cast-off clothes away ... My mother always gives hers to the *amah* of to the "boys" for their wives or to someone like that. It seems such a shame to allow good material to go to waste, especially when it turns out to be a perfect fit like the clothing I gave to Vera ...'

'Perhaps not *quite* a perfect fit, Miss Blackett,' said Vera

204

sweetly. 'I sometimes think that when I wear this dress it is a little tight across the chest. What is your opinion, Matthew? If I were a little more flat-chested would it not be an even more perfect fit? But then, even as a young girl, my breasts were rather well-developed. I find I sometimes breathe easier when I open these two top buttons. So!'

And Matthew, though the bungalow had for some time been rocking so badly that it was astonishing the vase of flowers could remain standing on the table, nevertheless snatched a moment to cast a hungry eye on Miss Chiang's exquisite chest, a good deal of which had now come to light as she fanned it, murmuring: 'Ouf! That's better.'

'A funny thing,' said Joan in honeyed tones, 'but my mother says the servants to whom she donates her old clothes are very often not in the least grateful! Would you believe it, Matthew? D'you think it is because they aren't of pure European stock or is it simply a lack of education and good breeding?'

'Well, good gracious!' exclaimed Matthew, gripping the arms of his chair for dear life as he was hurled this way and that. 'I should hardly ...'

While Joan had been talking she had been struggling with one hand behind her back, frowning with concentration. Now her expression relaxed and she, too, unbuttoned the front of her dress, though with difficulty because it was wet; having done so she began tugging away a shapeless piece of white cloth, saying: 'I must say, there's nothing more disagreeable than a damp bra.'

'Look, I really must go to bed now,' said Matthew, jumping to his feet. 'I feel dreadfully ill ...' The floor had now begun to tilt in different directions at the same time and it was a miracle that he could retain his balance at all.

'But Matthew,' exclaimed Vera, jumping to her feet. 'You must come and look at the "snaps" I have in my room.' And taking his arm she began to lead him from the verandah. But Joan, too, had got to her feet and taking him by the other arm started to drag him in the other direction, saying: 'First Matthew is coming to see something I want to show him outside in the compound ... and as it may take a little time, Vera, I think it would be best if you don't bother to wait up.'

'In that case it is better that I take him first to my room,' cried Vera tugging Matthew rather hard in that direction.

How long this embarrassing scene would have continued it was hard to say, but at this moment a torrent of blackness swept over Matthew's storm-battered brain and he sank diplomatically to the floor between the two young women.

'It's no joke being attractive to women, I must say,' he thought as he lost consciousness.

27

When Matthew came to he found himself lying on the floor exactly where he had fallen. The Major and Dupigny were kneeling beside him. The two young women had disappeared (Joan to fetch Dr Brownley, Vera to crack ice for a cold compress). The Major and Dupigny, seeing that he was conscious again, helped him to his feet and then supported him to his bedroom, one on each side.

'*Ça a l'air assez grave*,' remarked Dupigny to his friend over Matthew's swaying head. '*C'est la grippe de Singapour si je ne me trompe pas.*'

Matthew, however, felt a little better after a few moments and declared himself able to peel off his own clothes which were as sodden as if he had indeed plunged into the swimming pool. He dried his quaking body with a towel and then crawled under his mosquito net. A pair of wet footprints glistened on the floor where he had been standing. The Major handed him an aspirin and a glass of water; when he had swallowed them he lay back in the darkness, watching giddily as the room began to revolve slowly like a roundabout. Gradually, the bed, too, began to spin, dipping and rising, faster and faster. He had to cling on tightly, as to the neck of a wooden horse, or be hurled out against the walls by centrifugal force. Although the night was still, great gales of hot air poured in through the open shutters and tugged at the mosquito net. Time passed. The light was switched on. Now faces were swirling round the bed: he recognized the Major's anxious features and Dupigny's wrinkled face, pickled in cynicism like a walnut in vinegar, and Dr Brownley chuckling like a fiend, but then Matthew closed his eyes, knowing he must be delirious, and fell into a troubled sleep. In his dreams he was back in Geneva ... the pale, sorrowful ghost of Matsuoka appeared and whispered: 'Matthew, why do you persecute me like this? You know I am only trying to do what is best.' And then he smiled and his face turned into that of a cobra. Outside in the darkness some small creature uttered a cry as it was killed by a snake.

Now, a few miles away at Katong, Sir Robert Brooke-Popham also lay dreaming of the Japanese. Brooke-Popham slept on his back, legs apart, arms away from his body, wrists and palms turned upwards, an attitude of total surrender to sleep, perhaps, or that of a man felled suddenly in the boxing-ring by an unexpected blow. His honest, friendly face looked older now that sleep had allowed the muscles of his jaw to sag, older than his age indeed for he was not much over sixty; but this long Sunday had been spent in interminable conferences and he was exhausted. Moreover, these conferences still had not resolved the problem which faced him. Should he order troops across the border into Siam in order to forestall a possible Japanese landing there?

Malaya, very roughly, was carrot-shaped with Singapore at its tip and Siam, more roughly still, providing its plume of green leaves. The obvious place to defend Malaya's northern border with Siam was where the green plume grew out of the carrot, at the thinnest part, for there you would need least troops to do the job. Alas, there was a snag to this, because the border, although it obligingly started at the thinnest part on the western side of the carrot, instead of heading straight to the east to snip off the leaves neatly where they should be snipped off, wandered south for some distance into the pink flesh of the carrot itself at its fattest. Nor was the problem simply that Malaya's real border, by wandering hither and yon through the bulging part of the peninsula, was a good deal longer than it need have been: the fact was that there were only two roads south into Malaya through the jungle and mountains and both of them *began* some fifty miles across the border into Siam, one at a place called Singora, the other at Patani.

So what was he going to do? (Or, to put it another way, what should he have *already done*?) Should he order the 11th Division to invade Siam and occupy Singora before the Japanese could land? There was hardly still time to do so, anyway. Ah, but he did not know (although he might suspect) that the Japanese were even thinking of landing there. This was a terrible dilemma for a man who was not as young as he used to be. After all, one rash act might plunge Britain into war with Siam and her patron, Japan, when by abstaining it might be avoided. This was the fix which Brooke-Popham had found himself in. During the past week the Chiefs of Staff in London had authorized him to go ahead and launch his forestalling operation (which had been named Matador) into Siam if he thought a Japanese landing there was imminent. Well!

Nor was it only a question of occupying Singora. There was the other road, too, the one which began at Patani and ran south-west towards the Malayan border. To hold this road would also mean pushing into Siam, though it should not be necessary to occupy Patani itself. This time the idea was to seize the only defensible position on the road, at a place called 'the Ledge', where it entered the mountains near the border. The Ledge was vital, Brooke-Popham was in no doubt about that. If you did not stop an attacking force at the Ledge there was no knowing where you would stop it. Most likely you would have to take to your heels and try to halt it again some miles down the road at Kroh. But once the enemy (still hypothetical, thank goodness!) had reached Kroh they would have crossed Malaya's mountainous spine and reached the civilized and vulnerable western coast with its open rice fields and rubber plantations. And once there you would no longer have the jungle to inhibit their flanking operations. Somehow you would have to bottle them up, for if they once got loose in all that open country, well, it would be better not to think of what might happen ... ! He and General Percival, whose responsibilities began on the Malayan side of the border, had agreed therefore, that they should have a battalion waiting at Kroh, ready to sprint up the road into Siam and grab the Ledge: they might have some Siamese border guards to deal with on the way but that should not worry them. So everything was ready as far as the Ledge was concerned, more or less, though the troops could have done with more training, raw recruits as many of them were. Brooke-Popham knew, even in his sleep, what had to be done. What he did not know, and could not decide, was when, if ever, to do it. After all, by acting too soon he could start an international incident! And if he did that he would really look a fool. Because, frankly, that is the sort of thing that people remember about a chap, not all the hard work he has got through in his career.

Brooke-Popham lay pole-axed on his bed. Occasionally he gibbered a little or champed his moustache briefly with his lower lip. Although he was asleep his mind still bore the traces of the day's dilemma, printed on it like crisp footprints in the snow: the problems that faced him went on rehearsing themselves even when his conscious mind had been ordered to stand easy. If only he had known earlier what the Japanese were doing! (Mind you, he still did not know *for sure*, for absolute sure.) For the past week the sky over the South China Sea had been thickly carpeted with cloud, making air reconnaissance impossible. But then, late on Saturday morning, one of the RAF Hudsons, on the point of turning for home, had come across a break in the cloud over the sea some distance to the south of the tip of Indo-China. And there below had been first one Japanese convoy with three troopships, then another with twenty, both with an escort of warships. What he and his staff had found difficult to determine was where they were going. The first convoy was heading north-west into the Gulf of Siam, the second due west: therefore, the most likely explanation was that they were innocently rounding the tip of Indo-China from Saigon on their way to Bangkok. So more Hudsons and a Catalina flying-boat had been sent out to look for them where they *should* have been, in the Gulf of Siam. The Catalina had failed to return: nothing more had been heard of it. As for the Hudsons, that providential break in the cloud had sealed itself up again and they had seen no more, merely that endless fluffy carpet, white on top, grey below, stretching from one horizon to the other. Somewhere beneath that carpet were two sinister little herds of Japanese troopships, but where? They had cudgelled their brains all Saturday night to find the answer.

What was to be done? Last night he would have given a great deal to be able to ask General Percival and Admiral Phillips what they thought. But Percival was in Kuala Lumpur visiting iii Corps and Tom Phillips was in Manila. Moreover, with one's own staff one must be careful to display confidence and an air of decision; the important thing is to give the impression that you know what you are doing, even when in doubt: any commander will tell you that. But what a burden it had been that he had had to carry by himself! He remembered a cartoon he had seen in some magazine, making fun of the excesses of German discipline. A platoon of storm-troopers were marching over a cliff while their officer was trying to decide what order to give next. An NCO was pleading with him: 'Say *something*, even if it's only goodbye!' Brooke-Popham had chuckled heartily when he had seen that cartoon. But in the last few terrible hours it had returned to haunt him and he had been unable to get it out of his head. Say *something*, even if it's only goodbye!

The hours of Sunday had ticked away slowly until, at long last, at about the time when the first *pahits* of the evening were being sipped all around him in peaceful, unsuspecting Singapore, the Hudsons, skimming the wave tops, had found the troopships again. All his worst fears had been immediately realized: the troopships were on course for Singora and a mere hundred miles away. Others were steaming down the coast in the same direction. A Hudson had been fired on by a destroyer.

Brooke-Popham champed his moustache again and uttered a long, low sigh, aware that in a few minutes he would have to drag himself back to full consciousness to find out what was happening. The sighting of those troopships approaching Singora had meant another round of exhausting conferences. Percival had come back on the train from KL, displaying surprise that he had not begun 'Matador' and ordered the 11th Division into Siam yesterday when the troopships had first been sighted. But it was all very well for Percival, he did not have the wider responsibilities! Any fool could see that the political implications of 'Matador' could not be shrugged off lightly. Had he not just had a telegram from Crosby in Bangkok warning him against alienating the Siamese by violating their neutrality? As Commander-in-Chief Far East he was obliged to consider all sides of the matter.

While Matthew and the others had been at The Great World more exhausting conferences were taking place, and yet more after supper. By now Tom Phillips had returned from Manila. Percival asserted that 'Matador' should be abandoned as General Heath and 11th Division would no longer have time to reach Singora before the Japanese landed. Well, in a way this had come as something of a relief: it meant that, whatever else might happen, he would not involve his country in a diplomatic incident. Still, 'Matador' had been a good idea strategically and he was reluctant to abandon it altogether. It might still come in useful, though in what way, precisely, he could not quite say. So, before retiring to rest in the early hours, he had ordered that word should be sent to Heath to keep the 'Matador' troops standing by. He had noticed one or two raised eyebrows at this (what was the point, his staff might have been wondering, in keeping troops standing by for an operation which it was too late to execute?) and a ghostly voice had whispered in his ear: 'Say *something*, even if it's only good-bye!'

And yet ... and yet, perhaps he should have ignored Percival and ordered 'Matador' to go ahead and hang the consequences. Which was the greater risk, to start a military engagement at a disadvantage or to risk making an enemy of a potential ally? And what had happened to the poor devils in that Catalina which had gone out yesterday? A typewriter was clattering faintly two, three rooms away. Soon it would be dawn and he would have more decisions to wrestle with; he must sleep, if only for a while. Perhaps they were even now floating some-where in the warm, sluggish waters of the Gulf of Siam, hoping against hope for rescue. He felt old and tired: he, too, was floating in warm, sluggish waters, hopelessly, hopelessly. Life had been better when he was still Governor of Kenya: he had not felt so worn out there; the drier climate had suited him better than this humid heat. Well, he had retired once and now here he was back again in harness. Ah, but life had been best of all in France in 1914, the good fellowship and the sun-light and the smell of the country. What fun he had had with their liaison officer, Prince Murat, when the mayor of Saponay was making a fuss about Royal Flying Corps men stealing fruit from orchards: Murat had told the poor mayor that he would have him court-martialled and shot! That had quietened him down. And then there was another time at some little country restaurant near Fère-en-Tardenbois with Murat and Baring, yes, eating outside in the sunlight surrounded by roses and pear trees ... how golden the Montrachet had sparkled in their glasses! And the time Hillaire Belloc had visited them from England and the boxer, Carpentier, a colleague in the French naval air force; he remembered how Trenchard (he was a General in those days) had thrown his cigar into a carp-pond at some place, perhaps a monastery, where they were having lunch, and a carp had eaten it and for a while seemed to have poisoned itself but afterwards to everyone's delight staged a recovery. But above all there came to him now, as he lay troubled and sweating on his bed at Katong, the smell of cider echoing back over quarter of a century from that long, sunlit autumn of 1914, and the memory of Avros and Blériots and Farmans as they came grumbling through the translucent evening, one by one, towards the stubble of the aerodrome. Now the first ground-mist was beginning to form while the shadows reached out across the field and the Mess bell sang its clear note into the still air, calling them all to supper. Brooke-Popham sighed again in the darkness. Outside the window the breeze gently tossed the palms of Katong, making them creak and rustle. Beside him the menacing shadow of the telephone crouched like a toad in the gloom.

General Percival, too, had stretched out to snatch a little rest. And he also slept with his mouth open, snoring slightly from time to time. Were those his teeth in a glass by his bedside? No, his teeth, though they protruded, were perfectly sound: it was just a glass of water in case he should wake during the night and feel thirsty. Beside it glimmered the luminous dial of his watch. What time is it? Half past two, perhaps. It is difficult to make sense of those glowing, trembling dots and bars in the darkness. He was dreaming, partly of the defence of Malaya, partly of the Governor, Sir Shenton Thomas. Someone was whispering to the Governor that he, Percival, was not senior enough to take command in Malaya. Who is this sinister whisperer dripping poison into the Governor's ear? Percival can see the man's hands, knotted and heavily veined, emerging from the sleeves of a uniform, but the face remains in shadow. It must be someone who had known him when he was out here before in Singapore, in 1937, on General Dobbie's staff ... General Dobbie, there was a man for you! Over six feet tall, broad-shouldered, and with the quiet confidence of a man who has the gift of Faith. You had only to look into those steady blue eyes and to witness that calm, informal manner to know that Dobbie would support you through thick and thin. And yet the whispering continued: that face in the shadows was telling the Governor that Percival would be a nuisance, that he did not know how to handle civilians. But this was not true! He did know how to deal with civilians. It is just that one must be careful with them. With civilians it is all a question of morale, of what goes on in their minds. He had seen that in Ireland as a youngster. And civilians *get things wrong*! They take fright, like one of those herds of antelope dashing this way and that on the African plain. And no army on earth can save them once they start this blind dashing about. A snore back-fired and almost woke him, causing his sleep to stall like a cold engine, but somehow he managed to keep it going, and presently the rhythm picked up again and he slept on, breathing deeply.

At his bungalow opposite the Mayfair the Major, reclining in a cane chair in his pyjamas, had managed to doze off too, and was dreaming of Ireland twenty years ago and of a woman who might have been his. He woke up and cleared his throat despondently. How sad it all was! But no doubt everything had been for the best. He dozed again. Perhaps in sleep the past could be rearranged and things turn out better.

On one of the upper floors of Government House Sir Shenton Thomas slept uneasily, his handsome face unstirring, however, on the pillow. His difficulties were not near the surface of his sleeping mind but he was dimly aware of them, nevertheless, fluttering and darting shadows like sparrows in a leafy thicket. He got on well with the Asiatics, so it was not that ... They liked and respected him. No, of all his preoccupations the most disturbing was that in these troubled times unless he remained alert he might not be able to prevent the dignity of his office from being eroded. Duff Cooper and the Military watched the powers he held as Governor the way greedy schoolboys might watch a pie cooling on the window-sill. He did not mind for himself, he was not a selfish man, but for the Colonial Service and for his successors. And for the natives, too, lest they should be abused. Beside him the telephone dozed peacefully in its cradle. In a few minutes it would awaken and begin to shriek.

Not everyone was asleep, however. In the Operations Room at Sime Road a considerable amount of excitement was developing. When Sinclair had come on duty (at one a.m., not midnight as he had told Monty) he had found a discussion taking place between the GSO2 and the Brigadier General Staff as to whether the code-word 'Black-Out' should be sent out. The BGS, however, had declared that this was the Governor's responsibility. Not long afterwards the 'green line' telephone had suddenly started to ring. Sinclair, beside himself with excitement, had watched the RAF officer on duty pick it up. It was the aerodrome at Kota Bahru on the north-east coast near the Siamese border. Suspicious shipping had been detected standing off the coast. Pulford, the Air Officer Commanding, had been summoned. GHQ Far East had been contacted and asked to identify these ships because it looked as if they could only be ... Sinclair shuddered with the effort of maintaining an impassive appearance as he worked rapidly to assist the GSO2 in the preparation of the Situation Report. He was going to be present at the beginning of war in the Far East, he was certain of it!

Nor was General Gordon Bennett, the commander of the Australian Imperial Force in Malaya, asleep. As a matter of fact, he was not even in Singapore but hundreds of miles away in Rangoon. He had been obliged to stop there on his way to Malaya from Egypt where he had been visiting the Australian troops in the Middle East. Now, while waiting for an aircraft to convey him to Singapore, he was spending the night at the splendid old Strand Hotel beside the Rangoon River. Instead of sleeping, however, he was sitting in the dark beside the open window of his room, gazing out surreptitiously into the sweltering night towards the window of another room and holding his breath with excitement.

On account of the heat the window of this room, too, stood open and a light was burning there despite the lateness of the hour. Thanks to the angle of the building Gordon Bennett could see into it across the intervening courtyard. And what could he see in that room but four men who he was pretty certain were Japanese busy poring over maps which he was convinced were maps of Malaya. Japanese spies! What else could they be? He had already telephoned Military Headquarters in Rangoon and told them, guardedly at first, that he had uncovered a nest of spies. Then, since they did not appear very interested, he had had to make it explicit. Jap spies hard at it, spinning their toils practically under his nose! But although the blockheads in charge had told him, soothingly, that they would see about it, he had been watching for hours and they had still done nothing. Meanwhile, he had been staring so long and so fixedly at that nest of spies that he was finding it difficult to keep his eyes focused on them. He ground his teeth in frustration. Why didn't the police come? This heat was quite unbearable. Every now and then he was obliged to close his aching eyes. So the night wore on, the spies scheming, Gordon Bennett grinding his teeth.

Back in Singapore the Major had opened his eyes to find himself still in his cane chair with a burned-out cigar between his fingers. He must have dozed off for a moment. What time could it be? Presently he would go across the road to see whether Matthew's fever was any worse. He yawned. His limbs were stiff. He wondered whether all the claret he had left in Berry Brothers' cellars was surviving the Blitz. How wasteful and senseless was the destruction of war! He had hoped to have finished with all that in 1918. And the twins! Where were they under the bombing? Safely evacuated now, thank heaven. He had had a letter from Northumberland a couple of days ago. Wearing sensible shoes and lisle stockings, each with her brood of unruly, unnerving children (*his* god-children). It was just as well, too, since (husbands away at the war) they had taken to dancing with Free Frenchmen. He must write tomorrow, no later, and tell them not to flirt with the farmhands, not that he had much confidence that they would do as they were told. 'There'll be a lot to sort out, one way or another, when this one is over.' More to the point, was his Château Margaux and Château Laffitte surviving? It should be almost ready to drink by the time he got home. He had not meant to stay out in the East so long. And Sarah, where was she under the bombs? Married somewhere, no doubt. Oh well, perhaps it was all for the best in the long run. And Sarah? He dozed again. How sad it all was! Sarah ... The Major dozed despondently.

Not far away, in bedrooms looking out over the placid gleaming skin of the swimming pool Monty and Joan lay on their beds and slept. Joan was visited in her dreams by Matthew, but a slim, handsome, graceful, authoritative Matthew with a thin moustache and without spectacles; together, wealthy, powerful and admired for their good looks, they reigned in contentment over the Straits. As for Monty, in his dreams you might expect to find naked women jostling each other for the best position under the eye of his subconsciousness; surprisingly this was not the case. Instead, a young boy with a pure, loving face came to see him. He had known this boy at school, though he had never spoken to him. He had left school suddenly when his father had died and had never returned. Now, though, he at last came back, filling Monty's sleeping mind with a piercing tenderness; no doubt everyone carries such an image of purity and love without limit, hidden perhaps by the dross of tainted circumstances and the limits of living from one day to the next, but still capable of ringing through one's dreams like the chime of a bell on a frosty morning. It was this chime which the conscious Monty, fated to toil in sexual salt-mines throughout his waking hours, now faintly heard from an unexpected direction.

Who else? Walter and his wife sleep side by side, rather touchingly holding hands: it is too hot to get any closer than that. Walter's bristles lie smooth and sleek against his spine: he is at peace. He sleeps a calm and confident sleep, very black, and when he wakes he will not remember having had any dreams. Only deep down in the foundations of his sleep are there one or two disturbing shapes which slip or slither (the problem of palm-oil for instance crouches blackly in the blackness and watches him with blazing eyes) but nothing that would seriously disturb that towering, restful edifice. But it's all very well for Walter to sleep peacefully. He is used to the Straits, has spent most of his life here. It is not so easy for the soldiers scattered about the island in clammy tents or snoring barracks. The Indian troops sleep best, the heat is nothing to them, but what about the British and even the Australians? The whirrings and pipings that issue from the jungle close at hand are enough to make a bloke's hair stand on end, particularly if he has only been in the tropics for a week, and in the army itself for not much longer.

Somewhere in the dark waters far to the north, a certain Private Kikuchi (a nephew of Bugler Kikuchi who, as every Japanese schoolboy knows, died heroically for the Emperor not long ago in the war in China) waits tensely in the troopship bringing him closer to Kota Bahru and the north-eastern shores of Malaya. He has just finished reading a pamphlet called 'Read This Alone – And the War Can Be Won'. This work, issued to himself and his comrades on board, explains in simple terms how in the Far East a hundred million Asians have been tyrannized by a mere three hundred thousand whites sucking their blood to maintain themselves in luxury, the natives in misery. Private Kikuchi has read with drumming pulse how it is the Emperor's will that the races of the East shall combine under Japan's leadership for peace and independence from white oppression. In addition he has read about numerous other matters: about how to avoid sea-sickness in various ways, by keeping a high morale, by practising the Respiration Method, by use of bicarbonate and Jintan pills, and by willpower. He has learned how to cherish his weapons, what to eat, to treat natives with consideration but caution, remembering that they all suffer from venereal diseases, how to mount machine-guns in the bow of the landing-craft and to plunge without hesitation into the water when ordered. If he discovers a dangerous snake he knows he must kill it and then swallow its liver raw as there is no better tonic for strengthening the body. He knows that when it is very hot he must bind a cloth round his forehead beneath his steel helmet to prevent sweat from running into his eyes. He knows, too, that in the jungle he should avoid highly coloured, strongly scented or very sweet fruit. He must avoid fruit that are unusually beautiful in shape or with beautifully coloured leaves. Nor must he eat mangoes at the same time as drinking goat's milk or spirits. These and a thousand other useful things he has learned, but now, just for a moment, the motion of the ship gives him a queer sensation. And yet ... No! Fixing his mind on Uncle Kikuchi's glorious example he wills himself to feel normal for the Emperor.

Now a young Malay fisherman, dozing on the poles and planks of his fishing trap out in the sound off Pulau Ubin, suddenly wakes and hears a faint but steadily increasing drone from the north-east. He has heard aeroplanes before but this time they are coming in a great number. What an ominous noise they make when they fly all together like a flock of birds! But aeroplanes are the business of the white men: their comings and goings are nothing to him. His job is merely to catch fish: he wonders whether the fish in the swirling black water can hear this dreadful pulsing as it swells overhead.

When the bombs fall, as they will in a few moments, it will not be on the soldiers in their tents or barracks, who might in some measure be prepared to consider them as part of their duties, nor even on black-dreaming Walter whose tremendous commercial struggles over the past decade have at least played some tiny part in building up the pressures whose sudden bursting-out is to be symbolized by a few tons of high explosive released over a sleeping city, but on Chinatown where a few luckless families or individuals, floated this way by fate across the South China Sea, sucked in by the vortex of British capital invested in Malaya, are now to be eclipsed.

The starlight glints on the silver wings of the Japanese bombers, slipping through the clear skies like fish through a sluice-gate. They make their way in over Changi Point towards the neatly arranged beads and necklaces of streetlights, which agitated and recently awakened authorities are at last and in vain trying to have extinguished. In a dark space between two necklaces of light lies a tenement divided into tiny cubicles, each of which contains a number of huddled figures sleeping on the floor. Many of the cubicles possess neither window nor water supply (it will take high explosive, in the end, to loosen the grip of tuberculosis and malaria on them). In one cubicle, not much bigger than a large wardrobe, an elderly Chinese wharf-coolie lies awake beside a window covered with wire-netting. Beside him, close to his head, is the shrine for the worship of his ancestors with bunches of red and white candles strung together by their wicks. It was here beside him that his wife died and sometimes, in the early hours, she returns to be with him for a little while. But tonight she has not come and so, presently, he slips out of his cubicle and down the stairs, stepping over sleeping forms, to visit the privy outside. As he returns, stepping into the looming shadow of the tenement, there is a white flash and the darkness drains like a liquid out of everything he can see. The building seems to hang over him for a moment and then slowly dissolves, engulfing him. Later, when official estimates are made of this first raid on Singapore (sixty-one killed, one hundred and thirty-three injured), there will be no mention of this old man for the simple reason that he, in common with so many others, has left no trace of ever having existed either in this part of the world or in any other.

Part Three

28

The suburb of Tanglin where Matthew continued to thrash and sweat in the grip of his fever lay some distance from Chinatown and Raffles Place. The noise of bombs exploding over there on the far side of the river was not quite loud enough, therefore, to wake heavy sleepers like Walter and Monty. It was not until morning that they learned the astonishing news: Singapore had been bombed, Malaya had been invaded! Nor was that all, for the Japanese had simultaneously attacked the Americans, too, demolishing their fleet at Pearl Harbor. America was in the war at last. A strange elation took hold of the European community.

The United States suddenly became popular. The Stars and Stripes sprouted beside the Union Jack in the shop windows along Orchard Road. American citizens who had been ignored or even jeered for their country's neutrality found themselves welcome everywhere and were bought drinks whenever they showed themselves in the street or Club. Joan even considered revising her opinion of Ehrendorf, despite the tiring scenes which had led up to what she jokingly described to Monty as 'Ehrendorf's Farewell'. ('The lovesick glances he kept ladling over me like tepid soup!') Perhaps, carried along on the tide of goodwill, if Joan or Monty had happened to bump into Ehrendorf they would at least have bought the blighter a drink. But he did not put in an appearance anywhere. No doubt he was busy with his superiors, putting finishing touches to plans for obliterating the yellow aggressors.

Later in the morning Walter strolled the few yards from his office on Collyer Quay to have a look at the damage to Robinson's in Raffles Place. Around the corner barriers had been set up to keep back sightseers, but Walter showed his official pass and was allowed through. Broken glass and silk underwear from Gian Singh's window in Battery Road still lay on the pavement; part of Guthrie's had been reduced to a pile of rubble across the road. Walter surveyed with equanimity this devastation of one of his principal rival's buildings. Nevertheless he offered his sympathy to a Guthrie's man he saw standing nearby, and feebly tried to prevent himself thinking: 'It's an ill wind ...' His blue eyes glittered cheerfully in the sunlight as he watched the cautious efforts being made to search for unexploded bombs and to clear the rubble. Later, however, when he had returned to his office once more, a more sober mood took hold of him and he thought: 'This is a fine thing to happen in our jubilee year!' Moreover, this unexpected attack by the Japanese could prove troublesome to Blackett and Webb's commercial interests.

Forewarned of centralized buying by the Americans, Walter in a short space of time had committed himself to a great deal of forward business in order to escape the limitations of the new arrangements. He had been obliged to acquire rubber in substantial quantities from other producers as well as from the estates managed by Blackett and Webb in order to fill these contracts. Not that, under the Restriction Scheme, it had been enough to get his hands on the rubber: it had also been necessary to buy *the right to sell it*. Under Restriction each rubber producer, whether estate or smallholding, had been allotted a share of Malaya's total exports. Each producer's share, naturally, was less than his capacity to produce: that was the point of the Scheme. Even with light tapping, heavy replanting and recent high rates of release to the world market, there was still no shortage of rubber (inside Malaya, that is). Rubber was plentiful, the right to sell it was scarce.

Fortunately, however, export rights could be bought from Asiatic smallholders who, for one reason or another, were not using them to sell their own rubber. Smallholders were issued with coupons which were equivalent to their share of Malaya's export rights: these coupons had to accompany any rubber they intended to sell. However, many of the smallholders were illiterate, or simply baffled by the bureaucratic intricacies of the system. Others were swindled out of their coupons by unscrupulous clerks at the Land Offices which issued them or, believing them to be of no value, gave them away to Chinese or Chettyar pimps who lay in wait outside. Some even believed that these perplexing pieces of paper represented a new government tax and therefore willingly surrendered them to entrepreneurs who magnanimously undertook to pay on their behalf in return for some favour. A number of smallholders gave up tapping their trees and simply sold their coupons instead of rubber. Walter, in any event, had found it possible to enlarge the export quota of Blackett and Webb's estates to cover the considerable stocks of extra rubber he had accumulated. Blackett and Webb's godowns in Singapore on this first day of the war in the Far East were crammed with rubber destined for America and fit to burst.

Walter, at first, had been delighted by his success in arranging contracts which would evade the Americans' new centralized buying. He had secured this business at prices which none of his competitors would be able to match. This was surely a coup to rival those of Mr Webb's early days in Rangoon! It made him feel young again; it reminded him that business was an adventure. How angry old Solomon Langfield must have been when he heard of these deals which Walter had closed in the nick of time. It would have been obvious to old Langfield that Walter had been tipped the wink in advance. How bitterly he must have remonstrated with Langfield and Bowser's board of dimwits for not having got wind of it! Walter thought with satisfaction of their fat, complacent Secretary, W. J. Bowser-Barrington, trembling before the old man's anger. Every *stengah* they drank for a month must have tasted of bile. Ha! He had vowed to give Langfields and the rest something to remember Blackett and Webb's jubilee by ... and he had done so.

All the same, even at the height of his satisfaction with this state of affairs he had not been able entirely to conceal from himself certain misgivings about the sheer quantity of rubber he had awaiting shipment to various American ports. These misgivings had increased steadily week by week as shipping became more difficult to find. This morning, with the American Pacific fleet knocked out of action, or at best disabled, the prospects were that merchant shipping would become even more scarce. Hence, the chances of realizing Blackett and Webb's considerable investment in the rubber-crammed godowns on the wharfs in the near future had also diminished. Walter was not seriously worried yet. But he was beginning to wonder whether he might not have been a little too clever. Besides, there was another aspect of the matter on which he now began to brood and to which had not given sufficient attention earlier.

Walter, you might argue, must have always known he was taking a risk, given the ominous way in which the Far Eastern political climate had been developing for some time past. He must have known that there was a possibility that he might be left holding a great deal of rubber which he was unable to deliver to the buyers. But a businessman must sometimes take a risk, particularly if he hopes to make profits on a grand scale. So what is all the fuss about? Walter will get rid of his rubber sooner or later, particularly now that America is in the war. If instead of making his grand profit the risk causes his plans to go astray, it will not be the end of the world for Blackett and Webb, merely a nuisance and a dead weight that must be carried for a while. Well, the aspect of the matter on which Walter had begun to brood (not that it was easy to brood on anything in the hectic atmosphere of that Monday morning, and with the sudden vulnerability of Blackett and Webb's Shanghai and Hong Kong interests demanding instant attention) was this: although certainly a considerable risk was embodied in those rubber-crammed godowns, there was no chance of making a grand profit, nor had there ever been. Blackett and Webb, being British-registered, were subject to the one hundred per cent excess profits tax introduced in the summer of 1940. The most that could be made on Walter's risky initiative was 'a standard profit'. He had known this all along but had ignored it, dazzled by the prospect of an old-fashioned coup to celebrate his jubilee year. This was the first time in years that he had committed an error of judgement of this magnitude. It was clear that the prospective reward should have been on the same scale as the risk.

'Well, it may still turn out all right,' Walter told himself with an effort and, shrugging off this depressing line of thought, turned to the more urgent matters awaiting his attention.

'We have good reason to be proud of the RAF. In aircraft and efficiency it is second to none in the world!'

These words, echoing beneath the high ceiling of an upstairs room in the Singapore Cricket Club were sucked into the blur of the fan revolving above and scattered on the breeze to every corner. Half a dozen members of the Citizens' Committee for Civil Defence, of which the Major was founder, chairman, secretary, treasurer and most active participant, stirred and murmured: 'Hear! hear!' These members, and others not present, had been summoned to attend an emergency meeting of the Committee. Of the other members, three were absent without explanation (either they had not been successfully contacted, or were ill, or were dead ... death being a not uncommon reason for non-attendance, given the great age of most of the Committee members), three more were temporarily away in Malacca and Kuala Lumpur, another had not come on principle because he was having a feud with the Major: he was indignant at having been urged on a previous occasion to abbreviate his harangues to the Committee. There remained two other members whom the Major officially considered to be present although, in fact, they had been lost in the bar downstairs where they were performing the useful function of toasting the American entry into the war.

The Major, slumped in his chair at the head of the long table, did not join in the approval of the RAF; indeed, his eyebrows gathered into a gloomy frown. Although as loyal to the Forces as the next man, he had come to dread these patriotic remarks. He had found that even on a good day they badly clogged the proceedings of the Committee. On a bad day the wheels would not move at all. Besides, the Major reflected that he was surely not the only person in Singapore to wonder why the RAF had not managed to shoot down or drive off the Japanese bombers last night.

'The attempts to set fire to London from the air persistently carried out in the raids from 1915 to 1917 resulted in failure,' declared the speaker, an octogenarian planter called Mr Bridges, in a quavering voice. '*Why?*' He lifted his bespectacled eyes from the paper he held and glared round the table at his colleagues: this, however, was a mistake because he then had to find his place again, which took some time. The Major stirred restlessly and looked at his watch.

'Why? Because of the low efficiency of the incendiary bombs then used, the poor marksmanship of the enemy and the brilliantly effective fire-fighting services.' Again Mr Bridges was unable to resist looking up from the paper in his trembling hand and glaring at his audience over his spectacles. This glare did not mean that Mr Bridges was aroused: it was purely rhetorical, part of the old chap's habitual oratory learned in youth from some forceful speaker and displayed year after year before the boards of the various tin mines and rubber companies on which he had served. 'Let me say, gentlemen, that for courage and ability I doubt if there is a finer body of men than the London Fire Brigade.'

Once more his audience stirred and muttered: 'Hear! hear!' with the exception of the Major who ground his teeth and scratched his bare knee which had just been bitten by some insect.

'Out of 354 incendiary bombs on London only eight caused fatal casualties. The maximum number that fell during one raid

223

was 258 and these were distributed over a wide area averaging seven bombs per square mile ...'

'Seven bombs per square mile! Where on earth has the old blighter got all this from?' wondered the Major knocking out his pipe into an ashtray which had been filled with water to prevent the ash being blown about by the fan overhead. He stifled a yawn. Lunch, combined with Mr Bridges' statistics, had made him drowsy. It was hot here, too, despite the generous dimensions of the room. How he loved the tropical Victorian architecture of the Cricket Club with its vast rooms, high ceilings and ornamented balconies! Behind his chair a segment of the green *padang* could be seen through the window which was angled to face, not the Eurasian Club at the far end of the ground, but the Esplanade and the sea. In the small area of the field that was visible from where he sat a little group of Tamil groundsmen were peacefully at work moving the practice nets a few feet seawards to a fresh patch of turf. No doubt cricket would continue despite the bombing; important matches could not be expected to wait until the Japanese had been dealt with. While the Major was trying to recall whether the annual Civil Service and Law versus the Rest (Gentlemen v. Players some cynic had called it) had yet taken place, there came unbidden to his mind the recollection of a girl being shot at a cricket match in College Park, oh, years ago. He had read about it in the *Irish Times*: a young woman of twenty or so who had been watching the Gentlemen of Ireland playing the Army. Some Sinn Feiner had fired a revolver through the park railings and taken to his heels; the bullet, aimed at one of the Army officers, had struck her on the temple. She had been engaged to be married, too, if he recalled correctly; an innocent young girl killed by a scampering fanatic in a cloth cap. This recollection, echoing back over two decades, still had the power to numb the Major with indignation and despair. The uselessness of it!

'The total number of casualties in England from aerial attack during the Great War was 1,414 killed and 3,416 wounded ... Material damage costing three million pounds was produced by 643 aircraft dropping 8,776 bombs which weighed a total of 270 tons!'

This paroxysm of statistics was delivered with such vigour that it caused someone inopportunely to murmur: 'Hear! hear!' but the Major, profiting from the fact that Mr Bridges had once again glared round the table and lost his place, seized his chance.

'We're all grateful, I'm sure, to Mr Bridges who has spared no effort of research into the last war. The point he is trying to make, I believe, is that a great gulf exists between the bombing methods of then and now ... What we must decide is how best to combat by our civil defence procedure the *modern* methods of which we had a sample in the early hours of this morning. And in any case ...'

But here he was obliged to stop for Mr Bridges had now succeeded in hunting down his lost place and capturing it on the page with a long ivory fingernail: this permitted him to display indignation at the Major's interruption. He still had a great deal to say! He still had to delve into the question of the Zeppelin raids on London in 1915 and 1916! The question he wanted to consider was whether the amount of damage caused varied according to the amount of cloud cover. 'For example, on 31 May 1915, a fine moonlit night, Zeppelin LZ 38 dropped eighty-seven incendiary bombs and twenty-five explosive bombs, killing seven people, injuring thirty-two, and starting forty-one fires which caused £18,396 worth of damage *whereas* ...'

This information was greeted by a groan. It came, however, not from one of the Committee members, whose minds had wandered in a herd to other pastures, but from behind the Major's chair, to the leg of which a black and white spotted dog was tethered. This animal, a Dalmatian, did not belong to the Major but had been borrowed for a demonstration which was to take place later in the afternoon. The poor dog undoubtedly was bored, hot and restless. The Major, who was suffering similarly, without turning reached a sympathetic hand behind his chair to caress the animal's damp muzzle. An unseen tongue licked his open palm.

But the Major did not want to hurt the old man's feelings: he had clearly put in a lot of work on his Zeppelins. Alarmed by Dupigny's sombre predictions of a Japanese advance to the south the Major had formed the Committee some weeks earlier with the idea of putting pressure on the arrogant, inert administration of the Colony to do something about civil defence. A gathering of influential citizens was what he had had in mind, but in the event he had only been able to conscript a handful of retired planters and businessmen, one or two Chinese merchants who agreed with everything but kept their own counsel and an argumentative young man from the Indian Protection Agency who disagreed with everything and, fortunately, seldom put in an appearance: at the moment he was several *stengahs* the worse for wear in the bar downstairs.

The truth was, and even now listening to Mr Bridges (the Zeppelins had moved off, giving place to some curious information about the angle at which bombs dropped from various heights arrived on the earth) the Major was reluctant to face it, they were making no headway. At best the Committee provided a weekly airing for a number of elderly gentlemen who otherwise would not get out of their bungalows very often. The Major himself had been responsible for such positive initiatives as had been taken. At his own expense he had put advertisements in the *Straits Times* and *Tribune* calling for assistance from the general public. The response had been disappointing.

A Chinese company had tried to sell him a stirrup-pump, 'approved by ARP Singapore and now on show at ARP headquarters, Old Supreme Court Building, Singapore'. There had also been a long, mysteriously defensive letter from the sales manager of a firm manufacturing a patent rake-and-shovel for scooping up blazing incendiary bombs. It was *not true*, declared this letter, as had been stated 'in certain quarters' that, when tested, the incendiary bomb had burned a hole in the shovel. In most conditions this would not occur. It was the opinion of the sales manager that the people testing the shovel had used the wrong kind of incendiary bomb.

The other two replies had also had a commercial flavour, embroidering prettily on the initials ARP. One of them, addressed to Mrs Brenda Archer, urged him to Appear Rosy and Pretty under all conditions. 'War is horrible but preserve your composure and don't look terrible. Keep your colour by using Evelyn Astrova Face Powder.' Finally, a printed circular in a similar vein suggested that 'A Reassuring Packet of what is now a very popular brand, Gold Bird (Ceylon) Tea, will soothe and refresh you in your worried moments.' To sell people things, reflected the Major, is all very well, nothing in the least wrong with it (does nothing but good when you come to think of it and one might even say, as Walter did, that but for commerce Singapore would hardly have existed at all), but this commercial spirit needed to be leavened by patriotism and an interest in the community as a whole. For if Malaya were nothing more than a vast congeries of competing self-interests what chance would it have against a homogeneous nation like Japan?

Of course, there were patriots here, too, and in plenty. At this very moment Mr Bridges had paused again to pay tribute to 'the brave lads in khaki who had come from the four corners of the Earth to defend Malaya'. ('Hear! hear!') The trouble was that for the British this patriotism was operating at long distance: their real concern was not for Malaya but for a country several thousand miles away. As for the Indians and Chinese, the great majority of them felt more loyalty to their communities in India and China than to Malaya: they had, after all, simply come here to find work, not to die for the place. Moreover, Malaya's population, already divided by race and religion, was even further divided by differing political beliefs. Walter Blackett, the Major knew, was concerned by the existence of clandestine Communist groups in his enormous labour force. Where the Government was concerned, anxiety about the allegiance of the Chinese and of their various 'national salvation' organizations was chronic.

A few weeks earlier the Major had been summoned by some official to the Chinese Protectorate on Havelock Road and shown a list of patriotic Chinese associations believed to be under Communist control. But, he had wanted to know, what had these alarming associations to do with his own gentlemanly Civil Defence Committee, which was never likely to cross the path, at least he hoped not, of, for example, the 'Youth Blood and Iron Traitor-Exterminating Corps'? Blinking rapidly the official had replied that, in his 'humble opinion', the Malayan Communist Party would choose just such an innocent organization as the Major's for its subversive manoeuvres. The Major should know that Communists behaved in a society, particularly in a Chinese society, the way hookworm larvae behave in the human body, boring their way from one organ to another.

Startled by this image, the Major had looked at the official more closely: he was a bald young man with glasses, sweating profusely; in the draught of the fan thin wisps of hair flickered about his ears like sparks of electricity. He had said his name was Smith. The Major wondered whether this could be the same Smith who, Walter had told him, had incurred the wrath of old Mr Webb one day in Walter's office. The Major could not quite remember what it had been about ... something to do with Miss Chiang, though. Perhaps he had made some disparaging remark about her, or about the Chinese generally, and Mr Webb had taken umbrage.

Yes, the young man had continued, they ignored what one considered to be the natural boundaries of the separate organs, passing through the skin into the blood-stream, migrating from the pulmonary capillaries into the air sacs, into the alveoli and bronchioles and thence, as adolescent worms, into the intestines where, developing a temporary mouth capsule, they attached themselves to the wall to suck blood, pumping it through their own horrible guts. And from time to time they would abandon the old site, which they had sucked dry ... ('*dry*, Major, d'you understand, *dry* ...') ... and attach themselves to a new and more nourishing location.

'Steady on!' the Major had exclaimed, taken aback. 'These blessed worms don't have anything to do with civil defence. Nor with Communists, for that matter.'

'No, they don't,' agreed Smith calmly, but with the tufts of hair still flickering around his ears in a disturbing sort of way. 'Speaking of worms I'm trying to make you aware of how these men ... and women, too, Major, I believe you are friendly with a certain Miss Vera Chiang, are you not? Yes? I thought so ... of how they pass from one organ to another in our society. Did you know that Stalin has recommended infiltration of Nationalist movements in his *Problems of Leninism*? Ah, I see you did not! Did you know that the Comintern had opened a Far Eastern Bureau in Shanghai, Major, not to mention the Sun Yat-sen University and the University of the Toilers of the East in Moscow? Perhaps some of your so innocent Chinese friends are graduates, Major, had you thought of that? Did you know that in 1925 the head of the Comintern, Zinoviev, declared that the road to world revolution lies through the East rather than the West ... at a time, mind you, when the Chinese Communists and the Kuomintang were still working hand in glove? What more natural, when Chiang Kai-shek turned on his Communist friends in 1927 and destroyed their power, than that they should seek other and more innocent organizations such as yours to *worm* their way into? That is why I speak of worms, Major! You lack experience in such matters. You'd do much better to leave civil defence to the proper authority.'

'If we had thought the Government was competent we wouldn't have considered it necessary to form the Committee in the first place!' the Major had retorted sharply, nettled by the young man's tone.

As it had turned out, he now reflected sadly, dropping a hand to soothe the Dalmatian again, for all the progress that had been made he might as well have taken Smith's advice. He had been faced at every turn by total indifference. But what, after all, could one expect of a society whose only culture and reason for existence was commercial self-interest? A society without traditions, without common beliefs or language, a melting-pot, certainly, but one in which the ingredients had failed to melt: what could one expect of such a place?

The Major now saw an opportunity for interrupting Mr Bridges again, and this time more successfully, by suggesting that the time had come for questions. From behind his chair there came a long, warbling howl of despair. The Major added swiftly that since there were no questions they would adjourn until the following week and, in the meantime, he would continue to press the administration for air-raid shelters in the populous quarters of the city and a proper distribution of gas-masks among the Asiatic communities. With that, he got to his feet, released the dog, and with a hasty goodbye made for the door. The emergency meeting had not been a success.

29

A clock somewhere was striking five o'clock as the Major's Lagonda turned to the right off Orchard Road on its way to the Tanglin Club. A few moments later the Major, followed by the dog, was making his way up the steps to the entrance. Here he unexpectedly came upon Dupigny, clad in billowing tennis flannels which the Major had no difficulty in recognizing as his own; moreover, it was the Major's old school tie which had been knotted around Dupigny's waist to serve as a belt. The Major's old school, Sandhall's, was not a famous establishment but the Major was attached to it, none the less, and it caused him a moment's distress to see his school colours wrapped like a boa-constrictor around a Frenchman's waist. But still, one must not make a fuss about trifles. This was war.

The Major continued to look preoccupied, though about something else, as he climbed the steps with the black and white dog trotting behind him, its tail waving back and forth like a metronome. At the top he paused and said: 'Well, François, do we have to fear the Communists in Singapore?'

'Until you have a government popular and democratical in Malaya, yes, you must fear them,' replied Dupigny after a moment's reflection. 'Your Government here fears, naturally, an anti-colonial revolution if the Communists are allowed to operate freely. It is true, there is a risk. Thus, your dilemma can be stated so: *with* them in danger ... *without* them, too weak to resist the Japanese!'

'Oh, François!' The Major shook his head and sighed but did not pursue the matter. Instead he asked Dupigny if he had heard any further news of the Japanese attack. According to the communiqué issued that morning by GHQ the Japanese had tried to land at Kota Bahru in the extreme north-east of the country but had been driven off. But in the meantime Dupigny had spoken to someone who had attended another briefing: the few Japanese left on the beach were being heavily machine-gunned, he told the Major.

'First we repel them. Then, though we have repelled them, they are on the beach and we are machine-gunning them!'

The Major shrugged and turned away, but continued to stand there for a moment, fingering his moustache gloomily. Dupigny surmised that he was exploring the worrying possibility of the Colony being attacked not only from the sea and the sky but also, as it were, being eaten away from within by a Communist Fifth Column. Beside him, sitting up straight, the dog looked worried, too, though no doubt only because his friend the Major was looking worried.

The predicament of the British in Malaya, mused Dupigny not without satisfaction, for like any good Frenchman he had suffered from the superior airs the British had given themselves since the fall of France, was strikingly similar in many ways to that which he himself and Catroux, his Governor-General, had had to face in Indo-China. How were they to make twenty-five million natives loyal to France and impermeable to enemy propaganda? Catroux, remembering that Lyautey, faced with the same problem in Morocco during the Great War, had solved it by practising what he had called '*la politique du sourire*', had resolved to do the same. Like Lyautey he had made it a rule that no one in authority should show the least sign of distress no matter how adversely the war might seem to be going. And so, Dupigny recalled smiling ruefully, their policy in Indo-China for the first few months of the war had been a display of nonchalance. Now, here in Singapore, the British had evidently decided on similar tactics to judge by their first cheerful communiqués.

Having invited Dupigny to attend the lecture he would presently deliver on 'ARP and Pets', the Major passed on his way leaving Dupigny to wait for his partner in the Club tennis competition: this was Mrs Blackett's brother, Captain Charlie Tyrrell. Dupigny had decided for his own self-respect and for the prestige of France to win this competition, come what might. He had already discovered, however, that his partner was a serious impediment to this ambition. Charlie had been retained temporarily in Singapore to replace a staff officer who had gone sick. Alas, Dupigny had been deceived by Charlie's athletic appearance into choosing him to share the spoils of victory. Not only had Charlie proved to be a highly erratic tennis-player, the man could scarcely even be depended upon to put in an appearance when a match had been arranged. Only grim efforts on Dupigny's part had allowed them to reach the third round. Now their opponents, two polite young Englishmen, were already waiting for them on one of the courts.

But presently Charlie arrived, looking flustered and clutching an impressive armful of tennis rackets. 'I say, I'm not late, am I?' he asked apprehensively. He was alarmed and dismayed by Dupigny's determination to win the competition, which seemed to him, at best, peculiar, at worst, deranged. And the further they advanced the more gravely unbalanced, it seemed to him, grew Dupigny's behaviour. Needless to say, he now regretted ever having agreed to become the fellow's partner. But with any luck they would be soundly beaten by the two sporting young men whom he could see waiting for them on a distant court beyond the swimming pool. On closer inspection their opponents both proved to have very blue eyes and hair glistening neatly with hair-oil. One of them stirred as they approached and called 'Rough or smooth?', spinning his racket on the red clay.

Dupigny was equal to this. 'Ah, you mean, as we say in French, "Pile ou face"'? he said swiftly. 'Alors, pile! Ah, pile it is,' he added, picking up the fallen racket and inspecting it. He showed it to the young Englishman. They glanced at each other but said nothing.

But today even Dupigny, reminded of Indo-China by the Major, found it hard to concentrate on the game, determined though he was to win it. He recalled how, when Catroux had been appointed Governor-General in 1939, he had taken the train from Hanoi to meet him in Saigon. The day after their return to Hanoi war had been declared with Germany.

'Mine! No, yours!' Dupigny shouted as a tennis ball hurtled down on them out of the steamy sky. 'Ah, well placed, sir!' he added as Charlie executed a perfect smash between their two opponents. Charlie's form today verged on the miraculous.

They were winning comfortably but Dupigny was over-powered by a sudden feeling of discouragement. He and Catroux had got on well together. Together, with one or two trivial adjustments to the course which events had taken, they might have brought off a splendid coup! They might have succeeded in detaching Indo-China from Vichy and have struck off on their own. Now, instead of standing here in a British colony in bor-rowed tennis flannels (ludicrously too long so that one of the Major's ties, which he had selected for its disagreeably clashing colours with the idea of unsettling their opponents, encircled his body not round his waist but just below the armpits) he and Catroux might have been navigating an autonomous country like some great vessel into a new era.

Indo-China, self-supporting in food, was not a difficult country to administer, as Catroux had been pleased to discover. All their difficulties, indeed, had stemmed in one way or another from their confused and fitful contacts with metropolitan France. From time to time baffling instructions would reach them from one ministry or another. Supplies in vast quantities, they were instructed, were to be sent to France under the general mobilization scheme. As a result he and Catroux had presently found themselves presiding over great quantities of rice, maize, rubber, coffee and other commodities, rotting on the quays at Haiphong and Saigon for want of shipping.

And so it had continued throughout the *drôle de guerre*. Their contact with ministries in Paris had grown increasingly spas-modic. Urgent cables for instructions would be met by dead silence. But then suddenly, out of this silence, would crackle some insane command. The Ministère des Colonies, for example, in order to meet some whim of the European coffee markets, had abruptly ordered them to increase the area of the country under coffee. Catroux had had to point out that coffee would only start producing at the end of the fourth year of growth ... and so, once again, the Ministry had lapsed into silence until, presently, there had come some other eccentric command ... and another, and another. But by then it had become clear to both Catroux and Dupigny that, because of the lack of shipping to Europe and the need to trade instead with China, Japan and Malaya, the country in their charge was growing autonomous with every passing day.

Meanwhile, as to what might be going on in Europe nobody

had bothered to inform them. Dupigny had two memories of that stifling early summer in Hanoi: one was of sitting with Catroux in the Governor-General's palace. There, beneath the Sèvres bust of 'Marianne' on the mantelpiece, they had discussed the long official telegram containing news of the German offensive and of Gamelin's counter-manoeuvre in Belgium: they had realized that unless there was a quick French victory in Europe their own position in Indo-China would be made precarious by the threat from Japan. Dupigny's other memory was of the arrival of a second telegram, after four weeks of total silence, announcing that a request for an armistice had been made to the Germans.

'Mine! No, yours! No, mine!' howled Dupigny as their opponents once more lobbed high into the hot evening sky. But Charlie, ignoring these instructions, continued to crouch like a toad with his head in the air and a fixed expression on his face, precisely where the ball was about to return to earth. Dupigny knew better than to trust Charlie with that fixed look in his eyes posing gracefully beneath the ball. So, thrusting him aside he managed to usurp his place and scramble the ball back over the net with the wooden part of his racket. The two young Englishmen, who had already retreated to the back of the court in expectation of Charlie's smash, hammered their legs with their rackets and looked tense.

Yes, all was going well ... at least on the tennis court. Back in Hanoi, however, their position had become hopeless once France had fallen. Nevertheless, for two desperate weeks he and Catroux had not for a moment stopped looking for support. They had cabled Washington seeking American help, in vain. They had made a last appeal to Bordeaux (whither the Government had retreated) begging that war materials should be sent to Indo-China rather than handed over to the enemy. This had produced no result either. In the end everything had depended on Decoux, Admiral of the Far Eastern Fleet at Saigon. Decoux, who was not subject to the Governor-General's authority, had been wavering as to whether he should order his fleet to fight on with the British or submit to orders from defeated France. At first he had seemed inclined to reject the armistice, sending a signal to Admiral Darlan in France to the effect that the universal feeling in Indo-China was for continuing the struggle with the help of the British. Darlan's cunning response was an offer to make Decoux Governor-General in place of Catroux.

And so to Saigon where a last-resort conference had been arranged with the British represented by Admiral Sir Percy Noble, an old acquaintance of Decoux's. The whole of Saigon, Dupigny recalled, had been simmering with excitement and patriotism. On the Rue Catinat every shop and café displayed French and British flags interlaced. Fervent crowds of *anciens combattants* held meetings to protest their loyalty or gathered in front of the British Consulate on the Quai de la Belgique. On the way to the quays for the conference on board his flag-ship, the *Lamotte-Picquet*, Decoux had shown signs of weakening in his determination to resist, hinting darkly that secret meetings were being held in Saigon at which 'extreme solutions' were envisaged. He had been approached by certain hot-headed young officers who wanted to join Noble in Singapore. Very soon it had been evident that, despite his protestations of friendship for the British, Decoux would not resist Darlan's tempting offer. Catroux, even with the promised support of the Army and of the French community would clearly be unable to retain control of Indo-China against both Decoux and the Japanese.

During the conference with Noble they had discussed the possibility of defending Indo-China in case of attack by the Japanese, but that was out of the question. How could they possibly resist the two hundred modern Japanese planes on Hainan Island with the handful of obsolete aircraft at their disposal? The British were too weak themselves to send reinforcements. At the dinner to mark the end of the conference there had been an air of disillusion and hostility beneath the formal politeness: when Decoux proposed a toast to *Le Président de la République* there was a moment of hesitation, then Admiral Noble declared that because of the armistice he could not drink to the President but would simply drink to *La France*. Decoux had turned pale but said nothing.

Two days later, at a formal leave-taking on the quay, another moment of bitterness had occurred. In the full hearing of the officers standing around, Admiral Noble had remarked grimly: 'As a friend, Decoux, I advise you not to stay on board the *Lamotte-Picquet* in future. If she were on her way back to Europe we might have to sink her and I should prefer to know that you were not on board.' With that, he had turned away to board the British cruiser *Kanimbla* leaving Decoux, angry and shaken, standing on the quay in the sunshine. Thus had the French Far Eastern Fleet been lost to the Allies.

A year and a half later Dupigny found himself standing on a tennis court in the sweltering Singapore evening, watching a dense cloud of tiny birds swirling against the dying blaze of the sky. Their two opponents, overcome without difficulty, had trailed away to the changing-rooms with a baffled air and one or two backward glances at Dupigny, who struck them as decidedly odd. Charlie had followed them to stand them a drink at the bar. Dupigny, still brooding, drifted after them. Now the Major's voice, floating down from the open deck-like structure above, reminded him of the ARP lecture. Feeling his years, he climbed the flight of outside stairs to where the Major, with his spotted dog slumbering at his side, was addressing a handful of people, mainly women. Out here, Dupigny had been told, dances and cinema-shows were sometimes held when the weather was considered too hot to use the ballroom inside the building. Dupigny himself never attended dances, seeing no interest whatsoever in grasping an adult woman and trotting with her fully clothed in the tropical evening.

'It is most important that your animals should remain calm ... A box of five-grain potassium bromide tablets from any chemist ... one tablet for a cat or small dog, such as a Pekinese, two for a terrier, three for a spaniel ...'

Stranded in an alien culture, surrounded by British dog-lovers, Dupigny suffered an acute pang of nostalgia for the pre-war days in Hanoi, or better still, Saigon ... How pleasant to be sitting now as the light was beginning to fade on the *terrasse* of the Hotel Continental, drinking beer and watching the evening crowds swirling round the corner of the Rue Catinat towards the Boulevard Bonnard, the women so graceful in their slit tunics and flowing black silk trousers! Or to wander through the great flower market set up in the Boulevard Charner on the eve of Tet. Later, having eaten at one of the excellent restaurants in the city he might move on to take coffee at the Café Parisien in the Rue de l'Avalanche or, even better, at the Café du Théâtre from where he could look out across the square and listen to the night breeze in the tamarinds.

'Gas masks are not suitable for animals ...' (Was this a joke? No, the Major was serious. He looked discomfited by the chuckles of his audience) ... 'but instead you can put them in a box with a hole covered in wire netting and a blanket soaked in a solution of bicarbonate of soda, four pounds to the gallon of water, or permanganate of potash ...' The spotted dog at the

Major's feet stirred and looked up enquiringly for it had heard the Major's talk many times before and had come to recognize the moment when its services would be required.

Ah, Dupigny's nostalgia became deliciously acute as he remembered Saigon mornings, walking in a vast airy room, treading the waxed tiles of the Continental's long corridors which had a special, indefinable smell of France about them, on the way to a quiet inner courtyard to a breakfast of coffee and croissants and small, succulent strawberries from Dalat, sitting there in the open air surrounded by flowering shrubs. Later in the morning, perhaps in the company of Turner-Smith, a friend from the British Consulate and a pederast of refinement, he would make his way up the Rue Catinat past the looming red-brick Basilica de Notre-Dame. At the corner of the Rue Chasseloup-Laubat he and Turner-Smith would part company, the latter to take up his station outside the boys' Collège, while he himself would find a vantage point near the gates of the girls' school, the Lycée Marie-Curie: he had done this so often while on leave from Hanoi that the sly little creatures had come to recognize him and had even (one of them had confessed in a gale of childish laughter) given him a nickname . . . Monsieur Marie-Curie!

Yes, at any moment now it would be noon and the gates would open to release a flood of beautiful young girls, their bodies so lithe and graceful in their school uniforms, their skins so smooth, their black eyes sparkling with mischief. Why, he mused, his nostalgia bordering on ecstasy, if homosexuality was *le vice anglais* the Frenchman's great temptation was *le ballet rose*! Of all the pleasures which he missed here in dull British Singapore he missed none so much as the *ballets roses* which an indulgent madame of Saigon would organize for his distraction from the cares of office. The British, *hélas*, would never understand. How, for instance, could he begin to explain such a joy to the Major?

The Major was concluding his address with the advice that his audience should get their animals used to seeing them in their gas-masks. 'The point is,' he explained, fumbling with his own gas-mask case, 'that your dog may get frightened when he sees you wearing one and your voice, which means so much to him, will sound completely different. Let me show you what I mean.' The Major, with the skill of long practice, drew on his gas-mask, transforming his mild face into that of a monster with round glass windows for eyes and a snout like that of a pig. He turned to the spotted dog beside him and the dog, recognizing its cue, barked loudly three times and then, pleased with its performance, wagged its tail. The Major's talk was over; now they could both go home and have supper.

Dupigny, exiled among the British, uttered a sigh and longed to go home, too.

30

HOUSEHOLDERS: No lights showing seaward or upward. Remove bulbs so that your servants cannot put on a light you have considered unnecessary.

MOTORISTS: Headlights and sidelights have got to be darkened. It is the beam that is the danger. A sheet of brown paper entirely covering the whole headlight glass with a double thickness on the top half kills the beam and upward glare but gives a reasonable light on an unlit road. Wind down window before leaving car to prevent glass fragments in a blast.

Now darkness had fallen on Singapore, this first evening of the war in the Far East. While it was still daylight the coming of war had remained difficult to grasp, at least for those who had not been living or working near where the bombs had fallen. Even those who, like Walter, had looked at the roped-off bomb damage in Raffles Place and Battery Road had found it hard to see the rubble as being in any way different from some civilian catastrophe, the exploding of a gas main, say, or one of China-town's periodic tenement conflagrations. But this evening when it grew dark, it grew very dark indeed. The dimming of street lights, the motor-cars creeping along with masked head-lights, the blacked-out shops and bungalows and tenements and street stalls (not perfectly blacked-out, admittedly, because in that sweltering climate windows must be kept open, but still a shocking extinction of light and life) ... all this came as an unpleasant surprise to the city's population, reminding them that History had once more switched its points; this time most abruptly, to send them careering along a track which curved away into a frightening darkness, beyond which lay their destination.

But if the first evening of the war was bad, the second was even worse. The first had been a novelty, at least. People were excited by the prospect of another air-raid. They thought of the Blitz and felt that they were participating at last, that unusual demands were being made on them. But when it grew dark again on the second evening it gradually became clear that this new way of life was not a passing fancy: it had come to stay for as long as it liked and when it would end nobody could say. Walter, who had arrived at Government House in daylight and normality for a conference with the Governor's staff and the Colonial Secretary on the subject of new freight priorities to take effect on the other side of the Causeway, experienced the darkness as a physical shock when his Bentley crept away down the drive once more and out into the shrouded city. Moreover, he was disturbed by what he had just heard for, just as he was on the point of leaving, the Governor, who had not himself taken part in the conference, had asked to see him for a moment.

Walter was no longer as frequent a visitor to Government House as he once had been. In his younger days he had been on more friendly terms with the Governor of the time than he now was with Sir Shenton and Lady Thomas. It was not that he found Sir Shenton Thomas more formal than his predecessors: if anything, it was the reverse. Walter had felt more at ease when the *man* was masked by the dignity and ceremony of the office. Walter and his wife had often been invited to formal dinners at Government House in days gone by. It had not seemed to him in the least unsuitable that the guests on such occasions should be assembled in a respectful herd while waiting for the Governor and his wife to make an entrance; nor that, when the entrance was made and an aide announced 'His Excellency the Officer Administering the Government ...', a regimental band should strike up the National Anthem on the verandah a few yards away. This was exactly what Walter required in a Governor. It did not even seem to him ridiculous, though he would have had to admit that it was ridiculous if you had taxed him with it, that the Governor and his wife, who were followed by a private secretary in a tail-coat with gilt buttons and blue facings, should be presented by the latter to the assembled guests as if they had never met before, although in fact they knew each other quite well. Walter had simply felt that it was *right* to proceed, as they had proceeded, in strict precedence, the Governor having given his arm to one of

238

the ladies, across the marble hall (which he was now treading accompanied only by a secretary) to *The Roast Beef of Old England*. It was the way things *should* be done, because that way it did not matter who the Governor was. He wore his office like a uniform. And he could not give himself airs any more than a uniform could. So Walter thought, glancing for reassurance at the statue of Queen Victoria presented by her Chinese subjects which stood at the end of the hall. That, at any rate, was still unchanged.

He had expected to find the Governor in his office; instead, the secretary led him up the main staircase to the first-floor reception rooms. There he found Sir Shenton standing beside his wife, the pair of them oddly silent, motionless and disaffected in this vast room scattered with crimson sofas and gilt chairs. The room, indeed, was so large that it seemed to dwarf the two small figures. Walter found himself thinking of two weary travellers stranded without explanation in a deserted railway station. They stirred at the sight of Walter's squat, energetic figure and appeared to revive a little.

There was something about the Governor's good looks, or about his voice, or perhaps just about his manner which made Walter feel ill at ease. He was faintly conscious of an effort to make him feel inferior, the slightly patronizing air of the diplomat to the businessman. Or was he just imagining it? Did he have a chip on his shoulder? No doubt it *was* just imagination. Nevertheless, the bristles along his spine began to puff up involuntarily as he advanced, and he thought: 'Who does the *real* work, the work that pays the wages of stuffed shirts like this chump!' Sir Shenton asked him whether he would like a drink and, when he asked for a beer, set off wearily towards a table against one of the distant walls to pour it himself. 'Where on earth are the "boys"?' Walter asked himself, amazed by this lack of circumstance. Meanwhile, he exchanged a few words with Lady Thomas who was enquiring politely after Sylvia and Joan (Walter stared at her suspiciously with his bulging blue eyes, examining her for traces of condescension and trying to make out what she *really* might be thinking) and saying that the Blacketts really must come over one of these days ... 'once everything is back to normal,' she added, smiling bravely. When her husband, looking more exhausted than ever, had trudged back again from a distant part of the room, she said goodbye graciously to Walter and withdrew, leaving the two men alone together. Walter peered with suppressed irritation at the Gov-

239

ernor's handsome features; the blighter looked tired, certainly, but his manner was as urbane as ever. He explained that he had been up most of the night, that he would not keep Walter long, that . . .

At this point he appeared to get stuck, for he paused, his eyes vaguely on Walter's chin, for a considerable time, until even Walter, who was by no means ready to let himself be outstared by this powdered, pomaded, well-tailored but otherwise nugatory symbol of His Majesty's authority in a foreign land, began to grow uneasy. But just as he was about to clear his throat to remind the Governor of his presence he started up again of his own accord, at the same time putting an end to his long contemplation of Walter's chin . . . That, he continued, looking Walter now straight in the eye, he wanted Walter's opinion on how the native communities would respond to 'the current situation' if the Japanese effectively established themselves on the peninsula . . . 'as they look like doing', he added sombrely. He knew, he went on, that Walter kept a close eye on his work force and for that reason had felt that his opinion . . . the opinion not of an office-bound administrator but of a man in daily contact with the people of Malaya . . . would be of particular value.

Walter, by no means sure that this reference to his qualifications as an adviser was not subtly but slightingly intended, followed with a suspicious eye the distinguished figure of the Governor as he retreated a few steps to perch with a weary, languid air on the arm of a chair. Extending a neatly creased trouser leg which terminated in a brilliantly polished shoe, Sir Shenton began to move it back and forth in a very deliberate imitation of a casual manner. However, Walter was obliged to give his attention to the Governor's question which was precisely that which he himself had not ceased to ponder ever since he had learned of Sunday night's air-raid.

'Not to mince matters, sir,' he replied, 'I would expect apathy towards both us and the Japanese until it becomes clear that either one side or the other is likely to get the upper hand. A possible exception, and one in our favour in most cases if not all, would be the politically-minded Chinese. Fortunately, the Japanese are even less popular with them than we are, thanks to their war in China. But as you know, discontent among the Chinese and even the Indians has been increasing steadily over the past four or five years, to judge by strikes . . .'

'Then you take a pessimistic view? Did you read this?'

Walter took the paper which the Governor handed to him. It was the *Order of the Day*, published that morning. '... We are confident. Our defences are strong and our weapons efficient. Whatever our race, and whether we are now in our native land or have come thousands of miles, we have one aim and one only. It is to defend these shores ...' Not knowing quite what was expected of him Walter nodded gravely as he handed the paper back; but this pronouncement, when he had read it earlier, had seemed to him to be futile and inept. It simply served to draw attention to the fact that the different races in Malaya did not have one aim only, however ardently the Administration might wish that they did.

The Governor was evidently satisfied with his nod and did not pursue the matter further. He looked at his watch: the interview was at an end. Walter now found himself obliged to gulp off a large glass of beer while the Governor waited for him, tapping his foot. 'No hurry,' he said, noticing that Walter was becoming breathless, but at the same time stared about the room as if contemplating already the important matter which he would attend to as soon as he had got rid of his guest. Again Walter felt that he was being patronized and wished, having at last drained his glass, that he had simply put it aside with dignity, untouched.

To Walter's surprise, however, the Governor courteously set out with him on the long trek back across the deserted room: this gave him an opportunity to ask if there was any news of the fighting in the north. The Governor replied grimly that he had heard nothing definite, that the Military, as Walter could imagine, were inclined to keep these things to themselves, but that he suspected that they were not very much wiser than he was, as to what was happening. And a grimace of pain passed fleetingly across the Governor's handsome features, for Walter's question had touched on a raw nerve: Sir Shenton had known of the plan to launch an attack over the border into Siam to forestall Japanese landings at Singora and Patani. He had assumed, therefore, that if the Japanese had been obliged to land on Malayan soil at Kota Bahru it was because British troops had denied them Singora and Patani.

But this had proved not to be the case. They had landed successfully at all three places and were threatening not only the difficult and inhospitable east coast but also the fertile and vulnerable west coast. It was the west coast that mattered, after all! But, in theory at least, the Japanese should only be able to get at the vulnerable west coast by using the road from Singora. And on that road defences had been prepared to deal with them, protecting the rich, rice-growing area of Perlis and Kedah, the important aerodrome at Alor Star, a staging post for aircraft reinforcements from Ceylon, and, some way farther south, Penang itself. So a great deal would depend on these defences which had been set up a little to the north of Alor Star, at Jitra.

There did remain, however, just one other way in which the west coast might be threatened: that is to say, along the road from Patani that led through the mountains. Luckily Brooke-Popham and Malaya Command had thought of this and had sent two battalions up the road into Siam to occupy the only defensible position on it (The Ledge) before the Japanese could get there. The Governor was grateful for their foresight because even he, though no military expert, could see that if the Japanese started coming down the road from Patani they would be coming in behind the defences at Jitra and would be able to cut their communications. And if Jitra had to be abandoned, the important aerodrome at Alor Star would be lost, and perhaps even Penang into the bargain.

The two men had reached the door now and had paused on the point of saying goodbye. Or rather, it was the Governor who had paused: in the middle of some valedictory remark he had got stuck again in the contemplation of Walter's chin ... For it seemed to Sir Shenton that, simply stated, the situation was this: if the Ledge went then the Jitra defences would be untenable; if the Jitra defences went then Alor Star would go, too; if Alor Star was lost then Penang and another important aerodrome at Butterworth would be in danger; and if ... but, of course, it had not come to that and the Army was there to see that it never did. Why then had Blackett touched a raw nerve when he had asked for news of the fighting in the north? Precisely because the absence of news was beginning to be a cause for concern. The Japanese had landed at Patani in the early hours of Monday morning. Very well. But it was now Tuesday evening and he had still had no confirmation that the Ledge had been successfully occupied although more than thirty-six hours had elapsed. Sir Shenton did not know off-hand how far it was from the Malayan border to the Ledge but it could hardly be more than fifty miles. And the distance the Japanese would have to travel along that same road from Patani to reach the Ledge would not be much greater. In other words, by now both sides had had ample time to get there. Sir Shenton did not like to admit even to himself the possibility that the Japanese might have got to the Ledge first. Most likely there had been some breakdown in the communications which linked the Army with the Government.

'... For giving up your time. I know how busy you must be at the moment,' he said, concluding an earlier remark and at the same time releasing Walter's chin from his gaze. 'I hope you're doing something about that cough, Blackett,' he added, realizing that for the last few moments Walter had been trying to clear his bronchial tubes. 'They can be the devil even in this climate.' His eyes once more shifted towards Walter's chin as he said vaguely: 'Yes, yes ... A jubilee? What jubilee?'

'Ours, sir ... Blackett and Webb's,' said Walter patiently, but at the same time wondering whether it would be regarded as treason or merely as common assault to knock down His Excellency the Officer Administering the Government; he was also annoyed with himself for having twice in the course of the interview addressed the Governor as 'sir'. 'You and the Colonial Secretary both agreed that it would be of benefit to the morale of the Asiatic communities if we made a bit of a splash with our jubilee. You may remember our slogan: "Continuity in Prosperity" ... Well, I just wanted to reassure you that we would keep steadfastly to our plans regardless of the Jap invasion.'

'That's the ticket, Blackett,' said the Governor with rather hollow enthusiasm. 'That's the spirit. Wish everyone had your ... Well, I must be getting on ...' His eyes settled on Walter's chin again like two butterflies, but just for an instant, then they were away once more, chasing each other this way and that.

'You know, Walter,' he said suddenly and with unexpected warmth, 'we don't see enough of you and Sylvia. We're all too busy, I suppose. What lives we lead! Well, we must make amends one of these days! Goodbye.'

'Thank you, sir. Goodbye.'

'The Governor's not such a bad chap when you get to know him,' Walter was thinking as he descended the staircase, humming *The Roast Beef of Old England*, towards the marble hall. 'Rather out of touch, perhaps.'

31

Walter's more cheerful frame of mind was not fated to last much farther than the drive of Government House: sitting in the back of the Bentley as it crept out into the darkened city he recalled the Governor's distraught air and his mind filled with foreboding. If the Japanese became established on the peninsula, he had said, 'as they look like doing' ...

Slowly they made their way up Orchard Roard in the gloom; the other cars they passed loomed up simply as dark shapes, headlights masked with metal grilles or paper. A steady rain had begun to fall. If it were like this in the north it would not be much fun fighting the Japs in the jungle. The Malay *syce* peered ahead into the darkness through the swirling, flowing windscreen wipers. Walter sighed and sat back, folding his arms impatiently. It irritated him to be driven at this speed: he had a great deal to do. Before he got down to work, however, he must look in at the Mayfair to see whether Matthew was showing any signs of recovery. And that was another important matter which must be seen to: Joan must be married off without any further delay. The many uncertainties which faced international commerce over the next few months and years required that a business should have the strongest foundations. He was fairly confident, however, that Joan could be left to deal with that side of things. It was true that so far, by her own account, she had not made as much progress as either of them would have hoped. At first, as she now admitted herself, she had underestimated the difficulties of attracting a young man like Matthew. For one thing he spent so much time talking about 'unreal things' ... yes, she meant abstract ... that it had been hard to get him to fix his attention on *her* rather than whatever it was that was passing through his mind. Hard, not impossible. Right from the beginning she had noticed him staring at her legs, which was encouraging. 'For another thing,' she had explained to Walter, 'half the time I believe that he can't actually *see* me ... physically, I mean. Which makes things difficult. I often feel like snatching off his spectacles, giving them a good polish, and then putting them back on his nose again. He does *peer* at you terribly! And if he can't see me properly, I have to get him to *touch* me. Fortunately, he seems quite keen on the idea of *that* ... but it's not all that easy to find opportunities. And now he's got this dratted fever just as I was beginning to make some solid progress. Oh, and incidentally, we must send Vera Chiang packing before he's up and about again. She's a distraction. We must keep his mind on *me*. No, Daddy, of course she isn't ... at least, not a serious one.'

Well, so much for Matthew. He would be dealt with. There remained the Japs. It was intolerable that they should have been allowed to land at Kota Bahru. What did the Army think they were up to? Or was it the RAF's fault? His mind went back to the tedious disputes of the previous year between Bond and Babington as to who should be responsible for the defence of Malaya. It had been decided, had it not, that it was to be the RAF's job and that the Army would protect the northern airfields, of which there was one at Kota Bahru, the very place where the Japanese had succeeded in landing! Could it be that the years of endeavour that had gone into the building of Blackett and Webb into a successful enterprise were now to be put at risk by a handful of pig-headed officers and snobbish emissaries of the Colonial Office? 'Thank heaven that at least with the *Prince of Wales* and the *Repulse* in the Straits we have some protection for shipping!'

'Watch, Mohammed!'

The Bentley had braked suddenly, narrowly missing some dim object that had lumbered across its path, perhaps a rickshaw, it was impossible to tell in the swirling darkness. Walter sighed with irritation and his hand closed over the door handle. For a moment he was tempted to step out and finish his journey on foot despite the rain. He mastered his impatience, however, and sat back again.

Well, what of the enemy? Walter knew better than to accept the general view in Singapore that the Japanese were either ridiculous or incompetent. Indeed, the skill with which the Army had gradually tightened its grip on Japan's economy over the past decade was impressive. The policy of girding the economy for war, begun in Manchukuo under the sinister auspices of the South Manchuria Railway Company, had in due course spread back to Japan itself, leaving the *zaibatsu* (the old capitalist groups like Mitsui, Mitsubishi, Yasuda and Sumitomo which now found their enormous shipping, textile and trading industries beginning to flag) to compensate themselves as best they could with increased profits from their munitions and armaments factories. This diversion of resources from the *zaibatsu*, which had become even more pronounced since the beginning of the Sino-Japanese war, had provided Blackett and Webb with some relief in their Far Eastern trade as they struggled to recover from the Depression. Nevertheless, Walter had watched apprehensively the rise of the '*new zaibatsu*', the firms like Mori and Nissan whose fortunes had been derived from the manufacture of armaments and whose future prosperity would depend, perhaps, on the successful use of the weapons they manufactured.

At last the car was edging its way off the road by the dim glow of its masked headlights. They had evidently arrived at the Mayfair. Walter continued to sit huddled in the back of the car, however, while the *syce* groped for his oiled-paper umbrella. Sometimes, in his rare moments of depression, Walter would imagine the whole of Malaya spread out before him with its population of Malays, Indians and Chinese all steadily working away. He would see the rubber and oil-palm plantations, the tin mines and rice fields, combining to produce a strong-flowing river of wealth. Above the mines and plantations, each of which sent its tributary to the main current, he would see a little group of Europeans ... he saw himself and his family, he saw his colleagues from the Singapore Club, the men from Guthrie's and Sime Darby and Harrison's and Crossfield and the Langfields and Bowsers, all of them, the whole pack, he saw the police and the Government and the Military, the Shenton Thomases and Duff Coopers, the Brooke-Pophams and the Bonds and the Babingtons ... he saw them all, herded together in a tiny élite group directing the affairs of the country. And then he would ask himself what would happen if, perhaps, some higher force removed this tiny élite group and replaced it by another ... say, the South Manchuria Railway Company's executives ... Would the Colony then, as one might expect, wither away promptly, like a plant whose head has been cut off, or would it, on the contrary, continue exactly as it had before, producing that steady, strong river of wealth exactly as if nothing had happened? Experience had taught him that the answer which condensed in his mind in response to this question varied according to his frame of mind. Thus it provided him with a useful barometer to his health and spirits.

'You blighters don't know how lucky you are, Mohammed,'

growled Walter to the *syce* as the door beside him opened to the streaming blackness. The *syce*, who was used to having cryptic fragments of Walter's inner debates addressed to him, nodded and smiled politely, holding out the umbrella for Walter to step under and ignoring the rain that hammered on his own unprotected shoulders.

'Why don't they oil that damn thing?' Walter wondered a few moments later, standing in almost total darkness just inside the verandah door. There were distant sounds of movement and a scampering near the floor in the obscurity. He became aware than an animal of some sort was leaning forward to sniff him cautiously. A few seconds passed during which neither Walter nor this creature cared to make a move. Then an electric light was switched on, revealing a large Dalmatian. It wagged its tail briefly and then whisked away into the jungle of rattan furniture. Presently it returned followed by the Major.

'Ah, Major, I see you have a dog.'

The Major, who appeared to have just awoken, stared somewhat dubiously at the Dalmatian and said: 'Actually, it's not mine. It goes home tomorrow with luck.' After a moment he added: 'Watch out, there's another one behind you,' causing Walter to give a violent start; it was true: another shadowy animal had crept out of the furniture and with its head tilted on one side was running its nose over his ankle. It uttered a yelp as Walter aimed a kick at it; then promptly waddled away to take shelter behind the Major. As far as Walter could make out in the dim light it was an elderly and decrepit King Charles spaniel: its coat, which had plainly come under attack from some worm, was in some patches bald, in others matted and filthy; its tail hung out at a drunken angle and was liberally coated in some dark and viscous substance resembling axle-grease.

'I found it here when I got in this evening. Someone had left it tethered to the gatepost, with five dollars and a note. Probably someone who had heard of my lectures. Here, have a look.'

The note, typed with a great number of mistakes and unsigned, declared that the writer had been recalled to Europe at such short notice that he had had no time to settle his affairs. He urged the Major 'as a lover of dogs' to be so kind as to have this one destroyed. The money was enclosed to cover mortuary expenses. A harrowing postscript asserted: 'He was a faithful friend.' As if this were not enough the dog, perhaps divining that its fate was under discussion, set up a doleful whine and turned its bulging, bleary eyes up at the Major.

'It's a bit thick, frankly. I have enough on my plate already without having to deal with this poor little brute,' said the Major gloomily, stooping to tickle the animal behind one cankerous ear.

'Does it have a name?' asked Walter, retreating as the repulsive creature, reassured, made to approach him.

'The note doesn't say. François has taken to calling it "The Human Condition" for some reason. I think he means it as a joke.'

'Well, you'd better have it done away with before it gives us all rabies,' said Walter. He became brisk again: 'I just came to enquire after young Webb. How is he?'

The two men set off down the corridor towards Matthew's room, the Major explaining that since the fever still had not abated they were continuing to give him large quantities of liquid. Dr Brownley was optimistic that the patient would soon be over the worst. The Dalmatian loped cheerfully after them, followed, groaning and gasping, at some distance by The Human Condition.

After a brief look at Matthew, who appeared to be still too busy thrashing and sweating beneath his mosquito net to recognize him, Walter took the Major by the arm for, as it happened, visiting the sick had only been part of his purpose in coming to the Mayfair. He also wanted to discuss Blackett and Webb's jubilee parade with the Major and, if possible, to conscript him to play a more active part in it. 'You'll be lending us a hand, won't you, Major?' he asked with a winning smile, and he went on to emphasize the great importance which the Governor himself was placing on this event, as he happened to know for a fact, just having come this moment from Government House. To cut a long story short Sir Shenton was absolutely relying on this parade to keep up the morale of the Straits Settlements at this dire turning-point in their history ... 'And he expects every one of us, Major, to put his shoulder to the wheel,' he was obliged to add, seeing that the Major was still showing signs of reluctance. Although work on the floats was well in hand there was still a great deal to be done in the way of organization. As soon as Matthew Webb had come to his senses again, every pressure must be exerted on him in order to persuade him to take the place that his father would have occupied had he lived: that is to say, he would have to sit on the throne as the symbol of Continuity and, no less essential, deliver a keynote speech on Prosperity as it affected workers of all races in the Colony.

Since the Major still hesitated and hung back, murmuring that he had a great deal to do in organizing his AFS unit and carrying the burden of his Committee for Civil Defence, Walter launched into an enthusiastic description of the way in which their plans for a parade had evolved into something more impressive: Blackett and Webb's jubilee parade would not only be a patriotic cavalcade of a magnificence rarely seen, it would also be a living diagram, as it were, of the Colony's economy in miniature, since the company was involved at least to some extent in every one of Malaya's principle trading and productive activities (though only indirectly in tin-mining and no longer to a great extent in the entrepôt business) ... 'With the exception of palm-oil,' he muttered as an afterthought, looking uneasy. The Major was surprised to notice the look of uncertainty which passed fleetingly over Walter's commanding features. Walter coughed in a harassed sort of way and scratched the back of his head ... but the next moment he was off again, brimming with confidence as he explained his 'grand design' to the Major.

The old idea, as the Major might remember, had been to have a series of floats depicting Blackett and Webb's commercial ventures, plus a few of the dragons that are *de rigueur* in any Chinese festival, a brass band or two and the usual fireworks. But, one of his brighter young executives had suggested, since the idea of the parade was partly to instruct, should they not broaden their scope in order to include some of the hazards which these commercial ventures had had to overcome, and still *were* having to overcome? A brilliant notion! In this way the idea of a counter-parade to accompany the parade had been born. And so what was now projected was to have Chinese acrobats, schoolboys, and volunteers of all races dress up in appropriate costumes as devils and imps accompanying the main procession, tumbling and turning cartwheels and playing pranks on the crowd, squirting water over them and so forth. Did the Major not think that was an idea of genius? These imps and devils would carry pitchforks to prod maliciously at the characters of Continuity and Prosperity, throwing banana skins in front of them and so on. And, of course, they would wear placards identifying them as the particular enemies of Continuity and Prosperity. Thus there would be imps and devils representing: 'Labour Unrest', 'Rice Hoarding', 'Japanese

Aggression', 'Wage Demands' (what a fearful lot of banana skins this devil would scatter in front of Blackett and Webb's proud floats!), 'Foolish Talk', 'International Communism', 'Fraudulent Accountancy' (a great trick of the Chinese businessman who habitually keeps two sets of books), 'Racial Enmity', 'Corruption and Squeeze', 'Slander Against Government and British Empire', 'Slander Against Private Enterprise', 'Irresponsible Strikes' and many, many more: indeed, there were so many possibilities that they must be careful not to bury the floats completely ... Well, what did the Major think? Would he enter into the spirit of the thing and perhaps wear one of the devils' costumes not yet allocated? Would he mind personifying 'Inflation', for example, which would mean dressing up in a fiery red costume with horns and a tail and lashing about with a tennis ball tied to a stick?

'Well, Walter, I'm not sure that I ...'

'The Governor and Lady Thomas will be personally grateful to you, I happen to know,' said Walter, pressing his advantage as he saw the Major begin to weaken. 'He sets particular store by having a mixture of races. What we must have above all is Europeans! That is crucial to the whole exercise. We've even considered having an additional slogan: *"All in it together!"'*

'Well, I suppose, in that case ...'

'Good man! I knew I could depend on you ... Well, Major, I think it should be a success but sometimes I do have the feeling that there's something missing, that we still need a single float representing Singapore herself. We've thought of all the usual things, the Lion City and so on, but it's weak, it's been done before ... We need to show Singapore in her relationship with the other trading centres of the Far East, holding them in a friendly grip. It's deuced hard to think of anything suitable, I can tell you! All we've managed to think of so far is to have Singapore at the centre of a float as a sort of beneficial octopus with its tentacles in a friendly way encircling the necks of Shanghai, Hong Kong, Bombay, Colombo, Rangoon, Saigon and Batavia. Of course, the snag is that the octopus does not have a very good reputation whereas ...' Walter fell silent.

They were standing in the corridor. From a few feet away they could hear the springs of Matthew's bed as he thrashed and muttered and groaned in his fever. From the dim depths of the floor The Human Condition peered up at Walter in perplexity with its bulging eyes. The Major cleared his throat. 'Forgive me mentioning this, Walter, but I noticed a moment

ago that you had a spot of something yellow on your chin ...
a spot of, well, egg, I suppose.'

'What?' cried Walter, clapping a hand to his chin in horror.

'Oh, it's nothing,' said the Major hurriedly, taken aback by
the effect of his words. 'Just a spot of something ... You can
hardly see it.' Walter spat on a handkerchief and began to rub
his chin violently. Watching him at work the Major could not
help thinking: 'Walter *is* getting rather odd in some ways.'

32

Poor Matthew! What a terrible fever he had to endure! Every
two or three hours he would be roused from his churning
dreams and would find himself surrounded by a circle of
Oriental faces, for Cheong had summoned assistance from his
relatives. Then he would become aware of many hands hoisting
him into the air while other hands dragged away the sodden
sheets and replaced them with dry: these dry sheets would be
wringing wet too, though, within a few moments. At intervals
he would find a glass of cold liquid held to his lips: then he
would gulp for his life, while faces flared up before his eyes.
'Hello you!' said Joan brightly, puffing away at a long cigarette
holder, to be replaced in a moment by Charlie informing him
that there was a huge demand for cheap coolie labour during
the rice-milling season from January to May, or by an unknown doctor, an Englishman wearing a linen jacket and a
striped tie. This man, he found, was talking to him cheerfully
and evidently had been doing so for some time, encouraging
him to swallow some white pills which lay in his yellowish,
horny palm. As Matthew took them the doctor opened his
mouth and gulped sympathetically, as if he too had some pills
to swallow; then, satisfied, he beckoned Cheong forward with
a pitcher of iced lemonade. Matthew gulped down glass after
glass, before sinking back into his dreams ... only to find a
moment later that the Major's worried countenance was looming over him. He could tell by the Major's expression that
something had gone dreadfully wrong. What was it he was
trying to say to Dupigny on the other side of the bed? The
Prince of Wales had called but had been repulsed! Matthew

could just reach consciousness with his fingertips. If he could only drag himself up a little further! 'I had no idea he was even in Singapore,' he just managed to say before losing his grip and tumbling back head over heels into his churning dreams again.

Hours passed. Some time later, in a moment of lucidity which occurred while he was trying to thrash his way out of a net that German spies were throwing over him to prevent him rejoining the League 'somewhere in the Atlantic', Matthew found himself hanging upside down out of bed, neatly trussed up in a cocoon of mosquito netting which he had somehow dragged off its frame. From this odd position he had an excellent view of a number of neatly swept floorboards in diminishing perspective. Standing on these floorboards under the bed was what he at first took to be a chamber-pot ... a moment later he realized that it was simply a basin which had been put there to collect his own sweat which was soaking through the mattress and steadily dripping into it. The basin was already brimming.

A faint clicking sound approached him across the floorboards and suddenly he found that his own eyeballs were a mere inch or two from another pair of eyeballs; these ones, bulging and bleary, were set in the hairy face of a Chinese demon, of a kind he had hitherto only seen sculpted in stone outside temples. Matthew was on the point of howling for Cheong to come and drive off this horrid little creature (it was not exactly sweet-smelling, either) but at this very instant the German spies, one of whom bore a stern resemblance to the portrait of his father in Walter's drawing-room, abruptly caught up with him and he was off again like a hare, twisting now this way, now that. His sweat continued its steady drip, drip, drip through the mattress.

When he finally returned to his senses the fourth day since he had been ill was just beginning. He lay half awake, listening for the drip of sweat beneath the bed. But now the silence, except for a distant creaking from outside the window, was complete. He crumpled the sheets in his fist: they were dry. Thank heaven for that! He wondered how many basins of his sweat had been poured away since his fever had begun; he felt so exhausted that it was as if he himself had been poured away.

The distant creaking, he noticed, was punctuated by an occasional thump. Creak, creak, thump! He dozed for a moment and woke again. Creak, creak, thump! Curiosity at last gave him the strength to make a move. Beside him lay a 'Dutch wife', a long narrow bolster whose purpose was to allow the air to circulate: he fought with it weakly and at last overcame it. Then with great difficulty he negotiated the fish's gill exit from the mosquito net. The window shutters were open and he could see that it was already growing light in the compound outside. Somewhere on the other side of the house the sun must be just rising. It was pleasantly cool by the window.

The creaking was coming from the clearing beside the recreation hut where the abandoned vaulting-horse stood with its companion, a big horizontal bar tethered by rusting guy-ropes. A slender girl who appeared to be Chinese was swinging by her hands from this bar, attempting by a sudden kick and a stiffening of her arms at the elbow to bring her waist up to it. (Did she have red hair or was that just a glint of sunrise?) But what caused Matthew to blink and wonder whether this was still part of his feverish fantasy, now taking a more agreeable turn, was the fact that she appeared to be stark naked.

He scratched his head and set off in search of spectacles, but it was some time before he managed to find them: Cheong, afraid that he might damage them in his delirium, had removed them to a place of safety. He crammed them on and hurried back to the window just in time to see the girl (Vera! Good gracious! Naked!) at last succeed in bringing her shoulders above the bar. She steadied herself there for a moment, recovering from the effort she had made. In the early light her skin shone greenish-white against the dark foliage around her.

Matthew now realized that he was not the only spectator of this scene, for an elderly orang-utan with elaborate mutton-chop whiskers lay sprawled in a rubber tree on the edge of the glade watching the girl's gymnastics. And while it watched her it distractedly ate an apple, holding it up from time to time for inspection and meanwhile drumming absent-mindedly with the fingers of its other hand on its pale, bulging paunch. Still supporting her weight on her straightened arms, her body curved in a slim crescent, Vera managed to hook one leg over the bar and then, with more difficulty, the other, so that at last she sat precariously on top of it, hands between her thighs gripping the bar tightly to steady herself. When she was satisfied with her balance she let go of the bar with her hands, raised them above her head like a diver and threw herself backwards.

The orang-utan, on the point of taking a bite of apple, paused with its mouth open to watch the outcome of this reckless manoeuvre. The girl's flexed knees were still bent over the bar as she swung down through three-quarters of a circle trailing a stream of red-black hair behind her. Reaching the top of the arc she released the bar by straightening her legs, dropped to all fours on the grass, staggered a little, recovered her balance, stood up on tip-toe and marched smartly forward for three or four paces before returning to lean wearily against one of the perpendicular supports. Knitting its ginger brows the orang-utan returned its attention to the apple and, having smoothed its mutton-chop whiskers, took a bite.

Vera had her back to the orang-utan and perhaps had not seen it. She was leaning all her weight on the upright as if punting a boat and her chin rested charmingly on her raised arm. The orang-utan paused again in its eating and watched her. Then, holding the apple core delicately by its stalk in the fingers of its left hand it slipped from the branch on which it had been sitting, hung from it revolving by one finger for a few moments, then dropped silently to the ground. Now it hesitated for a moment, clearly in two minds as how best to proceed. It scratched its head, fingered the ginger hair that sprouted between its eyes, and at last began to move circumspectly towards the girl. Matthew watched as if in a dream (perhaps he was indeed in a dream).

She remained in exactly the same position, resting, lost in thought. The orang-utan moved towards her using the knuckles of its right hand to assist its progress, still holding the apple core in the other. Matthew would have called out but his vocal chords had ceased to work; besides, the animal did not appear aggressive in the least. As it drew near Vera another access of doubt overcame it. It halted, it looked around and rubbed its stomach dubiously, it plucked a blade of grass and threw it away. At length, however, it could wait no longer and, taking another step or two forward, it reached out to place one timid, hairy hand on the girl's naked bottom. Without turning she slapped the hand smartly. The orang-utan sprang back, shocked, and returned in haste to its rubber tree. There it set about nibbling with renewed energy at the apple core until presently there was nothing left of it but an inch of stalk which it threw away.

Vera, meanwhile, had turned and seen the pale and haggard Matthew watching her from the window. She waved. For a moment she seemed about to shout something to him but thought better of it, smiled, shook her head, picked up a white bath-robe which she threw over her shoulder and walked away from the house, shaking her finger at the orang-utan as she passed. The orang-utan watched her glumly from the tree.

Before she was quite out of Matthew's line of vision she threw the robe away again, poised for a moment, and then plunged forward headlong over the brilliant viridian lawn ... which here astonishingly turned out to be water, for she landed with a great green splash and the lawn rippled about her in every direction and even lapped the edge of the tennis court. A moment later she had vanished from sight altogether and though Matthew waited by the window in case she should re-appear there was no further sign of her.

Matthew left the window in a state of considerable excite-ment, not because he believed what he had just seen with his own eyes, but, on the contrary, because he was inclined to doubt it. Like everyone else he had, in his time, enjoyed a fair number of sexual dreams. Could it simply be another of these? The orang-utan, a clear symbol of male sexuality, had very likely been furnished by his own sub-conscious. The only trouble with this theory was that when he looked out of the window the symbol was still there, sprawled in the rubber tree and once more drumming idly with its fingers on its bulging abdomen ... but never mind, there was no reason why it should not linger after the main vision had evaporated. He began to stride up and down, although rather weakly because of his state of exhaustion, discussing aloud with himself the implications of the strange hallucination from which he had just emerged. He must remember to mention it to Ehrendorf. No doubt the fever had heightened his sensibility, made porous the outer brickwork of his conscious mind!

Presently, though, he found himself climbing weakly back through the slit in his mosquito net, assisted by Cheong who was cooing reprovingly in Hokkien (or in Cantonese, for all Matthew knew), convinced that he had struggled out of bed in his delirium. And Matthew himself was obliged to conclude as he fell asleep again that his fever, far from subsiding, had perhaps taken a graver though not altogether unpleasant turn. But now he dreamed vividly that an old gentleman with a white beard was throwing a net over him: and he made such a good job of trussing Matthew up that for the next few hours he lay there unconscious, hardly moving a muscle. This un-natural stillness puzzled Cheong who looked in on Matthew from time to time throughout the day. But then, with 'foreign devils' one never knew what to expect: they were doubtless constructed on different principles from normal, beardless, small-nosed, odourless human beings like himself.

Cheong's father and two uncles had been shipped to Singapore as indentured coolies before the turn of the century in conditions so dreadful that one of the uncles had died on the way; his father had survived the voyage but the memory of it had haunted him for the rest of his life. He had transmitted his anger to Cheong, describing to him how agents had roamed the poverty-stricken villages of South China recruiting simple peasants with promises of wealth in Malaya together with a small advance payment (sufficient to entangle them in a debt they would be unable to repay if they changed their minds), then delivered them to departure-camps known as 'baracoons'; once there they were entirely in the power of the entrepreneur for use as cargo in his coolie-ships (each person allotted, as a rule, a space of two feet by four feet for a voyage that might take several weeks). No wonder Cheong was angry when he thought of how these simple people had been swindled and abused, of the thousands who had died like his uncle from illness or by suicide before reaching Malaya and beginning their years of servitude! But what affected him more deeply still was the knowledge that so few people in the Chinese communities of Malaya and Singapore now seemed to remember or care about the exploitation and suffering of their ancestors on these criminal voyages. These things must not be forgotten! Justice demanded that they should be known. With this in mind he had taken in the past few months the first laborious steps in educating himself at a night-school in the city, helped oddly enough by old Webb who had once, as it happened, shipped coolies himself, though only as deck-cargo with the other commodities in which he traded.

'How strange these people are!' he thought, looking at Matthew's immobile form.

'My dear chap, the way the war is going could hardly be better for us! There is no doubt about it. This time the Japanese have bitten off more than they can chew!'

It was the Major, standing beside Matthew's bedside with a cheerful expression on his normally anxious face, who had just made this confident assertion. Matthew had just woken feeling much better after his long sleep. Dr Brownley had had a look at him and pronounced himself satisfied: another day or two's rest and he should be back on his feet again. However, Dr Brownley had taken the Major aside on his way out to whisper one or two additional comments. He explained that a patient can suffer a serious depression after such a high fever: the system has to recover from the shock imposed upon it. Well, he happened to know that Matthew was a young man of great sensibility, excitable, given to sudden impulses. He did not, of course, consider it likely that Matthew, on hearing the news of the last few days, would snatch up a razor and cut his throat. There was, fortunately, no prospect of his doing anything so foolish (though it would probably be as well not to leave any sharp instruments lying about). It was simply that having just emerged from a debilitating illness a young man who, unlike himself and the Major, had been spared some of the buffets of life, was more likely to take things to heart which a more seasoned campaigner would shrug off without a second thought. For this reason the Major's tone was cheerful as he recounted the reverses of the past few days.

Matthew listened in some surprise, first to the Major's re-assuring description of the first Japanese air-raid on Singapore, which had barely disturbed the slumbers of those living near where the bombs had fallen, then to his account of Japanese landings at Kota Bahru and elsewhere: where the latter were concerned the Major could inspire himself directly from the sedative communiqués issued by General Headquarters and did not have to fumble for words. So things were going along splendidly on that front but there was even better news to come! The Major, becoming more pleased than ever with the way things were going, explained that after the *Prince of Wales* and the *Repulse* had been sunk off the east coast a remarkably large ...

'Sunk!' cried Matthew, lifting his large fist and waving it as if ready to fell the Major, not out of hostility but out of a need for a physical expression of his excitement, and at the same time rolling his eyeballs in a way which gave the Major to believe that perhaps his precautions in the breaking of bad news had not been exaggerated.

'Sunk! But that's dreadful! Our most modern battleship and cruiser ...'

The actual sinking of these two capital ships, the Major agreed hastily, was not altogether good news, but what he had been going to say was that a remarkably large proportion of

257

the officers and ratings of the two ships had been saved, some two thousand men.

'But surely, the Japanese Navy isn't . . .'

'It wasn't their Navy. It seems they were sunk by torpedo-bombers. But the thing is that . . .' The Major paused, unable to think what the thing was. There was no disguising the fact that this was a terrible blow. Without those two powerful ships, and taking into account the loss of the American Pacific fleet at Pearl Harbor, the Japanese would have control of the South China Sea, and perhaps even of the Indian Ocean as well. The Australian and Dutch Navies surely had nothing to challenge them.

'But what was the RAF doing?' demanded Matthew, sinking back weakly against his pillow, extenuated by this sudden surge of emotion. The Major made no reply however, and silence fell. It was very hot in the room. The shutters were partly closed for the sake of the black-out (or 'brown-out'); the only illumination came from a bedside lamp whose shade had been swathed by Cheong in heavy cloth so that it shed an oblique light against the wall. At the edge of this pool of light a tiny brown lizard of the kind known as a 'chichak' had stationed itself on the wall, motionless, its fat little legs flexed like those of a Japanese wrestler. Presently it emitted an oddly metallic clicking sound and the Major explained that the Malays believed that chichaks brought good luck to the houses where they appeared and that, moreover . . . He sighed and silence fell again.

'What's that noise?'

A roaring sound had begun outside and was steadily increasing in volume.

'It's just the rain,' said the Major, wondering how the rest of the British warships might be faring in the wet darkness. It was on just such a night as this, in April 1905, that Admiral Rozhdestvensky and his forty-five elderly, barnacle-clad Russian warships and supply ships had steamed in a tepid downpour through the Straits of Malacca on their long journey from the Baltic, too late to lift the siege of Port Arthur, aware that they were hopelessly outclassed by the Japanese fleet. What brave men, all the same! Sent to the other end of the world by the incompetents in the Ministry in St Petersburg; with crews untrained in war manoeuvres; without enough ammunition to practise gunnery; obliged to coal at sea as often as not for lack of a neutral anchorage that would accept them; continually obliged to stop as the engines of one ship after another broke down; and at the end of their long voyage only the prospect of being sent to the bottom by the superior Japanese fleet. The capture of Port Arthur and the Russian naval defeat at Tsushima, the Major reflected, should have been a warning not to underestimate the Japanese.

'François had gone up to Penang for a few days. He may have some news of how things are going in the north when he gets back.'

'Just listen to the rain!'

Now another grim possibility had occurred to the Major: if the Japanese Navy did get control of the Straits there would be nothing to prevent them landing troops behind the British lines at any point they wished. No doubt there were fixed defences already established at the most vulnerable places, but with such a long coastline to defend it was bound to be difficult. Still, they had the RAF to reckon with.

Now from another part of the house there came the plaintive cry of the door's rusty hinges and, a moment later, voices on the verandah.

'I wonder who that can be? I'd better go and see.' The Major stood up.

'Enter two drowned rats,' laughed Joan, putting her head round the door before the Major could reach it. 'We were halfway through the compound when it started to come down in torrents. It's no good trying to shelter, either. You get just as wet standing under a tree.'

Matthew and the Major stared at her in wonder. Her hair had turned a shade or two darker and stuck to her forehead and cheeks in wet ringlets: water was still gleaming on her neck while her sodden dress clung to her so intimately that one could make out on her heaving chest the two little studs of her nipples and the flutter of her diaphragm where the ribs parted: evidently she had been running.

'Come and sit down,' said the Major genially. 'But I can only see one drowned rat. Where's the other?'

Matthew smiled wanly at Joan as she came to sit beside him, clearly not in the least abashed to be seen in wet and semi-transparent clothing. Indeed, she was positively sparkling with health and high spirits after sprinting through the downpour. 'How attractive she is!'

'The other is Papa. He's just gone to get a towel from the "boy". But here he comes now.'

Walter, too, seemed to be in exceptionally good spirits, as if the sudden downpour had revived him. Of late he had a careworn air, as if his manifold responsibilities were at last beginning to get the better of him: he had begun to hesitate in a way he had never done before, to speculate too exhaustively about the possible consequences of his decisions. The absence of old Mr Webb's strong character in the background, the uncertainty which clouded the political future of the Colony, the blunder he had made over those huge stocks of rubber he had waiting on the quays, all these matters had combined to sap his strength of purpose. But Walter was not the sort of man who could be kept down for very long. What were all these difficulties but the biggest challenge he had had to face since the Depression? Having decided to define his problems as a challenge he found that a weight had been lifted from his mind. Now he stood there laughing, his stocky figure radiating energy, quite oblivious of the puddle of water which had formed around his shoes. Snatching up a rattan chair he set it down by Matthew's bedside saying:

'Soaked to the skin! That's what comes of trusting your daughter, Major. Well, Matthew, you look a hundred per cent better ... You've lost a bit of weight, perhaps, but there's no harm in that for a man of your size ...' And on he went, his voice reverberating confidently above the roar of rain drumming on the roof.

Matthew and the Major stared at him, hypnotized. The Major, who had become accustomed to seeing Walter despondent or full of bitter nostalgia for the old days, was delighted to see the change that had come over him. Matthew lay back against his pillows looking somewhat bewildered but pleased that everyone should be in such a good mood despite the sinking of the *Prince of Wales* and the *Repulse*.

'Now, my boy,' said Walter affably, 'these are momentous days we're living through and it's time we had a serious discussion about what's to become of you. No, now wait a jiffy, you'll have your chance to say your piece in a moment. What I want to say is this ... Now that your poor father is no longer with us I feel I have a special responsibility not just to my own family but to you as well ... Well, m'lad, I've had my eye on you and if you don't mind me saying so it's become pretty clear to me that you've taken a bit of a shine to my daughter Joan here and, frankly, young man, I can't say I blame you because she's a good young woman even if she does get her old Papa soaked to the skin from time to time, ha! ha! ... and, between you and me, half the young fellows in Singapore are after her ...'

'But, Walter! Well, I mean, good heavens ... !' cried Matthew and began to struggle agitatedly with his sheet and the 'Dutch wife' and a fold of the mosquito net which had come adrift, as if he meant to spring out of bed and start pacing up and down. The Major, indeed, jumped up to restrain him, very concerned by the stare of excitement in which the patient had been thrown by Walter's curious preamble about his daughter. But the Major's intervention was not needed for Matthew had somehow got himself so entangled in his sheet that in his weakened state he could scarcely move and presently subsided again.

Walter, meanwhile, ignoring this commotion, held up his hand and, nodding towards his daughter, went on steadily: 'And she, if I'm not talking out of turn, has a bit of a soft spot for you. Isn't that right, m'dear? Well, in these circumstances I think that there's only one course for sensible people to take ... And I think we all know what *that* is! There now, I've said my party piece.' Walter sat back, thoroughly satisfied with the way the interview was going.

'But Mr Blackett ... That's to say, Walter ...' exclaimed Matthew, still bound to the bed by the folds of his sheet but rolling his eyeballs excitedly. 'What can I say? I mean, I'm certainly very fond of Joan, that's true, but never for a minute ... I mean, such an idea has never even ... but perhaps I've got the wrong end of the stick ... Well, I simply don't know what to say.' He gazed at his companions, quite overwhelmed by this unexpected development. Once again it seemed to him that reality had taken a dream-like turn, for while Walter had been making his extraordinary speech Cheong had stolen up behind him with a towel and had set to work, his face perfectly impassive, briskly rubbing down Walter's head and patting his pink, commanding cheeks, so that an occasional word here and there in Walter's discourse had been muffled by a thickness of towel, causing Matthew to be not altogether sure that Walter *was* saying what he appeared to be saying. When Cheong had finished with Walter he started to rub no less briskly at Joan's damp ringlets, but after a moment she motioned him away.

Although Joan had not assented very vigorously when her father had declared that she had a 'soft spot' for Matthew (instead she had gazed calmly at the floor where another puddle was beginning to form between her feet) neither had she uttered any word that might be interpreted as a disclaimer. Now, when she spoke, it was merely to ask, looking round: 'Has the "boy" gone? If so, I'm going to take off this wet dress if you don't mind. You don't mind, do you, Papa?'

'I don't mind in the least, m'dear, but you'd better ask these gentlemen ... though I'm sure they're men o' the world enough not to mind seeing a fat little piglet like you in your underwear ... You don't mind, do you, Major?'

'Oh, me? Not at all, not at all,' mumbled the Major, laughing and clearing his throat; and he puffed with embarrassment at his pipe, stopping and unstopping its bowl with two fingers to make it draw. He might have been thinking, as he cast a hasty, sidelong glance at Joan's agreeable figure, that even with advancing years a man might still be troubled by thoughts of ... well, never mind ... who knows what he was thinking as he puffed at his pipe, for presently he had disappeared into a blue haze of tobacco smoke?

As for the patient, despite his weakened condition and his confused state of mind, his eyes wandered appreciatively over Joan's gleaming skin as she stepped out of her sodden dress and he seemed to be thinking: 'Well, a body's a body, for all that,' or something of the sort.

'You don't mind, Papa,' asked Joan, smiling mischievously, 'if I climb into bed beside Matthew until the rain stops? I'll be much more comfortable. We can have the "Dutch wife" between us.'

'Oh, the little rascal,' chuckled Walter. 'Oh, the little hussy! What d'you think of that, Major? And before her own father's very eyes! And *what*, I should like to know, young lady, would your mother say if she could see you now?' And while Joan hung her dress on a coat-hanger to dry before climbing into bed Walter beamed at Matthew more expansively than ever. 'Well, there you are, my boy,' he seemed to be saying. 'There are the goods. You won't find better. You can see for yourself. It's a good offer. Take it or leave it.'

Presently, when the rain had stopped, Walter and Joan made their way back through the compound beside pools of rainwater which were now reflecting the stars. Father and daughter did not speak as they made their way through the drenched garden but they did not have to: they understood each other perfectly. Abdul, the old major-domo, was waiting for them, concerned that they should have got such a soaking.

'What news, Master?'

'Good news, Abdul!' replied Walter in the conventional manner, but as he went upstairs to change his clothes he thought: 'Yes, good news!'

33

'Well, I suppose it *might* be true,' the Major was saying doubtfully. 'One never knows. I was in Harbin in 1937 and there was still a lot of White Russians there at the time. A lot of the poor devils were starving, too.'

The Major and Matthew were sitting in the office which had once been old Mr Webb's. Matthew, drained of all energy, had at last managed to leave his bed and drag himself as far as his father's desk where he sat drowsing over an untidy pile of reports, accounts and miscellaneous papers concerning the rubber industry. The Major, filled with concern by the young man's sombre and listless frame of mind, attempted from time to time to engage him in cheerful conversation. But these days what was there to be cheerful *about*? Only the subject of Vera Chiang had aroused a tiny spark of interest in the patient: Matthew had remembered a dream conversation between Vera and Joan in which Vera had claimed that her mother was a Russian princess and her father a Chinese tea-merchant ... or something of the sort. What did the Major think of it? The Major, it turned out, had heard the same story from Vera with one or two added details and had politely suspended disbelief. After all, far-fetched though it sounded, one never knew. Stranger things had happened in that part of the world in the last few years.

'By the way, where is she? I thought she was supposed to have a room here still.'

'One of Blackett and Webb's vans came to pick up her belongings the other day. Not that they needed a van, mind you. There was only a small bag and a parcel or two. I gather Walter wanted her moved out for some reason, he didn't say why. But she's a friendly sort of girl and I expect she'll look in to say hello one of these days.' The Major stood up. 'I must go and do some work. Monty said he'd be dropping in to see you presently.'

Matthew had begun to drowse over his papers once more when Monty suddenly appeared.

'Congratulations,' he said. Monty was looking preoccupied for some reason.

'How d'you mean?'

'Well, I hear you and Joan are thinking of teaming up.'

'Oh, it hasn't quite come to that, has it? I mean, I know your father did say something the other night about it being a good idea, or something on those lines. But I don't think anything, well, *definite* was decided, you know ... At least that was my impression. After all ...'

But Monty merely shrugged; he did not seem particularly interested in the matter. He said vaguely: 'I expect I got hold of the wrong end of the stick ... But from what they've been saying I thought they were planning a wedding ... You know, bridesmaids and all that rubbish.' Monty collapsed into a chair and put his feet up on Matthew's desk, upsetting a tumbler full of pencils as he did so but making no effort to gather them up again. 'I suppose this means you aren't going to want to come in with me and the other two chaps in sharing this Chinese filly,' he said morosely, 'that, is, if you and Joan *are* teaming up. It's going to make it damned expensive for the rest of us,' he added accusingly.

'But Monty ...'

'The other two are regular fellows. Great sports. And it's not as if there were enough white women to go round (if there were I'd tell you). I don't suppose you know that there's only one to every fifty white blokes.'

'I told you ages ago, Monty, that I wasn't interested. It's not my cup of tea.'

'Oh, all right, all right. Don't go on about it. It doesn't matter to me whether you come in or not, though you'll be missing a splendid opportunity. That's your look-out, though.' Monty sighed heavily. 'I really came over to explain about the replanting of rubber trees on your Johore estate. The Old Man said I ought to keep you in the picture though you're probably not interested. The answer is simply that it's more profitable to replant now than to go on tapping.'

'But how can it be? I thought there was someone clamouring for every scrap of rubber we produce.'

'It's to do with the excess profits tax ... You don't want me to go into it, do you?'

But Matthew evidently did want him to, and so, with a much put-upon air, Monty removed his feet from the table and began to explain. When the war had broken out in 1939 a sixty per cent excess profits tax had been slapped on all sterling companies either at home or abroad. Blackett's hadn't minded too much at first. Propitious years, as far as they were concerned, had been chosen for the calculation of 'standard profits'. 'We found we could still keep our hands on a satisfactory chunk of the profits. All well and good. But then I'll be damned if they don't increase the excess profits tax to one hundred per cent! Can you beat it?' Monty, his eyes blue and bulging like his father's, stared at Matthew in disgust.

At the same time the price of rubber had risen and more of it could be released under the Restriction Scheme. 'The next thing we find is that we can make the bloody "standard profits" (all we're allowed, the British Government confiscating the rest) by producing a *smaller amount of rubber* than we're actually allowed to release to the market! Can you beat it? What's the point in producing more when we don't make any profit by doing so?'

Monty's gaze had momentarily become troubled for, although on the whole he believed he did understand his father's commercial strategy (and admired it, too, his father was hot stuff when it came to spotting opportunities), there was one of Walter's initiatives for which a sound commercial reason had so far eluded him: the signing of contracts with the Americans, for huge quantities of rubber for which no shipping could be found. The accumulation for this rubber on the quays directly contradicted, as far as Monty could see, the other policy of not producing rubber from which no profit could be made. The excess profits tax would apply just as much to the American contracts. It was a mystery which Monty could not explain ... though there must be an explanation. Monty had even, for want of anything better, come close once or twice to suspecting his father of patriotism. But no, it surely could not be that. He had, of course, asked Walter for an explanation, but he had shown signs of extreme exasperation and had declined to reply. However, the truth was at last beginning to dawn on Monty in the past few days following the Japanese attack. It was a terrible truth, if Monty had guessed correctly, but was there any other explanation? Walter, in his omniscience, had foreseen the Japanese attack. More than that, he had foreseen the capture of

Malay or destruction of Singapore. He was actually wagering on the capture or destruction of all that rubber and planning to demand compensation from the Government in some more healthy part of the world! True, this did seem, even to Monty, an extravagant wager, but what other reason could there be? His father never did anything in business without a sound reason.

'Anyway,' he said, returning his attention to Matthew, 'we decided that the only sensible thing to do was to replant ... Why? Because replanting expenses are allowable against tax.'

'Even if it means replanting perfectly healthy and productive trees!' exclaimed Matthew.

'Certainly! Because we're replanting them with these newly developed clones I was telling you about. When they're mature in a few years time they'll produce almost twice as much per tree.'

'But what about the War Effort? Everyone's crying out for rubber *now* not in a few *years'* time. And we're cutting down the trees that produce the stuff and planting seedlings in their place. And we aren't even slaughter-tapping, as far as I can make out! It's madness.' Casting off his apathy Matthew had sprung to his feet and now gripped Monty's arm with one hand and the lapels of his jacket with the other. Monty uttered a hoarse cry of alarm and flinched away under this onslaught, convinced that he was about to be assaulted by Matthew whose reason clearly swung on very fragile hinges. Monty was not surprised: he had suspected as much for some time. Next time he would see to it that his father dealt with this madman.

'Well, it wasn't my idea,' he murmured soothingly. 'Don't blame me. You'll have to take it up with Father, though I must say ...' he added more confidently as Matthew released him and began to pace up and down the room, waving one fist certainly, but otherwise not looking so dangerous, '... that I really don't think you should take this pious attitude the whole time. People don't go in for that sort of thing out here. As a matter of fact, they think it's deuced odd, if you want to know. But of course, you must suit yourself,' he went on hurriedly, as Matthew turned towards him once more.

'But it's not that, Monty ... it's a matter of principle.'

'Yes, yes, of course it is,' agreed Monty. 'Anyway, I must be on my way now. I've a lot to do. You don't want to change your mind about that Chinese girl ... No, no, I can see you don't. It's quite all right. Well, goodbye!' And Monty beat a hasty retreat, thankful to have escaped without any broken bones.

Matthew sank back into his chair, exhausted once more. He poured himself a drink of iced water from the vacuum flask on his desk and gulped it quickly; he must soon have a talk with Walter and try to persuade him to stop all this ridiculous re-planting. How much had already been carried out? He searched in vain among the papers on his desk but he could not find the figures he wanted before lethargy once more stole over him. With an effort he roused himself and went outside to the tin-roofed garage where the Major was performing a laborious inspection of the trailer-pump. He intended to discuss the re-planting issue with the Major and installed himself in the Major's open Lagonda nearby: but the heat and his lassitude were too much for him and soon he was drowsing again with his feet poking out of the open door while the Major inspected and cleaned the pump's sparking-plugs. The Major suspected that it would not be very long before this machine found itself in service. Meanwhile, The Human Condition, diminutive, elderly and frail, dozed perilously under one wire-spoked wheel of the motor-car which was on a slight gradient and might decide to roll forward at any moment, putting an end to its miseries.

The Major was thinking of Vera Chiang as he worked, and of Harbin in 1937. 'How hard life can be for refugees!' he mused, squinting at a sparking-plug (his eyesight was no longer what it had been). 'We don't realize in our own comfortable, well-ordered lives what it must be like to lose everything in one of these political upheavals that bang and clatter senselessly round the world like thunderstorms uprooting people right and left.' He sighed and the sparking-plug which lay in his palm grew blurred and changed into a picture of Harbin ... what was it? ... four, no, five years ago almost. Harbin had surely been one of the most depressing places on earth.

That had been on the Major's first trip out East ... when he had suddenly, on an impulse, decided to give up the settled, comfortable life he was leading in London and see the world, visit François in Indo-China, visit Japan, too, and see what all the fuss was about ... see what life itself was all about before it was too late and old age descended on him. You might have thought that Harbin was a Russian city from the great Ortho-dox cathedral towering over Kitaiskaya and Novogorodnaya Street, and from the Russian shop-signs you saw, the vodka, the samovars, the Russian cafés and the agreeable sound of the

Russian language being spoken everywhere. But it was a Russian city which had turned into a nightmare of poverty for the White Russians who had been washed eastwards on the tidal wave of the Revolution. How helpless they were! How few human beings, the Major thought with a sigh, can exert by hard work, thrift, intelligence or any other virtue the slightest influence on their own destiny! That was the grim truth about life on this planet.

Until Manchukuo had bought the Chinese Eastern Railway from the Soviet Government the year before the Major's visit, there had at least been a large contingent of Soviet railway employees in Harbin to patronize the Russian shops and cafés, but by the time he had arrived even this flimsy economic support had been pulled from under the refugees. The railwaymen had returned to Russia, leaving the refugees to destitution. At one time there had been 80,000 of them; by the time the Major had arrived this number had dwindled by half. Those young and strong enough had gone south to look for some means of support in a China which was itself ravaged by famine and bandit armies. Those who stayed in Harbin very often starved. The Major himself had seen ragged white men pulling rickshaws in Harbin.

Vera Chiang had spent her childhood and adolescence in Harbin: that much was certainly true for when the Major had questioned her about it she had known every corner of the city. Her mother had died there, 'of a broken heart', she said sometimes; 'of TB' she said at others. She had only been a child then. Her father had gone south to try to establish another business to replace the one he had lost in the Revolution in Russia, leaving her in a school run by American missionaries. Thus she had learned to speak English. How sad and lonely she had been! she had told the Major with a tear sparkling in her eye, while the Major murmured comfortingly; he had never been able to resist a woman in distress. But how much worse her life had become when a message, long-delayed, had reached her from her father. He was lying ill, broken by poverty, in Canton. 'Selling the last of my mother's rings I set out . . .' Easily affected by feminine distress though he was, the Major had been assailed by misgivings at this point . . . But still, one never knew. One thing was certain: you had to account for Vera Chiang *somehow*! Her Russian recollections were not very convincing, though. Furs, and icicles on window-panes, and snow on the rooftops, steam hanging in the 'biting air' from the horse's nostrils, and jewels winking at the throat of the noble-women who had leaned over her cot, for she had been a baby at the time of the Revolution, of course, the sleigh's runners hissing in the snow as they glided east to escape the Bolsheviks, her own little black almond-shaped eyes completely surrounded by fur, gazing out over the interminable, frozen wastes of Russia. That sort of thing. It was not impossible, of course. Above all, it was the mother's rings that made the Major uneasy. The reason was this. In a Shanghai nightclub the Major had found himself talking to one of the hostesses, a beautiful Russian girl, also a princess, who after one or two decorous waltzes had confessed her predicament to him: the following morning, as soon as the pawnbroker's shop opened for business, she would have to pawn her mother's wedding ring in order to prevent her younger sister from selling herself as a prostitute. Good gracious! What a business! What could the Major do but try to help avert this calamity? Well, you see, the Major's dilemma was that *sometimes these stories were true*. Not very often, perhaps, but *sometimes*.

The Major had frozen into an attitude of despair, staring unseeing at the sparking-plug in his hand. Perhaps sensing that his thoughts had taken a bleak turn, The Human Condition left its perilous couch under the wheel of the Lagonda and crept over to lean its chin on his shoe, revolving its bulging eyeballs upwards to scan the Major's gloomy features. Could it be that the Major was brooding over the best way to have a dog done away with? But no, the Major was still thinking of refugees, this time of those who had managed to escape from Harbin, moving south to where there were other cities with foreign concessions, to Tientsin and farther, to Shanghai. But even in Shanghai there were many Russians who found themselves starving side by side with the most wretched of Chinese coolies, obliged to sleep on the streets or in the parks through the bitter Chinese winter, candidates to join the grim regiment of 'exposed corpses'. These gaunt scarecrows for a few years had haunted the foreign concessions. But time is cruel: people get shaken down into a society or shaken out. History moves on and the problem gets solved, one way or another, without regard to our finer feelings.

And Vera? Her father, she said, had had a stroke and was half paralysed. She had gone to Canton to support him as best she could (the Major had tactfully refrained from asking how). They were in destitution. Presently he had died and she had moved on to Shanghai. She had lived there for a couple of years until there had been some trouble with a Japanese officer. Then, with the help of some friends, she had come here to Singapore.

Well, was she indeed the daughter of a Russian princess and a Chinese tea-merchant? Was it likely that a Russian princess would marry a Chinese tea-merchant? No, but many strange alliances had been bonded in the bubbling retort of the Revolution in its early years. Vera, now in her early twenties, would be just about the right age, certainly, to be the product of such a desperate union. In Harbin, he recalled, it had been a common sight to see young women of noble blood sweeping out the Russian shops on Novogorodnaya Street or waiting at café tables beneath the inevitable, gradually yellowing portrait of the last Tsar. In such desperate circumstances people will do whatever is necessary to survive. Moreover, as the circumstances grew more desperate it had turned out, like it or not, that an attractive Russian girl, princess or dairy-maid, had at least *something* to sell ... if only herself. In Harbin, he had heard, British and American visitors were sometimes approached by destitute Russians inviting them to abscond with the wives they could no longer support. The Major himself had been approached in that nightmare city by a young Russian girl in rags, anxious to exchange the use of her body for a meal. He sighed. Sometimes in Harbin he had wished he had never left London; if this was what finding out about 'life' entailed he would rather have remained in ignorance.

In Shanghai things had not been quite so bad. Attractive Russian girls could do better there, it transpired, because white taxi-girls were very popular with wealthy Chinese and could earn a reasonable living in the city's dance-halls and cabarets. They earned, he had been told, two Chinese dollars commission on every bottle of champagne they sold. Moreover, in the brothels of Shanghai, while a Chinese girl was available from one Chinese dollar upwards, the minimum price for a white girl had been ten dollars. And for the princely sum of fifty dollars, so the Major had been informed on good authority, you could have a nude dance performed in the privacy of your own home or hotel room, by six Russian girls. The Major, despite the urgings of his informant, had not been tempted: it was not that he had been daunted by the expense; it was simply that he could not visualize himself cloistered in his hotel room with six naked White Russian ladies ... perhaps even unclothed members of Russia's fallen aristocracy. Besides (he found himself calculating providently), even for the libidinous it did not seem such very good value since, for another ten dollars, you could have enjoyed the six girls severally at the going rates.

Now in turn the nightclubs of Shanghai grew blurred and were replaced by a sparking-plug lying in a wrinkled palm and by a pair of bleary, anxious eyes. The Major turned the palm over to look at the watch on his wrist. The light was beginning to fade and it was a little cooler. Matthew, still looking weary, was struggling out of the Lagonda. With a sigh the Major replaced the plug in the pump and went to wash his hands. He had accepted an invitation to eat with Mr Wu, the Chinese businessman who had joined the Mayfair AFS unit. As he climbed the steps to the verandah he paused for a moment to look up while a single Blenheim bomber droned acros the opal sky in the direction of Kallang aerodrome. Later, he picked up the *Straits Times*, while waiting for Mr Wu, to read about how black things were looking for the Japanese.

34

From the beginning the Major and Mr Wu had conceived a great liking for each other. Each, indeed, recognized in the other a person so much after his own heart that it swiftly became clear to Mr Wu that the Major was simply an English Mr Wu, and to the Major that Mr Wu was nothing less than a Chinese Major. Mr Wu had even, some ten years earlier, served in what the Major supposed must have been the Kuomintang Air Force in China, for on one occasion he had given the Major a card on which, beneath a sprinkling of Chinese characters, one could read in English: 'Captain Wu. Number 5 Pursuiting Squadron.' The Major, in any case, since his arrival in the East had realized that there was no other race or culture on earth that he admired so much as the Chinese, for their tact, for their politeness, their good nature, their industry and their sense of humour. And Mr Wu combined all these virtues with a great warmth of character. He and the Major got on like a house on fire, a friendship conducted as much with smiles as with words because while Mr Wu's grasp of English was loose the Major, for his part, could get no purchase on Cantonese at all.

Now they were sitting together smiling in a companionable silence in the back of Mr Wu's elderly Buick on the way to some restaurant. Meanwhile, the Major was once more pondering the question of whether the Chinese community would remain loyal. If all the Chinese were like Mr Wu they would certainly help defend Malaya against the Japanese as staunchly as if it were their own country. For the Straits-born Chinese, of course, it really *was* their own country, but did they regard it as such? For the Major, no less than Walter, was worried about the prospects for Malaya's plural society when faced with the homogeneity of Japan. What chance would muddled, divided Malaya have against the efficiency and discipline he had seen everywhere on his visit to Manchukuo and to Japan itself?

After several months in the Far East the Major had been amazed to find trains running more regularly than they did in Europe: on his way to Harbin from Dairen he had taken the *Asia*, the 60-m.p.h. luxury express that was the pride of the South Manchuria Railway Company. Why, it had even had a library of books in English for the delectation of its Anglo-Saxon passengers! But you should not, for all that, think that you were in an imitation Western country: if, as the train began to pull out of the station, you happened to look out at the people on the platform who had come to see their friends off, you would see no emotional waving or shouting: you would see instead that they folded themselves to the ground and bowed low to the departing train, all together like a cornfield in a sudden gale. The Major had received a little shock when he had seen that; he had allowed himself to forget just how different the Japanese were from Europeans.

Yes, the Japanese, thought the Major beaming at his friend, Mr Wu (where were they going, by the way?), were an astonishingly determined and disciplined people. They believed in doing things properly, even in Manchukuo. In the barbers' shops there they even went so far as to wash clients' ears in eau de Cologne! You only had to see what they had accomplished ... the rebuilding of Changchun, for instance, formerly a mere collection of hovels, into a modern city with electric light, drains, parks, hospitals, libraries and even a zoo. There was, besides, that which no civilized modern city could possibly do without: a golf course!

272

Some young Japanese officers, seeing that the Major, from force of habit, was travelling with his ancient wooden golf clubs in his luggage, had invited him to play a few holes with them at the golf links on the outskirts of the city. He had declined the opportunity to play but had gone along to watch. For half the year, the officers explained, one was obliged to drive off into the teeth of the Siberian winter, for the other half into a Mongolian dust-storm. The Major had watched from the club-house, intrigued, as his new friends, wearing respirators, vanished gamely into the clouds of dust, driven here for hundreds of miles over the plains by the never-ceasing wind. Here and there the Major could see a patch of snow but not a single blade of grass (grass had been imported, he was told, but had not survived). Certainly, the Japanese were determined to do things properly!

In due course the young officers had returned, having surrendered a prodigious number of golf balls to the Mongolian plain, true, but with the obligations to civilized modern living thoroughly satisfied. Next they had whisked the Major, whom they had now identified not only as golfer and gentleman but as a brother officer into the bargain, off to a nearby inn for a meal of raw fish and eggs washed down by gallons of warm *saké*. With the utmost sincerity and good fellowship they explained to the Major as best they could in a mixture of English, French and German, how distressed they had been by certain apparently anti-Japanese *démarches* taken by the British in their China policy. They themselves, they explained, did not feel the ill-will towards the British that many of their young comrades felt. No, they felt more sorrow than anger that Britain should support the Nanking Government in its anti-Japanese behaviour and believed it was because the respected British people were so far away that they did not fully understand what the bandit war-lords of the Kuomintang were up to.

The Major, at the best of times, had trouble making up his mind about these perplexing international issues; but squatting on the floor of the inn with his new friends, some of whom wore military uniform, others kimonos, he soon found that the *saké* had stolen clean away with even those few elements of the situation which he believed he had grasped. To make matters worse, just as he felt he was beginning at last to get his teeth into the problem, a geisha girl dressed and painted like a charming little doll suddenly appeared and sang a song like that of a lonely wading-bird in a remote Siberian river, so charming, so melancholy, on and on it went, reedy, lyrical, moving, and sad ... the Major was transfixed by its sadness and beauty and could have gone on listening for hours, but wait, what was it he had been about to say about the Nanking Government?

'It is sincere wish, Major Archer,' declared one of his more articulate companions, throwing off yet another thimbleful of *saké*, 'that when we have cleared away bad China policy Japan and England co-operate in friendship for economic develop of China.'

'Well, I must say ...' the Major agreed affably, while someone else was saying that they were not interesting in helping Osaka merchants attack Lancashire merchants ('Well, that's splendid!' declared the Major heartily). They were against Big Business and their only desire was to spread Japanese National Spirit, although for the moment they might be obliged to make use of Big Business for their own ends such as develop of Manchuko. Yes, it was the Japanese National Spirit which was the important thing!

'I must say I thoroughly approve of your Japanese National Spirit,' said the Major holding his thimble of *saké* aloft and smiling.

'Ah so?' His companions looked surprised and gratified by this remark. The Major, who had merely been attempting a pleasantry, was a little disconcerted but thought it best not to explain. It was not the first time that one of his jokes had failed to find its mark.

Encouraged by the Major's approval, his friends now began to enlarge on National Spirit though this was not easy to define. There were many aspects of it: Loyalty to Emperor: the Major had perhaps visited Tokyo and seen ordinary citizens stand beside the huge moat surrounding the Imperial Palace and bow towards the gate which the Emperor sometimes used? Then there were Morals, too: not long ago a group of patriotic young students had burst into a dance being held at a fashionable Tokyo hotel and obliged all Japanese couples to leave the floor as 'a disgrace to the country' ... ('I say, that's a bit steep, isn't it?' murmured the Major) ... but, of course, foreigners were not molested. It was, the Major should understand, to protect national ideals and national customs against the taint of foreign influence that such action was necessary. In schools, too, it was most important that national purity and loyalty to Emperor should be maintained. An officer on the Major's right, who took a particular interest in education, now withdrew a book from the folds of his kimono and began to talk with great emphasis, his dark eyes burning.

The Major had noticed this particular fellow earlier because he had made a bit of a scene out at the golf club. While his comrades had been teeing up their balls and peering at them through the windows of their respirators before driving off into the swirling dust-clouds on a compass bearing for the first green, this man had begun shouting at them from a distance and waving his arms, making quite a din despite the howling of the wind. Since they paid no great attention to him he came, presently, to stand directly in front of where they were shifting their feet and waggling their wrists over their golf balls, in the very direction in which they were about to drive off. Not content with that, he even unbuttoned the tunic of his uniform to expose his naked chest to the bitter wind. And he had gone on standing there, still shouting, until two or three of the golfers had thrown down their clubs and led him gently aside. He had watched them morosely then from a distance while they began their ritual once more, shouting at them from time to time.

'Ah Scotland tradition bad Japan tradition,' muttered the officer who had stayed behind in the club-house to keep the Major company, and he had looked quite upset about something or other.

This man who had tried to stand in the way of the golf balls was the fellow who had now launched into a passionate discourse. Although, his companions explained, he had mastered several Western languages 'as a mental discipline' and spoke them fluently, he declined to use them, even speaking with a foreigner ... so one of his brother-officers was obliged to interpret for the Major as best he could. This book in his hand was, he explained, a text book used in schools: he began to translate what the Major supposed must be chapter headings: Tea Raising, Our Town, The Emperor, Healthy Body, Persimmons, Great Japan, Cherry Blossom, Getting Up Early, The Sun and the Wind, Loyal Behaviour ... and so on. ('Charming,' said the Major, 'but I don't think I quite ...') These subjects in book were designed to make good loyal Japanese citizen working hard for good of Japanese nation!

The officer at the Major's elbow, his eyes (no doubt refuelled

275

by the *saké*) smouldering more fiercely than ever, was now reading excitedly from the chapter on Military Loyalty, only pausing occasionally to aim a look of hatred and loathing at the Major. 'The object of lesson is to arouse Loyalty-feeling and foster purpose of self-sacrificing for Emperor. He tells story of how in war with China our soldiers fall into ambush at dead of night and enemy fire on them at close range. Instead of cowardly retreating they are full of Self-Sacrifice-feeling and rush on and Bugler Kikuchi, who badly wounded, keep bugle to lips and sound bugle with dying breath . . .' ('Well, upon my word . . .' said the Major.)

'If at any time Emperor give command, he who is Japanese must bravely advance to battle-place. When he has reach battle-place he must carefully obey command of superior officer. Bugler Kikuchi, who offer life, perform duty nobly and manifest magnificent Loyalty- feeling to Emperor!'

The Major, not used to squatting for long periods, was becoming decidedly stiff in the joints and felt it was time to return to his hotel and sleep off the *saké* he had consumed. But the officer at his elbow kept on and on reading from the school text book. Presently, he had finished reading the chapter on Persimmons and was declaiming exultantly from that on Great Japan. At length, however, he was quelled by his brother officers who wanted to say something to the Major, they had a most sincere request to make of him. Would he kindly give them permission to sing old school song?

'Why, certainly!' said the Major, unable to think what a Japanese old school song might sound like (perhaps a chorus suggesting a whole flock of wading-birds standing in a lonely Siberian river).

But no, the Major had not understood. They wanted to sing *his* old school song. 'You go perhaps to famous academy like Eton and . . .' The officers groped for a name and consulted each other . . . 'Eton and Harromachi.'

'Something like those but smaller,' agreed the Major cautiously. 'Mine was called Sandhall's.' The young officers looked very pleased at this information and, smiling at the Major, rolled the word on their palates to savour it. And so it was that, in due course, after a great number of rehearsals and false starts, the Major's old school song, sung by one light, not very certain tenor and a chorus of wading-birds which included even the officer with the burning eyes, had begun to echo out over the lonely expanses of Manchuria.

'Alma mater te bibamus,
Tui calices poscamus,
Hanc sententiam dicamus:
Floreat Sand ... ha! ... ha! ... lia!'

Now, although he was at war with them, the Major, sitting beside his friend Mr Wu, could not help but think of the young officers with pleasure. The Major admired their idealism: what splendid young chaps they were! But at the same time one had to admit that their National Spirit had its disquieting side: he had felt it even at the time: he felt it all the more strongly now. One expects a patriotic spirit from military officers, of course. The British officer, though less voluble on the subject, was probably no less determined to do his duty. But what had struck the Major was that *even in peacetime* the entire Japanese nation seemed to be imbued with this fervour. Later in that same year he had visisted the vast Mitsui industrial and mining centre at Miike in Kyushu and had seen other signs of the nationalistic spirit which pervaded Japan. He had seen, for example, the entire staff of a factory, several hundred men, bow down three times in the direction of the palace in Tokyo. He had been shown a laboratory where special phosphate pills were prepared to make the miners work harder, each man being given a pill to swallow before he went down the mine-shaft. And if it had been like that in Japan in 1937 what must it be like now that the country was at war with the British Empire and America? The Major uttered a gloomy sigh as he climbed out of the Buick. For in the meantime they had arrived.

While the Major had been engrossed in his melancholy thoughts they had entered the maze of Chinese streets which lie between Bencoolen Street and Beach Road. They had only reached their destination, it transpired, to the extent that the Buick would no longer fit into the streets along which their route lay. The Major found himself following Mr Wu down a series of very narrow and strong-smelling alleys until, beaming and murmuring: 'This way, please,' his host led him into an amazingly dingy restaurant. It was deserted except for a rickshaw coolie who sat, barefoot, on a bench, his knees to his ears, quickly shovelling fried *mee* from a bowl propped against his lower lip into his mouth. An elderly woman mopping the floor paused to gaze impassively at the Major. Chuckling, Mr Wu led the way upstairs. But even as he climbed the stairs the

Major had to deal with a final disquieting recollection from his visit to Japan. One of the young officers had told him that the readiness of the Japanese to die for their country may be compared to the ants in the 'Japanese Alps' which, when threatened by fire, mass themselves round it and extinguish it with their burning bodies so that it will not destroy their nests. Had not the Japanese infantry defied the Russian machine-guns at Port Arthur in exactly such a way? 'But surely no one is threatening your nest,' the Major had replied. The officer, after a moment's pause, had explained ominously that an attempt to deprive Japan of raw materials and markets was just such a threat.

The room into which Mr Wu was now ushering the Major was densely crowded and very, very hot. The table to which they were shown was already occupied, at least in the sense that a young Chinese was sprawled over it in a stupor, whether the result of weariness or narcotics it was hard to tell. He was swiftly dragged away, however, and the table was given a swift polish with a damp cloth. It was evident that Mr Wu was a respected client. Meanwhile, the Major had been unable to resist putting to Mr Wu that same question which had been gnawing at his mind earlier (and apparently, elsewhere in Singapore, had been disturbing the peace of mind of the Governor, and of other prominent citizens): what would be the response of the Chinese, Indian and Malayan communities to the invasion?

Mr Wu, who had been smiling cheerfully, became grave instantly. The Major, unable to hear what he was saying because of the noise from the other tables, craned forward, but he still could not make out what it was, though Mr Wu's round face grew steadily longer as he spoke. Ah, now he was looking cheerful again, thank heaven for that!

It soon became clear, however, that Mr Wu's change of mood derived from the preparations being made for their meal rather than the state of the Colony ... a rickety gas-burner connected to a rubber pipe had been set on the table and lit. On top of it was set a concave metal ring forming a bowl which was swimming with a clear broth. Then the gas jet was turned up so that blue flame roared out of the open funnel at the top of the metal bowl and the soup inside it began to bubble.

'We call ah steam-boat,' explained Mr Wu.

'No wonder it's so hot up here,' thought the Major who was suffering from the heat. Similar blue flames roared at other tables and the noise from the men sitting around them was deafening. He sipped the hot tea which had been set before him and longed for a cold beer. A young waitress who had joined them at the table busied herself with chopsticks, picking morsels of raw meat, chicken and fish off a plate and dropping them into the seething soup. When they were cooked she fished them out and dropped them now into the Major's bowl, now into Mr Wu's. The Major, anxious to be polite, struggled to maintain a conversation on fire-fighting of which it was all he could do to make out his own words, let alone those of Mr Wu.

The noise from the other tables continued to grow in volume. The Major was astonished; he was accustomed to think of the Chinese as quiet and well-behaved but these Chinese were shouting their heads off. Mr Wu himself appeared not to notice his fellow-diners until the Major drew his attention to them. He had to shout to make himself heard ... Who were these young men at the other tables?

'National anti-enemy society of ah Kuomintang!' shouted Mr Wu. 'They drink ah whisky for defeating ah enemy!' And he roared with laughter while the Major had a look. Mr Wu was quite right: each young Chinese had a half-bottle of whisky planted on the table in front of him and from time to time he took a swig from it to moisten his gullet before resuming his shouting.

The evening pursued its course. The heat and the noise grew steadily more acute. This, the Major decided, his brain reeling, could only be a local chapter meeting of the Youth Blood and Iron Traitor-Exterminating Corps. He could not help but make a dubious comparison between these wild and vociferous young men and the disciplined Japanese officers he had met. What chance would they have? Why, none at all. Their eyes bulged, their faces grew red, though not as red as the Major's, and the veins stood out on their temples. Many of them wore string singlets over their stomachs and as they got drunker they lifted them to cool their navels. Presently, tired of shouting their lungs out at each other they gathered round the Major and Mr Wu instead and shouted their lungs out at them.

Meanwhile, unconcerned, Mr Wu, continued to pick delicately with his chopsticks in the bubbling soup, searching for choice fragments of squid and sea-slug to drop in the Major's bowl. Only when he had finished this search did he notice the Major's harassed expression. Then he tried to explain something but the Major, deafened, could not hear. Mr Wu turned to the shouting young men and with a barely perceptible frown murmured something under his breath. Instantly, the young men stopped shouting and fell back, watching the remainder of the meal in eerie silence from their own tables.

'They make you member society,' explained Mr Wu genially. 'Society call ah Prum Brossom Fists Society.'

'Good heavens!' exclaimed the Major, touched. 'Please thank them on my behalf. He wondered why the name of the society should stir some distant recollection in his mind. It was only later that it came back to him. Was it not something to do with the Boxer Rising in 1900? Surely one of the factions pledged to drive foreigners out of China had been called the Plum Blossom Fists Society? He was almost certain. He must remember to ask Mr Wu.

35

'My dear Herringport, nothing could give me greater pleasure now that your country has entered the War than to accede to your request.' Thus it was that Brooke-Popham, ambushed by Ehrendorf as he was leaving a conference, gave him the opportunity to satisfy his most pressing need: to leave the city in which Joan lived without delay. Brooke-Popham had spoken in what was, for that kindly gentleman, a somewhat surly tone: he was tired of being ambushed by people; he was tired of conferences, too; he was tired of the War, even, although it had only just begun. In a few days from now, however, someone else would be stepping into his shoes as Commander-in-Chief and he would be able to return to Britain. Not a moment too soon, as far as he was concerned.

Noticing that Ehrendorf was looking somewhat taken aback by the brusqueness of his tone, Brooke-Popham relented and placing a friendly hand on the young man's shoulder he walked with him a few paces down the corridor for, after all, this was the charming young Herringport, not one of the aggressive blighters on the War Council.

'What would you suggest, Jack?' he said over his shoulder. 'This young man wants a closer view of the action.'

'I should think a spell on Heath's staff in KL would be the

place for a ringside seat,' came the amiable reply.

'Good idea! Clear it with Percival and Heath, will you? I take it,' he went on, this time to Ehrendorf, 'that your own chaps have no objection. After all, now that we've got allies we don't want to get off on the wrong footing with them, do we?' And the Commander-in-Chief strolled on, still with a paternal hand on Ehrendorf's shoulder but with a wary eye open lest one of the Resident Minister's minions should choose this moment to pounce on him. 'By the way, Jack,' he said over his shoulder again. 'Have you come across a fellow called Simson? No? Obsessed with tank-traps. Says Japanese tanks could be through Malaya like Carter's Little Liver Pills and we'd have no way of stopping 'm. Still, one never knows, he could be right. One must be fair, after all. What d'you think? All I can say is, thank heaven that's Percival's pidgin! Nothing to do with me. Quite a presentable looking fellow, actually. Says he's an Engineer. No reason to doubt it, of course ...'

Seeing that the Commander-in-Chief's attention had moved on to another problem, Ehrendorf seized the opportunity to escape, though not before having made swift arrangements with another member of Brooke-Popham's train for the necessary documents. Then he hastened out to where his car was waiting ... but on the way, something rather curious happened. He had been aware for some days of a growing strain running in a line down the centre of his body. This strain, since his last meeting with Joan, had become steadily stronger. Suddenly now on his way to the staff-car (it was most unexpected) he split into two Ehrendorfs. While one Ehrendorf gave brisk instructions to the driver, who seemed not to have noticed anything unusual, the other took his seat in the back, shaking his head sadly, as if to say: 'It doesn't matter in the least where you tell him to drive you, because one place is exactly like another.' And while the first Ehrendorf, ignoring this, tried to decide whether to send a last 'final letter' to Joan (there had already been one or two), perhaps mentioning that he was 'off to the Front' (a slight exaggeration since the HQ of III Indian Corps, where he was going, though the centre of operational command for northern Malaya, was actually situated in reasonable comfort and security in Kuala Lumpur, but never mind) and wishing her well for the future with Matthew or the guy with the stammer, the second Ehrendorf continued to watch him with detachment and contempt, as if to suggest that the writing of such a letter was quite as useless as any other course of action he could take and a sign of weakness into the bargain, the aping of noble sentiments which he did not feel in the least.

Passing across Anderson Bridge the car's progress was slowed by a convoy of armoured troop-carriers; glancing down at the river, Ehrendorf saw the cluster of *sampans* and *tongkangs* riding the slime: here entire families of Chinese were fated to spend their lives. For a moment the misery of this waterborne population caused the two Ehrendorfs to merge into one again. But they separated once more on the other side of the bridge. One can hardly be expected constantly, day in and day out, to measure one's own slender but personal misery against the collective misery of the world! That is asking too much. And about that letter, would it really be self-pitying to send Joan a note wishing her future happiness with Kate's Human Bean, who was also his own best friend, after all? Yet the truth was (was it not?) that under the guise of these silken good wishes he would really have liked to send Joan a rasping sarcasm. Admit it! Thus brooded the two Ehrendorfs sitting in the back of the car.

When he had returned to his apartment in Market Street, he packed his kit and left it by the door; then he wandered aimlessly from sitting-room to bedroom and back again, now and again picking up a small object (a bottle of ink, a comb, a cotton reel of khaki thread), inspecting it and putting it down again. He stared for a long time at a section of the wall by the window where the whitewash, thickly applied, had begun to flake away: he examined it with great attention as if for some hidden significance, but at length, with a shrug of his shoulders he moved away, unable to make anything of it. He paused to look down into Market Street for a moment. Normally this was one of his favourite occupations: he loved the smell of cummin, cinnamon and allspice which drifted up to his window when sacks and kegs of spices were being unloaded at the spice merchant's below. On the other side of the street were the money-lenders' shops: there Chettyars in white cheese-cloth *dhotis* dozed over their accounts in dim interiors, lounging or squatting on polished wooden platforms while they waited for business, or poring over ledgers at ankle-high desks whose wood was as dark and gleaming as their own skins. They reminded Ehrendorf of somnolent alligators waiting until chance should bring them a meal on the current of passers-by flowing down the street. He smiled at the thought but the street, too, had grown oppressive and he moved on, this time picking up a snapshot of himself and his brothers and sisters. On an impulse he put it in an envelope and scribbled Matthew's name and address on it: he explored his mind for some friendly comment he might write on the back of it but could find nothing, his mind was perfectly empty. In the end, unable to think of anything suitable, he simply sealed it, stuck a stamp on it and put it in his pocket. 'What time is it?' he asked himself aloud. An overwhelming desire to sleep came over him, although he had slept soundly all night and most of the preceding afternoon. 'This won't do at all. If I leave now I could catch an early train and be in KL by ...' Instead he picked up a newspaper and began to read an article on the developing friendship between Chinese and Indian ARP wardens. 'Perhaps I should eat something?'

'... This little incident is typical of the comradeship now to be found every day of the week in the streets of our city among Asiatic and European volunteers in the "Passive Defence" services ...' What little incident? Ehrendorf, though he began doggedly to read the article again, was unable to find 'the little incident'. He even counted the pages of the newspaper; he must have lost a page somewhere. But no, it was all there. He threw it aside. What did it matter? Should he go to sleep again or should he go to the railway station? He went into the kitchen and opened his refrigerator: it contained eggs, milk, a lettuce, some corned beef on a saucer (frozen on to it), a boiled potato that for some reason had turned a dark grey colour, some beetroot and the manuscript of a novel he was writing about a gifted young American from Kansas City who goes to Oxford on a scholarship and there, having fallen in love with an English girl who surrounds herself with cynical, sophisticated people, goes to the dogs, forgetting the sincere, warm-hearted American girl whose virginity he had made away with while crossing the Atlantic on a Cunard liner ... et cetera ... 'How could I write such rubbish?' Still, he could not quite bring himself to tear it up ... ('All I need now is the sincere, warm-hearted American girl.') He left the novel where it was but transferred the food to the table, having fried the eggs and the grey boiled potato.

Then he began to eat. He still did not feel in the least hungry but his Calvinist conscience would not allow him to leave the food to spoil while he was away from Singapore. It would have been a better idea, he realized, to give it to some hungry Singaporean but he was unable, in his present frame of mind, to face the problem of finding and communicating with a suitable recipient. He ate his way remorselessly through the food on the table, trying to make himself belch from time to time to lessen the strain. When he had finished he obliged himself, as an extra penance, to eat his way through a wedge of cake he discovered in a biscuit tin. As he ate, taking frequent swigs of milk to reduce the cake to a gruel he could swallow, he mused on the natural tendency, observable in human affairs, for things to go wrong, a law which in his blind optimism he had not perceived until this moment. Since nobody else appeared to have given it much thought, either, he felt justified in christening this discovery: Ehrendorf's Second Law. It asserted: 'In human affairs things tend inevitably to go wrong.' Or to put it another way: 'The human situation, in general or in particular, is slightly worse (ignoring an occasional hiccup in the graph) at any given moment than at any preceding moment.' This notion caused him to smile for a moment: he must pass it on to Matthew. The reflection which caused him to wince immediately after having smiled (namely, that as Matthew was a rival he had most likely lost not only Joan but his best friend into the bargain), he saw merely as a demonstration of the universal application to Ehrendorf's Second Law.

Ehrendorf, having overcome with great difficulty a desire to retire to bed and sleep for several more hours, finally persuaded himself to take the evening train to Kuala Lumpur: it was Thursday, 11 December. By the time he set out he was already very tired; he also felt bloated and ill from the unwanted food he had consumed. The cavernous Railway Station in Keppel Road was already thronged with bored, weary or resigned-looking troops: British, Australian, Indian and Ghurka; their kit and rifles lay piled haphazardly; men shouted orders but without apparently diminishing the chaos, causing Ehrendorf, who for some weeks had been contemplating the conversion of his novel into an epic of Tolstoyan dimensions, to wonder whether war was of interest to anyone but the commanders who were conducting it. Was it not, for the troops themselves, a matter of standing around for hours on end speechless with boredom, perhaps with now and then a moment of terror?

The train, when he succeeded in finding it, was already crammed with troops. He forced his way into a first-class compartment with a number of British officers who eyed him with hostility; one of them reluctantly removed his kit from a seat by the window, the only place unoccupied. It was extremely hot in the compartment and the atmosphere of ill-will among its occupants showed no sign of dissipating, nor the train any sign of moving out of the station. The insignia of the Federated Malay States Railway, palm-trees and a lion, had been engraved on the window beside Ehrendorf: he gazed at it, thinking of the vanished comfort and security of earlier days in Malaya, and found it beautiful. At last the train began to move; they crept out of the station, passing the General Hospital and the old Lunatic Asylum on their right and then curved away across the island towards the Causeway. Almost immediately the red-tiled roofs of Singapore gave way to jungle, so astonishingly dense that one might not have known that a great city lay just on the other side of it a few hundred yards away; after the jungle, mangrove swamps, a wretched Malay village scattered with rusting tin çans, a banana grove, a rubber smallholding or two, a few frail-looking papaya trees, then more jungle and mangrove until they reached the Causeway and the flashing water on either side.

Once out of the dilapidated streets of Johore Bahru the jungle returned, a solid green wall in which it was hard to distinguish individual leaves and fronds; Ehrendorf had the impression of travelling through an interminable dark green corridor. Presently, it grew dark and began to rain heavily, making it necessary to shut the windows. The heat quickly grew intolerable. The only illumination was a single light-bulb painted blue in deference to the black-out: in the faint glow that it cast it was barely possible to make out the faces of the other men in the compartment. Time passed. The rain stopped and it was possible to open the windows again. When, for no apparent reason, they halted, Ehrendorf could smell the steam from the locomotive which hung in the saturated air and refused to dissipate.

They crept forward again, then stopped. A man ran back along the train blowing a whistle and shouting 'Air-raid!' his feet crunching noisily on the cinders as he passed. One of the officers switched off the blue light and the others groped for their helmets. Nothing happened; they sat in silence, waiting. The night sounds of the jungle rose in volume around them, eerie and frightening. Something, perhaps a moth, brushed against Ehrendorf's face in the darkness and he flailed at it in sudden horror. Still nothing happened. Feeling drowsy he leaned his head against the side of the coach, his helmet tilted to form a comfortable support. After a wait that seemed interminable the train began cautiously to advance once more.

Ehrendorf slept now, shaken this way and that by the motion of the train. A smell of tobacco, remembered from his childhood, flirted with his scarcely conscious mind, a smell not of burning tobacco but of the empty cigarette tins his father used to give him. In his dream he thought: 'How close we are to things when we smell them!' Then his restless mind meandered away in a long, meaningless series of half-thoughts about Joan. He saw her walking ahead of him in a blue cotton dress, flaring and fading rhythmically in time with the motion of the train. 'It would never have worked in any case. We had nothing in common.'

The train had stopped, evidently in some small station, perhaps Segamat or Gemas. There were no lights on the platform so it was impossible to make out. There was a storm grumbling nearby: lightning flickered over the surrounding tree tops. He wondered what time it was. A flash of lightning illuminated the compartment for an instant and he saw his travelling companions; they were still silent but no longer sitting erect: now they slumped as if mysteriously gassed. Another train travelling in the opposite direction had stopped beside their own. One of them began to move: at first he thought it was the one he was in but it proved to be the other: a brief, sickening impression of immobility took hold of him as he realized. One darkened compartment after another slipped past. And then, surprisingly, a compartment which by comparison with the rest seemed brightly lit. Ehrendorf, still drugged with sleep, glimpsed a little cluster of illuminated brigadiers poring over a map which they had spread on a table between them. He sat up quickly, but the other train had already vanished into the darkness.

'Wasn't that General Heath in the middle?' he asked the man opposite him, but there was no reply. Heath was in command of III Corps. After all, he mused, things might not be going too badly if Heath was paying a visit to Singapore.

36

Dupigny had spent the past two days very pleasantly in George Town, the only town of consequence on the island of Penang. He had come here partly because he felt he needed a change from Singapore, partly in the hope of borrowing some money from a French acquaintance. Although, as it had transpired, he had not succeeded in borrowing the money, in all other respects his visit to Penang had turned out well. He had managed, despite his threadbare clothing, to persuade the management of the Eastern and Oriental Hotel that Monsieur Ballereau, the French Consul in Singapore whom Dupigny considered, for no particular reason, his sworn enemy, would redeem all his bills and chits ... a decidedly satisfactory state of affairs, given the excellence of the hotel's cuisine. Now the problem which was exercising him as he strolled along the esplanade giving himself an appetite for a substantial lunch in prospect, was this : would his residence at the E and O be a sufficient sign of affluence for him to buy new clothes at a superior outfitter's on credit ? In normal times a European would have expected to be given credit in any case without difficulty, merely signing a chit to be redeemed in due course. But of late things had been growing more difficult. Dupigny had already been rebuffed more than once in his efforts to fit himself out in a suitable manner.

This was a thorny problem but he did not intend to let it spoil his stroll. This promenade, he considered, had something of the atmosphere of a seaside resort in Normandy ... Deauville, say, or Cabourg. Here, on one rounded elbow of the island, the town hall and municipal offices presided in peaceful dignity over a stretch of open ground giving on to the ruined earthworks of Fort Cornwallis. In Deauville, of course, there would have been a bracing smell of the sea and the Tricolour would have been galloping on a flag-staff; here there was a flag-staff, certainly, but the Union Jack hung limp from it in the humid heat. No, it was not bracing here, far from it, but by half closing your eyes and very vigorously exercising your imagination you might, for a moment or two, think yourself in a tropical Balbec on your way to meet some dark-skinned little Albertine.

George Town, he was thinking, as he followed the elbow of the coast road where it turned sharply to head back south-west along Weld Quay towards the ferry, though not the most exciting place in the world, was certainly one of the most peaceful, even with the war so close. Yes, it even seemed peaceful this morning when Weld Quay was thronged with Chinese and Indians, come to watch the Japanese bombers attacking Butterworth across the water as they had on the previous day. Undoubtedly there had not been such excitement in Penang, apart from some race riots between Chinese and Indians, in the hundred years since the government of the Straits Settlements had passed to Singapore ... But Dupigny hardly had time to finish this thought: the next moment he looked out to sea, looked again, hesitated, then began to run.

It is unusual to see someone running in the tropics; now and then Europeans, in defiance of the heat, may be seen playing football, cricket or some other sport, but not running the way Dupigny was (as if his life depended upon it, as perhaps it did). People turned to stare at him as he raced back the way he had come towards the ruined walls and grassy banks of Fort Cornwallis. At first he shouted at them, but they paid no attention to him; he decided immediately it was useless, a waste of breath, so he ran on in silence, passing a Chinese ARP warden who realized immediately why he was running and started shouting wildly at a little group of Indians nearby, trying to marshal them in one direction or another. Although he tried to point in the direction of what was approaching from the mainland as he ran, it made no difference: one or two of the strollers even grinned at each other at the sight of a middle-aged European running for all he was worth in the steaming midday heat. Now Dupigny paid no attention to them, hardly even saw them. He ran and ran and, wiry though he was, the sweat poured off his face and neck.

Here and there the crowds were so dense that there was hardly room to move, but Dupigny shoved people rudely aside in his determination to get where he was going, too breathless to apologize, though again he tried to point across the water. One or two of those he shoved aside shouted angrily after him; nobody cares to be barged into the gutter while taking a stroll. An elderly English gentleman shook a walking-stick after him: this was the sort of ill-mannered fellow one found coming out

East in recent years: not enough breeding to wrap in a postage stamp! But still Dupigny ran and ran for his life. There was an expression of fierce concentration on his face as he ran, looking neither right nor left, head down, elbows working. The sole of one of his shoes, which he had been obliged by poverty to wear ever since leaving Saigon and which he had been nursing anxiously for some weeks, now detached itself and began to flap ridiculously. But he did not even stop to attend to this, merely kicked the shoe off as he was running because already, above the thudding of his own pulse in his ears, he could hear the drone of the approaching bombers.

As he drew near the corner of Light Street where the seafront turned towards the fort and the esplanade, the crowds became thinner and several people were looking up at the sky, their attention drawn by the steadily increasing sound of motors. One or two of them, concerned as much to see Dupigny running as by the thought that these approaching aeroplanes might be a source of danger quickened their pace, but with the air of people who do not want to be thought ridiculous. Dupigny ran on with open mouth and staring eyes, for now it seemed to him that he was running in a dream and in semi-darkness through which there penetrated, wriggling into his consciousness like little silver worms, the sound of ARP whistles, followed by the undulating wail of the siren from the roof of the police station.

He was no more than sixty yards from the protection of the green banks of earth by the fort but moving in slow motion. He ran and ran but the fort seemed to come no closer; the muscles of his thighs no longer obeyed him. Half-way across the intervening open space he stumbled and fell on the gravel. He could no longer hear the engines but looking up at last he saw that one of the bombers flying very low was almost on top of him and appeared to be hovering over him like a bird of prey, blotting out the sun. Getting to his feet he staggered forward again in desperation and finding himself on the edge of a grassy bank of earth he hurled himself over it and tumbled head over heels down and down into the shady depths of a gully full of sand and stones. And as he did so he was followed by a great tidal wave of sound that swept over his head and tore savagely at the flag hanging limply from the flag-staff a few yards away.

He lay there quaking for some moments with his head in his hands, flinching as one aeroplane after another roared overhead, each one followed by a series of resonant explosions which shook the ground and created a miniature landslide of pebbles a few inches in front of his nose. Simultaneously with the explosions there came what might have been the pattering of fingernails on a metal table, very thin and trivial compared with the violent beating of big drums and the grinding of masonry. Machine-guns!

Again and again he heard the crump of falling bombs. Some of them fell very close, and with each bomb there was the same dreadful shudder of the earth and a trickle of gravel by his face. A spider, horribly agile, galloped away in a panic. When he looked up he could see that the godowns along Swettenham and Victoria Piers were blazing briskly and beyond, on the peaceful and shining waters towards the mainland, smoke was rising from several of the anchored vessels, swelling from slender trunks into canopies that hung over them, giving them the appearance of monstrous elms.

For some minutes, while he recovered a little from the effort he had made, he lay where he was, thinking of nothing; then he climbed unsteadily out of his refuge. Without considering where he was going, though perhaps with some dazed notion that he might escape from this catastrophe by taking the electric tram which ran from the railway jetty along the Dato Kramat Road to Ayer Itam Village, he began to wander back the way he had come. But, of course, such an escape was out of the question: even if there had been anyone left to drive a tram the tracks were cratered and the overhead wires lay tangled on the ground amid the rubble of masonry.

Despite the crackle of burning buildings and the shouts and screams of those who had been injured, to Dupigny it suddenly seemed very quiet as he retraced his steps towards the Railway Jetty. It seemed that it was only a moment earlier that he had been running in the opposite direction; yet of the crowds through which he had had to force his way there was no sign: they had melted away mysteriously leaving only, dotted on the pavement here and there, bundles of clothes: from many of these bundles, however, blood was flowing

One of the bundles was of pure white muslin and from it there issued such a lake of blood that Dupigny found himself marvelling that the human body could contain that quantity. He was obliged to make a considerable detour to avoid splashing through it, which, considering that he had lost one shoe, he believed he might find disagreeable. But even the sight of the blood nauseated him and he was obliged to shift his gaze to something more comforting: in the event this was the smoke pouring prettily out of the window of a burning building across the street.

He took a closer look. This time he noticed that the smoke did not have a long slender trunk and a canopy like an elm, as with the ships burning in the anchorage, but a short, fat stalk like a cauliflower. And also like a cauliflower this smoke seemed quite green below, billowing out into white flowerets above. Someone was shouting at him from the window.

No. There was someone at the window but she was dead, hanging out of it with gracefully trailing arms in the manner of someone in a rowing-boat idly trailing fingers in the water. At the same time there was someone shouting at him from the road: a short, fat man with no neck: his red, flustered face appeared to be set directly on his shoulders, his arms emerging from just below his ears.

'Come on, now, I want you to take care of me,' he was shouting. 'You'll have to shift things so that I can drive my car. Come on. Yes, you. You're the only person here so you'll have to do.' He was standing beside a little Ford without a windscreen. As Dupigny made no move he added pleadingly: 'There's a good fellow. You aren't going to leave me in the lurch, are you? Those bloody bombers may come back any minute.'

'Very well,' said Dupigny and having brushed the glass from the front seat he got in beside the fat man, who said: 'No, no. You must crank!' and produced a starting-handle which he handed to Dupigny. Dupigny got out again and with much difficulty found the hole in which to insert the end of the starting-handle. 'Ready?' But he could barely see the man in the driving-seat for the smoke which was drifting around them from the burning building nearby.

The motor fired immediately and Dupigny got back into the car. As he did so he noticed that a picture advertising a round tin of Capstan cigarettes had been painted on the side of the vehicle. 'Do you have a cigarette, please?' he asked, but there was no reply. They set off jerkily down the road following the tram-lines, weaving in and out between craters, bodies and rubble ... in places, because of the drifting smoke, it was impossible to see what lay ahead. The fat man drove, muttering to himself and tears cascaded down his plump cheeks, but whether they were caused by grief, alarm or simply the smoke it was impossible to say. Now their way was blocked by a mess of twisted girders and high-tension wires. The fat man peered ahead uncertainly.

'Drive up on the pavement.'

'But that is against the law,' said the fat man unhappily. 'We must go back.'

'Drive on the pavement,' repeated Dupigny harshly, 'or we'll never get out of this place. Go forward. I see where you can cross the storm-drain.'

They drove on, managing with inches to spare to find a way through. Looking to his right Dupigny searched for some sign of life from the fire station in Chulia Street but all he could see was the unbroken curtain of smoke: perhaps the station itself had been hit. Turning inland to follow Maxwell Road they saw that a hysterical crowd had gathered around the dead and wounded in the market, which itself was a shambles in which carcasses of animals and humans had become indistinguishable.

'We'll never get through there,' whimpered the fat man. 'They'll kill us like dogs.'

'Don't be stupid. Drive up Magazine Road instead. It looks more clear.'

At a junction with another road they crossed over the tramlines again. Here there was not so much damage and the overhead cables had not been brought down. Macalister Road was crowded with excited people but otherwise the way was clear. Presently they turned north, then west on to Burmah Road. Now they found themselves in almost deserted countryside. 'Where are we going?' Dupigny wondered.

Suddenly the fat man stamped on the brake pedal and the car drifted sideways, locked tyres screaming, until it came to a halt by some sugar cane. Dupigny could see no reason for stopping. The road ahead was empty. But the fat man had bounded out of the car and with his little arms working vigorously on his rotund body he scurried across the road and plunged into the sugar cane. The foliage swallowed him immediately and he gave no further sign of life.

'Ah!' Dupigny now saw why he had taken to his heels. A two-engined Mitsubishi bomber had crept into view following the coastline in a westerly direction but already beginning to turn inland towards the stalled motor-car where Dupigny was sitting. It was flying very slowly and very low. He could see every detail of it. Its wing dipped and it began to turn on a wide curve that would bring it back over George Town and the shipping once more. Dupigny sat there too tired to move and watched the nose of the aeroplane coming towards him, looking, he thought, like the cruel head of a pike. For a moment he could see the four bomb-doors under the belly of the plane and one wheel, half tucked into its undercarriage like an acorn in its cup. Now its camouflaged surface was hard to follow against the dark green flank of Penang Hill but then, as it banked more steeply, the underneath of the plane was eclipsed and the sunlight flared first on one facet of the glass cockpit, then on another, to be picked up in turn by the machine-gun turret just above and behind the wing; as the glare died Dupigny saw the dark silhouette of the gunner's head and of the gun itself with its barrel swivelling and he realized that the pilot was banking to give the gunner a view of the ground. Now he, too, felt like running for the sugar cane but he knew it was too late: he sat perfectly still, hoping that the gunner would think the car was abandoned. The bomber came curving nearer, only a few feet above the church and market at Pulau Tikus and the rooftops along Cantonment Road. Dust and gravel spurted from the road and seemed to hang there printed on his retina like a formation of stalagmites. A great roar of engines and a draught of wind rocked the car and then the plane had passed over, leaving him with a singing in his ears. Silence fell again. Nothing stirred. Dupigny continued to sit there where he was. In the glove compartment there was a tin of Capstan cigarettes and a box of matches. Dupigny lit one and waited. There was no sign of the fat man.

After he had finished the cigarette, he put the gear lever in neutral and got out the starting-handle again. When the motor was running he sounded the horn, waited for a while, then drove away, thinking that he might find some sheltered and isolated place to stay until the 'all clear' sounded. He was obliged to drive slowly because in the absence of a windscreen he could not see properly. Soon, however, he was on the coast road to Tanjong Bungah. Several civilian cars, an Army lorry and a bren-gun carrier passed him, driving quickly in the direction of George Town. He saw a sign then for the Swimming Club and turned off the road into some trees on the right, parking the car in the shade of one of them.

The Swimming Club's doors and shutters were open but it seemed deserted except for a frightened looking Chinese at the bar. Dupigny ordered a beer and told the boy to serve it on the verandah. While he was waiting he paused to examine a couple of framed photographs on the wall. One of them, dating from about 1910 to judge by the clothes, showed the ladies and gentlemen of the Penang Swimming Club attending what was evidently an annual prize-giving. The ladies, wearing long dresses and broad-brimmed Edwardian hats swagged with silk and taffeta, sat demurely in the foreground beside a small table laden with silver cups and trophies. The gentlemen, meanwhile, were disposed in studied little groups here and there at the windows and on the verandah of the club-house, suggesting the crowd-scene of a musical comedy when the members of the chorus in the background talk to each other with animation, roar with laughter or slap their thighs with delight ... but all in silence, while some other matter is being dealt with by the leading players in the foreground. 'Ah, what a great deal can change even in a place like Penang in thirty years!'

The other photograph, from about the same period, also showed a group of ladies and gentlemen, assembled this time for a picnic, perhaps. The padre was there looking young and vigorous, a watch-chain visible against his black waistcoat and with a white sun-helmet on his head. The ladies were still sitting in the rickshaws that had brought them; but only one coolie had remained to appear in the picture and there he was, still gripping the shafts as if he had only just trundled his fair cargo up. The European standing beside the rickshaw had reached out a hand as the photograph was being taken and forced the coolie's head down so that only his straw hat and not his face should be visible in the picture.

With a sigh Dupigny stretched out on a comfortable rattan chair on the verandah, musing on the confident assumption of superiority embodied in that hand forcing the coolie to hide his face. He himself had often seen Europeans in the East treating the Asiatics in that way in his earlier days but now it looked ... well, slightly incongruous when seen with the modern eye of 1941. Imperceptibly ideas had been changing, the relative power of the races had been changing, and not only in the British colonies but in the French and Dutch as well. Even without Vichy it would have been attempting the impossible to continue governing Indo-China from Hanoi for very much longer. Both he and Catroux had been aware of it at the time without acknowledging it. Whatever happened with the Japanese the old colonial life in the East, the European's hand on the coolie's straw hat, was finished. The boy had brought his beer. He took the chit and, not without pleasure, signed it 'Ballereau'. The Chinese boy had lingered on the verandah looking east to the vast canopy of smoke that hung over George Town.

37

'In human affairs things tend inevitably to go wrong. Things are slightly worse at any given moment than at any preceding moment.' This proposition, known as the Second Law, its discoverer now had the opportunity of seeing demonstrated on a remarkably generous scale. His vantage point for watching its operation was III Corps Headquarters in Kuala Lumpur where a strong smell of incipient disaster hung in the air, like the smoke that hangs in a theatre after the firing of a blank cartridge. Not only, he discovered, had a great deal gone wrong before his arrival but almost every message which now arrived in the Operations room signified that something else had just gone wrong, with the probability of more to follow.

Ehrendorf had arrived at III Corps Headquarters shortly after nine o'clock in the morning, very weary after his night in the train. His arrival coincided almost to the minute with a crucial development in the struggle for northern Malaya, for General Murray-Lyon, commander of the 11th Division which had been given the principal rôle in its defence, had just telephoned. Murray-Lyon had been trying to contact General Heath, to request permission to withdraw from the preordained defensive position he had occupied at Jitra. He was afraid that unless he did so the 11th Division might be destroyed. General Heath, however, could not be found: Ehrendorf had not been deceived when in the middle of the night he had seen that illuminated compartment with its little cluster of brightly lit officers around General Heath vanishing into the jungle darkness. Heath had gone to Singapore to confer with General Percival. Ehrendorf also learned on arrival that Japanese bombers had given Penang and Butterworth a pounding on the previous day. Since there were no ack-ack guns on the island it had been defenceless.

'But what about the RAF at Butterworth?'

'Partly damaged, partly withdrawn to Singapore,' he was told.

Somewhat surprisingly in the circumstances Ehrendorf found that he was given a warm welcome by General Heath's staff. During the lengthy period he had spent in Singapore he had become accustomed to being treated with reserve by the British staff officers he had come across in the course of his duties, even sometimes in recent months with veiled contempt. But now he was warmly shaken by the hand, found a billet and given some breakfast. It was a little time before he realized that this was probably because he was the first American officer to be seen in KL since America had entered the war. The welcome was symbolic. Perhaps, too, since the unfortunate start to the campaign in Malaya a feeling was beginning to take root that the power of the United States might well become necessary if the Japanese were to be contained and subdued in the Pacific. It had been the habit of British officers to scoff at the Japanese Army. Had they not been battling fruitlessly with a rabble of Chinese since 1937, unable to get the upper hand? The military engagements of the last three or four days, however, had revealed that the Japanese invaders were far from being the ineffectual enemy they had expected. Finally there was another, more human reason for the warmth of Ehrendorf's welcome: he had arrived at a moment when General Heath's staff was secretly heaving a collective sigh of relief.

For a moment, half an hour earlier, it had seemed possible that in the General's absence they might *themselves* have to come to a decision on Murray-Lyon's request to withdraw the 11th Division from Jitra to a new position behind the Kedah River. Only III Corps HQ had detailed knowledge, after all, of the grave way the situation had developed. But think of it! After a night without sleep (for in KL the lights had been burning, too, while men pored over maps) to be presented with such a dilemma! To be asked at a moment's notice when a telephone rang to sanction the abandonment of a defensive position established months, even years, in advance ... and that in favour of a position not yet prepared!

No wonder, mused Ehrendorf, enjoying toast and marmalade and a welcome cup of hot coffee, that this particular potato which Murray-Lyon had just raked out of the embers and presented to HQ III Corps, after some moments of frenzied juggling from one hand to another should be got rid of with relief into the less sensitive palms of Malaya Command. When

Murray-Lyon's request had been considered, however, and judgement passed on it by Percival and Heath in Singapore, their verdict being that the 11th Division should stand its ground and fight the battle at Jitra as planned, gloom descended on the staff once more, in time for lunch ... for it had turned out that there was, after all, a drawback to passing this crucial decision on to Malaya Command, which was simply that Malaya Command had made the wrong choice. That much was clear, even to Ehrendorf who had studied the positions and managed by tea-time to get the hang of what was going on. And what he saw on the battlefield in his mind's eye as he sat eating cherry cake and drinking tea, and even enjoying them in the rather bleak sort of way of someone who considers that he might as well be dead, was everywhere the Second Law triumphant.

But even in terms of the Second Law the tribulations of the 11th Division were to be wondered at, for they had spent two whole days (while Brooke-Popham inspected his thoughts) waiting at the Siamese border under a tropical downpour for the order to spring forward and give the Japs a sock on the jaw as they were trying to land at Singora. And when Brooke-Popham had at last decided not to push forward into Siam, after all, helped out of his dilemma by the fact that it was now too late, anyway, the Japanese in the meantime having completed their landing satisfactorily, the two brigades of 11th Division (there was another brigade waiting in the wings somewhere, Ehrendorf had not yet discovered where) had trudged back to find their prepared defences at Jitra flooded out and far from 'prepared' ... for the key part they were supposed to play in defending Malaya from the main Japanese thrust across the border.

What this amounted to, he was thinking as he said, yes, he would like another cup of tea, thanks, to the saturnine and upper-class young captain at his elbow, was that the British had been caught half-way between one plan and another and were in imminent danger of not succeeding with either. But in the meantime the plot had been thickening ominously elsewhere, for the column of two battalions under Lieutenant-Colonel Moorehead which was supposed to dash forward into Siam and deny the Japanese the road through the mountains from Patani by capturing the only defensible position on it: the Ledge ... had not managed to do so. The Japanese had got there first. What could one say about this except that it was a pity?

It was worse than a pity, it was a catastrophe, for it meant that even if the 11th Division succeeded in baling out their flooded defences, repairing the barbed wire and putting down their signals equipment in time to meet the Japanese attack, they would still have to face the prospect of having their lines of communication with the rest of the British forces severed by a Japanese column coming along that road through the mountains.

The best that one could say of the situation, as Ehrendorf saw it, was that one catastrophe (unprepared defences at Jitra) more or less cancelled out the other catastrophe (failure to secure the road through the mountains) because, after all, you could only lose Jitra to the enemy *once* and it was immaterial whether you did so by unprepared defences, or loss of a road behind you, or most generously of all, by both at the same time. Although, mused Ehrendorf, if it *were* possible to lose Jitra twice, these guys would certainly stand a good chance of doing so. All the same, they were treating him very hospitably and someone in their outfit clearly knew how to make a good cup of tea.

To make matters just a little worse, the 'prepared' position at Jitra was even at the best of times a long way from being the ideal place to make a stand, scattered as it was over a front of a dozen miles or so on each side of the main road from the Siamese border. Probing attacks by Japanese infantry and tanks had already put to flight or partly destroyed two reserve battalions sent forward to delay them, thereby rendering the defences even more shallow than they had been to begin with. Ehrendorf, whose favourite bedside reading since boyhood had been military strategy and who considered himself an unrecognized military genius obliged to fritter away his talents on diplomatic and administrative matters, shook his head over the lack of reserves; there should have another battalion of the reserve brigade (the 28th) but it had been left behind to guard the airfields at Alor Star and Sungei Patani against a possible parachute attack. There was, therefore, nothing serious in the way of reserve which could be used for a counter-attack. During the night, while he had been dozing in the train, the Japanese advance guard had attacked twice, the first time straight down the road against the position held by the Leicesters, who had succeeded in driving them back, the second time to the east of the road where they had managed to find a slight opening between the Leicesters' right flank and the Japs' left, thus threatening them both. Attempts to dislodge them and restore the integrity of the line had so far failed.

The day was unbearably hot and sultry with intermittent downpours and thunderstorms. Ehrendorf, whose digestion had barely recovered from the strain of eating up the odds and ends of food from his refrigerator in Singapore but who was still obliged to rely heavily upon eating, both as a comfort to keep up his own leaden spirits and as a means of social contact with the staff officers of III Corps, by tea-time had begun to feel dangerously bloated once more. So presently, while news was circulating that the Japs had attacked again and driven yet further into the already dented line between the Leicesters and the Jats, he asked to be directed to the 'bathroom' so that he could 'wash up', a locution which caused some of his new comrades to titter vaguely while they considered this new in-stalment of bad news from the front. Once in the 'bathroom' he forced himself to throw up: this was a disagreeable sensa-tion but he soon felt somewhat better and found that on his return he could manage another slice of cake and cup of tea.

Over supper, which began with rather dry *ikan merah* fried in butter with lemon, there was talk of a counter-attack, but also of straightening out the line by withdrawing the Leicesters to a position farther back along the Bata River. While drinking beer and eating a creamy chicken curry whose fire was some-what moderated by the fresh grapefruit and papaya with which it was served, Ehrendorf discovered, by a heroic effort of con-centration on what his fellow-diners were saying, that some of them believed it had been decided that the Leicesters and East Surreys were to counter-attack, while others believed that the identical units were to retreat. He tried to draw attention to these discrepant opinions but found it hard to get anyone's attention and was rewarded only with one or two baffled, toothy grins and, when he persisted, signs of offence being taken. It was true that he himself had had one or two beers ... 'But what a gang of clowns, all the same!' he thought in wonder.

In due course, as the evening advanced, the first signs began to appear that the confusion at III Corps HQ was mirrored among the troops at Jitra. It also became clear that if the 11th Division was having such difficulty containing the advance guard of the Japanese force they would have little prospect of resisting the main assault which was bound to come in a matter of hours. Between the pudding, which was prunes and custard, and the cheese, things continued to go wrong at a comfortable rate. News came that Penang, still defenceless to air attack, had been heavily bombed for the second day running and that the docks and much of George Town were on fire. There was also word that the force commanded by Moorehead, which had failed to reach the Ledge in time and which had instead retired to take up a defensive position at Kroh, had suffered considerable losses. Would it have any chance now of resisting a Japanese thrust through the mountains led by tanks?

On the heels of this bad news of Moorehead's force came the word that Murray-Lyon had telephoned again for Heath's permission to withdraw; once again he had been referred to Singapore. 'This time,' thought Ehrendorf, 'either they agree or the entire 11th Division will be cashing in its chips.' For some minutes the Brigadier at the end of the table, none too sober, had been eyeing Ehrendorf with a sardonic and petulant expression. This man, who was short of breath and getting on in years, had a distressing habit of moistening his toothbrush moustache with a long and pendulous lower lip, an idiosyncrasy which he repeated at regular intervals. Now, as if guessing Ehrendorf's thoughts, he said in a loud and condescending tone: 'Perhaps our Yankee visitor would give us the benefit of his appraisal of the situation based, I've no doubt, on long experience of warfare in this part of the world.'

'I'm afraid, sir,' replied Ehrendorf in a neutral tone, 'that in such a complex matter ...' And he shrugged diffidently.

But the Brigadier was enjoying himself. 'Come, come ... No need to be bashful, Captain.'

And he stared at Ehrendorf sardonically while the other officers grew quiet waiting to see how he would deal with the situation. This was by no means the first time they had seen the Brigadier making sport of a newcomer. But Ehrendorf replied unruffled: 'If you really want to know what I think, sir, it's this ... I think the 11th Division is in serious trouble if it stays where it is, that it should have been withdrawn from Jitra this morning by a competent commander in full possession of the facts, and that it must, at any rate, be withdrawn now before the main Jap attack and preferably behind a river wide enough to stop their tanks. Surely, sir, nobody is in any doubt about that?' And he gazed with equanimity at the Brigadier.

Gradually, despite the temperature, the glistening brows and necks, and the sweat-darkened shirts of the officers sitting round the table, the atmosphere grew chilly in the room. It was felt that Ehrendorf, who had been not only tolerated but treated rather well during this long day of battle, which had been felt no less keenly at III Corps HQ than at Jitra two hundred and fifty miles away, had displayed ingratitude by this low assessment of their efforts. They waited for the reply which would put this brash, too-clever-by-half American in his place. They waited and watched and, in due course, the Brigadier's lower lip climbed towards his nose and moistened his neatly-clipped moustache. Whether, given time, he would have made any other reply it was impossible to say, because at this moment news came that Malaya Command had authorized Murray-Lyon to disengage and withdraw behind the Kedah River. And most likely he would do so tonight under cover of darkness.

'Thank God for that!' said Ehrendorf, smiling bleakly at his companions. The battle of Jitra was over but at least the 11th Division had been saved. This might be a good time, if it were not raining, to take a stroll in the fresh air before the Second Law, eating away steadily like worm in the rafters, brought another section of the roof crashing down.

38

'Cheong, what thing trouble?'

Even the Major, by no means the most observant of men, could not have failed to take note of the Chinese servant's deep sighs and of the glances of despair he dispensed to right and left as he went about his duties. Moreover, Cheong was the last person to make a fuss unnecessarily. 'Cheong, blong what thing trouble?' the Major insisted.

'My too much fear,' said Cheong grimly. 'Japanese just now catch Penang.'

'Nonsense, Cheong,' exclaimed the Major, relieved to hear that Cheong's worries were of such a chimerical nature. 'Japanese this fashion no can. This blong fool pidgin.'

But the servant did not seemed reassured. 'S'pose Japanese catch Penang, tomollow maybe catch Singapore! Japanese pay Blitish too much lose face!' And shaking his head sadly he marched off to the kitchen refusing all comfort.

'Cheong has some story about Penang falling to the Japanese,' the Major informed Matthew later in the morning. 'I don't know where he's got it from. But once these absurd rumours start buzzing around one finds that even a sensible chap like him is believing them. Nothing could be worse for the morale of the Asiatics than this sort of thing. Besides, where would he have got the news even if it *were* true?' the Major added a trifle uneasily. 'There's been nothing in the papers about the Japs being anywhere near Penang.' Undoubtedly the whole thing was nonsense and the Major now regretted even mentioning it to Matthew who looked depressed enough already. 'Are you all right?' he asked. For the past three or four days Matthew had been sitting listlessly at his desk, haggard, unwashed, unshaven, the very picture of despair. He no longer ate anything. He was growing thin. Even his appetite for the rubber business had disappeared. At first, when he had still been expecting a visit from Vera Chiang, life had seemed capable of striking one or two sparks of interest from the dull succession of hours. But as the days went by and there was no sign of her he had relapsed into apathy.

What did it matter? he wondered, scratching his itchy scalp. She was beautiful, certainly, but so what? Even the idea of being married to a beautiful woman like Miss Chiang which had once seemed to him a delightful and tempting fantasy had lost its appeal. Was there any point in possessing a beautiful woman all to oneself? The answer was: no, not really. For, after all, he reasoned, having the proprietorial rights over a woman that a husband has over his wife or that a lover has over his mistress *does not actually get you any further forward*! For, unless you are the sort of Mohammedan who keeps his wife heavily veiled, her beauty is scarcely less available to casual passers-by in the street than it is to *you*, whose job it is to foot the bill for her food, lodging and general maintenance. True, the husband or lover has the added gratification of a range of intimacies usually denied to the passer-by. But look here! The effect produced by a beautiful woman is *visual* ... touching her does not bring you any closer to her beauty than touching the paint of a Botticelli brings you closer to the beauty of his painting. It might even be argued that the closer you get to this painting or this woman the less you are able to appreciate its or her beauty, or even what makes each different from others of its kind. In the most intimate position of all, with your eyeball, so to speak, resting against the paint itself you would be hard put to it to tell any difference at all between this one and another. What had happened in the case of beautiful women, Matthew reflected, was that lust and aesthetic pleasure had got hopelessly mixed up. As a result, men felt obliged to marry beautiful women when in many cases they would have been better advised to marry a plain woman with a pleasant disposition and acquire, perhaps, some compensatingly beautiful object such as a piece of T'ang porcelain.

Matthew tried to engage the Major in conversation on the nature of feminine beauty. Very likely the Major had had more practical experience in these matters than he had. But the Major was distraught and plainly found it hard to give his full attention to disentangling the lustful from the aesthetic. The Major did try to cheer Matthew up, though, explaining to him that depression was bound to follow such a fever, never failed to do so. Matthew, unshaven, had taken to sitting all day with his feet on his father's desk, spinning the chamber of a revolver he had found in one of its drawers.

'A young man like you should think of getting married, you know,' said the Major who found the appearance of the revolver disquieting.

'Well, you never got married yourself, did you, Major?' asked Matthew accusingly.

'Ouf, well, no, I suppose not,' agreed the Major, taken aback by this frontal assault. 'Just between you and me, though, there have been moments when I've rather regretted it, just now and then, you know. After all, when all's said and done ...' The Major lapsed into silence and at the same time felt himself invaded by loneliness and despair, so that the muscles of his face which was still wearing a cheerful expression began to ache with the effort of holding the expression in place and, severely pruned though it was, the moustache on his upper lip felt as heavy as antlers. 'Anyway,' he said at last, 'if you don't want to get married I think it might be a good idea to mention it to the Blacketts in the not-too-distant future.'

Matthew could see that there was something in what the Major said. Monty had dropped in the previous afternoon, explaining that he had had to escape from his family whose conversation these days was limited to talk of wedding arrangements. Nor was it simply 'bridesmaids and all that rubbish'; now, a prey to this new and, in Monty's opinion, sickening obsession, his family really had 'the bit between their teeth' ...

There was endless talk of recipes for wedding-cakes, of patterns of wedding-dresses and of printers who would have to be consulted about suitable invitation cards. 'They really have it in for you, old boy,' Monty had warned him. 'Mark my words!'

'But I don't think I even said I wanted to marry her,' protested Matthew apathetically. 'I mean, good gracious ...'

It was true, he really must do something about it but just at the moment he felt he could not quite face having it out with the Blacketts. And, after all, why not get married? Matthew wondered, grimly scratching his itchy scalp with the barrel of the revolver. After all, it is what everybody does. He was thirty-three, no longer a young man, really. All his Oxford friends and contemporaries except Ehrendorf were long since married and many of them had swarms of children into the bargain. His life certainly had not amounted to much so far: he might as well settle for reproducing himself like everyone else ... at least that would be *something*. For a while, during his early optimistic years in Geneva pacing the deck of the League of Nations, he had believed he was playing a part, minuscule certainly but worthwhile none the less, in steering that great ship towards a hopeful shore. But then, torpedoed by the Axis Powers one after another, the League had sunk leaving merely a patch of oil and a few spars. The fact was that since the League had gone down, Matthew had been in a muddle; he had found it hard to bring himself to abandon ship, sunk though it was.

But sooner or later one must face reality. One must lay a solid foundation for one's life. The League had been like a pleasant collective fantasy of mankind, dreaming of a better life for itself the way a tramp asleep in a hedge might dream of living in a mansion. Yes, why should he not get married to Joan and begin to live a more practical sort of life? One must make up one's mind in the long run. And Matthew sighed, dejectedly scratching his ear with the revolver and pulling the trigger as he did so. The click caused the Major to start violently. 'I'll go over and see the Blacketts later on,' said Matthew in a more resolute tone, taking his feet off the desk, putting down the revolver and sitting up straight.

On his way to the Blacketts' compound Matthew paused on its threshold in the green antechamber lit with rare tropical flowers. Here, on his way to propose marriage to Joan (a spurious proposal, if Monty was to be believed, since she appeared to think it had already been made), standing beside the African mallow and crêpe myrtle, cassia and rambutan, Matthew suddenly found himself captured like a bird in a net by the heavy perfumes that wavered invisibly over the dripping leaves and glistening flowers. And while he was still lingering there to sniff and marvel at the new sensations which were flooding into his mind, one, two, three butterflies, astonishingly beautiful and of a kind he had never seen before with pink and yellow on their wings and long, trailing tails like kites came fluttering around him, as if they had taken a liking to his freshly ironed linen suit and were considering settling on it. He watched them, filled with wonder, noticing how the beat of their wings, slower than that of European butterflies, made them rise and fall as if in slow motion, and swoop and glide almost like birds. And presently these three butterflies, which had finally decided to forsake the elegant suit in which Matthew was going to make his proposal for the scarlet flowers of the Indian coral tree, were joined by a fourth, even more beautiful and languorous in flight, and larger, too, with black and white embroidered wings which suggested the scribbles of the batik shirts he had seen the Malays wearing. This butterfly Matthew was tentatively able to identify, thanks to a manual the Major had lent him while he was convalescent, as a Common Tree Nymph.

To have a profound spiritual or sensual experience, he was thinking as he strode on into the corridor of white-flowered pili nut trees, one must rupture one's old habits of feeling. That was it, exactly ... and that was what he would be doing by marrying Joan. You have to burst through the skin of your old life which surrounds you the way a bladder of skin surrounds the meat and oatmeal of a haggis! He paused on the white colonnaded steps which led up to the Blacketts' house, pleased to find himself in such a positive frame of mind at this important moment of his life. Then, straightening his shoulders, he plunged into the shade of the verandah in search of Joan.

Inside, however, he found himself unexpectedly baulked. Miss Blackett was not at home, though she was expected back shortly. Would Mr Webb wait for her in the drawing-room? Matthew surveyed the old Malay servant, Abdul, feeling some of his resolution draining away: the old man's eyes, dim and watery with age, were expressionless. Matthew said he would wait and was shown into the drawing-room. It was cool in here and a great stillness prevailed. A patch of whiteness stirred on the white sofa and Matthew recognized a friend; Ming Toy,

Kate's Siamese cat was taking its afternoon nap in the coolest and quietest room it could find. Matthew went to sit down beside it, feeling in his pocket for a letter the Major had handed to him as he was on his way out. He opened it: it contained only a photograph. Matthew gazed at it, moved, for it was a photograph he remembered having seen once before, years ago, when he and Ehrendorf had been at Oxford together.

They had been taking an evening stroll by the Cherwell, he remembered, towards the end of their last summer term. It was one of those hushed, damp, rather chilly June evenings that seem to go on for ever before darkness falls. The knowledge that they would soon be coming to the end of this phase of their life, saying goodbye to friends and launching out into careers that were still barely imaginable, had cast an air of melancholy over them. There had been a smell of damp grass, perhaps the flutter of a water-hen in the thicket overhanging the river bank. Ehrendorf had been saying how he felt he had changed during the time he had spent in Europe, how difficult he believed he would find it returning to his home town in America. 'Why don't you stay here then?' Matthew had asked. Ehrendorf had handed him the photograph then, saying with a smile: 'My brothers and sisters. They'd never understand if I didn't go back.'

Matthew was now studying the photograph again. It showed Ehrendorf looking younger, as he had looked at Oxford, but otherwise not much changed. He was tall, handsome, smiling as ever. The absence of a moustache made him look younger, too. He was standing in the middle of the picture looking directly into the lens of the camera: grouped around him was what looked like a brood of dwarfs and hunchbacks, all gazing up reverently at their brother with gargoyle faces.

Well! Matthew still remembered how surprised he had been by the contrast between Ehrendorf and his brothers and sisters: it was as if every virtue and physical grace had been concentrated in him to the detriment of his adoring siblings. And Ehrendorf adored them, too, that was the point ... or why else would he have gone back to Kansas City (or wherever it was) when all his interests and the people who understood him were no longer there but in Europe? But in the end Kansas City had not quite managed to claim him ... nor Europe either, come to that. Poor Ehrendorf! Thanks to the Rhodes scholarship that had taken him to Oxford the poor fellow had split in two like an amoeba! Half of him had now fetched up in Singapore and had made itself unhappy by falling in love with the English girl whom he, Matthew, was about to marry. Matthew sighed, wondering whether it might not be a better idea to put it off until another time. The last thing he wanted to do was to hurt Ehrendorf's feelings.

While he was considering this he seized Ming Toy and dragged that furry creature nearer; he had been interrupted by Walter on a previous occasion while trying to find out what sex the cat belonged to: this would be a good opportunity to pursue his researches. Ming Toy lay there, still half asleep and unprotesting, while Matthew once again lifted his magnificent tail and inspected his copiously furred hindquarters for some sign of gender. Finding none he picked up a pencil and began to rummage about with it. Ming Toy began to purr.

'Oh hello . . .' Walter was standing in the door, giving Matthew a very odd look indeed

'Oh!' exclaimed Matthew, startled. He hurriedly dropped Ming Toy's tail and shoved him aside, deciding it was probably best not to try to explain. 'I was just waiting for Joan,' he said, recovering quickly, 'but perhaps I could have a word with you about this replanting business . . .'

'I can only give you five minutes, I'm afraid. Come into my study.'

Matthew had not been in Walter's study before and was somewhat surprised to find that the room had an unused air. Walter himself had the air of a stranger as he looked around: indeed, he seldom used this room, preferring the tranquillity of his dressing-room on the first floor. He was looking impatiently at his watch, so Matthew explained that he thought it was wrong for the rubber companies managed by Blackett and Webb to be replanting healthy trees. Mature trees produced rubber badly needed for the War Effort; replanting them with immature rubber which yielded nothing simply did not make sense.

'Monty told you, did he, about the excess profits tax? You realize that we make the same "standard" profit whatever we do?'

Matthew nodded.

'And that replanting expenses are allowable against tax? Yes. Well, I agree that if we were the only people in the rubber industry there would be something in what you say. But alas, we're not. We have rivals and competitors, my dear boy! If we don't replant now with this new high-yielding material, particularly now when there's a clear financial advantage in doing so, while our competitors *do* replant, where shall we be when it reaches maturity? Not on Easy Street, I can tell you! Because we'll find ourselves producing half as much rubber per acre as, say, Langfield and Bowser at the same cost, or perhaps even a higher cost. It simply won't wash, I'm afraid. Now does that answer your objection?'

'Well, not really, no, Walter,' said Matthew becoming physically restless as he always did when excited but controlling himself as best he could. 'Because I don't deny the commercial advantage. How could I? I don't know anything about these things. But this is a matter of principle. Your argument is the one that businessmen always use when asked to make some sacrifice in the public interest: "We would like to help but it's out of the question if we are to remain competitive." The business community in Rangoon said exactly the same thing years ago when asked to make some contribution to the welfare of the coolies who were in the most dreadful state of poverty and dying like flies. But no! Spending money to help those poor devils would have made us vulnerable, Blackett and Webb included ... You see, I've been reading about our dealings in the rice trade in my father's papers and frankly ... Ah!' he grunted as the cat, which had taken a liking to him and followed them into the study, suddenly sprang into his lap.

'The fact that an argument is often used, by businessmen or anyone else,' replied Walter calmly, 'does not unfortunately mean that it is any the less true. Would that it were! As for using all our resources now, as you recommend, for the War Effort and finding ourselves as a nation without any means of support when the war is over, well, I doubt if that is a very good idea. A nation, Matthew, is roughly speaking as strong as it is wealthy. And it's as wealthy as, again roughly speaking, its individual businesses are healthy. And they are healthy only as long as they are able to compete with the industries and firms of other nations in their line of business. If we follow your advice the big Dutch estates in Java and Sumatra (which, incidentally, got on to new clones before we did) will have put us out of business by 1946 or 1947 when their new stock matures.' Walter beamed at Matthew who, for his part, found himself at a loss for words, partly because this was an arguement he had not yet considered, partly because Ming Toy was kneading his trousers in order to test out his (or possibly her) claws, evidently not realizing that Matthew's sensitive skin lay just underneath.

Walter got to his feet.

'But wait, Walter ...' Matthew sprang up and the cat, which he had forgotten about, in turn had to spring for its life. Matthew hurried after Walter. 'It's madness! With the Japs in the north of the country we should be producing every scrap of rubber we can. Who knows but that in a few months they won't have taken over a lot of the estates?' Matthew clapped a hand to his brow as he tried to catch up with Walter. Wait, what was he doing arguing with Walter? He had planned to ask Joan to marry him and here he was instead, arguing with her father.

'There's no shipping, anyway,' said Walter, scowling for the first time in their discussion. 'The wharves are packed with rubber already that we have no way of shifting. Well, now I really must be going, old chap. Duty calls. You and Joan are getting along all right, are you?' he called back over his shoulder as he hurried down the steps to where his car was waiting. 'Come and have supper. Bring the Major, too. We don't dress, as you know.'

'Well, that was another thing I wanted to ... about getting married and so on ...' cried Matthew. But Walter, with a final wave, had disappeared into the back of his Bentley and it had moved off.

39

Matthew sat down on the steps, rather disconsolately. Joan still had not returned. Perhaps this was just as well, for he was by no means sure that he was all that keen on marrying her, after all. It had certainly seemed a good idea earlier in the afternoon, though. Besides, he had gone to the trouble of shaving and putting on a new suit. 'Perhaps she will refuse,' he thought hopefully; that would settle the matter without his having to make a decision. (But no, there was no chance of her refusing.) He sighed, and for some reason felt as lonely and as unwanted as if she *had* refused him.

Meanwhile, four bright eyes were surveying him from behind a dazzling cascade of bougainvillaea. One pair belonged to Kate Blackett, the other to a friend of Kate's called Melanie

Langfield. This Melanie Langfield, who was of an age with Kate, belonged to the detested Langfield family and was, in fact, a grand-daughter of old Solomon Langfield, the mere thought of whom was enough to make the bristles on Walter's spine puff up with loathing. The raid which the two girls had just performed on the larder had been partly foiled by the vigilance of Abdul, the major-domo. Before being discovered, however, they had each managed to get a spoonful of Kate's 'Radio Malt' and Melanie had had the presence of mind to slip a jar of lemonade crystals into the pocket of her frock. Now she and Kate, hidden by the bougainvillaea, were alternately dipping moistened fingers into the jar and licking off the crystals that stuck to them, enjoying the tingling acid taste on their tongues.

What was a member of the hated Langfield family doing at the Blacketts' house? Kate and Melanie, as it happened, had been sent to the same school in England and neither of them had any other friends of her own age in Singapore. Since neither of their respective sets of parents could be convinced that the other children who abounded in the colony were quite the social equals of their own daughter both families had found themselves in a dilemma. The result was that though the Langfields and the Blacketts did not for a moment cease to speak ill of each other or to detest each other any the less heartily, they did sometimes grudgingly agree to the smaller children playing together 'unofficially'. This was fortunate because otherwise Kate and Melanie might have had to spend their childhood totally immured, as so many unhappy children do, behind their parents' snobbery. Kate and Melanie would be allowed to be friends for as long as they could be thought of as 'children'; in just such a way Monty and Joan had been allowed when small to play with little Langfields they would now scarcely acknowledge in the street even if the rickshaws they were travelling in happened to pull up alongside each other at a traffic light. Thanks to this fiction that a child did not exist or, at worst, like an immature wasp had not yet grown its sting, Walter could even, and often did, reach out a paternal hand to fondle Melanie's charming blonde curls and without suffering any ill effects whatsoever. But if you had insisted on telling him that this was not a child but a *Langfield* he would certainly have sprung back in horror. He would have been as likely then to stroke the slimy head of a toad as little Melanie's curls.

Melanie, as it happened, was a pale little creature who looked younger than Kate though they were the same age. But her pallor concealed a powerful personality and a restless inventor of schemes. As for obeying rules, at school she had more than once spat in the eye of authority (she had practised spitting in the garden in Singapore). Rules were made to be broken, in Melanie's view. Yes, Langfield blood ran in her veins all right; if Walter could have read her school report he would have been in no doubt about that. But perhaps she had mellowed a little, had she not, in the course of the past few months as her body began the upsetting change from that of a child to that of a woman? Well, no, not really, no, she had not mellowed at all. All that had happened was that her preoccupations had begun to change, and Kate's with them: both girls had become more curious about *men*. A few months earlier those four eyes observing Matthew would have passed over him without really noticing him, as over a potted plant or a chest of drawers. But now they remained on him attentively as he sat on the steps with his head in his hands.

'Darling, whatever is the matter with the Human Bean?'

'Darling, I haven't the faintest.'

'Haven't you, darling? Let's go and ask him.'

Matthew was quite glad to see the girls, though surprised that Kate, who usually called him 'Matthew' should call him 'My dear darling Human Bean'. When she had introduced him to her dearest friend in the whole world, Melanie, he asked her to explain and she told him how Ehrendorf had called him a 'wonderful human bean'. 'Ah, poor Ehrendorf,' he thought. 'Where is he now, I wonder?'

While this was being settled Melanie's eyes had been examining Matthew's face in a way which was every bit as calculating as one might have expected even of a senior Langfield. And now she had a suggestion which to Kate seemed staggering in its audacity: the Human Bean should take them to the cinema! This was daring: neither girl was allowed to go to the cinema until she had forced her way through a veritable thicket of preconditions: an eternity of good behaviour was demanded, not to mention school reports which were favourable almost to the point of fawning ... and, most thorny of all, a preliminary inspection of the film by an adult member of the family.

But if Melanie's first suggestion was daring, her second was breathtaking in its temerity. For, fixing her bright, unblinking eyes on Matthew's face like a lizard watching a moth, she added: 'We want to go and see Robert Taylor in *Waterloo Bridge*.' Kate grew very tense; she held her breath and her heart began to pound. She had difficulty in preventing herself from gasping at this. *Waterloo Bridge* was a picture for grown-ups. It would never have qualified as suitable in a million years! It spoke (so they had been told by Mrs Langfield's Irish maid) of intimate and romantic relations between men and women. It was about all *that* sort of thing (for Kate 'all that sort of thing' was a churning vat of dark and still mysterious experience from beneath whose tap-tapping lid there issued an occasional whiff of intoxicating steam). She suddenly began to feel rather sick with excitement and dread. One moment it had been an ordinary, rather boring afternoon, the next she was walking along the edge of a dizzy precipice with the gravel crumbling from under her feet.

Matthew, meanwhile, was looking rather bemused, like someone who has just been roused from a heavy afternoon nap. He looked vaguely at his watch, shook his wrist and looked at it again. But it was working, after all.

'Go on, be a sport,' said Melanie. 'We could go to the four o'clock show and be back for supper,' she added persuasively.

'No one would know,' put in Kate, and received a vicious, warning pinch from Melanie: she would arouse the Bean's suspicions by making stupid remarks like that.

Matthew was not all that keen, anyway. It was too hot to sit in a picture-house. 'I really came over to see Joan, you know. There was something I wanted to ask her.'

'She won't be back for *ages*!'

'Probably not before supper!'

'Oh, won't she?' Matthew looked rather baffled and again consulted his watch. 'Couldn't we go another time? Say, the day after tomorrow, for example?'

'But that's *Sunday*!' screamed Melanie. 'Nobody goes to the pictures on *Sunday*. It's simply not *done*!'

'Oh, well then ...' Matthew hesitated. He really wanted to return to the Mayfair to ponder his conversation with Walter and perhaps discuss it with the Major. 'You're sure Joan won't be back till supper?'

'Of course we're sure, you dumb-bell!' shouted Melanie, beside herself with excitement and frustration. By now she had sized Matthew up and she could see that he needed a *firm hand*.

'Wouldn't you like instead just to go and eat ices at John Little's?'

'No we bloody well wouldn't!' declared Melanie emphatically: she had noticed Kate brightening at the idea, just like a little girl, and knew it must be scotched immediately.

Matthew scratched his head uncertainly and looked around. Then he again looked at his watch but that still offered no assistance. The girls stood there like coiled springs.

'Well, in that case ...' he murmured and came to a stop again. Melanie rolled her eyes to heaven at these hesitations. 'All right then,' he said at last. 'I'll ask the Major if I can borrow his car.'

The girls gave a great whoop of delight.

'But you must bring your gas-mask cases.'

'Have we got to?' They had been issued, by some stroke of bureaucratic insensitivity, with (of all things!) Mickey Mouse gas-masks! As if they were little kids! It was too, too shaming! They tried to explain this to Matthew. They would rather be *gassed*! But Matthew was adamant ... No gas-masks, no pictures. The girls were so overwhelmed, however, by the startling success of Melanie's boldness that in the end they were prepared to concede gas-masks. Curiously, as they dashed back into the house to get them they were holding hands tightly like two little children, having forgotten to be sophisticated in their excitement.

Accompanying Matthew back through the compound to the Mayfair, Kate and Melanie were inclined to be furtive at first. They were afraid of being spotted at the last moment by some interfering adult. But once they had plunged into the corridor of pili nut trees they considered themselves fairly safe, barring some coincidence. Mrs Blackett never ventured this far.

Unfortunately, while borrowing the keys of the Lagonda from the Major, Matthew could not resist mentioning the conversation he had just had with Walter about replanting. And the Major, who was also concerned about this matter, mentioned the interesting fact that two or three of the other small rubber companies manged by Blackett and Webb had attempted, in the interests of the War Effort, to stop this replanting in order to maintain the highest possible rate of tapping. But faced with Blackett and Webb's orders to the contrary they had been unable to do anything about it. Matthew was astonished. 'But that's absurd, Major! How can they stop a company doing what it wants? They only manage it, don't they? They don't own it.'

So, while the minutes ticked away and the girls grew fretful, the Major explained. Blackett and Webb were responsible not only for the daily management (buying of equipment and supplies, selling of produce, tapping policy, hiring of labour and so on) but for the investment of profits as well. For some years now they had made it their policy to invest the profits of one company in the shares of the other companies for which they acted as agents. The result of this incestuous investment as far as the Mayfair, to give an example, was concerned, was that the Mayfair's shares were concentrated in other companies controlled by Blackett and Webb, while the shares of each other company were held by the Mayfair and other Blackett companies. Thus, a revolt against Blackett and Webb's tapping policy by the directors of any single company could be easily quelled by marshalling proxy votes from the others. The only way in which Blackett and Webb's grip on the destinies of individual companies could be loosened would be by a simultaneous uprising, so to speak, of a majority of them acting in concert. But since the investment had taken place not only in rubber but in all sorts of other companies, shipping, trading, insurance and whatnot ... such a simultaneous uprising was naturally out of the question. The beauty of this system from Blackett and Webb's point of view was that they had not invested a penny in many of these companies and yet they lay as firmly in their grip as if they owned them lock, stock and barrel.

'Oh, do let's go!' pleaded Kate. 'We'll miss the beginning.'

'But good gracious! Can that be legal?'

'Perfectly, it appears.'

'Do get a move on. There's no time for all this *talk*!' Melanie seized the dazed Matthew by one arm and began to drag him physically towards the verandah door. But she was very slight and Matthew was very heavy: she only managed to drag him one or two reluctant paces.

'Well I must say ...' Matthew might have gone on standing there until they had missed the newsreel had not the Major noticed the girls' anxiety and said: 'But I can see these young ladies don't want me to waste any more of your time. What are you going to see, by the way?'

'Oh, wait,' said Matthew. 'Something or other called ...'

'A picture with Robert Taylor and Vivien Leigh,' gabbled Melanie, interrupting him with the presence of mind for which Langfields were notorious in Singapore. 'Now we must *go*!'

And go they did, at long last. Hardly had they turned out into the road than they passed Joan's open Riley tourer just returning from the Cold Storage. Joan caught sight of them as they passed and the girls saw her head turn. But by that time they were away. Matthew, who managed to be both a cautious and a reckless driver at the same time, was peering with grim concentration through his dusty spectacles at the road ahead. He did not see her.

40

One hour, two hours passed. The sun dipped towards Sumatra in the west. Now Matthew was once more peering at the road ahead with a grim expression but this time the Lagonda was going along Orchard Road in the opposite direction, to drop Melanie at the Langfields' elegant house on Nassim Road. It was cooler. The city was bathed in a gentle golden light which, for a little while before sunset, came as a reprieve from the dazzling hours of daylight. But still, Matthew had the dazed and vulnerable feeling, the slight taste of ashes, which he always experienced when he came out of a cinema into daylight. The girls sat crammed together beside him, for the Lagonda was only a two-seater, each busy with her own thoughts. As far as Kate was concerned these had a somewhat apprehensive cast. She was afraid there might be a row when she got home. She was also afraid that she might have got Matthew into trouble by taking advantage of his innocence.

For the most part, however, Kate's thoughts were concerned with the film they had just seen. As they were coming out of the picture-house Melanie had whispered: 'Isn't he divine?' Kate had nodded vehemently, but with closed lips. She was not certain whether Melanie meant Matthew or Robert Taylor and was afraid of agreeing to the wrong one. But after a moment Melanie added condescendingly: 'She's not *bad* ... but I don't think that sort of woman is *really* attractive, do you?' This time Kate shook her head vehemently, still with set lips. Melanie could only mean Vivien Leigh, that much was settled at least. But whether or not that sort of woman was 'really attractive' was something that Kate had not even considered. Nor was she even sure how to begin to have an opinion. Melanie was simply amazing! While she herself had been struggling to understand what was happening in the story (which had suddenly grown puzzling with Vivien Leigh dressed in a beret, a sweater and high-heeled shoes hanging around Waterloo Station and saying hello to soldiers for no obvious reason), Melanie had clearly been coming to the conclusion that if Robert Taylor had had to choose between her and Vivien Leigh he would have chosen Melanie!

Kate was also afraid that Melanie had been rather rude to Matthew. For Matthew had grown restless once the old newsreel was over (he had been gratified to see a hundred thousand Italian prisoners being marched along in North Africa by one British Tommy). He had sat placidly enough through the beginning when Robert Taylor in uniform said to his driver: 'To France ... to Waterloo Station,' and even through the air-raid on Waterloo Bridge when he bumped into Vivien Leigh with the sirens going and the wardens blowing whistles and said: 'You little fool, are you tired of life?' and she had said, as they were walking to the air-raid shelter: 'Would it be too unmilitary if we were to run?' and gave him a good luck charm to stop him being killed, which seemed to be made of Bakelite.

During all that part Matthew had not been too bad: he had only begun to fidget during the scenes when the strict sort of headmistress who ran the ballet was being beastly to Vivien Leigh who wanted to flirt with Robert Taylor who had not had to go to France after all, but then he had had to go before they had time to get married. Matthew had fidgeted worse and worse during the scene in the Candlelight Club with all the violins when they danced to the 'Farewell Waltz' which sounded very like 'Auld Lang Syne', and worse still during the scene where Vivien Leigh, who had been sacked from the ballet and had run out of money, read in the paper that he had been killed, while she was waiting in the Ritz to have tea with his mother, Lady Margaret, who turned up late and found her drunk.

'Are you sure you want to stay for the rest?' Matthew had asked suddenly in a loud voice at about the time when Vivien Leigh had started hanging around Waterloo Station saying things like 'hello' and 'welcome home' to soldiers. It was at that moment that Melanie had asked him to be quiet, she was trying to concentrate, and a man in the row in front had said shush. Kate had turned once or twice to look at Matthew after that. He had sunk very low in his seat with his shoulders to his ears: she could tell by the light from the screen that he was unhappy.

Meanwhile, Vivien Leigh was getting more and more unhappy, too, and spending more and more time with her beret and handbag and high heels saying hello to soldiers even though it did not seem to agree with her. There was something wrong, that was obvious, but what was it? Kate had no idea but could not bring herself to ask Melanie. And when Robert Taylor had suddenly appeared again at the station with some other soldiers she was about to say hello to, instead of looking pleased to see him she had looked quite upset and had said: 'Oh Roy, you're alive,' and gone on acting in the same peculiar way. Even Robert Taylor did not seem to know what ailed her. He had taken her up to his castle in Scotland, and she had got on quite well this time with Lady Margaret and they were going to be married, but she still had moments of being peculiar and finally she had told Lady Margaret, who had become very understanding, that she had something to confess though without saying what it was. But Lady Margaret had seemed to guess (which was more than Kate could!) and said something like 'Oh my poor child' and then had seemed to agree that she should run away to London again which she did and then threw herself under a lorry on Waterloo Bridge and that was the end apart from some moping by Robert Taylor on Waterloo Bridge. Still, Kate, though she had not understood it, had found it a shattering experience. She only wished that Melanie had not been quite such a bully with Matthew. At the same time, in some strange way, a part of Kate *did* know what the film was about ... the explanation, she knew, lay just below the surface of her mind, and when she uncovered it, it would seem perfectly familiar.

But now they had reached Melanie's house on Nassim Road. Matthew would have driven up the drive and into this Langfield stronghold like some innocent wayfarer straying into a robber's den, had not Kate had her wits about her and stopped him at the gate. Melanie gabbled a quick formula of thanks at Matthew, turned her bright, beady eyes on Kate for a moment and then bolted up the drive. Kate somehow knew that if their visit to the cinema were discovered Melanie would be ready with a story to divert all blame from herself to Matthew or to the Blackett family. But then, what could òne expect of a Langfield? Even Kate was not too young to have learned that it made as much sense to reproach a Langfield for treacherous behaviour as it would to condemn a fox for killing a chicken.

Unexpectedly, Kate and Matthew became cheerful once they had dropped Melanie, and although it was almost supper-time they decided to buy mango ice-creams at the California Sandwich Shoppe to eat on the way home. As she sat in the Lagonda beside Matthew trying not to let the ice-cream drip on to her frock, a profound feeling of happiness stole over Kate. At first she thought it was because of the ice-cream, but even when she had finished the ice-cream it persisted. Besides, it was not just happiness, it was a feeling of relief to find herself alone with Matthew : she felt that she had no need to explain anything to him, that he understood her immediately and that somehow he even understood her without her having to say anything at all. This feeling of being understood, though it only lasted for the ten minutes or so it took them to return to the Mayfair, came as a shock and a revelation to Kate. It abruptly opened up all sorts of new possibilities, not just with the Human Bean, of course, though now she understood why Joan wanted to marry him, but of a much more general kind. It was as if she had suddenly realized *what human beans are for*! To understand each other without speaking, that was what they were for! ... She felt she wanted to touch Matthew, but did not quite dare. As they reached the Mayfair she began to worry again about the row which might await her. How peaceful it was here beneath the green arching trees of Tanglin! She clutched her gas-mask case and hoped for the best.

The car had hardly come to a stop when they saw the Major signalling to them from the verandah. They could tell from his expression that something was wrong. Kate's heart sank : her parents must have found out already what she had been up to. But it turned out to be something else which was troubling the Major. He waited until they had got out of the car and come quite close. Then he said grimly : 'Penang has fallen. François has just got back from there. It seems incredible but I'm afraid there's no doubt about it.'

As Kate walked home through the compound she thought : 'With all the fuss nobody will worry about me going to the cinema, at any rate.'

When Matthew and the Major followed her to the Blacketts' house a few minutes later they found an atmosphere of despondency and alarm. Mrs Blackett was worried about her brother, Charlie, who had returned to his regiment only three days earlier after a spell of comparative safety in Singapore. Had there been a big defeat and, if so, had the Punjabis been involved in it? Nobody knew, of course. For all anyone knew the Punjabis were still safely lodged in some barracks in Kuala

Lumpur. Walter, though showing concern for his wife's anxiety, was less worried about Charlie than about the general situation: Penang was such a familiar part of his life in Malaya that it seemed inconceivable that it should fall to the Japanese. Moreover, he was indignant that he should have had no prior warning from the authorities that such a disaster might occur. As for Monty, he was worried about his own prospects: he was afraid that unless he was careful he might end up having to fight Japanese himself. Everything was going wrong these days. All this ghastly wedding furore and now Penang. He could hardly even find anyone to talk to! Even Sinclair Sinclair seemed determined to give up his staff job and rejoin his regiment, the Argylls, if he could wangle it. Why he should want to go and get himself killed was more than Monty could fathom. Monty had been hoping that Sinclair might be able to use some influence on his behalf if the worst came to the worst, but he only seemed interested in getting shot at.

Of all the guests who assembled for supper at the Blacketts' only Dr Brownley and Dupigny did not seem dismayed by the fall of Penang. The former went around shaking hands with everyone politely and murmuring to them in a soothing voice, as if in the presence of a mortal illness. 'Sad news, I'm afraid,' he whispered to Matthew, who was startled to see him winking and nodding. But this was only a nervous idiosyncrasy, it appeared. The Doctor had entered accompanied by Dupigny whose wounds he had been dressing. Despite these wounds Dupigny seemed in good spirits. A dressing had been applied to one side of his face with sticking plaster and there was another dressing on the back of his skull where the hair had been partly shaved away to accommodate it. Nevertheless, his eyes glinted with malicious pleasure as he surveyed the despondent scene in the Blacketts' drawing-room. This was for two reasons: firstly, the Blacketts had behaved so condescendingly towards him since the fall of France that he found it agreeable to see them in a humbler frame of mind; secondly, it vindicated all the sombre predictions he had been making for the past few months concerning the Japanese to the general amusement of Singapore. Moreover, in a general way it reinforced all his deterministic beliefs about the way nations behave.

For Dupigny a nation resembled a very primitive human being: this human being consisted of, simply, an appetite and some sort of mechanism for satisfying the appetite. In the case of a nation the appetite was usually, if not quite invariably, economic ... (now and again the national vanity which at intervals gripped nations like France and Britain would compel them to some act which made no sense economically: but in this respect, too, they resembled human beings). As for the mechanism for fulfilling the appetite, what was that but a nation's armed forces? The more powerful the armed forces the better the prospects for satiating the appetite; the more powerful the armed forces the more likely (indeed, inevitable, in Dupigny's view) that an attempt *would be made* to satiate it; just as heavyweight boxers are more frequently involved in tavern brawls than, say, dentists, so the very existence of power demands that it should be used. His own failure in Indo-China had merely confirmed him in his cynical views. The League of Nations? Nothing but a pious waste of time!

'Never mind, he's had a good innings,' the Doctor observed soothingly to no one in particular, while Matthew, who was sitting on a sofa nearby, gazed at him baffled by this remark for which he could see no sane explanation. Joan came to sit beside him and he realized with a mild shock: 'People must now think we're *a couple*!' He could not think of anything to say to her, however. She said in an undertone: 'Poor Monty, they keep trying to call him up for the F.M.S. Volunteers. But, of course, he's doing essential war work and can't possibly go. Besides, they can hardly be "volunteers" if they're forcing him to join, can they?' Matthew had to agree that, strictly speaking ... She ignored him, however, and went on: 'I do believe that François is wearing new clothes.'

It was true. After months of appearing in the threadbare suit he had managed to salvage in his flight from Saigon Dupigny was now smartly dressed in a new shirt, new trousers, and a new linen jacket, not to mention a splendid pair of gleaming shoes. This elegant attire he had succeeded, not without difficulty, in looting from a burning shop in George Town. The bandages which swathed the fingers and palms of both hands were the result of this gallant effort, though he did not say so when anyone remarked on them, implying diffidently instead that he had been obliged to rescue someone (himself, as it happened: he had spent too long searching for clothes that were the right size) from a blazing building where he had been trapped by a beam which had fallen across his foot. 'With the roof about to fall,' he was explaining modestly to Mrs Blackett as he gingerly accepted a *pahit* from the Chinese boy's tray, 'it was necessary to pick it up with the bare hands, otherwise he would not have had a chance, the poor fellow.'

Walter, overhearing this, frowned at Dupigny, not because he disbelieved this story, but to indicate that he should speak guardedly in front of the 'boy'; because if news of the disaster which had befallen Penang, a town which had been British for centuries, should circulate among the natives, what would be the state of their morale? The Major noticed Walter's frown and knew what he was thinking. But he also knew that Walter's precaution was futile, for had not Cheong told him of the fall of Penang that morning before anyone else had heard of it? The Major was doubly distressed to think that the Europeans had been evacuated from Penang while the rest of the population had been left to make the best of it.

Joan's place beside Matthew on the sofa had been taken by Monty, who said gloomily: 'You've heard they're trying to shove me into the bloody Volunteers?'

'Joan just told me.'

'They're being frightfully sticky about it. And now all this about Penang. If you ask me they're making a complete mess of things.' Monty sighed, wondering if he could get himself sent on a trade mission to Australia or America. To think that a few days ago life had seemed perfectly OK!

Dupigny, surrounded by a sombre group, was describing the nightmare journey he had made from Penang to KL. The last fifty miles he had travelled in a lorry belonging to a Chinese rubber dealer who had been out collecting rubber from small-holdings. One of the drawbacks to this vehicle was that there had been nothing to screen the engine from themselves. It had been right there with them in the cab, so that every time the driver accelerated there had been great flashes of flame from the fuel chamber, not to mention spurts of water from the radiator. The only seat for both himself and the Chinese had been a plank on a wooden box. To make matters worse there was no way of fastening the door: at every turn he risked plunging out into the rainy jungle. From time to time, when the engine faltered on an incline, the Chinese had leaned forward to grope encouragingly in the entrails, putting his hand on the carburettor to supply a choke or pinning a raw wire against the metal of the cab to sound the horn. The wiring festooned everywhere had sparkled like a Christmas tree and every few miles he, Dupigny, had been obliged to cool his heels while the Chinese crawled into the lorry's intestines with a spanner to perform some major operation. By the time they had reached KL, thanks to the flames, the boiling water and the steam from the engine, he had been grilled, boiled and finally poached, like a Dieppe sole! How glad he had been to come upon young Ehrendorf having a drink by himself at the Majestic Hotel opposite the railway station.

'Did he say how the fighting was going?'

'He was not cheerful. But he did not say anything specific.'

'Well, we had better eat,' said Walter, ushering his guests towards the dining-room. 'Perhaps things are not quite as bad as they seem.'

Penang, after all, was almost five hundred miles away. There was still plenty of territory between themselves and the Japanese. Still, although of little importance commercially, Penang had always been a part of the Blacketts' world. Now they felt the ground beginning to shift under their feet.

The meal would have been lugubrious indeed if Dr Brownley had not been there. At first he had been uneasy, inclined to think: 'Good gracious, this makes it twenty-two times in a row that they've invited me here and I still haven't invited them back!' But he was a doctor, after all, and could see that this evening the Blacketts needed the comfort of some more familiar topic to occupy their minds. And what better than the Langfields? A long time ago he had discovered that there was nothing that could make a Blackett feel himself again so swiftly as a Langfield (or vice versa, of course, for both these eminent Singapore families were the Doctor's patients). Should a Blackett find himself suffering from depression, insomnia or loss of appetite, it would usually take no more than a faintly disparaging remark about the Langfields' style of life, their furniture or curtains, say, to effect a cure. On other occasions, when a thorough quickening of the blood was indicated, as in cases of migraine, back-ache, severe constipation or the loss of concentration which Mrs Blackett increasingly suffered as she grew older, stronger meat was sometimes required. Then the Doctor would disclose some more serious matter, the Langfields' reluctance to pay their bills, or their attempts to claim they had paid when they had not, or requests for medical attention on social occasions. As he had dined regularly with both families over the years and with each had concluded that the only topic of conversation guaranteed to please was the other, he had, perhaps, not been as sparing with this drug as he should. It had come about, indeed, that nowadays, just to maintain the family in normal health, he felt it necessary as a matter of course to prepare one or two choice bits of gossip and bring them to the table, the way a zoo-keeper brings herrings in a bucket when he visits the sea-lions.

'Walter, you'd hardly believe the latest about a certain family (I won't say who, mind, but it's no secret they live on Nassim Road)! Well, it seems that they've really outdone themselves this time!' And the Doctor chuckled conspiratorially, looking round the table. The Blacketts, shocked though they were by the loss of Penang, disturbed by thoughts of the future, felt nevertheless a slight alleviation of their burden. The Doctor cut away busily at his veal cutlet, taking his time but still chuckling, while the Blacketts put aside thoughts of Penang in flames and focused their attention on him. 'Yes,' thought the Doctor as he began to enlarge on an example of the Langfields' shortcomings, 'that's what they need. Something to take their minds off it.'

In no time at all one herring after another was describing a glistening arc over the dining-table to be deftly plucked out of the air by one whiskered Blackett head after another. Presently, only the Major, Dupigny and Matthew were sitting there without the head and tail of a fish protruding from their mouths. What was all this about? they wondered. And what did it have to do with Penang?

Matthew, in his excitement and concern over this serious news from Penang had not been paying proper attention to the amount of alcohol he had been drinking. He had been absent-mindedly swallowing one glass of wine after another and now he was far from sober. He was bored with the Doctor and his chat about the Langfields: it seemed to him ridiculous and unworthy that they should be chatting in such a suburban vein at this historic moment when great events were brewing all around them, when a new and terrible link was being forged in the chain of events which reached back to the first betrayal of justice at the League. Instead they should be talking about, well ... no matter *what*, provided it expressed one's real feelings. This was a moment to discuss matters which one does not normally mention on social occasions for fear of making oneself ridiculous or embarrassing one's friends; love and death, for example. Presently, inspired by Walter's claret, he decided that this might be a good moment in which to make the proposal of marriage to Joan which he had intended to make earlier in the afternoon. He looked at her: never had the modelling of her cheekbones seemed so exquisite! Never had her sable curls glowed more richly! He felt moved by her beauty, or perhaps it was simply by the wine and the spice of risk which had been added to life by the news from Penang. Suddenly, he pushed back his chair and stood up.

Silence fell around the table. The Blacketts gazed at him in surprise. He stood there for a moment without saying anything, leaning forward slightly with his knuckles on the polished surface of the table. 'A sad occasion,' muttered the Doctor at his side, looking rather put out, for Matthew had interrupted a choice anecdote by so boorishly rising to his feet. Matthew, while his audience waited, combed his mind for the various things he wanted to say ... he knew what they were (they had been there only a moment ago), and he knew he must say them from the heart.

'Monty has told me,' he began at last, 'that for the past few days certain plans for Joan's wedding have been discussed and that these plans have included me. Well, this evening, it seems to me, we should for once in our lives speak out about our innermost feelings ... And that's why I suddenly got up just now, I suppose it may have looked a bit odd, now I come to think of it ... I think we should say, well ... I think you see what I mean ...'

The Blacketts stirred uneasily, by no means sure that they did see what he meant. Besides, Matthew had plainly had a few drinks too many. But still, he did sound as if he might be on the right lines as far as the wedding was concerned. Until now he had seemed thoroughly apathetic about the whole business, indeed, had not mentioned it at all, and that had been a strain, particularly for Walter and Joan, who could not quite decide whether to go ahead with final arrangements on the strength of what had been agreed already, or whether to wait for a more positive sign from Matthew.

'To you sitting around this table who knew my father rather better than I did, I'm afraid ... I hope you don't mind if I call you "my dearest friends" ... Well, I just wanted to say ... and assure you that I do mean it ...' Matthew, who had got a bit muddled, had to pause for a moment to straighten out exactly what *was* in his mind, to run a hot iron over his thoughts and smooth out any final contradictions in them. This was not difficult. He had to say what he really felt about the prospect of marrying Joan. And so it was that a moment later, to his own surprise he heard a rather far-off voice saying: 'I suppose I should have spoken up before in order to prevent a misunderstanding but, although I like Joan very much, I don't really want to marry her, if you see what I mean. Well, that's all I wanted to say.' And with that he sat down, feeling distinctly uncomfortable.

Part Four

41

I returned to Singapore on the morning of 20 December and shortly afterwards issued a paper containing information of the Japanese tactics and instructions as to how they should be countered. In this I stressed that the first essential was rigid discipline and absolute steadiness and secondly, that the enemy's out-flanking and infiltration tactics must not lead to withdrawals which should only take place on the order of higher authority. I suggested that the best method of defence might be for a holding group to be dug in astride the main artery of communication with striking forces on the flanks ready to attack as soon as the enemy made contact with the holding group. With a view to trying to curb the many wild rumours which were flying about, aggravated by the difficulty of finding out what really was happening, I ordered that the spreading of rumours and exaggerated reports of the enemy's efficiency must be rigidly suppressed.

Lieutenant-General A. E. Percival,
The War in Malaya

JAPANESE BURNING KORAN IN NORTH

Refugees who have made their way out of Trengganu since the Japanese occupation bring a shocking story of sacrilege. They state that the Japanese broke into the Mohammedan religious school at Kuala Trengganu, capital of the state, ransacked it, threw the kitab-kitab (holy books) out of the window and desecrated the holy Koran. Further, they have set up their own idols in the Police Suran (place of worship) in Kuala Trengganu. This news, following on the bombing of the mosques in Penang and Kuala Lumpur, is causing Malays to recall bitterly that it is only a few weeks since the Tokio radio was broadcasting nightly assurances of special solicitude for Muslims and Muslim places of worship in Malay and elsewhere.

According to last night's official communiqué, the Japanese have not been able to maintain their pressure on the Perak front, where our patrols have been active.

RAIDS ON KUALA LUMPUR

Since their first raid on Kuala Lumpur town on Friday the Japanese have returned regularly every day. On Tuesday there were five alerts. The raiders are always met by heavy ack-ack fire. As a result they have not dared appear directly over the town and have not dropped any bombs since last Friday.

Straits Times Thursday, 1 January 1942

Now the New Year of 1942 began and life in Singapore underwent yet another frightening metamorphosis. Little by little people had grown accustomed to the darkness of the blacked-out streets and the military road-blocks, though they had not ceased to be an inconvenience. But now air-raids, sporadic at first and usually aimed at the docks and airfields, came to remind Singapore's inhabitants of the dangers they ran. And yet, when you thought about it, only a few days had passed since Singapore had been still enjoying the comfort and security of peace-time. How far away those pleasant days already seemed! These days, unless your character was unusually imperturbable, you found it hard to enjoy dining on the lawn of Raffles Hotel in the tropical night surrounded by the fan-shaped silhouettes of travellers' palms. By now people preferred to dine inside: for one thing there was no light to read the menu by if you stayed outside; for another, although it was still just as enchanting to listen to the sighing of the warm breeze as it tossed the ruffled heads of the nibong palms against the stars high above you, you could no longer be quite sure that the dark shape of a Japanese bomber was not lurking like a panther in those tossing palms and watching you with yellow eyes as you put your spoon into a *soufflé au fromage*. Besides, sitting out there by yourself, could you be altogether certain that you would not find yourself sharing your *soufflé* with a Japanese parachutist?

For Europeans, these days, work swallowed up everything. For no sooner had you finished at the office than you were obliged to report for an evening's training with the passive defence and volunteer forces. If you were over the age of forty-one you now found yourself, unless exempted for some other

327

essential work, serving with the volunteer police or firemen or with the Local Defence Corps. Nevertheless, it had taken Singapore's second air-raid on 29 December, and those that followed in ever more rapid succession, to make a real dent in Singapore's way of life. Sporting activities on the *padang* came to an end (to Matthew's inexperienced eye not the least astonishing thing about Singapore had been the sight of thirty grown men engaged in a violently energetic game of rugby a mere few miles from the equator): the municipal engineering department had erected obstacles to deny such open spaces to aircraft or paratroops. Supplies of tinned food were brought up and people began to improvise air-raid shelters in their gardens or in the less fragile parts of their homes.

Outwardly, perhaps, not so much had changed. You could still pause almost anywhere in the city, just as you had always done, and buy a refreshing slice of pineapple, or a bunch of tiny, delicious bananas no bigger than the fingers of your hand, or even, if you were adventurous, scoop out the fragrant, heavenly, alarming flesh of the durian. Some people, no less adventurous, occasionally managed a round of golf under the air-raids, at least until golf links and club-house were taken over to be fortified by the Military despite a gallant rear-guard action by the Club Committee to save it for its members. Others sported and splashed in the wavelets at Tanjong Rhu while Japanese bombers raided Keppel Harbour across the water. Was this bravado or simply an illustration of the time it takes to change from the reality of peace to the new reality of war? Well, you were probably no less safe and a great deal more comfortable having a swim during an air-raid than sweltering in an improvised shelter.

The Major took tiffin one day in the first week of January with Dr Brownley at the Adelphi Hotel and was surprised to find that the hotel's orchestra was still playing its usual lunch-time concert of old favourites. The only interruption to his conversation with the Doctor, whom he was trying to persuade to provide a mobile medical service for the Mayfair A.F.S. unit, came when a drunken Australian journalist blundered into their table, asked: 'How's the tucker?' and blundered away again. The Major later glimpsed him vomiting into some palms in the lobby while the Swiss manager wrung his hands nearby. Still, considering it was wartime, it was not too much to put up with.

One thing, however, did come as a shock to the Major. He had expected that resentment towards the Forces, endemic for the past few years among European civilians, would be dissipated immediately by the opening of hostilities on the mainland. But on the contrary, it grew even more acute. The Military, it was felt, who were supposed to be defending Singapore's commercial activities, vital as a source of produce for the Empire and for the earning of dollars from America, were doing everything to make business impossible by their high-handed requisitioning of land and property. If the Army had had its way it would have made off with a sizeable part of the labour force into the bargain, to build the camps and fortifications which they should be building for themselves! What indignation would presently be caused in Singapore when (in the third week of January) the *Sunday Pictorial* in Britain published what the *Straits Times* called 'absurd allegations regarding whisky-swilling planters, indolent officials and greedy businessmen who refused to pay taxes.'

But as January pursues its course the civilians and the Military are at least united in one pastime in the increasingly devastated and dangerous city ... they go to the cinema. They go to see *Private Affairs* with Nancy Kelly and Robert Cummings at the Cathay, or *Bad Men of Missouri* at the Alhambra, or Charlie Chaplin in *The Great Dictator* at the Roxy. Battered troops from up-country or new arrivals from Britain, Australia and India watch John Wayne in *Dark Command* at the Empire beside anxious and forlorn refugees from Penang and Kuala Lumpur. Together in the hot darkness they watch Joe E. Brown in *So You Won't Talk?*, *Mata Hari* with Greta Garbo and Ramon Novarro, and Henry Fonda in *The Return of Frank James* which, despite the boom and thud of bombs and anti-aircraft guns filtering into the cinema, has had all traces of gun-play removed by the Singapore censor in order not to give ideas to the city's Chinese gangsters. Perhaps as they sit there they are a little re-assured by 'the first drama of Uncle Sam's new jump fighters': *Parachute Battalion* with Robert Preston and Edmond O'Brien ... but no doubt they find parachutes too close to reality and prefer Loretta Young in *The Lady from Cheyenne*: 'It was a man's world until a low-cut gown took over the town.' They watch in silence with the light from the screen flickering on their strained faces. The week it is shown (by that time people will be wearing steel helmets in the stalls during air-raids) will see, on Tuesday, a massive raid by eighty-one Japanese Navy bombers on the Tanglin and Orchard Road district and, on

Wednesday, an even more devastating raid on Beach Road.

'*Pakai angku punia sarong muka!* Put on your gas-masks! *Jangan tembak sampai depat hukum!* Don't fire until you receive orders!' exclaimed the Major, stifling a yawn that threatened to have its way with him. '*Jaga itu periok api ... bedil itu sudah letup.* Beware of bombs: the shell has exploded!' Such was the heat and humidity that a prodigious effort was required merely to keep one's eyes open. His head began to droop once more on to his chest. He forced himself to straighten up and say: '*Gali parit untok lima kaki tinggi. Kapal terbang tedak boleh naik sabab musim ribot.* Dig a trench about five feet high. The aeroplanes can't go up owing to stormy weather ...' Again his head began to droop. There was a sudden crash and he sat up with a start. Dupigny had just hurled a book across the room at a fat, ginger cockroach which was making its way, glistening with health and horribly alert, across the wall of the outer office where they were sitting. The book had missed, however, and the cockroach darted away at an unnatural speed.

Revived by the noise, the Major put down the list of useful Malay phrases he had been trying to master and walked across to the window. The rain was pelting down on the broad, green banana leaves and sweeping down the drive in a river towards the storm-drain.

'Listen to this, Brendan,' chuckled Dupigny, who was sprawled in a rattan chair reading the *Straits Times*. ' "Newly arrived. Sandbags! Only a limited quantity available. Apply Hagemeyer Trading Company Ltd.' They have a vigorous commercial instinct, the people of Singapore!'

'Undoubtedly, François, the Japanese have gained some initial advantage,' said the Major who had been following his own train of thought. 'But I doubt if they will get much further.'

'*Sans blague!*'

'They had the advantage of surprise and that counts for a great deal. But the further they drive our chaps back, the more concentrated our forces become ... like a spring which is being compressed. In due course we'll spring back all the more powerfully.'

'*Sans blague!*'

'Would you mind not saying "*sans blague*" all the time? It gets on my nerves.'

'Sorry.'

330

It had grown very dark outside and the rain fell so heavily that it filled the room with a noise like a roll of drums. Through a crack in the floorboards the Major could see a sheet of rainwater sliding under the bungalow between the pillars on which it stood. From time to time a flash of lightning lit up Dupigny's face across the room, a cynical mass of wrinkles. He had put down the newspaper which he could no longer see to read.

'What a storm!' said Matthew, wandering in from his office next door and joining the Major at the window.

'They don't usually last very long,' said the Major. He added presently: 'By the way, Mr Wu was here earlier and said he had heard there had been more trouble up-country.' The Major, though he did not say so, was afraid that Malaya might be beginning to fall to pieces. Nor was it simply a question of the military situation. He explained to Matthew what he had heard.

Last week there had been talk of Australian troops wrecking a hotel somewhere. Now rumours had reached Mr Wu, who had business contacts in Penang, Kuala Lumpur, Ipoh and Kuantan, that civil disorder, looting and inter-racial strife was spreading like a shock-wave in front of the advancing Japanese bayonets. In some places the retreating British troops, instructed to destroy stores that might be of value to the enemy, had set the example by looting jewellers and liquor shops, eagerly assisted by the local population and even by the police who had discarded their uniforms and joined in with a will. Open season had been declared on anything of value left behind. A cloud of locusts descended on every abandoned European bungalow: in no time it was stripped of everything down to light-bulbs, door-handles and bathroom fittings. When European bungalows had all been stripped the looters turned to those abandoned by rich Chinese, Indians and Malays ... and, presently, to those that had *not* been abandoned, stripping them regardless and, if the owner did not promptly produce his valuables, torturing him until he did. Sometimes, according to Mr Wu's all too circumstantial and convincing account, Chinese looters would wear masks, or pretend to be Japanese soldiers; sometimes two rival bands of looters would arrive to sack the same premises, which now included Government rice godowns, Land offices and Customs premises, and do battle with each other for the right to pillage. And all this accompanied by wholesale violence and rape, not to mention old scores being paid off. The country was foundering in anarchy!

'What do you expect to happen?' asked Dupigny, dismissing the matter with a shrug. 'I do not see why you should be surprised.'

'But wait, François. The laws of a country are merely the wish of people to live in a certain way. Remove the laws for a few days and you don't expect anarchy to result overnight, any more than by abolishing road regulations you would expect motorists to pick at random which side of the road they would drive on. Laws aren't a means of coercing a population of wild animals but an agreement between people ... D'you see what I mean? But in that case why has this moral vacuum appeared in the space between the two armies where the rule of law is suspended? It must mean that all these people looting and raping don't consider themselves to belong to our community at all!'

'But exactly!' cried Dupigny and a flash of lightning lit up his sardonic smile. 'In a country like Malaya such an ideal community is impossible because people belong to different races and only have self-interest in common. A brotherhood of man? Rubbish! But let us not complain, self-interest is the surest source of wealth as your Mr Smith has so brilliantly demonstrated.'

'Do you really believe, François, that until now our British laws have merely been preventing people here from doing what they would most like to do, namely: attack, rob and rape their neighbours? Come now!'

'Certainly. Today you have the proof!'

Instead of replying, the Major stooped and held out his fingers to The Human Condition who was hesitating prudently a few feet away, as if afraid that the Major might be about to scoop him up and drop him into an incinerator. After some moments of interior debate the animal crept a little closer and faintly wagged its wretched tail. The Major sighed. Outside the window the first thin shaft of sunlight broke through the cloud and hung quivering in the murky gloom of the drive, at the same time striking emerald sparks from a dripping banana leaf.

Matthew, who had spent a little time with his hands in his pockets at the window, staring out in a gloomy reverie at the drenched foliage, had become interested in this discussion. He remembered with what pleasure he had watched the mingling of races on the dance-floor at The Great World. It was surely true that to build a nation out of Malaya's plural society some greater ideal than the profit of plantation owners, merchants and assorted entrepreneurs combined with the accumulation of wealth by the labour force, was required. What was needed was *a new spirit* ... the spirit that had animated people at Geneva in the early days before everything had turned sour. Matthew began, haltingly, to explain this to the Major and Dupigny. It was simply a question of breaking out of old habits of thought! It was so easy, given the right atmosphere, for people to change the way they approached each other! Even apparently self-interested people were capable of it. It was like ... like ... He groped the air with his fingers, searching for an example. Yes, it was like someone in the empty compartment of a train who pulls down the blinds and puts his suitcases on the seat to prevent another passenger sharing it with him. Yet if, once installed, the newcomer should become ill the original occupant will spare no effort to help him, will take off his jacket, perhaps, to spread it over him, will stop the train and bully officials into coming to his companion's assistance, and go to all manner of trouble! It was a fact! And truly there was no earthly reason why all human affairs should not be conducted in this manner! It was just as available to people as conduct based on suspicion and self-interest. Even with the Japanese it would have been possible if they had not been infected with our own cynical approach to power.

'I refuse to believe that self-interest is the best source of prosperity. It only *seems* that way because we've never been able to break out of this bad habit with which we've been shackled by our history. Men are capable of becoming brothers, whatever you say, François. And I'm sure you'll find, once this dreadful war is over, that thousands of people of different races have been willing to risk their lives for each other!'

While Matthew, stuttering with excitement, had been stating his belief, his companions had been listening, the Major dubiously, Dupigny with derision. Now Dupigny got to his feet: it was time for his late afternoon siesta on the table in the Board Room, the only room in the building which possessed an efficient fan. On his way out he paused to pat Matthew on the shoulder, saying with a laugh: 'You might just as well expect stockbrokers to be ready to die for the Stock Exchange!'

42

It was in these days that members of the Mayfair AFS unit first began to be seen at fires here and there in the city with their glistening new trailer-pump. Nothing spectacular at first while they were learning the business; a shop-house or a godown, perhaps, set on fire by an air-raid on the docks. A tiny convoy would set off led by the Major's Lagonda driven by the Major himself, keeping an eye on the trailer-pump dodging and swaying in the rear-view mirror, and followed by Mr Wu's ancient Buick, crammed with helmeted figures and equipment. Sometimes, as the fires grew bigger, they would find a number of other units there, too, and as they arrived they would have to bump over several hose-ramps while trying to locate the officer in charge of the fire. Quite often this would turn out to be a man called Adamson who, they learned from some of the regular firemen, had an unusual reputation for skill in beating back or outflanking fires that threatened to get out of control ... the reputation of a general, one might have thought. His appearance, though, was disappointingly ordinary ... a rather anonymous-looking individual in his forties with bristly grey hair and a manner that suggested more a curious by-stander than a general on a battlefield. Matthew, in particular, surveyed him with interest, wondering how it was that so many legends had attached themselves to him.

At one godown fire, while Matthew was talking to a man called Evans from the Central Fire Station in Hill Street, there came a shout of 'Stand from under!'

'That means the façade is about to topple,' Evans explained and together they joined the other men drifting back to a safer distance. Evans, however, was watching Adamson who still lingered beneath the building, staring up at it, hands in pockets. There was a story, he told Matthew, that Adamson had once been caught at just such a moment under a tall façade as it toppled outwards over him. Because it had been too late to run he had calmly estimated where an open window would fall, had changed his position slightly and then stood still. The façade had fallen neatly around him, leaving him untouched.

'Great Scott!' Matthew gazed at Adamson, deeply impressed by such sang-froid, but at the same time half suspecting that this might be just a story which old hands told to new recruits like himself.

Despite the satisfaction Matthew experienced these days in the knowledge that he was doing his bit for the Colony, and even putting himself at risk for it, he was still not altogether pleased with himself. His relations with the Blackett family had been seriously clouded by the unfortunate manner in which he had announced that he did not want to marry Joan. How could he have done such a thing? The Blacketts were his father's life-long friends! Now he flushed with embarrassment at the mere recollection of his dreadful behaviour. Naturally, he had written notes of apology to Walter, to Mrs Blackett, and to Joan herself (how could he have been so insensitive as to reject the poor girl in public!) ... but he had heard nothing and did not expect to be forgiven for his appalling lapse.

He would have written a note to Monty, too, but Monty had turned up in person before he could do so and, as a matter of fact, did not appear to be particularly put out. Monty, indeed, was inclined to look on the bright side and said, chuckling: 'Boy, you've really put your foot in it this time. They aren't very pleased with you at home, to put it mildly! But at least you've got rid of all the bloody bridesmaids! Frankly, old chap, I hand it to you ... I didn't think you had it in you.' But Matthew was not to be consoled. It was true that he did not now have to marry Joan ... but such was his remorse that he would almost have preferred to have done so.

Presently, a hastily written message from Walter did arrive and Matthew opened it expecting recriminations. But to his surprise the message did not even mention his lapse and one might even have supposed, reading it, that Walter had already forgotten about it. The note begged Matthew, in the name of his country and of everything he held dear, to reconsider his refusal to impersonate Continuity in Blackett and Webb's jubilee parade. 'Since the loss of Penang,' wrote Walter, 'it has become more necessary than ever to shore up the morale of the Asiatic communities in the Colony by a display of firmness and a reminder of our past association which has been so fruitful to them.' Because of 'recent events' it had been necessary to postpone the jubilee parade and celebrations, but 'any day now' final arrangements would be made. In the meantime, Matthew was asked to come with the Major and Dupigny to a dress rehearsal for the parade to make sure that everybody knew what was expected of him.

This note had been dictated in a rather discursive style and typed on Walter's office note-paper. Walter had added a cryptic postscript in ink, however, which stated: 'I hear young Langfield has not been doing *too badly* as a fireman. What d'you think? Perhaps he is not as bad as the rest of *that gang*?' Matthew was relieved to get Walter's note, though a little puzzled by the reference to Nigel Langfield: Walter musing aloud, it seemed. He hastily sent a note in return, agreeing to do anything Walter wanted. After his lapse there was nothing else for him to do, after all.

His conscience lightened somewhat by this exchange, Matthew decided to take the afternoon off. His efforts to grasp the complexities of the rubber business took second place these days, in any case, to his duties as a fireman. Besides, he still hardly knew Singapore.

The Major, who had to pick up an order of books from Kelly and Walsh's, dropped him near Raffles Place and he set off, hands in pockets, with no particular destination. First he walked down Market Street. It was here, he remembered, that Ehrendorf had his flat but as to which number it was in the street he had no idea. As he strolled along he was suddenly enveloped in a delightful smell of cloves and cinnamon which hung outside a spice merchant's. On the opposite side of the street his eye was caught by the money-lenders shops and he paused for a moment to stare in wonder and dismay at the white-garmented figures lurking in those dim interiors. What did this glimpse of money-lenders remind him of? Yes. He moved on once more, pondering the assertion that self-interest is the most efficient producer of wealth, that what an undeveloped tropical country most needed were entrepreneurs like his father and like Walter. Many people believed, he was aware, that no matter what an individual entrepreneur might accomplish in the way of exploitation or abuse of native labour, his presence was still beneficial to the country as the most effective means by which the local population could begin to accumuate capital of its own. This paradox, which was no doubt true within limits, was accompanied by a cynical companion in the form of another assertion: namely, that human beings would only produce their best efforts when they were working, not for the community in which they lived, but for themselves. This Matthew *refused to believe*!

336

He had paused, muttering under his breath, in the doorway of a metalwork shop where he found himself gazing at his own perspiring, bespectacled face upside down in a gleaming concave bowl. Inside the shop he could see a man on his hands and knees cutting out a long strip of metal to make a bucket; another man, cross-legged, sat on the floor hammering rivets into another strip which had been bent into a cylinder. Beside them glistened a pile of newly minted buckets. To produce such handsome buckets without even a work-bench, using only primitive tools, seemed to him miraculous.

He walked on at random, now northwards, now westwards. He passed a sign which read Nanyang Dentist and the dentist himself, perhaps, sitting in his white coat on the pavement smoking a cigarette. A ginger cat with a docked tail crossed his path and slipped hopefully under the bead-hung entrance to the North Pole Creamery. A Chinese song blared tinnily from a wireless somewhere above his head in the forest of poles and washing; two voices gabbled in different languages riddled with atmospheric from two other wirelesses nearby. He passed on to the street corner where a Chinese funeral, which he at first took for a parade, was getting down to business outside a shophouse. A framed photograph of the dead man had been set up on a table on the pavement, a prosperous-looking fellow wearing the most formal of Western blue suits and white shirts; two tall lamps swathed in sackcloth for the occasion flanked the photograph: piles of oranges and apples and bundles of smoking joss-sticks stood in front of it. At the side of this table was another; Matthew found himself confronted with a great lobster-coloured pig's mask complete with ears and flaring nostrils, crabs, whole naked chickens, some squashed as flat as plates, very greasy-looking, others with their yellow waxen heads horribly bent back over their bodies.

Matthew looked at his watch: he would soon have to be getting back to the Mayfair for something to eat before the night's watch. He lingered for a moment, however, to inspect the paper models of a motor-car, a wireless, a refrigerator and other useful articles that the dead man would be taking on his journey, thinking: 'After all, if these are the things people want and entrepreneurs like my father help them to get them ...' He wondered what the head man had thought of it all, whether he had been satisfied. Here he was, presumably, in this impressive coffin which might, to judge by its size, have been hollowed out of a substantial tree trunk, each end swept up like the prow of a ship and standing on trestles which advertised, in English and Chinese, the name and telephone number of the undertaker. A line of professional mourners dressed in crudely stitched sackcloth sat on the kerb, smoking cigarettes and looking disaffected. A small boy hammered on a tin drum and was now joined by a rather down-at-heel brass band of elderly men in white uniforms who struck up raggedly for a few moments. An aeroplane roared by very low overhead and the mourners looked up apprehensively ... but it was British, a Catalina flying-boat. Matthew walked on thoughtfully. As he walked, hands in pockets, he felt someone take his arm. Looking round he saw Miss Chiang's smiling face.

'Vera! Where have you been? Why haven't you been back to the Mayfair?'

Vera's smile disappeared; she looked a trifle upset. She said with a shrug: 'They told me not to come back.'

'Who told you?'

'A man from Mr Blackett's office.' She shrugged again. 'It does not matter. It is not in the least "pressing". Tell me about yourself ... I'm so glad to see you are now well again. What a terrible fever! You gave me such a fright. I was afraid you might "kick the bucket".'

'But why did they tell you not to come back?'

'They say my job has been finished. They bring me suitcase and money and a letter of thanks signed by Miss Blackett. I think it is because she is jealous of my beauty.'

'D'you really think so? Lumme!' Matthew mopped his perspiring face with a handkerchief.

'Yes,' went on Vera, looking pretty and malicious, yet at the same time more innocent than ever, 'it is because also she does not have my command of foreign languages and because my breasts are bigger than hers. She does not have my poise, either, which I have probably inherited from my mother ... I think I told you my mother was Russian princess, forced to show "clean heels" during Revolution. Well, there ... it is not worth bothering about.'

Meanwhile, they had strolled on together and, after a moment's hesitation, Vera had taken his arm again and her light hand resting in the hollow of his elbow caused a delicate warmth to flow into him. Some women, he could not help thinking, were extraordinarily good at touching you, while others did so as if they had had a recently dislocated arm (no doubt women found the same about men). Vera's touch was as distinctive as her voice. At the end of the street, however, they discovered that they were obliged to go in different directions, which seemed a pity. They lingered there for a moment.

'You must halt ...' said Vera with a sigh. 'I must go on because my silk-worms are hungry.'

'What? You have silk-worms?' cried Matthew, thinking: 'How delightfully Chinese!'

'Oh no, here in Singapore it is too hot for silk-worms.' She smiled flirtatiously. 'It is a line from an old Chinese song about a woman who is separated from her lover.'

'Well, let me see ...' Matthew again looked at his watch. 'Can I invite you to a cup of tea?'

'Thank you, but first I must visit a friend who is dying. Will you come with me?'

Presently, Matthew found himself standing in a vast dimly lit shed, blinking and polishing his spectacles; but even when he had put them on again, such was the contrast with the brightness outside, he still could not see very well. Vera had set off down a sort of aisle on each side of which rose tier after tier of shadowy racks, as in a store-house or wine-cellar. Matthew followed her, stepping uncertainly. There was a smell of humanity here and a faint, twittering murmur of voices.

As his vision improved he saw that the racks on either side were occupied by recumbent forms, some of which stirred slightly as he passed but for the most part lying still ... Eyes followed him incuriously, the sunken eyes of very elderly, emaciated people; here and there he made out a somewhat younger face. Vera explained to him that this was a Chinese 'dying-house' where lonely people came to die. He had not wanted to come; he had tried to explain to Vera that he had only just finished watching a funeral. It seemed to him that his life had taken a decidely lugubrious turn all of a sudden. No, he would definitely prefer to wait for her outside.

But as they were walking Vera had told him a little about the old man she was going to visit. He had befriended her on the boat that had taken her from Shanghai to Singapore (that same boat on which Miss Blackett and her mother had been travelling), had given her a little money and had helped her to find her feet; his own children had died or disappeared in one of the civil wars that had swept back and forth over China since the fall of the Manchu dynasty. While talking about this man, to whom she was bringing a little parcel of food, Vera happened to mention that until he had grown too old to work he had lived by tapping his few rubber trees on a smallholding near Layang Layang in Johore. Matthew had pricked up his ears at this and exclaimed: 'That's near my own estate!' And so, despite his misgivings, he had decided to enter the dying-house with her. Now, blundering between these racks of moribund people in the gloom, he felt like Orpheus descending into the underworld.

It was not only the lonely who came to die here, explained Vera in a low voice, grasping him by the sleeve, but a great many others, too. People were brought here to die by their families in order to spare the home from the bad luck that comes when somebody dies there ...

'I must say, that sounds a bit heartless!'

Yes, and yet it was accepted by the person who was dying as the best thing to do and the custom had been carried on, perhaps, for generations. And no doubt those who came here from the land of the living to bring food and water to their dying relations would in due course come to spend their own last days or hours here, rather than take up room in one of the crowded tenement cubicles or boats on the river ... It was very sad, certainly, but it was moving, too, to see the way these shelves of dying people accepted their fate. Vera's dark eyes searched Matthew's face to see whether he understood. He nodded cautiously though, as a matter of fact, he was not very keen on hearing of people 'accepting their fate'. Vera seemed to him extraordinarily full of life by contrast with the trays of shadowy expiring figures on either side. 'What a dismal way to end up though!'

'How attractive he is!' Vera was thinking. 'How stooping and shortsighted! What deliciously round shoulders and unhealthy complexion!' She gazed at him in wonder, reflecting that there was no way in which he could be improved. Indeed, she could hardly keep her eyes off him. For the fact was that Vera had been brought up, as Chinese girls had been for centuries, to find stooping, bespectacled, scholarly-looking young men attractive, and the more literary the better; no doubt there was an economic motive originally buried somewhere beneath this tradition of finding attractive qualities in poor physical specimens like Matthew (although, actually, *he* was quite strong): for until recently with the fall of the Ch'ing dynasty all China's most powerful administrators and officials, a source of prosperity and glory for their families as well as themselves, had been chosen traditionally by competitive examinations in literary subjects open to rich and poor alike. Already though, a willingness to have their heart-strings plucked in such a way was beginning to seem old-fashioned to the young women of the New China. Yes, already by January 1942, young men with rippling muscles, fists of steel and a good posture were beginning to barge these spindle-legged weaklings aside and leave them grovelling in the dust for their spectacles while *they*, instead, installed themselves in maidenly dreams from Shanghai to Sinkiang. How lucky then for Matthew, who was just in time to catch Vera's eye. He would not have cut much ice with one of these others. As a matter of fact, she had already begun to notice one or two young men with fists of steel who perhaps did not look *too* unprepossessing.

43

Vera had paused for a moment to talk to a middle-aged man sitting on his heels beside someone on the lowest rack; he was wearing a cheap, crumpled European suit whose pockets were bulging with packages of various kinds; a stethoscope hung over his open-necked white shirt. As he was talking he looked up briefly at Matthew and smiled: his face, which was deeply lined and cross-hatched, conveyed a strong impression of sensitivity and strength of character. As they walked on again, it occurred to Matthew that if you could tell someone's character by his face, even without sharing a culture or language with him, perhaps people of different nations and races were not so deeply divided from each other as they appeared to be, that whatever Dupigny might think, there *was* such a thing as shared humanity, and that with one or two minor adjustments different nations and communities could live in harmony with each other, concerning themselves with each other's welfare.

The doctor she had just spoken to, Vera explained, devoted all his spare time and money to treating the inmates of the dying-house who could not otherwise afford medical attention.

'Of course he does!' exclaimed Matthew excitedly. 'You only

have to look at his face to know that!' He would hardly have believed her if she had suggested anything else. Oppressed as he was by Dupigny's cynical views on human nature, he felt quite delighted to have stumbled on this lonely philanthropist. Vera, meanwhile, was indicating in a whisper that those inhabitants of the dying-house who were actually expiring were brought down to the floor level because it was believed that anyone below a dying person would be visited by bad luck.

After a moment of uncertainty while she peered in the gloom at one elderly Chinese face after another (each shrivelled and puckered like an old apple and, to Matthew, almost indistinguishable) Vera had made her selection and was kneeling by a frail figure where it was darkest at the end of the row. Matthew approached, too, and gazed with interest and sympathy at the wizened head which lay, not on a pillow, but on a small bundle, perhaps of clothing. At the touch of Vera's hand on his arm, the old man's eyes opened slowly. He surveyed her calmly, remotely, showing no sign of surprise or animation. But presently he murmured something. A faint conversation ensued. Once, very slowly, his eyes moved towards Matthew. Vera's parcel contained a small bowl of rice, mushrooms and sea-slugs. A boy appeared with a pot of tea and Vera gave him a coin. Meanwhile the old man's withered hand had been groping feebly at his bedside and presently closed over a pair of chopsticks. Vera took them from him and helped him to eat a few mouthfuls from the bowl.

When he had finished eating the old man again looked at Matthew and said something to Vera. Vera, too, looked at Matthew and replied with a smile, saying then in English: 'I tell him you are in rubber business.'

The old man spoke again, this time to Matthew, in a faint, grumbling voice.

'What does he say?'

'He ask you where your estates are ... I tell him you son of Blackett and Webb.'

Matthew nodded and smiled winningly at the old Chinese, delighted to think that he was at last, thanks to Vera, coming into contact with the real roots of life in Malaya, not just its top dressing of Europeans.

But despite Matthew's winning smiles the old fellow on his death-bed did not altogether give the impression of being won over. Indeed, he had begun to fidget restlessly on his tray, muttering indignantly. Matthew was not sure but he thought he could make out the words 'Brackett and Webb' recurring in the old chap's mutterings. Vera was listening attentively: her face showed concern.

'Well, oh dear ... He say you swindle smallholders. He says European estates swindle him and other smallholders ...'

'Oh really, Vera!' scoffed Matthew. 'The poor old blighter's just wool-gathering. But I can see my presence is upsetting him so perhaps I'd better ...' He was afraid that the elderly Chinese, who was now searching crossly with trembling, skeletal hands for something in the pile of rags he was using as a pillow, might suffer some terminal seizure brought on by excitement and indignation. To judge by his wasted body and blue lips it would not take very much to capsize the frail craft in which the old chap was now trying to navigate the final stages of his life's voyage. Still, something caused Matthew to linger. Until now he had not given much thought to native smallholders. Their smallholdings seldom amounted to more than a few acres, at most. And yet, now he thought about it, these native smallholdings together produced nearly half of Malaya's rubber and covered almost a million and a quarter acres! 'What's he saying now?' he asked uneasily.

'He says British steal money from his rubber trees.'

'How did they do that?' asked Matthew dubiously. Vera turned back to the old man who had fallen back now, exhausted by his efforts to find whatever it was he had been looking for. He was no longer looking at Matthew but into the distance; his chest hardly seemed to move but still that faint, grumbling voice went on and on, rising and falling, almost like the wind when it sighs under a doorway.

'He says the inspector did not give him proper share of rubber to sell when he came to look at his trees for Restriction Scheme ...'

'I suppose he means when his production was being assessed before the scheme started ... to see what his share of the total export rights would be. All right, go on.'

'It was the same with other smallholders in this village, too. Inspector says he tells a lie how much rubber his trees are making, that they are too thickly planted to make so much rubber. He says inspectors are Europeans who work for the estates and do not want smallholders to get their proper share ...'

'Well, good gracious! Tell him ... tell him ...' But Matthew could not think what Vera should tell him. 'What a disagreeable old codger!' he thought, taken aback by this list of complaints. 'You'd think that at death's door he'd have better things to think about. There might be some truth in it, mind you ... but all the same!' Matthew had discovered that he did not mind being critical of the British himself, but when a foreigner was critical, that was different. And, after all, he had ventured into this decidedly creepy place merely to pay his respects to the old blighter!

But in spite of natural feelings of indignation that the old chap should pick a quarrel with him on what was really a social occasion (paying of respects to someone on the point of cashing in his chips), there was an aspect of the matter which Matthew, in spite of himself, did find rather interesting. For he had already been struck by the fact there there was one significant difference between the production of rubber and the production of most other things ... namely, there was little advantage in cost to those who operated on a big scale with several hundred or more acres. Those who produce corn, say, or motor-cars on a large scale can usually do so more cheaply than their smaller competitors. Not so with rubber where a method of mass-production using machinery had yet to be discovered. If anything, the native smallholder, who as well as tapping his few rubber trees could very often keep himself by growing fruit and vegetables and raising a few chickens, should be able to produce rubber *more* cheaply than the European estates which were obliged to pay and feed a large work-force of tappers, weeders, foremen and other estate workers, not to mention the even more expensive European managers, agents, secretaries and, ultimately, company directors and shareholders.

Matthew now remembered the discussion he had had with Ehrendorf (it seemed ages ago but was, in fact, only a few days) at The Great World, when they had been trying to decide to what extent the coming of Western capital to Britain's tropical colonies had had the benefits that were claimed for it. Well, the relationship between the European estates and the native smallholders seemed to throw an interesting light on that discussion. It was obvious that in most cases, although natives could be employed by Western enterprise, they lacked the knowledge, skill and capital to compete directly with it. But in the case of rubber, by a happy coincidence this was not so. There was nothing in the growing and tapping of trees, in the coagulation of latex by adding acid, or in the mangling and smoking of the resulting rubber sheets, that could not be done as easily by an illiterate Malay or Chinese as by a graduate of a British agricultural college. If the Colonial Office and the Government here really had the interests of their native subjects at heart, and not merely their exploitation as cheap labour, they could hardly have been presented with a better opportunity of demonstrating it by promoting and defending their interests! But wait! What was this he was hearing (for the old man's quavering sing-song, while Matthew had been brooding on these matters, had not ceased its gentle sighing like the wind coming under the door)?

'He says that European estates were given an extra share for trees that were too young to make rubber ... Smallholders were given nothing.' Vera looked at him helplessly, embarrassed by this litany of complaints. 'He says European inspectors never looked properly at trees. He says there were only twenty inspectors for whole of Malaya. He says nobody inspected the estates. The estates told the Controller of Rubber how much share they wanted and Controller did as they say. He says Controller of Rubber was friendly to estates, not friendly to smallholders!'

'Quite true, sir,' piped up another quavering voice at Matthew's elbow, causing him to start violently and peer into the gloom where another of the shadowy cadavers, hitherto lying supine on the lowest rack and displaying no signs of life, had now collected up two sets of bones and thrown them over the side of his tray; after dangling uncertainly for a while they anchored themselves to the floor and proved to be legs; then, with a further scraping of bones, their owner levered himself politely to his feet and stood swaying beside Matthew. 'Quite true, sir. Controller of Rubber listen only to European estates. He have five men on his committee from estates ... only one smallholder! On his Rubber Regulation Committee he have twenty-seven men from estates, still only one from smallholders. And yet smallholders produce half country's rubber! That is not fair, sir. It is disgusting. Quite true, sir.' And he sank back with a moan into the shadows and a moment later there came a faint rattling sound. 'Oh dear,' thought Matthew, 'but still, he's probably had a good innings.'

Meanwhile, the speaker's place had been taken by other shadowy figures and Vera, tugging at his arm, was anxious to gain his attention because the sighing, sing-song voice of her friend had not ceased all this time and by now had built up a considerable backlog of complaints. 'He says Rubber Research Institute run by Government does not help smallholders, it helps only estates. He says smallholders pay for Institute from taxes just like European estates, but Institute only gives new, very good rubber plants to estates! What they call 'budwood'' ...'

'He means these new high-yielding clones?'

'Yes, budwood ... he means new clones ... He telling truth!' sang a chorus of skeletons and moribunds who had crowded around Matthew and were tugging at his garments to attract his attention ...

'He says smallholders producing more rubber per acre than estates but given much smaller share!'

'Look here, Vera, I'm afraid I shall have to be going now. I'm on duty this evening and I'm late already ...'

'He says bloody big swindle ... he says ...'

For the past few moments, extenuated though he was by his long list of complaints, Vera's friend had resumed his petulant search in the bundle of rags he was using as a pillow; now, with a final effort which seemed as if it might capsize him completely, his trembling fingers had fastened on what they were looking for. This proved to be a yellowing page of newsprint which he held up, quivering, to Matthew. Matthew took it, straining his eyes in the half-light to see what it was. He could just make out that it was the editorial opinion of *The Planter* and that the date on the top of the page was June 1930. 'I'm afraid I can't quite see what it says,' he murmured apologetically. But one of the skeletons at his shoulder, with a prodigious effort which seemed to drain him of his last resources of energy, had succeeded in dragging the head of a match against the sandpaper of a matchbox held in the shaking hands of two of his companions. The match flared. Matthew read aloud as rapidly as he could ...

' "In the hands of the producers of budwood ..." '

'He means Government Research Institute ...'

'I say, please don't interrupt me because otherwise I won't be able to finish this before the match goes out,' protested Matthew. 'Well where was I ... "In the hands of the producers of budwood lies the decision whether rubber planting will, in the far and remote future, become a native industry, or remain an asset of immense value to those European races to whose administrative skill and financial acumen ... (Oh dear, I don't like the sound of this) ... the development of Malaya and of the

Dutch East Indies has been due ..."'

'More, sir, more!' croaked his audience.

'"... It is the honest unbiased opinion of many leading men outside the rubber industry that the less the smallholder has to do with rubber the better it will be in the long run for himself and for all others engaged in rubber production ..."' The match died. Matthew was left with the piece of paper in his fingers. He sighed.

All around him in the semi-darkness, as if summoned by the last trump for a final dispensation of justice over the doings of this imperfect world, supine figures were sitting up and casting off their shrouds and bandages, while others were clambering down from the tiers of shelves on which they had been stretched. He sighed again and looked down at his watch as they crowded round him.

44

Towards the end of the year Sir Robert Brooke-Popham had been replaced as Commander-in-Chief Far East by General Pownall. Although he had been on friendly terms with Brooke-Popham and his successor was unknown to him, Walter was nevertheless relieved to see the departure of his friend for it had grown increasingly clear that Brooke-Popham was not comfortable in the rôle to which he had been assigned. But if this change of commanders had been expected to exert a beneficial effect on the course of the campaign there was no immediate sign of it, at least to the eyes of a civilian onlooker. By now, in any case, the most crucial military decisions had to be taken within the borders of Malaya itself, and thus the responsibility for making them fell to General Percival and his staff at Malaya Command.

The departure of Brooke-Popham did have a disadvantage for Walter, though, in that it removed the one person from whom he could have found out, in general if not in particular, how the campaign was going. If there was going to be trouble in Singapore, and despite the confident tone of the daily communiqués it was growing increasingly clear that there *was* going to be, Walter wanted to make sure that his womenfolk were removed to a place of safety in plenty of time. But he was not only worried about his wife, Joan and Kate: he was also worried about the rubber which still crammed his godowns at the docks, for the greater part of which he had still been unable to arrange shipping. To make matters worse, this rubber was increasingly in danger from air-raids. He would have liked to have taken Brooke-Popham for a stroll round the Orchid Garden and asked him, man to man, when RAF reinforcements were going to arrive and do something about these raids. Because something would have to be done about them, that much was clear. Otherwise the whole of Singapore would go up in flames and nobody could do a thing about it. He would have liked to approach, if not Brooke-Popham, then someone on Percival's staff. But Malaya Command did not have much time for Walter these days. They were too busy doing whatever it was they were doing up-country. 'Not like it was a few months ago,' he grumbled to his wife, 'when they were willing enough to drink my *pahits*.'

Mrs Blackett herself was frantic with worry for her younger brother, Charlie, who had gone to rejoin his regiment across the Causeway and had not been seen since. This was not such a bad thing, in Walter's view, but he did what he could to allay her fears, pointing out that it was perfectly normal for soldiers not to be heard from when they were fighting the enemy, particularly in the jungle. Could he not approach General Percival and ask him to have Charlie sent back to Singapore? she wanted to know. 'My dear, I don't even know the fellow,' Walter replied, showing signs of exasperation, 'and even if I did I could hardly ask him *that*. It might just be possible, if I knew Percival, to ask him to move Charlie towards the enemy, but I couldn't possibly ask him to move him in the opposite direction. He's a soldier, my dear. That's his job. That's what he's there for. I can't see why you should want him not to do his blessed job!'

'But surely, Walter,' cried Mrs Blackett, close to tears. 'There must have been some terrible fighting ... I hear that wounded men are arriving every day at the railway station by the hundreds and if the Japanese have captured Penang ...'

'Percival has too much on his mind, Sylvia, and there's an end of it,' said Walter crossly.

'But you don't know if you haven't tried!'

Walter, however, was quite right. General Percival did have a great deal on his mind. After the débâcle at Jitra the British forces had withdrawn behind the Perak River. But there was a snag about the Perak River, for it flowed in the wrong direction from north to south in the direction of the Japanese advance rather than from east to west, across it. Unfortunately for Percival, however, a position any farther north would have been made untenable by that same Japanese unit which had landed at Patani and, by snatching the Ledge, had earlier threatened the communications of the doomed position of Jitra. This force, by continuing to advance parallel to the main Japanese thrust, which was coming down the trunk road, had maintained its threat of turning the right flank of any new defensive line. As the Japanese Army advanced, therefore, so did this menacing shadow beside it.

But why had this second force been allowed to shadow the main force along the trunk road? The reason was that the British commanders had considered that the terrain did not permit such a manoeuvre, omitting from their calculations a certain unmetalled road which they thought unsuitable for mechanized transport (and so it was, though by no means impassable for infantry advancing on foot or on bicycles). This road headed straight in the direction the Japanese wanted to go, towards Kuala Kangsar. The fact was that from the very beginning of the campaign this force from Patani had supplied the loose thread which was causing the British defences to unravel right down the peninsula.

At last, however, at Kuala Kangsar this particular loose thread came to an end and the British right flank was secured by the solid stitching of Malaya's mountainous spine. But even now, with the mountains at his elbow, Percival felt another retreat was necessary because, alas, the Japanese could use the Perak River to penetrate any defences established north of Telok Anson. And so, in due course and after a further withdrawal, new defensive positions had been prepared in the region of the border between Perak and Selangor on the Slim River, and also to the north and south of it.

It sometimes happens in a dream that you find, as if by coincidence, that all the fears you have when awake are improbably realized one after another. This dismaying sensation of events having tumbled together *not really by accident* but in a way specially designed to deprive you of all hope, which normally only takes advantage of a dreamer's gullibility, for the British commanders had moved out of a nightmare into reality: having at long last escaped from what had been threatening them hitherto, they now found with relentless dream-logic that this apparently secure position on the Slim River was threatened from a completely different direction.

That very circumstance which the Major had feared in the first week of the campaign on hearing that the *Prince of Wales* and the *Repulse* had been sunk had materialized. Thanks to their virtually complete control of both sea and air the Japanese were now in a position to land as they pleased on the thinly defended west coast (on the east coast, too, come to that). To make matters worse this fragile military situation had to be contained in some way by the men of the exhausted 11th Division although, as it happened, Percival had at his disposal the fresh troops of the 9th Division on the other side of the mountains on the east coast: their job was the defence of the airfield at Kuantan and the denial of Mersing against possible landings, both tasks rendered pointless in the event by the collapse in the west. It was this same unfortunate 11th Division which had been obliged to wait in the rain at the very start of the campaign three weeks earlier while Brooke-Popham pondered his pre-emptive advance into Siam. Those fresh and confident troops waiting for the signal to advance and give the Japanese a thrashing would have been hard to recognize in the somnambulant men wearily digging themselves in and putting up anti-tank obstacles at the Slim River; even Mrs Blackett's brother, Charlie, though his stay in Singapore had spared him the first part of the retreat, was looking decidedly the worse for wear as he worked with a company of Punjabis at wiring the road.

Yet if these fighting men were weary, so was General Percival, and he was worried, too. Does it strike you as odd that whatever iniative was planned by Malaya Command invariably turned out to contain a flaw which would cause it to fail? It was beginning to strike Percival as very odd indeed. At times he could see the flaw well in advance but even so ... it always happened that he could do nothing about it. He could not find fault with General Heath, though it was true that Heath was 'Indian Army' and hence, in Percival's view, not a great deal could be expected of him. As a matter of fact, it could even be argued that Heath was being miracuously successful in preserving his retreating 111 Indian Corps from being destroyed. And so, who was to blame? He could not, in all fairness, blame himself or his staff for the flaw that kept appearing. Very often it was simply the lie of land that caused his plans to go adrift ... or perhaps it was the result of that earlier bungling by poor old Brookers. Whatever the reason, the flaw kept on appearing. It was most peculiar. Or worse than peculiar.

On the night of 4 January, worn out by the constant strain and worried by the prospect of an important conference with General Heath and General Gordon Bennett at Segamat on the following day, Percival fell into a deep sleep. Almost immediately, it seemed, he plunged into a confusing dream about some interminable dinner-party at Government House. But it was not *now* that it was taking place, in the New Year of 1942, for there, opposite, was the decent, blunt, straightforward countenance of old General Dobbie, the GOC. So it must then be 1937 when he had been out here as GSO1 on Dobbie's staff. At the end of the table he could see the Governor's handsome, slightly supercilious face: behind the Governor again there was someone standing in the shadows speaking into his ear. Percival knew there was someone there because whoever it was had rested his hand on the back of the Governor's chair in a familiar sort of way while he was whispering. He could just make out that the hand emerged from the sleeve of a uniform, but belonging to which of the Services he could not say.

Suddenly, and with spirit, he challenged this man in the shadows. After a moment the hand on the Governor's chair was withdrawn. A period of confusion and darkness followed, of which he could make no sense. Presently he sat up, sweating and suffocating inside the mosquito net. The image of the Governor, gazing at him with a condescending smile, slowly faded. It was still dark.

Percival looked at his watch, took a swallow of water from the glass beside his bed and lay back again. It was very hot. The fan slogging away above him could make little impression on the air inside his mosquito net. He would have liked to tear away the net and sleep in fresh air again, but he could not possibly risk an insect bite that might lead to malaria or dengue fever, not at this stage. 'I'll never sleep like this, though,' he told himself. Yet, despite the heat, he fell asleep again almost immediately and this time he dreamed that he was back at Staff College and he was doing some exam or other on which his whole career in the Army would depend. Wait, he had remembered now what it was. He had to prevent the Japanese from seizing the Naval Base on Singapore Island and they had already got almost as far as Kuala Lumpur. He was no longer at Staff College. He was in Malaya and it was the real thing. He began to sweat and worry again in his sleep.

But towards dawn Percival received a welcome visit. The shades of Clausewitz and Metternich came to his bedside to offer their advice. Presently they were joined by the spirits of Liddell Hart and of Sir Edward Hamley, author of Hamley's *The Operations of War, Explained and Illustrated*. These gentlemen considered a number of solutions to the difficulties which faced him. Metternich recommended that everything should be wagered on a rapid strike north to disrupt the Japanese lines of communication, Hamley spoke vaguely of flanking movements (and also, less pertinently, of cavalry), Clausewitz wanted Percival to withdraw his troops intact to Singapore Island to conserve them until reinforcements could arrive from Europe and America. Ah, that was interesting! Percival listened eagerly to these ghostly advisers and found each more persuasive than the last. But presently their voices grew fainter and they fell to arguing among themselves. All too soon came the tread of the orderly's heavy boots in the corridor outside.

Conscious again, Percival decided, at his meeting in Segamat with General Heath and General Gordon Bennett, that although in most respects the narrowness of the Slim River position lent itself well to defence, the threat of amphibious landings further down the coast would make it untenable in the long run unless reinforcements could be brought up to cover the coastal area. The Slim River defile, however, provided the last chance of stopping the enemy short of Kuala Lumpur ... or indeed, south of it for a considerable distance. For as you went south the knobbly spine of mountains sank back beneath the peninsula's fair skin, which itself became pleasantly wrinkled with roads. There would be little chance in such favourable terrain of stopping the Japanese in Malacca. And so, if not in Malacca, it would have to be in Johore ... if not on Singapore Island itself. In the meantime, the Japanese must be denied the airfield at Kuantan on the east coast, at least until the reinforcements of troops and planes expected in mid-January had arrived. Moreover, if the defence of Johore was to be properly organized, the Japanese must be halted for a time and the capture of Kuala Lumpur postponed. Everything pointed therefore to the critical defensive stand being made at the Slim River. The Japanese must be stopped there or the defence of Johore would be hopeless. That was why the Punjabis and the Argylls had to keep on digging themselves in even after dark on the following nights. Everything would depend on them.

45

As the late afternoon shadows were beginning to lengthen over the Mayfair's increasingly neglected and overgrown compound, two figures could be seen making their way along the well-trodden path towards the Blacketts' house: one of these was easily recognizable as Matthew, normally dressed, looking some-what pensive, but who was the other, this individual wearing what looked like a scarlet boiler-suit, a scarlet balaclava helmet from which horns protruded, and carrying a large toasting-fork? This, as it happened, was only the Major who with great reluctance had put on the suit which he had been sent by Blackett and Webb Limited for the dress rehearsal of their jubilee parade. He was now regretting the decision because he felt much too hot: you cannot expect to wear a balaclava hel-met and horns in the tropics without discomfort. Besides, he was afraid that he might be the only person who had decided to dress up, and he now regretted having yielded to Walter's in-sistence that he should personify Inflation. The Major swiped irritably with his toasting-fork at one of the giant thistles grow-ing beside the tennis court and the air filled with drifting white down.

The Major, however, had a reason for wanting to keep in with Walter. Several of Blackett and Webb's vans had been set aside for conversion into floats for the jubilee parade and the Major, to whom it had been perfectly clear for some time that the parade would never take place, was anxious that his AFS unit should be able to call on them in an emergency to supplement what scanty transport was available: this amounted to the Lagonda, Mr Wu's Buick, a motor-cycle belonging to the estate manager and a couple of bicycles.

A site for the building of the floats had been chosen adjacent to the Blacketts' compound in a yard surrounded by a cluster of dilapidated godowns which at some time in the last century had been used as storage sheds for a nutmeg plantation but for the past many years had been disused, at least, until recently when Walter's excessive buying of rubber to circumvent the new American regulations had filled all Blackett and Webb's other godowns to overflowing and obliged these tumbledown buildings, hastily restored, to accommodate some of the surplus. Walter had originally bought the former nutmeg plantation, which still boasted pleasant groves of lofty, evergreen nutmeg trees, in order to cushion his own property from its acquisition by disagreeable neighbours. But now it seemed to him that he could hardly have made a better investment. Where better could he have found to prepare in secret the floats for Blackett and Webb's triumphant parade?

The Major had been waiting patiently over the past three weeks for the reality of Singapore's increasingly precarious situation to put paid to Walter's jubilee parade. At least, he had assumed, work on building the floats would have been abandoned. With a continuing shortage of labour at the docks and with the Forces trying desperately to recruit men to build defences and accommodation that should have been built years ago it was inconceivable that labour should be diverted to something as trivial as Walter's floats. Yet although the building of them had been considerably delayed he was astonished to find now that work was still continuing; moreover, twice as many men were working on them as before. The explanation was simple: the men in question, Asiatics normally employed as carpenters, painters or welders at the docks, very naturally preferred the comparative safety of this nutmeg grove to working on coastal defences, at the docks, or the Naval Base under the threat of air-raids.

In other respects, however, there were definite signs that reality was making substantial inroads into Walter's dream. The only Europeans who had decided to attend this dress rehearsal were Monty, even more bizarrely dressed than the Major, and a few of the younger executives of Blackett and Webb who had presumably found it impossible to refuse; none of the latter had seen fit to dress up for the occasion. Less than half of the Chinese who had been summoned to animate the dragons had turned up. Not more than three-quarters of a Chinese brass band was perched on some rusting machinery at one end of the yard, occasionally banging or blowing at their instruments but for the most part watching dubiously as Walter, looking impatient and out of sorts, shouted at his helpers and tried to marshal enough volunteers to get one of the dragons moving. As he saw Matthew and the Major arrive he broke off, however, and came over to them.

'It's good of you to come,' he said. 'I appreciate it. Most people haven't, though, and I doubt whether we're going to be able to do very much with what we have ...' He paused gesturing vigorously. 'Not there, you ass! Over there with the others! How many times do I have to tell you?' He sighed with exasperation, stuck his hands in his pockets and surveyed the chaotic scene spread before him. He was perspiring freely, and looked squat, formidable and slightly demented. 'It's no use,' he muttered, more to himself than to the Major and Matthew, 'what can you do with such people?'

The Major cautiously lifted a finger to scratch one of his horns which was itching. He was a little surprised to find that he felt sorry for Walter. He said nothing, however. Together they set off to inspect the floats, Walter explaining that he *had* hoped to get the whole parade together and into motion and to take a couple of turns around the swimming pool and back here again to iron out any last minute difficulties. That was now out of the question unless the absentees presented themselves double quick. They passed two floats parked in the shade of a nutmeg tree: on one of them Joan sat, wearing a plumed Roman helmet and a flowing white garment of Grecian appearance which displayed her lovely arms and shoulders to advantage; in her left hand she held a trident, her right hand secured the Britannic shield. She was gazing impassively ahead and when Matthew murmured 'Hello' made no reply (perhaps she had not heard him). Kate sat on the other float with her arm around a gigantic cornucopia: she brightened up when she saw Matthew and waved her free hand.

Kate's cornucopia had a few minutes earlier been the cause of a furious row between Walter and Monty. From out of its gaping mouth there spilled an abundance of everything made of rubber: motor-tyres of all shapes and sizes, bicycle tyres, inner tubes, shoes and wellingtons, rubber gloves, sou'westers, batting gloves, rubber sheets and tiles, shock absorbers, rubber-tipped pencils, cushions, kneeling pads, balloons, elastic bands, belts, braces and a hundred and one other things, not all of them recognizable. To this magnificent array Monty, as a joke, had attempted to add a packet of contraceptives. As ill luck would have it, Walter had noticed his son chuckling gleefully as he arranged something conspicuously on the very lip of the cornucopia. His display of anger, even to Monty who was accustomed to it, had been frightening. Walter was incensed, not simply that Monty should have done something that might have made the cornucopia look ridiculous, but that he should have

355

paid so little heed to the modesty of his younger sister. Monty had retired, disgraced, and was at present slouching glumly in the shade of another tree.

'Why don't you get off your behind and do something to help,' Walter shouted at him roughly as he passed. Monty stirred uncomfortably but evidently could think of no way in which he could improve on what was being done already, for presently he sank back again. Monty, the Major noticed, like himself had been allotted a rôle in the counter-parade which was to accompany the parade proper, harassing it symbolically to represent the pitfalls that a thriving business might have to face in its passage over the years; as a matter of fact, the Major was quite looking forward to tormenting plump and cheerful little Kate with his toasting-fork, though he could see no real reason why inflation should carry a toasting-fork at all. Monty's costume came no closer than the Major's to suggesting the part that he was to portray: it consisted of an old striped swimming-costume with shoulder straps, striped football socks rolled right up his hairy thighs and a fanged mask which bore a disturbing coincidental resemblance to General Percival: at the moment this mask and an inflated bladder tied to a stick lay on the ground beside him; the final and most frightening touch in Monty's costume were the awe-inspiring, curved talons which had been grafted on to a pair of batting-gloves for the occasion. Walter had alloted Monty the rôle of Crippling Overheads in the parade and had refused all his requests for a more heroic part.

The Major was now gazing with misgiving at one or two of the other floats which Walter, his spirits reviving a little, was showing him (Matthew had sloped off for a chat with Kate and perhaps was even hoping to make it up with Joan). Despite all the difficulties and postponements, Walter was saying, certain advances had been made in Blackett and Webb's preparations: it would be a great shame, and the most bitter of disappointments to him personally, if the jubilee should 'for one reason or another' now fail to take place. These advances, the Major had to agree, were considerable: four of the vans which had been set aside for the jubilee had already been crowned with the harnesses of wooden spars and metal brackets on which would be placed, when the time came, the floats which the committee had decided upon; other harnesses and floats were still under construction here and there, and in due course other vans would

356

be temporarily commandeered to support them. Here was the towering dome-shaped head of the octopus which, instead of the more usual lion, had been selected to symbolize Singapore herself: this octopus, smiling genially, had been fitted out with amazingly lifelike rubber tentacles specially made for the occasion in Blackett and Webb's local workshops with the participation of local craftsmen 'of all races' (as Walter explained). The advantage of rubber for this purpose, he went on, was that it was flexible and the ends of tentacles which were twisted normally into rings could be pulled open to allow someone to be 'captured' in a friendly grip: in this way young women with banners proclaiming them to be Shanghai, Hong Kong, Batavia, Saigon and so forth could walk along beside the float and appear to writhe in the tentacles, which would fit round their necks, in 'a very naturalistic manner'. An elegant solution to the problem, as the Major must agree.

Next to the octopus came another float with eight more arms, this time human. These arms, immensely long, stretched forward over the cab of the van which was to carry them, and had been painted variously dark brown, light brown, yellow and white to represent the four races of Malaya stretching out side by side to reach for prosperity above massive signboards reading, in Tamil, Malay, Chinese and English: ALL IN IT TO-GETHER.

'Wouldn't it be better if it read simply "All together" or "All working together"?' suggested the Major. 'It seems to me that there's something a bit odd about "all *in it* together".'

'Oh, I don't think so, no,' replied Walter vaguely. 'It seems all right to me ... Not inside the bloody van, you idiot, *on top of it!*' he added in an indignant howl at an impassive Chinese carpenter who was trying to drag a large sign bearing the words 'Continuity in Prosperity' into the driving seat of one of the vans.

'Still no sign of the rest of the so-and-sos who said they'd come!' Walter inspected his watch, looking defenceless all of a sudden. 'Well, come on, we'll give them another few minutes and then if they haven't turned up we'll call it a day.'

They walked on. A pink-faced youth, one of Blackett and Webb's younger executives, hurried up with some problem for Walter. After a hasty conference Walter said: 'if you don't mind, Major, this young man will show you the rest. I'll be with you again in a few minutes.' He strode away, summoning an

Indian secretary with a clipboard to accompany him. Once he was out of sight the prospective participants in the parade relaxed visibly.

The Major, with the pink-faced young man at his side, now found himself standing in front of Prosperity herself, depicted by sandwich boards as long as the van which was to carry them and twice as high. These boards had been skillfully painted to imitate Straits dollar bills, enormously magnified: on one side the blue one-dollar, on the other the red ten-dollar, and both with the oval portrait of the King which you would find on the currency itself, beautifully painted to show every detail of his wavy hair and high ceremonial collar, though perhaps with eyes more slanted than usual, for this, too, was the work of a Chinese artist. 'Blackett and Webb 1892–1942. Fifty Years of Prosperity for Workers of All Races.'

'I hope you approve, Major Archer,' said the young man politely. 'We in the Firm happen to think it's a rather valuable contribution.'

'I must say,' said the Major dubiously, 'that I wonder whether this is quite the moment to go in for all this sort of thing.'

But no! didn't the Major see that it was precisely now that such a jubilee parade was needed, now more than at any other moment in the history of the Colony?

They had moved on to yet another float in the form of a crown composed of vertical wooden laths painted silver to simulate metal and tipped with arrowheads. This float, which was entitled 'The Blackett and Webb Group of Companies', also carried the slogans 'Continuity in Prosperity' and 'All in it Together'. The Major paused, fascinated, for behind the bars of the crown, as if in a cage, were a number of rather sulky-looking young women with marcelled hair and bright red lipstick wearing glittering silver lamé dresses. Each of these women was evidently intended to represent one of Blackett and Webb's interests for although their dresses were identical they wore a variety of silk sashes proclaiming 'Shipping', 'Insurance', 'Import-Export', 'Rubber', 'Engineering', 'Pineapple Canning', 'Entrepôt' and a great many more. The Major, eyeing this float, was recalling uneasily his conversation with Matthew about how Blackett and Webb controlled the rubber companies under its management by means of incestuous investment, when the young women on the float spotted his companion; they appeared to recognize him for they crowded to the bars of the crown and began to shout abuse, including certain expressions which the Major was surprised to hear coming from such attractive young ladies. 'When you give us bloody-damn money?' they shrieked at him, among other things. 'We waiting here all bloody-damn afternoon!'

The young executive, however, blushing furiously, averted his gaze and hurried the Major along, explaining in an undertone that these young women had possibly been 'a bit of a mistake': they were a singing group called the Da Sousa Sisters temporarily stranded in Singapore for want of nightclub engagements. Although the terms of their employment in Blackett and Webb's jubilee parade had been carefully explained to them in advance, it had turned out that they had expected a certain amount of special treatment as 'professional artistes'. However, he went on, panting slightly, what he had been about to say was that the important thing was *continuity* in the Colony's prosperity. All races must realize that there was no earthly use in a long period of poverty followed by a quick and unreliable fortune, like a big win at roulette. That sort of thing got a country nowhere! What you wanted was a slow and steady enrichment over the years ... the very thing, as it happened, that firms like Blackett and Webb had been supplying for the past fifty years or more. While he was enlarging excitedly on this aspect of prosperity, using expressions like 'infrastructure' and 'economic spread' which, however, only served to numb the Major's brain, an air-raid siren sounded. Some moments of chaos followed. Men dashed here and there. Steel helmets were clapped on. Some people peered apprehensively at the sky, others dived for shelter. The Da Sousa Sisters set up a terrible shrieking to be let out of the crown in which they were imprisoned. 'I suppose we'll have to let them out,' muttered the young executive, 'but I don't know how we'll ever get them back.' But already Monty was unfastening the door of their cage in an effort to ingratiate himself, though not before 'Import–Export' had taken off one of her shoes to join 'Wireless and Electrical' in hammering on the bars. The Major's companion dragged him hurriedly towards a makeshift shelter, more, it seemed, for protection from the Da Sousa Sisters who were now running loose than from possible bombs.

In due course the Major found himself crouching down in a sort of igloo made of rubber bales which was the nearest approach that could be devised to an air-raid shelter; while he crouched there democratically with 'workers of all races' he noticed that his companion had clapped on a steel helmet. The

Major regretted that he had not brought his own helmet: clearly it could not have been expected to fit over his horns. Never mind, it was too late to do anything about it now! Nevertheless, while the young executive began to explain that by 'infrastructure' he meant such things as roads, railways and other services which, though they do not produce wealth *themselves*, are crucial to its production in the long run, not least by enticing investment from overseas, the Major continued to finger his horns uncertainly, wishing that he had not been such a bally fool. He had not brought his gas-mask either.

But, the young man went on, you could not build roads and railways on a 'here today, gone tomorrow' basis ... for such investments you need a steady volume of trade over a number of years! That was the substance of the magic phrase 'continuity in prosperity' which, as the Major had no doubt noticed, was painted everywhere in Chinese as well as English characters.

Would it not have been better, though, replied the Major, if both vans and workers of all races had been employed on the more urgent tasks of, say, preventing Singapore from burning to the ground, repairing the bomb damage or unloading the ships which lay in the docks with cargoes of urgently needed ammunition and supplies?

After all, it was absurd that soldiers who were needed to man the defences should have to unload these ships because the labour force had decamped to build Blackett and Webb's floats. But even as the Major spoke there came the crump of exploding bombs from the direction of Keppel Harbour and he was obliged to admit that the labour force, ill-paid as it was, and without adequate air-raid shelters, would most likely have decamped anyway, and one could hardly blame them. At length, the 'all clear' sounded and the Major crawled stiffly out of the rubber igloo and got to his feet. It was time he was getting back to the Mayfair in case his services should be needed.

But there was still something that the young man from Blackett and Webb wanted to show him before he went and the Major, protesting weakly, allowed himself to be diverted towards one or two floats which had been designed to portray the social benefits which had attended these fifty years of successful commerce. Here was a papier mâché teacher beside a gigantic blackboard on which was written in the usual languages 'All in it together' and these small grey lumps which had still to be painted severally in dark brown, light brown, yellow and ...

'Yes, of course, "children of all races",' said the Major who was getting the hang of it by now.

'And this figure on a horse which is meant to be a sort of Chinese Saint George is using his lance to kill ... no, not a dragon, the Chinese are rather fond of dragons ... but a hook-worm, very much magnified, of course. But now, and this is what I really wanted you to see, we come to the most ambitious float of all from a technical point of view ... though it doesn't look much, I agree, until you see it working. Yes, it represents a symbolical rubber tree ... It had to be symbolical because real rubber trees look so uninteresting ... producing wealth for all races. If you look closely, Major, you'll see that a hole representing the cut made by the tapper's knife has been made in the bark. Now when I pull this switch here liquid gold pours out into this basin ...'

'Liquid gold?'

'Well, actually, its just coloured water ... now what's the matter. Oh, I see, the pump's not plugged in. Here we go!' He pulled the switch and the tree began to spurt noisily into the basin.

'It looks as if it's ... well ...' said the Major.

'Yes, I'm afraid it does rather. But it was the best we could do. At first we tried a little conveyor belt inside the trunk which kept spilling coins through the opening in the bark and that looked fine, but the blighters kept pinching the coins. Still, it wasn't a bad idea.' He sighed and looked momentarily discouraged. 'Anyway, don't you agree that once we get this jubilee parade on the road it should make it clear to everyone what they will have to lose by exchanging us for the Japanese?'

46

There was an area of unusually dense jungle in that part of the Slim River region where General Percival had decided that a stand must be made if southern Malaya were to be given the time to prepare its defences: it lay a little to the north of the village and rubber plantation at Trolak where, incidently, one branch of the river flowed under a bridge. To cross this stretch of dense jungle both the trunk road and the railway were obliged to squeeze together and run side by side through a narrow defile which resembled the unusually long neck of a bottle. If the Japanese tanks were to continue their southward advance they would have no alternative but to come through this narrow defile. But just beyond its long neck the bottle opened out into the wider chamber (more like a decanter than a bottle) of the Klapa Bali rubber estate and of Trolak village. If the Japanese tanks once managed to pass through that long neck and get loose among the rubber trees, well ... then there would be no stopping them. The only chance then, perhaps, might be to delay them by demolishing the bridge at Trolak and the Slim River Bridge some five miles down the road. And so, demolition charges had been set against these bridges, just in case.

The Brigadier in command of the 12th Brigade, which had been given the task of defending the defile, had established his Brigade HQ some distance into the Klapa Bali estate on the western side of the road. In the rubber on the other side of the road was the 2nd Battalion of his own regiment, the Argyll and Sutherland Highlanders, known since Balaclava as 'The Thin Red Line'; the presence of the Argylls was naturally a source of comfort to the Brigadier for unlike many of the other troops at his disposal, who were ill-trained and inexperienced, they had proved an effective fighting force against the Japanese, thanks largely to his own efforts in training them for jungle warfare before the campaign began. The Brigadier was a tall man with a long, lean, intelligent face which wore, as a rule, a somewhat grim and determined expression. A luxuriant moustache flourished on his upper lip, as surprising on those craggy features as a clump of wild flowers lodged on a rock face. His arms were thin, his body was thin, his knees under his shorts were thin, all of him was thin. It was surprising then that, despite this lack of manifest strength, he should radiate such purpose and such confidence. Even now, exhausted though he was by three weeks of retreating, digging in, fighting, and again retreating, invariably under appalling conditions, his confidence appeared undiminished.

Nevertheless, as darkness now began to fall on 6 January and he awaited developments, the Brigadier was seriously concerned. Because of the eerie quietness which had prevailed all day he had dared to hope that the Japanese might have been halted by the severe blow they had received in an ambush sprung by the Argylls on the railway the previous day. General Paris, on the other hand, whom he had contacted by telephone, had gloomily postulated a wide flanking movement through the dense jungle which would suddenly develop into an attack in the rear. It had happened before.

The Brigadier had pondered the problems of fighting in the jungle and had noticed that instead of a wary advance on a broad front the Japanese preferred a swift and violent attack down the narrow corridor of the road itself to a considerable depth. For whoever had control of the road, as the Brigadier had already realized, in a situation where maps and wireless were scarce, had control of the only practical means of communication. In dense jungle or in a trackless ocean of identical rubber trees it was hard, or impossible, to calculate your exact position; without an accurate idea of where you were it was out of the question to organize an effective manoeuvre. If you had the road, on the other hand, you had everything.

The Brigadier, therefore, was expecting the Japanese to attack straight down the road: given the position they could, in any case, do little else; only if this assault were stopped could they be expected to leave the road and attempt to encircle its defenders. He had, therefore, disposed his 12th Brigade in depth along the road and railway where they ran together for some distance, with two battalions in the defile: one, the Hyderabads, in a forward position to take the first assault and then fall back; the other, the Punjabis, to deal with the main attack. He was counting on the Japanese being stopped at this point and finding themselves committed to encircling through the jungle. To deal with this eventuality, at the southern end of the defile four companies of the Argylls were positioned on either side of the road to meet flanking attacks at the point where the Japanese would emerge from the jungle into the rubber.

But what made the Brigadier's long face look even sterner than usual as he awaited developments was the knowledge of the weakened state the brigade was in. Even his own Argylls were reaching the end of their physical resources: what they needed, and the Indian battalions even more so, was just a little time to recover ... even a few hours would make a difference. But throughout the campaign the Japanese had, time and again, followed up their attacks more quickly than expected. The Brigadier was hardly surprised in consequence when Captain Sinclair presently informed him that Chinese refugees filtering through the British positions ahead of the advancing Japanese had brought news of a large column of tanks they had seen moving up the trunk road.

'They say their engineers have been suh ... suh ... suh ... warming like ants at every demolished bridge for miles back, sir,' stammered Sinclair excitedly. He was surprised and deeply impressed that the Brigadier should remain his imperturbable self at this news of approaching tanks. *He* knew, and the Brigadier knew, just how much could be hoped for from the anti-tank defences in the defile ... In the four days that had elapsed since the decision had been taken to make a stand here, work on the defences had continued whenever the constant Japanese air-raids permitted. Weapons pits had been dug and wire had been strung by Chinese and Indian coolies supervised by engineers sent forward by 11th Division; no sooner had the troops themselves arrived, tired though they were by this latest withdrawal, than they, too, had been obliged to join in the work on the defences. But the only defences that could be found that might, at a pinch, stop tanks were a few concrete blocks and a couple of dozen anti-tank mines, both of which had been disposed in the defile. All well and good. Sinclair knew; however (he was a much keener soldier than he had been a diplomat), that tanks are distinctly solid objects: the only point in stopping them with your concrete blocks, which you won't do for long, in any case, with these improvised methods, is to allow your anti-tank guns to get in a good shot at them while motionless. Unfortunately, the slender obstacles which the 12th Brigade had been able to erect in the defile were covered by a mere three anti-tank guns manned, into the bargain, by gunners who had, alas, never been trained to cope with tanks at all, even in daylight, let alone tanks most likely firing tracer at close range in pitch darkness. That should be enough to make even a seasoned gunner's hair stand on end, never mind a raw Indian recruit.

Well then, what else was there to stop the Japs? A railway bridge, forward, had been blown up (the Japanese had tanks with wheels that would run on the rails, it was thought). The Argylls, in common with the rest of the British forces in Malaya, had no tanks of their own, only armoured cars and bren-gun carriers; although these might come in handy on the estate roads to cope with a flanking movement by the Jap infantry into the rubber they were quite useless, of course, against tanks. Most serious of all, the British anti-tank rifles would not penetrate the armour of the Japanese medium tanks. And so what could be done? If the tanks once got through the defile there was only the bridge at Trolak and the Slim River Bridge, both prepared for demolition, which lay between the tanks and the open road to Singapore. And now, into the bargain, it seemed that the Japanese attack would come twenty-four hours sooner than expected.

If the Brigadier received this news of an impending attack from young Sinclair without making a fuss, it was partly because it was his business to be imperturbable, partly because he knew that one can never predict quite how things will turn out: battles cannot be decided on paper by subtracting the armour of one side from the armour of the other and giving the victory to the side which has the surplus. There was a probability, certainly, that the tanks would have the advantage ... but so much depends on the quality of the men and on what is going on in their minds. True, the Indian battalions were in very poor shape and the Argylls were not much better. But a quick success or two and who could tell? Thank heaven, anyway, for the few dozen reinforcements who had just arrived from Singapore on this dark, rain-lashed night, under Captain Hamish Ross, for they included some of the best men in the battalion. The few words he had had with Ross had cheered him.

'We had a wee spot o' bother, sir, at Tyersall Park,' Ross had said, eyeing the Brigadier slyly. 'I suppose ye might call it a mutiny.'

'A mutiny, man? Ye'll no expect me to believe that, Hamish Ross!'

And so Captain Ross had explained. When his party of reinforcements had paraded at the Tyersall camp in Singapore a number of Argylls on staff duty whom Malaya Command had specifically ordered him to leave behind had paraded too, demanding to return to the regiment to join in the scrap.

'Aye, now that's more like it,' nodded the Brigadier and, though his expression was no less forbidding, Hamish Ross could tell by the glint in his eye that he was pleased. These new arrivals would help put heart into the other men, given enough time for them to settle in.

Outside, the rain had slackened now. Making his way through the rubber trees back to the road to find out whether anything more had been gleaned from Chinese refugees, Sinclair paused, gripped by the sense of unreality which comes from excitement and lack of sleep. In the course of the afternoon he had gone forward with the Brigadier to inspect the progress that the Hyderabads and the Punjabis were making with their defences and there he had met Charlie Tyrrell, Mrs Blackett's brother. He did not know Charlie very well. In Singapore they had not met more than once or twice at the Blacketts' house and even then had scarcely exchanged more than a few words. But seeing each other now in these unusual, even desperate circumstances, they had immediately begun to talk as if they were old friends. Charlie had come back with him for an hour to the Argylls' area in the rubber.

Sinclair had been shocked to see the state that Charlie was in. His handsome face was hollow-cheeked with fatigue, dirty and inflamed with insect bites; even his khaki was in tatters. But it was not so much Charlie's physical appearance that had given Sinclair a shock, for in the middle of a jungle campaign one does not expect to see a soldier looking as if he has just turned out on parade: it was the feverish look in his eyes and the obsessive, fatalistic way in which he talked ... almost as if he were talking to himself, as if Sinclair had not been there at all. Charlie talked incessantly about his men: he had never seen them so apathetic and dejected! They were at the end of their tether, that much was clear! 'How can you blame them?' he had demanded without waiting for a reply. 'Most of them are barely trained recruits.'

Sinclair had nodded sympathetically. Unlike the Argylls down the road the Punjabis did not possess that extra strength for living and fighting in the jungle which comes from training in atrocious conditions, from discipline, from regimental traditions which, combining all together, temper each individual and form what Sinclair thought of as a collective willpower, imperious and inflexible (yet even some of his own Argylls were close to cracking).

He had watched his men for the past two days, Charlie went on, and it was clear that their only thought (though these were the bravest of men!) was to huddle in their slit trenches, the nearest approach to security they could find. But who could blame them? In the course of their long retreat through northern and central Malaya the battalion had lost two hundred and fifty men, of whom many had been killed. From dawn the day before yesterday, there had been a steady stream of Jap bombers and fighters blasting away at the edges of the jungle on both sides of the defile where, though hidden, they knew the British forces to be. These planes had robbed the Punjabis of any chance they might have had of resting before the next attack; they had also caused a further trickle of casualties. And yet, somehow, even that was not the worst of it ... It was ...

They were standing a little way off the road in the shade. Charlie was leaning his back against the trunk of a rubber tree. As he spoke he kept wearily slapping his sweating face with his hand as if to drive off insects but mechanically, with resignation (besides, Sinclair could see no insects around Charlie's face) ... Abruptly Sinclair was afraid that the Brigadier might come by and see Charlie in this state. He felt that that could not be allowed to happen, he could not quite say why, except that you only had to glance at the way Charlie was leaning against the rubber tree, talking and slapping himself, his gaunt and desperate face dappled by sunlight and shadow filtering through the leaves, to know that he had very nearly reached the point where he simply *would not care* any longer!

But still Charlie was trying to explain himself to Sinclair, with an almost pathetic determination that he should understand ... He was trying to say that, however bad it might be when the Jap Zero was roaring along the road machine-gunning the fringes of the jungle, it was no better when the plane had dipped its wing and swung away over the tree tops. Because within a few seconds an eerie silence had fallen, blanketing even the sound of the departing plane. 'When you've been in this bloody place a bit longer, Sinclair,' he said, grinning now as if there was something amusing about what he was saying, but at the same time scratching his ribs viciously through his tattered shirt, 'you'll understand exactly what I mean.'

'Well, I've been trying to get up here for the past three weeks,' said Sinclair defensively, for it was true that it was only four days since he had left Singapore, 'but I think I know what you mean.'

There was something about this silence, went on Charlie, ignoring him : it gave the sound of your voice a distant, unreal quality. Even quite sharp sounds, like the dropping of a mess tin on the metalled road, would be blotted up immediately by the dense green walls on either side. The sound did not seem to *go* anywhere, that was it. There was no resonance. It gave you a baffling sensation, like speaking into a dead telephone. Only at night did you begin to hear sounds again. But so disturbing were the night sounds that the silence was almost better. Another thing, action here seemed to have no more resonance than sounds. During the daytime when you stopped moving, everything stopped, as if you were on the floor of a dead ocean. Everything had to come from *you*, that was what was so intolerable. His men felt the same way, he could tell by watching them. For men already exhausted this need to initiate all movement from their own resources was unendurable.

The two men were silent for a few moments. Charlie had evidently come to the end of what he had wanted to say. Although he still leaned dejectedly against the tree, he had stopped slapping himself and appeared calmer. 'Sorry to go on like that about it,' he said presently. 'It's the same for everyone, of course. Besides, it's not much better for you blokes here in the rubber.' It was true, Sinclair reflected, that even at the best of times there was something unnerving about a rubber plantation; wherever you stood you found yourself at the centre of a bewildering maze of identical trees which stretched out geometrically in every direction as far as the eye could see. But in Malaya the eye, as a rule, could not see very far; you seldom found a place from where you could get a prospect over the jungle or rubber which covered the country like a green lid on a saucepan.

'D'you know Rilke's poem about the panther?' asked Charlie suddenly, smiling.

> Sein Blick ist vom Vorübergehen der Stäbe
> So müd geworden ... dass er nichts mehr hält ...

'Roughly translated it means: "His gaze from looking through the bars has grown so tired he can't take in anything more."

> Ihm ist, als ob es tausend Stäbe gäbe
> Und hinter tausend Stäben keine Welt.

"It seems to him as if there are a thousand bars and behind the thousand bars, no world." That's what I feel about all these bloody rubber trees.'

Sinclair thought of this again as, now in darkness, he strode on through the dripping ranks of trees, trying to shake off the premonition that if the Japanese attacked tonight it would be the end of the line for the Punjabis, no matter how strong the position they occupied in the defile.

As the night advanced the rain stopped and the moon began to appear, fitfully at first and then more frequently, between the clouds. From the jungle a dreadful odour of rotting vegetation crept out over the waiting Punjabis and hung there in the humid atmosphere. Now, more brilliant than ever, the moon hung like a great white lamp over the two black walls of jungle, shining so brightly that if you moved out of the covering foliage you could see your shadow clearly printed on the surface of the road. Behind them, a little way along the road, the Argylls guarding the exits from the defile into the rubber listened, skin crawling, to the steady churning of the jungle.

Charlie looked at the luminous green face of his wrist watch: it was midnight. From close at hand there came the metallic sound of some insect he had never been able to identify ... it resembled the winding-up of a clockwork toy. He was dreamily contemplating this sound and at the same time vowing to keep his eyes open when, like a paralysing blow from the darkness, there came at last the sound for which he had been listening for so long, the first thud of guns from the Hyderabads' position up the road. The shelling continued. For a while nothing else happened. One, two, three hours passed. He began to nod off again. Suddenly, he woke. The noise of gunfire had ceased. The Japanese were beginning their attack.

47

Not far away from where Charlie waited with the Punjabis, a small, bespectacled figure in battledress sat in the back of a lorry gripping his knees tensely, his rifle locked between them. This was none other than Private Kikuchi and as he sat there in complete darkness he was doing his best to concentrate his thoughts on the heroic example of his uncle, Bugler Kikuchi,. who had sounded his bugle with his dying breath. Private Kikuchi knew that in a few minutes, at a sign from his commander, Lieutenant Matsushita, he would have to hurl himself forward with his bayonet at the ready 'like a blind man unafraid of snakes', as Matsushita put it. Would he be able to follow Uncle Kikuchi's immaculate example? Huddled beside him in the lorry as it crept forward without lights he sensed, but could not see, his comrades of the Ando Regiment. Perhaps they too, were wondering what the hours before dawn would bring? Would they even live to see the daylight again? Perhaps they were hoping, if possible, to die gloriously fighting for the Emperor. Certainly, Lieutenant Matsushita would be. He was an officer with strangely burning eyes who had already served in the Imperial Army, mopping up bandits in Manchuria.

Kikuchi was astonished and awed by Lieutenant Matsushita. Every time he met those burning eyes it was as if he received an electric shock. The intensity of feeling in Matsushita, his utter devotion to the Emperor and to his country, had come as a revelation even to Kikuchi who, one might have thought, had little to learn about Japanese National Spirit with such an uncle. Yet there was something that Kikuchi found rather frightening about him at the same time ... Sometimes it almost seemed as if he wanted to get not only himself but everyone else killed, too. He would dash forward sometimes with bullets falling about him like a spring shower while he might easily have advanced in relative security by some other route.

To make matters worse (or better, depending how you looked at it) he had taken a particular liking to Kikuchi, either because of his glorious uncle or because he sensed Kikuchi's fascination with him. On one occasion he had taken Kikuchi aside and shown him some of the medals he had been awarded and which he carried everywhere with him in a little waterproof pouch, even on the most desperate sorties into the jungle. He had allowed Kikuchi to gaze at his Order of the Rising Sun, Fourth Class, at his Decoration of Manchuria, Fourth and Fifth Classes, at his Campaign Medal of the Chinese Incident, at his Campaign Medal of the Manchurian Incident and at several others, including an Order of the Golden Kite, Fifth Class. 'One day, Kikuchi, you too will have medals like these,' he had said, his eyes fastened on Kikuchi's and gripping them tightly as in two glowing chopsticks so that he could not turn away. 'Or you will be dead,' he added in a somewhat chilling manner, as an afterthought.

It was not that Kikuchi minded exactly dying for his Emperor if he had to; after all, like his comrades he had left some hair and fingernail clippings behind in Japan for funerary purposes in case the rest of his body did not return. He was not a Kikuchi for nothing! And yet, once or twice, observing Matsushita and his bosom companion, Lieutenant Nakamura, with whom he had graduated from the Military Academy, the thought had crossed Kikuchi's mind (indeed, it had had to be frogmarched across his mind under heavy guard and swiftly, like a deserter who must not be allowed to contaminate his fellows) that all things in human affairs, even battlefield glory, can be taken a tiny bit too far. Could it be that the High Com-

mand thought so, too? Well, no, that was unlikely. Yet despite
their heroism neither Matsushita nor Nakamura had as yet
risen very far in the Army. They were both still young, of
course, but perhaps something else lay behind their lack of
promotion ... Kikuchi had heard a vague rumour that they
might have been involved in an attempt to revive the November
Affair at the Military Academy with a new revolt of ultra-
patriotic cadets ... or perhaps it was that they had led an
assault on brother officers they suspected of aping European
manners, something of the sort ... Never mind, whatever the
truth of the matter it was an honour, Kikuchi assured himself,
gripping his knees more tightly than ever to take his mind off
his churning stomach (perhaps he should have swallowed a
couple of Jintan pills?), to serve under such fearless and
patriotic officers. Both of them, as it happened, were nearby at
this very moment: Matsushita was only a matter of inches
away in the swaying darkness: Kikuchi could not see him but
he pictured him sitting in his habitual pose, palms of both
hands resting on the tasselled hilt of his sabre, his expression
merciless.

As for Nakamura, he was leading the medium tanks and so,
you might have thought, could not possibly be anywhere near
this lorry full of infantry. Nevertheless, Nakamura was only a
few yards in front. What had happened was that Matsushita,
reckless as ever, had insisted that a platoon of picked infantry,
under his personal leadership, should come next to Nakamura's
leading tank in the assault column now moving down the road
towards the British positions. He had wasted no time in picking
Kikuchi to ride with him in his first lorry sandwiched between
the two leading tanks; more troops of the Ando Detachment
came in a position of somewhat greater security further down
the armoured column. Kikuchi, naturally, was deeply conscious
of the honour that had been done him. All the same, the leading
vehicles in the column would certainly bear the brunt of the
enemy fire. This would be bad enough for the tanks with their
armour; what would it be like for a vulnerable lorry-load of
infantry? Still, one must act heroically and hope for the best.

The tanks and lorries continued to creep forward head to tail,
without lights. It was very quiet, as if all the men in the lorry
were holding their breath; Kikuchi listened to the steady rattling
of the tank tracks on the road's surface but even this sound
seemed barely audible, soaked up instantly by the dark mass of
jungle on each side. How much longer would this go on for?
He was weary and wanted to sleep. He was also hungry. How

they had been driven! It seemed to him that this campaign, though it had lasted only three weeks, had been going on for ever. He sometimes found it hard to believe that he had ever known another kind of life ... on and on they had trudged, seldom eating anything but dry bread and salt, not even pausing to consume the munificent food supplies left by the British as they retreated.

And what terrible endurance the High Command demanded of them! In Kikuchi's mind one ordeal had begun to blur and blend into another and only now and then did some particular occasion stand out clearly in his mind: he remembered advancing through the jungle towards the bridge at Kuala Kangsar with nothing to eat but what fruit they could find (yes, he had remembered not to eat beautifully shaped or coloured fruit), and an occasional stew of snake-meat (and yes, he had dutifully eaten the snake's raw liver according to instructions whenever the opportunity presented itself), prepared from the dismal creatures that squeezed in and out of the undergrowth beneath their feet. He remembered a fierce attack by Scotsmen north of the Perak River; for a while they had been halted there unable to communicate with their headquarters. But then a light aeroplane had appeared over the jungle and had dropped them a communication tube. It was a message from Mr Staff Officer Okada. Matsushita had told Kikuchi what it contained ... 'Esteemed detachment, deep gratitude for several days' heroic fighting.' How pleased Matsushita had been for this praise from Mr Staff Officer Okada. He had been even more pleased when he had read on, for the message had ordered a raid on the southern bank of the Perak River. The bridge must be captured before it was demolished by the retreating British. How Matsushita's eyes had glistened at this desperate proposal!

Matsushita had grown thin as they made their way through the jungle, though none was more adept at killing snakes and swallowing their livers than he, gulping them one after another like oysters and leaving their disembowelled remains to be sucked and gnawed by his men as best they could for cooking-fires must not be lit lest the smoke give away their position. As he grew thinner, Matsushita's eyes grew larger and burned more fiercely than ever. Now he would be part of the glorious capture of the Perak River Bridge! And he had whipped his men forward to reach it and snip those glistening wires before the British engineers had time to press down the plunger. It would be done! For the Emperor!

Matsushita had asked for volunteers for this rash assignment. The men had all volunteered, of course. Even if any of them had not felt like doing so it would never have done to let Lieutenant Matsushita get it into his head that you were a coward ... 'Well then, I must pick the men for this patrol myself,' he had said, his eyes piercing each man in turn. And he had done so, while the troops waited in silence to hear their fate. Presently Kikuchi heard his name spoken.

At about midnight on 22 December while they had been camped some distance from the Perak River Bridge in a jungle of wild rubber, a tremendous boom had reverberated from the south. So astonishing was this noise that for several moments afterwards all the night-sounds of the jungle ceased, a dreadful silence prevailed: even small insects hesitated before eating each other and snakes paused as they squirmed in and out of their slimy homes. Kikuchi and his comrades had gazed at each other in consternation: this noise could only have come from one source. The British had demolished the bridge which they had been hoping to capture intact. White with shock at this lost opportunity Matsushita nevertheless had insisted on examining his maps to see whether the map reference of the bridge tallied with the direction from which the sound had appeared to come. It did. Matsushita uttered a groan and bowed his head to the earth. Later, he took Kikuchi aside and said in a low voice: 'Thoughts of self-condemnation overwhelm my heart, Kikuchi. Our lives will have to compensate for our error.' Kikuchi had nodded soothingly, though it had occurred to him that there seemed to be no particular reason why troops who had merely obeyed orders should have to take a share in the Lieutenant's error.

In front of them now Nakamura's tank had come to rest, bringing the column behind it to a halt. A whispered consultation was taking place: it was thought that they must now be very near the first position defended by the British. Matsushita had slipped off the tail of the lorry like a panther, invisible in the darkness. Kikuchi stood up carefully and managed to get a glimpse back down the road. Behind them stretched a column of some two dozen twenty-ton tanks, the moonlight glinting on their turrets; infantry lorries were interspersed with the more distant tanks. He knew that a detachment of lighter 'whippet' tanks came behind the medium tanks but he could not see them for a bend in the road.

Kikuchi sank back, a little reassured by this impressive sight.

Each of the medium tanks, he knew, carried a four-pounder anti-tank gun and two heavy ·303 machine-guns. But, in addition, a mortar had been fitted to each tank; although it was fixed so that it could only cover one side of the road, the tanks had been arranged so that the mortars alternated, now on one side, now on the other. There would certainly be a heavy enough fire from the tanks. Perhaps he might have a chance, after all. But even if he survived this battle there would still be another battle afterwards and another after that. How many weeks or months would this nightmarish life continue? He no longer had any idea whereabouts on the Malayan peninsula they were, or even what date it might be. The New Year had begun, that was all he knew for certain.

And what a New Year it had been; Matsushita had insisted on leading the unit on a wide detour through dense jungle and swamp to the west of the road to strike behind the position fortified by the British at Kampar. And so, while in Tokyo hundreds of miles away his family and friends had been exchanging greetings and celebrating with dishes of *soba*, Kikuchi and his comrades had been plunging through terrifying swamps, often sinking up to the chest in stinking slime which threatened to swallow them up and covered them with leeches fattening visibly on their tender flesh. Instead of listening to the temple bells on New Year's Eve as they rang out their message: 'All is vanity and unreality in this world!' and having a good time, Kikuchi had had to drag himself after Matsushita, his flesh lacerated by thorny vines, hair standing on end as poisonous snakes reared to right and left. And with nothing to chew but dry, uncooked rice and an occasional piece of snake dropped by Matsushita when he had gulped its liver in accordance with the pamphlet 'Read This Alone and the War Can Be Won'. As a matter of fact, it had been in the course of this particular ordeal that Kikuchi had first begun to wonder whether Matsushita was altogether sane. For, although he had always had a tendency to ramble on about Kikuchi's uncle, the legendary Bugler, he had now taken to making from time to time a slighting remark about him, hinting that in a contest of bravery and devotion to duty he, Matsushita, would by no means have come off second best to Uncle Kikuchi ... and even going so far as to suggest that, although to blow a bugle with one's dying breath was all very fine in its way, if you were dying anyway you might just as well blow a bugle with it as do anything else. And, as if this were not sufficiently dismaying, there was worse. For Matsushita, as he plunged relentlessly on through swamp and jungle, hacking vigorously with his tasselled sabre, eyes burning, would occasionally pause and chant half aloud, half to himself, a weird song in a language which Kikuchi had never heard before. Often Matsushita would press on so swiftly that he would leave his men behind and they would find him waiting impatiently for them when at last they caught up. One day Kikuchi, hastening after his commander who as usual had got far ahead of the rest of the squad, had come upon him unexpectedly in a sort of clearing. Matsushita had thrown off his uniform for some reason and was standing there stark naked except for the bulging leeches which covered him from head to foot. Moreover, he was surrounded by a little circle of poisonous snakes which had reared up around him as if to listen as he sang to them, conducting himself with his sabre. Kikuchi tried to make out the strange words ...

> ... Hanc sententiam dicamus ...
> Floreat Sand ... ha ... haa ... liaaaaah!

As this weird and chilling incantation came to an end, Matsushita took the sabre and with a swift, clean swipe beheaded one snake after another. Then he swiftly gathered up the writhing bodies by the tails, stood there for a moment with a fistful of lashing bodies spraying blood over his thighs as if deep in thought, and finally went to sit against the bole of a tree, prising them open one after another with two stubby fingers to search out the liver and pop it in his mouth. An enormous leech, Kikuchi could not help noticing, had battened on the Lieutenant's private parts. Kikuchi from a screen of fronds gazed in dismay at his leader, wondering what to do. But what was there to do, except report for duty as if nothing had happened?

However, as Kikuchi approached, Matsushita addressed him quite rationally and even, once the rest of the unit had arrived, delivered a short, invigorating lecture on Japanese National Spirit, enlarging on the virtues that this Spirit would bring to the oppressed races of Eastern Asia once the decadent Europeans had been thrust aside by the Imperial Army. While he spoke the members of his unit stood 'at ease' in an exhausted row, eyeing the leech which adhered to the Lieutenant's private parts and wondering whether they should bring it to his attention.

48

The column had again halted. On a whispered order the infantry stumbled out of the lorries and dispersed to the sides of the road. How stiff were Kikuchi's limbs from the hours he had spent sitting on his heels in the back of the lorry! Since that dreadful ordeal in the jungle and the subsequent capture of Kampar fortress he had been obliged to travel fifty miles or more without transport. The Okabe Regiment, which had made the frontal assault on Kampar, had suffered losses and so the Ando Regiment (and Kikuchi) had had to take up the pursuit again. Since the retreating enemy had taken care to demolish the bridges behind them Kikuchi and his comrades had found themselves travelling on bicycles. This had not seemed too unpleasant at first (anything would have seemed better than wading up to your armpits through leech-filled swamps) but in no time Kikuchi was exhausted; whenever they came to a stream or a river it had to be waded and this entailed carrying his bicycle and equipment on his shoulders. Presently too, his tyres had punctured in the heat like those of his comrades: they had been obliged to rattle along on the rims (this sound, like a company of tanks approaching in the distance, sowed alarm among the retreating British). But so rapidly was the 15th Engineer Regiment repairing the bridges behind them that in due course the Ando Regiment had once more been overtaken by the heavy vehicle, artillery and tank units. Now here they all were, ready to attack by moonlight! Kikuchi's bayonet caught a glint of the moon as he waited, his heart pounding, and he thought: 'How beautiful!'

But he hardly had time to consider this thought before the night erupted into a volcano spitting fire and projectiles. The tank cannons flashed and roared, tracer poured in fiery streams into the darkness and Kikuchi found himself charging forward. A moment earlier it had seemed that he could scarcely hobble, so stiff were his limbs ... but now he found himself running like a hare, with mouth open and lips curled back to emit a terrifying scream which, however, he himself could not hear at all, such was the noise of gunfire. Ahead of him galloped

Matsushita, sword in one hand, revolver in the other. A grenade flashed in front of him but the Lieutenant had thrown himself into the ditch beside the road which lay in the shadow of the jungle, or fallen into it, more likely. Kikuchi had reached the comparative safety of this ditch a moment earlier and now crept along it towards Matsushita. Ahead, rolls of wire and a few concrete blocks had been set up across the road. Already, as they watched, the leading tank, still raking the British position with tracer, had reached the first of these pitiful obstacles, had crushed and snapped the barbed wire and brushed aside the concrete blocks and earthworks as easily as if they had been matchboxes. But this was Nakamura's tank. Kikuchi heard Matsushita hiss respectfully between his teeth as he watched it.

Though the British had been driven back to the fringes of the jungle a steady drizzle of rifle fire punctuated by grenades still poured out of the darkness. Only a madman would consider showing himself on the road itself under such a fire, but the next moment Matsushita had leapt out of the ditch and was signalling to his men to follow the tank down the channel it had battered into the British defences The column must drive on deep into the British lines and seize the bridges before they could be demolished. Nakamura must not get all the glory for his tank company!

Kikuchi, hastening after the Lieutenant, stumbled over a dead Hyderabadi, and in doing so grazed the palms of his hands on the road surface. Picking up his rifle again he hastened on over the flattened wire. Nakamura's tank had turned aside to blaze away at a fortified position in the jungle from which, in the blackness, a machine-gun was still dribbling fire, striking sparks off the tank's armoured turret. Meanwhile, more tanks had surged past Nakamura's, motors roaring, down the road into the haven of peace and darkness on the other side of the road-block.

At this moment Kikuchi became aware that the infantry lorry had followed him and was gunning its motor at his back as it negotiated the ruined and abandoned British defences. He stood aside and swung himself aboard as it passed. Other members of his platoon, already inside, grabbed him and hauled him in. A few yards further on another figure loomed out of the darkness and sprang aboard like a panther. A mortar bomb exploding behind them lit up the face of this latecomer ... it was Matsushita, his lips working, eyes burning, speechless with excitement. Kikuchi sniffed carefully. Even if he had not seen the Lieutenant's face he could have told who it was by the strange odour, unlike anything he had ever smelled before, which came from him. He sniffed again. If electricity had a smell, that was what Matsushita would have smelled like at that moment.

Now the lorry had reached the dark haven which lay between the Hyderabads and the next British position. More tanks were following them, dark shapes on the moonlit road, and soon the sound of gunfire was left far behind. They drove on down the road as rapidly as they dared without lights in the wake of the two tanks which had taken over the lead. Nakamura's tank was now cruising immediately behind them.

On and on they went into the darkness. Kikuchi was in a trance, his mind whirling. He became aware presently that his mouth was open and that he was panting like a dog, his tongue hanging over his lower lip. It must be the heat, he thought. He closed his mouth and tried not to pant, afraid that Matsushita might regard it as a sign of fear. Now the word was passed back that the leading tank was approaching Milestone 61. Air reconnaissance had revealed further road-blocks at this point. The time was 4.30 a.m. It was still pitch dark. Kikuchi experienced a craving to see daylight once more.

Suddenly there was a flash and a violent explosion just ahead of them. The leading tank had struck a mine buried in the road: instantly the quiet night erupted into fire and uproar. Once more Kikuchi found himself tumbling out on to the road with his companions, screaming at the top of his lungs. Streams of tracer poured over his head from Nakamura's tank behind the lorry, so close that it seemed to scorch his cheek with its fiery breath.

In the darkness something hit him a sharp blow on the side of the head: perhaps the tail-gate of the lorry or the butt of someone's rifle. The blow dazed him; he stood still in a pool of darkness. It was like being in a cage of bright dotted lines criss-crossing each other ... it was like a firework display: amid the rushing streams of fire from the tracer there bloomed and died magnificent white and orange chrysanthemums. The white lights which flickered and dribbled from pillboxes set back from the road might have been merely the sparklers which children hold in their hands. The air was alive, too, with the hum and whir of insect wings just as when cherry blossom covers the branches with its lovely foam in the spring and all the hives are busy. 'How beautiful! he thought for the second time. And he continued to stand there while enemy bullets fell so thickly around him that it was just like a sudden hailstorm rattling on the slopes of Mount Fuji. 'Look at this!' he marvelled, contemplating the way the bullets furrowed the soft tar of the road-surface like thick worms in the moonlight.

Suddenly his arm was roughly taken and he was thrown down again into the ditch at the side of the road. The shock brought him partly to his senses and he thought that perhaps an Englishman was at this moment fumbling with his shirt before slipping a knife between his ribs. But the voice which spoke to him spoke Japanese and belonged to Corporal Hayashi. Another tank had been immobilized near where they crouched, perhaps even that of Major Toda himself : its track, struck by a shot from an anti-tank rifle, had unrolled and lay flat on the road; nevertheless, its guns continued firing into the jungle. A few moments later the leading tank, attempting once again to batter a channel through the defences, touched off another mine and was wrecked. Small, dark shapes rose and fell against a patch of moonlit sky. Grenades! Corporal Hayashi paternally gripped Kikuchi's head and thrust it down into the ditch; Kikuchi felt the ground shake all around him. But the Corporal's grip on his neck had loosened and when Kikuchi raised his head again, the hand fell away. Hayashi had been struck on the temple by a fragment of shrapnel but his spectacles, untouched, continued to glint in a friendly way at Kikuchi.

Meanwhile, other tanks had come up and grouped themselves so close to each other that it seemed as if a battleship, guns blazing, had moored here in the middle of the jungle, pouring a steady, concentrated fire at each side of the road. Time passed. Another tank was knocked out by an anti-tank gun firing from a fortified position. More time passed. Still tracer zipped into the jungle, still the cannon and mortar boomed. The British fire, though, had diminished. The anti-tank guns were silent. Now the tanks had left their solid formation and were nudging into the jungle. Kikuchi could make out other figures huddled not far away in the cover of the ditch; among them Matsushita crouched, giving orders to the men with him. Soon they would make a bayonet charge to put an end to the stubborn resistance of the Punjabis.

Only a few yards from where Kikuchi waited for the fateful moment when he would have to leap up from the shelter of the ditch, Charlie Tyrrell was kneeling behind a buttress of earth in a litter of spent cartridges trying to estimate from the flashes of their guns whether the tanks were making any progress in their efforts to force a way through the defences. If the tanks could be held until daylight there might be some prospect of a counter-attack, either by the Argylls or by the Punjabis of the 28th Brigade who were resting some miles further back. On the other hand, his own battalion had already suffered such heavy losses from the tank barrage that he doubted whether they would be able to hold off a determined assault by the Japanese infantry. Charlie himself had so far escaped unscathed except for a flesh wound in the calf which had soaked one sock with blood causing it to squelch disagreeably when he walked; but this wound, combined with the shattering noise of the guns and his own fundamental weariness, cast him into a dream-like frame of mind in which he found it hard to think constructively. But even if his state of mind had been more normal he would have found it no easier; it was almost impossible in the darkness, with communications within the battalion difficult and those between the battalion and the Brigade H.Q. now severed, to form a clear idea of what was happening.

The Brigadier, meanwhile, was anxiously prowling about his headquarters in the rubber plantation. All the telephone wires had been cut by this time but he knew that, as he had expected, the Japanese had broken through the Hyderabads and had been halted, at least for a while, by the Punjabis. He now summoned a despatch rider and sent him up the road to the Punjabis, ordering them to hold on to their positions by the road even if the Japanese tanks broke through. At the same time he ordered the Argylls to set up road-blocks.

It was the Argylls' habit to take breakfast early in order to fight on a full stomach. So, having breakfasted before dawn they set to work improvising road-blocks in the darkness, one where the trunk road first entered the rubber, the other a hundred yards in front of the bridge at Trolak (that is, the first of the two bridges the Japanese would reach): this road-block was covered by two armoured cars with anti-tank rifles; at the same time volunteers for a Molotov Cocktail party were called for and marshalled in readiness.

Though the sky was at last beginning to grow pale it was still very dark on the road. Sinclair, in his anxiety to find out how A and D Companies were faring in the rubber on the other side of the trunk road, borrowed a motor-cycle and set off on it rather unsteadily down the estate road from Brigade Headquarters. As he came careering out of the rubber trees, going rather faster than he intended and meaning to cross the trunk road and follow the estate road which continued among the trees on the far side, a vast shape suddenly loomed out of the darkness. A Japanese tank! Swerving violently he crashed into it, almost head on ... but luckily for Sinclair he was thrown clear. As the tank advanced, one of its tracks ran over the motor-cycle, flattened, it, chewed it up and dropped it on the roadway behind. Sinclair dusted himself off shakily as the tank disappeared on down the road into the darkness. 'Suh ... suh ... suh ... suh ... wine!' he shouted after it. 'You weren't carrying any bloody luh ... luh ... luh ... headlights!' But all he could see, as he stood cursing beside his flattened motorcycle, was the rapidly diminishing flicker of the tank's exhaust. And then he thought: 'But my God! A Jap tank isn't supposed to be *here* at all!' And although he knew that by now it was almost certainly too late to warn anybody he began to run as fast as he could back the way he had come.

But if the tank had already passed through the long neck and out into the bottle itself, this meant that the Japanese had not only broken through the Punjabis position but that the first of the Argylls' obstacles where the trunk road left the jungle and entered the rubber had also failed to stop it. What had happened was that the Japanese tanks, which had been successfully stopped by the Punjabis on the trunk road, had found a way round them: for it so happened that the line which the trunk road now followed was not the original one. The original road had snaked through the defile with a number of sharp bends. When the road, in the process of being improved, had been straightened out, the disused loops of the original road had been left and no anti-tank defences had been provided for them. Thus it was that Nakamura's tank had discovered one of the disused loops and used it to circle around the British position, emerging in the rear. The Punjabis' resistance now at last collapsed. Charlie collected those men of his own contingent who were still able to walk and retreated with them into the jungle, hoping that they might be able to make their way back to the Slim River Bridge and the British lines. It was just beginning to grow light as Charlie and his men were swallowed up by the great dark-green wall of jungle. Subsequently nothing more would be seen or heard of them.

Now the tanks of Major Toda and Lieutenant Nakamura with

two more medium tanks behind them (the very last of which had just flattened a motor-cycle) and a single lorry-load of infantry which included a dismayed Kikuchi and the reckless Matsushita, had brushed aside one pitiful road-block where the road left the jungle and surged on down the road. This was already a victory for they had broken through the defile and could now operate in the greater freedom of the rubber estate if it suited them. But Nakamura had his eye on an even greater feat of arms ... to capture the two bridges before they could be blown up!

In no time the leading tanks had reached the second road-block which the Argylls had set up a hundred yards in front of the bridge at Trolak. This second obstacle, prepared in haste, was scarcely more impressive than the first, but it was covered by the two Argyll armoured cars, together with the Molotov Cocktail party lurking in the ditch with brimming jam jars and petrol-soaked rags. It was now just light enough to make out the forms of the tanks as they appeared out of the darkness and came to a halt, checked by the concrete blocks and chains across the road.

Once they were motionless the officer in command of the armoured cars gave the signal and, one from each side of the road, they opened up with their anti-tank rifles. But their shots merely glanced off the tanks' armour and ricocheted howling into the rubber. Now the cocktail party galloped up, flung their projectiles and hared away again for cover. Flames leaped up here and there and it seemed for a moment that one of the tanks had been set ablaze: but only the petrol which drenched its armour was on fire and presently it died out and the early morning gloom returned. In the meantime the tanks had turned their squat heads, as if in surprise, to look at the pitiful armoured cars which were opposing them. Their guns spoke. Instantly one armoured car was a smoking wreck, the other disabled. Tracer stitched up and down the Argyll's hastily prepared defences. The tanks' main armament and machine-guns continued to fire: to the boom of the guns and grenades and the chatter of small arms was added the frightful cracking of rubber trees in the estate behind.

Kikuchi and his comrades lay as flat as they could on the floor of the lorry as bullets ripped through the canvas awning above them. Even Matsushita was crouching down. But at this moment some instinct told him that the time had come and suddenly, grabbing a light machine-gun from the man beside him, he sprang out into the road. He was just in time to see the turret of the leading tank some yards ahead open up and Nakamura's head appear. While Major Toda's tank continued to blaze away to give him cover the heroic Nakamura carrying his sabre clambered over the road-block. At the other end of the bridge it was now possible to make out the explosive charge which had been set against one of the pillars and even the wires which led back from it. With bullets kicking up the dust all around him Nakamura raced forward sabre in hand and Matsushita, dashing after him, was just in time to see a British soldier leap up to hurl a grenade: Matsushita cut him down with a burst of machine-gun fire. With a mighty slash of his sabre Nakamura severed the wires leading to the demolition charge, then turned and sprinted back towards his tank. It seemed impossible that he should get back alive through that storm of bullets but in a moment he had vaulted on to the nose of the tank and was slithering down like a snake into the safety of its hole. The turret-cover shut after him with a clang.

How long would it be before the tanks had burst through the roadblock in front of the bridge? With its motor roaring Nakamura's tank began to batter this light obstruction aside. In desperation the officer commanding the armoured cars, ignoring the fire from the tanks a mere hundred yards down the road, took the brake off the disabled armoured car and pushed it down the slight incline on to the bridge where he tried unsuccessfully to overturn it. But even this gallant effort could not hope to stop the tanks. With a grinding of metal and concrete Nakamura's tank had at last burst through on to the bridge, followed by that of Major Toda, guns still blazing. It took only a few moments to force aside the wrecked armoured car on the bridge. Once more the open road lay ahead.

On they raced in the direction of Kampong Slim, now in broad daylight. About a mile north of the village Nakamura, riding with head and shoulders out of his turret and surveying the road ahead like an eagle, saw movement. His eyes glittered. In an instant the turret-cover clanged shut again and the tank accelerated into a battalion of Punjabis of the 28th Brigade which had been hurriedly ordered forward by the Brigadier and were marching unsuspectingly up the road. The first company melted away under Nakamura's machine-gun fire; of the second company only a score of men escaped uninjured, while the two rear companies managed to dive into the rubber on each side of the road. At Kampong Slim the trunk road took a sharp turn to the left and ran eastwards through the Cluny Estate. Here Nakamura found further prey, a battalion of Gurkha Rifles moving along the road in column of route without the least suspicion that a Japanese tank might be in the vicinity: they suffered the same fate as the Punjabis, caught in close order by Nakamura's machine-guns and scythed down.

Next comes the turn of two batteries of the 137th Field Regiment dozing peacefully at the roadside in the Cluny Estate: one moment all is quiet and in good order, the next their camp is reduced to a smoking shambles and the tanks are moving on again. Major Toda would like to take the lead for already the greatest prize perhaps of the whole campaign is in reach: the Slim River Bridge itself! And so rapidly has the Toda tank company burst through the entire depth of the British defences that they find this vital bridge is defended by nothing more daunting than one troop of a Light Anti-Aircraft Battery equipped with Bofors guns, together with a party of sappers at work preparing the demolition of the bridge.

Just as one may sometimes see flights of terrified birds fleeing in front of a hurricane, now the Toda tank company is driving a random selection of vehicles in front of it. Men in lorries, in cars and on motor-cycles (even a man on horseback is to be seen galloping away though what he is doing there nobody knows); men pedal away furiously on bicycles and swerve up estate roads out of the path of the rumbling tanks. A party of signallers in a lorry rattles on to the bridge and shouts at the sappers who are putting the finishing touches to the charges laid against the far pillars and at the others who are unreeling the wire back to a safe distance to connect with the plunger: 'Jap tanks are coming! Jap tanks are coming!' Word is passed to the officer with the anti-aircraft guns. Only two of the Bofors will bear on the road. He prepares to fire over open sights and waits until he sees the first of the sinister vehicles surge into view, followed by another and another and another. At a hundred yards he opens fire on the leading tank but the light shells merely bounce off the tank's armour and depart screaming into the rubber. The tanks in turn open fire on the unprotected guns. In a few moments they are out of action; men lie dead and wounded around them in a cloud of smoke and dust.

Nakamura, cunningly, has refused to acknowledge Major Toda's attempts to take the lead and so the tracks of his tank are the first to thunder on to the long bridge. His eyes are on the explosive charge which is now so near; his eyes are on the sappers scattering into the rubber, two of them running with a reel unwinding between them. The hollow roar of the tracks on the bridge, the bridge itself seems to him to go on for ever. Nakamura, in the course of his earlier endeavour, has been wounded in the right hand and can no longer hold his sabre. Besides, rifle bullets are again zinging on the armour. He takes a machine-gun and directs it at the wire running along and away from the bridge until, yes, the bullets have severed it. The Slim River Bridge has been captured intact!

Major Toda orders one tank to remain guarding the bridge lest the British should return and try to demolish it. Then, Nakamura still in the lead, the other tanks move on a mile down the road in the direction of Tanjong Malim. It is now half past nine and the day is beginning to grow hot. Abruptly, the tanks find themselves in yet another formation of unsuspecting British troops moving up to the front line (which *they* still think is nineteen miles away). Nakamura at last has indulgently given up the lead to Lieutenant Ogawa. The British, although taken by surprise, will this time prove to be not such an easy prey, for this is the fine 155th Field Regiment. One detachment, working feverishly under a fusillade from the tanks, manages to unlimber its 4.5-inch howitzer; this gun opens fire from a mere thirty yards' range at the leading tank, smashing it. The advance of the tanks is halted at last.

A little later, once the British had retired, Kikuchi inspected the wreckage of this tank. He found Lieutenant Ogawa, although dead, still sitting upright and holding his sabre. So ended the engagement at the Slim River.

49

In spite of the difficulties he had encountered with certain of the inmates of the dying-house which he had visited with Vera, Matthew could now only think of that institution with pleasure, for it had created a definite bond between them. There is something about a large number of dying people, provided you aren't one of them, that can make you feel extraordinarily full of vitality. Matthew and Vera, once they had emerged from that shadowy world, had found themselves positively seething with high spirits. At the door of the dying-house, as soon as each saw the unwrinkled face of the other, they had fumbled for each other's hands and gripped them tightly. Unfortunately, the complaints of the moribund smallholders had taken up so much time that they had been obliged to part again almost immediately, but this time not without making arrangements to meet again. Thus it happened that, in due course, they found themselves standing at the curved entrance to The Great World.

Vera saw Matthew's seductively curved spine while she was still some distance away, and her heart went pit-a-pat (no young men with fists of steel for her!) He was wandering up and down muttering to himself and occasionally lifting his knuckles to nudge his spectacles up on his nose. Once, evidently having forgotten what he was doing there, he began to stride away purposefully, but presently, remembering, came back. By this time, however, Vera had decided that it was best to step forward and announce herself. She took his arm and they strolled into The Great World. A mysterious tropical twilight prevailed in which bats skidded here and there, squeaking and clicking. Matthew was surprised to find The Great World still open despite the war which, after all, was now not very far away. There had been changes, however. For one thing, there were no longer as many lights burning; now there was merely a faint glow here and there against which you saw milling shadows silhouetted in the dusk. But the sensation of tropical mystery, the unfamiliar aromas and sensations, had redoubled in intensity and the crowds at this hour seemed scarcely less abundant. That atmosphere of cigar smoke and sandalwood, incense and perfume, that stirring compound of food and dust and citrus blossom, of sensuality and spices filled Matthew with such excitement that his spirit began flapping violently inside him like a freshly caught fish in a basket.

Matthew was thirsty. Spotting a group of shadowy figures drinking something at a stall he steered Vera towards it. They were drinking from straws stuck in coconuts which had been topped like boiled eggs. How delicious! But Vera diverted him. Coconut milk was not good for men, she explained.

'How d'you mean?'

Well, the Malays said it had a weakening effect of them, she murmured evasively, and directed him instead to another stall, insisting that he should partake of a strange, meaty, spicy soup of which she would only tell him the Chinese name (it was monkey soup, a powerful aphrodisiac). He tasted it and found it, well, rather strange. What did she say was in it? But again she would only tell him the Chinese name. The elderly, wizened Chinese who brewed it, who looked as if he himself was only on temporary leave from the dying-house, cackled with amusement at this burly warrior sharpening his jade arrows before loosing them at the Coral Palace. He stroked his wispy beard and peered into his vat of bubbling soup, remembering not without melancholy how in days gone by he had enjoyed an occasional bit of 'fang-shih' himself.

Yes, it was not at all bad, Matthew decided when he had tasted it again. In no time he had finished the bowl and asked for a second helping. Delicious! He would have ordered a third helping but Vera thought he had probably had enough and so they strolled on through the smoky, crowded darkness. Here and there tapers glimmered, illuminating a circle of oriental faces and Matthew even noticed a few soldiers. One of the soldiers, however, had his arm in a sling; another had a thick bandage round his head; others were drunken but silent now, and morose. With dull eyes they watched the swirling cosmopolitan bustle around them, as if from the other side of a plate-glass window. No doubt these poor fellows had been invalided back from the fighting in the north. One could hardly expect them to look cheerful.

Vera was worried about the progress of the war. She had already told Matthew that she had first come to Singapore in order to escape the Japanese in Shanghai. Now, every day, despite what it said in the newspapers, the Japanese seemed to be coming nearer and nearer. Where would she go if they reached Singapore? she asked Matthew, looking innocent and defenceless, but perhaps wondering at the same time whether all the monkey soup he had consumed might not have put him in a protective frame of mind.

'Oh, don't worry, I'll look after you,' said Matthew protectively, folding her comfortingly in his arms (how light and lithe her body felt against his own!). 'Besides, I don't think we need to worry about them getting this far.' He nudged his spectacles up on his nose and added more cautiously: 'At least, I'll do my best. Let's talk about something more cheerful.' Vera agreed, aware that contact with this attractive man had caused her own *yin* essences to begin to flow in spite of her worries. They strolled on. Time passed in a dream. Presently, they found that The Great World was closing: these days, because of the war and the black-out, it was obliged to close early.

They spilled out of the gates in the departing crowd and sauntered through the warm darkness along a street of dilapidated shop-houses. A vast yellow moon was just rising over the tiled rooftops. A man with an ARP armband and a satchel over his shoulder flashed a torch in their faces and muttered something in Cantonese, but he did not try to stop them and they walked on. Matthew wanted her to return to the Mayfair with him but she refused with signs of indignation. She would not go where she was not wanted!

'But you *are* wanted! What are you talking about?'

'Mr Blackett and Miss Blackett have told me ...'

'But it's nothing to do with them. The place belongs to me.'

'It doesn't matter. They behave badly. I am not going to fall over backwards to please them!'

'Oh, really!'

But Vera had upset herself by remembering this injury done her by the Blacketts. For a few moments she became tearful, even blaming Matthew for having allowed her to be slighted, though she was by no means sure how he could have prevented it. 'You should tell them to behave properly towards me,' she said sulkily. 'I am not going to Mayfair again.' As it happened, it would have suited her quite well to go to the Mayfair since she felt too ashamed of her own tenement cubicle to take Matthew back there; having taken up such a strong position, however, she felt she could not now abandon it without loss of face. There was a drinking establishment round the corner: perhaps one of the booths there would be free.

They entered an open doorway where a number of men and women, all Chinese, sat at tables drinking and playing mah-jong, some on the pavement, some inside where there was a little light. They passed between the tables and entered an even dimmer corridor where a strong smell of garlic hung on the stagnant air. The proprietor hurried along beside them, chattering, but Vera paid no attention to him. The corridor was lined with curtained booths and as she went along she opened and closed one curtain after another to look inside; in each of them a man and a woman sat close together, drinking; despite a rich atmosphere of sensuality, however, nothing untoward appeared to be happening. Vera grimaced at Matthew. There were no unoccupied booths and she felt that he could have been a bit more helpful in suggesting somewhere for them to go. But as usual Matthew's mind had wandered from the immediate problem, that of finding a place for them to be alone. His own voice had

given him a shock a little earlier when he had heard it saying:
'The place belongs to me.' For it seemed to him that even this
simple sentence cast its own moral shadow. The problem was
this: could you own something like the Mayfair and still consider yourself a just man? But before he could properly get to
grips with this question he glimpsed something in the last booth,
where Vera had without ceremony opened and closed the curtain, which suggested a quite different line of enquiry. For in
the last booth there were two startled Chinese men giving each
other a rather peculiar handshake. What were they doing? he
asked Vera.

'I don't know,' she shrugged. 'Perhaps secret society?'

'D'you think that was the Singapore Grip?'

But Vera shook her head, smiling. She found his question so
entertaining that her impatience with Matthew melted away.

All the booths were full. There was nothing for it, therefore,
but to take Matthew back to where she lived. They set out once
more into the warm darkness of the city and as they went along
Vera tried to prepare him for the shock of seeing the tenement
where she lived which was not far from the river at New Bridge
Road. Presently, they were standing in front of it. She sighed
at the smell of drains and the peeling paint and the huddled
shapes you had to step over as you climbed the stairs, by no
means sure that she had not made a mistake in bringing Matthew here. How sweet-smelling the air of Tanglin was by comparison! Thank heaven that at least she did not have to share
her cubicle with several other people like her neighbours!

Still wondering about the Singapore Grip Matthew followed
her along what he supposed must be a corridor, but a corridor
in which people evidently made their homes; he found himself
stepping over an ancient man with a face like a road map,
asleep on the stairs over a pipe with a long metal stem. There
was no light to speak of, just one naked bulb at the head of the
stairs and a slender shaft of moonlight from a window in the
distance ... but there was enough to see the darker lumps of
darkness that lay in neat rows along the walls on each side. He
knew instantly, without knowing *how* he knew, which of these
bundles were property and which were people. There was a
smell in the air, too, besides the smell of drains that Vera was
worried about ... he recognized it, a vaguely smoky smell, as
of smouldering rubbish or rags, the smell of poverty.

These walls on each side, however, proved not to be walls at
all, but merely flimsy wooden partitions. Originally this floor

had comprised perhaps three or four large rooms, but in order to maximize the rent from it the landlord had subdivided it into a vast number of cubicles not much bigger than cupboards, separated from the corridor by hanging clothes or bead curtains. Matthew peered into some of these dark receptacles as he passed by, but one had to go carefully for fear of treading on the hand or face of an exhausted coolie who had slumped out into your path: in one of them a little old lady with her hair in a bun was on her knees, muttering prayers in front of a scroll of red ideographs with red candles and joss-sticks smouldering beside her; in another a family was grouped around a blue flame eating rice. Someone was coughing wearily nearby, a long, wretched, tubercular cough, the very sound of resignation or despair. So this was what life was like here!

Vera's cubicle, by comparison with the others, was comfortable: it was at the end of the corridor not far from where the only tap dripped into a bucket and it shared half a window with the next cubicle. It was very small (Matthew could have crossed it in one stride) but neat and had a little furniture: the iron bed which for Vera symbolized her Russian ancestry, a table made from the door of a wardrobe resting on a tea-chest, on which, in turn, rested a mirror and a few little bottles of cosmetics. There was an oil-lamp and a Primus stove; biscuit-coloured tatami covered the floor. The clothes passed on to her by Joan hung beside the window (her Chinese clothing had been packed away in mothballs under the bed) with a pair of wooden clogs and a pair of leather shoes neatly arranged beneath them. On the floor by the Primus stove were two bowls and a saucepan; a jam jar contained chopsticks and a porcelain spoon.

While Vera lit the oil-lamp Matthew stood uncertainly beside her with his hands in his pockets, touched by the simplicity of her home. When there was enough light to see each other by they both felt embarrassed. To conceal her shyness Vera began to rummage unnecessarily in her handbag. Matthew gazed at the pictures torn from magazines which were pinned to the partition by the bed: there was a picture of someone whom he supposed must be the last Tsar of Russia, looking very hairy, and another of King George VI and another of Myrna Loy. He sat down on the bed beside which there was a pile of movie magazines and some books. Three or four of the books were in Chinese (among them, though he did not know it, a treatise on sexual techniques, for Vera took such matters seriously); there was a copy of *Self-Help* indented with the stamp of the American Missionary Society, Harbin, and a tattered collection of other books in English, including Waley's 170 *Chinese Poems*, once the property of the United Services Club and Percy F. Westerman's *To the Fore with the Tanks*, much scribbled on in red pencil by a child.

Vera sat down on the bed beside him. She no longer experienced the slippery sensation she had felt before and which she usually felt when aroused. Concerned with the impression that her room might be making on her visitor the flow of her *yin* essences had declined to a trickle. She sensed, too, that Matthew's *yang* force had also been diverted into another channel and now lacked the fierce concentration of the unbridled *yang* spirit.

Indeed, Matthew, sitting quietly in this dimly lit cubicle, not much bigger, he supposed, than the closet where a man like Walter Blackett would hang his suits, was again brooding on the question of property and wondering whether it was possible to be wealthy and yet to live a just life. For, in a competitive society, how could you be wealthy in a vacuum? Were you not wealthy *against* other people poorer than you? No matter how justly you tried to behave, and did behave, no matter how honest and charitable and sympathetic to suffering, did not this possession of wealth, which allowed you to go to the opera and drink fine wines now and then, which made your experience of life less harsh in almost every way, cast a subtle blight over all your aspirations? Could someone live justly in Tanglin while at the same time people lived in this wretched tenement riddled with malnutrition and tuberculosis (he could still hear that weary, relentless coughing through the partitions)? This question was quite apart from the fact that the man coughing had been sucked into Malaya by the great implosion of British capital invested in cheap tropical land and labour, for it could certainly be strongly argued that he was a beneficiary rather than the victim of British enterprise, including that of Blackett and Webb among others. He put a comforting arm round Vera's shoulders, thinking that she must not stay here to catch tuberculosis from her neighbours and at the same time wondering how one should behave in order to live justly.

Vera, meanwhile, with Matthew's arm around her had begun to feel slippery again, so that presently, if you had tried to grasp her, she would have sprung out of your fingers like a bar of soap in the bathtub. She wriggled closer and put an arm around his waist. This, in turn, had a certain effect on Matthew for the monkey soup had not ceased to flow richly in his veins. The *yang* spirit, which had been dozing like a tiger in its cave, was abruptly awoken by that lithe yet slippery arm which had encircled his waist: now it came snarling out of its lair, determined to be satiated, come what might.

Without receiving conscious instructions from their owner, Matthew's hands began to wander over Vera's clothes and in due course found some buttons. But the buttons proved to be ornamental and so, after a considerable interval of pulling and tugging which was plainly getting his hands nowhere, Vera decided that they would have to be discreetly helped in the right direction, though this tended to undermine the impression of surprised innocence she had been hoping to convey. Even this did not really improve matters, however, because Matthew's fingers were made clumsy by theoretical instructions which began belatedly to arrive from his brain. Finally, Vera had to become thoroughly practical and take off all her clothes herself: they did not amount to much, anyway, and if crumpled up would easily have fitted into one of Matthew's pockets. Matthew also took the opportunity to remove his own clothes and, as he did so, a dense cloud of white dust rose from his loins and hung glimmering in the lamplight. Vera looked surprised at so much dust, wondering whether his private parts might not be covered in cobwebs too. But Matthew hurriedly explained that it was just talcum from his evening bath. Once this had been settled the twin rivers of *yin* and *yang* which, though flowing in the same direction, one in shadow, the other in sunlight, had been separated by a range of mountains, now begun to turn gently towards each other as the mountains became hills and the hills sloped down to the wide valley.

And yet before the rivers joined, one river flowing into the other, the other flowing into the one, there was still some way to go. Vera, who had carefully educated herself in the arts of love, did not believe that this sacred art, whose purpose was to unite her not only with her lover but with the earth and the firmament, too, should take place in the Western manner which to her resembled nothing so much as a pair of drunken rickshaw coolies colliding briefly at some foggy cross-roads at the dead of night. But in order to do things properly it was clear that she would have to give Matthew a hasty but basic education in what was expected of him. For one thing, a common terminology had to be established; Matthew's grasp of such matters had proved even more elementary than she had feared. Indeed, he seemed thoroughly bewildered as he stood there naked and blinking, for he had taken off his spectacles and put them down on the pile of books by the bed. So Vera set to work giving names to various parts, first pointing them out where applicable on Matthew, then on her own pretty person.

'This is called "*kuei-tou*" or "*yü-ching*" or, how d'you say, hmm, "jade flower-stem" ... or sometimes "*nan-ching*" or even "*yang-feng*", OK?' But Matthew could only gaze at her in astonishment and she had to repeat what she had said.

'Now d'you think you've got it?' she enquired, and could not help adopting the rather condescending tone which had once been adopted by the missionary who had taught her English years ago.

'You mean, all those words mean that?' asked Matthew, indicating the part in question.

'Well, not literally, of course. One, you see, means "head of turtle", another "jade stalk" and so on ... but they all add up to that, d'you see now?' Vera was becoming a little impatient.

'I'm not sure ...'

'Look, I just tell you names for things, OK? We talk about it later.'

Matthew agreed, still looking baffled.

'Here is called "*yin-nang*" or "secret pouch" and here on me is called ...' but Matthew had not been properly paying attention and all this had to be repeated, too. He was shown the '*yü-men*' or the '*ch'iung-men*' as it was sometimes known and that naturally led them on to the '*yü-tai*' and, from the particular to the general, to '*fang-shih*' or '*ou-yu*'. Vera held forth on all this with rapidity, certainly, but not without touching on the Five Natural Moods or Qualities which he might expect to find in himself, nor the Five Revealing Signs which should be manifested by his partner: the flushing pink of throat and cheeks, perspiration on nose like dew on grass in the morning, depth and rapidity of breathing, increase of slipperiness and so forth. And Matthew found himself obliged also to acquire a working knowledge of the Hundred Anxious Feelings (though there was no time to go through them one by one), the Five Male Overstrainings, and the medicinal liquor that he might expect to lap up from his lover's body at the Three Levels, for example, that sweet little cordial called Liquid Snow exuding from between the breasts at the Middle Level (good for gall-stones).

Vera could now see that the mighty *yang* spirit which, a little earlier, had seized Matthew and held him up by the ears like a rabbit, was no longer gripping him so firmly. She decided to content herself with once more running over the names of the most important parts so there would be no misunderstanding. And it was lucky she did so because it turned out that there was a part she had forgotten to mention the first time, namely, the '*chieh-shan-chu*' or 'pearl on jade threshold'. Drawing up her knees to her chin she pointed it out with a magenta fingernail.

Matthew peered at her, blinking. He could not for the life of him think why all this elaborate 'naming of parts' should be necessary. However, he bent his head obediently to look for the '*chieh-shan-chu*'. After some moments of inspecting her closely he brought the oil-lamp a little closer and put his spectacles on again.

'Oh yes, I think I see what you mean,' he murmured politely.

'Good,' said Vera. 'Now we can begin.'

Matthew brightened and after a moment's hesitation took off his spectacles again. But what Vera meant was that she could now begin to explain what he would need to know in order to bring to a successful conclusion their first and relatively simple manoeuvre, known as 'Bamboo Swaying in Spring Wind'. After that they might have a go at 'Butterfly Hovering over Snow White Peony' and then later, if all went well, she might wake up a girlfriend who slept in a neighbouring cubicle and invite her to join them for 'Goldfish Mouthing in Crystal Tank' if they were not too tired by then. But for the moment Matthew still had a few things to learn.

'What is it you don't understand, Matthew?' she enquired with the monolithic patience she had so admired in her missionary teacher. Matthew sighed. It was clear that some more time would elapse before the rivers of *yin* and *yang* reached their confluence at last. All this time the sound of weary coughing had not ceased for a moment.

50

No doubt there were many unexpected developments in Singapore in the first two weeks of January but few can have been as unexpected as that which affected the Blacketts and the Langfields. How could it have come about that these two families which had hitherto held each other in such abhorrence and contempt should, after so many years, establish amicable social relations? Any close observer (Dr Brownley, for instance, who had made what amounted to a hobby of the mutual detestation of one family for the other) would have found it most unlikely that the Blacketts would ever issue an invitation and quite improbable that the Langfields would accept it. Nevertheless, it did come about. It came about under the pressure of circumstances, as the head of each family became concerned for the welfare of his women-folk.

Walter and Solomon Langfield, bumping into each other by chance at the Long Bar of the Singapore Club, as they had done, indeed, week in, week out, for the better part of thirty years, happened at last to recognize each other. Recognition led to a wary offer of a *stengah*, made in a manner so casual that it was almost not an offer at all, and an equally wary acceptance. In a little while they were patting each other on the back and bullying each other pleasantly for the privilege of signing the chit. And, although each time one of them cordially scribbled his signature on the pad which the barman handed to him he might secretly have been thinking: 'I knew as much ... The old blighter is "pencil shy" (the quintessence of meanness in the clubs of Singapore), outwardly at least no ripple of discord was allowed to corrugate this new-found friendship. Soon Walter was confiding to old Langfield his anxiety for his wife and daughters. This, it turned out, exactly mirrored a similar concern, 'since the RAF did not seem to be putting up much of a show', that Solomon felt for Mrs Langfield and little Melanie beneath the bombs. The women should be sent to a safer place, it was agreed, perhaps to Australia where both firms had branch offices. But neither Mrs Langfield nor Mrs Blackett would be very good at fending for herself. Why should they not travel together? Together they would manage much better. Perhaps by pulling some strings it might be possible for Monty or young Nigel Langfield to accompany them And so in no time it had been agreed: it only remained to persuade the women that this was the best course.

'By the way, Blackett,' old Solomon Langfield was unable to resist saying with ill-concealed malice as they prepared to go their separate ways, 'it's bad luck about your jubilee. I suppose you'll have to call it off under the present circumstances.'

'Not at all,' replied Walter coldly. 'We've been asked to go ahead with it for the sake of civilian morale. I hope you don't mean to call yours off?'

'We aren't due to have ours for another couple of years,' Solomon Langfield, out-manoeuvred and cursing inwardly, was forced to admit.

'Oh? I didn't realize that we had been established longer than you and Bowser,' said Walter condescendingly.

'By that time, at any rate,' replied Solomon, trying to recover the ground he had lost, 'we should be at peace again and able to do things properly.'

'By *that* time,' retorted Walter, delivering the *coup de grâce*, 'another war will probably have broken out or heaven knows what will have happened.'

When Walter mentioned evacuation to Australia in the company of the Langfield women to his own family, however, his proposal was received with indignation and dismay. To travel with Langfields was bad enough, but to be expected to live cheek by jowl with them in Australia was more than flesh and blood could endure. Joan flatly refused to consider leaving with anybody, let alone a Langfield. There was a war on and plenty for an able-bodied young woman to do in Singapore! As for Kate, she was alarmed at the prospect of having as a constant companion Melanie, whom she considered capable of any outrage or excess. For there were times, particularly when there was some authority to be flouted, when Melanie's behaviour verged on the insane, so it seemed to Kate. Now, while she listened to her parents arguing, she remembered an occasion at school when the girls in her dormitory had planned a midnight feast. It had been agreed that each of them would contribute something to eat or drink, a couple of biscuits saved from teatime, say, or a bottle of lemonade crystals. She remembered how they had all crouched, shivering and breathless with excitement, on the waxed floor between two beds, each producing what she had managed to collect ... until last of all, Melanie, with an air of triumph had slapped something down on the floor with a dull thud. An enormous dead chicken! She had somehow broken into the caretaker's chicken coop, strangled a chicken, plucked it and here it was! Well, it seemed to Kate that someone who instead of a bar of chocolate or a couple of Marie biscuits brought a raw chicken to a midnight feast could hardly be called sane. What would she get up to in Australia with only her mother to restrain her?

Monty, on the other hand, brightened up when he heard that there was a prospect of either Nigel Langfield or himself accompanying the women-folk to safety. He believed he could count on Nigel to show the necessary courage and foolishness to insist on sticking it out at his post. Things had not been going well recently for Monty but now they might be looking better. In the meantime he was having to fight a determined rear-guard action with medical certificates from Dr Brownley to prevent himself being enlisted in the Local Defence Corps. The air-raids, too, increasingly alarmed him. Well, if there was a chance of escorting women to safety only an idiot would linger in Singapore to be bombed. He would crack off to Australia and take charge of the firm's office there ... as an 'essential occupation' that should keep him out of the beastly Army, with luck.

But after a day or two Monty's spirits sank again. No European men were being allowed to leave without special permission and it soon became clear that such permission would not be granted to either himself or Nigel under the present circumstances despite more string-pulling by both Walter and Solomon. Evidently some spiteful little official in some office was seizing his opportunity to pay off a grudge against the merchant community. And *he* had to suffer!

In due course it was decided that Kate and Melanie and their mothers should leave for Australia on the *Narkunda*, sailing in mid-January. Walter agreed provisionally that Joan should stay a little longer but insisted that she would have to follow her mother if the situation got any worse. The truth was that Walter had need of Joan in Singapore, not only to supervise the running of the household in the absence of his wife, but also to lend a hand in the increasingly frantic work involved in administering Blackett and Webb's affairs from temporary offices in Tanglin, for by now the air-raids on the docks, spasmodic hitherto, had made continued occupation of the premises on Collyer's Quay too dangerous. Moreover, Walter still had not quite given up hope that Matthew might suffer a change of heart and decide he must marry Joan, after all. This match was such a good idea! That was what upset Walter, to see a good idea go to waste. There persisted in his mind the feeling that in some way Joan's marriage could still be the foundation of Blackett and Webb's recovery. But how? It was an instinct, nothing more.

An impetus was needed, that much was certain! Whether or not Singapore might survive as a military strong-point in the Far East it was clear that as a business centre it was finished for some time to come. As a result all Walter's efforts were now directed towards the running-down of the company's Singapore operations, the transferring of business to branches overseas in Britain, America and Australia and the suspension of that which could not be transferred.

And there still remained as a reminder of his own weakness those vast quantities of rubber in his godowns on the Singapore River. He had barely been able to shift a fraction of it. Nor was it any comfort to tell himself that he was the victim of circumstances beyond his control. Difficulties are made to be overcome! A businessman must shape his own environment to suit his needs: once he finds himself having to submit to it he is doomed. Once, years ago, while leafing through a copy of *Wide World*, he had come across a blurred photograph which, for reasons which he had not understood, had made a great impression on him. Well, if he had not understood it then, he certainly understood it now! It was a photograph, very poorly printed, of some dying animal, perhaps a panther or a leopard, it was hard to tell. Too weak to defend itself, this animal was being eaten alive by a flock of hideous birds. Walter had never been able to forget that picture. He had thought of it not long ago while standing at old Mr Webb's bedside. And now, he thought of it again, reflecting that there comes a time, inevitably, when the strong become, first weak, then helpless.

Walter knew very well, mind you, that other rubber merchants shared at least some of his own difficulties. Even old Solomon Langfield had admitted in an unguarded moment that he had large stocks waiting on the quays for a carrier. This was no comfort, however: Walter had always held in contempt businessmen who excused their own failures by matching them with those of other people. There was a way of shipping that rubber, he knew, just as there was a way of doing everything. But the present state of the docks baffled and exhausted him: the quays were jammed with shipping still loaded with war material said to be urgently needed by the military. Yet nobody was doing anything about it: the labour force had largely decamped, doubtless because they were unwilling to risk their lives under constant air-raids; what unloading was taking place was being done by the troops themselves: Walter had tried to suggest to a military acquaintance that these same men should reload with rubber 'urgently needed for the War Effort elsewhere', but the man had looked at him as if he were out of his mind.

Walter, even in his weakened state, had been stubborn enough to keep on trying. He had paid another visit to the Governor, suggesting that he might intercede with the War Council to provide a labour company under military discipline (which might encourage them to turn up for work) in order to start reloading the great backlog of rubber before it was too late. But Sir Shenton Thomas had barely listened to him. Although he was normally sympathetic to the Colony's mercantile community, he had shown visible signs of impatience with Walter's difficulties. That stuffed shirt! He had hardly even taken the trouble to make an excuse, muttering something about it being all he could do to prevent the military from commandeering what labour was already available to the rubber industry ... Relations with Malaya Command and Singapore Fortress, already bad at the outbreak of war, had got worse ... Walter would kindly realize that the community had other needs, above all civil defence, besides his own ... Well! Walter had come close to asking him whose taxes he thought paid his bloody salary! Affronted, he had taken his leave. The bales of rubber, in their thousands of tons, had continued to sleep undisturbed in their godowns.

And yet this was the moment, Walter knew in his heart, to adopt some resolute plan, perhaps to conscript a labour force of one's own by closing down other aspects of the business, certain of which would soon close down anyway of their own accord, by transferring estate labour (such of it as had not yet been overrun by the advancing Japanese) to the docks, by offering double wages if necessary, anything provided that rubber was shifted. It was no good for Walter, isolated and overworked as he was, to tell himself that he must not let that rubber get out of proportion ... What was it compared to the rubber which had passed through his hands in his time? Nothing! ... It seemed to him like a tumour, disfiguring his career in Singapore. And like a tumour it continued to grow because, although diminished in quantity by the Japanese advance and by the increasingly chaotic state of the roads in Johore, new consignments of rubber continued to arrive from across the Causeway.

The fact was that all the options Walter considered were hedged around with administrative difficulties through which he could see no way. In desperation he even considered, though only for a moment, the possibility of forming a co-operative labour force with other firms in a similar, if less acute, predicament ... perhaps even with Langfield and Bowser. But that solution, which was probably the only one capable of realization in practice, was denied to Walter by the competitive habits of a lifetime. He could hardly enter into such an agreement without revealing the sheer size of his stocks to his rivals, who would know immediately by the amount of rubber he had waiting that he had made a grotesque miscalculation. To go cap in hand to old Solomon Langfield in Blackett and Webb's jubilee year to propose such a scheme was more than he could bring himself to do. But at this point fate, in the shape of a Japanese bomb, took a hand.

<h1 style="text-align:center">51</h1>

Even taking into account the new-found amity between the two families, you would hardly have expected to see what you now *did* see at the Blacketts' house, the extraordinary spectacle of lions lying down with lambs and scarcely even licking their lips. Walter found himself sitting at his own dining-table surrounded, it seemed, by nothing but Langfields. Even more unexpected was the fact that a similar scene had taken place yesterday and would take place again tomorrow ... though with the women-folk subtracted, for this was the eve of their departure for Australia. What then was the explanation? For this was not, needless to say, the company that Walter would have chosen for his evening meal, including as it did, old Solomon Langfield with a slightly condescending expression on his cunning old face and young Nigel, who looked almost human by comparison, sitting next to Joan.

The Langfields on the whole looked subdued, which Walter found reasonably gratifying. Nor was this simply because their family was about to be sundered. The Langfields had suffered a misfortune. A bomb jettisoned at random by a Japanese plane had fallen in Nassim Road, partly destroying their house. None of them had been hurt, fortunately, except for a few scratches. Since the damage had only been to property Walter had felt himself permitted at first to treat the matter as a joke. At the Club, chuckling, he had entertained his friends with what he claimed was an eye-witness description of 'the bomb on the bear-garden'. The rats and cockroaches that had poured out of the smoking ruins had been nobody's business! And poor old

Solomon wandering about howling with grief. Why? Because he kept his money under his mattress, as everyone knew, and it had been blown up with the rest of the bear-garden! After a while, however, Walter fell silent, having realized that some of his audience were not relishing his joke at Langfield's expense quite as much as he did himself. But Walter was fundamentally a kind-hearted man and he could see that, after all, having your house destroyed could have its unpleasant side. And so he had generously made amends by inviting the Langfields to stay at his house until they had managed to re-establish themselves in their own; besides, since the women-folk were going off together it made sense for the two families to be under the same roof for a while. Walter was considered at the Singapore Club to have emerged, after a shaky start, very creditably from the Langfields' misfortune, given the legendary antipathy between the two families.

Solomon, as it happened, was not looking particularly well. He was getting on in years and had reached the age when a person finds it hard to adjust to a sudden shock like the destruction of his house. Mrs Langfield had confided in Mrs Blackett (the two ladies, having swallowed the distaste of years in a few minutes, had discovered that they had everything in common and had quite as much gossip backed up over the years as Walter had rubber in his warehouses) that it had taken some time for the poor old fellow to be coaxed out of the ruins. He had wanted to stay on there, it appeared! With ceilings which might collapse at any moment! And when he had been told of the invitation to the Blacketts' he had grown more stubborn than ever. In the end Nigel had had to accept the invitation on his behalf and Dr Brownley had had to make a personal visit to the shattered house in Nassim Road to dislodge the old boy.

Dr Brownley, seated opposite old Solomon, might well have been thinking that the old man's face had an unhealthy cast, yellowish with brightly flushed patches. But as a matter of fact he was concentrating more on his supper which was exceptionally appetizing. Walter, drumming absently on the table with a crust of 'health bread', for to the indignation of Tanglin the Cold Storage had stopped baking white bread on Government orders, surveyed the table and reflected that tomorrow, when the women had sailed for Australia, he would at last have time to get down to some serious work. He would miss them, no doubt, but that could not be helped. Besides, there was always Joan.

At the end of the table Matthew had become involved in a heated discussion with Nigel, odd snatches of which reached Walter's distracted ears ... something about colonial policy during the Depression. Matthew, Walter had to admit, had turned out a disappointment. He had grown somewhat thinner during his weeks in Singapore but no less excitable and opinionated. Why, the other day he had even asserted that the European estates had swindled inarticulate native smallholders out of their share of Malaya's rubber exports under the Restriction Scheme. And how, Walter had enquired with an ironical smile, did we manage to do that? How did we manage to do that when assessment was under Government control? The estates had managed to do it through their creature, the Controller of Rubber! By packing the committee formed to 'advise' him ... that was to say, to give him instructions for whatever they wanted to be done so that he could apply the official stamp to them!

'Don't be an idiot!'

'I'm not saying you did anything illegal, just that you used your influence to bend the rules in your favour. Isn't that the way it's always done? Come to think of it, that's what my father and his cronies did in the rice trade in Rangoon all those years ago. I suppose that's what business out here consists of.'

Walter had spoken sharply at this point. He was not ready to listen to Matthew saying anything against old Mr Webb who had been the very soul of rectitude and one of the pillars of the Singapore community His was an example of honesty and industry which Matthew would do well to follow instead of ... of ... Walter had been about to say 'carrying on with half-caste women' but thought better of it at the last moment. He had heard reports that Matthew had been seen with Miss Chiang but did not want to bring the matter up until he was more sure of his ground, for it was out of the question for a Webb to be seen associating openly with a 'stengah', particularly in Blackett and Webb's jubilee year. '... Instead of wasting your time,' he had finished rather weakly. Matthew had abandoned the subject, looking depressed.

Matthew was now saying, 'Far from doing anything to help our colonies foster their own native industries the Colonial Office sees to it that any which begin to develop are promptly scotched!'

'Why should they do that?' scoffed Nigel Langfield, under the approving eye of his elders. 'I say, Mr Blackett, what d'you think, sir? Isn't that just the nonsense that the Nationalists are always spouting?'

'Why?' demanded Matthew heatedly. 'Because we want to sell our own goods. We don't want competition from the natives: we want to keep them on the estates producing the raw materials we need.'

'Absolute poppycock, old boy,' chuckled Nigel. 'Westminster has done a jolly great deal with grants to build up industry in the colonies.'

'Grants, certainly ... but what for? So that they could buy British capital equipment for bridges and railways. The only purpose of these grants was to deal with unemployment in Britain. Funds were produced so that the unfortunate colonies could buy equipment which they could ill afford and which was of dubious advantage to them, though it probably *was* to the advantage of the European businesses established in the colonies!'

Walter could not help glancing at old Solomon Langfield to see how he was responding to these unfortunate remarks. Ah, it was as he feared! On the man's sickly face an expression of amazement and disgust had appeared. Glancing up swiftly the wily old fellow caught Walter's eye before he had time to look away. Promptly his expression changed to one of sarcasm, even glee, as if to say: 'So this is the sort of degenerate talk that goes on in the Blackett household ... I might have known!' But perhaps Walter had merely imagined that his old rival was gloating over him: a moment later Solomon had dropped his chin wearily to his plate once more. He really did look rather ill. Perhaps it was just as well that the doctor was at hand. Much as he detested the Langfields Walter did not particularly want one to die under his roof.

'In Burma during the Depression there was such a high tax on matches that the natives started a flourishing local industry making cheap cigarette lighters. Guess what happened. The Government, disliking the loss of revenue, suppressed it by instituting heavy fines! Well, by an interesting coincidence the same thing happened in the Dutch East Indies. There, too, cheap cigarette lighters threatened the revenue from matches. But the Dutch allowed them to continue making the lighters on the grounds that it created employment. And the same goes for many other local industries, too ... The result is that the Dutch East Indies now have a spinning industry and instead of importing *sarongs* they make their own. The same goes for soap, cigarettes and any number of other things. There's even a native bank to finance native enterprises! And what have we been doing? We've seen to it that even basic things like nails still have to be imported from Britain!'

'Oh, that's all very well,' blustered Nigel. 'Anyone can quote isolated facts, but that just distorts the overall picture.' And Nigel flushed, nettled by Matthew's tone and conscious that he had not emerged from this arguement as well as he had hoped, particularly with the beautiful Joan Blackett sitting in silent judgement at his elbow. What a smasher she was! Nigel particularly liked the way the light fell on her curly hair, making it glow like ... like ...

'Matthew doesn't know anything, Nigel, about what things are really like here,' said Joan suddenly and in such a bitter tone that even Nigel peered at her in surprise, delighted, however, that she should take his side.

Walter had been listening attentively to the exchange between the two young men at the end of the table. As he listened his face had darkened and the bristles on his spine had risen, causing his Lancashire cotton shirt and even the jacket of his linen suit to puff up into a hump. Distracted though she was by her imminent departure, Mrs Blackett had noticed the warning signs and held her breath, afraid lest her husband explode at any moment. But just as it had seemed that an explosion of rage was inevitable, Walter's thoughts had abruptly been diverted into a more soothing channel by his daughter's defence of Nigel. And so promising was this new channel that within a few moments those horrid bristles had subsided and were nestling peacefully once more flat against Walter's coarse pink skin. Walter had begun to have ideas about young Nigel Langfield.

Walter had known Nigel since childhood; according to the general proposition that Langfields only became odious and unsuitable on reaching puberty, he had often been permitted to come as a child to play with Monty just as now Melanie came to play with Kate. And naturally, even after Nigel had made the change from acceptable tadpole to unacceptable frog, Walter had continued to see him here or there for they belonged, of course, to the same clubs and it was inevitable that the young man should crop up in Walter's field of vision over the years carrying now a tennis racket, now a briefcase, Singapore being a very small world, after all. Nevertheless it was only now that the bombed-out Langfields had assembled under his roof that Walter was at last really able to form an opinion about the young man: on the whole he had been agreeably surprised.

Nigel had the right ideas. He was not, like Monty, a wash-out. On the contrary, from what he had overheard passing between Nigel and his father the young man was already active in the affairs of Langfield and Bowser. Walter, preoccupied though he was this evening with other matters, had not failed to notice that every now and again Nigel's eyes would surreptitiously come to rest on Joan and contemplate her avidly. A young man's normal stirrings of lust, perhaps? No, Walter did not think so. He believed that there might be more to it than that. For Nigel was making every effort to be agreeable to Joan and once or twice, for no apparent reason, a deep blush had stained the young man's cheeks, which were, incidentally, still pleasantly freckled like those of a child.

Yes, Walter was still faced with the problem of finding a husband for Joan. How times had changed that he should now be giving serious consideration to an offspring of the Langfields! But a businessman must adapt his views to meet changing times; otherwise he will be left high and dry. Walter had not forgotten (how often had he not repeated it to little Monty when the lad was still in the nursery) the fate of the rice-millers in London who had gone to their doom because they had been unable to foresee the effects that the opening of the Suez Canal would have on their trade. A man must move with the times. If a union of the Blacketts and the Langfields was what the times called for, then so be it. Moreover, the more Walter thought about it, the more it seemed to him that this might be the master-stroke that solved all his problems simultaneously. If the two firms were merged into a new company, Blackett, Webb and Langfield, then the danger that Matthew Webb might one day use his holdings to force some independent, hare-brained, moralistic policy on the Blackett interest would automatically disappear. Matthew's stake would be diluted. Of course, he would have the problem of imposing his will on the Langfield interest but old Solomon would not last for ever and Walter was confident that with Joan's help he could deal easily enough with young Nigel. Why, a union of the two families might even help him solve the more immediate problem of shipping his rubber by putting him in a better position to suggest some joint solution of the difficulty to Solomon.

Mr Webb would not have approved of such a match as Walter was now contemplating. But no matter, Walter thought with a grim chuckle, old Webb was dead and from the grave a man's influence on the board of directors is much reduced. Nor would his wife approve ... but tomorrow Sylvia would be on her way to Australia. As for Monty, trained to detest Langfields the way a police-dog is trained to leap for the throats of burglars, he might not like it but then his opinion was of no account. For a moment Walter's eye rested sadly on his only son. Why could he not have turned out like one of Harvey Firestone's boys? As if aware of his father's disappointment Monty looked up at that moment. 'What's biting the old man?' he wondered. 'Perhaps there's something he wants me to do?' But the next moment his thoughts had returned to browse on his own problems which, like his father's, were manifold. How was he to get out of this hole, Singapore, with his skin in one piece? And, a more immediate problem, how was he to get through another dreary evening when he had seen almost every film in town? The only one poor Monty had not seen was Myrna Loy in *Third Finger, Left Hand*. Could you beat it! That was certain to be the sort of romantic rubbish to which he would normally have given a wide berth. But if that's all there was then there was nothing else he could do. He would have to put up with it. '*Third Finger, Left Hand* indeed!' he thought grimly as he tackled his pudding. 'Why am I being punished like this?'

52

'A businessman must move with the times!' Two hours had passed and calm had descended on the Blacketts' household once more, but Walter's train of thought had not made much progress. Now he and Solomon Langfield and the doctor sat on the unlit verandah smoking cigars; upstairs, after an abortive attempt to be allowed to stay up late on this their last night in Singapore, Kate and Melanie were lying almost naked on their beds complaining of the heat and calling each other 'darling' in affected tones: Melanie was still hoping to be rescued from this early banishment by an air-raid and planned to cause a sensation, if the Japanese obliged, by appearing in the Blacketts' improvised shelter wearing no more clothes than she was at present. Kate was less unhappy than she had expected to be at the prospect of leaving, partly because her father had agreed after a great deal of persuasion that her beloved cat, Ming Toy, might accompany her to Australia. Mrs Langfield and Mrs Blackett had both retired early. Matthew, after murmuring his good-byes to the ladies (only Kate had shed a tear at parting from the Human Bean), had made himself scarce. Joan and Nigel had wandered into the garden and were sitting by the swimming pool watching the moon sliding gently this way and that on its dark skin.

Walter was pondering the question of palm-oil as he had done time and again in recent weeks. Palm-oil was plainly a business for the future. It was also, all too plainly, one in which he had allowed Blackett and Webb to get left behind. Other matters had obtruded, preventing him from taking the decisive action that was needed: old Webb's illness, the war, worries about young Webb's holdings in the company .... and before all that there had been the Depression and its aftermath, the struggle for a Restriction Scheme and heaven knew what else. But while he had been hesitating what had happened? Guthries had been going from strength to strength with their new oil bulking company. Even the French had been at it, with Socfin (La Société Financière des Caoutchoucs) building a bulk shipment plant at Port Swettenham. Why, he had heard that Guthries now had twenty thousand acres under oil palms! To make the matter more galling, it seemed that Malayan palm-oil was considered superior to West African. One day, for all Walter knew, it might become as important as rubber ... or more so, if synthetic rubber developed. Then where would Blackett and Webb be?

Walter had been aware of all this for years, of course. It was useless to pretend otherwise. Younger, he might have taken the plunge, built a modern oil mill and bulk shipment plant, negotiated for estates. It was absurd to think you could compete by shipping the stuff in wooden barrels in this day and age; it would take a considerable investment. It was the sort of venture that might be undertaken, perhaps, by a firm as large as Blackett's and Langfield's combined. Walter was profoundly depressed by the thought that a good fifteen years had gone by since Guthries had gone heavily into palm-oil. In that time he had done nothing! There was one consolation, at least as far as Socfin were concerned: Port Swettenham must be in Japanese hands by now.

Dr Brownley stood up to take his leave, murmuring that one of these days Walter must ...

'Yes, yes,' muttered Walter impatiently, anxious for the

Doctor to leave without delay. There was a matter he wanted to discuss with Solomon Langfield. Discountenanced by the briskness of Walter's goodbyes, the Doctor retreated. Walter was left alone in the semi-darkness of the verandah with his old rival of many years.

'Well, Solomon,' he began cautiously, 'these are troubled times for Singapore and I have a feeling that things will never again be quite the way they used to be in the old days.' A grunt of assent came from the figure in the cane chair beside him. Encouraged, Walter went on: 'Soon it will be time for another generation to take over from us the building of this Colony. But still, I think we've done our bit, people like you and me ... and my sorely missed partner, Webb, of course.' He added as an afterthought: '... And poor old Bowser, too, we mustn't forget him.' Walter considered it generous of himself to include the incompetent, drunken Bowser and the crafty, even criminal Langfield among the founders of modern Singapore. All the same, he waited rather anxiously for Solomon's response which, when it came, was another grunt, somewhat non-committal this time. On the darkened verandah Walter could see little but the glow of his companion's cigar tip on the arm of his chair and a faint gleam of moonlight on the bald pate as it curved up to the long sagacious forehead where preposterous eyebrows rose like puffs of steam.

'I must say that it reassures me when I think that our work here will be in good hands when our youngsters take over from us. Mind you, my boy, Monty, has never been as interested in the business as I would have hoped ... not his line but, well, fair enough, we all have our rôle to play and he's more of ... I suppose you'd say he was more of an academic turn of mind,' proceeded Walter, fumbling rather. 'But my girl, Joan, now, she's as hard-headed as they come and one day she'll make a fine businesswoman. Why, she could buy and sell her old papa already!'

A faint snicker greeted this remark and Walter paused, disconcerted. Had he imagined a sarcastic note to it, as if one were to say: 'Well, *that* wouldn't be difficult!'

'Yes,' he continued, summing up, 'I don't think we need worry about those who come after.' And he added, almost as an afterthought: 'Young Nigel, he's a fine lad, too. I like the cut of his jib, I must say. Too bad there aren't more like him coming out East these days ... Someone at the Club the other day, just forget who it was, said to me: "Look here, Blackett, why don't you and Langfield marry that young pair off? That'd give Guthries and Sime Darby something to think about! And by Jove, you know, he wasn't far wide of the mark either when you come to think about it.'

A faint, enigmatic chortle greeted this last observation, followed by silence.

'Well, Solomon,' Walter ventured presently. 'What would you think of such an arrangement if the interested parties liked the sound of it? There need be no great changes on the business side during our lifetime, of course. Frankly, I think we could both do a lot worse. What d'you think?'

Now at last, after being immobile for so long that it might have been taken merely for a piece of furniture, the passive silhouette beside Walter began to move, to struggle to its feet with a creaking and shrieking of bamboo, accompanied by a most peculiar gasping sound which it took him a little time to recognize as laughter. At length, however, the wheezing and gasping died away. By now Langfield was on his feet in front of Walter and bobbing up and down. Again it took Walter a few moments before he realized what the dimly perceived figure was doing. Then it was suddenly clear: the old codger was executing an insulting little caper in front of him.

'So you're having trouble getting rid of her, are you, Blackett?' he crowed. 'Well, no son of mine would look at her in a hundred years. Never! Not if you gave him half Singapore with her! Ah, that's a good one ... That's the best I've heard for years ... Ha! ha! ... Your daughter and my son! He wouldn't look at her! Ha!' Solomon had paused in the half-open door which led back into the house and his old monkey's face, illuminated by a glow from within, was twisted with hideous glee. 'Good night, Blackett. Why, that's the best I've heard for years! You've made my day.'

The door slammed. Walter was left alone on the verandah but he could still hear Langfield's footsteps departing down the corridor. Then, from somewhere deep inside the house, faintly, a querulous voice cried out: 'He wouldn't touch the bitch! Never! Never!' A burst of frenzied laughter and all was quiet.

Not far away, in another and less elegant part of the city, Matthew was sitting on Vera's bed, apparently about to begin his second meal of the evening. For the past week Vera had issued repeated promises that she would one day cook him a meal, ignoring his protests that he was managing perfectly well for food already. Now here was the promised meal, balanced on his lap, and there seemed to be no option but to go ahead and eat it. He peered at what lay on the plate which was by no means easy to identify in the dim light of the oil-lamp. He prodded it suspiciously. 'What is it?'

'Baked beans.'

'I can see they're baked beans. But what are these two lumps of slippery stuff?'

'Chicken blood ... a Chinese delicacy. Taste. You'll like it very much, Matthew, I know.'

'And these two other lumps covered in sauce?'

'They are other Chinese delicacy ... They are white mice, poached Chinese-style. Taste. They are very good.'

'I'm not frightfully hungry, as a matter of fact. I've had one meal already this evening ... But I'm really looking forward to tasting all this,' he added hastily as Vera looked hurt, 'even if I don't quite manage to finish it all.' He captured a baked bean with his chopsticks and nibbled it cautiously.

'Oh, Matthew, you don't think I am a good cook, do you?'

'Of course I do,' protested Matthew, and in a fit of bravado lifted one of the white mice to his lips and began to gnaw at it, making appreciative sounds. He found that it did not taste too bad, but would have liked to have known which end of the mouse he was eating.

'You think Miss Blackett is better cook than I,' Vera said accusingly. 'I don't know how you can touch a European woman like Miss Blackett, they sweat so much. It is something horrible!'

'But ...'

'Yes, you prefer making love-making to Miss Blackett even though she sweats something horrible.'

'Don't be silly. You say that just because I'm not hungry when you cook me a meal! You know I only like to be with you. Come and sit beside me.' Putting the plate down, he murmured: 'I'll finish the rest later.'

'I know you think I am not a good cook but my mother could not teach me. Always she was used to servants here, servants there, because she was a princess. It is because my family has blue blood that I do not know how to cook.'

'But Vera, I think ...'

She had come to sit beside him and now put her hand over his mouth and said: 'If we stay together I'll learn to be a good

410

cook so that you can invite your friends and we will have a nice time.'

'I don't have any friends, except Major Archer and Dupigny ... and, of course, Jim Ehrendorf, but I don't know where he is.' He looked at his watch. 'Soon I shall have to be going, Vera. I'm expected on duty tonight.'

'Not just yet. Lie here with me a little while. "With so much quarrelling and so few kisses, how long do you think our love can last?" That is what it says in the Chinese song translated into English by Mr Waley. Shall I read you another verse? But first take off your clothes and lie down beside me.'

'Mrs Blackett and Kate are leaving for Australia tomorrow ... and I hear that lots of other women are leaving, too. Tomorrow we must try to arrange for you to leave, too. It isn't safe for you to stay in Singapore with the Japanese so close.'

> All night I could not sleep
> Because of the moonlight on my bed.
> I kept hearing a voice calling;
> Out of nowhere, Nothing answered 'yes'.

Matthew lay there inert, listening to the faint sounds which came from the other cubicles in the tenement and from outside in the street, above all, like the very rhythm of poverty and despair, that weary, tubercular coughing which never ceased. 'Tomorrow, d'you hear me?'

> I will carry my coat and not put on my belt;
> With unpainted eyebrows I will stand at the front window.
> My tiresome petticoat keeps on flapping about;
> If it opens a little, I shall blame the spring wind.

'What will become of us?' Matthew wondered, thinking how vulnerable they both were, lying there in the stifling cubicle and breathing that strange smell that hung everywhere in Chinatown, that odour of drains and burnings rags. And how strange it was that someone should have made up these verses, which he found extraordinarily moving, hundreds of years ago and yet they sounded as new and fresh as if they had been composed by someone who had been here in this cubicle only a moment earlier. And that this person should have belonged to a quite different culture from his own made it seem even

411

more moving. And slowly a peculiar feeling stole over Matthew, almost like a premonition of disaster. All the different matters, both in his own personal life and outside it, which had pre-occupied him in the past few weeks and even years, his relationship with his father and the history of Blackett and Webb, the time he had spent in Oxford and in Geneva, his friendship with Ehrendorf and with Vera and with the Major, his arguments about the League and even the one about colonial policy which he had had earlier in the evening with Nigel, and yes even his saying goodbye to dear little Kate ... all these things now seemed to cling together, to belong to each other and to have a direction and an impetus towards destruction which it was impossible to resist.

> I heard my love was going to Yang-chou
> And went with him as far as Ch'u-shan.
> For a moment when you held me fast in your
>   outstretched arms
> I thought the river stood still and did not flow.

'Vera, listen to me. We must make arrangements for you to leave, and no later than tomorrow.'

Part Five

53

AIR-RAIDS: TWO POINTS FOR THE PUBLIC

1 You *must not* crowd to the place where a bomb has dropped. The enemy may come back and machine-gun you. Moreover, crowds interfere with the Passive Defence Services.

2 In air-raids people are sometimes suffocated by dust and plaster. You can lessen this danger by covering your mouth and nose with a wet handkerchief.

In the past few days the Major, assisted by Matthew, Dupigny, Nigel Langfield and such of the other volunteer firemen who were at hand, had made an effort to convert the Mayfair into a more efficient fire station. Matthew's former office had become a dormitory where those on night-duty might rest between calls: half a dozen *charpoys* had been put against the walls and an extra fan installed. The room next to it, meanwhile, had been converted into a watch-room where the Major presided over the telephone and maps of Singapore. There was no way of protecting such a building adequately against bombs: constructed of wood on brick piles even the blast from a near miss would be likely to demolish it. Nevertheless, the two rooms most in use had been protected with an outer layer of sandbags while work on an air-raid shelter of sorts had begun in the compound where the ground rose conveniently in a slope up to the road at the rear. Into this slope a trench was dug, just long enough to accommodate the estimated maximum number of people likely to be found at the Mayfair at any one moment; it was then roofed over with timber and corrugated-iron sheets which the Major, without consulting Walter, commandeered from the construction of the floats in the nutmeg grove.

As the days went by, however, the shelter had to be dug further and further into the slope, on account of the Mayfair's steadily increasing population of volunteer firemen, of refugees from up-country who could find no other lodging, and of transients of one kind and another. Among the new arrivals in the early days of the New Year there were a number who did not stay more than a night, military people *en route* from one posting to another and very often with a bottle of whisky or gin in their trappings, anxious to celebrate a few hours of freedom before plunging back into the struggle. At such times the Mayfair took on a gay, even uproarious atmosphere: the piano was trundled up from the recreation hut, someone was found to hammer away at it and songs were bellowed out into the compound from the verandah where, though it was dark, at least the revellers could get a breath of air. Other people came and went according to a mysterious time-table of their own, sleeping on camp-beds in odd corners or even on the floor, perhaps not speaking to anyone but merely dropping in to use the lavatory, for the Mayfair, though dilapidated in certain respects, had one that flushed, a great luxury in Singapore.

With refugees pouring back in increasing numbers on to Singapore Island you saw new faces wherever you went, and even some people who had already been living in the city had adapted themselves to a new, nomadic sort of life. Thus, one day when the Major returned from the compound where he had been training some new recruits in a 'dry drill', he was not particularly surprised to find on the verandah an elderly gentleman who had not been there before. This old fellow, comfortably installed and drinking a cup of tea he had ordered from Cheong, gave no explanation of his presence but he did introduce himself in the course of the conversation. His name was Captain John Brown and he was eighty years of age, he informed the Major in the confident tone of a man accustomed to command. He had spent the greater part of his life in Eastern waters, fool that he was for he hated every inch, every last shoal and channel of 'em ... As a result his health was ruined and as for savings, ha! If the Major saw his bank balance he would be astonished, yes, flabbergasted that this was all a man had been able to put by for his old age after sixty-five years at sea. 'My health has been ruined by the climate out here, Archer, and that's a fact.'

The Major, inspecting Captain Brown, could not help thinking that he looked remarkably hale, considering his age. He was a wiry little man with unusually large ears. His thin neck and prominent Adam's apple were encircled by a collar several times too big for them and altogether his physical presence was too slight to explain the air of authority which clung to him. It emerged that the Captain had been living in a hostel for mariners near the docks; the air-raids on the docks had obliged him to leave and push further inland, a mile or two, as far as Tanglin. But he evidently had another billet as well as the Mayfair for after a day or two of holding forth to the young firemen about the hard knocks which life in the East had dealt him and adjudicating any other matters which came up in his presence he disappeared again, picking up his bag and slinging it over his shoulder as if he were a twenty-year-old. For three or four days there was no sign of him, but then the Major passed Cheong hastening towards the verandah with a sandwich and a cup of tea, peremptorily ordered by Captain Brown, and there he was, comfortably installed in his favourite chair once again.

'How are you, sir?' asked the Major, pleased to see him back.

'Very ill,' retorted the Captain grimly, and for some time held forth fluently on the state of his health, which did not prevent him bolting his sandwich in the meantime. For the better part of a week Captain Brown was in residence and whether he was on the verandah or in the outer office, which now served as the watch-room for the AFS unit, everything grew ship-shape around him; he could not abide slackness or muddle and he had strong opinions on how matters should be conducted. Indeed, if the Major had not at last spoken out bluntly he would have assumed command of the fire-service.

The Human Condition, with an instinct which drew him magnetically to pay homage to the most powerful source of authority within range, invariably installed himself beneath the Captain's chair whenever he was in residence. 'I really must have that poor animal destroyed,' mused the Major. But the Major had a great deal to do without having to deal with dogs as well. Although Captain Brown soon proved to be a considerable help in the administration of the AFS unit, the Major now had the added problem of refugees from the more dangerous parts of Singapore.

One day, for example, when he was going about his business as usual he received an urgent instruction to call on Mr Smith of the Chinese Protectorate. The Major remembered Smith as the rather supercilious young man who had summoned him once before, to warn him of the dangers of Communism and wondered whether he was to be given a further homily on the subject. But this time Smith, with his hair still flickering disconcertingly about his ears and showing no sign of having moved an inch in the weeks that had passed since the Major had last seen him, wanted to know how many vacant rooms there were at the Mayfair Building. The Major had no difficulty in answering that question.

'None.' And he explained about his refugees.

'How many rooms then which are not vacant?'

The Major told him.

'Excellent. Since these other lodgers you mention are not official evacuees you will be able to turn them out in favour of the girls we are going to send you from the Poh Leung Kuk.'

'From *where?*'

'From the Chinese Girls' Home.'

'But that's impossible. We can't turn people out when they have nowhere to go!'

'They'll find somewhere, Major, don't worry. Besides, it's an order. It has nothing to do with me. It's official, so there you are. Perhaps you'd like to know a little more about them?' And Smith began to explain that the Poh Leung Kuk was run by a committee of Chinese under the supervision of the Protectorate. There had been such an importing of young girls into the Colony to act as prostitutes, particularly before the brothels had been closed down in 1930, that it had been necessary to find a suitable institution to house them. Girls arriving from China were taken to an inspection depot and only released to genuine relatives or employers. Any employers with dubious credentials were obliged to post a bond for a sum of money that the girl in question would not be disposed of to someone else or made to work as a prostitute. Other girls found themselves in the home as a result of police raids on illicit establishments. Unfortunately, since the Poh Leung Kuk was situated in a vulnerable part of Singapore in buildings near Outram Road (next to the prison on one side and near the Teck Lee Ice Works on the other), it had been found necessary to disperse the inmates where possible. The Major had been specially selected as a man of probity to give temporary shelter to half a dozen of these girls.

'Oh, and one more thing, Major. You'll probably find that some, if not all, of your girls are on the "marriage list". I suppose you don't know the procedure in that eventuality ...'

'No, I don't, and frankly ...'

'No need to take that tone here, Major. You don't seem to realize that there's a war on and that we must improvise as best we can. Now, about the "marriage list" ...'

In due course the Major, accompanied for moral support by Dupigny, had driven over to the Poh Leung Kuk in one of the Blackett and Webb vans to take delivery of the half-dozen girls who had been assigned to the Mayfair. He found himself waiting in a sort of yard aware that from the windows round about him a multitude of eyes were appraising him. After a while, the official to whom he had explained his business returned, saying rather nervously: 'They'll be out in a moment, I think.' He stood in silence for a moment, then said brightly: 'None of yours have any venereal problems, as far as we know.' The Major cleared his throat gloomily, but said nothing. 'Ah, here they come now.'

'But there were supposed only to be half a dozen. Here there are twice as many!'

'That was only an estimate ...'

'What d'you think, François? They *look* well-behaved. Can we manage so many? I suppose they could help Cheong with the cooking and household chores ...' The Major surveyed the row of neatly dressed Chinese girls who had lined up beside the van as if for inspection, each with her little bundle of belongings. They kept their eyes meekly on the ground while the two men discussed what to do. Dupigny, who could see the Major already weakening and who, moreover, was experienced in the ways of civil servants, gave it as his opinion that they should return to the Mayfair and only accept those girls whom the Protectorate succeeded in billeting on them by force.

'But François, we can't possibly leave so many of them here! How would we feel if a bomb dropped on this building tonight? We could never forgive ourselves!'

And so, with the back of the van crammed with young women, the Major and Dupigny drove back to the Mayfair. 'I'm sure they won't be any trouble, François ... what d'you think?' There was silence from Dupigny and a raised eyebrow. 'Once we've got it sorted out which of them is on the marriage list and which isn't ... I mean, that's the only real problem.' Smith had explained that thanks to a shortage of women in the Colony, there was a great demand for brides from the Poh Leung Kuk among the less affluent Chinese who could not afford to find a wife in the usual manner, that is through a go-between, which could involve great expense. A man who wanted a wife, once he had given details of his circumstances, might look over the girls on the list and make his selection. The girl then would accept or reject him on the spot. He would then pay forty dollars for his bride's trousseau and undergo a medical inspection. And that was that.

'I shouldn't think there'll be many men wanting to get married in the present situation,' said the Major confidently. 'I don't think we need worry about it, François. What d'you think?' Dupigny smiled but still made no comment. From the back of the van there came one or two smothered giggles.

All the same, there was no question of the Major asking any of the refugees to leave so that he might accommodate the newcomers. He allotted the former Board Room to the girls as a dormitory, asked Cheong to make use of them for kitchen and cleaning duties and, having nominated Captain Brown to deal with any difficulties that might arise, he returned to his other preoccupations, hoping for the best.

And still, as the days went by, more refugees continued to arrive so that soon new arrivals were obliged to camp in the compound. Now the centre of the city was thronged with refugees from up-country, milling about aimlessly all day in the hot streets in the hope of coming across someone they knew who might be able to help them. Many of them were women with small children who had been separated from their men-folk in the upheaval and had no idea of how they could make contact with them again. The Major, gazing at these shattered-looking people, was appalled and angry at the inadequacy of the arrangements which had been made to cope with them. But at this late date, with the administration of the city already in chaos, what was there to be done?

There was, however, one newcomer to the Mayfair whom everyone was pleased to see. Returning early one morning from an exhausting night at the docks, Matthew saw a familiar figure sitting on the verandah chatting with Dupigny. It was Ehrendorf.

'You've got thin, Matthew,' he said with a smile, getting to his feet. 'I hardly recognize you.'

'So have you!' Matthew was taken aback to see the change that had taken place in his friend's appearance in the few weeks since he had last seen him. Ehrendorf's handsome face was deeply lined and shrunk, as if he were suddenly ten years older. His cheekbones stood out sharply and grim little brackets which Matthew had never noticed before now enclosed the corners of his mouth; as he was speaking his eyes kept wandering from Matthew's face, as if he were trying to estimate, by the sound of the ack-ack batteries, the course of the raid which at that moment was taking place to the south.

Ehrendorf's voice was firm, however, as he explained that he had been ill with dysentery in Kuala Lumpur. Later he had been to Kuantan on the east coast, then back to Kuala Lumpur to find that it was being evacuated. He had no specific idea of how the campaign was progressing but it was clear that it was going badly. The roads throughout Johore were jammed with reinforcements and supplies going in one direction and refugees going, or attempting to go, in the other. It had taken him many hours to get through the traffic by car to Singapore and there was a danger of the whole line of communication seizing up. It was already a sitting target during daylight hours for Japanese bombers. He had heard one piece of good news, though. Last Tuesday it had rained providentially and a convoy of reinforcements had managed to sneak in, thanks to the bad weather, without being taken to bits by the bombers which now prowled the sea approaches to Singapore. Provided there was some way of getting the new men and equipment into the line quickly enough ... Ehrendorf shrugged.

'I shall probably be going back to the States in a few days if I can get transport.'

'In the meantime, you can stay here and lend a hand at the pumps.' Noticing Ehrendorf hesitate he added: 'You haven't seen Joan, I suppose? Mrs Blackett and Kate have left for Australia. Joan's still here, I believe, but I haven't seen her recently. Come on, grab your kit and I'll show you the few inches that are your ration of floorboards. We'll soon make a fireman of you.'

54

LEARN TO DANCE AND DROWN YOUR WORRIES IN
CABARETS!
Success guaranteed to anyone after two and a half hours
private coaching at the
Modern Dancing School
5A Ann Siang Hill
(the road is diagonally opposite to the Hindu Temple
of South Bridge Road).

Straits Times, 16 Jan 1942

at the Sea View Hotel popular concert
11 a.m. to 1 p.m. by Reller's band

1 Overture ......The Beautiful Helena............Offenbach
2 Waltz ....Wine, Women & Song.........Strauss
3 Fantasia ....Faust ....Gounod
4 Selection ......Showboat ....Kern
5 Rhapsody ......Slavonic Rhapsody...............Friedman
6 Selection ......No, No, Nanette ....Youman
7 Medley ....Somers Scotttish Medley ......Rijf
8 Selection ......Tommy's Tunes ....Pecher

Tiffin special Curry served from 12.30–2.30 p.m.

MR SOLOMON R. LANGFIELD,
PEACEFULLY IN HIS SIXTY-THIRD YEAR.
NO FLOWERS PLEASE.

The death was announced today of Mr Solomon Langfield, co-founder of Langfield and Bowser Ltd and a familiar figure in Singapore business circles for many years. Mr Walter Blackett, paying tribute, said that although not the first in the field Mr Langfield's family firm had made a contribution.

So troubled were the times that for the general public the passing of old Solomon Langfield, who surprisingly had turned out not to be quite as old as everyone had thought, took place with scarcely a murmur. There were none of the official manifestations of grief which had marked old Mr Webb's departure, for example, none of the letters of regret from the Governor nor the flying of flags at half-mast over buildings frequented by rubber dealers, bankers and merchants. At best a few of his old colleagues from Club or committee found their way to the Blacketts' residence to pay their last respects and offer condolences to young Nigel Langfield on his bereavement. If there were not even as many of these as one might have hoped, considering the long and devoted service which Solomon Langfield had bestowed unstintingly on the Colony in a number of different fields of endeavour, it was partly because in these troubled times everyone had difficulties of his own. It was partly, too, because some of those who were among the first to make the sad pilgrimage to take leave of their friend, reported back that Walter was inclined to be moody and odd in his behaviour, feigning not to know why they had come and then, when they had explained, giving the impression that their journey had been a waste of time and that they were disturbing his peace unnecessarily for such a trivial matter. However, with a shrug of his shoulders he would direct them to the room where the body had been laid out (refrigerated fortunately) awaiting mortuary attentions.

No doubt Walter's moody behaviour would have seemed more explicable to the friends of the deceased if they had known the extent of his disappointment over Solomon Langfield's rejection of the match he had proposed between their respective children. Walter was bitter about this. It had been such a good idea. When you are in a pickle as complicated as that which Walter considered himself to be in, with a partner in your company you cannot depend upon with a daughter to marry off, and vast stocks of rubber to ship, it could only be expected that the rejection of a single elegant solution to these disparate problems would come as a blow. Add to that old Solomon Langfield's insulting behaviour and you have enough to make blood bubble in the veins.

A great deal of thought must be given to your daughter's marriage. Otherwise she will simply slink off like a cat on a dark night and get herself fertilized under a bush by God knows whom! Yes, even a sensible daughter will, there's no trusting them, particularly these days ... Or to put it another way, there are no sensible daughters. Not even with a girl like Joan, who had her head screwed on more tightly than most, could you be sure that you would not wake up one morning to find her entangled with some worthless adventurer. Now, although Walter was confident that sooner or later the present difficulties with the Japanese would be overcome and life in Singapore would return to normal, it was increasingly obvious to him that for some time to come the Singapore community would be scattered to the winds. Finding herself in a different environment, in Australia, say, or India, was there not a danger that Joan would lose the sensible perspective she had acquired in Singapore? Yes, there was, and that was why Walter felt he must see Joan married before she left Singapore. The last thing Walter wanted was to find her captivated by some mustachioed flight-lieutenant who happened to catch her fancy because he was serving his country so heroically.

The morning after Langfield had rejected his proposal so impudently Walter had discussed the matter with Joan. 'The old brute was against the idea,' he had explained grimly, 'and even if Nigel was so besotted about you that he was willing to go

421

ahead without the old man's permission, it still wouldn't do any good because if I know Solomon he'd just cut off the funds. Then we'd be stuck with Nigel but with none of the Langfield business which would be the worst possible solution.' Yes, it had begun to seem to Walter that he had left this question of marrying off his daughter until too late. Fate, however, had then taken a hand.

When, in due course, Abdul came to inform Walter, first that *Tuan* Langfield had not risen for breakfast, then that *Tuan* Langfield would not be rising again on this earth, Walter had merely said to himself: 'What a blessed nuisance! Trust that old codger to make a nuisance of himself!' But presently it did occur to him that provided Solomon had not discussed the matter with his son, his death might not be such a nuisance after all. Joan was inclined to share his opinion.

Walter was astonished to see the effect that the news of his father's death had on Nigel. The young man seemed positively afflicted to hear of it; he was visibly on the verge of breaking down. Walter inspected him with curiosity, marvelling at the resources of human nature that could inspire, even for such as Solomon Langfield, an affection so deep. But there was the evidence: Nigel sat before him with his head in his hands, overcome. Such grief could only be respected.

Walter gave Joan a nod and a wink and she advanced to place a comforting hand on the young man's shoulder. Walter himself retired then to brood in his dressing-room. He believed he had thought of a way to bring solace to Nigel in his hour of loss. Thus, later in the morning when Nigel had regained control of himself, Walter summoned him and said: 'My boy, I know how you must be feeling. I won't beat about the bush. Your father and I had our ups and downs but we always respected each other. When you get down to it, you know, we were very much alike in many ways. Well, I hesitate to tell you what I'm going to tell you because I know that he did not want you to be influenced in any way. I think that poor Solomon may have had some intimation that the end was not far away because the other evening, while we were chatting together about old times and the fun we'd had as youngsters in this Colony, he happened to say how concerned he was for the future ... Yes, to put it in a nutshell he told me that he would not be at all averse to seeing you settle down and start a family. "Well, Walter," he said to me, "this may come as a surprise to you, considering the ups and downs we've had in business matters, but there's only one young woman I'd like to see him married to and that's that young woman of yours, Joan." There it is, Nigel, and I was pretty surprised about it, I must say, but once I'd got to thinking about it, why ... Lord, are those the wretched air-raid sirens again?'

'But Mr Blackett!' cried Nigel who in the matter of a few seconds had flushed, turned pale and was now flushing again.

'Dammit! It's only five to ten. This is becoming too much of a good thing ...'

'I thought my father ...'

'Well, there we are. We'll talk about it later ... but of course, only if you want to. Maybe I've been speaking out of turn, maybe I should have kept mum about it: it wasn't an easy decision for me to bring it up. And mind you, I know he didn't want you to be influenced in any way and he even told me that if anything he would pretend to take a dim view of such an arrangement just so that ... Ah, there go the guns! Damn these air-raids! How can we possibly get anything done? By the sound of the guns they seem to be coming our way ... We'd better go to the shelter this time, I think. You go and get Joan and I'll tell the staff to get under cover ...'

There was no time for further discussion. Already the bombs were beginning to fall and the thudding of the anti-aircraft guns matched the thudding of young Nigel's heart as he dashed upstairs to get Joan and bring her to the shelter which Walter had had dug beside the Orchid Garden. This time, it seemed, the Japanese bombers were not going to be content with an attack on Keppel Harbour or the Naval Base: they were setting to work on the city itself and on Tanglin in particular.

Nearby at the Mayfair those of the Major's firemen who were awake after their night's work listened wearily to the sirens. Only when the guns at Bukit Timah opened up did they make a move to take shelter. Here, as almost everywhere else on the island, it was hard to see any distance, except upwards. And so as they struggled out of the building, still red-eyed and bewildered from lack of sleep, they looked upwards ... to see a densely packed wave of Japanese bombers flying at a great height and directly over Tanglin. In a moment the leading bomber would fire a burst of machine-gun fire: at this signal all the planes would drop their bombs at the same moment and there would be havoc on the ground. Meanwhile, a few hundred yards from where they stood the light ack-ack battery over the brow of the hill was blazing away quite uselessly, it seemed, for the bombers were flying well out of range.

Now the aeroplanes above, like monstrous insects, began to deposit batches of little black eggs into the sky and a fearful whistling grew in the air around the men fleeing through the flowerbeds. Soon the shelter was crammed and people flung themselves down in any hole or ditch they could find while the Major, wearing a steel helmet, bundled the girls from the Poh Leung Kuk and other latecomers into the recreation hut whose walls had been padded with rubber bales, mattresses and cushions, more as a gesture than anything else. As he did so the first bomb landed in the long-disused swimming pool sending up a great column of water which hung in the air for a moment like a block of green marble before crashing down again. Another bomb landed simultaneously in the road blowing a snowstorm of red tiles off the Mayfair's roof and out over the compound, and another in the grove of old rubber which lay between the Mayfair and the Blacketts' house. The last explosion, though some distance from both makeshift shelters, was strong enough to blow in one wall of the recreation hut, hurling those who had been huddled against it back into a jumble of cushions, mattresses and struggling bodies: the roof, too, began to sag and utter piercing cracks. In the deep hush which followed, the telephone could be heard ringing, very faintly, in the empty bungalow. People began to extricate themselves from the jumble on the floor of the recreation hut. Nobody seemed to be badly hurt.

Abruptly there was a roar overhead and everyone ducked. 'It's one of the RAF buses!' someone shouted as a Hurricane vanished over the tree tops. A ragged cheer went up. The telephone was still ringing: it seemed a miracle that the wires had not been brought down in the bombing. The Major ran towards the bungalow to answer it. He had to swing himself up by the verandah rail because the wooden steps had been carried away by the blast from the bomb which had fallen in the road and now sagged in a drunken concertina some yards from the building. As he had expected they were being called to a fire: houses and a timber yard between River Valley Road and the river had been set alight.

Shortly afterwards a strange cavalcade was to be seen setting out from the Mayfair. In the lead came the Major's Lagonda towing a trailer-pump, followed by Mr Wu's Buick crammed with passengers. Next came two Blackett and Webb vans commandeered from the nutmeg grove by the Major and it was these which lent the Mayfair unit its air of rather desperate carnival, for there had been no time to unbolt the bizarre wooden super-structure which had been fitted on top of them; besides, it might give added protection from shrapnel. The first van, tow-ing a second, newly acquired trailer-pump, still carried the gigantic facsimilies of red and blue Straits dollar bills, complete with slant-eyed portrait of the King. From the other van eight long arms painted dark brown, light brown, yellow and white, each pair supplied with a papier mâché head, emerged symboli-cally from the jaws of Poverty; since these arms, which were enormously long and stretched forward over the cabin of the van, were supposed to be reaching for Prosperity, it had been collectively decided that the van displaying the dollar bills should go first. Otherwise, as Dupigny remarked, it might almost look as if dollar bills were chasing the representatives of the four races and that they, arms outstretched, were fleeing in terror.

As they emerged on to Orchard Road they saw for the first time the extent of the havoc caused by the air-raid. A stick of high-explosive bombs had fallen along the upper reaches begin-ning near the junction with Tanglin Road and neatly distributing themselves, two on one side, three on the other, reducing a number of buildings to rubble, bringing down overhead cables and smashing shop windows so that the pavements of the covered ways glittered with a frosting of glass. The way into Paterson Road was blocked by a number of blazing vehicles which had been hurled across the road by the blast; a lorry lay upside down, its wheels in the air; everywhere people scrabbled desperately in the rubble searching for survivors. A greyish-white cloud of dust muted the blaze of the burning vehicles and turned the people struggling in the road into figures from a winter scene.

The Major continued down Orchard Road hoping to approach River Valley Road from the other direction; he looked back once or twice to make sure that the others were following. Behind the two vans a motor-cycle brought up the rear of the column, carrying Turner, formerly the manager of the Johore estate, but now obliged by military preparations across the Causeway to return to Singapore, and a Chinese friend of Mr Wu's whose name was Kee, a strong and taciturn individual, extremely courageous.

They had to proceed carefully here, sounding their horns on account of the people, many of them apparently still dazed, some wandering about aimlessly, others laying out the dead and wounded at the side of the road. Once they had to stop while an abandoned vehicle was dragged out of their path; then they came upon an oil-tanker that had collided with a tree but by a miracle had not caught fire. Not far away the Cold Storage had had a near miss and badly shaken shoppers were being helped from the building. Near the vegetable and fruit market next door a block of flats was on fire. A Sikh traffic policeman, still incongruously wearing the basketwork wings that gave him the appearance of a dragon-fly, waved his arms vigorously, trying to direct the Major towards the burning flats. But the Major would not be directed: he had his own fire to go to. As they passed by he saw the policeman sink to his knees and then fold up with his forehead on the sticky tar surface of the road, evidently overcome by shock or concussion: one of his basket wings had been neatly broken in the middle and bent back behind the shoulderblade. A moment later and he had been left behind in the swirling dust and smoke, motionless as a dying insect in the road.

By the time they reached the timber yard two Chinese AFS units were already at work under a detachment from the Central Fire Station but it was clear that there was no chance of saving either the yard itself or the adjoining saw-mills, both of which were well alight. To make matters worse a stiff breeze was blowing from the north-east in the direction of a group of slum tenements standing a little way back from the river: an attempt was being made to arrest the wall of flame advancing towards them.

When the suction hose had been dropped in the river and the delivery hose had been laid out the pumps were started up: the Major and Ehrendorf went ahead with one branch, Mr Wu and Turner with the other. Kee, who was a mechanic, had taken charge of both pumps, assisted by Captain Brown, while Matthew, Cheong, Dupigny and the others ran back and forth as the branches advanced, laying out extra lengths, signalling to the pumps, uncoupling and coupling again, dizzy and breathless with heat. His head spinning, Matthew watched the jets from half a dozen branches curving towards the fire but nevertheless it grew and grew. Flames were now rising over half an acre of piled-up timber and roaring a hundred feet into the air and the water seemed to evaporate before it had time to touch any part of it. Once, when he was accidently splashed by water from another branch on his way to relieve the Major, who was lurching drunkenly and seemed about to fall, Matthew gave an involuntary cry of pain: the water was scalding.

Now the fire, like some inadequately chained-up oriental demon, was roaring and raging on his left, occasionally making sudden darts forward as if to seize him by the leg and drag him back to its lair. Behind him was the river; on his right was a wooden fence and, beyond that, the tenements whose windows he could see were packed with round Chinese heads, like oranges in a box, watching the fire as if it were no concern of theirs. 'Why doesn't someone tell them to hop it?' he shouted at Ehrendorf beside him, but Ehrendorf was too bemused by the heat to reply.

Beside this ocean of flame hours passed in a dream. Every so often the men holding the branch were relieved and led back to splash themselves with the stinking water from the river. Again and again Matthew was scalded with water from another branch, but now he could hardly feel it. One moment he would be drenched from head to foot, the next his clothes would be dry and stiff on his body again.

Suddenly Matthew realized that this fire had a personality of its own. It was not just a fire, in fact, it was a living creature. He tried to explain this to Ehrendorf who was again beside him, holding on like himself to the same struggling branch: he gabbled away laughing at his insight but could not get Ehrendorf to comprehend. But it was so obvious! Not only did this fire have its own delightful fragrance (like sandalwood), it also had a restless and cunning disposition, constantly sending out rivulets of flame like outstretched claws to surround and seize the men fighting it and squeeze them to its fiery heart. But Ehrendorf, on whose forehead a large white blister had appeared, could only shake his head and mumble . . . meanwhile, the blister grew and presently burst and fluid ran down his face but dried instantly, like a trail of tears on his cheeks. These claws of flame which stretched out from the fire, Matthew noticed, very often overran the lengths of bulging hose that lay between the river and the fire and, presently, on one of his stumbling journeys back and forth, he saw that the canvas skin of the hose had already been eaten so thin by the fire that he could see the water coursing through, as if these were semi-transparent veins pulsing in the direction of the fire to supply it with nourishment. But what they were really trying to do was not to nourish it but to poison it. The fire chuckled and crackled cheerfully at this, and said: 'You won't poison *me* so quickly. You'd better watch out for your*self*!'

55

There was something odd about that fire, Matthew found. It hypnotized him. And not only him but everyone else round about. There was another air-raid before the end of the morning, but this time nobody paid it the least attention. The fact that somewhere above the smoke and heat some aeroplanes were dropping bombs seemed, beside that monstrous fire, altogether trivial.

The hours wore on without any appreciable change, except that the heat from the fire seemed to grow more intense. Early in the afternoon another AFS unit arrived and, without a word to anyone, they dropped their hoses into the river and set to work. This new team displayed even greater human variety than the Major's: if you looked at them closely you could see that it included Indians, Malays, Chinese, Europeans and even an African who spoke only French. But these men had been to another fire and their hands and faces were already so blackened and blistered that it had become difficult to tell them apart. They knew what they were about, though, and positioned their branches so that they could control and repulse the restless claws of fire that continually threatened to encircle the Major's men.

Matthew now found that he was present at the fire merely in excerpts with long blank intervals in between: one moment he would be holding the branch with someone else and trying to shield himself from the intense heat, the next he would be slumped on the river bank trying to explain to Ehrendorf how simple it would be for human beings to use co-operation instead of self-interest as the basis of all their behaviour. 'So many people already do!' he exclaimed, but Ehrendorf, who was not as accustomed to fire-fighting as Matthew, looked too distressed to reply. If you looked at teachers and nurses and all sorts of ordinary people, to whom, incidentally, society granted a rather reluctant and condescending respect, there were already many people whose greatest ambition was the welfare of others! Why should this not be extended to every walk of life? Ah, just you wait a moment, he protested, for Ehrendorf was opening and closing his mouth like a goldfish, I know that you want to say that such people, too, are motivated by self-interest but that they get their satisfaction in a different way. That is merely a psychological quibble! There's all the difference in the world between someone who gets his satisfaction from helping others instead of helping himself! Can you imagine how tremendous life would be? Look at all these men at the fire: they'd do anything for each other, though some of them don't even speak the same bloody language! But perhaps Matthew, instead of saying all this, had merely thought it, because when Ehrendorf at last managed to reply, his words did not seem to make any sense.

Ehrendorf, in case he should not survive, was urgently trying to pass on to Matthew his great discovery; Ehrendorf's Second Law! That everything in human affairs is slightly worse at any given moment than at any preceding moment. It was very important that this should be more widely known ...

'Say it again.'

Ehrendorf did so.

'What? But it's not true!'

'Yes it is, if you think about' it.'

'Well, let me see ... Certainly things seem to be getting worse for us in Singapore, but not for the Japanese.'

'Yes, they are getting worse for the Japanese. It only *seems* that they're not. Because things keep happening which don't do anybody any good!'

'Yes, but still there are lots of things ...' Before Matthew could finish what he was saying, however, he found himself back at the fire and feeling dreadfully exhausted. He inspected the person beside him, planning to give him a piece of his mind if it turned out to Ehrendorf. It was ridiculous that a man of his intelligence and culture should not be able to see how important it was that a vast, universal change of heart should take place. It was the only answer.

'You might just as well expect stockbrokers to be ready to die for the Stock Exchange,' chuckled the fire, trying to grasp his ankle with a fiery talon.

The man standing beside him, however, turned out to be not Ehrendorf but Dupigny. Dupigny's normally pallid face had been scorched an angry red by the heat and his hair, cut to about the height of a toothbrush where it flourished most stiffly on the back and sides of his head, appeared to be smouldering. He was about to ask for an explanation of Dupigny's presence when, pausing to blink his sore eyes, he suffered another irritating time slip and was once more holding the branch, but this time with a Chinese on whose face white blisters had risen where the skin covered bone. His face had become unrecognizable but it might have been Kee. Matthew had an urge to finger his own blisters which were becoming extremely painful, but he was afraid that if he removed one hand from the branch he would be too weak to hold it ... it would wrestle him to the ground and flail-out his brains.

From the fire there now came a series of dull reports, as of internal organs swelling and exploding. 'Paint chop!' howled the Chinese beside him, pointing to the depths of the fire where the skeleton of a fiercely burning hut could still be seen. It dissolved as Matthew watched, shielding his eyes. 'What about the tenements?' he asked, unexpectedly finding himself back in reality again. The tenements were still there, certainly, and so was the wooden fence, but the round Chinese heads had departed from the windows. Evidently someone had at last thought of evacuating them, which was just as well because the fire was still lapping in that direction.

Towards the end of the afternoon half a dozen huge cranes which had been towering over the fire in a semi-circle on its south-western fringe began to waver; then, one by one, they slowly buckled, toppling into the fire and sending up great fountains of sparks and burning debris which started fresh fires all around as they fell to earth again; these new fires threatened once more to cut off the men wielding the branches. The Major had become very concerned about the safety of his men and decided on a roll-call: even this was not easy to effect in the dense smoke and ever more intense heat. Finally it was completed. There was one man missing. Nobody had seen Mr Wu since he had been relieved at one of the branches some time earlier: an hour, half an hour? it was impossible to say. But just as they were deciding with dismay that Mr Wu must have been cut off by a subsidiary fire stemming from one of the fallen cranes and consumed, he suddenly reappeared again, as cheerful as ever, together with a lorry loaded with Fraser and Neave's mineral waters which he had somehow commandeered, hired or hijacked ... and not a moment too soon for everyone at the fire was suffering badly from dehydration. The Chinese driver of the lorry, which had evidently been on a delivery round, then volunteered to join the firemen and was promptly enrolled. Next time, the Major reflected, it would be as well to bring food and drink; it had not occurred to him that they might have to spend such a long time away from the Mayfair.

At dusk the fire grew steadily more magnificent. As the sky darkened they became aware that the air was full of drifting sparks which fell around them in a steady golden drizzle which now and again grew more heavy, so that they wondered uneasily whether their clothes might catch fire. Nevertheless, the beauty of this golden rainstorm was such that Matthew was filled with great exhilaration, no longer feeling the sting of sparks on his unprotected face and forearms but gazing about in wonder like a child.

For some time now the fire had ceased to make progress towards the tenements and it was easier in the darkness to spot new advances it tried to make before they had time to become established. But although the fire itself stopped advancing, and even fell back a little, its core in which thousands of tons of logs were being consumed, grew hotter and hotter so that even at a considerable distance it could no longer be faced and the men with the branch could only work for a few minutes at a time. In the gloom it could be seen that the drainpipes on the tenement buildings had begun to glow red-hot, standing out like blood vessels on the dark masses of the buildings. And now the wooden fence spontaneously burst into flame though the fire was nowhere near it: it blazed furiously for a minute or two, then melted away and a rich wine darkness returned.

Some time after midnight Adamson arrived, bringing two more units from another fire at the docks. He made a quick inspection, detailed the new men to hose down the tenement roofs and walls and then, after a word of encouragement to the exhausted men, returned to his own fire at the docks. Not long afterwards it was found that there were two men missing from one of the other AFS units: a frantic search for them began. One was found unconscious not far from the pumps, overcome by the heat and smoke: he was splashed with water from the river and given some lemonade from Mr Wu's lorry. Towards dawn the other man was found dead on the no man's land between the fire and the tenements where he had evidently collapsed. His scanty clothing had been burned off his back and his helmet was glowing a dull red. For some hours it was impossible to retrieve his body and when at last this was done and someone made to grasp his arm to lift him on to a stretcher, the arm came away from the shoulder like the wing of an over-cooked chicken.

The fire reached its zenith at about five o'clock in the morning and thereafter it became possible to drive it back gradually, a few feet hour after hour: the plan was to contain it and let it burn itself out. Abruptly Matthew realized that it was daylight again: standing so close to the fire he had not noticed the sky growing paler. In the darkness it had been difficult to tell the Mayfair men from the others, but in the daylight it was not much easier, so dirty and unkempt were the figures staggering drunkenly about on the uneven ground. Moreover, by now there was so much hose running between the river and the fire that when it became necessary to put in another length it was a laborious job to discover which hose belonged to the Mayfair and which to other units; the job was made even more difficult by the exhausted state that everyone was in, for by now they had been almost twenty hours at the fire and those who fell down found it hard to get up again. At one point, while engaged in a weary search to trace the correct coupling in the hoses which lay like a bundle of arteries half-buried in sodden wood shavings, Matthew stumbled against a man from one of the other companies lying on the ground. 'Thanks, mate, I'm OK,' he said when Matthew tried to help him up. 'I'll be all right in a minute.' He peered up at Matthew, recognizing him. 'You still all right then?' It was Evans, the fireman who had told him about Adamson some days earlier.

'Don't worry, I'll be OK in a minute,' Evans repeated. So Matthew went on searching for the hose he wanted. But half an hour later Evans was still lying there.

Presently Matthew, too, stumbled and fell into a pile of wood shavings: they had a pleasantly fresh scent: he lay with his cheek against them and his head spinning. He felt wonderfully contented, however, and despite his weariness, exhilarated by the sense of comradeship with the other men. After a while he made feeble efforts to get to his feet again, but the best he could do was to sit up. He sat there in the wood shavings between the fire and the river, waiting for the strength to move: the fire was quiet now, and in daylight appeared shabby and dull but it still radiated the same stupendous heat. 'This is the life I should have been living years ago,' he thought, again experiencing an extraordinary sensation of freedom and fulfilment, 'instead of which I've wasted my time with theories and empty disputes! When the war is over I shall make myself useful to someone.'

Presently Ehrendorf and Dupigny came looking for him and between them got him to his feet. The Mayfair unit was being relieved, they told him. He would do better to sleep in one of the roster beds at the Mayfair. As they left, Evans was still lying exhausted on the ground. Hardly had they passed through the shattered streets to the Mayfair when the sirens began to wail once more. Another raid, heavier even than the one on Tanglin, was just beginning on the crowded shop-houses and tenements of the Beach Road area.

56

An indication of communal co-operation was provided yesterday when Indian passive defence volunteers attended to the casualties in their area ... these casualties were mostly Chinese. One of the members of the Indian Youth League, Mr N. M. Marshall, was most helpful in providing a van for the removal of the casualties.

In a certain well-known hotel yesterday a bomb damaged the boys' quarters but this did not prevent patrons from having their midday meal. They went to the kitchen and helped themselves.

WORKERS, every hour counts in the battle for Singapore. Don't let the sirens stop your work. The enemy bombers may be miles away. They may never come near you. Carry on till the roof-spotters give the signal to take cover. The fighting men are counting on you. Back them up in the workshops, shipyards and offices. Every hour's work makes Singapore stronger.

'DIFFICULT TO TAKE SINGAPORE,' SAYS JAP.
'It would be risky to expect that the capture of Singapore will be an easy task to be fulfilled in a short time,' said the spokesman of the Jap War Ministry in a broadcast speech quoted by Rome radio.

Reuter.

In the course of this last week of January the city underwent a final metamorphosis: the peaceful and prosperous city of Singapore which Walter remembered from his early days had already been eroded by time and change, the way all cities are. But now there came a dreadful acceleration: in the course of a few days and nights many familiar parts of the city were demolished. Bombs fell in Tanglin, interrupting his important conversation with Nigel. They were sprinkled through the grounds of Government House and fell in a dense shower on Beach Road. They peppered the docks and the airfields and Bukit Timah. They fell all around the *padang* and the Municipal Offices, shattering windows in High Street and Armenian Street beneath Fort Canning Hill, and blowing out one face of the clock in the tower of the Victoria Memorial Theatre where, in years gone by, Walter had so often gone with other parents to watch the children of the European community in Mr Buckley's Christmas pantomime. 'What was all this, anyway,' mused Walter grimly, 'but the physical evidence of all the more fundamental changes that had taken place in Singapore in the last two decades?'

Walter did not often abandon himself to abstract thought and when he did so it was a sign that he was in a state of depression. He found himself now, however, brooding on what makes up a moment of history; if you took a knife and chopped cleanly through a moment of history what would it look like in cross-section? Would it be like chopping through a leg of lamb where you see the ends of the muscles, nerves, sinews and bone of one piece matching a similar arrangement in the other? Walter thought that it would, on the whole. A moment of

434

history would be composed of countless millions of events of varying degrees of importance, some of them independent, other associated with each other. And since all these events would have both causes and consequences they would certainly match each other where they were divided, just like the leg of lamb. But did all these events collectively have a meaning?

Most people, Walter believed, would have said 'No, they are merely random.' Perhaps sometimes, in retrospect, we may stick a label on a whole stretch of events and call it, say, 'The Age of Enlightenment' the way we might call a long hank of muscle a fillet steak, but we are simply imposing a meaning on what was, unlike the fillet steak whose cells are organized to some purpose, essentially random. Well, if that was what most people thought, Walter did not agree with them.

Certainly, it was not easy to see a common principle in the great mass of events occurring at any moment far and near. But Walter believed that that was because you were too near to them. It was like being a single gymnast in a vast stadium with several thousand other gymnasts: your movements and theirs might seem quite baffling from where you stand whereas viewed from an aeroplane, collectively you are forming letters which spell out 'God Save The King' in a pattern of delightful colours.

Well, what was this organizing principle? Walter was vague about that. He believed that each individual event in a historical moment was subtly modified by an intangible mechanism which he could only think of as 'the spirit of the time'. If a Japanese bomber had opened its bomb doors over Singapore in the year 1920 no bomb would have struck the city. Its bombs would have been lodged in the transparent roof that covered Singapore like a bubble, or bounced off it into the sea. This transparent roof was 'the spirit of those times'. The spirit of these times, unfortunately, allowed the bombs of an Asiatic nation to fall on a British city. Walter had seen the roof growing weaker even during the early thirties: such ruinous Japanese competition in the cotton trade would not have been permitted by the spirit of yet earlier times. Now the bubble no longer covered Singapore at all, or if it did, it let everything through.

Walter's own house had so far escaped damage though it had lost a few windows in the air-raid of 20 January. But the atmosphere of the place had changed considerably since his wife and Kate had left. It was not too bad during the daytime: there was always a good deal of bustle now that he had moved his office staff up here from Collyer Quay. Once the office had closed down for the day, however, an eerie solitude descended on the house. He would sit fidgeting restlessly on the verandah or stroll on the lawn, waiting for the sirens or watching the searchlight batteries fingering the sky. Now he was back sitting on the verandah in darkness.

He was surprised that the absence of his wife and Kate should make such a difference. There were still people about. Nigel and Joan were usually somewhere mooning about the house (thank heaven, at least, that that looked like coming off successfully!). There were still the 'boys' and Abdul, though some of the kitchen staff had made themselves scarce. He occasionally saw Monty sloping in from the direction of the compound. No, what upset Walter was not the absence of people but the absence of normality. Life had taken on an aspect of nightmarish unreality. If someone had told him a year ago that on a certain date in January Solomon Langfield would be found under his roof he would have dismissed the idea as ridiculous. Yet not only was Langfield under his roof (his mortal remains, anyway) but at this very moment he was in the process of being embalmed by Dr Brownley on the dining-room table . . . or would have been if Dr Brownley had known better how to proceed. As it was, for the last few minutes he had been on the telephone asking a colleague for instructions. The line was not a good one and he had to shout. So Walter's melancholy reflections had been punctuated by the medical instructions which Dr Brownley howled for confirmation into the instrument. Evidently he was concerned lest too much time should have elapsed since the old fox had gone to his reward. No wonder then if Walter felt that his grip on reality had loosened.

Embalming old Langfield at a time like this, what an idea! To embalm him at any time would have seemed to Walter an unprofitable undertaking, but with bombs raining on the city and corpses laid out everywhere on the pavements the idea of preserving the old goat was perfectly ludicrous. Yet his board of directors had demanded it 'for the sake of Langfield and Bowser Limited and its British and overseas shareholders' on whose behalf, they had explained, they were making 'this very natural gesture'.

'Very natural indeed!' grumbled Walter to himself. 'What could be more *un*natural? I should have had him stuck under the ground immediately. Mind you, with the sort of man they have on Langfield's board these days they would most likely have been out there in the graveyard at the dead of night helping the company secretary to dig him up again!'

Walter sighed, allowing his mind to wander on to the subject of graveyards ... Poor old Webb must be rotted away by now, he mused. His cane chair squeaked as he shifted about in it restlessly, trying to convince himself that the best thing would be to go inside and deal with some of the paper-work which awaited him. Abruptly he became aware that two wraith-like figures were moving in the shadows beyond the swimming pool. He stirred uneasily, trying to identify them. Nigel and Joan perhaps? But they had gone inside some time ago. The white wraiths shimmered nearer, growing brighter as they left the shadows of the trees and drifted into the open. Voices now reached Walter, raised in argument, and he relaxed for these were not the ghosts of old Webb and old Langfield returning to remonstrate with him from beyond the grave, but Matthew and Ehrendorf haggling over colonial policy well on this side of it.

'If by "progress" you mean the increasing welfare of the native then I'm afraid you're going to have a job proving the beneficial effects of these public works you make such a song and dance about ...' Matthew was saying: he had not forgotten his moment of illumination while sitting exhausted beside the fire at the timber-yard: he still intended to give up theorizing and devote his life to practical work of some kind. But there were one or two arguments he felt he had to finish first; besides, the mere presence of Ehrendorf, even mute, was enough to start his brain secreting theories and his tongue expressing them. As for Ehrendorf, he was peering ahead at the dark house with trepidation, half hoping, half dreading that they would bump into Joan. A moment ago he had bravely offered to accompany Matthew across the compound to see Walter about something, but he had not expected to feel quite so vulnerable.

'I suppose you're talking about railways ... In our African colonies something like three-quarters of all loans raised by the colonial governments are for railways. True, they're useful for administration ... but what they're mainly useful for is opening up great tracts of land to be developed as plantations by Europeans. In other words, it's done not for the natives' benefit but for ours! To which you will reply, Jim, that what benefits us, benefits them ... To which I reply ... "Not necessarily so!" To which you reply ...'

'Wait a moment,' came Dr Brownley's voice faintly to Walter on the darkened verandah, interrupting Matthew who had been

437

gripped by such a frenzy of abstractions that he had been obliged to commandeer both sides of the argument. 'Let me make quite sure that I've got the embalming fluid down properly ... I repeat ... Liquor formaldehyde, 13·5cc. Sodium borate, 5 grammes ... and water to make up to 100cc. Is that correct? Yes, I see ... And with what? A bicycle pump?'

'A bicycle pump!' thought Walter giddily.

Meanwhile, as a descant to Dr Brownley's rather anxious elucidations (the good doctor, though for years he had been medical officer to Langfield and Bowser Limited, had never been faced with such a problem before ... And just think of it! The Chairman himself! A heavy responsibility indeed!) there came Ehrendorf's reasonable tones, gently chiding Matthew for being selective in his view of railways in the colonies, for conveniently forgetting their positive aspects ...

'What we are doing is subsidizing the white man's business operations at the expense of native welfare ... Now, I agree with you, this would not matter if the profits stayed where they were produced, *but they don't* ... they're whipped off back to Britain, or France, or Belgium or Holland or wherever ...'

'A three-gallon bottle with two glass tubes passing through the rubber stopper, yes, I've got that ... One tube reaches the bottom of the bottle to take up the liquid and pass it out to a rubber tube and then to the injection canula. I see. The other glass tube through the stopper you attach to the bicycle pump ... Oh, I see, a foot pump ... I thought you might mean ...'

'Let's not forget that railways act as an instrument of civilization,' said Ehrendorf vaguely, his eyes probing the darkness for some sign of hope, 'bringing isolated people into contact with the modern world.'

'Slavery used to be defended in those very words! Besides, in Africa natives died by the hundreds of thousands just in building the damn things. Look at the Belgian Congo under Leopold! You see, what I'm trying to explain is how everything in a colony, even beneficial-sounding things like railways and experimental rice-growing stations, are set up in one way or another to the commercial advantage of the Europeans or Americans with money invested in the country ...'

'D'you mind if we just go over the sites of injection once more,' cried Dr Brownley in a voice of despair. 'No, operator, this is an important matter, a matter of life and death. I'm a doctor, will you kindly get off the line, please. Now, fluid equal to fifteen per cent of body weight into the arterial system?

450 cc to a pound, yes, I've got that. Two per cent body weight to be injected into each femoral artery towards the toes. One per cent into each brachial artery towards the fingers, yes. One common carotid artery towards head with two per cent. Inject same carotid towards heart with seven per cent. Total amount of fluid should come to fifteen per cent body weight. What happens, though, if the blood in the artery has clotted, as I'm afraid it might have by now, and you can't force the fluid in? Wait a moment, I'm trying to note it down, yes ... the extremity should be wrapped in cotton wool soaked in the fluid and then bandaged ... and you keep on soaking the cotton at intervals. Good. Another thing I want to know is whether one has to inject fluid into the thoracic and abdominal cavities?'

'How frightful!' thought Walter, and despite the heat his skin became gooseflesh and even the bristles on his spine rose in horror. Meanwhile, the two young men had reached the foot of the white marble steps which curved up to the portico and thence to the verandah. Still talking nonsense they began to ascend.

'How about the rights of the individual, imported along with a Western legal system? Isn't that worth having, Matthew?'

'Freedom of the individual at the expense of food, clothing and a harmonious life, of being swindled by a system devised to the advantage of those with capital? If you had asked the inmates of the coolie barracks in Rangoon, dying by their hundreds from malnutrition and disease, I'm sure they would have told you that wonderful though being free was, just at the moment so wretched was their condition that it wasn't much help. It's no good calling somebody free unless he's economically free, too, at least to some extent ... Is it? ... however much lack of individual freedom may horrify an English intellectual sitting at his desk with a hot dinner under his belt.'

'Yet even if one admits, and I'm not saying I do,' replied Ehrendorf, 'that the natives in British and other colonies have been placed at a disadvantage, or even swindled and abused, can you actually say that they would have been better off left strictly alone? You could say that the coming of Western capital is simply a bitter pill that they have to swallow if they are ever to achieve a higher state of civilization ... In others words, that capitalism is like a disease against which no traditional culture anywhere has any resistance and that, in the circumstances, in Malaya and other colonies it could have been worse and will certainly get better.'

'Perhaps,' said Matthew dubiously, 'at some future period

men will be able to look back and say, why, it was merely a bitter pill they had to swallow before achieving their present state of felicity, but for the moment, although it's clear what they've lost with their traditional way of life, it's not so easy to see what they've gained. Improved medicine in some places, but mainly to combat new illnesses we've brought with us. Education ... largely to become unemployable or exploited clerks in the service of our businesses or government departments ... And so on.'

'I say, Walter, are you there?' called Dr Brownley who had left the telephone and was peering uneasily out on to the darkened verandah. 'Oh, there you are, I didn't see you at first. What a business!' he added, mopping his brow. 'It seems we must wash the entire body with the fluid, including the face, ears and hair ... and we can get rid of any post-mortem staining of the face by massage.'

Walter did not reply. He was looking at the silhouettes of Matthew and Ehrendorf who had paused by the wire door to the verandah and were looking out towards the restlessly moving searchlights over the docks. Dr Brownley, distraught, began to think of a matter which had occupied his mind almost exclusively for the past few days: walking with an innocent mind and a serene, untroubled expression on his face along the street his eye had happened to stray to Whiteaway's window and there, alas, had found itself locked in the basilisk stare emitted by a certain article of an almost infinite desirability, agreed, but costing $985.50. How could a man afford such a price? Yes, but how could a man do without such an article? These were the horns of the Doctor's dilemma. But first he would have to deal with this dreadful business of embalming old Langfield.

'There's only one way, it seems to me,' said Matthew with a sigh, 'in which our colonies could begin to get the benefits of their contact with us ...'

'And what's that, I should like to know?' came Walter's forbidding voice from within, startling the two young men.

'Oh, hello, Walter. Well, by kicking us out and running the mines and plantations for their own profit instead of ours. In other words, a revolution!' He smiled wearily. 'The only trouble with a revolution is that it seldom improves things and very often makes them worse.'

'Obviously they too are subject to my Second Law,' smiled Ehrendorf.

'But it wasn't that that I wanted to see you about, Walter. I wanted to ask for your help in another matter entirely.'

'And what might that be?' Walter did not sound encouraging. Matthew explained that he was trying to help Miss Chiang to leave Singapore because she would run a particular risk if the city fell to the Japanese. It seemed impossible, however, to get her the necessary passport and permit to leave. Perhaps Walter could do something ...?

'I don't see how I can help,' said Walter testily. 'With all the red tape I can't get anything done myself these days.' Although there was some truth in this, Walter would not have felt inclined to help in any case. He considered it a sign of 'the spirit of the times' that Matthew should be seeking a favour for a Eurasian woman with little concern for propriety as if she were his wife.

'I thought it might be easier to get her an exit permit if she were travelling with someone who had a British passport. Presumably Joan will be leaving soon? Perhaps she could go with Joan if you have no objection?'

'That's up to Joan,' replied Walter shortly. 'You'd better ask her and Nigel.' From his tone it was plain that he did not want to discuss the matter further.

When the two young men had retreated, in silence this time, the way they had come, the Doctor cleared his throat. 'I say, Walter, d'you think you could give me a hand in the dining-room for a few minutes. I can't get hold of anyone to help me on account of these damned air-raids. This job shouldn't be too difficult, fortunately, but I've never had to do it before ... And by the way, please don't let me forget to plug the anus, mouth and nostrils with cotton soaked in the embalming fluid. Oh yes, and what I wanted to ask you was this: do you think that the Langfield and Bowser shareholders will want to keep the body a long time? I mean, they aren't thinking of keeping it in a glass case in the board-room or anything like that, are they? Because the thing is this: if they do want to keep it we shall have to rub it with plenty of Vaseline and bandage it to prevent it from drying out ... I say, Walter, is anything the matter?'

57

'I'll make sure that she has money, of course, and take care of the ticket. We think it may be easier to get her an exit permit if she is employed, at least nominally, by someone with a British passport. She won't be any trouble, Joan, I guarantee.'

'Nigel,' Joan called to her fiancé, invisible in the room behind her, 'Matthew wants to know if we can take someone with us? I don't think we can, can we?'

'I don't think you realize how urgent it is . . .'

'A Eurasian girl, you say? An *amah*? A servant? Really, it's impossible.'

'Not a servant . . . a friend.'

'I'm sorry.'

'Joan, this isn't just anyone. It's someone you *know*. She'll be in deadly danger if the Japanese ever take Singapore and she's still here. Vera has told me that you were there when the Japs arrested her in Shanghai . . . You know better than anyone what will happen to her if they find her here!'

'Nigel, there's nothing we can do, is there?'

A voice called something from the interior of the room which Matthew was unable to make out.

'Sorry, Miss Chiang should have thought about all this earlier in the day. There's nothing we can do, I'm afraid.'

'To hell with you then, you bitch!' cried Matthew in a voice that took even him by surprise.

Since the air-raids which had on successive days devastated Tanglin, Beach Road and the central part of the city, many Europeans had at last come to realize the extreme danger that they ran. Even if it were improbable that the Japanese would be permitted to land on Singapore Island itself, the fact remained that their air force, whose control of the sky was no longer seriously disputed by the few and rapidly diminishing fighters of the RAF, could inflict all the damage that was necessary. Such was the confidence of the Japanese bombers that they now droned constantly over the city in daylight, flying at a great height, twenty thousand feet or more, in enormous packs that for some reason were always in multiples of twenty-seven, causing Europeans below to think that there must be something sinister and unusual about Japanese arithmetic. At such a height they were well beyond the range of the light anti-aircraft guns which made up the greater part of Singapore's air defences. And so the truth had begun to dawn on the inhabitants of the city: if attacked from the air they were defenceless.

Many European women who had bravely declared that they would 'stay put' now had second thoughts or at least yielded to the demands of their men-folk that they should leave forthwith. The result was that every day crowds assembled at the shipping offices in search of passages to Europe, Australia or India. But, although earlier in the month many ships had sailed from Singapore with room to spare (Mrs Blackett and Mrs Langfield had marvelled at the deserted decks and echoing staterooms of the *Narkunda*) now, quite suddenly it seemed, you were lucky to find a berth on any sort of vessel going anywhere. Partly this was the result of the chaos in the docks, where unloading had almost seized up under the bombing; partly it was the result of the diminished ability of the RAF to defend incoming convoys in the sea approaches to the Island, now rendered hazardous to a distance of twenty miles or more by prowling Japanese bombers.

Matthew's efforts to help Vera had so far been frustrated as much by the perplexing regulations which governed departure from the Colony as by the rapidly swelling numbers of those who wanted to leave. Moreover, so much of his time was taken up by his duties as a fireman that he had little time or energy to spare to help and encourage her. One of the major difficulties was to find *somewhere for her to go*. After a series of tiring and time-consuming enquiries he had at length succeeded in discovering that it was government policy that women and children, irrespective of race, should be allowed to leave if they wanted to. To begin with he had thought it would be best to send Vera to Australia ... but Australia had agreed to accept only a limited number of Asiatics and Vera had returned empty-handed from their temporary immigration office, depressed and exhausted after many hours of waiting.

Why had she been refused? Were her papers not in order or was there some other reason? Vera shook her head; she had been unable to get any explanation from the harassed and impatient officials at the office. Her papers certainly did not look very convincing. Under the Aliens Ordinance, 1932, she had been given merely a landing-permit which she had been obliged to exchange for a certificate of admission valid for two years and renewable. Matthew nudged his glasses up on his nose and examined the document despondently: it identified Vera merely as a landed immigrant resident in the Straits Settlements. If she needed a passport would she be able to get one at this eleventh hour? And what country would give her a passport? Time was running out so quickly. He was somewhat heartened, however, by the knowledge that it was official government policy that Vera, in common with other women, should leave if she wanted to.

Next, Vera had gone to another office to enquire whether she would be permitted to go to India. She had again been obliged to wait for many hours and once more it had proved to be in vain. On this occasion, although there had been no racial difficulty as there had been with Australia, she had been asked for evidence that she would have enough money to support herself in India. She had had none and by the time Matthew had taken out a letter of credit for her with the Hong Kong and Shanghai Bank and sent her back again another two precious days had passed and she was once more obliged to join a long line of anxious people besieging the office ... it had closed before she had been able to get anywhere near the counter. To make matters worse, Matthew could see that with weariness and disappointment Vera had grown fatalistic: she no longer believed that she would be allowed to leave Singapore before the Japanese arrived. Matthew, who in the meantime had been waiting fruitlessly on her behalf in another equally anxious queue at the Chinese Protectorate to apply for an exit permit, had secretly begun to wonder whether she might not be right. However, he did his best to reassure her, saying that certainly she would be able to escape and that the Japanese would be most unlikely to take Singapore.

Matthew was so tired these days that his few off-duty hours were spent in a waking trance. If he so much as sat down for a moment he was liable to fall asleep immediately; it seemed that his mind would only work in slow motion. If only he had had time to sleep he felt he might have been able to think of some solution, some way of getting through this baffling maze of administrative regulations. Add to that the difficulty, under constant air-raids, of accomplishing the most simple formalities. In search of a document you went to some office, only to find that it had been evacuated, nobody knew where. Then further exhausting searches through other offices, which themselves might have removed themselves to a safer area outside the city, would be necessary before you could locate the office you wanted.

While in the queue at the Chinese Protectorate Matthew had been told by some of the other people waiting that Vera would need passport photographs in order to obtain her exit permit. She had none and these days it had become impossible to obtain them. Change Alley, which had once swarmed with photographers who were only too willing to snap you in any official pose you wished, or even in a grotto of cardboard tigers and palms, was deserted, for the photographers had all been Japanese and were now interned. So what was to be done? Matthew considered buying a camera and taking the photographs himself, but this was hardly a solution: he would still have to find someone to develop and print them. To make matters worse Matthew had heard from the Major, who had heard from someone at ARP headquarters, that the troopships, the *West Point* and the *Wakefield*, which were bringing the 18th Division, would soon be able to take a great number of women and children to safety, provided that they could avoid the Japanese bombers. To know that only bureaucratic formalities prevented Vera from having this chance of escape filled Matthew with bitterness and despair. After five days of roaming the hot and increasingly ruined city with her in the last week of January, obliged to take shelter at intervals in the nearest storm-drain, he felt utterly exhausted and demoralized.

'Don't worry, we'll find a way,' he told her as he was leaving her one evening after another unsuccessful search for a photographer. 'Didn't you once have a camera?' He remembered that she had wanted to show him some pictures of his father. Yes, but it had only been a box-camera and anyway it had been stolen. Vera was lying on her bed in an odd, crumpled position, the very picture of hopelessness. She gave him a wan smile however, and told him in turn not to worry. After he had gone, she would get up and go and see someone she knew who might be able to help. Some hours later, returning from the docks with the Mayfair AFS unit, he passed near where she lived and asked the Major to stop for a moment so that he could ask whether she had been successful. With refugees from across the Causeway the number of people living in Vera's tenement had greatly increased and he had difficulty making his way past those sleeping on the stairs and in the corridor. When he had at last reached Vera's cubicle he found that she was still lying on the bed in the same odd position, just as he had left her. It seemed that she no longer even had the will to move.

'You must come with me to the Mayfair,' he said. 'Bring a toothbrush and whatever else you need.

But Vera shook her head. 'No Matthew, I am better to stay here. Soon I will feel better.'

'But it's dangerous here. You're too near the river and the docks.'

Again she shook her head. Nothing he could say would make her change her mind.

'I must go. They're waiting for me outside. You stay here and rest ... I know how tired you must be. And don't worry about the photographs. I'll think of something ...'

Having returned to the Mayfair still, despite his reassuring words to Vera, without any idea of what to do next, Matthew was greeted by the smiling face of Mr Wu, to whom he had already spoken of the difficulty of finding a photographer. Mr Wu had thought of a solution to the problem in the meantime. He had an interest in a Chinese newspaper which would undoubtedly employ a photographer. It would take nothing more than a telephone call: by evening Vera would have her photographs. It seemed almost too good to be true.

Tired though he was, Matthew set off again, this time on a bicycle he had borrowed, to tell Vera the good news. The streets were just beginning to get light; in Chinatown the first shadowy figures were emerging after the night's curfew. On his way along Southbridge Road, however, he was astonished to see that a great crowd of women and children had already formed outside one of the buildings and he thought: 'Good heavens! What can they possibly want at this time in the morning?' But then he realized that they were waiting outside the passport office for it to open and his heart sank at the thought that the photographs were only the beginning.

Vera had been asleep: she gazed at him with dulled eyes as he told her about the photographs.

'Don't you see!' he exclaimed irritably. 'Now we'll be able to get the exit permit and everything else!' He was angry with her for not having reacted with more enthusiasm. It seemed that she had given up hope at the very moment that they had a chance of success. But his anger melted away almost immediately. 'You mustn't give up hope,' he said more gently. 'When did you last have something to eat?' He went out then to the food-stalls at the end of the street and presently returned with some soup and a dish of fried rice. He had to feed her with chopsticks, like a child: she was utterly exhausted. While he fed her he spoke to her encouragingly: when they had the photographs they would go to the Chinese Protectorate and get her an exit permit and whatever else was needed. After all, the Government wanted her to leave: they said so! Then they would get her a berth on a boat to Colombo or, failing that, to England. He would have money sent to a bank there for her. She could stay in a hotel and he would join her as soon as he could get away from Singapore. By tomorrow evening or perhaps the one after that, they should have all the necessary papers: then they could go together and register her name at the P & O office. They would certainly be in time to get her on one of the ships that were due to leave soon.

'I don't want to leave without you.'

'But you must. If the Japs take Singapore ...'

'You always said they wouldn't,' she said, smiling at last.

'Well, perhaps not. Who knows?' Matthew no longer knew himself whether he believed that Singapore would hold out. 'I must go now before the morning raids begin. Is there anywhere for you to shelter if the bombers come this way?'

Vera shook her head. 'Don't worry. I feel better now.' She smiled again and squeezed his hand. 'I'm sorry to have been "a weak link".'

'You're not a weak link,' said Matthew, delighted to see her more cheerful. 'Don't forget to eat something today, even if it's only a pair of white mice on toast.'

58

In these last days of January it had become General Percival's habit to rise before dawn and spend an hour in his office before leaving by car for Johore just over the Causeway where the fighting was now taking place. As a rule, therefore, it was still dark outside the bathroom window while he was shaving. But he had had a restless night and had reached the bathroom a little later than usual: the sky was already brightening as he rubbed a finger over his bristly chin. In the course of the night two matters of enormous importance had loomed-up over his half-sleeping mind saying: 'Remember us tomorrow!' But now, as he delved to drag them into the light, he could scarcely believe that he had taken them seriously. One of these anxieties had concerned transport: the prospect that every motor-car and lorry in his Army might have a simultaneous puncture causing the entire force to freeze up had afflicted him dreadfully. Was it nothing more than that? Evidently not.

Well, what was the other worry? During the night he had decided that he must issue orders to the effect that all dripping taps, both civilian and military, must be turned off at the main forthwith or provided with new washers. This was ridiculous too, but at least he knew what had caused it. The day before he had had a brief word with Brigadier Simson, the Director-General Civil Defence, who had made some gloomy observations about Singapore's water supply: it appeared that out here in the tropics where there was no danger of pipes freezing up, the municipal engineers did not bury them deep underground as they did in England: hence they were vulnerable to bombs. Already there had been considerable damage.

In a moment of intuition he realized, too, the source of his worry about punctures ... it was the fear that both the 53rd (British) Brigade and the Segamat force might be cut off by the Japanese before they had time to retreat through the bottleneck at Yong Peng. But that was a danger which was now in the past, thank heavens. Strange that it should continue even so to torment him in his dreams. But ... he brushed all that aside. He had more important things to think about.

As he began to shave, though, he did not think about them. He began to think about other things, about the Governor, and about oil dumps, and about his mother in Hertfordshire. What a terrible year 1941 had been! And yet it had seemed to start off so well with his appointment as GOC Singapore. In April, even before he had left England, his mother had died suddenly. She had been getting on in years, mind you, but it had been a heavy blow, nevertheless. All the same, once or twice recently when he had been in low spirits, it had occurred to him that perhaps, after all, her death had been a blessing in disguise, sparing her from unnecessary suffering on his account.

He stood poised, razor in hand, gazing at his lathered face in the mirror. A commander must be a man of strength of purpose and authority, like General Dobbie who had once no doubt shaved in this very mirror. But his own face with its thick white beard of lather looked encouragingly commanding and purposeful. With care, for he had been a staff officer long enough to know that one must be scrupulous in attention to detail, he began to attack the fringes of the lather, driving it inwards from its perimeter at ears and throat with tiny strokes of the blade in the direction of chin, lips and moustache. Here he would presently have it surrounded, if his experience was anything to go by, and would finish it off with a few decisive strokes.

Meanwhile, his mind had begun to feed once more on that run of bad luck which had assailed him so abruptly. His mother had not been dead a year and yet his whole career and perhaps even his life itself were in jeopardy. He had served on the Western Front in the Great War and had kept his eyes open. Yes, he knew what was what! For the truth was, if you were not on the Western Front you were *nowhere* ... at least as far as the Powers That Be were concerned. The same thing went for this war, too. Right from the start he had been in no doubt about that. You only had to look at the obsolete equipment and untrained men, the odds and ends and riff-raff from India and Australia, all speaking different tongues. You only had to look at the way his best officers had been milked off to lend tone to the Middle Eastern and European theatres to know that Malaya Command was not very much in anybody's thoughts in Whitehall. The big reputations would be made in Europe: it had happened before and it would happen again. Europe was the fashionable place for a soldier to display his skills. Out here a man could perform miracles of military strategy and much good would it do him! Nobody would pay the slightest attention. But make a blunder and, ah! then it would be different.

'Out here you can destroy your career in two shakes, but can you make one? Not an earthly.'

The door-handle rattled faintly as someone tried it discreetly from the outside, but it was locked. Could that be Pulford up and about already? Percival paused again, this time about to launch a flanking attack along his jaw from the direction of his right ear. If it *was* Pulford, he himself must be running even later than he had realized. He usually beat Pulford to the breakfast table. Poor Pulford! His career, too, depended on obsolete equipment ... fancy having to send up the poor old Vildebeeste against modern Jap fighter planes! He had taken a liking to Pulford partly through loneliness, for neither man had brought out his family; he had not for a moment regretted inviting him to come and live here. One needed a staunch friend in a place as full of intrigue and back-biting as Singapore.

'They're all watching out for their own interests, every man jack of 'em, beginning with the Governor!'

How could the GOC Malaya be expected to defend a country whose civilians devoted their every effort to baulking his initiatives? What had happened to the Straits Settlements Volunteer Force, for instance? You might well ask! Volunteer force indeed! When he had tried to call up part of it for training the civilians had created such a song and dance that the Government had insisted on his abandoning the rest of the training programme. Why? Because a rash of strikes on the plantations had been blamed on the fact that the Europeans were absent ... while the truth of the matter was that they were not paying their workers enough. Naturally, he had protested. A waste of time! The Governor had waved some instructions from the Colonial Office in his face: these declared that exemption from training should not be what he (the GOC) considered practicable 'but what he, the Governor, thought was necessary to keep up tin and rubber production'.

And now, when retreat to the Island had become inevitable (as you were! 'withdrawal' to the Island), would you believe it? He was up to his tricks again. This time Sir Shenton was declining to intervene with the Chinese Protectorate who were refusing exit permits to Chinese who wanted to leave the Colony. He had done his best to spell it out to the Governor: in a very short time they would find themselves under siege on an island already teeming with refugees. Non-combatants must not only be allowed but *encouraged* to leave, if necessary *made* to leave. But oh no, the Governor would not listen ... for him this exit permit business was just another chapter in a story which had begun long before the Japanese had invaded. Sir Shenton Thomas was too august a figure to consider explaining himself to the GOC. But Percival had heard the story anyway from other sources. It seemed that the Chinese community had conceived a violent dislike of two senior officials of the Chinese secretariat: this pair were obsessed by the need to root out Communist infiltrators and even with the Japanese sweeping through Johore the fervour of their anti-Communist mission remained undimmed. It would have been sensible to get rid of these men months ago, to get the Chinese population firmly on the British side, but this the Governor would not do. The dignity of the British Government was at stake. You could not, in his opinion, start giving way to demands from the local population. Well, so much the worse for everyone. Other people had remonstrated with the Governor: Simson, the DGCD, for example, and a number of influential Chinese businessmen. Many Chinese would be on the Japanese death-list if Singapore fell. But it had been to no avail.

Percival had been scraping steadily at his commanding, white-bearded face. Gradually, as the razor advanced and the white beard fell away, the features in the mirror had grown more uncertain: a rather delicate jaw had appeared, followed by a not very strong chin and a mouth not sufficiently assertive for the moustache on its upper lip. Nevertheless, it was the face of a man anxious to do his best. Percival washed it carefully and mopped it, gasping slightly. As he did so the door-handle turned again. 'Just a minute,' he called. Silence and a vague air of expectation was all that came from the other side of the door. But why, Percival wondered, should Pulford want to use this bathroom when he had one of his own? Perhaps it was simply that he had left his shaving-tackle here. No doubt this rather unimpressive toothbrush was his; Percival inspected with disapproval its splayed and wilting bristles; it looked as if his batman had been cleaning his cap-badge with it.

His eyes moved back to the mirror to study with sympathy his clean-shaven but drawn features. Weariness was becoming a disease of epidemic proportions in Singapore these days and the past week had, perhaps, been the most exhausting in his life, spent in long car journeys back and forth to the front for conferences with his commanders. He had decided, however, that if disaster were not to ensue he must supervise the defence of Johore himself.

Alas, even this, he reflected, scrubbing his prominent teeth with tooth-powder from the round tin by the mirror, had not been enough, for Gordon Bennett had blundered. In Percival's view it was not surprising that he had blundered, given his mentality and erratic behaviour. It was unfortunate that nothing could be done about Bennett without risk of offending the Australian Government. Bennett, moreover, had made a good impression on Wavell who had lately insisted on putting him in charge of the vulnerable west coast in the place of the battered III Corps. Good impression notwithstanding it was Bennett who had left the unfortunate, untrained 45th Indian Brigade to secure his communications on the coast from the Muar River southwards against amphibious attacks that were all too predictable. The Japanese had naturally made short work of encircling the 45th Brigade and all subsequent efforts to rescue them had failed. Indeed, one had to be thankful that in the end it had been possible to withdraw the rest of the force by the trunk road and railway without having a substantial part of it cut off by the Japanese strike from the coast. Percival heaved a sigh. By now it was clear in any case that a retreat to Singapore Island would be inevitable.

There had been moments since the opening of the war in Malaya when Percival had been visited by an exceedingly curious notion. Though he had done his best, as a pragmatic military man, to shrug it off, it had nevertheless returned more and more frequently in the past few days. Now it entered his mind again as he wearily threw his towel over his shoulder and unlocked the bathroom door. 'Good morning,' he said to Pulford who was hovering dejectedly in the corridor in a pair of pyjamas of Air Force blue. Pulford, too, had a thin face but more deeply lined than his own and with ears that stood out sharply from the side of his head; his moustache, moreover, was distinctly less generous ... a mere smudge around the channel beneath his nose, creeping a little way out along his upper lip. Still, his features gave the impression of a decent and dependable sort of man. 'You need a new toothbrush, old chap,' Percival told him as he continued along the corridor. 'Do I?' asked Pulford, somewhat taken aback.

This exchange, unfortunately, had not been quite enough to distract Percival's attention from his new train of thought, which could be summarized in one simple question. Had this entire campaign, in which tanks, ships and aeroplanes had taken part and in which thousands of men had already died, been staged or devised by Fate or by some unseen hand simply in order to make a mockery of his own private hopes and ambitions? Percival was not accustomed to think in such terms. He was a practical man. He did not believe in 'unseen hands'. That sort of thing was balderdash in his view. He still thought so ... yet the way in which, time and again, a flaw had appeared in his defences, first on one flank, then on the other ... the way in which there always proved to be just one missing element (the aircraft carrier, for instance, which would have prevented the sinking of the *Prince of Wales* and the *Repulse* but which had *gone aground* on the way to Singapore: how often in a man's lifetime does an aircraft carrier go aground that it should do so on the only occasion that he needed it?), a missing element which in due course would bring down a crucial part of the defensive edifice he had been trying to construct, this had begun to have its effect on Percival as it would on any reasonable man.

It was easy, Percival knew, when a fellow got tired for him to get things out of proportion. He was tired. He knew that, admitted it straight out. Still, he was aware of the risk and was determined to be objective. He was only interested in what the evidence had to say. Well, the fact was that all these apparently random acts of fate, all these strokes of bad luck, had now begun (for the man putting his thin legs into shorts wide enough to have accommodated not only the GOC but a member of his staff into the bargain) to appear suspiciously weighted against him. For if you looked at what had happened carefully enough and remained objective, you could see that some hidden hand had been tampering with what one might reasonably expect to have been the normal course of events. It was as if, to speak plainly, on life's ladder some unseen hand had all but sawn through a number of the more important rungs.

The defence of Malaya had been organized before the war on the assumption that the RAF would deal with enemy forces before they had a chance to get ashore. But, in the event, the RAF, suffering from a suspicious lack of planes, had been quite unable to do this. Well, never mind. They were busy elsewhere. Such things do happen. But if, having put your foot on the RAF rung and heard it snap under your weight you thought, well, you still had your other foot on the strike across the Siamese border, here, too, you would have found yourself treading all too firmly on thin air, for the man in charge of that operation had been poor old Brookers, an actor quite improbably cast in the rôle of Commander-in-Chief, Far East.

A commander, as Percival very well knew, cannot always have things his own way. But when *everything* is designed to frustrate him he may well begin to wonder. To be expected to fight against trained men with untrained men, to fight without naval or air support worth mentioning through a sweltering country of apathetic natives and exasperating Europeans whose only aim is to obstruct him, frankly that is too much: he begins to see that he is the victim of some pretty curious circumstances.

Consider for a moment the defence of Johore that he had been trying to organize. When he had been GSO1 to General Dobbie in 1937 fixed defences had been planned for Johore to protect Singapore Island from overland attack. But where were they now that overland attack had developed? They were non-existent. Very well. Consider now Gordon Bennett, the man in command of the Australian Imperial Force in Malaya on whom he had to rely for the defence of Johore (with 'Piggy' Heath, of course, and his Indians). It was common knowledge that Bennett had been repeatedly passed over for the command of Australian forces sent to the Middle East; he was considered too difficult and erratic. There was no prospect, you might have thought, of such a man (a man of whom both the Australian War Minister and the Chief of the General Staff disapproved) being given command of the Australians in Malaya. So you might have thought. But already the sound of discreet sawing could be heard and presently these two influential men who disapproved of Bennett (the War Minister and the Chief of the General Staff) trod simultaneously on another weakened rung and the plane in which they were both travelling crashed in Canberra. They were replaced by men partial to Gordon Bennett. Aha! Bennett had wasted no time in promoting in turn Lieutenant-Colonel Maxwell, an 'amateur' militia soldier and peacetime doctor, over the heads of more senior battalion commanders to take command of the 27th Australian Brigade on its way to Malaya. Maxwell, by the way, liked to keep his HQ near to Bennett's in case he should need a spot of assistance. Maxwell, a rank outsider!

Or consider how Johore had been lost: that is to say, as a result of their inability to secure either flank against amphibious landings. The fortunes of war? But this would not have come about if that aircraft carrier had not gone aground in Jamaica and if the *Prince of Wales* and the *Repulse* had not in consequence been lost. But no, let us not be difficult. Let the carrier go aground! Sink the ships! It was a cruel and unexpected blow but never mind, he would bow his head. A commander sometimes had to put up with cruel and unexpected blows. Yes, but what he should not have to put up with is that faint rasp of metal teeth on wood! For if he followed the naval situation a little further back and strained his ears Percival could hear it again, quite clearly, that discreet rasping sound. He was now thinking of the French Far Eastern Fleet and how eager it had been to join the British in Singapore. It would have made all the difference, too, no doubt about it. But beneath the loyalty of Admiral Decoux, that friend and admirer of the British, that most patriotic of men (you might have thought) a sinister little cone of sawdust was beginning to pile up. The only man who could prevent the French fleet joining the British had, by an unfortunate coincidence (rasp! rasp! rasp!), a secret ambition to become Governor-General of Indo-China.

Percival stifled a groan and stood up to draw in the double-pronged buckle of his Sam Browne belt, passing the shoulder-strap beneath the flap on the right shoulder of his shirt; as he did so his groping fingers touched the solid little crown on his shoulder-flap and the sensation brought with it a sharp reminder of his rank and duties. If it was his job to fight not only the Japanese but an unseen hand as well, then so be it. It was his duty to get on with the job and leave the speculation to future historians who, he did not doubt, would not fail to find something fairly fishy about the way events had coincided against him. He glanced at the rectangular face of his wrist-watch. How late it was! No wonder Pulford had been trying to get into the bathroom. On his way down the corridor he glimpsed Pulford through the half-open door of his room in the act of adjusting a sock-suspender around a grey calf.

Breakfast. A cool and succulent slice of papaya, tea and toast. When he had finished he went directly to his office to study the latest situation reports and evaluate the night's events. Then, with the balding, long-nosed, rather grim figure of the Brigadier General Staff, he went through the agenda for the daily meeting of the War Council: he must remember to have a final shot at getting the Governor to do something about exit permits for the Chinese if it were not already too late. Should he not be back from Johore Bahru in time the BGS would have to attend the War Council meeting in his place. Today, 28 January, was going to be another crucial day on the other side of the Causeway.

By 08.40 he was speeding across the island on his way to confer with General Heath at III Corps Headquarters, now located just on the other side of the Causeway in Johore Bahru. As he sat in the back of the car, his face beautifully shaven but expressionless, he swiftly reviewed the plans that had been made by Heath and his staff for the withdrawal of his entire force across the Causeway to Singapore Island. He had hoped until yesterday not to have put this plan into operation, particularly now that the 18th (British) Division was about to arrive. But alas, there was nothing else for it. Were his men to remain in Johore their flanks would still be threatened by amphibious attack, as Singapore Island itself would be, of course. Moreover, communications would depend on the narrow Causeway, all too vulnerable to air attack.

To withdraw is a delicate business at the best of times, but to withdraw such a disparate collection of forces from across a wide front back into the narrow neck of a funnel in the face of such a rapidly advancing enemy would require a degree of accuracy and discipline verging on the miraculous. Should one contingent withdraw too quickly it would automatically expose the flanks of its neighbours. General Heath's 11th Division was to cover the crossroads at Skudai where the roads from east and west converged, (pinching in the funnel to its narrow neck) until the forces from the west coast had passed through. Meanwhile, yesterday afternoon the 8th Brigade of General Barstow's 9th Indian Division had begun to withdraw down the railway in the direction of Layang Layang, passing through the 22nd Brigade under Brigadier Painter who had been ordered to hold his ground in concert with the phased withdrawal elsewhere.

'These manoeuvres can be a sticky business,' mused Percival, raising a hand to shield his eyes from the sudden glare reflected from the surface of the water as the car emerged from the foliage of the island and sped out over the Causeway. Yes, such a delicate operation, mismanaged, could result in the most fearful mess. He sighed. The car hurtled on over the water.

If you had been watching it from the island you would have seen that camouflaged staff-car gradually diminish in size until it became merely a moving dot in the distance; the next moment it had disappeared altogether as it plunged into the streets of Johore Bahru. One hour, two hours passed. The sun changed its position so that the glare from the Strait of Johore became even more dazzling. At last a tiny moving dot appeared again on the mainland side of the Causeway cutting in and out of the slow line of traffic and rapidly growing larger until it revealed itself as the same car carrying Percival back from his conference with Heath. Heath had been worried about the ability of the 11th Division (the poor devils who had been in the thick of it since Jitra) to hold out much longer against the Japanese Imperial Guards. As a result the crossing of the Causeway had been moved forward twenty-four hours. At least, Percival reflected, again shielding his eyes, he would not get into hot water with the Chief of Staff, for Wavell had given him permission to withdraw to the Island at his own discretion. That old warrior had seen in the end that there would be nothing else for it. Unlike Churchill who a week earlier had sent instructions that they were to fight in the ruins of Singapore if necessary,

Wavell had some conception of what they were up against.

How drab and dismal Singapore Island looked at a distance! And yet it would be here on this grey-green slab of land surrounded by glaring water that the most important events of his life would undoubtedly take place, providing he got his troops back to it safely. This thought reminded him that there had been one slightly disturbing piece of news at III Corps. Nothing too serious for the moment, just that contact had been lost temporarily with 22nd Brigade: that was the one which had been ordered to hold firm in front of Layang Layang. General Barstow was going forward now to find out what was the matter.

Later in the day, while Percival was in the Operations Room in Sime Road, he was observed by Sinclair who now found himself back there, much chastened and perplexed by his participation in the action at the Slim River: this in the end had amounted to a brief and disagreeable traffic accident and a good deal of even more disagreeable crawling through miles of jungle to get back to a British-held position. To make matters worse he had broken his wrist in his collision with the tank, although he had not realized it at first in the heat of the moment: this had soon become extremely painful, and all the more so as two hands are needed for making one's way through the jungle. He would probably not have got through at all without the help of a little party of resourceful and determined Argylls who, like himself, had been over-run by the enemy attack, and were also making their way back. It had been gruelling enough, certainly, but there was no use trying to conceal the fact: he had hoped for more from his first active engagement. If only he had been at the bridge he could have joined in some real fighting. But he had gathered from his brother officers that even there it had not lasted very long. Sinclair could not help wondering whether warfare had not been a little spoiled by all the modern equipment that armies had taken to using. What fun was there in fighting with tanks? A cavalry charge would have been more his cup of tea. In any case, now he was back where he had started, and with his wrist in plaster into the bargain. Thank heaven that at least they had allowed him to do something useful!

Sinclair, busy though he was, was deeply interested in the comportment of the GOC at this critical point in the campaign and every now and then he would snatch a glance in his direction. Percival's face wore a rather blank expression, rather like that which senior staff officers affected when on duty. Sinclair thought of it as a professional man's face ... where the profession is of the kind which expects you to keep a careful watch on your dignity. Sinclair found it fascinating, though, to think that this was the man who was conducting the defence of Malaya; behind that expressionless face, even while Sinclair's eyes rested on its outer crust, the molten lava of history was boiling up!

Now some rather disturbing news was coming in: the 22nd Brigade had been cut off. Aghast though he was, Sinclair could not help keeping a surreptitious eye on the GOC to see how he was taking this news. Percival merely frowned slightly and looked annoyed, waiting for more details. It seemed that the 8th Brigade had retired further than planned, allowing the Japanese to move through the rubber around Painter's eastern flank and seize Layang Layang. More serious still, General Barstow had gone up the railway with two staff officers to investigate, had been ambushed and was now missing, having hurled himself down one side of the railway embankment while the two staff officers, who had escaped, had thrown themselves down the other. Barstow, an experienced and able soldier, would be sorely missed if, as seemed likely, he had been killed or captured. Now the question was whether it would be possible to rescue the 22nd Brigade without prejudicing the evacuation of the entire force. All too soon it became clear that Painter and his men would have to be left to fight their own way out through the jungle as best they could. And what hope was there that, having done so, they would then be able to get across the Strait?

Presently, Percival came to stand quite near Sinclair, talking something over with the BGS but in a voice too low for him to hear. Sinclair considered that he had taken the bad news about the 22nd Brigade with admirable composure; but, of course, one had to remember that Percival was a professional and one would no more expect him to throw himself on the floor in a tantrum at the loss of a brigade than one would expect a grand master to utter a howl of anguish whenever one of his pawns was taken. That blank face of Percival's, Sinclair realized, was the face of a man who has excluded all unnecessary emotion from the job in hand because he knows that it will only hinder him. Sinclair watched and approved. But then, quite unexpectedly, despite his blank expression, Percival began to shout. He suddenly shouted that men could not work properly in such conditions.

The Operations Room at Sime Road consisted of a wooden hut about the width of a tennis court but longer, more than half as long again. Tables ran from one end to the other and supported a bewildering mass of maps, charts and documents. Here and there telephones were shrilling in little herds, all together like frogs in a pond. Add to this the overcrowding, for this room housed the RAF as well as the Army Staff, the jostling to get a look at wall maps and aircraft availability charts, the shouting into telephones and hammering of typewriters and all the other commotion one would expect in the central nervous system of that clanking, mechanical warrior which the modern army has become, as the campaign in which he is engaged begins to near its climax, and yes, one could very well see that General Percival, who after all had the main responsibility to bear, might find it something of a nightmare to conduct his campaign from such a mad-house.

But in due course it emerged that Percival was not complaining of the noise from inside the hut but from *outside*, where, in order to remedy the serious overcrowding at Sime Road, a party of Engineers were working to provide some further accommodation. The BGS scratched his balding head but showed no more surprise at Percival's outburst than he did at anything else. But all the same, to Sinclair it did seem peculiar. The fact was, you see, that with the noise *inside* the hut, a considerable racket, you could barely hear anything at all from outside. Sinclair cocked an ear and listened ... but all he could hear was the faint whisper of a saw on wood as the men worked on the construction of the new hut.

59

The number of people, mainly men, who had taken up lodging at or near the Mayfair Building had continued to grow day by day. Now there were people there whom the Major barely knew by sight, others whom he did not know at all. Certain of these newcomers merely came to hang about during the day-time, for thanks to the fire-fighting the Mayfair was a centre of activity and news, or, if not news, rumours. The latest rumour asserted that a gigantic American force of several divisions had passed through the Straits of Malacca during the night and landed near Alor Star in the north. When asked to confirm this rumour, however, Ehrendorf merely shook his head sadly.

Of all the new lodgers, none pleased the Major so much as the girls from the Poh Leung Kuk who were quartered in the Board Room. They were so helpful, so good-natured and polite! The Major was delighted with them: they appealed strongly to his paternal instincts. He was somewhat surprised, however, when one day Captain Brown, whom he had put in charge of them, asked him what was supposed to be done about their prospective bridegrooms? What bridegrooms? The ones, Captain Brown said, that kept calling to inspect the girls with a view to matrimony. He had paraded them himself, looked them over, and given them short shrift: not good enough. But the girls had been upset: they wanted a go at the bridegrooms themselves! They did not want Captain Brown who was used to having everything ship-shape and had spent a lifetime on the water-fronts up and down the China coast selecting crews with the jaundiced eye of experience, they did not want him to make their decisions for them!

This was a difficult problem. The Major was surprised, as a matter of fact, that at such a time, with the city being progressively smashed to bits from the air, there should be any prospective bridegrooms at all, but perhaps it was the very uncertainty of the situation which was causing single men to make up their minds. Well, there was no doubt in his mind, provided the men had some sort of credentials to prove that they did not want the girls to stock brothels and could produce the forty dollars for the trousseau, the girls themselves, not Captain Brown, must choose.

Captain Brown was indignant. He was not accustomed to having his decisions questioned: it was only out of politeness that he had mentioned the matter to the Major at all. Since he had obtained his Master's ticket all those years ago he had made it plain, as quite a few Owners had discovered to their cost, that he was not the sort of man who would countenance being interfered with in the correct exercise of his duties. The Major, taken aback, had tried to suggest to Captain Brown that this was note quite the same thing, that these girls, after all ... But Captain Brown was adamant. Either they were under his command or they were not! And he had departed in a huff, leaving the Major to cope with the problem as best he could.

Dupigny, consulted, was of the opinion that the girls should

460

be left to deal with the matter themselves. Although the Major would have liked and indeed intended to exercise some sort of supervision over the bridegrooms, he had so much on his mind these days that really he had no time to spare, and neither did anyone else. At best half an hour now and again could be set aside by Dupigny or Ehrendorf to inspect credentials, but in the existing conditions it was impossible even to do this properly. The girls were naturally delighted by their victory over Captain Brown and became more helpful than ever to the Major, showering him with little attentions, sewing on buttons for him and polishing his shoes. What splendid little things they were! It was all he could do to prevent the little darlings from bringing him cups of tea whenever he sat down for a moment. Indeed, when they were not interviewing bridegrooms in the Board Room, which they were doing a lot of the time, they brought cups of tea to everyone at all hours of the day. The only thing that made the Major a little uneasy was the fact that though there was a constant and increasing supply of bridegrooms waiting to be summoned to the Board Room (now and again the door would open releasing a gale of giggles) they never actually seemed to *choose* one. Still, that was hardly his business.

Now the Major and Dupigny were making their way to the verandah for some fresh air, picking their way among sleeping firemen; the Major noticed as he passed that many of them had simply thrown themselves down on the floor with a cushion or a jacket under their heads, faces and clothes still blackened by the fire they had just been to. Weariness now affected everyone, causing men to stumble about as if they were drunk, or forget to deal with the most urgent matters. 'Really,' he thought, 'we can't be expected to go on much longer like this!'

To replace the wooden steps to the compound which had been carried away in the raid a week earlier a ladder had been improvised. The Major descended it stiffly, his movements made clumsy by fatigue.

'And who on earth is this?' he asked Dupigny rather petulantly, for even more people had arrived since he had last made a tour of inspection and had installed themselves in a sort of gypsy encampment among the score of brick pillars on which the bungalow was built. Here in the shade woman and children sat mournfully among piles of suitcases and other belongings. Some of them dozed or nursed crying babies, others stared blankly at the Major and Dupigny as they passed, red-eyed and seemingly in a state of shock.

'Refugees.'

'Of course, but why is nothing being done by the Government to take care them? *We* can't possibly be expected to feed them all. And what about sanitary arrangements? We'll have an epidemic in no time if they stay here. I thought schools had been taken over to house them. Perhaps you could enquire, François, and see if there's somewhere for them to go ... The poor things are obviously too exhausted to find out for themselves.'

Dupigny smiled at his friend and made a gesture of helplessness; his experience of administration in Hanoi told him that even in the best conditions it would take several days or even weeks before Singapore was again able to cope adequately with its administrative problems, of which the refugees were only one. What about the water supply? The burial of the dead? The demolition of damaged buildings? The repair of damage done to vital roads, to gas, electricity and telephone installations? And then there was the storing and distribution of food, the struggle to prevent an epidemic of typhus or cholera, and a hundred and one other difficulties ... None of these matters, Dupigny knew without any doubt, would be dealt with adequately, for the simple reason that there were not enough experienced men to do the job ... some of them, he explained to the Major, would not be dealt with at all unless people took matters into their own hands ... 'Like this fellow here,' he added.

They had passed through another little community, this time living in army tents scrounged from somewhere, and had come with a certain relief to an open space which led presently to the little wilderness of rare shrubs beyond which lay the Blacketts' compound. Beneath the shade of a rambutan a Chinese was digging a grave, or rather he had already dug the grave and was now shovelling earth back into it. On closer inspection the Chinese turned out to be Cheong who, for the past few days, had been working with astonishing energy and fortitude to provide meals at intervals for the ever-increasing number of volunteer firemen and their dependents. And now, not content with feeding people, here he was burying someone single-handed.

'Ah, Cheong,' said the Major peering into the grave where, however, nothing could be seen but the well-polished toes of a pair of stout English shoes. 'Good show,' he added, wanting to make it clear how much he appreciated Cheong's efforts.

'Whose grave is that?'

Cheong, without pausing in his digging, muttered a name which the Major had to cup his ear to catch.

'Not old Tom Prescott!' cried the Major in dismay. 'Why, François, I knew him well. He used to do a trick at parties with an egg.' And the Major gazed into the grave in concern.

Dupigny shrugged, as if to say: 'What else can one expect, the way things are?'

They moved on a little way. The Major, upset, mopped his brow with a silk handkerchief. 'Poor old Tommy,' he said. 'What a card he was! He used to have us in fits. Mind you, he was getting on in years. He'd had a good innings.'

The Major, too, Dupigny could not help thinking, was beginning to look his years; the lack of sleep and the ceaseless activity of the past few days had given his features a haggard appearance, accentuating the lines under his eyes; even his moustache had a chewed and patchy look, perhaps singed by drifting sparks at one of the fires he had attended.

'People are like bubbles, Brendan,' declared Dupigny in a sombre and sententious manner. 'They drift about for a little while and then they burst.'

'Oh, François, please!'

'Not clear bubbles which sparkle, but bubbles of muddy, blood-stained water. Prick them and they burst. Moreover, it is scientific,' he added, narrowing his eyes in a Cartesian manner. 'We are made of ninety-nine per cent water, we are like cucumbers. So what do you expect?' If you prick a cucumber it does not burst, the Major thought of saying, but decided not to encourage his friend in this lugubrious vein.

Having returned to the bungalow they found Ehrendorf who had disappeared for an hour to drive some of the women refugees from up-country to Cluny to join the queue of people trying to register for passages at the P & O Agency House. He reported a scene of despair and chaos. Now, with what might be the last passenger ships for some time preparing to leave, men, women and children were braving the heat and the air-raids in an attempt to get away.

'Perhaps you should be on one of them yourself, Jim, unless you expect your army to arrive and rescue us and are merely waiting to welcome them ashore.'

'While François is still in the Colony I know it must be safe,' replied Ehrendorf with a smile.

'You surely do not expect me to leave on ... *quelle horreur* ... a troopship. If you have ever been on such a vessel you will know that there is at least one instance in which it is better to arrive than to travel. Besides, I am curious to see how it ends, this Singapore story.'

Matthew, too, arrived presently. He had spent the morning at the Chinese Protectorate trying to get an exit permit for Vera. They now had everything that was needed including photographs and had both been hopeful that at last they would be able to tackle the next obstacle of getting Vera registered with the P & O. But the exit permit had been refused without explanation. Matthew was still shocked by this set-back: he had been so certain that they would succeed. Curiously enough, this time Vera had seemed to be less affected than he was by the disappointment, had comforted him as best she could and had come back with him to the Mayfair.

'I know someone at the Protectorate,' said the Major suddenly. 'I think I shall go and have a word with him.'

It was not until later in the afternoon that the Major found time to telephone Smith at the Chinese Protectorate, asking to see him. Smith was discouraging. 'We're very busy here, Major. We have a whole lot of Chinese on our plate. What's it about?'

'I'm coming to see you now, Smith,' the Major told him sharply, 'and you'd better be there or else you'll find a dozen young women camping in your office tomorrow.'

'You'll never get through. Traffic jams.' There was silence for a moment, then Smith's voice asked suspiciously: 'What's it about?'

The Major rang off.

Word had now spread that two, or even more, of the troop-ships that had brought the 18th Division would be sailing that evening after dark. This was a further blow for Matthew, made no better by the knowledge that even if they had managed to get the exit permit they still would not have been able to complete the other formalities in time to get Vera on board. From early in the afternoon those prospective passengers fortunate enough to have been granted passages on the ships that were due to sail had begun to converge on the docks, with the result that delays and traffic jams soon began to develop. Eventually those who were trying to approach Keppel Harbour along Tanjong Pagar Road found that they could no longer move forward at all: so many cars had been abandoned in the road by passengers who had driven themselves to the docks that the stream of traffic had become hopelessly blocked by them. The situation both there and in the other approach roads was made even worse by the bomb-craters, the rubble from destroyed buildings which had not yet been cleared away, and by the efforts of the newly arrived 18th Division to unload their equipment and force a passage through for it in the opposite direction. Everywhere desperate people were sweltering in cars which crept forward at best only a few feet at a time through clouds of smoke or dust, thin in places, dense in others, between rows of heat-distorted buildings, accompanied by a nightmare braying of car-horns, the hammering of anti-aircraft guns and the crump of bombs falling ahead of them. Nearer the docks a number of buildings were on fire: there were godowns with roofs neatly carpeted with rectangles of flame and shop-houses with flames sprouting like orange weeds from every window. Some passengers began to realize that they would never reach the docks in time, but the greater the panic the worse the situation became. It was obvious, even to the Major, arriving after a considerable delay at the Chinese Protectorate on the corner of Havelock Road, that the embarkation had turned into a shambles.

The Major had half expected not to find Smith in his office but there he was at his desk, peering intently into one of its drawers which, however, contained nothing but a few whiskers of perforated paper left over from a sheet of postage stamps, a much-bitten pencil, and one or two wire paper-clips. Ignoring the Major's entrance he put the pencil between his teeth and after some deliberation selected one of the paper-clips. Sitting back he asked blandly: 'Well, what can I do for you, Major?'

The Major explained that he wanted an exit permit for Vera.

'Does she have a valid certificate of admission? Why doesn't she apply herself?'

'She *has* . . . and has been refused without explanation.'

'I'm afraid in that case . . .' said Smith, beginning to clean his ear with the paper-clip and inspecting it at intervals.

'She'll be in grave danger should the Japanese gain control of Singapore.'

'Can't do much about that, I'm afraid. But as a favour we'll have a little look at her file, shall we? If she's properly registered we should have her photograph and thumb-print, I should think . . . Just a moment.'

Smith got to his feet and made his way to a door leading to an inner office. He left the door ajar and the Major could hear whispering but could not make out what was being said. He looked around. Nothing in the office had changed since his first visit except that strips of brown paper had been pasted over the window as a precaution against flying glass-splinters. It was some time before Smith reappeared; when he did so he was wearing spectacles and carrying a file. The atmosphere in the office was stifling despite the fan thrashing away above his desk. He sat down and for a while studied the file suspiciously, occasionally making a clicking sound with his tongue. From time to time he lifted the paper-clip and twisted it in his ear like a key in a lock. At length he looked up and said sharply: 'What's your interest in this case, Major?'

'She's a friend of mine . . .'

'I believe we've discussed this woman before, haven't we? I told you she wasn't reliable, perhaps even a whore. Surely now you don't mean to tell me that she's a friend of yours!'

'Even if your evil-minded suggestions were true,' replied the Major coldly, 'it would be no reason to refuse her an exit permit when her life is in danger if she remains in Singapore.'

Smith had once more dropped his eyes to the file and was champing his lips in a disagreeable manner. How little had changed, the Major reflected, since the first time he had sat in this office! Smith was still blinking and sweating profusely: wisps of hair still flickered on each side of his bald crown like electric sparks, dancing weirdly in the draught of the fan. The Major had been too busy fire-fighting to give much thought to earlier days when his Civil Defence Committee had lobbied the various departments of the Government for distribution of gas-masks and for air-raid shelters in the populous quarters of the city. But now his sense of frustration with petty officials returned in full force, combined with bitterness at the results of their ineptitude which he had witnessed in the last few days driving about in the defenceless, shelterless city.

'This woman once had connections with the General Labour Union,' pursued Smith, unaware of the Major's anger. 'I suppose you know that that was a Communist organization?'

The Major said nothing. Outside the air-raid sirens yet again began their rise and fall, rise and fall. Smith cocked an ear anxiously to them, then went on: 'We have information that she was also implicated in some criminal affair in Shanghai before the war in which a Japanese officer was killed. That was also Communist-inspired without doubt. So you see . . .'

'I see nothing except that she'll be on a Japanese black-list if she remains in Singapore!' shouted the Major, losing his temper.

'Don't raise your voice with me, Major,' said Smith nastily. 'You'll find that it doesn't get you anywhere.'

466

'From the way you talk it sounds as if you're on the side of the Japanese. Let me remind you that they and not the Chinese are the enemy!'

'Look here, old man,' said Smith in a condescending tone. 'I happen to know a great deal more about this business than you do. Of course, the Japs are the enemy, of course they are! But that doesn't mean the Chinese are on our side, particularly the Communists. You don't know, as I do, how dangerous they are to the fabric of our society. Well, they're like ... I always say ... hookworms in the body. They don't respect the natural boundaries of the organs ... They pass from one to another ...'

'So you said before. But I want an exit permit for that young woman and I don't mean to leave without one.'

'Out of the question, old man. Here in Singapore we have the Communists isolated and under control. We can't allow them to spread all over the place. The way I describe it, which many people have been kind enough to find illuminating, is that they're like millions of seeds in a pod. If we allow that pod to burst in India, say, or even in Australia, why, they'll be scattered all over the Empire in no time ... Oh Lord!' he added hurrying to the window and throwing it open. 'It looks as if they're coming this way. We'd better go down to the shelter.'

The Major joined him at the window. The office was on the top floor of the building and looked eastwards over the city towards the sea. At this hour the stretch of water between Anderson Bridge and the horizon was a delicate duck-egg blue, extraordinarily beautiful. The Major, however, was looking up at the minute formation of silver-black planes flying towards the city at a great height. As the bombers passed over Kallang little white puffs began to appear in the sky beneath them, as if dotted here and there with an invisible paint-brush. After a moment the thud of guns came to them at the window. 'Yes, they do seem to be coming this way,' he agreed.

'Well, we'll have to continue this chat another time.' Smith picked up the file, snapped it shut and clamped it under his arm very firmly, as if he expected the Major to snatch it from him. He eyed the Major warily, his head on one side.

The Major was surprised to hear himself say: 'I'm not leaving this office without that exit permit and neither are you.' He advanced on Smith threateningly, sensing that despite his advantage of years Smith was afraid of him; perhaps Smith sensed how deeply angry and resentful the Major was after the days he had spent working in the chaotic streets. The Major

467

gripped the back of a chair and Smith fell back a pace. Outside an alarm-bell jangled.

'That's the roof-spotter,' cried Smith in alarm. 'Look, be sensible. I don't even have the proper forms here. You must come back later, come back some other time.'

'Just write it out on official paper, sign it and stamp it!' The Major advanced a step. 'I've had about enough of this,' he added, taking off his jacket. 'Put up your fists.'

'What d'you mean?' asked Smith, staring at him in amazement.

'I mean I'm going to give you a punch on the nose,' replied the Major.

'This is absurd,' muttered Smith. He had turned very pale. Tufts of hair continued to flutter above his ears. A hideous whistling sound had begun from outside; it grew higher and higher in pitch, ending in an explosion that shook the building. 'Don't be ridiculous,' said Smith, ringing the bell on his desk sharply. But nothing happened. Evidently the people in the next office had departed to the shelter by another exit.

'Now look here ...' said Smith, making for the door and delivering the Major a paralysing hack on the shins as he passed. But the Major caught him by the arm and yanked him back into the room. 'Just a minute,' he said. 'Put up your fists.'

'At least let me take off my glasses,' said Smith, giving the Major another mighty hack on the shins and punching him in the stomach for good measure.

'I'm afraid you've gone too far,' gasped the Major and, glasses or no glasses, drew back his first. But before he could strike, Smith was at his desk, writing busily.

'Why didn't you tell me straight away that she was your tart?' he demanded in an aggrieved tone. 'For chaps' tarts we can make exceptions.'

Smith had finished writing. The Major picked up the paper, read it carefully and put it in his pocket. 'One more thing. If I hear you've done anything to countermand this ...'

But Smith had already fled for safety from the bombs and from the Major.

60

The first week of February was a week of frantic activity for General Percival. Such was the swiftness with which the Japanese had followed up their attacks throughout the campaign that he knew he could not count on more than a week's grace before they launched their attack on Singapore Island itself. There was so much to be done, so little time in which to do it. He no longer even returned to Flagstaff House to sleep. Instead he would stretch out in his office at Command Headquarters in Sime Road and, within a few moments, would find himself plunging into a torrent of anxieties even more distressing than those he had to face while awake. And so, tired though he was, he preferred to remain conscious, taking cover in his work as if in a fortified position.

Moreover, he now sometimes had the impression that his luck was about to change, that the unseen hand had ceased to wield its influence over his affairs. For if you looked at matters objectively you would see immediately that the situation could have been a great deal worse. After all, was it not the case that the major part of his forces from the mainland had withdrawn unscathed across the Causeway and had been redeployed successfully to their defensive positions on the Island? They were there now, digging in as best they could under the shells which had started coming over the water from Johore. True, the 22nd Brigade had been lost, apart from a few stragglers who had managed to find their way across the Strait in small boats or who had been picked up at night by what was left of the Navy. On the other hand, the remainder of the (British) 18th Division was due to arrive on the 5th. It was Percival's belief that it would arrive just in the nick of time.

Singapore Island in shape somewhat resembled the head of an elephant lumbering towards you, with both its flapping ears outstretched and with Singapore Town about where the mouth would be. On the extreme tip of the elephant's left ear (on the east coast, that is) were the great fixed guns of the Johore and Changi batteries. On the other ear there was Tengah airfield and the coastline of creeks and mangrove swamps. As it happened, neither ear was now of very much use to Percival. Tengah was within easy range of observed artillery fire from the mainland and could no longer be used by the few remaining Hurricanes, detained on the Island for the purposes of morale and for the escorting of the last convoys: they now had to use the civil aerodrome at Kallang. As for those enormous, leopard-striped fifteen-inch guns at Changi which had contributed so much to Singapore's reputation as a fortress, they had been sited to deal with an attack by ships from the sea, although some of them could indeed be traversed to fire into Johore; their ammunition (in short supply, incidentally) since it was armour-piercing, was also intended for use against ships and was expected to bury itself too deeply to be effective against targets on land.

No, although the ears must also, of course, be defended against an enemy landing, it was really the head itself that mattered, for it was in this central part of the Island that everything of importance was located. On the crown of the elephant's head the Island was (or rather, had been) joined to the mainland by the Causeway which was a little over a thousand yards in length. When the last of the Argylls, who had been given the risky job of covering the withdrawal, had crossed safely back to the Island a considerable hole had been blown in the Causeway ... or so it had seemed at first. Percival had been quite pleased with it, seeing the water flowing through at such a speed. But after a while even the hole had proved a disappointment, for what he had seen at first was the hole at *high tide* ... at low tide it was a different story. It no longer looked as if it would provide such an effective obstacle. Still, it was a great deal better than no hole at all.

The important road which, in normal times, came over on the Causeway and landed on the crown of the elephant's head continued straight down towards its mouth and trunk where Singapore Town was ... that, is in a southerly direction, more or less. Two-thirds of the way across, it reached Bukit Timah Village, thereafter calling itself the Bukit Timah Road for the last lap into the city itself.

This principal road across the Island was straddled by not very impressive hills: Bukit (which means 'hill') Mandai, Bukit Panjang, Bukit Timah and Bukit Brown, the only hill terrain on the Island, by a nondescript area called Sleepy Valley, by a race course, a golf club and a cemetery (the latter on Bukit Brown), all grouped around Command Headquarters in Sime

Road where Percival was now swatting at flies which were relentlessly trying to land on the backs of his sweating hands as he pored over the maps.

A little further to the east, right between the beast's eyes, lay the reservoirs which would become vital if the siege were prolonged, and, further east again, the pumping station at Woodleigh. Apart from the water in the reservoirs, great stocks of food retrieved from the mainland had been dumped on the race course. Beside the race course two large petrol dumps had been established, not to mention other food, petrol and ammunition dumps which were located in the Bukit Timah area. Yes, altogether this was an area that Percival knew he must defend at all costs. But then, 'at all costs' was how he would have had to defend it, anyway, since Singapore Town was only just down the road.

In the plans which had been laid for the defence of the Island it had been decided that if the worst came to the worst and the Japanese got a solid footing ashore, the eastern and western areas (the elephant's ears) might à la rigueur be abandoned and that the forces defending them might withdraw to second lines of defence. These second lines of defence, known as 'switch lines', followed very roughly the sides of the elephant's head where the ears were stuck on to it: on the eastern side the 'switch line' was obliged to bulge out a bit from the side of the head in order to include Kallang aerodrome; also, the big guns at Changi would have to be abandoned. On the western side the 'switch line' was particularly easy to define, thanks to two rivers or creeks, the Jurong and the Kranji, which flowed north and south respectively just where the ear joined the skull. It was simply, then, a question of joining one creek to the other with a defensive line from north to south across the Island to isolate the western ear completely. Nothing could be simpler.

This 'switch line', known as the 'Jurong line', was accordingly reconnoitred but no effort was made to install fixed defences. This was for two reasons. One was that the troops were already frantically digging themselves in around the northern coast in order to prepare for the Japanese attack across the Strait of Johore and did not have time. The other was that Percival did not really think that the Japanese would come that way. He was pretty well convinced that they would attack somewhere along the top of the other (eastern) ear between Changi and Seletar.

Percival considered that the Japanese attack would fall on the north-east coast of the Island partly because Wavell, when they had discussed the prospect a couple of weeks earlier, had taken a different view: Wavell thought it would fall on the north-western. Nor was Wavell the only one: Brigadier Simson, the DGCD, clearly thought so, too, because he or his Deputy Chief Engineer had been dumping quantities of defensive material west of the Causeway on their own initiative. Ever since December it had been piling up: booby-traps, barbed wire, high-tensile anti-tank wire, even drums of petrol with which to set fire to the water surface and searchlights to illuminate it at every possible landing site. He had even dumped anti-tank cylinders, blocks and chains by the sides of the roads. No doubt Simson meant well. The fact remained that, in Percival's view, he had the makings of a confounded nuisance. Ever since he had arrived he had been demanding that fixed defences should be built on the north shore of the Island. He simply had not wanted to realize what such defences would have done to the morale of the troops fighting up-country, or of the civilians either, come to that. Simson's latest was to start stripping the headlights off cars to augment his searchlights! The Governor, however, had soon put a stop to that. He himself, aware that there would no longer be much time left to prepare for the Japanese assault, had seen to it that the defensive material was shifted from west to east of the Causeway where, he was pretty sure, it would be needed.

Tormented by flies, light-headed from lack of sleep, Percival sat in his office at Sime Road, brooding over his maps and listening to the distant, monotonous thudding of the guns. The Japanese had wasted no time in moving up their heavy artillery, they were good soldiers, there was no denying it. Now they were laying down a heavy bombardment of the northern coast ... particularly, as it happened, *west* of the Causeway. Ah, but Percival was not about to be fooled into thinking that that was where the attack would come! To bombard one sector and attack another was the oldest trick in the game. There was something almost pleasant, he found, in this constant thudding of guns, which included his own artillery shelling Johore and the hammering of ack-ack guns ... it reminded him curiously of his youth, of the endless artillery exchanges of the Great War. Terrible though that had been, it now seemed almost a pleasant memory. He thought for a moment of mentioning it to Brookers ... he, too, would have enjoyed the reminiscence. But then he remembered that Brooke-Popham had already returned to England. Just as well, really. The old chap was no longer quite up to this sort of thing.

It occurred to Percival that what had gone wrong in the campaign until now was that he had never been able to act *positively*. Time and again he had been obliged to react. Thanks to Brooke-Popham's hesitations the Japanese commander had taken the initiative from the beginning and had never let it go. True, he himself had been the victim of the most extraordinary (indeed, suspicious) series of misfortunes. But the fact was that that unseen hand had led him by the nose. When Wavell had expressed the opinion that a Japanese attack would fall west of the Causeway, when, independently, it seemed, the Chief Engineer had started dumping material west of the Causeway, how easy it would have been to have made the assumption that this was where the attack *would* fall! But something inside him had rebelled. He had sensed that once again that unseen hand was trying to lead him by the nose. He had told himself: 'Be objective!' And so he had cleared his mind of prejudices and looked at the map again, asking himself what he would have done if he had been the Japanese commander. The answer was: he would have launched his attack on the north-east coast using Pulau Ubin, the long island which lay in the Strait of Johore, to shield his preparations from the view of Singapore Island. Accordingly, Percival had allotted to the recently arrived British troops of the 18th Division whose morale had not been dented in the long retreat down the Peninsula the sector which he considered most critical ... though the whole of the northern coast must be defended, of course.

There was, however, still the possibility that he was wrong in expecting the Japanese attack to fall east of the Causeway. The Intelligence wallahs in Fort Canning, for example, were predicting an attack to the west. But what did they know about it? They knew no more than he did: they had no reconnaissance planes to help them. All the same, to be on the safe side, he had ordered Gordon Bennett to send over night patrols to the mainland to get a better idea of what the Japanese were up to. Bennett had been dragging his feet over this. He would have to give him some plain speaking.

He reached out for some papers on his desk and as he picked them up a photograph fell out of them: they were private papers of no great importance which he had brought with him from Flagstaff House with the intention of having them destroyed. The photograph, by a coincidence, was of Gordon

Bennett and himself standing, by the look of it, outside Flagstaff House. They were both 'at ease', identically dressed except that Bennett was wearing a short-sleeved shirt while he himself had rolled his sleeves up to the elbow. But what struck Percival now was the difference of expression on their faces: while he himself was smiling pleasantly at the camera, Bennett, a short, plump fellow whose belt encircled a by no means negligible corporation, standing a few inches further back, was looking disaffected, was even glancing at him sideways out of the corner of his eye in a manner which could almost have been contemptuous. But perhaps he was simply imagining it ... photographs are notorious for giving the wrong impression, for catching people with misleading expressions on their faces. Still, he had to admit that he no longer had the confidence in Bennett that he had once had. While many of the Australian troops had fought heroically and effectively, Bennett as their leader had proved a liability. Altogether Percival was glad that Bennett would be covering the north-western area which was least likely to be attacked.

Presently Percival's thoughts were interrupted by the GSO1 on duty in the War Room, and not with good news. An urgent message had come through from Kallang aerodrome by way of the RAF staff: one of the convoy of four ships transporting the remaining units of the British 18th Division, the *Empress of Asia*, had fallen behind the other three and had not managed, under cover of darkness, to reach the (relatively) safe umbrella of Singapore's air defences. She had been attacked by dive-bombers off the Sembilan Islands and was in danger of sinking. Efforts were being made by the Navy to rescue survivors.

For some moments, while he considered this news, Percival was speechless. He had been so confident that the unseen hand would play no further part in his affairs ... and now this! He had been counting on the 18th Division arriving intact. At length, however, he collected himself and said mechanically to the GSO1: 'We must count ourselves lucky that that's the only ship we've lost.' Then, becoming brisk, he turned to other business. There was still a great deal to be done. He wanted to know in particular what progress was being made with the demolition of plant at the Naval Base; almost unbelievably, it seemed to him, Naval personnel had decamped to Ceylon on Admiralty orders, without even bothering to inform him that this demolition would have to be undertaken by his own hard-pressed troops.

A little later there was further news of the *Empress of Asia*: although both the liner herself and the equipment she was carrying had been destroyed, the loss of life had been small. This undoubtedly was a good omen: Percival immediately summoned his driver and had himself conveyed to the docks to greet the survivors. True, they would not be much help without their equipment, which had included anti-tank guns (if only there had been more of those at the Slim River!) but it was still a step in the right direction. And every able-bodied man might prove useful in the end, provided there was sufficient time to establish satisfactory defences.

Then, however, an even more disturbing piece of news reached him; at last, on 7 February, Bennett had seen his way to sending the night-patrols he had asked for over to the mainland. On their return they had brought the dismaying report that Japanese troops were concentrating opposite the north-*western* sector. Could it be, Percival wondered, that his prediction was wrong?

61

In the first days of February it seemed to Matthew that the dock buildings were permanently ablaze. There the Mayfair unit would be sent whenever there were no fires to deal with in their own district, and so frequently did this occur that presently it became almost a ritual: they would report to Adamson and set into a hydrant, or if there were no hydrant, drop their suction hose into the filthy water of the dock itself and start up the pumps. No matter when they arrived, or where, it seemed that it was always Adamson who was in charge of the fire they had been sent to. It was a mystery when he found time to sleep. He would emerge from the drifting smoke, never in a hurry, strolling almost, as if perfectly remote from the fire raging close at hand.

At some time in the past few days Adamson had acquired a dog, a black and white sheepdog which had mysteriously adopted him at one of the fires he had attended and which added to his air of detachment. Very often when the Mayfair party arrived the dog would appear first out of the smoke, would examine them, sniffing and wagging its tail, and then disappear into the smoke again, returning presently with Adamson. Then Adamson would briefly explain the nature of the fire to the Major and the plan for fighting, or at least containing it ... for the bombs which caused the fires continued to fall with ritual precision, day after day, very often at ten or eleven o'clock in the morning and again in the afternoon, but always more rapidly than the fires, death and destruction which they brought about could be dealt with. The truth was that although the staff at the Central Fire Station in Hill Street continued to map the new outbreaks as best they could, there were likely to be as many 'unofficial' fires burning briskly in the docks or elsewhere in the city as those which had been reported and mapped. But somehow Adamson and his dog found out about these fires, sifted them and matched them against the pumps and fire-engines available, deciding which were the least dangerous and could be left to burn, and which had to be stopped then and there.

Once or twice, when the Major happened on an unattended fire on his way to the docks, he anxiously sought out Adamson to report it, only to find out that Adamson already knew about it. 'Let it burn, Major,' he would say with a curious, ironic smile and then go on to explain in his casual manner where the Mayfair pumps might come in useful. At times Adamson was to be seen in a jeep he had found somewhere, manoeuvring in and out of the piles of rubble and masonry that lay in the streets, while the black and white dog sat up on the seat beside him looking around with keen interest as if ready to alert his companion to any new fire that broke out. But more often, because of the dense traffic of military vehicles unloading equipment and trying to move food stores from the threatened godowns to some safer location in the city, Adamson and his dog moved about on foot. Matthew, in particular, watched them with keen interest.

Despite his weariness, the hectic life he was leading, the constant danger, and his worries lest Vera should be trapped in Singapore, Matthew had not ceased to feel that novel sense of fulfilment which he had first experienced at the timber-yard fire. The satisfaction of doing something practical, the results of which were visible and practical, in the company of friends seemed to him so powerful that he was amazed that he should never have considered it before. While he had been cudgelling his brains with the question: 'What is the best way in which to live one's life?' with no other result than that a substantial part of that life had gone by in the process, the answer had been all around him, being demonstrated by the most ordinary of people.

Watching Adamson and his dog, calm but determined, going about their business, Matthew thought: 'Surely there are people like this all over the world, in every country, in every society in every class or caste or community! People who simply go about doing the things that have to be done, not just for themselves but for everybody.' Such people, whether they were Socialists, or Capitalists, or Communists, or paid no attention to politics at all, because they were entirely committed to whatever job it was they were doing were bound to be the very backbone of their society; without them people like himself who spent their days in speculation and dispute could scarcely expect to survive. Matthew was anxious to know Adamson's thoughts, to know whether he had consciously decided to behave in the way he did. But he found it difficult to corner Adamson and even more difficult to get him to say what he thought about anything. He would merely answer with a smile or a shrug when Matthew tried to sound him out on some political question. Once he admitted, reluctantly in reply to Matthew's question that, after the war, if he got back to Britain, he would vote for a Labour Government 'to change all this' and he gestured vaguely with a stick at the smouldering warehouses around them. After a moment's silent reflection he added: 'I read somewhere that the boatman who rowed King William back across the river after the Battle of the Boyne is supposed to have asked the King which side won ... To which the King replied: "What's it to you? You'll still be a boatman."' Matthew had to be satisfied with this.

In the course of the past few days Adamson had hurt his foot and now limped rather, but he still managed to convey the impression that he was merely out for a stroll among the burning buildings; his casual air was increased by the fact that he had taken to carrying a walking stick he had picked up somewhere. Once Matthew came upon him unexpectedly. Not far from one of the dock gates there was a sad little parcel of tattered clothing and personal odds and ends, abandoned by someone unable to carry them in the stampede to reach one of the last ships to leave. Other similarly abandoned suitcases had in the meantime vanished or been rifled of their contents. Now Adamson, leaning on his stick, was contemplating a battered old hairbrush with bristles splayed by use, a sponge-bag, a couple of books including a child's picture-book, what might have been a cotton dress or apron and several other indeterminate pieces of cloth or clothing. He continued to gaze at these things for a moment with raised eyebrows and a grim expression on his face; then he limped on, swiping with his stick at a tennis ball he saw in the gutter with a shoe and one or two other things. The dog, which had come back to see what was the matter, went racing off again to seek out more fires. Matthew would remember for a long time to come that bitter, ironic expression he had glimpsed on Adamson's face as he limped away down the empty street after the dog which had already disappeared into the rolling smoke.

But already the Mayfair unit had gained so much experience that its members depended less and less on Adamson's advice and directions. The Major himself had become a hardened fireman and no longer would have dreamed of taking the risks he had taken in the beginning. Not that fire-fighting had become any less dangerous. Quite apart from the heavy carpet-bombing raids by gigantic formations of bombers (still in multiples of twenty-seven) which continued and intensified in the first week of February, now lone fighter-aircraft would appear suddenly out of nowhere, zooming up and down the main thoroughfares of the city and machine-gunning anything that moved, even rickshaws or Cold Storage 'stop-me-and-buy-one' tricycles ... one day they passed an overturned tricycle with a Chinese youth beside it, his brains spilling into a pool of milk or ice-cream in the road. Anywhere, coming and going to fires, you might suddenly have come upon a row of bodies stretched out on the pavement following the appearance of one of these aircraft.

The city of Singapore which, in unison with the rise of Blackett and Webb, had grown from a small settlement into the greatest trading port of the Far East had been the home of something over half a million people in peacetime. Now in the space of a few weeks the population had suddenly doubled to over a million as refugees poured across the Causeway from up-country. By the time a hole had at last been blown in the Causeway and the flow of refugees had dried up, the Island, and Singapore Town in particular, was swarming with people who had nowhere to go. From now on, almost everywhere you went you would see people with suitcases or bundles sitting by the roadside in whatever shade they could find, under trees or on the pavements of covered ways, clustering around water-taps or begging food from passers-by. To Matthew and the Major and even to Dupigny who had spent so many years in the swarming cities of the East, this sudden increase in Singapore's population was quite unnerving. Among these aimless crowds of refugees they themselves felt a loss of identity and purpose. They felt themselves losing their accustomed rank as Europeans, their special status, in that great, amorphous, anonymous herd of humanity trapped there in a burning city and unable any longer to exert any control over its own destiny.

Even after the demolition of the Causeway more refugees still continued to appear in Singapore Town, evacuated from the northern part of the Island by the Military who were preparing their defences. From the beginning of February a curfew from nine p.m. to five a.m. had been in force, but you cannot confine people to their houses if they have no houses to go to; it was not very long before the city's population, abnormally swollen by refugees and demoralized troops, had begun to show signs of getting out of control. The first sporadic cases of looting occurred in bombed-out districts. Rumours of the excesses of un-disciplined troops, for the most part Australian, circulated among the alarmed Europeans: someone had had his car hi-jacked at gun-point by drunken soldiers carousing with prosti-tutes from Lavender Road, and someone else had heard of a rape of English nurses on waste land near the biscuit factory. This sudden collapse, which you could almost feel in the air, of *normal standards of behaviour* was the most frightening thing of all, more frightening even than the Japanese bombers. As a result, anyone who had still hesitated over leaving, and who had permission to do so, now made up his mind.

Thanks to the Major's influence at the Chinese Protectorate, Matthew had at last succeeded, after more anxious hours of waiting, in having Vera's name registered at the P & O's temp-orary office in Cluny Road. But Vera, though she had seemed in mortal fear of the Japanese while they were still hundreds of miles away in the north, now that they had come to within a few miles, and could even be seen with the naked eye (so one of the transient officers at the Mayfair asserted) strutting on the sea front at Johore Bahru, had grown calm and apparently re-signed. When every day, Matthew telephoned the P & O to find out if there were any ships sailing and, again every day, he received a negative answer she did not seem to be particularly disappointed. She merely shrugged her shoulders and smiled. In any case, he had less opportunity to see her now. While most of his waking hours were spent at fires, Vera had taken to working equally long hours as a volunteer nurse at one of the makeshift hospitals which had sprung up on the fringes of Chinatown to cope with the steadily increasing civilian casualties. Matthew continued doggedly to telephone the P & O, however. He was determined that she should not be in Singapore when the Japanese arrived. But would there be any more ships leaving? So the first week of February came to an end.

They slept side by side. Matthew was dreaming deeply, anxiously about Geneva. Things would go terribly wrong unless he was careful: he knew that Vera's life would be at stake unless he could persuade someone of something, whom and of what was not clear. He uttered a shout, waking himself up. But no, someone was there, hammering against the wall, telling him to wake up. He sat up immediately in the stifling darkness. He could see someone standing there in the faint glow from under the rolled-up bamboo window blinds, and he thought: 'They *have* come to arrest her, after all.'

'Sorry, I think you were having a nightmare,' said a familiar voice. It was the Major. He wanted to say that someone in the Control Room in Hill Street had told him that a Free French ship, the *Félix Roussel*, was due to sail for Bombay in a few hours and anyone who wanted to sail on her was advised to reserve a passage without delay. The P & O office was already besieged. There was no time to waste.

The following morning a cheerful crowd sat amid the jumble of mattresses and chairs in the Mayfair. Everything had at last been arranged. Matthew, jubilant, sat reading again and again the printed instructions they had been given at the P & O office. Vera was to report to Collyer Quay at eight o'clock that evening, bringing only what luggage she could carry herself. Matthew had been given a pass which would allow him to drive home after seeing her off, which would necessarily be after the curfew. As for Vera, though she smiled from time to time, she said nothing. Matthew was puzzled by her calm. Was she upset by the prospect of finding herself alone in Bombay?

'A little,' Vera agreed. 'But no, not really.' She had been used to this sort of thing from childhood, being uprooted from one place after another.

'You've got the address of the Hong Kong and Shanghai Bank, haven't you?' Matthew asked anxiously, not for the first time. 'It's in Churchgate Street. I'll write to you there and join you when I can.' Vera smiled again and squeezed his hand. Matthew suspected that she still did not really believe she would get away from Singapore.

While they sat around talking they were startled by a whirring sound like a great bird passing over the house, followed by an explosion, perhaps a quarter of a mile away.

'I didn't hear the sirens, did you?' They stared at each other in surprise. Only the Major knew immediately what had caused the explosion. He had heard that sort of noise before. He sighed but said nothing, bending his ear politely to listen to what his neighbour was saying. This man, a purple-faced planter from the Kuala Lumpur area, was one of the many refugees who had wandered in unannounced, having heard somewhere that there was shelter to be found at the Mayfair; he had brought several bottles of whisky with which he fortified himself at intervals, waving a roll of paper. On this roll of paper, he said, were the plans of a new type of anti-aircraft gun he had invented in the long evenings on his estate. It would fire twice as high as anything they had at present. He had written to General Percival about it but his letter had gone unanswered. 'Save the whole of Singapore, old boy,' he was now explaining huskily to the Major. 'But the blighters won't look at it ... Save the British Empire, come to that!' And he waved his blueprint despondently.

Again there came that whirring, whistling sound, followed by another explosion, more distant this time.

'What on earth is it?'

'I'm afraid they've started shelling us now,' said the Major. 'They must have moved up some heavier guns to reach this side of the Island.' He felt a sudden compulsion to jump to his feet and start walking about, because if you kept on the move ... well, more than once in the trenches in the First War a shell had exploded where he had been sitting or standing a moment before. Nevertheless, he obliged himself to sit still, staring somewhat glassily at Matthew and Vera opposite him. He did not want to start all that again at his age! It had taken him years after the war to get over this compulsion to be always on the move. How many years had he not spent with invisible shells exploding in dining-rooms and drawing-rooms he had just vacated!

'At this range they'll only be able to send over the small stuff,' he added, lighting his pipe.

'The Major means that if you are lucky you will only be hit by a small shell,' observed Dupigny wryly from the doorway.

'Ah, François! I suppose you know there's a French ship sailing tonight for Bombay? Will you be aboard?'

Dupigny shook his head. 'I shall stay a little longer, I think.'

'This may be your last chance.'

Dupigny, however, merely shrugged.

'I saw Walter a little while ago. He said that Joan and Nigel would be leaving tonight. They're to be married in Bombay and then go to Australia to join the others as soon as they can ... Joan would have left the other day but could not get on the boat. It seems that ...' The Major paused. Matthew, with his finger to his lips, was signalling in the direction of Ehrendorf who lay sprawled on a mattress at the far end of the room with a folded newspaper over his head.

'What are you going to do about this poor fellow?' Matthew asked in order to change the subject.

Each shell that had exploded had produced a groan from beneath an elegant lacquered writing-desk which supported a field-telephone 'for emergencies' which no one could get to work and an ordinary telephone, as well as several other things. Presently the author of the groan crept out and wept to slump down under the Major's chair. With his refined sense of imminent danger The Human Condition had evidently sensed that these strange new explosions boded ill for his chances of survival.

'I'm afraid I'll have to take him to the vet this evening. We may as well bring him along at the same time as you go to the boat, poor creature.' At these words The Human Condition rolled his eyeballs up to the Major's face and uttered a piteous whine, licking the Major's hand at the same time.

'I think that dog must be rotting internally,' remarked Dupigny objectively.

62

Ehrendorf made his way, carrying a towel and swimming trunks, towards the Blacketts' compound, lingering for a moment among the exotic blooms which glowed like lamps amid the dark leaves. For a while he watched the butterflies which still swooped and fluttered in this little glade, impervious to the bombs that had fallen round about. Then, with a melancholy sigh which was partly counterfeit because he was now seeing himself as the ill-starred hero of his novel in its first version (innocent American abused by cynical Europeans), he moved on in the direction of the swimming pool.

Although he had paid a brief visit to Walter by darkness the other evening, it was several weeks since Ehrendorf had last seen the Blacketts' house by daylight. It seemed to him to have a forlorn and deserted air. During the raid on Tanglin a bomb had fallen at one edge of the lawn, uprooting the 'flame of the forest' tree beneath which, several months ago, he had been standing with Joan when she had thrown wine in his face at the garden-party. No effort had been made to fill in the crater on whose raised lip the grass lawn continued peacefully to grow; in the façade of the house itself several of the windows which had once been glazed for the air-conditioning now gaped darkly where once they had sparkled with reflections from the pool.

He plodded past the tennis courts whose white lines, washed out by the monsoon rains and not repainted, were by now scarcely visible. Normally, too, there would have been several Tamils working in the flower-beds or cutting back the *lalang* but today he could not see a soul. He paused to stare uncomprehendingly at an untidy mass of broken spars and tattered paper which stood at the margin of the nutmeg grove and which he failed to recognize as the remains of damaged floats for the jubilee celebrations. Can Walter and Joan have left already? he wondered and, resigned though he already was to the fact that he was unlikely ever to see Joan again, he was nevertheless surprised by the intense and chilling sadness which suddenly enveloped him.

The summer-house, in which the Blacketts in happier times had invited their guests to change their clothes, remained undamaged; Ehrendorf changed rapidly and plunged into the pool which was full of dead leaves and other flotsam. He dived and swam under water for a few feet but the water was murky and disagreeable. How different everything was! Surfacing he bumped into a piece of floating wood on which the words '... in Prosperity' were written. He took a deep breath and dived again; this time he dragged himself on and on through the silent grey corridors, counting the grey tiles on the bottom, inspecting weird grey objects which lay there: a broken flower-pot from which still trailed a slimy grey plant which wavered slightly at his passage, a brick, a rusting metal golf club, a slimy, swollen, disintegrating grey head, horribly merry, which had once belonged to one of the floats and which he also failed to recognize. He would have liked to drag himself on and on through that grey world but his lungs insisted that he should return to the surface. Shaking the water out of his eyes he saw that Joan was walking rapidly towards the pool. Her face was flushed and agitated.

'Oh, hiya. I hope you don't mind me using the pool. I didn't see anyone around. I thought you'd all gone.' He was aware of an extraordinary stiffness of the muscles of his face as he spoke.

Joan had stopped at the edge of the pool and was gazing down at him with an odd expression on her face, restlessly fingering the turban she was wearing. She ignored his greeting, turned away, looked at her watch, turned back to him. At last she said: 'You must help me get to the boat. I've been trying to ring people but everyone else has gone. There's only Abdul here and he's too old ... They say there's already a terrible traffic jam beginning ... All the "boys" have cleared off, even the kitchen "boy", and Father has gone off somewhere ... and Monty, I don't know where he is ... Nigel had to go and settle some business at the last moment and I'm to meet him at the boat but unless you help me ... You see, they've all gone! Father was supposed to be back ages ago to take me down to the docks himself, but even the *syce* isn't there and it's getting late ... Jim, I can't manage the luggage by myself, d'you see? Oh, go away! You're completely useless!' she screamed at Abdul suddenly for the elderly servant had followed her out on to the lawn and was rubbing his hands anxiously. Shocked, he fell back a few paces but continued to watch Joan.

Ehrendorf had turned over on to his back and was no longer looking at Joan but straight up at the sky which was cloudless though covered with a white haze. Floating with arms and legs outstretched he thought: 'From above I must look as if I'm floating like a star-fish ... or perhaps like a piece of flotsam.' In spite of the water bubbling in his ears he could still hear Joan's voice, though quite faintly now. He could tell from its pitch that she was panic-stricken. And this was the girl who had refused to help Matthew get Vera away! He said to himself, floating placidly: 'I wouldn't help her even if my life depended upon it!'

When he turned over to swim to the side he could no longer hear her voice, but she was still there, kneeling in tears of rage at the side of the pool, hammering at it with a piece of broken wood. As he gripped the rounded lip of the pool and heaved himself out of the water he glanced at her, musing on the wonder of a beautiful woman with a disagreeable personality. Such a woman, he mused, was like a lovely schooner with a mad captain. The custodian of this lovely body was a hard-hearted bitch. It was altogether astonishing.

'Of course I'll help you,' he said. 'Just wait a moment while I get changed.

Mr Wu's Buick, which had been under repair for some days, was now on the road again and heading towards Wilkie Street where The Human Condition was to be left at the vet's *en route* to Collyer's Quay. The dog sat on the front seat and stared out uneasily at the darkening streets. But when they reached Wilkie Street they found a large crowd of harrowed-looking people grasping dogs, cats and birds of all shapes and sizes already waiting. It seemed that these doomed creatures had sensed the anguish of their owners, too, for they were setting up the most distressing din of shrieking, whining, miaouwing, barking and piping. The Major had no appetite for this and said: 'We'll call on the way back from the boat. There won't be anyone there after the curfew. Besides, we'd better not waste any time.' The Human Condition, who had been staring with dismay at this frantic queue of fellow-victims, uttered a heart-rending groan. For how long had he been reprieved?

When they reached Collyer's Quay they were thankful that they had not delayed any longer for already the quay itself and the surrounding area was jammed with cars full of anxious people. Holding the paper that Vera had been given at Cluny Matthew plunged into the crowd of people trying to get tickets and embarkation instructions. He was gone for a long time; meanwhile the traffic jam around them had worsened considerably. When he at last returned he had Vera's ticket but he was looking worried: he explained that they still had to drive to the P & O wharf some three miles away and the traffic by now was scarcely moving. To make matters worse, passengers were only allowed to board the ship in groups which had been staggered alphabetically in order to prevent everybody arriving at the dock at the same time. Because Vera's surname began with C this regulation should have worked to her advantage, but by some error the official who had taken her name, perhaps assuming that she had given her surname first in the Chinese fashion, had reversed her names and allotted her to the last group. In any case passengers were not arriving at intervals as had been expected and some of those who had arrived too early were being made to wait, blocking the quayside. Nevertheless, although the boarding arrangements were no longer achieving what had been expected of them and were, indeed, only adding to the confusion, they were still being rigidly adhered to by the authorities in charge of the embarkation.

'We should still make it all right. The boat doesn't sail till one o'clock. We can always walk if the worst comes to the worst.'

It took several minutes before there was even an opening that allowed them to pull into the line of traffic crawling along Collyer's Quay; then, for long stretches, they were obliged to stop altogether. Sometimes they discovered the reason for these delays, a car that had overheated or run out of petrol perhaps; then they would overtake a demented man peering at his engine in a cloud of steam, or a weeping woman sitting by herself with a pile of luggage, while those behind cursed and hooted at her to get her car out of the way.

'This is dreadful.' The Major's face grew increasingly grim as the minutes ticked by. Presently a whole hour had fled. They still had not reached the shell of the Sailor's Institute at the end of Anson Road.

'Perhaps they'll delay the time of sailing.' But this, Matthew knew, was unlikely for if the *Félix Roussel* was to escape the Japanese bombers she would have to be well on her way from Singapore before dawn.

For some time now they had been following a large open Bentley which contained a party of elegantly dressed young ladies sitting on pigskin suitcases plastered with gaily coloured steamer and hotel labels. Since it was already quite dark and all street-lights had been extinguished in accordance with the blackout regulations there only remained the Buick's papered-over headlights to cast a faint glow on the party travelling in front. But from time to time a match would flare as a cigarette was lit ... (it appeared that the young ladies in the Bentley had no inhibitions about smoking in public) ... then a cheerful little scene would be briefly illuminated, for to celebrate their departure from Singapore the ladies had brought two or three bottles of champagne and some glasses. And so, while another hour went by, the grim party from the Mayfair, with their doomed little dog sitting on the front seat, sat and watched the beautifully marcelled tresses in front of them and listened to the clink of glasses and the giggles, shrieks and popping of corks.

Presently it occurred to the Major that there was something familiar about the Bentley.

'Isn't that one of Walter's cars?'

'I've been wondering the same thing. But what are those young women doing in it? There's something familiar about them, too. But it surely can't be Walter driving, nor his *syce* either, come to that.' The driver, whoever it was, remained invisible slumped far down in the seat in a manner which by contrast with the exuberance of his companions, was almost furtive.

'I have an idea it's that singing team,' said the Major, 'the Da Sousa Sisters ... the girls Walter wanted to have in his jubilee procession. He must have arranged for someone to take them to the boat in his car.'

After a while, in support of this theory as to their identity the young women sitting on their luggage in the back of the Bentley put their marcelled heads together and their arms round each other's shoulders and began to sing:

> Singapore, hulloa, hulloa!
> In silk and satin and boa
> We are the girlies from Goa!

The Major was too preoccupied, however, to be greatly concerned with the identity of some tipsy young women in Walter's car. He was more worried by the glowing clock on the dashboard (had it stopped or was it a quarter-past eleven already?). It was true that they had now almost reached the corner of Trafalgar Street but the nearer they came to the docks the slower their progress. Now increasingly they found themselves halted in the same place for several minutes at a time. The heat, the exhaust fumes and the ever-present drifting smoke from burning buildings made it hard to breathe. Vera lay with her head slumped against the back of the seat, her eyes closed. The minute hand on the dashboard crept on.

In the car ahead of them as time went on the gaiety of the Da Sousa Sisters was replaced by a rather sullen silence: evidently they, too, were becoming anxious about reaching the boat in time. Soon a squabble erupted and they began to scream, either at each other or at their driver, it was hard to say. Then they began to shriek abuse at the car in front of them which for some reason was being abandoned by its passengers. Eventually the Bentley managed to pull round it and the column advanced a few more yards. On the sea side of the road a warehouse which had been damaged in an earlier raid had been left to burn, casting a red glow over the line of cars ahead and bringing an intolerable increase in the temperature for some distance round about. It now became clear that a number of the cars ahead had been abandoned and were blocking the road beyond redemption.

'I think we'd better walk,' Matthew said. Vera said that she felt well enough to do so but it was obvious that the smoke, the heat and the fumes were making her feel ill.

'You go ahead,' the Major said. 'I'll see if I can get rid of the car and then come back and help.'

Matthew opened the door, threw out Vera's suitcase and helped her out into the road. As he was doing so The Human Condition suddenly sprang off the front seat into the darkness and vanished. 'Hey! Come back!' called the Major feebly, but this was no time to worry about a lost dog. Matthew picked up Vera's suitcase and, supporting her as best he could, set off with her into the flickering night. As they were passing the Bentley another squabble suddenly broke out between the young ladies and their driver. It was clear that they considered him to be responsible for the traffic jam in which they found themselves.

'You said you taking us to bloody boat!' they screamed. 'You damn well better take us to bloody-damn boat, OK!'

'Matthew!' called a despairing voice from the Bentley and Matthew stopped, peering at the car in astonishment, for there, slumped in the front seat, his face weirdly illuminated by the flickering light of the burning building nearby as if by infernal flames was Monty Blackett.

'I say, you couldn't give me a hand with some of this luggage, could you, old man? It's so heavy I can't manage it all. Go on, be a sport!'

'Impossible! I have all I can manage already.'

'Look here, Matthew, there's a good fellow,' pleaded Monty in a more confidential tone, 'these young ladies here, who are simply charming, by the way, will let us hide in their cabin till the boat has sailed, in return for helping them, I mean to say ... We'll be in Bombay in two shakes and no one will be the wiser. And they'll probably let us have some fun with them into the bargain. It's our only chance. Don't be a chump! Singapore's done for! It's common knowledge. And I promised these girls that I'd get them on board, you know, and they'll be frightfully sticky if I don't! We just go on board saying we're helping them with their bags and stay there. Things are in such a mess that no one will know the difference!'

'Sorry, Monty, I can't help you. But you're nearly there. I'm sure you'll make it. Goodbye.'

While Monty had thus been pleading for help two of the Da Sousa Sisters, who had begun to pummel him and pull his hair in their indignation, had desisted and fixed their glittering, anthracite eyes on Matthew, allowing their victim to make this last appeal. In the meantime, other Da Sousa Sisters had come hopping forward over the suitcases to perch like leather-winged harpies on the back of the seat, on the door at his side, and even on the windscreen, clutching on with long red fingernails and staring down at him with their cruelly glittering eyes, one or two of them already beginning to dribble from scarlet-lipsticked mouths.

'Be a sport!' wailed Monty.

But Matthew was already on his way with Vera towards the distant P & O wharf. He looked back once, just in time to see Monty's flickering, terror-stricken features disappear under a tide of biting, scratching, hair-pulling Da Sousa Sisters. In a moment there was nothing to be seen but an inner circle of feeding marcelled heads and an outer circle of tight-skirted bottoms. 'Poor Monty!' thought Matthew. 'What a fate!' But he hurried on with Vera, for by now it was getting close to midnight and the *Félix Roussel* was due to sail in a little over an hour.

As they advanced they saw that the road was jammed, not only with empty cars but with all sorts of other objects as well. Clearly no one had taken seriously the instruction to bring only hand luggage. Household goods of all sorts had been abandoned with the cars that had been conveying them: tables, chairs, chests and boxes were to be seen strapped on to car roofs: rolled-up carpets poked through windows. In places, abandoned possessions had been disgorged into the road, which was gradually coming to take on the appearance of a nightmare furniture store: some of them had been dragged by their reluctant owners a little distance in the direction of the wharf; in other cases their owners had not yet been able to make up their minds to forsake them: here and there a man with bulging eyes and swelling veins could still be seen wrestling with some possession too precious to leave behind, a mahogany dining-table perhaps, or a set of carved Chinese chairs, while at his side his wife groaned under a heavy brass Buddha or some other such fearful fardel.

Matthew and Vera now began to find that the litter of furniture and packing-cases, trunks and suitcases had become so dense in places that there was nothing for it but to climb over. They found themselves having to squeeze between wardrobes or clamber over pianos, their path lit only by the distant light of burning buildings, now seeing themselves faintly reflected in long mirrors, now listening to the sobs and groans of shadowy figures on their knees by the wayside. On one dark stretch they found themselves crunching through a tea-set of finest bone china; in another, stopping to rest because Vera was tired, they groped their way to a chesterfield sofa and sat down on it without realizing that a man and his wife, one at each end, were still trying to trundle it towards the wharf.

At long last they began to near the dock gates and could even make out the funnels of the Félix Roussel silhouetted against the pink glow of the night. Suddenly a rickshaw loomed out of the darkness along Keppel Road in the jostling crowd that flowed towards Gate 3 and the Empire Dock. Matthew, astonished, just had time to glimpse Joan sitting in it amidst a pile of luggage while Ehrendorf, stripped to the waist and streaming with sweat, galloped onwards as best he could between the shafts. Unable, like Matthew and Vera, to get through in the car Ehrendorf had wanted to abandon it, but Joan had refused to leave her luggage, which included a number of valuable wedding-presents, a set of pewter mugs, bed-linen, material to be made up into curtains according to a colour scheme she had already devised for her first home, a canteen of solid silver and other things. What was to be done? Ehrendorf had happened to spot an abandoned rickshaw beside the road and now here he was, head down and gasping for breath, scattering people right and left as he charged for the open gates.

'Darling! I was afraid you wouldn't get here in time,' cried a voice almost in Ehrendorf's ear. A pink-faced young man in a white linen suit and a trilby was addressing Joan. 'I have someone keeping me a place near the front. I say, who's this johnnie?' he added, noticing at length that there was something unusual about Joan's rickshaw-wallah. For a moment Ehrendorf stared into the slightly popping blue eyes of his successful rival. Then a lock of blonde hair dropped like a curtain from Nigel's forehead and only one blue eye was visible. Nigel reached a hand to his brow and removed the offending lock, allowing the silky hair to sift through his fingers to the knuckle while he contemplated the half-naked Ehrendorf with distaste. Ehrendorf dropped the shafts of the rickshaw and reached for his shirt, murmuring: 'I'll leave the rest to you, if you don't mind.' He hesitated a moment, examining Nigel without hostility. 'What on earth can she see in a chap like this?' he asked himself in wonder ... but then, women had appalling taste in men, he had always thought so. Without a further glance at Joan he slipped away, forcing his way back against the stream of people.

'I say aren't you going to stay and help with the luggage?' came a faint, indignant voice following him through the darkness.

When at last Matthew and Vera had passed through the gates and saw the state of the quay, they looked at each other in dismay. Between where they stood and the narrow corridor through which the passengers were channelled there swayed a densely packed mass of people. Beyond, sat or stood half a dozen harassed officials examining tickets, remonstrating, copying names into a ledger, shouting, shrugging shoulders, looking impatient. Every now and then someone tore himself away from this dense mass and pursued his lonely way through the corridor then up the canvas-sided gang-plank to disappear at last into the looming vessel watched all the way by the boiling throng below. As Matthew and Vera thrust their way into the crowd they saw a woman make her way up to the ship's side sobbing with nervous exhaustion and dragging by the hand a little girl with a pretty, open face and with a ribbon in her hair, herself carrying a doll in a long infant's dress; behind walked a boy with a Meccano-set looking self-conscious and wearing a sun-helmet. After them there was nobody for a while, then Nigel and Joan, heavily laden with suitcases, made their way aboard and disappeared from view. Once, a powerful searchlight from the ship's superstructure was switched on, swept over the packed crowds on the quay for a moment, then died.

As the hour drew nearer one a.m. and signs of activity began to appear at the ship's side the crowd pressed forward more anxiously than ever. People shouted and waved tickets above their heads, hoping to attract the attention of the officials and let them know that ticket-holding passengers still remained on shore. The rate at which they were passing up the gang-plank hardly seemed to quicken, however, even though the officials must have realized that there was a danger of people being left on the quayside. Meanwhile, still later arrivals continued to flood in from behind, straining and pushing forward with all their might.

Abruptly, after an age of being jostled back and forth in the densest part of the crowd, as if by a miracle Vera and Matthew found themselves within reach of the nearest desk and, lunging forward, Matthew managed to slap down Vera's ticket. The official picked it up, looked at it and handed it back with a shake of his head. 'Alphabetical order, sir. Sorry. We aren't ready for this lot yet.'

'But the ship is leaving in five minutes!'

'I can't help that. Next please.'

Matthew had released his hold on Vera in order to deal with the man at the desk. Looking round, he saw that she had been caught in a cross-current of shoving passengers and thrown back. But this man behind the desk! Matthew reached out to take the official by the throat, but the people behind who had been shouting abuse at him for wasting time now seized his clothes and dragged him out of the way. As he struggled to reach Vera, something darted between his legs and away towards the gang-plank. It was an elderly King Charles spaniel. One of the officials tried to grab it as it passed but it swerved and eluded him; head down it battled its way up the gang-plank, darted past a surprised seaman and, plunging on to the crowded deck, vanished from sight just as the order was being given to raise the gang-plank (thereafter, some instinct directed The Human Condition unerringly towards the bridge where the captain, though worried by Japanese bombers and the anxious hours that lay ahead, at that moment happened to be contemplating with regret and longing his own little dog which, by a fortunate coincidence, had died, smothered in comfort, only a few days earlier).

Again a searchlight was switched on and swept hastily over the crowded quays, hesitating for a moment on a great net cradle containing a large motor-car that was being winched aboard. Matthew stared in disbelief: surely it was the Bentley which Monty had been driving! But how had it managed to get to the quayside? There was no sign of Monty. Perhaps he was lying on the floor. There were Da Sousa Sisters perched everywhere, however. A French sailor, looking handsome, clung on to a rope with one foot on the Bentley's running-board and with the scarlet claws of one of the Da Sousa Sisters round his neck. Suddenly, like song-birds struck by a beam of sunlight, the Da Sousa Sisters put their marcelled heads together and trilled:

> Matelot, hulloa, hulloa!
> In silk and satin and boa
> We are the girlies from Goa!

The searchlight was switched out. Blackness and a sudden silence descended. The next moment a roar of outrage erupted from the disappointed passengers on the quayside. The gang-plank was beginning to go up.

Again the crowd pressed forward, pinning Matthew's arms to his sides and squeezing the air out of his lungs. He at last managed to free an arm and reach out towards Vera ... but as he did so, he saw the back of her reddish-black head vanish beneath the thrusting mob. In a rage he shoved his way through the crowd to where he had seen her go down, shouting at people to stand back from her. But nobody seemed to hear. As he groped for her on the ground his hand closed over a piece of wood and he picked it up, flailing about with it until he had driven everyone back from where she lay on the paved quay. He picked her up then and barged his way back towards the gates, still hitting about him with the piece of wood. Blood from her face began to trickle down his back. To the north the thud of guns continued. The Japanese assault on the island was only a few minutes away.

63

On his way home from the docks the Major, having given up the attempt to find Matthew and Vera in the crowd, had called in to see a friend at the Rescue Control Room in the Municipal Offices; together they had gone up to watch the bombardment from the flat roof of the building where a number of other people had already gathered. The flashes of the British guns, the noise, the restless glimmer of the Japanese batteries to the north, all combined to bring back memories of his younger days which he would have preferred to forget. After a few minutes he said goodbye to his friend and returned to the Mayfair. In the early hours of the morning Matthew and Vera returned, shocked and exhausted by their ordeal. Vera, though cut and bruised, was not badly hurt. The Major was sorry but he was not particularly surprised when he heard of the crowds left on the quayside.

Despite the lateness of the hour a sympathetic audience had assembled to hear what had happened at the docks. Everyone had found it hard to sleep, perhaps because there was a feeling in the air that a crisis was at hand. The terrific Japanese barrage from Johore suggested that it would not be long before they attempted to land on the Island. Earlier, in response to a rumour that all the alcohol in Singapore was soon to be destroyed lest Japanese troops, in the event of a successful landing, should go on the rampage among the civilian population, a party led by Dupigny and Mr Wu had slipped over to the Blacketts' house and returned with several cases of wine from Walter's cellar. Since there were not enough glasses to go round a separate bottle had been uncorked for everyone. Soon a party was getting under way.

Gradually, thanks to Walter's fine claret, a mood of elation came to replace the sombre atmosphere which had prevailed. Festive sounds also issued from the board-room where the girls from the Poh Leung Kuk, under orders from the Major to accelerate the process of selecting bridegrooms, appeared to be having an all-night sitting. They had asked the Major if they could borrow his gramophone. He had responded dubiously to their request, wanting to know why they should need a gramophone for such a purpose? They had looked so disappointed and abashed, they had blinked their long eyelashes so submissively (and, after all, they had behaved themselves jolly well of Château Ducru Beaucaillou he was holding, hoping that to put up with) that the Major had found himself yielding in spite of himself. So, not without misgivings, he had handed over the gramophone, the only two records which remained unbroken and a box of needles with strict instructions that they were to change the needle *every* time before playing a record and not to wind the instrument too hard or they would break the spring. 'And I want to see every single one of you with a husband by tomorrow at the latest,' he had added sternly. 'This choosing business has gone on long enough. If you don't make up your minds I shall ask Captain Brown to do it for you.'

As a matter of fact, the Major had expected to find the

bungalow quiet by the time he returned from the docks, but evidently the girls, in order to hammer out their final decisions, had found it necessary to retain their prospective bridegrooms even after the curfew. Now from behind the closed door of the board-room came the sound of laughter in the silence which followed Noel Coward singing 'London Pride'. The Major tried to estimate whether there was enough time for them to have changed the needle before the other record began.

> The moon that lingered over London Town,
> Poor puzzled moon, He wore a frown ...

The Major, too, wore a frown. He took a swig from the bottle of Château Ducru Beaucaillou he was holding, hoping that nothing untoward was happening in the board-room. He really should have insisted on the bridegrooms leaving before the curfew: he could hardly expect them to leave now. Perhaps he would turn them out at five o'clock.

> How could he know we two were so in love,
> The whole darn world was upside down?
> And as we kissed and said goodnight
> A nightingale sang in Berkley Square ...

Soon, the Major did not doubt, it would again be the turn of Noel Coward.

Presently, Cheong, who was also finding it difficult to sleep, joined the circle and he, too was given a bottle of claret. Cheong's status had undergone a remarkable change in the past few weeks. He was no longer to be considered a servant. On the contrary, he had now become a figure of considerable authority, organizing meals on a large scale and allotting space to transients who needed shelter both inside and underneath the bungalow. The Major depended on him heavily. On his own initiative he dealt with a variety of matters which, but for him, would most likely not have been dealt with at all. Had the Major not come across him burying someone quietly in the compound? To bury someone between breakfast and tiffin was nothing these days to Cheong. Sometimes the Major could not help wondering, such was the man's initiative, whether Cheong might not secretly be a graduate of the University of the Toilers of the East. Not that it mattered, of course.

Under the influence of the wine the conversation grew animated. Matthew, still full of bitterness after his experience at the docks and quite unable to put it out of his mind for more than a moment, began to discourse volubly in an anguished tone on the kind of society which must follow this one. It was the injustice which he saw all around him that maddened him! Why should privilege and self-interest rule in everything instead of justice and reason? There was no need for it. A society *based* on justice would get the best out of its members by appealing to their better instead of their worse natures! Dupigny shook his head sadly but did not bother to explain that this view of human psychology was hopelessly ingenuous; he could see that Matthew was upset. But, in due course, when Matthew had turned, as he often did when in a state of nervous excitement, to Geneva in order to make extravagent claims for those such as Emperor Haile Selassie and himself who had foreseen years ago that the devious, unprincipled behaviour of the Big Powers would end in wholesale carnage, Dupigny, pausing only to gargle blissfully with a mouthful of Haut-Brion, could not resist challenging him. 'I can't believe, even with the Italian invasion of Ethiopia to inspire him, that Haile Selassie could foresee in 1936 the troubles that we now are facing ... unless at his court he had a fortune-teller with the crystal ball.'

'Aha!' cried Matthew. 'And yet, François, in 1936 he said: "Do the peoples of the world not yet realize that by fighting on until the bitter end I am not only performing my sacred duty to my people *but standing guard in the last citadel of collective security*. I must hold on until my tardy allies appear. And if they never come then I say prophetically and without bitterness, the West must perish.' "

But Cheong, and perhaps Mr Wu too, had had difficulty in following the Emperor's words and now he was looking enquiringly at the Major. Apologizing for the poor quality of his pidgin, which contained odds and ends picked up here and there on his pre-war Eastern travels, the Major interpreted as best he could. 'Empelor talkee this fashion ... My fightee long time but world people no wantchee savee. My makee number one pidgin my people, same time makee all-piecee nation pidgin. Empelor talkee: Whobody come? My must stop look-see fliend no come by and by. Spose fliend no come, Blitain, Flance, Melika, all catchee too-metchee bobbery! All catchee die, chop-chop! ... Er, I'm afraid that's about the best I can do,' and the Major sank back, puffing his pipe.

'It's always the same, François. Your Foreign Office and mine, instead of making a principled stand on the Covenant of the League of Nations, always preferred some private horse-trading behind the scenes.' Matthew tipped up his bottle and indignantly swallowed half a pint of Laffitte: almost immediately he suffered the odd delusion that he was a lighthouse and that his indignation was a small boat rowing steadily away from him. The thought of Lord Halifax, however, caused it to row back a little way.

With the Major desperately trying to keep up with him in pidgin he described what it had been like in Geneva when Haile Selassie had come with the Ethiopian delegation to protest about the Italian annexation and to demand that the Council of the League should not recognize it. On that occasion Halifax had risen to make what was surely the most grossly hypocritical speech in the history of international affairs: this, too, but involuntarily, Matthew knew by heart, simply because he had been unable to forget it.

'Halifax said: "Here two ideals are in conflict: on the one hand the ideal of devotion, unflinching but unpractical, to some high purpose; on the other, the ideal of some practical victories for peace ... I cannot doubt that the strongest claim is that of peace ... Each of us knows by painful experience how consistently it is necessary to recognize that which may be ideally right and what is practically possible ..." And so on. If the League was not prepared to use force then it should submit to the "reality" of the Italian conquest in the interests of peace. Is that not outrageous, François?'

'Lord Halifax talkee this fashion,' explained the Major, struggling to find some way of abbreviating Matthew's harangue. '"League of Nations idea blong plenty proper, plenty fine maybe, but League idea all-same plenty fine motor-car buggerup, motor-car no walkee. League of Nations no sendee soldier-man, no can do. Blitish Government idea yes can do."' ('Oh dear, I'm afraid that was a bit complicated,' apologized the Major.)

'Ah so,' nodded Cheong thoughtfully. 'League Nation idea no walkee ... Howfashion Lord Ha Lee Fax no wantchee League idea? *Maskee,** this blong all-same fool pidgin!' And with a shrug of disgust he, too, took a long pull at his bottle of Margaux (making a face, he preferred rice wine).

'The Emperor replied to Halifax: "The suggestion of Great

*Never mind.

Britain is to favour general appeasement by the sacrifice of a people. This is contrary to the ideals of the Covenant and those ideals so constantly proclaimed by Great Britain and France," and he ended, "It is sheer hypocrisy to attempt to strangle a people by procedure!"'

'Empelor plenty angry,' summarized the Major. 'Empelor talkee: "You buggerupim League of Nations!"'

Cheong nodded gravely. He had assumed that such would have been the Emperor's reaction, for what other complexion could be put on Lord Ha Lee Fax's preference for 'realism', the gospel of the corrupt, entrepreneurial diplomats of the West, over principle? What could be expected, in any case, Cheong wondered, of such strong-smelling diplomats? He had more than once, in his previous employment in Shanghai, had occasion to take the coat of a second or third secretary from one Legation or another and he knew what he was talking about. When the new China arose, as he did not doubt that it would, a new type of diplomat, odourless and strong-principled, would strut the world's stage. Then at last things would be different.

'Will we never be able to loosen the grip of the self-interested and corrupt on human affairs?' demanded Matthew, springing to his feet, his eyes flashing.

'By the way, that reminds me,' remarked Ehrendorf, who had just been splashing himself from the Shanghai jar in the bathroom and now came in drying his hair to join the company, 'it seems that the expression, "the Singapore Grip", refers to the ability acquired by certain ladies of Singapore to control their autonomous vaginal muscles, apparently with delightful results. The girls from the Poh Leung Kuk agreed to tell me what it was for a dollar. They hinted that for ten dollars it might be possible to arrange a demonstration. Er ... of course I didn't accept,' he added, seeing that the Major was looking upset.

'No, Jim, that's not what the Singapore Grip is,' cried Matthew, his eyes flashing more than ever. 'I *know* what it is! It's the grip of our Western culture and economy on the Far East ... It's the stranglehold of capital on the traditional cultures of Malaya, China, Burma, Java, Indo-China and even India herself! It's the doing of things *our* way ... I mean, it's the pursuit of self-interest rather than of the *common* interest! But one day we shall have a new League of Nations to conduct the world's affairs with reason and justice and humanity! A League of Nations not made up of cynical power-brokers but of philosophers and philanthropists whose only desire will be to bind the nations and the races together!'

Ehrendorf sighed, thinking that in any case the Singapore Grip was about to be pried loose, if that was what it was. After some moments of hesitation and comparing of vintages, he selected the Laffitte. Altogether it had been a hard day.

Part Six

64

If you follow the Singapore River, from its mouth where it bulges and curves beneath the Fullerton Building, back along its many twists and turns, between sampans and barges so tightly packed that in places there is scarcely a channel wide enough for the flow of water-traffic, back almost as far as The Great World, then you will see an unusually handsome godown on the right bank, taller than any of the other godowns that line the river at that point, taller than any building of any kind for some distance and made taller by the familiar sign on its roof: Blackett and Webb Limited, painted white for the jubilee ... Or rather, you would have seen it in those days, for now it no longer exists. The place where it once stood is now dominated by several many-storey apartment buildings where the resettled inhabitants of former Chinese slums now live, and even The Great World itself is mostly shuttered and empty, trembling on the very brink of no longer existing: its fortune-tellers, quacks and *ronggeng* dancers, its Chinese actors and mounte-banks, its brewers of monkey-soup and sellers of fruit, its pimps and soldiers and whores, have all been dumped in the dustbin of history and the lid clapped firmly on top of them. Their place has been taken by prosperous-looking workers from the electronic factories out for an evening stroll with their children, by a party of polite Japanese tourists with cameras who have strayed here by mistake, and by the author of this book writing busily in a small red notebook and scratching his knuckles where some lonely, last-remaining mosquito (for even they have mostly departed or been done away with), ignoring his dignified appearance, has not hesitated to bite him as he scribbles.

This particular godown was the one to which Walter had taken Joan to propose that she should marry Matthew (how far off that seemed now!): it was the oldest, the biggest, Walter's favourite, the replica of that first warehouse in Rangoon which, in happier times, he had been so pleased to point out to visitors when he was showing them the paintings that hung in his drawing-room. To that first godown in Rangoon who knows what happened? No doubt it was knocked down, or fell down, or a fine offer was made for it, or perhaps it was even turned into a cinema. Walter did not know. But he was glad that this one still existed. For Walter had learned something important from his life in commerce : that business is not simply a matter of making profits.

A successful and respectable business, on the contrary, is deeply embedded in the life of its time and place. A respectable business supports the prevalent beliefs of the society of which it is a part. If society at large considers it immoral for a woman to smoke a cigarette in the street or for a man to wear a hat at· his dining-table, then you will certainly not find Blackett and Webb countenancing such behaviour in their staff. Not only at Blackett and Webb but at every other business of standing in Singapore the clerical staff, despite the temperature, were expected to wear white suits and black ties. Even the better Asiatic houses followed this custom. Respectability is important in business because it generates more and better custom : it means you will pay your debts and deliver the goods, resisting the temptation to make a bolt for the hills. Better business in turn generates more respectability. But in order to be respectable you do have to know what society approves of. Provided you know *that*, then there is no problem : your business can play its full part in the community. It is only at a time like the present when it is hard to be sure what society at large believes, or if it believes anything at all, that a businessman grows baffled and uneasy and perhaps with a shrug of his shoulders gives it up and limits himself to a dogged pursuit of his profits.

Walter certainly had not reached that stage; witness the effort and expense he had consecrated to his jubilee celebrations. But already, it seemed to him, Blackett and Webb was beginning to stand out as an oasis of old-fashioned virtues in a desert of less scrupulous businesses. It was 'the spirit of the times' again, that is what it was! Wherever you looked you saw it at work. Now, Walter had heard, in England women were no longer wearing hats and were going into pubs. Some women, even in Singapore, had taken to wearing trousers, not something he would have permitted to his own women-folk. Well, continue along that road and one fine day you would find that a gentleman's word was no longer his bond, but more likely an attempt to talk you into something. Why was this godown important to Walter? Because for him it symbolized the old-fashioned virtues and beliefs which were melting away all around him, progressively, in concert with the decaying spirit of earlier times to which he had been accustomed.

And yet ... a man must move with the times. Think of those rice-millers in London for whom the Suez Canal had proved a banana skin on the road to prosperity! This godown was also important to Walter for the great qualities of raw rubber that it contained. A business cannot embody the highest aims of society without trading profitably from its warehouses. What they contain must not be wasted or abandoned. It was out of the question to allow these warehouses not to make the profit which lay piled up within their shadowy walls.

Now on Monday, 8 February, came the news that the Japanese had succeeded in landing on the Island in the course of the night. Walter found himself faced with a disturbing prospect: the contents of this building on the river and of several other godowns nearby would most likely be destroyed in accordance with a contingency plan for the denial of useful materials to the Japanese. He had long expected something of the sort if the Japanese pursued their advance. Reports had reached him in recent weeks that officials from the Public Works Department had been snooping about making enquiries as to the contents of his various godowns. Their first visits had been discreet: the authorities had been anxious not to sap morale by making too obvious preparations for a capitulation ... Lately they had become more officious.

Today there came word that the Governor had authorized destruction of British-owned engineering plant, oil and rubber stocks, liquor supplies and various others goods and materials that the Japanese might consider valuable. Well, he had expected that it would come to this ... But above all it was the selective nature of the Governor's denial plans that stung Walter: Blackett and Webb (Engineering) Limited would be razed while neighbouring Chinese enterprises would be left untouched! It was an outrage. He promptly telephoned the Governor ... but could not get through. He tried to arrange an appointment with the Governor's staff: he had never had any trouble doing so before, yet now when it was necessary he found himself being headed off by pipsqueaks of secretaries. He would be left for minutes at a time holding a telephone receiver, obliged to listen

502

to baffling electrical interference: strange hiccups, faintly tink-ling xylophones, the ringing of distant telephones on other lines, and ghostly voices speaking gibberish which, however, sometimes held a queer sort of significance.

'Old men must die. They'd not be human otherwise,' some-one remarked cheerfully in the middle of a blizzard of clickings and buzzings. 'We're all on a conveyor belt, each one of us. We all must fall off at the other end. Does that answer your question?' Walter strained his ears but only to hear what sounded like a whole office full of telephones ringing. He put the telephone down, shattered. He was not used to making his own telephone calls at the best of times: that was his secretary's job. He picked up the receiver again: this time he heard what he was convinced was a stream of Japanese followed by high-pitched laughter. But they had only been on the Island since the previous night: they would hardly be using the telephones already. He tried to summon one of his assistants who under-stood Japanese but by the time he arrived the voice had been replaced by silence and, eventually, by the ominous ticking of a clock.

'Would you mind getting off this line, please?' demanded a woman's voice rudely.

'I certainly would!' snapped Walter. 'Blackett here ... of Blackett and Webb. I want to speak to the Governor and I've been kept waiting forty minutes already.' A click. No answer.

Walter was abruptly seized by a dismaying thought: he had surely recognized the woman's voice. Had it not been Lady Thomas herself? He was almost sure of it. But no, wait a moment. Lady Thomas was ill. He had heard someone saying so at the Club and he himself had even sent one of his staff to Government House with a basket of orchids and a note signed by ... by his wife, a forgery to which he was well accustomed and to which she had never raised any objection. He had forgotten for the moment that his wife was now in Australia. Moreover, Lady Thomas would certainly know she was there and would be perplexed to receive a note from her in Singa-pore ... But the man he had sent had returned still with the basket of orchids and the note (why had he not grabbed it back, oh fool!) saying that he had not been allowed past the gate, that the place was a shambles. How a shambles? Bomb-craters everywhere. Walter had flown into a rage, suspecting that the fellow had not bothered to go to Government House at all, that he considered such a messenger's job beneath his dignity.

Bomb-craters indeed! Walter had ordered him back to Government House and told him not to show himself again until he had delivered the orchids. Neither the messenger, nor the orchids, nor the note had been heard of since. Lady Thomas must consider him completely mad ... a note sent by his absent wife ... he himself rude to her on the telephone ...

'Things do not look particularly rosy,' agreed the telephone. And then: 'Thy sex to love!' Or was it: 'Three sets to love!'? Walter strained his ears but could not be sure.

Never mind. Never mind all that. It was of no great importance what she thought. Besides, it was clear to him that he was being deliberately baulked by the Government House staff, with or without the Governor's permission. All right, all right, he thought, making a feeble effort to look at both sides of the question, it was true that the Governor must have a lot on his mind with the Japanese on the Island ... but not to be able to get hold of him for such an important matter, that was an outrage! 'And whose taxes go to paying the salaries of these stuffed shirts I should like to know!'

But never mind. Even if he succeeded in buttonholing the Governor, he doubted whether he would be very helpful. Sir Shenton would be too conventional to entertain seriously the proposal which Walter had in mind. For, to Walter, the matter was plain: the Japanese were going to get more rubber than they had a use for, whatever happened. They already had under their control the entire production of Indo-China and Malaya. The Japanese would very likely agree that it was senseless to destroy the rubber in Walter's godowns. Well then, why should it not be kept pending the end of the war or, even better, sold under a strict guarantee to some non-belligerent nation such as Mexico or Portugal? Here Walter would have trading contracts and experience which the Japanese could put to good use: an understanding beneficial to all could certainly be reached with one of the *zaibatsu*. Walter had, he considered, an advantage over the Governor. He had had dealings for years with the Japanese. They were not ogres to him, as they undoubtedly were to Sir Shenton. Hard competitors they certainly were, but for that Walter could only admire them. Yes, an advantage could be won for Blackett and Webb in concert with, say, Mitsubishi, which would do no harm to anybody, least of all to the British War Effort. But Walter knew he must be realistic. There was little prospect of the Governor accepting such a plan.

Again he picked up the telephone. 'Who's there?' he demanded. For a while there was only that distant cascade of cymbals. 'You see,' said the telephone suddenly, 'capitalism *used to mean* a competitive export of goods, but that's all a thing of the past, I'm afraid. We now export cash instead ... sending it out here where it can make a bigger profit, thanks to low wages and the land available for estates. The result is that we've become a parasite on the land and labour of Malaya and our other colonies. Did you know, Walter, that bond-holdings brought in five times more revenue than actual foreign *trade* for Britain?'

'What?' demanded Walter. 'Are you talking to me?' But the voice had faded once more into the ghostly plucking of a harp. And anyway, it must have been someone else called Walter.

On the other hand, Walter realized suddenly, there was probably no need to worry about the rubber, at least for the moment. For there was so much of it, several thousand tons. Unless they had some mad idea of burning down the buildings as well, which was surely not the case, the PWD busybodies would need several weeks merely to shift the rubber from the godowns to a suitable site for burning. The same was probably true of other commodities which Blackett and Webb held in their godowns. It was evident that what was most at risk was the investment in engineering and motor-assembly plants. It was that which would need protection. It was that which the PWD men would go for first.

But oddly enough, as it turned out, they did not. They went for Walter's liquor godown at the docks. A telephone message chased him round the city, warning him. He could no longer bear to sit in the improvised offices in Tanglin surrounded by a staff which had by now shrunk, thanks to the demands of the passive defence services, to an efficient young Cantonese, a couple of elderly Englishmen who but for the war would long since have been put out to grass, and two or three Eurasian typists. So, despite the danger, Walter had himself driven about the city inspecting the various Blackett and Webb premises and offering a word of encouragement to whatever staff remained (for here, too, the number of his employees was shrinking daily, almost hourly). Mohammed, his *syce*, did not seem to mind: he, too, seemed anxious to pursue his normal life.

Although he seldom stayed for more than a few minutes at each place he visited, it now took so long to cross the ruined city that the better part of Walter's day was spent in the car, an ancient Alvis which Mohammed had found somewhere. Monty had evidently succeeded in getting both himself and the Bentley away on the *Félix Roussel*. Apart from faint surprise that the boy should have had sufficient initiative, Walter had no strong feelings about his son's desertion. On the whole he was better out of the way. Once or twice, though, staring out with sightless eyes at the boiling streets, the thought of Harvey Firestone's five efficient sons made him clench his fists and caused the bristles to stir on his spine. How promising life had once appeared, how disastrously it had turned out!

Even the city now was hardly recognizable any longer as the place where he had spent such a great part of his life. The roads were clogged with military vehicles, there were gun emplacements every few yards, each crossroads seemed to have its own traffic jam which sweating military policemen were trying to free. And everywhere he looked he saw bomb-craters and rubble, shattered trees, uprooted lamp-posts, tangled tramway cables, and smoke from the buildings burning on every side. With the smoke there came, barely noticeable at first, a disagreeable smell. Old Singapore hands like Walter were used to unpleasant smells: they came from everywhere ... from the drains and from the river above all, but also from less likely places, from Tanglin rose-gardens for instance, where the 'boys' sometimes failed to bury properly the household excrement, or someone's spaniel dug it up again. In Singapore you could never be quite safe: even while you stood smiling fixedly under the great candelabra in the ballroom at Government House, once a gift from the Emperor Franz Josef to the third Duke of Buckingham, you might suddenly get a distinct whiff of something disagreeable. But this was different. This was altogether more sickening. It seemed to cling to your hair and clothes. When you took out your handkerchief to blow your nose it was there, too. Presently, it became stronger and not even the swirling smoke could disguise the fact that it came from the bodies stretched in rows on the pavements which no one had yet had time to bury.

Tired of the endless delays and traffic jams on the way to Tanglin, Walter had a camp bed and a desk installed in the disused store-keeper's office in the godown on the river where he had brought Joan one day not very long ago. Thank heaven that she and Nigel had got away, at any rate! This little office, which was really just a box of wood and glass without a roof other than that of the godown itself way above, had strong associations for Walter, reminding him of the old days. It was peaceful here, too, and very quiet. The dim light, the smell of the raw rubber which rose in tiers, bale upon bale, to the dim heights of the roof, he found infinitely soothing. There was a window, too, in the office from which he could contemplate the river, not so very different even now from the river he had gazed at as a young man from this spot. He needed this tranquillity to restore and refresh himself after his wanderings in the city.

And still the city's collapse had not yet reached a limit which one could consider, however dreadful it might be, a stable state. On the contrary, familiar streets continued at an accelerating pace to be eaten away by fire and to crumble beneath the bombs and shells. A huge mushroom of black smoke had risen to the north: he paused to look at it from a window of the Singapore Club where he went for lunch. It issued, he was told, from the oil storage tanks at the Naval Base, to which fire had been set to prevent the Japanese capturing the fuel they so badly needed. From the Fullerton Building you looked over Anderson Bridge and the river, then an open space with an obelisk and the solid pile, now distinctly battered, of the Victoria Memorial Hall and Theatre and, away to the right, what might have been the two friendly onion domes of the Arab Community Arch. The smoke had risen on a fat, black stalk which, from where Walter was looking at it, grew just beside the clock tower though in fact its source was on the northern coast: its mushroom cap was growing steadily and spreading to the south-east. Soon it would cover most of the city and, indeed, of the Island itself, snowing as it came a light precipitation of oily black smuts which clung to everything, blackening skin and clothing alike.

When they set out to make another journey after lunch, this time to the docks, Mohammed had to switch on the windscreen wipers on account of the black film of soot that crept over the windscreen. But nowadays one needed to be able to see, not only forward, but upwards as well, because of the Zeros that continually tore in over the shattered palms or floated like hawks up and down the main roads, waiting for something to stir beneath them. Mohammed, therefore, opened the sliding roof of the Alvis so that while he drove he could keep an eye out. He also glanced into his rear-view mirror once or twice, half expecting Walter to protest. But Walter sat mute. It was not very long before one or two black spots of soot began to appear on Walter's white linen suit. He tried to brush them off, but that only made them worse. Soon his suit, his shirt and his face were covered in oily black smudges.

65

The Japanese fighters were now flying so low in search of people or vehicles to machine-gun that troops, and sometimes even civilians who had picked up a weapon somewhere, would very often fire back from whatever cover they could find. Several times Walter and Mohammed were obliged to leave the Alvis in the road and dive for cover. On one occasion, before they had had time to take shelter, a two-engined Mitsubishi bomber blocked the sky and a burst of machine-gun bullets from its rear turret stitched along the brick wall above their heads, showering them with fragments. Meanwhile, from a sand-bagged gun emplacement beside them a steel-helmeted corporal blazed away with a bren-gun. It jammed. Cursing, he struck off the magazine with a blow of the back of his hand and clipped on a new one. Nearby stood a shattered army lorry in which sat a headless soldier still grasping the wheel.

Once Walter saw one of the fighter-planes hit by a fusillade from the streets and go out of control, crashing with a roar some way away into a steep wooded bank beside the Bukit Timah Road. Yet although he nodded to the jubilant Mohammed and smiled grimly at the cheering Tommies beside the road and muttered: 'Well done ... Good show!' he was not really interested. He was too preoccupied with other matters to care greatly whether a Japanese plane crashed or did not crash. And when one of the two elderly Englishmen on his staff came running after him as he was leaving for the liquor godown where the PWD men were about to start demolition work and asked him whether he would like to take a gun with him 'just in case', he replied sharply: 'Don't be absurd, man! We aren't going to take the law into our own hands.'

'But I meant ...' stammered the assistant, astonished.

In the matter of the destruction of liquor, Walter did even

better than not taking the law into his own hands: he lent it his active support, ordering one of the remaining secretaries to telephone the *Tribune* and the *Straits Times* with instructions for them to send a photographer. His intention was to have himself photographed smashing the first bottle of whisky. In the event no photographer appeared. Nevertheless, he still insisted on smashing the first bottle.

'We aren't here to launch a bloody ship, sir, you know,' said the Volunteer Engineers sergeant who had been seconded to the PWD. 'We've got to get through all that lot and several more bonded warehouses as well. Not to mention the shops, clubs and hotels all over the place.' Walter nodded: he knew better than anyone how much liquor there must be on the Island. After all, Singapore was the distribution centre for the entire Far East. Blackett and Webb alone must have several tens of thousands of crates containing gin, whisky and wine; he could only guess that altogether there would be well over a million bottles of whisky belonging to various merchants and institutions in store or awaiting despatch from the Island, perhaps even more when one considered that the flow of spirits from Singapore into a number of Far Eastern ports had been dammed up for the past few weeks by the outbreak of war and the freezing of Japanese assets.

The demolition squad set to work on the cases with crowbars. Walter, thinking grimly of his jubilee year, obstinately grabbed a bottle out of the first case to be opened and smashed it violently at his feet.

'Not here, sir, the fumes will do us in,' said the sergeant, assuming he wanted to help.

Walter fell back then and watched silently as the bottles were carried outside and smashed against the wall. Presently, in a sort of daze from the heat and the noise of the ack-ack guns, that distant slamming of doors that followed you everywhere in the city, he too picked up some bottles and smashed them against the wall. And he went on doing so, despite the heat. Soon he was obliged to take off his jacket: the sweat fell in salty drops from his chin and his shirt clung to his back. The other men had stripped to the waist but this Walter could not do, because of the bristles on his spine.

The smashing of these bottles filled him with a strange exultation. He felt he could go on doing it for ever. Whereas the other men, conserving their strength, merely made the effort required to break the bottles, Walter dashed them violently against the wall. Once, as he turned too quickly, he thought he saw two other men exchanging a sly grin at his expense, but he did not care. He went on and on. He ground his teeth and smashed and muttered and smashed until his head was ringing. A mound of glittering broken glass rose steadily against the wall and in no time he found himself sloshing back and forth through deep pools of whisky which had gathered on the concrete surface. Even here outside the alcohol fumes soon became oppressive. Once, as he was sloshing through a pool of Johnny Walker, he lost his balance and sat down, cutting his hand on one of the bottles he had been holding and which had broken. He got up immediately, revived by the sharp stinging of alcohol on the wound, and went on with the job, but more carefully now. He was getting tired.

A telephone had been ringing for some time in the storekeeper's office. A whispered conversation took place between Mohammed and the store-keeper who had been eyeing Walter uncertainly. Mohammed finally approached Walter to tell him that his office had rung, afraid that Walter might forget that he had an appointment with the directors of Langfield and Bowser. Mohammed would have liked to ask Walter if he was feeling all right, but did not quite dare. He stared blankly at Mohammed for a few moments. Then he said: 'Oh yes, so I have. What time is it?'

When he had washed his face under a tap, and bound a handkerchief round his cut hand, he picked up his jacket and went outside to the car where Mohammed was waiting, holding the door open. As he made to get in he caught sight of his own reflection in the window. His shirt and trousers were black with smuts from the burning oil on the other side of the Island. He hesitated a moment, wondering whether he should first have driven himself to the Club to shower and change. But he was already late. Besides, there was a war on.

Langfield and Bowser's headquarters were in the Bowser Building on the corner of Cecil and Cross Streets. Had Solomon Langfield's house in Nassim Road not been devastated in the January air-raids they would most likely have moved their offices there, away from the centre of town, as Walter had done with his offices. As it was, on account of the sudden flowing back to Singapore of so many troops who had to be found billets, they had been unable to find convenient premises out of the danger zone. 'All the safe places appear to have been hogged by the bloody Army,' the Secretary had explained to those anxious members of the board who had remained on the Island. They might have managed to find somewhere even so, thanks to old Solomon's cunning and contacts, had the Chairman not been abruptly called to his reward. That had thrown everything into confusion. The result was that here they still were, holding uneasy board meetings in the Bowser Building 'in the thick of the action' as the Secretary put it. He belched dejectedly; for some reason everything he ate these days seemed to cause flatulence.

Meetings were now held as infrequently as possible, but unfortunately they could not be discontinued altogether: there was so much of importance that had to be discussed. They had been astonished and dismayed to hear of Nigel Langfield's proposed marriage to Joan Blackett and had spent many perilous hours attempting to predict its implications for themselves and their firm. If Walter Blackett got his hands on Nigel's stock or, what amounted to the same thing, got his hands on Nigel, then the future looked black indeed for Langfield and Bowser Limited. Walter would surely waste no time in diverting Langfield's most profitable business into Blackett and Webb's coffers, no doubt doing so with a wealth of plausible-sounding arguments about 'rationalization'. But Langfield's worried directors, sitting around their board-room table in steel helmets and quivering with alarm at the menacing sounds that filtered in from outside, had no appetite for a dose of rationalism administered by Walter ... at least, not if it meant what they thought it would mean.

They racked their brains, wondering what Solomon would have done in such a situation, though really they knew the answer all too well. Soloman would not have got himself into it in the first place. But one thing, above all, puzzled them. Why had Solomon given his blessing to the marriage? *He must have known* of the danger of Nigel's being annexed, shares and all, by the Blackett family. Yet he had given his consent. This was altogether baffling. For they had known Solomon well enough to realize that he would not have done so without having some clever plan worked out in advance in the manner of a chess master who sacrifices a piece willingly in the knowledge that, in the long run, it will be to his advantage. Again and again this had happened in the past, though never on such a momentous scale. Solomon had proposed some apparently rash manoeuvre which had then unexpectedly matured before their delighted eyes so that they could hardly prevent themselves clapping their hands with glee. But in this case what was it that Solomon had foreseen? What could it be?

They took off their steel helmets and scratched their heads and then put them back on again, all in vain. If only Solomon had still been there to answer this one question! Well, as it happened, Solomon *was* still there, various freight carriers and passenger ships alike having refused, even at full fare, to transport him home to his grateful shareholders at such a time. He even looked very little different from the way he had looked in life: his eyes had always had a hooded, half-closed appearance. But though he might still appear to be listening to questions, he no longer gave any answers. Had Solomon pulled a fast one after all? Or had Blackett pulled a fast one? Or, just conceivably, had both of them? It was too much for the worried board to make head or tail of. The best they could do in the circumstances was to hope that the young couple would be torpedoed on the way home. That, at least, would solve this particular problem.

After Nigel's departure from Singapore Walter had telephoned, saying that he wanted to discuss a combined approach to the demolition problem. The directors had eyed each other uneasily (what was he up to?) but they could hardly say no. And so now he was on his way, though already an hour late for some reason. As the minutes ticked by, one or two of the more sanguine members of the board began to have tempting visions of Walter lying riddled with tracer bullets in a ditch. But then, just as their optimism was beginning to increase, he was announced. And when they saw him they could hardly believe their eyes.

Instead of the brutal self-controlled ogre that they knew Walter to be, it was someone more resembling a down-and-out who now reeled through the door and stood gazing at them, wild-eyed. They all knew Walter, of course, at least by sight and reputation, if not personally, and there was not a Langfield man in Singapore (unless it were old Solomon himself) but had not found the mere presence of Walter daunting. Even if you passed him quietly drinking a beer at the Long Bar in the Club you could feel the electricity that charged the air around him. But the Walter who had now appeared was, well, pathetic. How could they ever have felt daunted by this dishevelled individual with a bloodstained handkerchief bound round one fist as if he had come straight from a waterfront brawl, this fellow whose suit could have done with a visit to the laundry? ... no, not even the laundry could have done anything with it; it was fit only for the rubbish dump. The board of Langfield and Bowser

Limited gazed long and hard at Walter and they liked what they saw. The Secretary, W. J. Bowser-Barrington, smirking politely, rose and offered him a chair.

Walter was wasting no time. Even before he had taken his seat he had begun to talk rapidly and somewhat incoherently about the destruction of engineering plant ... selective, mind you, they were not going to do a bloody thing to the Chinese. What did this mean? It meant that when the war was over the Chinese would have a head start in engineering throughout the Far East. Well, they knew the situation as well as he did, he did not have to spell it out for them! What they had to decide, without more ado, was how they were going to respond. One firm alone standing out against the demolition order was not going to cut any ice at all. Together there might be a better chance, not good but better, of making the Governor see reason. The question was, how were they going to get the Governor to rescind the order *in time!* '*In time!*' Walter repeated, stifling a groan, while the Langfield men gazed at him, hypnotized. They had not so much been listening to Walter's words as marvelling at his appearance and manner.

'In time!' he groaned again, striking the table with his damaged fist and causing the blood to well up between his bandaged fingers.

While Walter had been speaking, W. J. Bowser-Barrington had surreptitiously scribbled a little note and passed it along to his colleagues; *Blackett has been on quite a binge!!!* They nodded gravely to each other as this note was passed along. The truth of it was undeniable. Moreover, as Walter talked an overpowering smell of whisky permeated the airless atmosphere of the board-room. Yes, the fellow had without doubt been on a considerable bender. He looked as if he were going to pieces.

At length, Walter's speech became halting and eventually dried up altogether. None of the Langfield men had anything to say and for a considerable time they sat in silence in the gloomy little room, listening to the distant rattle and boom of the guns. W. J. Bowser-Barrington wore a pink carnation in his buttonhole and he had turned his head so that his nose rested among its petals; the sweet fragrance was a relief after the smell of sweat and alcohol from Walter. Since a reply was clearly expected, however, he stated his opinion, in terms as vague as possible and subject to all subsequent changes of mind and circumstances that there was little that could be done to resist, either severally or in concert, these admittedly undesirable developments, but

513

that no time should be lost in bringing pressure to bear in the appropriate quarters in London for adequate compensation for everything that was destroyed.

'And that is something,' he added cautiously, 'which would certainly benefit from a combined operation, perhaps with other Singapore firms who find themselves in the same predicament. And what's more ...'

'Ah, I see,' said Walter, cutting him short before he had a chance to finish. But instead of arguing or protesting, as they had expected (such a noisy scene, my dears, you have no idea! they had already imagined themselves saying to certain old cronies at the Club), Walter simply continued to sit there, breathing heavily, his eyes straying vaguely round the room.

'By the way, where's Solomon?' he asked suddenly. And then, seeing that the Langfield men were taken aback by this question, he added: 'I mean, did you ship him home or is he in a godown somewhere?'

'Well, no, he's here actually,' said Bowser-Barrington, pointing at a long wooden box beneath the table, on which, as it happened, Walter had a moment earlier been resting his feet. 'We'll probably take him with us when we leave. It's pretty clear that things will collapse here in a matter of days. We have a motor-launch waiting at the Telok Ayer Basin to take us to Sumatra when the balloon goes up. You'd better think of coming with us, old boy,' he added, his eyes narrowing insultingly, while the rest of the board gazed at him in consternation.

'Thanks, I'll bear it in mind,' replied Walter shortly. He despised Bowser-Barrington who was not even a real Bowser but had married one of the Bowser women and then changed his name to give himself face. He sighed. Then he got to his feet heavily, paused to look round the table, and with a shrug of indifference blundered out of the room without any further comment.

When the door had closed behind him an excited babble broke out among the Langfield men. What had the Secretary been thinking of! To invite Blackett to come with them, what an idea! Bowser-Barrington sat calmly and with a complacent expression on his face until the excitement had died down a little. Then he held up his hand for silence and began to explain. He now had the answer to that crucial question which had eluded them hitherto; namely, what could have been in old Solomon's mind when he had agreed to the marriage between

Nigel and Miss Blackett? For Solomon, with his customary perspicacity, had seen that the real situation was, in fact, the exact reverse of what they had imagined it to be. It was not Nigel and Langfield and Bowser Limited that were in danger of being swallowed up by Walter Blackett, it was Blackett and Webb which had become temptingly vulnerable to Langfield's, thanks to the fact that *Walter was going to pieces*. The old Chairman must have seen the tell-tale signs of Walter's imminent downfall and, with a clarity of mind which took your breath away, had drawn the appropriate conclusions.

It was true! What else could it be? It was suddenly so obvious now that it had been pointed out to them that they wondered why they had not seen it before. What a noise of jubilation rose from around the board-room table! So loudly did they cheer their Secretary and Chairman-elect that even Walter heard it and paused grimly on the way to his car, reflecting that the first thing he must do once he had taken control of Langfield and Bowser was to purge the board of its dimwits. But just for a moment, accepting the congratulations of his colleagues, Bowser-Barrington had a frightening feeling, almost as if he had heard what might have been a faint grunt of exasperation and a tapping against wood from beneath the table. But no, he was, of course, imagining it. It was merely one of his directors drumming with his shoe on the lid of the box in his excitement.

66

Singapore Island (which, if you recall, resembled the head and ears of an elephant on the map in General Percival's office) was now under siege. Late on Sunday night the first Japanese landing-craft had crossed the Strait to attack the north-western shore. This had come as an unpleasant surprise to General Percival because it meant that the Japanese were attacking the top of the elephant's right ear. In other words, they were attacking the *wrong one!* He had confidently expected them to attack the other ear, using Pulau Ubin to shield their approach. Even when the reconnaissance patrol sent across the Straits by General Gordon Bennett had reported large troop concentrations opposite that right-hand ear General Percival still had not ceased to hope that they might nevertheless attack the other one ...

where they would find the fresh, newly arrived British 18th Division waiting for them. After all, it might just be that this attack in the north-west was merely a diversionary move, intended to make him commit his reserve to *that* front while the main attack would still come in from the north-east to deal him a stunning blow on the left ear while he was looking in the other direction.

Percival, trying to snatch some sleep in his Sime Road office while waiting for news of the fighting, simply could not bring himself to believe that what Gordon Bennett's weakened 22nd Australian Brigade was now having to repel was the main attack. Communications had been severed by the heavy bombardment from the mainland before the attack: as a result there was a long delay before reports at last began to reach Sime Road. At first it seemed as if things might not be going too badly. There was word of tough resistance by the Australians and of Japanese landing craft being destroyed in large quantities. But that coastline was too long and too thinly defended. Gradually Percival's hopes began to melt away. By the early hours of the morning it had become evident that this was indeed the main Japanese attack and that, by daylight, the right-hand ear would be virtually lost to the Japanese.

At 8.30 a.m. Percival at last committed his only Command Reserve, the 12th Indian Brigade consisting of Argylls and Hyderabads who had survived the Slim River, to come under Gordon Bennett's orders for the defence of the crucial north–south line where the elephant's ear was attached to its head. This was the Jurong line, the shortest and the last line from which it was conceivable that the Japanese might be prevented from seizing the all-important central part of the Island and the high ground at Bukit Timah. Because from Bukit Timah, if they reached there, they would not only be occupying that part of the Island where the main food, fuel and ammunition stocks were held but also be looking down on Singapore Town itself. Then it would be all over: the city would lie in the palm of the Japanese hand.

Nevertheless, although this north–south line was in fact the last truly defensible position before Singapore Town itself, Percival was naturally obliged to draw up a contingency plan; after all, even if defeat is a foregone conclusion you still have to do *something* (otherwise you would look a fool). Accordingly, after a visit to Gordon Bennett's HQ near Bukit Timah village to discuss how best to defend the head from the lost

516

ear (that is, the Jurong line from an attack from the west), General Percival and his staff set to work with their maps drawing up the positively final perimeter beyond which there could be no further retreat unless to fight through the city streets.

Of necessity this perimeter closely hugged the fringes of the city itself, beginning in the east at the Tanjong Rhu Swimming Club to include Kallang Aerodrome, heading north from there to embrace the vital pumping station at Woodleigh, across country to include the reservoirs and the Bukit Timah depots and then down to the coast again at the village of Pasir Panjang. It was, of course, essential that knowledge of this emergency, last-resort perimeter should not filter down the chain of command, thereby encouraging a retreat beyond the last position from which a serious defence could be offered, the Jurong line. Percival gave details of the final perimeter to Generals Heath and Simmons when they visited him at Sime Road on that Monday evening. It was sent to Gordon Bennett in the early hours of Tuesday morning with instructions that it was to be kept secret. Bennett, however, promptly passed on as an operations order to his brigadiers those aspects of it which might concern them. Once again, and now for the last time in the campaign, if Percival had listened carefully he would have heard the discreet sawing of wood.

On this Tuesday, while Walter was smashing whisky bottles four or five miles away, General Percival at Sime Road was doggedly trying to get a clear picture of where the leaks had sprung in his line of defence. This was not easy. The heavy shelling of the north shore had to a great extent destroyed telephone wires; wireless reports, when they came in at all, were confusing. In the course of the morning a flying-boat dropped out of the cloud-covered sky and landed in the harbour, bringing General Wavell, the Supreme Commander, from Java. Percival, therefore, now found himself having to deal with the tricky job of reorganizing his defences with the gloomy glass eye of his Supreme Commander fixed on him. Together they drove to Gordon Bennett's new HQ on Ulu Pandan Road, just off Holland Road to the south of Bukit Timah village. Wavell's lined and rugged face grew increasingly sombre as Percival passed on what he knew of the night's events. The deep furrows which ran from his nose to the corner of his mouth grew deeper, his brow puckered, and his good right eye seemed to recede further into his skull. His lips were slightly parted as if he were on the point of making some bitter remark about the competence of Malaya Command and of Percival himself. He remained silent, however.

Nor did he brighten up at the sight of Gordon Bennett whose optimistic and aggressive spirit had cheered him earlier in the campaign on the mainland. Indeed, his gloom deepened as Bennett began to explain that he had little information about developments in his area. Bennett himself was much subdued. How had the Japanese broken through the Australian troops with such comparative ease? This had come as a great shock to him. He could still hardly believe it. Consequently there was little sign of his normal ebullience as the three generals began to survey the situation.

But hardly had they begun their discussion when anti-aircraft guns started up all around them like waking guard-dogs. Within a few moments the whistling of bombs could be heard. 'Take cover!' yelled someone outside and each of the generals dived under the nearest table. Instantly the room erupted in a blizzard of flying glass and plaster. The foundations of the house quaked as more bombs fell all around. As he crouched under the table Percival noticed something bright and gleaming roll towards him. For a moment he thought: 'My God! It's Wavell's glass eye!' but on closer inspection it turned out to be only a fugitive from a box of child's marbles left in a corner!'

When the three men stood up and dusted themselves off it was discovered that none of them had been hurt. Moreover, although one corner of the building had been demolished by a bomb (which fortunately had failed to explode) and both Percival's and Wavell's cars had been wrecked, there had been no casualities at the HQ itself. This seemed a miracle. The generals shook the plaster and broken glass off the map they had been studying and resumed their conference. 'Really,' declared Wavell presently, 'these constant withdrawals won't do, you know. You must attack, you must attack.

Percival and Bennett nodded thoughtfully, but what was in their minds as they stood there, all three of them, in this suddenly shattered room, as if in a tiny vessel tossed here and there in a mounting sea of confusion?

More cars were found. Wavell, determined to find out what was happening in the Causeway area, had decided to go forward to see General Heath at 11th Division. Just as they were leaving the Australian headquarters Percival was dismayed to see a group of Indian troops in filthy uniforms shambling along the road, rifles held any old way and not even properly formed up into column of route. He could not help glancing at Wavell: that merciless glass eye betrayed no emotion but Percival guessed what must be in his mind. How dreadful! Undisciplined men shambling about under their GOC's nose, that is the sort of thing that can have a bad effect on a fellow's chances if the rumour of it gets back to the Powers That Be. Of course, compared with everything else that had gone wrong this was a minor matter. The trouble was that this column of Indians was not alone by any means. Behind them, like a wound filling up with pus, Singapore Town was harbouring an increasing number of stragglers and deserters; in particular, it was reported that deserters from the untrained Australian reinforcements at the General Base Depot were running wild.

Exhausted though he was, Percival maintained a stoical determination to do his best with whatever opportunities the military situation offered. He was determined to show no sign of defeatism in front of Wavell. It was, however, only when they reached General Heath's headquarters that the really heavy blows began to fall. From Heath they learned that the 27th Australian Brigade under Brigadier Maxwell had withdrawn during the night. Maxwell? Was he not that same militia officer, a doctor by profession, whom Bennett had promoted as his protégé to the command of the 27th Brigade despite his lack of experience and seniority? This withdrawal had left a crucial gap between the Causeway and the Kranji River: this meant in turn that the most important road on the Island (that which began at the Causeway and headed south for Singapore Town by way of Bukit Timah village) lay open for the Japanese to push southwards *behind* the Jurong line which Percival had been hoping to hold. This was simply disastrous. Why had Maxwell withdrawn from his crucial position? He asserted that Gordon Bennett had authorized the move. The result, in any case, was that Percival now found his entire defensive edifice crumbling. He promptly ordered Maxwell to counter-attack to recover Mandai village and reoccupy his former position. He also ordered three battalions of the 18th Division to come under Bennett's command on the Bukit Timah Road, concentrating them at the racecourse to act as badly needed reserve. But these, as Percival well knew, were desperate measures.

It was half past two in the afternoon before Wavell and Percival returned to Gordon Bennett's headquarters. Here Bennett denied having authorized Maxwell's withdrawal during the night. In any event, there was worse to come. Brigadier Taylor's 22nd Australian Brigade, already shattered in the fighting which had taken place during the night, had been obliged to fall back to the Jurong line. Now, while Percival and Wavell had been visiting other units, news had reached Bennett that in the meantime Taylor had received the secret contingency plans for the last-resort perimeter round the city itself, including details of the sector south of the Bukit Timah Road which had been allotted to his brigade. Taylor had interpreted these plans as an order to fall back to this position. Accordingly, the last defensible position before Singapore Town, failing a successful counter-attack, had been abandoned without having been seriously put to the test by the Japanese. Given the confusion which now reigned behind the British lines, however, the units out of touch with their headquarters, the traffic jams, the communications difficulties and the hazards of organizing resistance with heterogeneous forces in territory that was unfamiliar to them, there seemed little prospect that a counter-attack would succeed.

By the time they had returned to Command Headquarters it was four o'clock in the afternoon. Now Percival was met by a worried Brigadier Torrance: a report had come in that the Japanese were approaching Bukit Timah village. Apart from its alarming general implications this news also indicated that the large reserve petrol depot to the east of the village was in danger of being captured. Percival ordered its immediate destruction and by six o'clock it had been set on fire. Wavell, meanwhile, had himself driven to Government House to see Sir Shenton Thomas. He was tired himself after the long day of visits and conferences. What must it be like for Percival and the others who had had no respite for days or weeks? Passing through the gates of Government House his eyes happened on a great basket of orchids decked with bright ribbons lying on the grass a few yards inside the railings. They had evidently been hurled over by some well-wisher too shy to present them. Most likely a sign, he mused, that the British were still popular among the native population in spite of their military reverses. He sighed as the car came to a stop and the door was opened for him. He must make a point of persuading Lady Thomas, who was sick, to return with him to Java in the Catalina.

At nine that evening, before leaving Singapore, Wavell went to Flagstaff House to say goodbye to Percival. The day, which had begun with at least some cards still held by the defenders, had ended with the defence a shambles. Nevertheless, before leaving, he had Ian Graham, one of his ADCs, type out a final exhortation for Percival to pass on to his troops; this was inspired by a signal he had received earlier in the day from Churchill comparing the British resistance unfavourably to that of the Russians and the Americans elsewhere and instructing the British troops to fight to the bitter end. Then, having ordered the last remaining squadron of Hurricanes to be evacuated from the Island, he shook hands with Percival and set off through the dark streets to the waterfront in the second of two cars, accompanied by Count Mackay, a member of his Java staff, and by Air Vice-Marshal Pulford. On the way they heard occasional shots. Looters, sensing the imminent collapse of the city, were already beginning the sack of shops and stores in the less frequented areas.

The Catalina was moored in the middle of the harbour. The car stopped beside the sea wall in the darkness and Pulford got out to look for a motor-boat to take Wavell and his party out to it. He was gone such a long time that Wavell, in frustration, suddenly opened the door on his left-hand side, the side of that blank, glass eye which throughout the long day had been picking up reflections of the British collapse. He sprang out ... but the car had parked so close to the sea wall that there was no ground left on this side of the car. He fell several feet in the darkness on to some rocks. He lay quietly where he had fallen for a little while, breathless with the shock and pain, thinking: 'Singapore is done for,' until presently he managed to shout and his ADCs, groping anxiously, located him and carried him to the motor-boat. He was laid in the bottom of the boat and presently they forged out on to the black waters, lit here and there by the fires burning on the shore all around. When they at last reached the flying-boat it was found impossible to lift Wavell into it without unshipping the machine-gun which had been mounted at the door. The Dutch crew of the flying-boat, unfamiliar with the mounting, set to work on it as best they could. At last they succeeded in removing it and Wavell was hoisted up from the swaying boat. But even when Wavell was safely aboard and had been given whisky and aspirins to dull the pain he was suffering and the sacks of government documents which Sir Shenton Thomas had entrusted to him to take to safety had been stowed beside him, the flying-boat still could not take off. The pilot reported that such was the number of small craft trying to escape from Singapore under cover of darkness he was unable to find a long enough stretch of clear water.

It was not until it at last began to grow light that they eventually managed to take off for Batavia, leaving the chaos and destruction of Singapore as nothing but a tiny smudge on the horizon, insignificant compared with the vast, shining sea beneath them.

67

Matthew had returned from fire-fighting to find a note from Vera saying that she had gone to Bukit Timah village to look for a friend who might be willing to hide her from the Japanese. Matthew clasped his brow in horror when he read this. Had she gone mad? Did she not realize that she was going to what must be the most dangerous part of the Island? Neither Matthew himself, nor anyone else he met, had any clear idea of where the front line might be, but it seemed likely from the noise of the guns that the Japanese were already advancing towards Bukit Timah. He hoped that there would be road-blocks to prevent her going forward, as seemed likely. But after some minutes spent pacing about, uncertain what to do, he decided to go and look for her himself. Even though he knew that his chances of finding her in the darkness and confusion were slim, at least this would give him something to do. And so, in due course, he set out on Turner's motor-cycle.

Matthew had only ridden a motor-cycle once or twice before and felt by no means confident that he could control this one, particularly on a pitch dark night with a masked headlight and the prospect of bomb-craters in the roads. But after five minutes practice in the compound under Turner's tutelage, wandering a couple of times round the tennis court and through the flower-beds in the darkness, he gripped the knob of the hand gear-lever on the petrol tank and prepared to release the clutch. The machine pounced into the road like a tiger.

In a flash he was careering up Stevens Road through the warm tropical darkness in the direction of the Bukit Timah Road. As he charged onwards his searching foot kept finding an outcrop of metal which ought to be the brake ... yet when he trod on it he only seemed to go faster, and the more alarmed he became, the faster he went, not realizing that in his excitement he was involuntarily twisting the throttle with his right hand. Dark objects loomed and vanished on either side with horrifying speed. On he sped, foot still searching for the brake-pedal. At the junction with Dalvey Road he at last realized that his frenzied grip of the throttle was what was causing the machine to bolt with him. He relaxed it and managed to slow down a little, and not a moment too soon, for here there was a road-block. A masked flashlight waved to him to stop. He drew near, his foot searching more desperately than ever for the brake as he wobbled towards it.

'I can't stop!' he shouted at the dim figures standing in the road ahead. In his excitement he again forgot not to twist the hand-grip; again he found himself hurled forward. The figures scattered to right and left.

'Silly bugger!' one of them shouted furiously after him as he shot by. But already he was at the corner of the Bukit Timah Road. Then, just as he was certain that he must hurtle to his doom in the stream of traffic ahead, his foot alighted on another outcrop of metal which this time proved to be the brake. By a miracle he avoided ramming a lorry that loomed across the end of Stevens Road.

It was hard to see what was going on. The road appeared to be full of shambling, cursing figures, some going one way, some going another. A military policeman was shouting hoarsely at drivers from the middle of the road beside the storm-canal. Beyond the canal an occasional flicker of light betrayed another vast military column on Dunearn Road struggling in the opposite direction. Someone flashed a torch in his face and shouted at him hoarsely: 'You're going the wrong bloody way, mate. That's the way to the war!' There were no further road-blocks and nobody tried to stop him, but all along the road men and vehicles continued to thrash in the obscurity like the limbs of some stricken, fettered giant.

Matthew soon became skilful at directing his motor-cycle into narrow gaps between the labouring vehicles but his progress was slow, nevertheless. Near the racecourse a huge fire was flaring a hundred feet into the sky: this was the reserve petrol dump which General Percival had ordered to be set on fire an hour before dark. Against its glare Matthew could see the long-shadowed silhouettes of men and guns, for the most part struggling in the direction of Singapore Town but constantly being arrested by traffic breaking into the stream or forcing a way through it. He, too, soon found it difficult to make any progress, wedged in now between two lorry-loads of silent, apprehensive Indians. Meanwhile, desperate-looking figures continued to pour in the opposite direction, their faces transfigured by the glare. One of these men staggered against him, breathing whisky fumes into his face. 'What's going on?' Matthew asked anxiously. 'Are we retreating?'

'You're damn right we are, sport!' And the man heaved himself away, laughing hysterically.

Even by the light of the burning petrol dump it was impossible to see clearly enough to recognize someone. 'How will I ever find Vera in all this?' Matthew wondered hopelessly. From time to time, among the soldiers fleeing from the direction of Bukit Timah village, there were little pockets of civilians with bundles on their backs or dragging hand-carts; at the side of the road he could see the shadows of men jogging with poles across their backs from which hung boxes, suitcases or other burdens, but they all slipped by, heads averted: only by their clothes could you make a guess as to whether they were Indian, Malay or Chinese. Yes, it was hopeless. He considered turning back, but by now he had passed the racecourse on the right and Bukit Timah itself could not be more than half a mile up the road, so he decided to press on a little further. He rode on in a daze, travelling more freely the further he went. He passed a road junction to the left. This road was quiet and tempting but he ignored it and presently, as the ground rose on either side, he knew that Bukit Timah and the junction with the Jurong Road must lie just ahead in the obscurity.

Suspended between two rows of houses above the wide road a bundle of electric cables spluttered a cascade of white sparks over a scene of such confusion that Matthew's heart sank. Lorries and turreted Quad cars were wedged together at all angles with a tide of men flowing by on each side of them; military police, bawling at drivers and at each other and at the same time trying to marshal a squad to drag away an abandoned or broken-down vehicle, seemed unable to make any impression on the jammed traffic. In the very middle of this chaos, four brigadiers in an open staff-car were trying to read a map by torchlight and occasionally peering about them into the seething darkness as if wondering where they were.

Matthew turned the motor-cycle and allowed himself to be swept back the way he had come for some distance in the middle of a cantering mob of Indian troops, some of whom had discarded their rifles and boots and were running barefoot, jabbering to each other hysterically as they ran. Matthew, infected by their alarm, kept looking over his shoulder as if expecting to find the Japanese at his heels. Abruptly he found himself at the quiet road he had seen before; he accelerated out of the chattering Indians and turned into it. For some distance after he had left them he could still hear them calling and chattering as they passed on down the road towards Singapore Town.

The road he had turned into was Reformatory Road which led down to Pasir Panjang on the coast. He could not be sure that it would not lead him into the Japanese lines ... for where *were* the Japanese lines? However, provided the road did not turn towards the thud and flash of the guns on his right, he was prepared to follow it, though cautiously. A few tepid spots of rain began to fall.

Some way ahead in the darkness he saw the flash of a torch. He stopped the motor-cycle immediately and held his breath, his heart pounding. The torchlight reappeared a moment later, shining on the front of a car. It did not seem to be coming any closer so he left the motor-cycle and advanced stealthily on foot. As he approached he saw the shadow of a jeep with a man in uniform peering under the bonnet; after a moment he slammed down the bonnet, said something to another man in the back and then began to jog away down the road in direction of Pasir Panjang, evidently to summon assistance.

Matthew moved forward cautiously, listening to the diminishing sound of the driver's boots on the metalled surface of the road: he did not want to be shot by mistake. When he was within a few yards of the stationary jeep the torch was switched on again and its glow revealed a portly little man with a moustache wearing a general's uniform; he, too, was consulting a map. Surely there was something familiar about that round, discontented face with its bulging eyes! This plump little fellow sitting abandoned in the darkness with raindrops beginning to patter on his red-banded hat and on the map he was holding was surely General Gordon Bennett, the Australian Commander! Matthew had seen a photograph of him in a newspaper inspecting troops. And now here he was, stranded in a broken-down jeep at what might be a crucial moment in the battle for Singapore. Perhaps he, Matthew, thanks to his motor-cycle, might be able to bring help to the General at a vital moment. He hesitated, wondering whether to spring forward and offer his services.

Gordon Bennett, sitting in the jeep, had not heard Matthew's approach. He had been too preoccupied with other, desperate matters. These last few hours had been among the worst he had ever experienced in his life. He had been shaken that morning when he had heard the news that the Japanese had broken through his Australian troops on the north-west coast, a failure that had earlier seemed to him inconceivable. Then there had been the bombing of his headquarters while Wavell and Percival had been visiting him. As if that had not been enough he had later been made to look a fool in front of Wavell by not knowing what Maxwell had been up to in his sector at the Causeway. No, things had not been going well in the past few hours. Perhaps the only crumb of comfort was that earlier in the campaign the Sultan of Johore had taken quite a liking to him and behaved most generously. He had even been given to understand by the Sultan that in the event of a total British collapse some help with an escape to Australia might not be altogether out of the question.

Yes, Gordon Bennett had recognized in the Sultan a really high-class person, and the Sultan, for his part, he felt sure, had not altogether failed to notice his own qualities of good breeding. Not long before, so he had heard, a guest of the Sultan, a titled English lady, had expressed a caprice to swim in the shark-infested Strait of Johore. For many a host this would have been too much, but not for the Sultan. What had he done? He had instructed several hundred of his palace guards to enter the water and link bands to form a shark-proof enclosure in which the lady could safely bathe. That, Bennett knew, was class. He could tell a classy act a mile off. He sighed and reluctantly returned his thoughts to the map. It was just at this moment, as if the breakdown itself were not bad enough, that some wild-eyed civilian sprang out of the darkness at him like a werewolf. As Matthew emerged from the surrounding darkness Bennett shrank back with a gasp of alarm, showing the whites of his eyes.

'Who the devil are you and what d'you want?' he demanded furiously.

'I have a motor-cycle,' said Matthew, taken aback by this hostile reception. 'I just wondered whether you might like a lift ... But I expect you don't,' he added as the General's cheeks grew purple. With an embarrassed cough he sank back again into the darkness. Presently a motor-cycle engine roared not far away and grew fainter. The General was left alone to the rain and the night.

When Matthew reached the Mayfair he learned that Vera, unable to get through to Bukit Timah, had returned to the Mayfair but had almost immediately set off again, nobody knew where.

68

Walter had long since ceased to believe that the surrender of Singapore to the Japanese could be averted. If it had not been possible to stop, or even delay, the Japanese up-country with the help of prepared defences and relatively fresh troops, it was improbable that they would be stopped now at the gates of the city. Curiously, he gave little thought either to escaping or to rejoining his family. After all, they were safe. His wife and Kate were in Australia. Monty was heaven knew where ... India perhaps. Joan and Nigel should soon be in Bombay. Joan's capture of Nigel, certainly, was a cause for satisfaction and boded well for the future of Blackett and Webb. In that respect everything had turned out even better than if she had got Matthew Webb in her grip: once the two companies had merged, any attempt by Matthew to use his stake in the company to influence its policy could be comfortably out-voted.

Yet what a lot had been lost for Blackett and Webb in the past few weeks! It would be a long time (he himself might even be an old man, a grumpy old figurehead to whom the young executives took it in turns to make polite remarks at garden-parties!) before Blackett and Webb was again the commercial force in the Far East that it had been over the past thirty or forty years. All Malaya's rubber, tin and palm-oil were already in Japanese hands; in Java and Sumatra they probably soon would be. All the agencies ... the shipping, the insurance, the import–export and entrepôt, the engineering and banking, were either in suspended animation or had been withdrawn to Australia or Britain, their management and staff scattered to the winds. Something on that scale is not built up again overnight! In so far as these enterprises had a physical presence (godowns, goods and produce in stock, engineering plant, vehicles and so forth) it was being demolished with equal enthusiasm by Japanese bombers and British demolition teams. Perhaps it was this

527

single-minded approach to the demolition of everything that had gone to make up the presence of Blackett and Webb in Singapore, amounting almost to collusion, it seemed to Walter, that he found so disorienting.

His family had left Singapore. He no longer had any responsibilities, except to the people who worked for him ... but even his duty to them had grown nebulous under the bombs. In any case, he could no longer exert any real influence to help them. He passed these few days, therefore, roaming the city aimlessly and alone, almost as he had done in his youth when he had lived in a mess run by one of the big merchant houses, with a lot of other young lads. So Walter drifted about the city like a shadow or brooded alone in the store-keeper's office in the godown on the river which he had made his temporary home. Once or twice, rather than walk or use a car, he hailed a *sampan* from where they clustered several deep with the *tong-kangs* at the Blackett quay and had himself conveyed downriver to the Club. But the Club itself was unrecognizable, crammed with refugees, sick and wounded, and he left again immediately without speaking to anyone. On the Wednesday afternoon he made a sudden appearance at a bonded liquor warehouse where the same demolition team which had destroyed Blackett and Webb's stocks had now begun work. Without a word he took off his jacket and set to work with them. They were grateful: they needed all the help they could get. Walter smashed bottles doggedly until it grew dark and then retired once more to brood alone in the godown on the river.

As he wandered along the narrow corridors between the bales of rubber he tried to explain to himself what had happened. If he succeeded in understanding what had gone wrong then perhaps he would once more be able to gain control of events instead of drifting helplessly, now this way, now that. It was surely not the Japanese alone who were to blame for the way things had gone. One of the first signs, undoubtedly, that Blackett and Webb's hitherto secure grip on its own destiny was beginning to loosen had come with the labour unrest on the estates five years ago ... not just his, but other firms', too, of course. Could the Japanese be blamed for that? Well, perhaps they could. They had certainly been behind a number of strikes in Shanghai against British firms. The strike in 1939 at the China Printing and Finishing Company in Pootung which had gone on for six months and for which British marines had had to be landed to keep order had certainly been engineered by the

Japanese. One had only to look at all the anti-British propaganda that had accompanied it, the wall-posters, the demonstrations, the pamphlets, the slogan-shouting ... even the sympathy strike organized at the British-owned Yee Tsoong Tobacco Factory. And then there had been a rash of strikes against other British concerns: the China Soup Company, the Asiatic Petroleum Company, Ewo Brewery and Ewo Cotton Mills, Ewo Cold Storage (Jardine Matheson had been a favourite target) and Paton and Baldwin's wool mill. But there was a difficulty here that Walter had to acknowledge. Although it was most likely that some, if not all, of these strikes *were* Japanese-inspired, it was extremely difficult to argue that they would not have broken out spontaneously, even without Japanese encouragement.

In a sense it did not matter whether these strikes had been encouraged for political reasons by the Japanese, or by the Communists, or had sprung up independently among disgruntled workers who happened to identify all employers with the British. Because given that huge reservoir of cheap labour with attendant 'exposed corpses' *pour encourager les autres* a mixture of the two extremes of submission and resistance was about what you would expect, in Walter's view. Thus the disadvantage of labour unrest was bonded indissolubly to the advantage of cheap labour.

In Malaya, however, which had lost its pool of cheap labour when immigration was curtailed as a result of the Depression, there were no 'exposed corpses' on the streets in the morning and the extremes to which the labour force had been driven were less stark. In Malaya it was clearly unrealistic to blame the Japanese for the growth of labour unrest. Purely political agitation by Nationalists and, above all, Communists against the British had caused a number of strikes which, because they were not based on genuine labour grievances, would not otherwise have occurred. Walter sensed that it was here that Blackett and Webb in common with other British firms had begun to lose its grip on the country and on its own destiny. A worker with a genuine grievance you can do something about. You can give him more pay, or sack him, or improve his living conditions. But what can you do with a worker who wants you to leave the country or, just as bad, wants to run the business himself?

'I suppose they expect me to dye my face brown and wear a *sarong*!' grumbled Walter aloud, pausing to lean wearily against a bale of the 'ribbed smoked sheet' that had made his fortune. He groaned. He had no difficulty in recognizing what it was that he had been up against. It was 'the spirit of the times' which had stolen up on him again.

Presently, feeling hungry, Walter went out into the streets again. He did not eat, however, but instead went to the Cricket Club for a shower. His clothes were filthy but so were everyone else's he met: nobody seemed to find anything remarkable about his appearance. He was shocked, however, to see what he looked like in a mirror and while he was taking a shower sent someone to fetch Mohammed from Tanglin with some clean clothes. He felt better then and ate a sandwich.

Mohammed, waiting for him outside in the car, wanted to drive him back to Tanglin but Walter told him to go to the godown on the river. He was very tired. To reach the store-keeper's office he had to climb the swaying ladder some forty feet up into the shadowy vault of the building to the ledge which formed a rudimentary loft some way out from the wall. Two-thirds the way up the ladder he dropped the electric torch he was holding. He saw its light revolve once in the air as it fell. Then it went out and he could see nothing at all. Fortunately, Mohammed, concerned for his safety, had been watching his unsteady ascent from the entrance to the godown. He shouted up to him not to move and hurried away to fetch another torch from the car.

While he waited on the gently creaking, bending ladder, too unsure of his balance to go either up or down in the almost total darkness, he nevertheless thought how easy it would be to let go, to allow himself to pitch out from the ladder and plunge into the silent, peaceful depths beneath. Mohammed was taking a long time. So much rubber! It was all around him. He could not see it but he knew it was there. He thought of oil palms again but no, that was merely a detail ... A man must move with the times, otherwise he is done for. Clinging to the ladder in the darkness he began to muse on this business of moving with the times. In Shanghai he had managed to do so with skill, why had he not succeeded in Malaya? In Shanghai it should have been more difficult. Surely no commercial city could have undergone so many drastic changes in such a short time as had Shanghai in the past five years: the Japanese war on the mainland, their blockade of the coastal ports, the ending in consequence of the Open Door policy and the decline of the Chinese Customs, not to mention all the deliberate Japanese attempts to strangle British trade with restrictions and mono-polies. Yet he had not only moved with the times and managed to survive in that beleaguered, monstrously over-populated city, he had positively thrived.

Ah, but he could be objective about Shanghai. It was difficult with Malaya. Malaya he regarded as his own country. He had lived here most of his life, had raised a family here. He had a preconceived idea of what the place should be like. He did not want it to change. He liked it the way it used to be. 'I'm begin-ning to sound like old Webb,' he thought. Well, he had accom-modated himself as best he could to the new labour disturbances. Perhaps he had not done so badly, after all.

Mohammed returned and Walter pursued his way upwards among the tiers of rubber bales by the light of the torch-beam from below. When he had reached the top Mohammed followed him up, carrying a basket with some provisions he had brought. Walter thanked him, took out his wallet and gave him a few dollars, adding that he would not be needed for some time, that he should lay the car up wherever he found convenient, prefer-ably immobilized and concealed, and that he would be well advised to return to his own *kampong* until the situation became normal.

'A man must move with the times, Mohammed,' he said with a faint smile. Then he conducted him back to the ladder and held the light for him while he descended.

'Goodbye, *Tuan*.'

'Goodbye, Mohammed.' And the *syce* departed, feeling more concerned than ever. It seemed to him that only a madman would want to stay in this place by the river where rats fidgeted in the darkness and mosquitoes settled on you in clouds. And then, of course, there were the bombs.

From the little window of the store-keeper's office Walter had an unobstructed view, thanks to the river, for a considerable distance to the east and south-east in the direction of Raffles Place. Over the low roofs on the far bank some of the taller buildings around Raffles Place stood out in silhouette against other buildings on fire behind them. The looming shape of the Fullerton Building was visible, too, thanks to some vessel burn-ing furiously in the inner roads behind it. Searchlights swept the sky, criss-crossing with each other; occasionally he could see the flashes of guns. Of the docks nothing was visible but it was clear from the pink-tinged clouds above them that they were still burning in several places. Nearer at hand yet another great conflagration had started in the godowns which lined the river between Clark Quay and Robertson Quay and on the opposite bank, too, between Magazine Road and part of Havelock Road where it ran beside the river. Walter, sometimes muttering something to himself, more often in silence, stood leaning against the side of the window for most of the night watching the progress of these fires.

69

It was to this fire beside the river that the Mayfair unit had been directed by the Central Fire Station. They sped towards it through a corridor of fire; on every street they passed through there seemed to be buildings ablaze. The major hunched wearily over the wheel, listening anxiously to the Lagonda's motor and sniffing the odour of petrol that was leaking somewhere. The Lagonda had broken down once or twice but somehow had been restored to the road; it now bore a jagged tear along one side from a piece of shrapnel and the paint on the bonnet was blistered in several places by the heat of previous fires. It had done good service, certainly. All the same, perhaps it was not wise to go to a fire in a car that was leaking petrol.

In spite of the curfew the streets were full of people, many of them refugees from the threatened area. The Lagonda raced past figures struggling with bundles and belongings, crashed and slithered over rubble strewn in the street, passed a crowd of looters dragging goods out of a shop window like entrails out of a dead animal. Matthew, beside the Major, turned to see a shadowy battery of guns pointing skywards which flashed and gulped one by one as they went by. Evidently another air-raid was in progress.

It was a relief to arrive at the fire by the river and set to work. This, at least, was familiar: the search for a water supply, the laying out of the hose, the starting of the pump. While they were busy looking for a convenient place to drop the suction hose into the river a dog came dashing up, inspected them and hurried away again. 'Adamson must be here somewhere!' And they all smiled, for this was comforting and familiar. And sure enough, presently Adamson appeared; he was still limping and walking with a stick; his manner was as casual as ever but for once even he looked tired. He said: 'I'd knock down that fence if I were you and do it from there. If you get in any closer you'll have one of these walls come down on top of you.' Presently he limped away again, vanishing into a trembling haze of heat and light with the dog at his heels.

Kee, Turner and Cheong were left to get the pumps ready, the others set off for the fire unreeling hose as they went. Evidently it had been burning unchecked for some considerable time for at its centre it was no longer possible to distinguish the individual riverside godowns: these had now become the fuel of a gigantic furnace. As they approached, they converged with other men, heads lowered into a glittering blizzard of sparks, dragging their hoses towards the fire's heart. Matthew was among the helmeted figures struggling through this brilliant storm, his pulse pounding with excitement and trepidation as it always did when he went to a fire. Had he touched wood? Yes. Or was that yesterday? He had lost his hold on the passage of time; events telescoped into each other. Soon the water was crackling through the hose and they were directing their branch against the outer walls of a vast arena of heat and light. For beyond the burning buildings which they were trying to contain, the fire possessed an inner core of other buildings which seemed to stretch over several acres and which by now could hardly be looked at with the naked eye.

Time passed. It could have been a few minutes but, looking at his watch, Matthew saw that two hours had elapsed since their arrival. Occasionally, hurrying back for another length of hose, he glimpsed the glowing inner core as he crossed a street leading into it. Then he would be buffeted suddenly by a wave of heat until he reached the shelter of the next wall. Once, as he hurried across one of these rivers of light, arm raised to shield his face, he saw two lamp-posts, whose elongated shadows almost reached him along the cobbles, buckle and wilt as they began to melt. An instant later he had plunged gratefully into the next dark shadow, unable to believe what he had just seen.

How strange it was to stumble from one of these avenues flowing with light into the black darkness of a side street! Here in the shadows an exhausted fireman sat on the kerb and used his steel helmet to scoop up the water running to waste and pour it over his head; when you looked more carefully you saw that he was not alone: other firemen sprawled here and there, driven back into this dark haven to recuperate. Surprisingly a mood of good humour, almost of elation, prevailed among these exhausted men: they called cheerfully to Matthew in whatever language they happened to speak ... in English, Tamil, Dutch, Cantonese ... they laughed and teased each other, put their arms around each other's shoulders and when, presently, the roof of a nearby godown fell in with a roar and another wave of sparks eddied over them illuminating the darkness of their refuge, a great cheer went up and someone began to sing 'Roll out the barrel'. Laughing uncontrollably, he did not know why, Matthew set off with the new length of hose he had been sent for, following the fire's perimeter. He was astonished at how quickly the fire changed its character from one sector to another. In one place it would be a cheerful blaze, gay with sparks, in another a sullen inflammation beneath blankets of acrid smoke; here, where the fire was spitting great streams of burning liquid towards a row of dark tenements, the firemen were fighting it with a desperate tenacity; nearby, where a bonded warehouse was in flames, they staggered about playfully, falling over each other like a litter of puppies, drunk with the alcohol fumes which billowed around them.

The night wore on. Matthew and Mr Wu were together at the branch, directing its jets at some gentle blue flames that prettily trimmed the roofs of a row of shop-houses, when they heard a sinister hissing above them. Behind them the men who had been singing fell silent. The hissing grew rapidly in volume and changed into a low whistle. Matthew and Mr Wu at the same moment dropped the branch and sprinted for the darkness. The next instant Matthew found himself lying face down in a pool of water issuing from a burst main; the road was quaking beneath him and he was being pummelled by flying fragments of brick and clods of earth. After a few moments a hand tugged his arm: he opened his eyes to see the ever-smiling face of Mr Wu. Together they began to search for the branch they had been holding and which they presently found, thrashing about by itself in the darkness. As Matthew tried to grasp it, it flailed up and dealt him a blow in the chest that robbed him of his breath; but Mr Wu had managed to throw himself on top of it and hold it down while they got a firm grip on it once more. A van now arrived, miraculously, from the Central Fire Station with hot, sweet tea in a metal fire-bucket.

While Matthew was sitting at some distance from the fire drinking tea with his back against a wall, Adamson and his dog approached. Two godowns containing rubber, engine-oil, copra, palm-oil and latex stored as a liquid were on fire only a few feet back from the river. Although there was no hope of saving the godowns themselves Adamson was afraid that burning liquid might flow from them into the river and set the crowded *sampans* and *tongkangs* on its surface alight. He wanted Matthew to relieve one of his men who was directing a jet from the roof of a tall building nearby. 'Can you manage the branch by yourself? I'll send someone to help as soon as I can.' Matthew nodded. The dog eyed him dubiously and then looked up at Adamson, as if afraid that Matthew might not be up to it.

It seemed to take an age of climbing ladders up through the dark warehouse before he finally emerged on the roof. He immediately saw the silhouette of the man he had come to relieve: he had lashed the branch to an iron railing, but loosely enough so that he could still turn the jet a few degrees, and was slumped against the parapet which ran round the roof; he found it hard to get up when he saw Matthew. 'I've been up here all night,' he said. 'I thought they'd forgotten me.'

'Tea is being served down below: if you hurry you might get some.'

'Enjoy the view,' called the departing fireman, leaving Matthew alone on the roof. He turned his attention to the fire. From this position he could look down over the godowns and he wondered whether Adamson realized how far gone they already were; it seemed unlikely that a single jet could make any difference. However, he played the jet over the roofs on the river side, trying to let it stream down the outside walls to cool them and keep them standing as long as possible.

Soon he began to savour the strange sensation of being marooned above the city in the hot darkness; he was pervaded by a feeling of isolation and melancholy. The occasional drone of a bomber in the black sky above him, the slamming of distant doors from the ack-ack guns, the dull thud, thud, thud of bombs falling, the rapid popping and sighing of the Bofors guns, even the deep bark of the artillery ... all this seemed perfectly remote from his vantage point over the rooftops. Up here he was only conscious of the moaning and creaking of the branch against the railing and the faint steady hiss of the jet as it curved down towards the fire. He could see a considerable distance, too: he could see the rapid flashes advancing along Raffles Quay ānd the Telok Ayer Basin as a stick of bombs fell, and the hulk of what might have been a barge burning near Anderson Bridge at the mouth of the river and another vessel blazing brilliantly in the inner roads, and yet other fires scattered here and there in the densely crowded residential quarters to the south and east of New Bridge Road. 'If a bomb fell here,' he thought suddenly, 'nobody would ever find me,' and he peered anxiously down towards the street to see if anyone was being sent up to join him, but with the smoke he could see nothing.

After a while he grew calm again, soothed by the regular creaking of the branch. He was so remote from what was happening down there, after all. It seemed impossible that anything happening on the ground could touch him. Below was the fire, and beyond the fire and all around lay the city of Singapore where two hostile armies were struggling to subdue each other in the darkness. Up here it made no difference. All that concerned him was the fire raging below him: he must concentrate on playing the jet where it would do most good. But soon he found himself wondering whether his efforts might not be superfluous. With a change in the tide, burning oil from a stricken vessel at the mouth of the river was already beginning to flow up towards the tightly packed *sampans* and barges in the heart of the city. As the sky grew pale on the eastern horizon Matthew watched in dismay the leisurely advance of this fiery serpent.

70

'The Blackett and Webb godown is threatened. Walter's inside and refuses to leave. Someone on his staff got in touch with Hill Street and they passed it on to us. Perhaps you wouldn't mind having a shot at persuading him?'

Matthew and the Major were sitting on the kerb beside the Blackett and Webb van which had once carried eight outstretched arms in various colours reaching for prosperity. These arms had not proved very durable and most of them had broken off going over bumps or pot-holes, some at the shoulder, some at the elbow. Only two still remained intact as far as the grasping fingers: Matthew suspected that they were the white ones but could not be sure. The steady precipitation of oily smuts from the sky had rendered white, yellow, light brown and dark brown and even the van itself a uniform black colour. Everything else in sight appeared also to be black, or grey like the sky and the smoke.

'I'd go myself,' said the Major, 'but I must get all this lot back to the Mayfair for some rest and food.' He stared vaguely at the palms of his hands which were raw and bleeding from handling hose in which the broken glass which littered the streets had become embedded. Matthew's palms were similarly flayed. They were waiting their turn while one of the regular firemen went about with a pitcher of iodine, dripping it on to the other men's wounds to a chorus of jokes, curses and cries of anguish. Adamson sat with them, holding out his own raw palms for this painful ritual. The dog slept with its head on his shoe. When, presently, Adamson got up to go for breakfast at Hill Street, the dog had to be shaken awake.

Matthew set off past a dismal row of buildings which had burned during the night: now they loomed, dripping, gutted shells in the grey light. Turning a corner he came upon half a dozen hoses lying side by side, still swollen into thick veins by the water coursing through them. A little further on the branches, perhaps abandoned during a raid, were rearing and flailing like a many-headed monster in the deserted street. He walked on, wondering where Vera was. He hoped that by now she had returned to the Mayfair. It might still be possible, somehow or other, to get her away from Singapore before the Japanese took over.

Matthew had visited the Blackett and Webb godown on the river once before, in the company of Walter himself, as it happened, in the first days after his arrival in Singapore. He had glimpsed it again when with Vera he had visited The Great World (now bleak and deserted except for an ARP post) for it lay close by. But he had found nothing particularly interesting about it, except that it had his own name painted on it in large white letters. Now, strangely undamaged amid the bomb-shattered buildings on either side, it looked somehow more impressive than he had remembered it.

Inside it seemed very dark at first, and quiet. What little light there was came from above, falling from a great height into the dim amphitheatre in which he stood. And there was a pleasant smell in the air, perhaps from the bales of rubber that mounted around him, if not from the old building itself.

'Walter?' he called uncertainly, his voice sounding very small in this great space. It seemed for a moment that there would be no answer but then there came the sound of footsteps from the half-floor above and a familiar voice asked impatiently: 'What is it?'

'It's me, Matthew Webb. I want to talk to you.'

'Who? Oh, it's you. Well, all right ... I suppose you want to destroy all this rubber, do you?' Walter uttered a grim laugh. 'I don't know what your father would have thought of all this madness that's got hold of everyone.'

'It's not about that. D'you mind if I come up there?' Without waiting for an invitation Matthew began to climb a ladder which he dimly perceived nearby. He found Walter waiting at the top, looking restless and irritable. He paused to recover his breath, peering at him uncertainly. 'Could we go somewhere where there's a bit more light?'

'All right. Come this way.' Walter led the way down corridors of rubber. At a turning an old rat stood in their path and stared at them insolently for a moment before limping away down a side alley. Around the next corner grey daylight issued from a little cubicle of wood and glass. A row of huge fruit bats, neatly folded, hung from a rafter overhead and slept. Walter ushered him inside and offered him a chair. Before taking it Matthew went to the window, anxious to see what progress the fire had made towards them. But although it faced east, the direction from which the fire was being driven, his view was so obscured by smoke that he could see nothing. He knew that it must be very close.

'You can't stay here, Walter, you know. Have you made no arrangements to leave Singapore?'

'I suppose like everybody else you want to get me out so you can burn the place down,' said Walter grimly.

'Don't be absurd. It's going to burn down without our help, I'm afraid. In any case, we're trying to stop fires, not start them.' He paused, noticing for the first time Walter's dishevelled appearance. The clean clothes he had put on the evening before were already covered in dust and even his hair was thick with it; both his eyelids were red and swollen, perhaps from insect bites. His eyes kept wandering restlessly from one place to another, without meeting Matthew's gaze for more than a moment.

'I'm glad your father didn't live to see this,' he said presently with an air of resignation. After a silence he added with a sigh:

'There was some fool here yesterday, an army chap ... D'you know what he said to me?'

'Well, no ...'

'I'll tell you. He had the gall to tell me that we were leaving the troops to do the fighting while we only thought of feathering our nests! Can you beat it? He tried to claim that civilians have been trying to stop his demolition squad from doing its work ... He actually said ...'

'But Walter, it's true. That *has* been happening in some places ... Look, we must go now. We'll talk about it another time.' Matthew got up and again looked anxiously out of the window: this time a bright banner of sparks was floating by. 'Have you no way of getting out of Singapore? It's obvious we aren't going to hold out much longer.'

'As a matter of fact, I have,' said Walter, chuckling grimly. 'Certain business acquaintances are anxious to share their boat with me. What time is it now? They talk of leaving this evening from Telok Ayer Basin. You'd better come too, I should think. They wouldn't refuse to take a Webb, even if it meant throwing someone else overboard!' And Walter gave a sudden shout of laughter which rang in the rafters high above them. The row of bats slept on undisturbed, however.

'After all,' he went on presently, following some train of thought of his own. 'War is only a passing phase in business life ... No, it was Lever of Lever Brothers who said that, not me! Yes, it seems that in the Great War he wanted, naturally enough, to go on selling his ... what did he call it? Sunlight Soap to the Germans ... He made quite a fuss when they wouldn't let him. He argued that the more soap they let him make the more glycerine there would be for munitions ... which is true enough when you come to think about it. If you want my opinion there's nothing like a spot of patriotism for blinding people to reality. Now they'd do far better to leave certain things in Singapore as they are ... Though destroy the oil the Japs need by all means, I don't hold with people standing in the way of demolition squads if they're acting sensibly ... But no, you can't argue with these people. You can't say, look here, let's discuss it sensibly! They swell up with patriotic indignation. They refuse to believe that in due course, probably in a matter of months, we'll have come to some understanding with Japan and everything will continue as before. Except that in *this case* it won't continue as before ... why? Because a lot of self-righteous bloody fools will have destroyed our investments, lock, stock and barrel ... and we shall have to start again from scratch!'

'Walter,' exclaimed Matthew, standing up excitedly, 'it's not self-righteous fools who are destroying your investment, it's the bloody Japanese bombers! My God! Look at this ...'

A momentary shift in the wind had peeled the smoke back from the river like a plaster from a wound. Near at hand a row of blazing godowns pointed towards their window like a fiery arrow whose barb had lodged in a shed burning directly beneath them. It was not this, however, but the river itself which had caused Matthew's dismay for it seemed to be nothing but flame from one bank to another. The blazing oil which had surged up on the tide from the mouth of the river had enveloped the small wooden craft which clustered thickly over almost its entire length and breadth except for the narrow channel in the middle. Fanned by the breeze from the sea the fire had eaten its way up the twisting longbow-shaped course of the river, past another fire at Ord Road, under the Pulo Saigon Bridge and almost as far as Robertson Quay.

Matthew turned away, shocked, hoping that Adamson had managed to evacuate the thousands of Chinese families who lived on the river. Walter had joined him at the window, staring at the shining snake twisting all the way back to Anderson Bridge. He muttered: 'Terrible! Terrible!' and then turned away. 'But look here,' he went on, after a moment, 'you forget the heavy responsibility that a businessman has to carry ...'

'Oh, Walter, please, not now. We must go.' Matthew sniffed, certain he could see smoke eddying up between the bales of rubber. One of the sleeping bats stirred uneasily. But Walter had slumped heavily in his chair again.

'You may think a responsibility to one's shareholders is nothing of importance but I can assure you ... Think of the poor widow, the clergyman, the spinster who has trusted her savings to your hands and whose very life may depend on the way you conduct your business. I can assure you, Matthew, that it makes you think twice when you have the well-being of other, perhaps vulnerable, people to protect. In the early days your father and I often used to work long into the night after everyone had gone ... Yes, I sometimes used to fall asleep at this very desk here from sheer exhaustion ... And what made me do it? I was quite simply afraid that Blackett and Webb, on whom so many poor people depended for their living, might

540

have to pass their dividends! Yes, scoff if you want to, I don't care!'

'I don't want to scoff, Walter. Of course I don't! I just want us to leave here before it's too late. We may be trapped.'

Walter again ignored him. 'Well, I suppose the world was a different place in those days. The spirit of the times was quite different from the way it is now. Singapore was different, anyway, I can tell you that much! We had none of the comforts when I was a boy that people seem to expect these days. You would hardly believe it but we didn't even have water you could drink out of a tap ... In those days when my dear mother was alive she always used to filter it through a muslin dripston ... you don't see them any more but in those days ... And did we have these fine roads and storm-drains and whatnot? Of course not. We had to put up with the monsoons as best we could. Sometimes the only way you could get about was in a rowing boat! Not like today when down comes the rain and it's all over in a few minutes.'

'Walter, I can hear a crackling sound from down below ... Listen!'

Walter nodded sadly. 'It was fun for us children, of course. Oh yes, we used to think it was great fun to have a change from the rickshaw. Mind you, we had fun in the rickshaws, too. Each of us kids had his own rickshaw and a coolie to himself. Yes. We used to make 'em race with us and see who'd win and we'd have a grand time. Yes ... Grand! Grand!'

Matthew wafted the smoke away so that he could see Walter better. Then he took off his glasses, polished them with a dirty handkerchief and put them back over his smarting eyes. Walter's massive head was bowed on his shoulders and he might almost have been asleep. He raised his head presently, however, and said: 'Mind you, they were strict with us, too. Not like your father, Matthew, and his new-fangled ideas. Boys and girls all twined up together in the bath like a mess of snakes! That's what they call education these days! And then they wonder why the kids go wrong. Well, I don't know. When we children had our tea in the afternoon we had a Chinese "boy" to supervise us. And we had to be properly dressed into the bargain. Ah, how the girls hated to wear their stockings in the heat! But they had to, not like today when they run about practically naked. Any talking or nonsense and the "boy" would give us a sharp rap over the knuckles, I can tell you!'

'Walter!' cried Matthew, but was interrupted by a fit of coughing. The bats had left their rafter now and were swooping about the godown squeaking unpleasantly. Matthew's skin crawled: he did not care for bats.

'Yes, my mother used to hold court with a circle of young men around her ... young lads who would come out East and get themselves into debt, silly beggars, by signing chits. My mother used to take charge of them just as if they were her own children. She'd see that they ate proper meals and didn't spend all their money drinking. She used to say to them: "What would your mother in England say if she could see you now? Think how her feelings would be hurt!" Ah, they adored her. Many of 'em were secretly homesick, you know, but didn't like to admit it because they thought it wasn't manly. They'd have done anything for her.'

Matthew again wafted his arm feebly to clear the smoke between them which grew thicker by the minute. 'Yes, it must have been pleasant here in those days,' he agreed with a sigh.

There was silence except for a crackling of wood from downstairs. Presently, Walter cleared his throat, then stood up abruptly. He pawed the smoky air in surprise.

'What's all this smoke?' he demanded irritably.

71

That afternoon Matthew, the Major, Mr Wu and Adamson went to the cinema. The Mayfair unit's last pump had broken down near the Gas Works and the water pressure throughout the city had fallen so low, thanks to burst mains, that it was no longer possible to use hydrants. On their way back from the Gas Works they passed two cinemas beside the Volunteers' Drill Hall on the sea side of Beach Road. Surprisingly, one of the cinemas, the Alhambra, a small and rather shabby-looking place at first sight, was still open and was showing a film called *Ziegfeld Girl*. This seemed such a cause for wonder that they stopped and consulted each other. Why not? Just for a minute or two. They had such a craving for normality, even if only a glimpse of it ... even if only for a few minutes. So they went inside, and once inside in the darkness they kept falling asleep and waking up, paralysed by weariness and comfort. With one thing and another they found it difficult to leave, now that they were inside.

When the light dimmed a newsreel, cheerful in tone, showed housewives with their hair tied up in handkerchiefs collecting pots and pans on the Home Front; next, iron railings were being harvested from parks and gardens. Matthew found this ridiculous and touching and was surprised to find himself in tears. The newsreel was followed by *Ziegfeld Girl*. He fell asleep for a few minutes and when he awoke it took him some time to fathom that the film concerned the destinies of a number of chorus girls. One of the girls, played by Hedy Lamarr, was beautiful, grave and sad. Her husband, a violinist of temperament, took a dim view of her being a chorus girl.

'Well, what is it you want me to do? Give up the job? I know it's a rather foolish way to earn money, but Franz, we need it!'

'Do you really imagine that I would stand by while you showed yourself to other men?'

Matthew sighed, his head dropped on to his chest and it seemed to him that he slept for a while. But when he awoke the same conversation still seemed to be going on.

'So we never really had the thing I thought we had,' Hedy Lamarr was saying. 'Faith in each other. If you have that you don't mind about the other things. You don't even know you haven't got them.'

'All right, take the job! Be a showgirl!'

'But Franz!'

A plane roared low overhead and the heads of the audience, many of them wearing helmets, wilted in silhouette against the flickering screen. 'I suppose it would be as well to put one's tin hat on,' mused the Major, returning his attention to the screen. But he put the matter out of his mind. He was too susceptible to the cold, rather sad beauty of Hedy Lamarr. He had never been able to resist that sort of woman: she reminded him of someone he had known, oh, years ago ... That melancholy smile. 'What's she like now?' he wondered. 'Getting on, of course. Water under the bridge,' he thought sadly. Yes, Hedy Lamarr was very much the Major's cup of tea.

Now it was the dressing-room before the first night.

'Nervous?'

'Oh, Jenny, I ... I can't even put on my lipstick.'

'Relax, honey. They won't be lookin' at your mouth.' A breathless, manic Judy Garland burst in. The girls chattered excitedly. They were quelled by a man who said: 'Listen, kids – I've got something important to say to you ... in a few minutes you're going on in your first number. D'you know what that means? It means you're a Ziegfeld Girl. It means you're going to have all the opportunities of a lifetime crowded into a couple of hours. And all the temptations ...'

'Oh dear,' said Matthew, drowsing with his chin on his chest. 'Soon I shall go and look for Vera.'

'The "Dream" number. Places for the "Dream" number.'

'All right, girls. And good luck.'

The music swelled and, as it did so, a bomb falling not far away caused the building to shake and one or two small pieces of plaster fell from the ceiling. In the warm darkness the audience stirred uneasily and one or two silhouettes, crouching under the beam from the projector, made their way to the exit.

But this was the 'Dream' number. A plump, sleek tenor wearing a voluminous pair of Oxford bags began to sing:

> You stepped out of a dream,
> You are too wonderful to be what you seem.
> Could there be eyes like yours?
> Could there be lips like yours?
> Could there be smiles like yours?
> Honestly and truly,
> You stepped out of a cloud
> I want to take you away, away from the crowd ...

Matthew fell asleep, woke, fell asleep, woke again. His limbs had grown stiff from sitting so long in the same position. He longed to stretch out and sleep ... in clean sheets, 'in safety. The palms of his hands, raw and weeping from the glass splinters that clung to the hose, had begun to throb unbearably; on the screen one glittering scene followed another: he could no longer make sense of them. The screen filled with balloons from the midst of which Judy Garland emerged dressed in white. Then there were girls dancing on moving white beds, girls in white fur, girls with sheepdogs. Meanwhile, the plot was begining to thicken beyond Matthew's powers of comprehension with Lana Turner forsaking a truck-driver for an older man with an English accent, identified as a 'stage-door johnny', who offered her a meal in a French restaurant, jewels, minks. This man bore a very slight resemblance to the Major. Judy Garland danced frantically and sang:

They call her Minnie from Trinidad,
And all the natives would be so sad,
Ay! Ay! Ay! . . .
If Minnie ever left Trinidad!

She was wearing a turban, three rings of big white beads and a striped dress, through the open front of which there was an occasional glimpse of her childishly muscled legs. Matthew found something distressing about her manic innocence. He fell asleep and woke again.

Now there was the shadow of the fat tenor thrown on to the sail of a yacht. As he spun the wheel he sang:

Come, come where the moon shines with magic enchantment,
High up in the blue sky above you.
Come where a scented breeze caresses you with a lovely melody.
While my heart is whispering 'I love you.'

Then Hedy Lamarr, reflected in a mirror misted over with steam, was getting into her bath, but Matthew could no longer make sense of it all and the others were asleep: even the Major missed this important development. Again and again the girls drifted up and down brilliant staircases wearing elaborate constructions of stars on twigs, of stuffed parrots, of spangles, trailing miles of white chiffon . . . and outside, beneath the music of the sound-track, the thudding of the guns continued without a pause. The girls now appeared to be clad only in flashing white beads. On and on they went filing up and down staircases. Their clothes grew ever more elaborate. One girl had an entire dead swan strapped to her chest with its neck round hers. Lana Turner, descending yet another staircase, but not so steadily now, for in the meantime she had taken to drink, at last pitched over senseless while supporting a whole flight of stuffed white doves.

'Gosh! How can a girl do that to her career?' asked one of the other girls.

'I must go and find Vera,' whispered Matthew to the Major. But the Major was still asleep. Matthew did not wake him but made his way stiffly out to the foyer. He stood there for a few moments gazing out in bewilderment as the last glittering stair-case faded from his mind and was replaced by half a dozen motor-cars blazing fiercely in a car park a hundred yards away.

Although Matthew had no clear idea where he should look for Vera, it seemed to him quite likely that he would find her sooner or later. After all, the space in which they could avoid each other was shrinking rapidly; they were like two fish caught in a huge net: as the net was drawn in they were inevitably brought closer together. The difficulty was that a million or more other people had been caught in the same net and now here they all were together, like herrings in a flashing bundle dumped on the quayside ... it was difficult to see one herring for all the others. Finding himself across the road from Raffles Hotel he went inside and telephoned the Mayfair. But Vera still had not returned and there had been no word of her.

In the past few hours a movement of refugees had developed from west to east across the city as the Japanese pressed in towards the outskirts of Tanglin and from Pasir Panjang towards the brickworks, Alexandra Barracks and the biscuit factory. As the fighting drew nearer, the Asiatic quarters emptied and people fled towards the Changi and Serangoon Roads with what few belongings they could carry, rushing together in a dying wave that would presently wash back again with diminished force the way it had come.

Matthew allowed himself to be carried along by the tide of refugees flowing from the direction of the *padang* and the cathedral. His watch had stopped and he had no idea what time it might be ... It had grown dark while he had been in the cinema and it was no longer possible to make out clearly the features of the people he saw in the street ... strained, blank, Oriental faces, men and women with swaying poles bouncing with the rhythm of their steps. Matthew felt sorry for them. What business was it of theirs, this war conceived hundreds of miles away and incubated in Geneva!

He plodded along mechanically, so tired that time passed in a dream. The palms of his hands continued to throb, but at a distance, as if they scarcely belonged to him any more. Presently he reached a place where the macadam road-surface, melted by the heat of the day, had been set on fire by an incendiary bomb and was burning bright orange. He hurried past it, aware that it must create a dangerous pool of light to attract the planes which still lurked in the black sky above. There was evidence of looting, too: he found himself trudging through sand-dunes which lay across his path and turned out to be sugar from a nearby store. He saw men and boys crawling in and out of shattered shop windows and a shadowy figure with a rickshaw full of bottles offered to sell him a bottle of brandy for a dollar. Half a mile further on he stumbled into a twenty-five-pounder field-gun halted in a prodigious traffic jam at a fork in the road: there were other guns, too, a little further on, and a great deal of cursing could be heard. A young officer sat on the wheel of one of the twenty-five-pounders.

'You don't happen to know where we are, do you?' he asked Matthew. 'We spent the afternoon over there firing on a map reference given us by the Sherwood Foresters, but the Japs landed a mortar on our OP truck and our maps went up with it.'

'I think this must be the Serangoon Road,' said Matthew. 'If you take the left-hand fork you go to Woodleigh. I don't know where the other one goes.'

'We're trying to get to Kallang.'

'Kallang should be over there somewhere,' said Matthew vaguely, pointing into the blackness with his throbbing hand. 'Those gun-flashes must be the ack-ack from the aeodrome, I should think. But you'll have to go back into town to get there. I don't think there's any road across. Are the Japs somewhere about?'

'No idea, old chap. To tell the truth I doubt if I'd know one if I saw one. I've only been here a week. You'll probably find them up the road somewhere. Well, thanks a lot.'

Matthew walked on into the darkness. Now there came a trickle of refugees from the opposite direction. He could just make them out as they flitted by with their bundles, some dragging carts, others steering monstrously overloaded bicycles. A party of men with rifles passed by: his pulse raced at the thought that this might be a Japanese patrol. The houses dropped away now; for a while there was a lull in the traffic and he could hear the guns grumbling for miles around. He wondered now whether it would be unwise to stretch out and sleep by the roadside, but plodded on, nevertheless. He was very thirsty, too, and his mind dully contemplated the thought of cold water as he walked. At length, however, he could walk no further: his legs would no longer carry him. An abandoned cart lay nearby at the side of the road. He crawled into it and fell asleep immediately with his arms over his face to protect it from mosquitoes. The battle for Singapore eddied and flowed around him while he slept.

72

When Matthew awoke day was breaking: the country round about was already suffused in a dismal grey light that reminded him of winter in England ... with the difference that here it was sweltering hot still. While he had been asleep a lorry had parked a few yards away in the sparse shade of a grove of old, healed-up rubber trees. A British officer and an Australian corporal sat beside it, swigging alternately from a khaki water bottle. Matthew's thirst had revived with horrible and astonishing power now that he was awake and he could hardly avert his eyes from the water bottle. The corporal noticed and said: 'You look as if you could do with a drink. Come and have some water for breakfast.'

Matthew took the water bottle and drank. He was so thirsty that he had to force himself to hand it back before he finished it. The officer's name was Major Williams. He said: 'You look a mess, old boy. What have you done to your hands?' Matthew told him. He nodded sympathetically and said: 'Come back with us and we'll get you a dressing.'

They climbed into the lorry's cabin and set off. Major Williams commanded a mixed battery of 3·7-inch heavy AA guns and 40-mm Bofors on the airfield at Kallang. He explained that the Japanese planes were at last flying low enough to be in range of the Bofors. Until the past week only the 3·7s had been able to get near them. He added: 'We lost half a dozen men, though, in a single raid yesterday. It's not as if there are even any bloody planes left on the aerodrome. I don't know why they bother.' They drove on some way in silence, Matthew beginning to feel thirsty again.

'None of this makes any sense to a chap like me,' Williams said after a while, gesturing at the rubble-strewn streets. 'I used to work in an insurance company before the war.'

They had barely reached the aerodrome when a siren began to wail. The corporal, who was behind the wheel, accelerated down one of the supply roads, slamming to a stop some fifty yards short of the nearest gun emplacement: all three sprinted for cover. 'We have ammo in the back,' the corporal said when he had recovered his breath. 'It wouldn't do to be caught in the open sitting on that lot.'

Now, all around the aerodrome the guns began to thunder. A squadron of Japanese bombers was approaching. This was not a high altitude carpet-bombing raid; the planes were coming in low and had split up before reaching the target to confuse the ack-ack guns. A scene of frenzied activity confronted Matthew in the sandbagged emplacement where he now found himself. He had no idea what was happening and hung back, anxious not to get in the way of the frantically working gun crew. He gazed in wonder at the great 3·7-inch gun looming above him; its two enormous, tyred wheels rearing off the ground gave it the appearance of a prancing prehistoric monster. Meanwhile the range was read off on the predictor, shells were brought up, their fuses were set and they were stacked into the loading trays. At a little distance on either side an appalling shrieking and popping had begun as the Bofors guns poured their small, impact-fused shells into the sky at the rate of two a second. To this shrieking and popping was added the prodigious roar of the heavy guns and the crump of bombs that made the ground ripple beneath his feet.

Matthew had never seen a gun fired at such close quarters and was overcome by enthusiasm. 'There's one, get it down!' he shouted, pointing and even climbing on to the sandbagged parapet in his excitement. 'Here it comes!' But the gunners paid no attention to him. They worked on grimly, for the most part not even looking up at the sky. They seemed to be working in a daze, automatically. Their hands were blistered and in some cases as raw as Matthew's own. The sweat poured off them. Sometimes they staggered under the weight of the shells as they handed them up. 'Magnificent! What splendid men!' thought Matthew, shouting and waving them on like a boat-race crew.

But now another bomber was clumsily droning towards them over the field, very low at no more than a few hundred feet, perhaps, coming from the direction of the river. Matthew leaped up again on to the parapet of sandbags and pointed, speechless with excitement, for evidently the gunners had not seen it. They continued to fire, not at this plane which lingered tantalizingly almost on their muzzle, but at some other aircraft which drifted miles above them and was scarcely to be seen through the canopy of smoke and cloud. Matthew, who did not know that the huge 3·7-inch would have been useless against a hedge-hopping plane, it was too slow (what you needed was a fast-swinging, rapid-firing gun like the Bofors, a glorified machine-gun), jumped up and down, almost having a fit. 'Look at this one!' he cried in a frenzy and again he pointed at the bomber which was still crawling steadily and now rather menacingly towards them, barely skimming the row of wooden huts on the far side of the field.

'Fire!' howled Matthew, gesticulating. 'It'll get away. Oh, my God! Quick!' But the men continued to serve the gun not placidly, no, but steadily, grimly, and the gun continued to fire at the other plane, remote, maybe twenty thousand feet above them and no longer even visible but obscured once more by the canopy of smoke.

'Can they be deaf?' groaned Matthew, looking, it seemed, into the very eyes of the oncoming bomber-pilot, and concluded that perhaps they were deaf as anyone would be, standing beside those guns all day. 'This may be dangerous,' he thought, jumping down from the parapet. But his excitement was too much for him and he promptly sprang up again, to see the Bofors on each side of him firing over open sights at the plane which was now a mere hundred yards away. For a second the two streams of shells formed two sides of a triangle whose apex was the bomber itself. The glass cockpit suddenly vanished, as if vaporized. Matthew ducked involuntarily. A dark shadow covered him, like a lid on a pot. An appalling rush of air and a quaking of the ground, in complete silence, it seemed.

Matthew again jumped up, in time to see through the smoke the bomber departing peacefully over the flat, marshy ground in the direction of Geylang, but very low ... and suddenly it seemed to trip on some obstruction, and then tumble head over heels with a tremendous explosion. Now it became several independent balls of fire that raced each other onwards over the flat ground burning brilliantly as they went and leaving the main hulk of the aircraft behind. Even the great noise this had caused had only reached Matthew faintly. The crew of the 3.7 had stopped firing, they were grinning, their mouths were working and they were waving their fists, Matthew swallowed and the sound suddenly came back. He, too, joined in the cheering. Around them all the guns had fallen silent for the moment. Williams appeared presently, having detailed one of his men to find Matthew a dressing. 'I'm glad we got another one before we give up,' he remarked.

'How d'you mean "before we give up"?' Matthew asked

vaguely; he now felt shaken and disgusted with himself for having exulted over the death of the Japanese bomber-crew; even though they had presumably wanted to kill him and his companions it did not seem right to have allowed himself to get so excited.

'The rumour is we'll surrender some time today.' Williams shrugged. 'It can't be much longer, anyway. A few of us here are thinking of trying to make it to Sumatra by boat once the surrender is official. We've got hold of a motor-launch over by the Swimming Club on the other side of the field.' He gazed at Matthew sympathetically. 'There's room for you if you care to join us.'

'Could I bring a Chinese girl? She's on the Japanese black-list.'

Williams nodded. 'It might be a squeeze. The plan is to leave as soon after nine o'clock as possible if we surrender today. If not, then tomorrow.'

'I may not be able to find her in time but I'll try. Don't wait for me if I'm not here.'

Presently Matthew set off on foot back towards the centre of the city but shortly after he had left the aerodrome gates he was given a lift by a taciturn young Scot driving a van. There was barely time for the vehicle to start moving, however, before there was the roar of an aero-engine overhead and bullets began to furrow the tarmacadam. A moment later the plane, a Zero, had overshot them, was climbing and turning. The driver accelerated and the van began to sway violently from side to side. Matthew craned out of the window, trying to follow the path of the plane as it circled round behind them.

'Damn! He's coming back.'

The van screeched to a stop beside the Kallang bridge, slewing round in the road so that it was sideways on to the direction they had been going. Matthew and the driver plunged out, one on each side of the road. Matthew took cover in the doorway of a deserted shop-house and sank to the ground with his back against the wall, feeling sick and exhausted. The Zero came back. Another rattle of machine-gun fire and it zoomed over again. Then all was quiet for a while. Nothing moved on the road or on the bridge. There was no sign of the young Scot. Matthew continued to sit where he was, staring at the buildings across the road.

Beside the canal was the Firestone factory: a long, cream, concrete building with green windows which had a slight air of a cinema, perhaps because of the name 'Firestone' in red gothic lettering attached to its façade. Matthew remembered now that Monty had pointed this building out to him on the evening he had first arrived. There had been some strike or other there. Some distance further along, sandwiched between the Gas Company gas-holder and the Nanyang Lights Company, was a bizarre little temple. Its outer wall was painted in red and white stripes and supported a multitude of strange, sculpted figures painted silver: a plump silver guru held up three fingers and gazed complacently back across the street at Matthew; beside him silver cows relaxed; the head of an elephant supported each gatepost while, on the arch above, a Buddha-like figure sat on a lotus flower and was saluted by two baby elephants with their trunks; on each side of the elephants, most curious, winged angels played violins and blew trumpets. Beyond, on the roof itself, an elephant-headed god rode a cow and a cobra rode a peacock. In front of the temple, like an offering, a dead man lay in the gutter under a buzzing, seething black shroud.

'I must get us both on to that boat tonight, come what may,' he thought, longing to go home himself and forget the cruel sights he had seen. With an effort he forced himself to stand up and go in search of the young Scot and find out why he had not returned to the van.

73

The last position from which a defence of Singapore might have been successful had been lost but still the city had not surrendered.

On the previous day, Saturday, 14 February, General Percival had found himself at last having to wrestle with the problem he had been dreading for weeks: how long would it be possible to fight on. The water supply was on the verge of failing. On higher ground it had failed already. Drinking water especially was in short supply. Because of the damaged mains there were fires burning out of control on every hand. Twice he had visited Brigadier Simson at the Municipal Offices to inspect the figures for the city's water supply for the previous day: he had found that two-thirds of the water being pumped was running to waste and that the situation was getting rapidly worse.

This was clearly a matter which must be discussed with the Governor who had, in the meantime, moved out of the bomb-damaged Government House and had taken up residence in the Singapore Club. This meeting with the Governor had left a distressing impression on Percival's mind. Sir Shenton Thomas was alarmed by the prospect of a serious epidemic in the city. Why then did Percival still hesitate to surrender? Wavell, now back in Java, had made it plain that he was expected to fight on as long as possible, if necessary by fighting through the streets. Behind this reluctance of Wavell's to countenance surrender there was undoubtedly the voice of Churchill himself. On the other hand, surrender was clearly the only way in which the civilian population might be spared some great disaster, either from an epidemic or from the fighting.

It is distressing to have to act under the impulsive orders of someone who, in a situation which concerns you deeply, does not know what he is talking about. Percival, as a deeply loyal soldier, was sufficiently nimble to dodge the notion that Churchill, trying to tell him what was best at a distance of several thousand miles, was nothing but a blockhead who had, moreover, already committed his full share of blunders with respect to the Malayan campaign. But no sooner had Percival dodged this disloyal thought than he found himself having to elude the grasp of another, even more cruel conviction: namely, that the Governor now sitting opposite him *was not real*. Nor was it only the Governor who suffered this disability: his wife did, too, and his staff, and indeed, everyone here in the Singapore Club and, come to that, outside it. For it had suddenly dawned on Percival that he was the victim of a cruel and elaborate charade: that the moment he left the Governor's presence the fellow would cease to exist. Percival passed a hand over his brow and tried to collect himself. Could it really be that Churchill, Wavell, Gordon Bennett, even his own staff, had no real substance, that they were merely phantasms sent to test and torment him, incredibly lifelike but with no more reality than the flickering images one saw on a cinema screen? Wherever he looked, yes, these deceptive images would spring up, but the instant he looked away again they would vanish. What evidence was there that they continued to exist when he was not looking at them? Why, he doubted whether the Governor, relying on the dignity of his office to deter Percival from touching him, even bothered to cloak himself with a tactile as well as visual semblance. He could probably poke a finger through him! For a moment, staring at the Governor suspiciously over the little table between them, Percival had an urge to experiment, an urge to reach out and grasp him by the throat. With an effort of will, however, he mastered himself and muttered: 'While we still have water we must fight on. It is our duty.' But he continued to stare at the Governor until the latter grew uneasy.

'Whatever ails the fellow?' Sir Shenton wondered while Percival's eyes, which for some reason had become unusually piercing, bored into him like the bits of two drills. 'He's been under a frightful strain, of course. But then, we all have.'

The Governor was somewhat relieved when Percival at last stood up to leave. Before he did so, he took the opportunity of returning once more to the subject of the epidemic he feared, but less with the hope of persuading Percival to surrender than of making sure that there was no doubt about his own position should the epidemic in fact occur. Percival nodded, licking his lips in an odd manner, and then asked unexpectedly: 'What will you do now ... I mean, immediately after I have left this room?'

'What?' The Governor was taken aback by this question which seemed to him peculiar, even impertinent. What business was it of Percival's what he was going to do now? Or ... wait. Wait a moment. Did Percival suspect that what he was about to do was to send a cable to the Colonial Office putting all responsibility for the decision not to surrender on to the Forces? He replied shortly that he must now visit his wife, who was sick. Percival nodded at this information, smiling in a rather offensive and knowing way, as if to say: 'I'll bet you are!' and then took his leave.

Still, the Governor could not help wondering about Percival's odd behaviour, even while drafting a cable to the Colonial Office to point out that there were now over a million people within a radius of three square miles. 'Many dead lying in the streets and burial impossible. We are faced with total deprivation of water which must result in pestilence. I have felt that it is my duty to bring this to notice of General Officer Commanding.' There! His flanks protected, the Governor felt a little better. Still, there was no denying it, they were all in a pickle.

That night Percival dreamed not about the war but about an epidemic. 'What has your epidemic got to do with me?' he demanded indignantly. The Governor replied: 'If you don't understand, it's not much use trying to explain.' Then the Governor faded and Percival slept in peace for a while, until presently a little group of military advisers assembled round his bedside led by Hamley, author of *The Operations of War Explained and Illustrated*. They were less confident than they had been on previous nights, but nevertheless, recommended a bold stroke: the million people who now crowded into Singapore Town should arm themselves as best they could with whatever lay to hand and all charge simultaneously at the same point of the Japanese lines. When they had finished with one point they might turn to another, and so on until the Japanese were defeated. 'An attack by a million people,' declared Hamley pompously, 'is not to be shrugged off lightly.'

Now Sunday dawned, ominous, unbearably hot. Percival took communion and prayed fervently: he found it hard to masticate the wafer he was given: his mouth was too dry. However, his frame of mind was somewhat better. Only once, noticing the chaplain gaze at him with interest and compassion, did he find himself wondering whether this cleric had any other existence beyond the walk-on part of lending verisimilitude to his own Sunday devotions. He shrugged the thought off hastily. There would be time enough to worry about the existence of other people. The campaign was almost at an end.

He had called a conference of all his commanders for nine-thirty a.m. Brigadier Simson now reported that a complete failure of the water supply was likely within twenty-four hours. In the light of this news there were only two possible courses of action. One was to counter-attack and recover the reservoirs and the food depots at Bukit Timah. The other was to surrender.

It was agreed unanimously that there was no real alternative. The meeting was over within twenty minutes and Percival immediately set to work on the delicate and humiliating task of negotiating Singapore's surrender. It was not until late in the afternoon that, after much difficulty, Percival found himself at the Ford factory, sitting opposite the Japanese Commander, General Yamashita. Although a cease-fire had already been ordered for four p.m. it was agreed that hostilities should officially cease at eight-thirty p.m. Yamashita conceded that his three fighting divisions should remain outside the city that night to prevent any disorder or excesses. At no point during this trying interview did General Yamashita seem anything but completely real to General Percival (only Torrance, his

Chief of Staff, who sat on his right, occasionally dimmed like an electric light in a thunderstorm).

This Sunday, then, was the last day of the defence of Singapore, the last day of freedom for the British who remained on the Island ... almost, you might say with hindsight, the last day of the British Empire in these parts. It took time for news of the impending surrender to percolate through the stricken city, particularly since the bombing, strafing and shelling continued unabated all morning and afternoon. Matthew still had not heard the news as he struggled in the mid-day heat near the Firestone factory to get the body of a young Scot into the back of the van ... as a matter of fact, by now he had lost count of the days and could not have told you that today was Sunday. Nor had the Major heard the news as, after a rather odd tiffin of tinned sardines and tinned pears, he and Captain Brown held a cut-rate auction of the remaining girls from the Poh Leung Kuk in the presence of the handful of bridegrooms he had persuaded to assemble, thanks to the good offices of Mr Wu. The bridegrooms were apathetic and uneasy and bidding was not brisk. But the Major comforted himself with the thought that to get them husbands of any description in the circumstances was not bad going. How would those girls who had declined to accept one or other of the Major's bridegrooms fare during the inevitable Japanese occupation of Singapore? He suspected that some of them, to judge by the lipstick and nail-varnish that was beginning to reappear, might fare all too well.

Matthew was now delivering the young Scot's body to the General Hospital in Outram Road. It had taken an age to get the body into the van (a corpse is heavy and Matthew was weak) and it was two o'clock exactly as he reached the hospital. There, beside one of the paths leading up the slope to the main building, a mass grave had been dug. He looked up, afflicted by the sight of so many bodies laid out on the lawn for burial, and noticed the white clock tower above the portico of the main block with its four small, black clock faces. It came as a shock, somehow. The clock looked so peaceful nestling there beneath drooping classical garlands while on the ground below there was nothing to be seen but carnage and violent death. Two o'clock.

Two, three hours passed in a dream. The guns had fallen silent at last and bombs ceased to fall on the city. At the Mayfair there was no sign of Vera. Matthew longed to lie down there and sleep but time was slipping away and he must find her soon if they were to escape that night. A little later, without remembering how he had got there, he found himself sitting on his heels and gazing down at the wall of the storm-drain that ran along Orchard Road; part of it had fallen in, revealing a great wedge of neatly packed pink bricks, like the roe of a gutted fish, each with the word Jurong neatly printed on its back.

Later again he passed Dr Brownley scurrying along Battery Road in the direction of Whiteaways': he called to him but the Doctor paid no attention. His eyes were shining, his pulse was racing, he suffered a painful, joyful constriction of his respiration. In his ears, instead of Matthew's greeting, a celestial music sounded, while in his pocket rested $985.50 cents which in a moment he would be exchanging for the only true object of his desire, that article which had fixed him with its basilisk stare from Whiteaways' window, whatever it was. Dr Brownley was flying as if to greet a lover (but let him pass on, for which of us is so poor in spirit that he has never experienced the delights of being united in bonds of ownership with a piece of merchandise?).

Then Matthew, having wished the Doctor well under his breath, was standing in the cathedral grounds inspecting a collection of furniture that had been carried outside. The pews, he noticed, were made of solid wood, such as one might find in any English church, but with woven rush seats and backs as a concession to the tropics. Inside, a hospital had been improvised. The shuttered sides of the building stood open, as did another row of shutters just beneath the timbered roof. Rows of wounded had been laid on the brown stone flags beneath a couple of dozen silently revolving fans which hung from elbowed brackets along the aisle. Nearer to the altar, a number of men and women knelt in prayer, some of them in uniform. From a distance this scene, like that in the grounds of the General Hospital, appeared relatively peaceful. It seemed to Matthew that the human beings in it looked quite insignificant compared with the great building which rose above them. The fans, revolving like propellers some distance below the dim heights of the roof, gave him the restful impression that he was under water ... It was only when he looked with more particular attention at the wounded on the floor that he realized that here, too, people lay shattered and dying. Shocked, he fell back, intending to continue his search somewhere else. But then, at last, he saw Vera working among the patients not far away.

Vera saw him at almost the same moment. She hurried

towards him but, at the last instant, hung back. He had thought at first that she was wearing a red and white dress. Now he saw that it was an overall and that she was soaked in blood from head to foot.

'I know,' she said immediately. 'I'm going to change as soon as I can.' She smiled at him then and burst into tears.

They went outside for a moment. 'D'you notice something odd?' he asked suddenly. 'There are no birds. They've all gone. That's why it seems so quiet.'

'Tell me where you'll be later,' Vera said. 'I can't talk to you now. I must go.'

'I'll come back here just after seven. There may be a boat leaving tonight which we could both take.'

Vera borrowed his handkerchief, dried her eyes, smiled at him and hurried away. He retired a little way into the grounds but lingered for a while, watching her as she moved from one patient to another.

Later, after lying down for some time on the cathedral lawn, he joined the crowds milling slowly about in Raffles Place. A strange hush had fallen over everything: in it the occasional crash or crackle of a fire not far away in Battery Road or Market Street could be clearly heard. People drifted, for the most part aimlessly, in and out of the shops that were still open, or simply stood about talking in little groups. Many people had suitcases or bundles, evidently refugees from up-country or from districts lying outside the British-held perimeter. There were a number of forlorn-looking children: some of them had been bedded down on the street or in doorways by their parents. There were a great many soldiers: some of them, in defiance of the supposed destruction of liquor, were drunk and belligerent.

A dense crowd had gathered at the far end of Raffles Place in front of the Mercantile Bank. There, under a thick stone colonnade, someone was shouting. Matthew pressed forward into the crowd to see what was happening. A sculpted stone flame resembling an ice-cream cone twirled up over the grandiose entrance to the Mercantile Bank. Above that, two fluted, indigestible stone pillars supported four more twirled ice-cream cones set in dishes. It was beneath this important façade that a ragged British Tommy had chosen to address the crowd. Matthew strained to hear what he was saying.

'A dirty capitalist war!' he was shouting. 'We've no reason to be here at all. Listen, mates, which of us gives a damn for the bleedin' Chinese? Let 'em sort it out for themselves with the bloody Japs ... What's it to do with us? I'll tell you what ... It's greedy profiteers in London, that's what it is ...'

A drunken shout of approval rose from the troops packed together in front of this vociferous figure. There were jeers, too, and bitter laughter. Matthew muttered: 'No, that's all wrong ...' and tried to force his way through the mob. But now, abruptly, a fight flared up just beside him and in the sudden thrashing of fists and boots Matthew was shoved backwards and somebody's elbow caught him a blow in the face. He fell and for a moment, dazed, was afraid that the crowd would surge over him before he could get up. He could still hear the Tommy ranting as he scrambled to his feet and worked his way round to the right by the Meyer Building, muttering to himself as he went.

Now he had shoved his way in under the colonnade and was almost within reach of the table on which the soldier was standing, still declaiming wildly against the profiteers and their native henchmen. At this moment a missile, perhaps a bottle, hurled from the crowd, struck the speaker and he fell suddenly to his knees, crouching on the table like a wild animal, blood pouring from his temple. Matthew saw the glinting studs of his boots as he knelt there with his head between his knees. Then someone helped him off the table and Matthew immediately jumped up in his place, holding up his hand and shouting:

'No! Don't you see? Things don't have to be like this ... Please listen to me! It's just a question of how we approach each other. People seem to think that self-interest ... No, what I mean to say really ... Wait! We're no different from each other, after all! We don't have to have ... yes, I believe it, and one day we won't! We won't have them ...! We shall live ...!' He tried to say more but a great wave of jeering and yelling surged forward from the crowd and his voice broke. 'Oh, don't you see, you're playing *their* game ...' he muttered, gazing down in distress at the baying crowd in front of him until, a moment later, a bottle came winging end over end towards him and struck him a numbing blow in the ribs. He staggered back with a gasp. A hand gripped his arm firmly and dragged him off the table. He found himself looking at the grinning face of Dupigny.

'François,' he muttered. 'What are you doing ...?'

'D'you want to get yourself killed?' asked Dupigny. 'Now is not the moment for such nonsense.'

74

At the Adelphi Hotel beside the cathedral someone had had the foresight to fill several baths before the water supply had failed. Although these baths had already been used by several people and the water in them had taken on a dark grey colour, both Matthew and Dupigny took advantage of them and were feeling distinctly refreshed as they emerged from the hotel into the twilight and crossed the road to the cathedral grounds. Dupigny himself had decided not to try to escape. He was too old, he had explained with a shrug, and besides 'avec la Boche en France' ... He would stay and keep his friend the Major company during the internment which no doubt awaited them. He had agreed to drive Matthew and Vera to the boat waiting at Tanjong Rhu, however.

A great crowd had gathered around the cathedral in the dusk, and seeing it Matthew began to feel anxious again, lest they should not be able to locate Vera. A service was in progress and these people standing in devout silence several deep around the building were those who had been unable to find room inside. As Matthew and Dupigny searched the fringes of this crowd the congregation began to sing:

> Praise, my soul, the King of Heaven,
> To his feet thy tribute bring.
> Ransomed, healed, restored, forgiven
> Who like me his praise should sing?
> Praise him! Praise him!
> Praise the everlasting King!

Suddenly a young woman detached herself from the crowd and took Matthew's arm. It was Vera. He gazed at her, smiling with relief, remembering how he had first seen her come up to him in the twilight at The Great World just like this.

'Come,' said Dupigny.

It was very dark by the time they reached the aerodrome. They left the car near the entrance, having decided that in order not to attract attention it would be best to complete their journey on foot. It seemed to grow even darker, however, once they were on the airfield itself and they had to grope their way forward with the utmost caution to avoid bomb-craters and other obstacles. This wandering in the blackness seemed to take an age. Once, not far away, they saw a party of men with a powerful torch, also moving across the field. They crouched down and held their breath while the men went by, talking among themselves. It was impossible to tell what language they were speaking. The wavering light of the torch moved on for another hundred yards, then was switched off suddenly. A little later it was switched on again and some distance further away and played for a moment on the shattered barrel of a spiked anti-aircraft gun. Then the torch vanished once more. Matthew, Vera and Dupigny continued their laborious journey. At last they could hear the lapping of the water and a voice spoke to them quietly from the darkness. Matthew answered. It was Major Williams.

'Glad you made it. There are some other people about so we'd better be quiet. They may be Japs or other escapers. You just got here in time, as a matter of fact, because we're about ready to leave. The boat's out here.'

Ahead of them a shaded light appeared for a second or two on a gang-plank. Matthew glimpsed the Australian corporal he had seen that morning with Williams; behind him it was just possible to make out the shadow of a boat against the water. 'Come along, the sooner we shove off the better.'

Matthew and Vera said goodbye to Dupigny and they wished each other luck. They shook hands. Matthew and Vera crossed the gang-plank followed by Williams. Dupigny waited to help them cast off and was just stooping to do so when a powerful beam sprang out of the darkness and played over the launch, then fastened on Dupigny. The figures on the deck froze. The Australian corporal who was holding a lamp switched it on. It illuminated a ragged party of soldiers wearing Australian hats. One of them had a revolver, another a tommy-gun. There were about a dozen of them.

'Sorry, sports, we're taking the boat,' the man with the torch on Dupigny said. 'Hop it.'

Nobody moved or spoke. Dupigny, however, reached down for the mooring-rope to cast off. There was a shot and he began to hop about like a wounded bird, clutching his leg.

'Why don't you find your own bloody boat?' shouted the Australian corporal in a sudden rage.

'Hop it. You, too, cobber.'

'There's nothing for it, I'm afraid,' said Williams. One by one they came back over the gang-plank.

'Right now. Clear off and take him, too, before we do him in.'

They picked up Dupigny who had now fallen over and was struggling to get up again. He said he was not badly hurt but Matthew and Williams had to take his arms over their shoulders and support him; one leg of his cotton drill trousers was already soaked in blood. Speechless with anger and frustration they made their way wearily back across the aerodrome in the darkness.

From elsewhere on the Island other parties bent on escape were also groping about in the darkness. General Gordon Bennett found himself at the docks searching for a boat in which he might sail to Malacca in search of a bigger boat which in turn might carry him to Australia and freedom; he had thought it best not to mention his departure to the GOC and had left an inspiriting order for the Australian troops under his command to remain vigilantly at their posts ... but in the meantime, where was that damn boat he needed?

As for Walter, he was making his way along a quay at Telok Ayer Basin where the *Nigel*, a handsome motor-yacht, was waiting for him and his companion, W. J. Bowser-Barrington. Poor Bowser-Barrington had fallen some way behind and was gasping under the tarpaulin-wrapped burden he carried on his shoulders. Bowser-Barrington was feeling anything but pleased, for his intention had been that Walter should carry this burden which consisted of his deceased Chairman who, though not a heavy man, was not a light one either. Walter, however, had flatly refused to have anything to do with carrying old Solomon's remains and had even gone so far as to recommend that Bowser-Barrington should simply throw his Chairman away somewhere. This, naturally, was altogether out of the question.

'Well,' thought Bowser-Barrington uneasily as he struggled along the quay in Walter's wake, 'once we're out at sea I'll show him who's boss.' Or rather ... wait. Perhaps that was something he should discuss with the rest of the Board. Might it not be better to wait until they had reached Australia?

'Ahhhh!' He stumbled in the darkness and, as he did so, it was almost as if his Chairman deliberately ground his sharp knee painfully into his ear. But, of course, that was out of the question. 'Where are you, Walter?' he cried feebly into the darkness. 'I say, old boy, please don't leave me!'

Once Dupigny, whose wound fortunately had proved none too serious, had been returned to the Mayfair, Matthew had to consider what to do next. With only a few hours left before the Japanese occupation of the city it had become urgent to find a place where Vera might be able to lie low and conceal her identity. She needed a Chinese family willing to take the risk of hiding her, but neither Vera nor Matthew knew one. The Major suggested that they should ask Mr Wu. But Mr Wu was nowhere to be found. Either he had managed to escape during the early part of the night or else he, too, in danger as a former officer in the Chinese Air Force, had decided to lie low. Matthew and Vera wasted two precious hours in a vain search for Mr Wu. Such was the confusion in the city that nobody knew where anybody might be. As they made their way once again through the city centre Matthew gazed with envy at the troops who had stretched out to sleep on the pavements. By now both he and Vera were too tired to think constructively: they just wandered aimlessly, hand in hand, full of bitterness and discouragement as a result of their abortive attempt to escape and longing to be at peace.

At last, in desperation, they went to visit the tenement where Vera had lived before. The building was half deserted and there was no longer anyone sleeping on the stairs or in the corridors. Evidently many of those who had lived there formerly had moved to *kampongs* outside the city to avoid the bombing and shelling. Vera's little cubicle was still as she had left it. Nothing had been touched in her absence.

'You can't stay here. Someone in the building would inform on you sooner or later.'

'Where else is there to go?' Vera put a soothing hand on his shoulder. 'They're simple people here. They don't know about what happened in Shanghai.'

'They'll think you're suspicious. They'll have seen you with me.'

'They will just think I'm a prostitute. To them all Englishmen look alike,' she smiled wanly. 'Really, I shall be all right. I have been in a situation like this before.' She shrugged. 'Besides, we have no choice.' After she had rested her head against his shoulder for a little while in silence she said: 'You must go now, Matthew. It would be best if we weren't seen together any more. When you have gone I shall cut my hair and take off these European clothes.'

'Is there nothing else I can do for you? Let me give you some money, though it may no longer be any use once the Japanese have taken over. Perhaps it would be best to buy some things tomorrow, then exchange them later when they get rid of our currency.'

Vera nodded and took the money. She began to weep quietly, saying: 'I'm sorry to be like this. I feel so tired, that's all. Tomorrow when I have slept I shall be all right.'

'We'll see each other again, won't we?'

'Yes, one day, certainly,' she agreed.

Early on Tuesday afternoon European civilians were at last marched off to Katong on the first stage of their long journey on foot to internment in Changi gaol. They had been assembled on the *padang* all morning under the tropical sun. Many of them were already suffering from the heat, weariness and thirst. The Major and Matthew walked one on each side of Dupigny who, despite his injury, insisted on walking by himself. Matthew carried a small bundle of Dupigny's belongings as well as a water bottle and a suitcase of his own. They walked in silence at first. The Major, in addition to his suitcase, carried a folded stretcher they had improvised, lest it should become necessary to carry Dupigny.

The ruined, baking streets stretched interminably ahead. In some of the shops they passed Matthew noticed that crude Japanese flags had already appeared. Dupigny noticed them, too, and said with a cynical smile: 'Well, Matthew, do you really believe that one day all races will decide to abandon self-interest and live together in harmony?'

'Yes, François, one day.'

They struggled on in the heat, stopping now and then to rest for a few moments in whatever shade they could find. Once, while they were resting, an elderly Chinese came out of a shop-house and offered them cigarettes from a round tin of Gold Flake, nodding and smiling at them sympathetically. They thanked him warmly and walked on, feeling encouraged.

The Chinese and Indians who had vanished from the streets after the surrender were beginning cautiously to reappear. By a row of burned-out shop-houses a group of young Indians had gathered to watch the column of Europeans as they straggled by.

When Dupigny, limping painfully, came abreast of them they laughed and jeered at him. Delighted, he turned to smile ironically at Matthew.

'One day, François.'

They walked on. As time passed, Dupigny found it increasingly difficult to keep up with the others. His face was grey now and running with sweat. The Major insisted on having a look at his leg: his wound had opened again and his shoe was full of blood. He told the others to go on without him; he would get a lift from one of the Japanese vehicles which occasionally passed on the road. But the others considered this too risky. Ignoring his protests the Major unfolded the stretcher and made Dupigny lie down on it. Then he and Matthew picked up the stretcher and they went forward again, leaving their suitcases to volunteers in the column behind them; meanwhile, another volunteer searched through the column for a doctor, but presently he returned saying none could be found: it seemed that the doctors had been detained to look after the wounded in the city. They moved on once more: Dupigny seemed hardly to have the strength to brush the flies from his lips and eyes. They spread a handkerchief over his face to keep off the glare of the sun.

Time passed. At last Katong was no longer very far ahead. Dupigny lay with his eyes closed and seemed to be scarcely conscious. Again they passed a crowd of jeering Indians. Hearing them, Dupigny opened his eyes for a moment and his mouth twisted into a smile.

In the weeks, then months, then years that followed, first in Changi, later at the Sime Road civilian camp, Matthew found that his world had suddenly shrunk. Accustomed to speculate grandly about the state and fate of nations he now found that his thought were limited to the smallest of matters ... a glass of water, a pencil, a handful of rice. Hope had deserted him completely. It came as a surprise to him to realize how much he had depended on it before.

In the first weeks after his internment, news began to filter into Changi of mass executions of Chinese suspected of having helped the British. 'Will all men still be brothers one day, Matthew?' asked Dupigny when he heard about these executions.

'I think so, François.' And Matthew shrugged sadly.

'Ah,' said Dupigny.

Many of the Chinese who were killed were towed out to sea in lighters and made to jump overboard, still bound together in twos and three. Others were machine-gunned wholesale on the beaches. According to the rumours which reached the camp, in every part of Singapore where Chinese lived they were forced by the Japanese to leave their houses at dawn and paraded in front of hooded informers. Matthew had a chilling vision of the scene . . . the hooded man, of whose face nothing could be seen but a glitter of eyes behind the mask, moving like Death along the row of waiting people, without explanation picking out now this person, now that. What chance would Vera have? No wonder hope had deserted him and that he preferred to restrict his thoughts to simple things. A glass of water, a pencil, a handful of rice.

But then one day in his second year of captivity, while he was out with a working party on the road, a young Chinese brushed up against him and pressed something into his hand. He looked at it surreptitiously: it was a cigarette packet wrapped in a handkerchief. When he opened it he put his head in his hands: it contained a lump of sugar and two cooked white mice. And he thought: 'Well, who knows? At least there's a chance. Perhaps she'll survive after all, and so will I.'

But more years pass and yet more. Let us suppose that Kate Blackett, now a woman with grown-up children of her own, is sitting at her breakfast-table in a quiet street in Bayswater. Kate has a pleasant, kindly, humorous look (as characters tend to have when their author treats them well) and this is an agreeable room she is having breakfast in: on the wall there is a charming painting by Patricia Moynagh of a curled-up cat, and a delightful, serene painting by Mary Newcomb of several people standing on a ferry, and another of a dog peacefully asleep surrounded by red flowers. Through the window, from where she is sitting, there is a glimpse of garden in which a cat is trying to catch butterflies . . . Or rather, no. Let us suppose that it is winter. Rub out the cat, erase the butterflies and let us move back inside where it is warmer.

Opposite Kate at the table is a man reading *The Times* for 10 December 1976. Kate can see nothing of this man (her husband, let us hope) but some grey hair on top of his head and two hands holding up the newspaper. Does he wear glasses? It is impossible to say. His face is hidden by the newspaper. The fingers which are holding it are long and slender and he is wearing a green sweater ... (we can see part of its sleeve) and that is all there will be of him until he decides to put down the newspaper. Well, not quite all, however, for presently he speaks to Kate with a slight drawl. An Australian perhaps? From his voice he could be English, though, or even an American who has lived a long time in England. Perhaps, then, Kate has married Ehrendorf, that incorrigible Anglophile, who has at last come to his senses and realized which was the most attractive of the Blackett girls.

'Listen to this, Kate,' he says. 'Here's something that might interest a rubber tycoon's daughter: "Plantation work pays less than one dollar a day." From Our Correspondent, Geneva, 9 December. "Millions of workers on rubber, sugar, tea, cotton or coffee plantations are earning less than $1 (62p) a day, according to the International Labour Office." Let me see, what else does it say? Trade union rights ... et cetera ... malnutrition ... disease .. Yes ... "Many migrant workers on rubber or sugar plantations live in conditions of acute overcrowding. Sometimes there are up to 100 workers in one large room." Daily wage rates ... And so on. There.'

Kate looks around the room vaguely but says nothing. Singapore seems very far away to her now, and no longer quite real ... a magical place where she spent her childhood. Why, Malaya is no longer even called Malaya. Things that once seemed immutable have turned out to be remarkably vulnerable to change.

Or have they? That man behind the newspaper, if it were Ehrendorf, let us say, and if he happened to remember his arguments of years ago with Matthew about colonialism and tropical agriculture, might he not, as his eye was caught by that headline 'Plantation work pays less than one dollar a day', have said to himself that nothing very much had changed, after all, despite that tremendous upheaval in the Far East? That if even after independence in these Third World countries, it is *still* like that, then something has gone wrong, that some other, perhaps native, élite has merely replaced the British? If it *were* Ehrendorf might he not have recalled that remark of Adamson's (passed on to him by Matthew) about King William and the boatman who asked who had won the battle ('What's it to you? You'll still be a boatman.')?

But Ehrendorf, with his good manners, would surely have put down the newspapers by now or would at least have given part of it to Kate to read. Instead of which this individual has by now moved on to read about some other matter in some other part of the world, leaving Kate to gaze out of the window at the garden where it is suddenly summer again and a cat is trying to catch a butterfly. In any case ...

In any case, there is really nothing more to be said. And so, if you have been reading in a deck-chair on the lawn, it is time to go inside and make the tea. And if you have been reading in bed, why, it is time to put out the light now and go to sleep. Tomorrow is another day, as they say, as they say.

Afterword

Among those works listed below which have been most valuable in this attempt to recreate the Far East of forty years ago I am particularly indebted to Professor P. T. Bauer's work on the rubber industry and especially to his classic report on small-holdings prepared for the Colonial Office in 1946 which, with J. S. Furnivall's *Colonial Policy and Practice*, first suggested to me another angle from which to consider the British Empire. The passage from *The Planter* in 1930 read by Matthew in the dying-house is quoted in Bauer, *The Rubber Industry*, p. 285. R. C. H. MacKie's *This Was Singapore*, the most evocative description of Singapore between the wars, also exerted a considerable influence on certain scenes. For Chinese love terminology I have relied chiefly on the fascinating *Yin Yang, The Chinese Way of Love* by Charles Humana and Wang Wu, though here and there I have been unable to resist taking a hand in it myself. Finally, no one could consider writing about the military campaign without making use of the outstanding work of the official historian, the late Major-General S. Woodburn Kirby.

Books apart, I am grateful to old Singapore hands, particularly Mrs Enid Sutton and Mr Richard Phelps, who have enlightened me about life there in those days, as well as to those inhabitants of modern Singapore who gave me their hospitality and help, especially Mr Nick Bridge of the New Zealand High Commission, and Mr Donald Moore. I would also like to thank: Mr Lacy Wright and Miss Thé-anh Cao who kindly showed me Saigon in the last few weeks before it became 'Ho Chi Minh City', Mr Ian Angus of King's College Library, London, my brother, Robert Farrell, of the University of Victoria Library, a constant source of good ideas and information, and Giorgio and Ginevra Agamben, from whom I first heard of the 'Singapore Grip'. Lastly, without a generous contribution from Booker McConnell Ltd for an earlier novel it would have been financially difficult for me to write this one.

Bibliography

Abend, Hallett, *Chaos in Asia* (London 1940)

Abend, Hallett, *My Years in China* (London 1944)

Allen, G. C. and Donnithorne A., *Western Enterprise in Indonesia and Malaya* (London 1957)

Anon., *The Bells Go Down* (London 1944)

Attiwill, K., *The Singapore Story* (London 1959)

Barber, Noel, *Sinister Twilight* (London 1968)

Baring, Maurice, *Flying Corps Headquarters 1914–1918* (London 1968)

Barnett, Robert W., *Economic Shanghai* (New York 1941)

Bauer, P. T., Colonial Office: *Report on a visit to the Rubber Growing Smallholdings of Malaya* (London 1946)

Bauer, P. T., *The Rubber Industry* (London 1948)

Catroux, G. A. J., *Deux Actes du Drame Indochinois* (Paris 1959)

Clune, Frank, *All Aboard for Singapore* (Sydney 1941)

Connell, John, *Wavell* (London 1969)

Cooper, Duff, *Old Men Forget* (London 1953)

Dalton, Clive, *A Child in the Sun* (London 1937)

Decoux, J., *A la Barre de l'Indochine* (Paris 1950)

Dixon, Alec, *Singapore Patrol* (London 1935)

Donahue, A. G., *Last Flight from Singapore* (London 1944)

Fauconnier, H., *Malaisie* (Paris 1930)

Federated Malay States, *Annual Report of Labour Department 1941*

Firestone, Harvey S. and Crowther S., *Men and Rubber* (New York 1926)

Furnivall, J. S., *Colonial Policy and Practice* (London 1948)

Gilmour, O. W., *Singapore to Freedom* (London 1943)

Glover, E. M., *In Seventy Days* (London 1946)

Gull, E. M., *British Economic Interests in the Far East* (London 1943)

Gunther, John, *Inside Asia* (London 1939)

Hahn, E., *Raffles of Singapore* (Singapore and Kuala Lumpur 1968)

Hastain, R., *White Coolie* (London 1947)

Hobson, J. A., *Imperialism* (London 1938)

Humana, Charles and Wang Wu, *Yin Yang* (London 1971)

Kirby, Major-General S. Woodburn, *The War Against Japan* vol. I (London 1957)

Kirby, Major-General S. Woodburn, *Singapore, The Chain of Disaster* (London 1971)

Lief, A., *The Firestone Story* (New York 1951)

MacKie, R. C. H., *This Was Singapore* (London 1942)

Maxwell, Sir G., *The Civil Defence of Malaya* (London 1944)

Mills, L. A., *British Rule in East Asia* (London 1942)

Morrison, Ian, *Malayan Postscript* (London 1942)

Onraet, R., *Singapore, A Police Background* (London 1947)

Owen, Frank, *The Fall of Singapore* (London 1960)

Percival, Lieutenant-General A. E., *The War in Malaya* (London 1949)

Playfair, Giles, *Singapore Goes Off the Air* (London 1944)

Priestley, J. B., *Postscripts* (London 1940)

Richardson, M. L., *London's Burning* (London 1941)

Rose, Angus, *Who Dies Fighting* (London 1944)

Schumpeter, E. B., *The Industrialisation of Japan and Manchukuo* (Cambridge, Mass. 1940)

Simson, Brigadier Ivan, *Singapore: Too Little, Too Late* (London 1970)

Stahl, K. M., *The Metropolitan Organisation of British Trade* (London 1951)

Stewart, Brigadier I. M., *The History of the Argyll and Sutherland Highlanders, 2nd Battalion 1941-2* (London 1947)

Teeling, L. W. B., *Gods of Tomorrow* (London 1936)

Tsuji, M., *Singapore, The Japanese Version* (London 1962)

Willis, A. C., *Singapore Guide* (Singapore 1936)

Acknowledgements

The author and publishers are grateful to the following sources: Constable & Co. Ltd for permission to quote from *170 Chinese Poems* translated by Arthur Waley; Eyre & Spottiswoode for permission to quote an extract from *The War in Malaya* by A. E. Percival; Metro-Goldwyn-Mayer Inc. for permission to quote from the MGM release *The Ziegfeld Girl* © 1941 Loew's Incorporated. Copyright renewed in 1967 by Metro-Goldwyn-Mayer Inc.; and Leo Feist Inc. for permission to quote from three songs: 'You Stepped out of a Dream' by N. H. Brown and G. Khan © 1940 renewed 1968 MGM Inc., all rights administered by Leo Feist Inc.; 'Minnie from Trinidad' by R. Edens © 1941 renewed 1969 Leo Feist Inc.; and 'Caribbean Love Song' by R. Edens and R. Freed © 1941 renewed 1969 Leo Feist Inc.; to EMI Music Publishing Ltd for permission to quote an extract from 'A Nightingale Sang in Berkeley Square' by Eric Maschwitz, © 1940 Peter Maurice Music Co. Ltd.

J. G. Farrell

Troubles

J. G. Farrell's brilliant evocation of Ireland in turmoil and the British Empire in decline.

'Subtly modulated, richly textured, sad, funny and altogether memorable.'   *The Times Literary Supplement*

'A tour de force . . . sad, tragic, also very funny.'   *Guardian*

The Singapore Grip

'A brilliantly idiosyncratic and funny novel . . . Farrell's imagination is remarkable for its depth and intensity . . . his relaxed prose is both ironic and warm . . . Farrell's characters are as unique as the densely imagined worlds in which they move.'   *New Statesman*

The Siege of Krishnapur

Winner of the Booker Prize.

'A novel of quite outstanding quality.'   *The Times*

Flamingo

Anthony Powell

A Dance to the Music of Time

'The most significant work of fiction produced in England since the last war.' *Clive James*

A Question of Upbringing

A Buyer's Market

The Acceptance World

At Lady Molly's

Casanova's Chinese Restaurant

The Kindly Ones

The Valley of Bones

The Soldier's Art

The Military Philosophers

Books Do Furnish a Room

Temporary Kings

Hearing Secret Harmonies

Flamingo

Flamingo

Flamingo is a quality imprint publishing both fiction and non-fiction. Below are some recent titles.

Fiction
- [ ] Home Thoughts *Tim Parks* £3.95
- [ ] Human Voices *Penelope Fitzgerald* £3.95
- [ ] Offshore *Penelope Fitzgerald* £3.95
- [ ] Nelly's Version *Eva Figes* £3.95
- [ ] The Joys of Motherhood *Buchi Emecheta* £3.95
- [ ] The Thirteenth House *Adam Zameenzad* £3.95
- [ ] My Friend Matt and Hena the Whore *Adam Zameenzad* £3.95
- [ ] Night Night *Sharman Macdonald* £3.95

Non-fiction
- [ ] The Dancing Wu Li Masters *Gary Zukav* £4.95
- [ ] The Book of Five Rings *Miyamoto Musashi* £3.95
- [ ] Home Life *Alice Thomas Ellis* £3.95
- [ ] More Home Life *Alice Thomas Ellis* £3.95
- [ ] In the Ditch *Buchi Emecheta* £3.95
- [ ] Uncommon Wisdom *Fritjof Capra* £4.95
- [ ] The Turning Point *Fritjof Capra* £3.50
- [ ] The Tao of Physics *Fritjof Capra* £3.50
- [ ] Feeding the Rat *Al Alvarez* £3.95

You can buy Flamingo paperbacks at your local bookshop or newsagent. Or you can order them from Fontana Paperbacks, Cash Sales Department, Box 29, Douglas, Isle of Man. Please send a cheque, postal or money order (not currency) worth the purchase price plus 22p per book (or plus 22p per book if outside the UK).

NAME (Block letters) _____

ADDRESS_____

_____

_____